KRISTY MARIE

A 21 RUMORS NOVEL

For my daughter.
With every turd you encounter, know your prince awaits you.
Just remember to have patience and pepper spray.

IOU
/ˈˌī ˌō ˈyo͞o/
noun

A signed document acknowledging a debt.
Late 18th century: representing the pronunci-
ation of *I owe you*

Merriam-Webster.com Dictionary, s.v. "IOU,"
accessed March 2, 2020, www.merriam-webster.
com/dictionary/IOU.

Copper.

Formaldehyde.

Insulin.

Rat poison.

What do all these things have in common?

Come on, you know.

I bet you have an idea but don't want to say because it sounds crazy. That's okay, I won't judge if you jump to conclusions. At least not until you've heard the whole story.

Rumor has it I'm clingy and naive with a heavy dose of crazy.

But my mother taught me not to believe everything I hear.

She also taught me that every story has two sides—the reality—which is obviously my side of the story—and the rumors—which is *his* side of the story and exactly how this whole shitshow started.

I take that back. This story *really* started with a shit*head* and his girlfriend. . .

IOU

Chapter One

Ainsley

Rumor has it she's a psycho.

Contrary to what you might hear, I'm not crazy. I swear it.

"Are you out of your goddamned mind?"

It's a rhetorical question.

"The fucking apartment is on fire, Ainsley!"

Tucker has always been the more dramatic one in our relationship, and if I weren't so pissed off, I would bring it up, but there's no point. He's not my problem anymore.

"Fuck you!" I shout over the smoke detector, glaring at the cheating scumbag who was my boyfriend up until sixty seconds ago.

He's only half right, by the way. The apartment isn't on fire, the curtains in the living room are. It's a small flame, but a flame big enough to set off the smoke detectors, which triggered the neighbors to pull the fire alarm.

At this point, though, you're probably wondering why I'm screaming, 'Fuck you!' instead of grabbing some water and helping Tucker pull the curtain rod down. It's simple. I hate Tucker and hope his dick catches fire.

And I hate the girl standing next to him. Taylor. My roommate and, currently, my boyfriend's side piece. But that's not even the fucked-up part. The real fucked-up part is the fact they decided to use *my* candles to create this ambiance of adultery.

I aim a glare at Taylor, who's been quiet during this entire meltdown, but I'm guessing that's because she's naked, shivering in our living room as her hideous curtains go up in flames. "I did Taylor a favor by burning those curtains," I continue, undeterred by Tucker's panic and the wailing of sirens in the distance. "That's what good roommates do! They rid you of the ugly things in your life."

I force out a devilish smile like Taylor did me a solid tonight by porking Tucker, showing me what a real piece of shit he is. And in return, I paid her back by setting our apartment ablaze. Okay, so ablaze sounds like I ripped the sofa cushions and lit a match. That's not what happened. I meant to hit Tucker with a lit candle and missed.

He deserved it, and so did she.

Even if Taylor and I weren't the greatest of friends, we made being roommates work. I mean, sure, she's a twat twenty-five days out of the month, but the rest of those six days, she's kind of decent. But she had to go and ruin our fickle relationship.

Taylor glares back at me, not bothering to cover her flawless tits. I used to think the rumors about her perfect tits were a drunken observation and not a real fact. But now that I'm looking at them, I mean, *really* looking at them, they are pretty perfect. The perfect handful guys fight over. Guys like my boyfriend, who's also naked. At least Tucker is covering his junk. Wait.

"Why are you covering yourself, Tucker? Your dick has to be more useful than fucking my roommate. Pee on the fire, why don't you? Do at least one redeeming thing tonight."

Tucker grits his teeth and snatches a throw from the floor where the love nest of soft blankets is rumpled from their fuckfest. "Get some water!"

I don't move at his frustrated shout. He lost the right to tell me what to do the minute I walked through the door tonight.

"Ainsley! Put aside our issues for a moment. Innocent people are in the building."

Our issues. Pfft. He makes it sound like we have a weekly appointment with a marriage counselor. Not like we were so in love that I followed his med-school bound ass to this college, giving up all of my dreams so he could chase his.

"Ainsley!"

Okay. Fine. He's right. Even if I would like for his dick to sizzle,

I don't want anyone to die or be responsible for any lung complications just because he crushed my heart tonight.

I look at Taylor, the traitor standing next to me. Her eyes are laser-focused, searing me with hate. It takes all I have not to tackle her and snatch those thousand-dollar extensions from her hair. But that would show I give a crap about their betrayals.

And I do.

But no one needs to know the truth.

This whole fire thing is a throwing mishap. But if I took Taylor down to the ground in a tangle of bitch slaps. . .? That would seem like I completely lost my shit and care that my roommate has been banging my boyfriend for who knows how long.

The message I want to send is they can live happily ever after for all I care.

I have options, dammit.

I have respect.

At least for now, until I can get to somewhere private and wallow in my heartbreak.

I tear away from Taylor's glare and rifle through the cabinet for a pitcher. I find one I bought when Taylor and I threw a spring break party last year. It has cute little watermelons on the side that reminds me of happier days.

I scoff.

Those days are over.

Taylor and I are over.

Tucker and I are over.

Hell, screw the whole complex. Havemeyer University can suck a big fat dick for all I care.

I snatch the pitcher from the cabinet, and to be petty, I slash at the plasticware alongside it, sending it all down to the floor. Kicking the containers out of my way, I fill the pitcher with water before traipsing over to Tucker, who has pulled the curtains down and is attempting to smother the fire with the throw blanket he was probably fucking on.

My earlier fury bubbles to the surface, and I pull back and slosh the water over the curtains and Tucker, who is still naked.

"Dammit, Ainsley! Is your aim that bad tonight?"

My aim has always been poor. I'm not known for my throwing skills, but had I known twenty minutes ago I would be sent home early from my shift at Studs and Spuds, I would have practiced a little in the parking lot before I came in.

I was in a good mood, dammit!

Nothing felt better than knowing I had a few free hours to soak in the tub and play Who Wants to Be a Millionaire on my iPad. But I had to come home and find Tucker ass up, humping my roommate in the middle of the coziest mound of blankets, surrounded by my candles. It looked like I had walked into a ritual sacrifice: moans and jerky movements combined with Taylor speaking in tongues. Honestly, I wasn't sure what I was witnessing until Taylor said, "Oh, God, Tucker. Harder." That's when all chaos broke loose.

I gasped.

Taylor screamed.

Tucker sprang from the floor with a noteworthy litheness.

I was the epitome of calm after that. I merely dropped my purse, grabbed one of the candles they were burning, and hurled it as hard as I could at Tucker. I was aiming for his balls, which I missed, but I think we can all agree I was upset and deserve a pass on that mistake.

The water, however, I purposely doused on his ass.

"Screw you, Tucker!"

Okay, so my vocabulary has not been vast in all of this. But what can you say to the two people who you were supposed to trust? They betrayed me, and—A loud knock breaks our heated stare. I mouth, "I hate you," at the bastard before going to the door and swinging it open. The smoke detector is still going off, so I'm not at all surprised to see the three firefighters standing in the doorway.

"We received a call about a fire."

I don't even bother explaining. I simply step aside and allow the firemen to address the remaining few sparks that Tucker hasn't been able to put out. I should have known he couldn't finish off anything but himself—selfish asswipe.

The firemen push through the apartment and spray Taylor's curtains with the fire extinguisher before turning off the alarm and filling the space around us with silence.

Well, it was silent for a minute. But rest assured, Frank, the landlord in all his terry-cloth glory, remedies that quickly. "What the hell happened in here?" He looks at Tucker—who has grabbed a blanket—before swinging his gaze to Taylor, who is now covered too.

How nice of them to finally show some decency.

"Taylor," he barks. "What is going on here?"

Frank isn't the easiest landlord to deal with, but I imagine when you own an apartment complex that mainly rents to college students, you don't have the luxury of being a nice guy.

Taylor narrows her eyes at me. "She tried to kill us, Mr. Frank!" Tears fall from her smudged face. "She lost it and tried to burn us alive!"

Now she decides to be dramatic.

I roll my eyes and address Frank. "It was an accident. I knocked over a candle."

Taylor wails, and Tucker wraps his arm around her, shushing her with a sweetness I've never seen from him.

Oh, hell no.

No, he didn't. What about me, huh? I'm the victim here! I am the one who came home and found the love of my life ravaging my roommate.

Me! Not her.

I grab another candle and go to hurl it when a massive body steps in front of me and plucks it from my hand. "Let me take that," he says softly. The name on his uniform reads Bostic. "Why don't you step outside with me and get some fresh air, huh?" His eyes are gentle. He's probably a good dad—even better—a faithful husband.

I crane around Bostic's massive shoulders and take one last look at what my life was. Tucker is holding Taylor's sobbing body to him, smoothing his hands down her back.

Fucker.

Good riddance. Taylor can have him. I'm out.

I nod to Bostic and follow his lead through the door when Frank grabs my arm. "You're done here, Ms. James. I don't want you back on the property anymore. If I see you again, I'll file a restraining order."

Bostic makes a noise deep in his chest like he wants to say

something but can't. It doesn't matter anyway. I wouldn't stay here with Taylor if you promised me my very own pet sea lion. I nod. "Understood. But I'll need to come back for my stuff."

"Don't bother," shouts Taylor. "We'll pack it up and leave it outside the door."

The hell she will. Tomorrow, when everything settles down, I'll talk to Frank and get my stuff. I have a class, and I'll need my laptop.

Bostic pats a brawny hand on my shoulder. "Come on. Let's get you out of here."

My shoulders slump as we descend the stairs, the adrenaline of the past twenty minutes petering out.

"Here, eat this." I stop mid-step and look at the mini pack of Skittles Bostic shoves at me. "You need the sugar." I must still look skeptical because he adds, "It'll help with the post-adrenaline crash."

Oh. "I'm fine. Thank you, though." I flash him a tired smile. "Are you waiting until the police come for me?"

He arches a brow. "What would the police want with you?"

"Because I lit the apartment on fire?" I suggest. I'd be a terrible criminal.

His lips twitch as if he's holding back a smile. "It was a candle accident. Last I heard, accidents aren't associated with jail time."

He pulls us down the sidewalk and motions for me to sit on the step of the firetruck.

"Do you have a Dalmatian in the cab?" I ask. I could go for some puppy love right now.

Bostic chuckles. "No. No dog on this rig."

"That's a shame," I mutter. "Everyone needs a dog." And a sea lion. But I don't add that comment. Bostic already thinks I'm crazy.

The sigh that leaves Bostic's chest is deep and heavy. "You want to tell me what happened in there?"

Not really. "I think I'll take those Skittles now." I could use the comfort food.

He hands them over, and I waste no time ripping into the bag and throwing back a few of the sugary pieces.

"Was that your boyfriend?" He prompts again.

I swallow and meet his warm and friendly brown eyes. He looks concerned. Not like he's trying to weasel a confession out of me. It's probably safe to answer him with the truth. I can't possibly screw tonight up any more than I already have. "Yeah."

"He cheat on you?" Bostic is a good man, I can tell. I mean, I used to be able to tell. I thought Tucker was a good man too. Look how that turned out. But Bostic seems different, and if I were into older men in their forties with a healthy obsession with dumbbells, I probably would turn on my charm and dial back the crazy, but I don't do rebounds or men who could be my daddy. Plus, I'm reasonably sure I have this man concerned for my mental well-being.

"Yeah." I throw back a few more Skittles until the bag is empty and crinkle it between my fingers. Too bad it was snack size. "All I wanted to do is take a bath and play Who Wants to Be a Millionaire. I didn't plan on causing a scene, but he was there, and neither of them looked the slightest bit remorseful when I walked in. I just reacted."

I shrug like my reaction was uncontrollable. It was. I'm not making excuses for endangering lives. I'm merely saying I didn't think at the time—being blinded by rage or whatever you want to call it. The fact is: Tucker and Taylor made a stupid decision tonight. And now, so have I.

Bostic nods, his jaw twitching as he glares at the third floor where his coworkers are probably filling out paperwork.

"I'm sorry you guys had to come out this late in the evening. I'm sure it's dinner time at the station, huh?" I've watched *911*. I know the firemen have big meals and big screen TVs and twenty-four-hour shifts. The last thing they want to do on a Tuesday night is to break up a ridiculous catfight.

"It's our job," he gruffs out.

"I know, but you should be saving lives in like forest fires and such. Not putting out a small candle fire." I downplay the flames just in case he's reconsidering turning me over to the cops.

A low noise rumbles out of Bostic's massive chest before he opens his mouth—probably to correct me on the size of the fire—but his crew descends the stairs and cuts him off.

I stand. "Thank you for the Skittles, and you know"—I wave to the third floor—"saving lives. There's probably a few you saved from shooting straight to hell." I grin. "I'm joking. Kind of."

The big man stands and tilts his head down to look at me. "You have somewhere to stay tonight?"

Right. Because I'm homeless now.

I swallow and manage a smile. "Yeah. I have some friends I can call." It's a complete and utter lie, but I can tell Bostic is a fixer, and well, I did this to myself. No one made me go crazy and set my apartment on fire, even if it was warranted.

"Are you sure?"

I don't want to lie to this man. "I'll be fine. I promise."

One of the other firemen claps Bostic on the back. "Ready to go?"

He doesn't move—only stares at me like he can somehow extract the truth with his eyes.

"I'll be fine, big guy." I encourage when his buddies start loading up.

He sighs. "I'm at Station 764 if you need anything."

He really is a nice man. I check his hand for a ring. Bare. Good, my mom could use a good man in her life. We both could, but she's been single longer, so she gets dibs.

"Thank you. I appreciate everything." I mean it. Bostic could have made my night a lot worse, and he didn't. He's a rare find.

The big man frowns but tips his chin in resignation, and I reassure him, once again, with a smile. I can handle myself. Granted, I've never been homeless, but how hard could it be? I have a car. It's not too hot out. And I have about ten hoodies in my backseat that will make the perfect pillow. Then, in the morning, I will find another roommate—easy-freaking-peasy. It'll be like camping all those years ago with Mom.

I wave at the firetruck as it pulls out of the complex. Everything has returned to normal, at least here in the parking lot. I don't know about inside the building because I'm banned.

Who needs an apartment anyway?

Or a roommate?

Certainly not me. I'd rather have my morals than to room with more liars.

Unzipping my purse, I dig out my car keys and head toward my parking space. The 2005 sedan that awaits me is dirty with a small ding in the bumper where I bumped into a gas station pole, but it's mine, and it's free of cheating scumbags and lying roommates, so I call that a win and home for possibly the rest of the semester.

I open the back door and get in, locking the doors behind me. Frank said he was kicking me out of my apartment. Not out of the parking lot. Surely, he won't bother checking to see if I've vacated the premises. Frank's lazy and considering he was already in his bathrobe, I imagine he's two beers from beddy-bye-time.

My phone buzzes—it's a text from my mom.

I hope you had a great day! Call me in the morning. Love you!

She thinks I'm still at work, and that's okay. We'll let her believe that. I don't want to talk to her right now anyway. If I do, I'm sure I'll cry at the sound of her voice. Through this whole disaster of a night, I've yet to let one single tear fall, and I typically cry when I'm mad.

I'm a passionate person, and therefore tears come a little more frequently for me than others. But that's to be expected, right? Or maybe it's my birth control because sometimes that shit fucks me up, and I feel like a raging psycho. But not today. Today was a good day.

I boot up the Who Wants to be a Millionaire app and choose my city. I'll take on London and Sasha, the other online player. Games have always been my source of comfort. I guess when you're an only child, you learn to entertain yourself. My grandmother used to love watching Who Wants to Be a Millionaire on TV and she got me addicted. So you can imagine when the app came out, I was freaking ecstatic. I am determined to become a virtual millionaire. I'm smart and well-versed in trivia. Well, I'm not *too* bright. Clearly.

But I had thought Tucker was different. Yes, I know. Let the shit go. But the betrayal is still raw. It's not that I had a whole lot of boyfriends in my lifetime. Admittedly, Tucker has been my only one. We met in high school, and it was love at first sight for me. He was the smartest kid in our entire class. Not only that, but he was also tall, much taller than me, which was something since I always felt like a giant with my five-foot-ten frame. I wasn't the tallest girl in our freshman class, but I might as well have been.

Most of the guys hadn't reached my height by ninth grade and therefore shunned anything to do with me. I got it. I made them look short. But not Tucker. Tucker was a beast, even though it seemed as if he stopped growing right around junior year. His height was one of the things that made him perfect for me. He was also fun and confident.

So I held on for the ride through high school, following him to Havemeyer, where he received a scholarship for pre-med. A school where I didn't receive an award. But we couldn't be apart—we were soul mates.

Wetness smears my phone screen and makes the trivia question unreadable. I watch as the countdown dwindles to zero, claiming Sasha as the winner by default. But I can't make myself care. The tears have finally come.

Tucker is gone.

My first kiss.

My first love.

Gone.

How long had he and Taylor been sleeping together? Was it just physical or—I gag—are they in love?

They can't be.

Tucker and I are destined to be together.

And Taylor, well, she's . . . I'm not going to stoop that low and take a dig at her just because I'm feeling sorry for myself. I'm better than that. At least I think I'm better than that. But I guess Tucker sees something in her that he didn't see in me.

I blink through the watery tears, the lights still on in my former apartment where Tucker is probably showering the soot off Taylor, using my body wash.

A sob catches in my throat.

How did this happen? How did I become this girl?

I can remember all these big dreams I had growing up. I wanted to save the sea lions. Save the otters and whales. Discover a cure for dementia. I wanted to be the best family counselor this state had ever seen.

Granted, I'm working on the counseling degree, but the rest of it . . . those poor sea animals? I gave up that dream and scholarship when Tucker was accepted to Havemeyer. Although Havemeyer has a marine biology program, it has a waiting list longer than Tucker's lies.

Counseling is still a good career, though, and the odds of making it in marine biology are slim to none. I needed to be realistic. I couldn't travel from coast to coast if Tucker had a staff position at the hospital. I would have never seen him, much less been able to have a family.

I tear my eyes away from the window when the lights to my old apartment go off. They're going to bed. Tucker and Taylor are snuggling down in her room, consoling each other from my madness.

Pfft. Who am I kidding? Knowing Tucker and his need for a release before bed, I'm positive they are celebrating their newfound freedom of not having to hide their affair anymore.

His chain has been cut free.

I turn off my phone and tuck it into my side like it's Lawrence, my poor stuffed sea lion that I left in the apartment, and close my eyes.

In the morning, things will be different.

In the morning, I'll go back to Lawrence.

In the morning, it'll be a new beginning.

Chapter Two

Maverick

Rumor has it the price of my company is a cold, lifeless soul.

"You're either in, or you're out, Tweener. Make a decision or go giggle with the girls next door."

Rowan is two seconds from hauling Jacob, aka Tweener, out of his chair and shoving his head through the felt table. The newbie is working his last frazzled nerve.

I pass him a joint. "Relax. Tweener is new." Precisely why the fresh-faced kid shouldn't be here. Guys like Tweener look like they should be out playing croquet while downing light beers. They don't look like they should be sitting around the poker table, testing my friend and game enforcer's patience.

Wednesday night poker is not amateur night. I created it that way. The cutthroat game of Texas Hold'em at my table is not some drunken card game that every half-decent solitaire player at Havemeyer University can play. With a two-thousand-dollar buy-in, you either have the cash or you don't play. There is no in-between. Poker, at my table, is invite-only, and if Sebastian, the grinning idiot across from me, weren't my closest friend, I wouldn't have let him bring this newbie.

"You may want to wipe that fucking smile off your face," I say, aiming a stern look at Sebastian, "because if he goes belly up, you're not leaving here until you cover his debt." I know he covered his buy-in too. No way did this kid have two grand to piss away.

Sebastian plucks the joint from Rowan's mouth and takes a long drag, his smirk never wavering. "You know what you need, Mav?"

Yeah, I'm not biting. Sebastian is the last person I would take advice from, even *if* he had any valuable information to offer.

Sebastian is Havemeyer's celebrity. He's semi-talented with a guitar, but he's mostly known for his outlandish reality clips. Basically, he's all show. Nothing in his life is real. It's all an act—all for the fake fame and publicity.

I ignore Sebastian's smirk and follow Rowan's glare to Tweener, who has yet to make a play. I'm not sure how high Rowan is at this moment, but I don't think it's enough to keep him from tossing the kid out of here in the next few seconds. Rather than goading me, Sebastian should focus more on helping his cameraman survive the night. What was he thinking bringing him here anyway?

"What you need, Mav, is a bad fuck or mediocre blow job. Wait, no, I got it!" He shuffles in his chair excitedly. "A sloppy rim job! That would loosen you up."

I don't make eye contact. Poker is a game of timing and knowing your opponent. You can have the shittiest hand at the table, but if you know your opponent, you can bluff your way to a win. For example, Sebastian is running his mouth. I know he has a semi-decent hand— probably chasing the straight if my theory is correct.

Every player has a tell.

Talking shit is Sebastian's. By running his mouth, he can get you so worked up and pissed off that you forget to pay attention to the players around you. He knows I won't fall for it, but that doesn't stop him from attempting to distract Rowan.

"See, you don't need a good dick sucking, just a simple, mediocre, wet the tip and fondle the balls until you're so frustrated you come just so you can send the pretty little thing home. You need to loosen up, Mav. Accept that people aren't perfect and need to learn."

He's not just talking about my empty bed at night. He's attempting to tell me that I shouldn't expect every player who comes to the table to be a pro. I don't. I know not everyone is perfect. The issue is, I enjoy simplicity and predictability in my life—something Sebastian doesn't understand. But I guess when you're always putting on a show for the public, you can't grasp that some people don't want their lives on display. Faking a persona is exhausting. I should know. I live a lie.

Most days, I can't remember who the real Maverick is anymore. Does he even like poker? Or was poker a matter of survival at the time? I'll never know because, at this point, I can never give it up. It's who I am now.

Unlike Sebastian, I don't thrive on drama or overshare one hundred percent of the time. I merely choose to keep my lies to myself and refrain from participating in his cesspool of nightly debauchery. I appreciate boundaries and enjoy time to myself. Respecting my sanity and choosing never to have overnight guests is how I've gotten through this past year. I don't need—or want—a sloppy rim job or a lackluster fuck. More than that, I don't want to forget to hide my shit, and my secrets get out.

Also, I genuinely don't trust people. And after all the favors I've doled out, I don't trust anyone. Everything can be bought. Even the most moral soul can be sold for a price. Life is a contract. Friendships. Marriages. Employment. It's all there in black and white. Once time has been served, or the contract hasn't been fulfilled to their standards, it's over.

I will never not have a contract. I learned early on that people will shit on you the minute they feel it is socially acceptable. It doesn't matter how many years of friendship or love you've had together.

All this to say, Sebastian, my closest friend, knows this. He knows my preference—or jaded insanity as he likes to call it—so him saying all of this right now is worthless and is only to buy Tweener more goddamned time to make a play.

Sebastian pauses, waiting for me to acknowledge his joke.

I lift a brow in warning, but it doesn't deter him. He's long lost his fear of me. Unlike most people, I knew Sebastian before I became *the Maverick Lexington*.

"I'm telling you, man. You haven't lived until you've come to the worst fuck ever."

Tingling starts in my lips as I fight the involuntary twitch. A lip twitch is my tell. One that everyone, apart from Tweener, knows.

I tap out a cigarette I'll never smoke and shove it between my lips.

The feeling of the filter not only calms the twitch, but the scent reminds me of calmer days—days when I used to sit here for hours in a cloud of smoke, winning one hand after another until the sun came up.

I cared about nothing.

But that was before—before everything changed.

"Sebastian," I finally meet his gaze, "if your friend doesn't check or bet, I'm going to shove this beer bottle up your goddamned ass and see how you enjoy a sloppy rim job."

Sebastian spews his beer with his boisterous laugh. "And here I thought you were in a bad mood today," he gurgles out between chuckles.

"Dammit, Bash. You got the cards wet."

I sigh, watching Rowan wipe off the cards, a low growl aimed in Tweener's direction.

"Check or bet. Now!"

Tweener jumps as Rowan's burly fist slams down on the table.

I sigh. It's been a long night, and honestly, my head isn't in the game tonight. Instead, I'd rather they all just get the fuck out.

Tweener locks eyes with Sebastian.

"I swear to God, I will—"

My words cut short as Tweener rushes out, "Check. I check."

Fucking finally.

I nod, rolling the cigarette between my lips. "Row?"

He looks at me and then at Sebastian. He knows we both have good hands, but he doesn't. How do I know? His aggression flares, and he worries his ear, the tips turning a light shade of red. Yep, he has shit.

"Fuck you both," he says, slamming his cards down. "I fold."

Good. He was never in this game anyway.

Sebastian, acting as the dealer tonight, throws down the river card, the last card in a hand, and tosses a handful of chips into the pot. He raises the bet. I'm right. He's after the straight. That's fine because I have the nuts, the best possible hand.

I grin and tip my chin at Sebastian. "Straight on the river?"

He doesn't look as cocky as he did a minute ago.

"Fuck." He groans.

Fuck is right. Fucking up happy endings is what I do best.

I toss my cards out on the table. "I got the boat. Now get the fuck out of my apartment."

Sebastian leans back in his chair, rocking on just two legs. "Let me win it back?"

"No." I stand, tossing the unlit cigarette onto the table. I was serious when I meant for them to get out. I need time to sort out my shit—sort out the text burning through my phone screen all evening.

I walk back to my bedroom, ignoring the pile of cash and chips on the table. No one is crazy enough to steal from me. When they're gone, and I've dealt with this text, I'll go back and clean it up.

Tugging my shirt off, I sit on the bed and grab my phone from the nightstand. I swipe away all the requests for meetings and favors, looking for the only text that matters. The one that turned my night into shit.

IOH-MB: I'm ready to cash in my favor.

My chest clenches. It did the same thing when I read it earlier. Owing someone a favor is a rarity for me. Sebastian would tell you it should be documented. I will tell you what it truly is. A mistake. One that will never happen again. But I'm not one to go back on my promises, so whether or not I can buy off this favor, I will complete it personally. I got myself into this mess, and this favor will be the end of it.

I take a deep breath, and my fingers tap across the keys.

Me: I thought you didn't want a favor from me.

The dots appear at the bottom of the screen, and my stomach begs for the cigarette I left on the poker table.

IOH-MB: I reconsidered. The offer has no expiration date, correct?

My hand clenches around the phone. This is not good. So not good.

Me: That's how it works. What do you need?

I lean over my knees and rake a hand through my hair. Am I fucking sweating?

IOH-MB: Tomorrow. 11 am. You know the place.

So goddamned careless. If I weren't so tense, I'd go to the gym and ask Rowan to beat the shit out of me so that I remember never to let this happen again. Me—owing someone else a fucking favor. Unbelievable.

Me: I'll be there.

I will fucking be there. Fuck me.

I spring from the bed and throw open the door. I need a beer. I need anything; at this point, a sloppy rim job doesn't sound too horrible.

Banging my head on the refrigerator a few times, I let out an angry growl and snatch open the door, grabbing a beer. I won't drink the fucker, even if I want to down it in one go. That would be too easy for me. Instead, I'll punish myself for getting into this situation by holding the cold glass in my hands, allowing the aroma to tempt me with its promise of washing away the stress with one long pull. I don't owe favors. I haven't since . . . it doesn't matter. I can handle whatever it is. If I can't, I'll know someone who can.

It's simple.

It's fine.

I pop the top on the bottle, the releasing hiss calming as I sulk through the living room and plant my ass in one of the plastic chairs on the balcony. It's pitch-black, save for a few porch lights. I like it that way. I feel secluded—at ease even. I'm an introvert by nature, but ever since I've been at Havemeyer, I've retreated even more.

My life is messy and complicated. And I'm not sure how to fucking fix it. Realistically, there's nothing to fix. I'm doing fine in all my classes. My family is taken care of. They haven't had to worry about sending me any money, thanks to my poker nights. So what if I can't sleep and my mind is in constant overdrive? Boo-fucking-hoo.

I take a longing look at the beer bottle clutched in my hand, swaying it back and forth until I have the angle just right, and pour the stream between the slats of wood down to the balcony below me.

"What the hell?" A female voice shrieks.

An errant smile tugs at my face. It feels suitable for once—relieving.

"Shh. Be quiet!" My neighbor below scolds. I don't know his fucking name and don't plan on learning it. He's a decent guy—has a cute girlfriend that he takes out on date nights every Friday, which inevitably leads to them cooing bullshit words like love and forever. It grates on my nerves and ruins my shitty mood. Hence the beer interruption.

I hear the sliding glass door click closed, and I can't even find it in me to relish the win. I need a distraction—another game, perhaps. Lately, though, the competition has been laughable. A trip deep into the city maybe? I check my watch. I have time. I could make it to Gigi's and catch a real game.

My fingers twitch.

No.

I dial another number instead.

"I swear to God you're worse than a girlfriend about these late-night cuddle calls."

I bark out a laugh, pouring out the rest of my beer. "What the hell is a cuddle call?"

"You know," his voice goes all high-pitched, "you wanna talk before bed? Tell me how your day went and all that shit."

The laughter feels good—distracting even. "Why don't you want to talk to your girlfriend at night?" Clearly, he gets this statement a lot.

Shuffling sounds on the phone. "Who the fuck do I look like? Dr. Phil?" His tone is incredulous. "If I wanted to spend two hours on the phone listening to drama, I'd ask Pops how his day was. Phone calls with girlfriends should be restricted to phone sex only."

"Agreed. So how often do you do it?"

He groans. "All the damn time. Why does pussy have to be so good?"

Even though my brother's tone is whiny, he's serious.

"Because something had to make us lose our sanity."

Pussy has never been enough for me to lose focus, though.

"Yeah, yeah. So, what's up? You lose tonight?"

My brother has never been someone to beat around the bush.

I shrug to no one, looking out into the night air.

"I just called to see how it went today."

I start laughing before he adds, "Fucking cuddle calling."

"I'm serious," I add soberly. "You had that big game today."

The hesitation and crunching in the background tell me I interrupted him mid-chew. Is he just now eating dinner?

"Decent. My bat was cold. I couldn't get anything out of the infield."

"Your arm still sore? You've been icing it like I told you?"

He groans. "Yes, *Dad*. I'm just distracted, that's all."

My brother is such a little shit, but I guess we both are. It comes with the last name.

A familiar ache tickles beneath my ribs. "Scouts not coming to games?"

He pauses, the crunching subsiding for a moment. "No, but it's fine. Carter and I were talking about working for his dad doing landscape once we graduate. I could try out when they hold open tryouts. I don't need to go to college to get into the Major Leagues."

True but. . . "It's the best way. You'd get better offers, and you'd have a degree to fall back on if you end up with a career-ending injury. It's a solid plan, Coop. Don't give up on it just yet."

My brother scoffs into the phone. He's never been set on going to college. He wants to go straight to the Major Leagues—arrogant little fucker. "I'm not giving up, Mav. I'm realistic. Kingston High hasn't seen a trophy in two decades. Scouts have no reason to come here. Maybe Dad was right. A professional athlete is only a loser's dream."

Michael Lexington is a fucking idiot. Greed and power are his motivation in life. If he can't buy or sell it, he doesn't bother with it. Example: my brother and me. When my mother was diagnosed with Multiple Sclerosis and could no longer be the beautiful wife on his arm, he bought another. Candi is her name. She's ninety-five pounds and my age.

And when my mother died at the young age of forty-five from pneumonia, he dumped my brother and me off at my pops's for the summer and never returned. I was fifteen, my brother thirteen. In a matter of months, we went from a family of four to a family of two. Motherless and fatherless all in a summer's break.

Again, contracts. My mother's was up, and so was ours.

Pops is cool, though. With a plush apartment in Atlanta, he took us in, let us sleep in his bed while he took the couch, and looked for a bigger place. He moved us out of the city after that first year, moving us into a subdivision with other kids, complete with a cul-de-sac. We lived a good life. Pops worked from home, hiring a vice president for his brokerage firm so he could spend more time with us.

Everything was looking great until my freshman year at college. Pops suffered a stroke that left him with left sided weakness and neurological deficits. He thinks he's perfectly fine and doesn't need us boys looking after him, but it's not true.

I know my brother is tired, and instead of spending his days partying with his senior friends, he's watching *Jeopardy* and tying the old man's shoes. I wanted to move back home and help, but Cooper wouldn't hear of it. He insists he's fine and Pops is no trouble. I'm not sure if I believe it, but the guilt as the older brother gnaws at me daily.

"Everything out of Dad's mouth is garbage. You're better off asking your Magic 8-Ball for advice. It's probably more accurate."

Both of us chuckle for a second, lightening the mood.

"How's the old man?" I ask like I do in every conversation.

"Still senile and full of shit." My brother laughs good-naturedly. "He told me last night that I should join FarmersOnly.com and meet a nice girl."

A real smile finally emerges. "Caught you with another girl again?"

My brother might stay home and take care of Pops, but his bed stays warm. "Hell yeah. Damn old man busted in yelling he was looking for mongrels."

I laugh a deep belly laugh. "Mongrels? Had he been drinking?"

"No, dude. Fucking Melissa was scratching the headboard with her goddamned bracelets. Pops thought I had rats in my room."

"Dude." I grin, leaning back against the chair. "You have got to clean your room occasionally. Maybe then he'll stop thinking it's a shithole that attracts vermin."

No joke. Last time I was there for Christmas, Pops told me he had to wear a mask to walk in and wake Coop up for school.

"It's fine. I'm a teenage boy. If it were clean, he would think I was sick."

True. He probably would.

"So," I go for a subject change. "You dating Melissa? I've heard you mention her a few times now." Fuck, I'm turning into my mom keeping tabs on my little brother's love life. But it helps knowing he's happy and doing normal teenage things since I'm gone and can't look after him like I used to.

During my entire high school years, I devoted myself to becoming my little brother's keeper. It was a hard change when Pops pushed me out the door, paid my first-year tuition, and told me I was not allowed to come back home until the break.

I knew Pops was pushing me for my good. He knew I wouldn't leave them, but I couldn't bear my little brother thinking that I too had left him. Pops has been an exceptional stand-in as a father, and his sarcastic personality is a lot like our mother's. Life with Pops was good. Normal even. But I would have held off on college for a few years until Cooper graduated, but Pops wouldn't hear of any delays in my education.

"I don't know." He sighs into the phone, answering my earlier question about his status with Melissa. "She's moving to Boston when she graduates. There's no need to get involved. As soon as we graduate, we'll be over."

That means he likes her, right?

"It won't matter when you can afford a flight every weekend. Or get drafted to Boston. They have an outstanding team, you know."

I'm not usually such an optimist, but I don't want Cooper to give up his dream of playing professional baseball. It was something he and my mother always bonded over. It wasn't my father who taught him how to throw a ball. It was my crazy supportive mom whom I caught awake late one night watching how-to videos. She was the one who, when he was four, signed him up for tee-ball and ran the bases with him when he wanted to run from first base to home and bypass the remaining plates. She was his biggest fan, and I know that deep down, making it to the Major Leagues is not only for him but for her too.

She would be proud of him either way, but ever since she died, he's thrown himself into the sport. It went from a backyard hobby to total obsession. Cooper let baseball consume him, and I think, in some way, heal him. He's not giving up now. Not if I can help it. I don't care how many poker games I need to win. Cooper is going to get his shot at the major leagues. The boy deserves a chance to see if he has what it takes.

"We'll see," he tells me somberly.

Yeah, we'll see.

I need the pieces to align soon.

"Don't worry about it yet. You have time. Do you and Pops need anything? I looked at the accounts last night, and they looked good." Enough. They looked good enough. Income hasn't been steady for Pops since he isn't able to manage the company on his own. I've been sending him and Coop money when I can, hoping to lessen the strain of the company finances since Laurant—his VP—quit last year and the market took a complete shit.

"Yeah, yeah. We're fine. What about you? You doing okay?"

I nod, fighting the fatigue. "Yeah. I'm good. I've been winning."

He pauses. I know that pause. It's the same conversation we have whenever he thinks I'm getting in too deep. "Be careful, Mav. Gambling is addictive. You could lose it all."

Poker is a necessity—a job. The only way I can help the man who gave up his whole life for Cooper and me. It's the least I can do to keep what little family I have left, safe.

"I got it handled, Coop. Don't worry about me." And it's the truth. I do have it handled. Maybe not well but handled nevertheless.

"All right, dude. Whatever you say. Just know Pops will kill you if you get caught up in owing some bookie hundreds of thousands."

I grin. "You've been watching too much TV, little brother."

"Maybe so, but take care of yourself, Mav. You're only one person."

Don't I feel that every single day.

"I know. Take care of Pops. I'll see you guys soon."

"Yeah. Yeah. Later, bro."

"Later."

I end the call and blow out a big breath of anxiety. My legs are heavy as I stand and shut the sliding door. I'm exhausted as I bypass the pile of cash on the table, leaving the lights on and heading to the bedroom where I drop to the mattress in one exaggerated move.

My eyes close.

I just need sleep and a way out.

Chapter Three

Ainsley

Rumor has it she was arrested.

The sun rises, and I'm wide awake. Not from the most refreshing sleep ever but from being up two-thirds of the night praying every noise wasn't the next Ted Bundy coming to offer me his back seat. Or truck. Wait. He was the one who took them on dates first, right? That might not have been too bad. At least then I could have squeezed a shower and food out of him before he killed me.

A night in the back seat of a car is no freaking joke, let me tell you. Who knew the middle seat that everyone's ass cheeks hang off of could be the devil incarnate? I mean, really. Why can't the entire back seat be one level? Did carmakers think, "Hey! Let's be sure to make this back seat unsleepable just in case the owner gets desperate?" I think they did. My ribs will show you the beating they took from the hump and seat belt buckle—let's not forget those lifesavers.

Needless to say, although today is a new beginning, it is not a pleasant one. I stink, I'm exhausted, and I'm alone. And . . . I might have been a little scared. Okay, I was a lot scared, but what drove my fright to nuclear levels was the brutal banging on my window that sent me shooting upright and knocking my head on the ceiling about five seconds ago.

"I thought you had a friend you could call!" An angry man growls through the closed window.

Bostic.

I told you he was a kind soul. And for that, I'll forgive him for stopping my heart this early in the morning.

I roll down the window, mindful of my breath. "I did," I say, grinning at a freshly shaven face. "Her name is Jane Honda. She offered me her back seat in exchange for filling her tank up with gas—a real giver, she is."

He doesn't look amused. The twitching lip and the narrowing of his eyes give it away. Clearly, Bostic needs more coffee, and if I'm honest, I could use a cup or three, like yesterday.

"You've been out here all night?" His voice is stern, like a parent. My mom would be super proud of his glare. But we are never mentioning this to her, ever. She doesn't deal well with stressful situations. It was already hard enough convincing her to let me leave the proverbial nest and live on my own. Granted, I haven't done such a bang-up job thus far, but I have potential.

I sigh, noting the hard edge of his words. This can go down one of two ways. I could lie, or I could evade the truth, but there will be no complete honesty. Bostic came back here out of suspicion, so deep down, he doesn't expect the whole truth from me right now. He knew I wasn't wholly forthcoming last night, so we can check being smart on his list of good attributes.

"Yep." I let the P pop a little like it was no big deal for me to sleep in my car. "It wasn't as bad as I thought. I mean, I could have used a little lavender to settle my nerves, but all in all, it wasn't terrible." It was brutal is what it was, but there's no sense in dwelling in the past. It was a unique experience, and hopefully, I'll never need to repeat it.

"Come on, get out." He wiggles the door handle impatiently.

I narrow my eyes. "Are you turning me over to the police?" It's possible. I'm not giving him trusting vibes here.

His chest expands, and he looks at the sky. "No. We're going to get your things."

Right. Of course he isn't turning me in. It was a candle accident, after all.

"Oh." I eye the steps into the complex. "Maybe we should wait until they leave for class?" He knows I'm referring to the cheating trolls upstairs.

Bostic shakes his head and wiggles the handle once again. "No. We're getting your things now. Then you're going to follow me to the firehouse for a shower and some breakfast."

Oh. Well, that sounds lovely. "Okay." I agree quickly and roll up my window, grabbing my purse.

Shit.

"Uh, can you turn around for a minute?" Bostic's eyes do this fearful jump thing, but he turns around, albeit slowly. I hurry and pull my arms through the sleeves of my shirt. There was no way I was sleeping with an underwire and a seat belt buckle jabbing into my ribs. I'm no masochist.

When I've got the girls all under wraps, I sweep my hair up into a ponytail and check for drool marks. "Okay, I'm ready," I announce, tossing my flip-flops on the ground and sliding my feet in.

Bostic eyes my choice of footwear.

"I don't have clean socks, and the flip-flops were in my car." I shrug. Desperate times call for desperate measures.

He grunts but doesn't comment. I'm pretty sure he isn't judgy. Instead, he's assessing the general hot mess that I am. "Lead the way," I tell him with a sweep of my hand. I'm sure as hell not going first. Frank isn't the forgiving type, and well, I feel much safer standing behind two hundred and fifty pounds of muscle.

"How did you know I was here?" I ask, out of breath. If there is one thing I've learned about Bostic in a short amount of time is that he does not walk. For a big guy, he freaking hustles.

"I just knew."

Oh, well, that's not evasive at all. Maybe he's like a guardian angel. I saw this show once about this clumsy girl who kept avoiding death because her guardian angel stepped in and saved her time after time. Or wait, was that *Final Destination* where she kept avoiding death? Ugh. Now I can't remember. Anyway. "So you just knew, huh?"

Bostic raps on the apartment door, and I fail to swallow my nerves when I hear footsteps.

"Stay behind me and keep quiet," says my guardian angel—or Devon Sawa—either one is fine at this point.

I smile and make a zipping motion across my lips just as Tucker's assface opens the door.

"Can I help you?" he has the nerve to ask.

Punch him right in the face, Bostic! Do it for me. Do it for his future girlfriends!

"Get out of my way," Bostic growls out instead.

It wasn't punching him in the face, but it was still satisfying seeing Tucker rear back at his malicious tone.

"We're here for her things."

That's right, bitch. Move!

It occurs to me that Bostic doesn't even know my name. Or maybe he does. It's likely someone told him for his report. Do firefighters do reports, or is that just the police? Well, shit. Now I'm getting confused again. This lack of sleep is really messing with my head, or maybe being with Tucker made me stupid. Can that happen? Can guys make you stupid? I'm going with: possibly.

Tucker tries to peer around, but Bostic takes a step toward him. "Are we going to have a problem?"

Please have a problem, Tucker. I would so love to see you get your ass beat right now.

Tucker takes a step back. I should have known he would always look out for himself. Tucker has never really been a fighter. Not that I look for guys to fight, but you have to admit it's super sexy when they unleash the beast with all that grunting and sweating. Whew. I've never appreciated a grunt as much as I have when I watch a UFC fight.

"By all means," Tucker says, motioning for Bostic and me to come in. I try not to look around. I *really*, really do. I mean, do I need to see if they'd resumed their fuckfest on the floor? No, I do not. But I look anyway. And thankfully, it's all gone, and our once sparse living room is back to normal. Not ours. Theirs. As in, not mine anymore.

I push my way past Bostic to my room, where I start throwing everything I can into my suitcase without hesitation. No need to stay here any longer than I have to.

"Do you need any help?"

That's Bostic, not Asshole.

My head drops to my chest in a big sigh. "I don't know." This is all happening so fast. It's like I'm living someone else's life. My room. My things. I've spent the last two years within these four walls and in seconds it's all gone.

I take a seat on the edge of my bed with my head in my hands. "I don't have anywhere to take all this stuff. What am I supposed to do with my bed?" I mean, really. What's the point in packing? I have nowhere to put it. Maybe I should give it away? Or perhaps I should drop out and go home. Find a community college closer to home where I'll have food in my belly and a roof over my head.

I look up at Bostic through bleary eyes.

I'm not going to cry. I can handle this. Think of it like when you had a Father's Day event at school and no father to have doughnuts with you. The initial pain hurts, but you get used to it. Eventually, you won't even care.

"We'll figure it out, kiddo. Right now, just grab what you need for the next few days." Bostic says this like he has a plan, or maybe he's just saying what he thinks I need to hear, so I don't lose my shit again and cause another fire.

Either way, he's right. There's nothing I can do about the bed and the larger items. Essentials. I just need essentials until I figure out my next step. I don't really want to go home, but if I have to, I have to. The important thing is I can't let Tucker win. He can't know that he's turned my life inside out. He can't see that I have no idea who I am at the moment or what I plan to do with myself.

Tucker just needs to see me pack up clothes and makeup. Oh. And a toothbrush—definitely a toothbrush.

I nod. "You're right. I'll find a new roommate in no time. We'll just hope Taylor doesn't stash a dead fish in the mattress before I return."

Bostic's eyes go wide, like the viciousness of women is new to him. Ha. He has no idea.

I wave off my comment. "I doubt she will, though. She's a vegetarian. Touching a fish is like wearing drugstore foundation to her. Just forget I said anything."

His nod is slow and wary, but he seems to move on from it after a few pained seconds.

"We can load up my truck with as much as we can fit today. I can ask some of the guys to come back and help take the bed apart. I could store it in my garage for the time being."

Ah, shit. See? I knew I scared him with all the dead fish talk and watery eyes.

"Don't worry about it, Boss—" Ooh. I like that nickname. "It'll be okay. You've already done so much for me."

He scoffs, but I ignore it and go back to shoving the contents of my dresser into my suitcase. Stuffing in everything I can, I finally manage to zip up my suitcase with Bostic's help.

"All done," I say, taking one last look around.

Bostic nods, grabs the suitcase with one hand, and proceeds out to the living room with a firm grunt and a "Let's go."

Can we just note that he doesn't bother with engaging the wheels? It's like he doesn't want anything slowing our exit from this hellhole.

Let's also note that Bostic needs a stuffed sea lion named after him. Pronto.

I refrain from flipping Tucker and Taylor off as we pass by, but then I feel a soft touch at my elbow. "Ainsley. I'm—"

"Get your hands off of her."

And that's why his nickname is Boss.

I let a smirk stretch out over my face as Tucker slowly backs away with his hands up. Bostic's growl is pretty freaking scary.

"Do not come near her ever again," he threatens, looking from Tucker to Taylor. "Either of you."

They both nod but it's forced. They don't want to piss off the big man, but they haven't finished saying all they need to say to me, and that's fine. I sure as shit have more I would like to say to them, but I won't. Not now. Because whatever I did to deserve Bostic's help at this moment, I'd like to keep it. And him, because he's just amazing.

Without another word, Bostic turns and heads out the front door. I follow dutifully but not before placing my hand behind my back and flipping off the two love birds. Screw them.

"You can shower at the fire station," says Bostic, descending the stairs with a hundred-pound suitcase hanging from his fist.

"Are we eating breakfast there too?"

He pauses when we reach the bottom of the stairs. "Yes. Is that okay?"

Uh, yeah, it's okay—more than okay actually. I'm starving.

And okay, for those of you who are skeptical, I know all the talks about stranger danger, and I don't plan on getting a ride in Bostic's truck, no matter how helpful he's been. But the fire station can't be that bad, right? I mean, they do background checks on these guys. If there was any place I could shower and get some breakfast, the fire station should be on the list as being safe. I figure if the law allows you to leave your baby there, then they have to be good guys, right?

"Yep. That sounds good to me. I'll even wash dishes as payment for letting me squat for the morning." I'm not a taker. I'll do my fair share.

"That won't be necessary."

I shrug when he starts walking again. "The offer stands should you change your mind," I call out to his back.

Bostic shakes his head like he isn't sure what to do with me. And that's fine. Most people aren't. I've grown accustomed to it.

"Come on." He tosses my bag in the truck. "Do you know how to get to the station?"

"Nope." GPS could probably help, but there are several fire stations around here. What if I pick the wrong one? I doubt they have the station numbers listed on the map.

Bostic rubs his forehead like a headache is brewing. "Follow me then."

I can do that. "Yes, sir."

I'm betting he regrets offering me anything at this point. And while I'm still in a state of shock, I realize that maybe my eccentric personality could have been part of the issue between Tucker and me. Tucker is calm. Reserved. Well-bred, so to speak. Not that I'm not well-bred, but I can't tell you who is a pro golfer and what charity my mom donates to every year. Tucker is exceptionally well-rounded. That's it. Well-rounded. And well, I'm not.

An ache in my chest knots up under my underwire. Today is a new day, though. Today, I can be anyone I want to be. I can start over.

I don't have to worry about impressing anyone or worrying if they like me or not.

I simply don't answer to anyone anymore.

It's a freeing feeling.

At least I hope it will be a freeing feeling once the ache in my chest wears off.

"Are you coming?" Bostic's truck is running, and I've yet to get into my car.

"Yeah, I'm coming." Because I'm free and Tucker doesn't get to tell me if this is an awful decision.

"These are the best-scrambled eggs I've ever had," I mumble between chews.

The chef of the morning, Kyle, grins, finally sitting down at the eight-person table.

I've already showered, and I've had two cups of coffee. I feel almost human again.

"Thank you. It's an old family recipe," he returns.

Chokes and thinly veiled snickers echo around the table.

"Do not let the rookie lie to you, Ainsley. His first kitchen duty ended with us putting out a fire in our own house."

Kyle's cheeks redden as his coworker, Luke (super-hot, by the way), ribs him from across the table. "It was the first time we had a fire in the station. We caught shit from the other stations for weeks."

All the guys laugh, and I feel the need to let Kyle know he isn't alone. "I set my curtains on fire last night." I shrug, catching his gaze. "But you probably knew that already. I'm just saying people do it all the time. Set their kitchens on fire, I mean. If they didn't, I guess they wouldn't need you guys, huh? Job security and all that."

The table goes quiet until Luke pushes back in his chair, resting his plate of eggs on his chest, a pretty incredible balancing act to witness. "Tell me, Ainsley, did you at least get a hit in on the prick before we got there?"

It takes me a minute, but I finally understand what he's referring to. I grin. "You mean, did I hit Tucker before you arrived?"

Luke nods.

"Sadly, no. With all the chaos of the alarms, I just yelled at him, and it wasn't even a good yell."

Don't ask me what a good yell consists of. I doubt I really know, but I feel like it would make me feel better. Like, I wouldn't still feel this weight sitting on my chest—this sadness that feels like if I just stop for a minute, it'll take over and consume me.

I look at Bostic and notice his jaw working extra hard, chewing his eggs. I guess I'm done here. I've effectively ruined their breakfast. I shovel the last bit of eggs down and push out of my chair. "Thank you for breakfast and"—I finger my wet hair—"the shower." I look at Bostic. "I promise to find a place today and get my bag out of the storage closet."

Bostic grunts but doesn't pull his eyes from the table. "Give Kyle your plate."

I glance at Kyle, who looks like he's used to cleaning up the table. "That's okay. I can wash it."

"Ainsley. Give Kyle your plate." He pushes up from the table. "I'll walk you out."

Okay. I guess there is no room for arguing. Boss is all boss when we're at the firehouse. I nod to Luke and the others. "It was nice meeting you all. Thanks for letting me crash your night and your morning."

Luke is the only one who laughs. "Anytime. We could use some fun around here."

Or the crazy, but he's kind enough not to specify.

Bostic guides me down the hall—I certainly haven't gotten my bearings—and leads me to the parking lot. "You'll come by for dinner, and I'll help you take your things to your new place." It's not a question. His stare is a warning that I better not sleep in my car again.

"Will do. And if I don't—"

"You will."

I wave off his glare and bossy tone. "Let me finish." Geez. "If I don't find a place to stay, I promise I will actually call a friend and stay with them."

One of his eyebrows rises a fraction. He doesn't believe me. That's okay because I'm lying.

"I promise," I add for good measure.

Forgive me. I had to lie to him. I know it's an awful thing to do to your newfound guardian angel, but the fact is I don't have any friends to call. If I'm unsuccessful at finding a place today, I'll have to sleep in my car. I literally do not have anywhere else to go. I'm almost two hours from home: no family, no friends, and no money. I am up shit creek. And really, I could endure one more night in the car. It wasn't that bad. Now that I know not all the bumps in the night are killers, I'll sleep much better. Maybe I'll try the front seat, though, and recline. I doubt the hump in the middle will be any more comfortable than before.

Here's the thing. I tried. I really, really tried.

"I'm sorry, Ainsley, but we're full. Maybe try a hotel?"

Lauren is lovely. Don't get me wrong. She is. But right now, I want to push her down and charge through the door and flop down on her sorority's couch.

"I don't have the money for a hotel," I beg her. "I don't get paid until Friday." And she should know that's a couple of days away. "I just need a place to stay for tonight."

Have some freaking mercy on my soul.

I'm really the one to blame. I know this. If I didn't scare off most people, I would have plenty of friends, and this would be a non-issue.

"I'm sorry, Ainsley. I wish I could, but we aren't allowed guests."

I can't believe she was able to keep a straight face. No guests? This is a freaking college, not a nunnery. Isn't that like a common occurrence to have someone passed out on the floor or the couch on the daily?

I sigh, taking a step back. This is ridiculous. "It's okay. I'll try another friend." I mean someone I have a class with, but it sounds better saying friend.

Lauren smiles hesitantly. "I hope you find something."

The scoff claws at my throat. "Me too. Thanks. Have a great night."

The door closes, and the sound of the lock clicking into place is the epic conclusion to this shitty day. I grab the strap of my bag and adjust it up on my shoulder. I can't worry about where I'm sleeping tonight. The more significant concern is how I'm going to endure this first shift with Tucker, the fuckface, and Taylor, the backstabber.

I have a feeling Bostic and his crew need to be on standby.

This catastrophe is just the beginning.

Chapter Four

Maverick

Rumor has it he's worth millions.

"Where were you this morning? I came by, but you weren't home."

"I didn't realize you were my mother." My voice is sharper than it should be, but I'm in a shitty mood after this morning's meeting. There's a reason I don't make a habit of owing people favors. I like to be the one in control. I know what I'm getting into when I accept an offer for a favor. I don't enjoy being on the other side.

"I'm not, bitch. I was just coming by to see if you wanted Vance to take care of that thing for you." His voice lowers as he realizes we're in public and have some secrets we don't want to share with the world.

"Not right now." My jaw locks up as I try really fucking hard not to hit something.

"Okaaaayyy. You want to tell me what's up your ass? Why are you being extra Maverick today?" He says the *extra Maverick* part like it's a thing—a girly thing at that.

I sigh and pull open the door to the steakhouse just outside of campus, Studs and Spuds. "Can I just have dinner without a fucking interrogation?" I know I'm projecting my anger on Sebastian. Honestly, it makes me feel better.

"Damn. Let's get your ass some food then."

The smell of charcoal and grease hits my stomach as soon as we walk in. But as much as I'm craving food, I desperately want a drink. I won't order one, though.

"Is this where what's-her-name works?" I just stare as Sebastian scans around the restaurant. It's not the first time we've been here. I wouldn't be surprised if he left what's-her-name with a bad taste in her mouth and the check on the table when he was last here.

"You're going to need to be more specific," I mutter, already eyeing Rowan crammed into a booth. "You screw so many people I can't keep them all straight."

He scoffs. "I don't sleep around *that* much."

I cock a brow. "I didn't say sleep. I said screw." Where I exchange unsavory favors, Sebastian fucks people over for likes. We're a vicious pair. "Come on. Rowan's waiting."

Sebastian casts me a wary glance and cringes. "Are you sure you wouldn't rather go over to Gigi's and make a little money? Gigi will cook you a steak."

Tempting, but no. The money would be a good distraction, but I actually need to get some things done, and if I go to Gigi's, I will gamble the night away.

"I need the Wi-Fi here, and the steak is better than Gigi's."

Sebastian shrugs. "But I can get high at Gigi's, and you can win some money." He arches his brows, pleading. "Besides, you know someone will write your paper for you."

True, but it's not a paper and not the point. "What the fuck did you do here, anyway?" Soon, we won't be welcome anywhere, and I rather like it here.

Sebastian swipes a hand through his hair. "I can't remember, dude. It's a problem."

A big problem, apparently. "You better get your shit together before you get kicked out of college." His wealthy parents would have him hidden and shipped off to whatever school they could get him into. More than likely one overseas. He's the disappointment of the family—exactly why we're friends. Like me, he has little faith in the kindness of the human population. "Havemeyer doesn't give a fuck how internet-famous you are."

"Just two?" The hostess approaches, and immediately, I know

Sebastian has forgotten his rep at this place. His eyes turn greedy, and he drops his shoulder like he has some kind of swag.

"No," I tell her all shitty, casting Sebastian a stern look and brushing past her without a backward glance. Rowan already has a drink when I slide in next to him.

He tips his chin.

I tip mine and then lean down and pull my laptop out of my bag.

"Ugh." Sebastian groans, sliding into the booth in front of us.

"I need to do a few things," I answer him, already pulling up the stats I need to review. "Then we can leave, and go to Gigi's."

Now that he mentioned it, I want to go too. We deserve to wash this awful day down with a pile of cash.

"Deal," he says excitedly. "Besides, I need a few minutes. It looks like there are new faces around here. Maybe I can cap off my night at Gigi's with one of these hotties on my lap."

It's like the last few minutes never existed. He'll either end up in jail or some jealous boyfriend's bitch.

"Unless you have some outstanding favors for a good time? I'm not opposed to taking one for the team."

My gaze travels above the edge of my laptop, eyeing the insanity that is Sebastian. "No," I clip out, getting back to my spreadsheet. "Besides, the last time you handled that particular favor, it earned you a pregnancy scare. I can't afford for you to knock them up. It voids the favor. They pay for a good time, not an eighteen-year commitment."

Sebastian grins, not offended in the slightest. "It was *one* time, and I haven't used that brand of condoms since." Rowan scoffs. "What? You don't believe me?"

That's precisely what we think, and when neither of us responds, he takes it as his cue to convince us. "I swear. I switched brands. Even if family dramas are hot right now, I don't want to go down that road just yet. I like being able to switch up my material."

For fuck's sake. The baby isn't the issue—the material is. Everything in his life is for sale. No memory is sacred. No moment is truly alone.

"What are you doing?" The shrill sound snaps all of our heads toward the bar, where two girls have their hands on a pitcher of beer. "It's my table!"

The blonde squeezed into a button-up shirt with the top four buttons undone shoves at the brunette who has a tight grip on the pitcher's handle. "It's my table, Taylor. Check the chart out front. You can't have *all* my tables." Her voice is calm, but it has an edge to it, like any minute all hell is going to break loose.

"I have ten on the blonde," says Sebastian, already passing over a ten-dollar bill.

"I have ten on the brunette," counters Rowan, digging a couple of bills out of his pocket too. "You in, Mav?"

I watch the dark-haired girl dressed in the same white shirt hold her position. "It's my table," she reiterates.

"No, your tables are over there." The blonde nods to a group of high school kids who are known not to tip well. "Tucker reassigned your zone."

At the mention of said Tucker, the brunette drops her hold on the pitcher, and the one stuffed in the shirt smiles victoriously. "Don't try taking my tables again, or I'll tell Sam. No one needs you bringing your drama to work."

"I change my mind. I hope the brunette kicks this bitch's ass." I don't acknowledge Sebastian's comment.

"Is it wrong that I hope she slams her head on the bar?" That's Rowan. He's always the violent one of our group.

I turn and face him. "What do you think this is? WWE?"

He shrugs unapologetically. "A nice reality check never hurt anyone."

I scoff. If Rowan is the one giving you that reality check, it does.

I shake my head and turn back to the bar where the girls have now separated.

"Can I get you gentlemen something to drink?"

The dipshit waiter we were saddled with steps in my eye line, blocking my view of the door behind the bar where I assume the girls disappeared into.

"I'll take a Scotch, neat," says Sebastian. "He'll take one too." Sebastian tips his chin at me.

"No scotch, just water," I correct him.

"I am so sick of this virgin version of Maverick," he whines, kicking his foot onto Rowan's and my bench. Rowan knocks it off quickly. "Where's the reckless guy I once—"

I aim a glare right at his playing hand. One look. That's all it would take for Rowan to jump across the table and break it. Would I do that to one of my closest friends? Maybe.

"Shut the fuck up," Rowan growls for me.

We don't feed the rumors of who I used to be. We only feed the rumors about who I am now. The last thing Sebastian wants us to do is start talking about each other's pasts. His has more secrets than mine.

Our waiter clears his throat awkwardly. "Anything else for you right now?" Finally, I look away and at the waiter still standing here talking and not fetching our goddamned drinks.

"Ye—" I start but then read his name tag. Tucker. "Are you the manager, Tucker?" Underneath is his title in small words reading assistant, not manager. Is this who the girls were talking about?

He stands straighter, proud of his assistant title. "Assistant, yes. Is there a problem?" His tone is professional, but a level of fear bubbles just beyond his flat and dull affect.

The little sniveling shit in front me is a college student. I've seen him around. I didn't know his name, but that's not surprising. I don't know most people's names. I can't be bothered learning names. You're either in a contract with me or not. Those who aren't are at the table with me. No one else matters.

I glance back at the bar, waiting to see if the brunette has come back out.

She hasn't.

"Not yet," I say flatly. I dismiss him by swiping, waking up my laptop, and pulling up an email. The girl behind the bar is not my problem. In fact, she's not a problem. From the sound of it, this asshole and his bitchy little helper are the problem.

"Uh . . . Okay then. I'll get you those drinks now."

None of us acknowledge his existence.

I go back to my spreadsheet and Sebastian back to texting.

I don't know how much time passes. It seems like only minutes, but when Rowan's phone dings, it has me pulling my head up and realizing I now have a plate of food in front of me. "When did you order?" Where the fuck was I?

Sebastian snorts. "About twenty minutes ago. You were doing that weird, chanting thing."

My lips purse. "It's called brainstorming."

"It's called schizophrenia. We've asked you to stop talking to the voices, Mav. It's weirding us out." He's fucking lying, and his deep baritone laugh confirms it.

"I'm working out scenarios in my head, dick. I'm not answering voices."

Sebastian shrugs. "Seems like an awful lot of chatter going on in there. I'm telling you, clear the demons. Smoke a joint and get laid, it'll clear all the voices out."

It's pointless to attempt a conversation with him.

"I'll pass. I've seen the shit you do high."

He leans forward, a big stupid grin stretching across his face. "Did you see my video last week? The shit got removed because they thought it was porn. Got over three million views, though, before it was taken down."

Rowan makes a disgusted noise. "Dude, we told you we don't watch or heart your shit. Stop asking us, you're making it weird."

Unfortunately, it's not weird for me. Sebastian and I have been friends for too long. I've seen his strange, and it no longer fazes me.

"Did you see it, Mav?" He sounds like a little kid, eager for praise.

I cut him a really-do-you-think-I-would-watch-my-friend-fuck-a-girl look.

He waves me off. "It wasn't that bad. All over the clothes stuff, but the noises she made. . ." He bites his knuckle and makes this face of ecstasy. "So fucking hot."

I finger the collar of my shirt. Fuck. I've been sweating. I really did get consumed.

Sebastian catches the movement. "See? So fucking scary. I'm on my third drink."

"I just get worked up when I'm going through all these numbers. It's fine."

Rowan doesn't look convinced. "Aren't you taking the same Calculus as me?"

I shut my laptop and stuff it in my bag. "It's harder for me than it is for you."

Grabbing the knife from the rolled napkin, I cut into my steak. Perfect. "Thanks for ordering for me." I know it was Sebastian.

"You would starve if we didn't."

I doubt that.

"And I don't want to hear any excuses that you can't go to Gigi's after we leave this snooze fest."

Ah. How could I forget?

I take a bite of my steak, and Rowan's phone dings again.

"Do you have a problem I should be concerned about?" I nod at his screen, knowing he's playing online poker just by the sound of the ding. I know it because once upon a time, I played it.

"If I did"—he pauses, flashing me a smirk—"I wouldn't ask for your help." But he would get it anyway. "I'm a big boy."

"We know," chimes in Sebastian, never looking up from his phone. "And if you don't lay off all those fries, you're going to be an even bigger boy."

Rowan tosses a fry, and I try not to grin. I'm mid-bite of the only thing I wanted tonight when I hear Sebastian groan and throw his fork down. "Can we not eat without being interrupted?"

I chew the greatest steak ever and swallow. "This isn't a date. Relax," I aim at Sebastian before wiping my hands and meeting the eyes of the person who is crazy enough to interrupt us.

"I'm so sorry to bother you, Mr. Lexington."

Mr. Lexington. That one never gets old. It sounds like he's speaking to my father.

I eye this frat boy's shorts and Hawaiian shirt. "You have fifteen seconds to make your case."

I don't have time for this. My steak is getting cold, and I didn't finish my spreadsheet. Neither of which makes me happy nor puts me in a very receptive mood.

"I need a favor," he rushes out.

I hear Sebastian mumble into a mouthful of mashed potatoes. "Shocker."

"What's your name?"

I don't really care, but he's nervous, and I don't have all day for him to spit it out.

"Todd."

I nod. "Great. So, Todd, this is how this works."

He nods eagerly.

"You have exactly five seconds left before I pick up my fork and resume eating, after which my friend Rowan here will escort you away from our table."

His hands drop to his side.

"My suggestion is to speed the fuck up."

If you're desperate enough to interrupt my dinner, you're desperate enough to ask me for a favor in one breath.

"I'm short on rent money!"

Rowan rolls his eyes. This particular favor is common amongst college students. The first time away from home and they blow student loan money, Mom and Dad's money, etc. Sometimes for girls. Sometimes for drugs but never for actual bills.

"How much?" My fingers itch to grab the fork. Ever since that first bite, I'm starving.

"Fifteen hundred."

Huh. I expected more. Most of the time, they come to me when they are nearing eviction.

"I need the money by tonight," he adds, his thick neck working to swallow his nerves.

Frankly, I couldn't give a fuck when he needs the money. I'm never rushed. "I take thirty percent to be repaid in thirty days plus your IOU."

They aren't good terms for Todd, but they are very profitable terms for me.

He nods reluctantly. "I can do that."

I reach into my back pocket and fish out a card and a Sharpie, writing the words IOU across the back. I slide it to the edge of the table. "Give your number to Sebastian." I nod to Bash just in case this kid doesn't know him. "He'll send you the info."

"But I need the money by tonight!"

Again, I don't fucking care.

"You get the money when I say you get the money. Unless you want to add a rush fee?"

I finger another card. *Don't do it, kid. Don't get that desperate.*

He shakes his head. "I can wait."

They always can. Even if I do plan on giving him the money tonight—I do honor deals after all—I don't like being rushed, especially when I'm eating. "Number?"

He calls out the numbers, and Sebastian begrudgingly types it into his phone.

"We'll be in touch," I say, dismissing him by picking up my fork and taking a bite. Fuck. Now it's cold. I sigh into my plate just as Todd scampers off.

"Why do you let them ask for favors at any time of the day?"

I level Rowan with a look. "The best ones always come at the worst time. Nothing beats a desperate soul willing to do anything for a favor."

"Yeah, but . . ."

"Better here than my house." I wave off his annoyed look and move the food around on my plate. "This shit's cold," I whine.

"No one cares. If you hadn't been calling out for your demon friends earlier, you would have had most of it eaten by now."

Sebastian, always the smartass.

"Again, I was not chanting. I was brainstorming."

His eyes go squinty. "You were chanting."

I go to argue, but Rowan beats me to it. "Just shut up and eat. We're ready to leave."

Leave or play poker? I guess it doesn't matter. I accomplished the majority of what I needed to do tonight.

"Ask that waitress to reheat your food."

I catch Sebastian's half-assed concern and follow his finger to where it's pointing to the brunette we saw arguing earlier behind the bar.

"Excuse me, Miss," calls Sebastian. She turns, pausing just a moment like she isn't sure if she should acknowledge him. "Yeah, you. Come here."

I feign interest in her snug white top with a large brown stain down the front. Did she go to the back and throw down with the blonde? If so, I'm impressed.

"Can I help you, gentlemen?"

Rowan makes a disbelieving sound. We're no gentlemen.

"Can you have this reheated?" I ask.

Her eyes narrow at my plate before flicking up to meet mine. "I'll get your waiter."

I slide the plate to the edge of the table. "That won't be necessary."

There's something to be said for a gambling man. Risk is always our reward. I live by the challenge and die by the loss. And right now, I want to see the cards this girl is holding. Is she a doormat, or does she have some fight in her? I couldn't tell earlier, but now, I'm in the betting mood. Those stormy eyes of hers aren't submissive. So why shut down at the mention of her assistant manager? Is she scared she'll be fired?

Her finger slides the plate back toward me. "It will be necessary. Tucker will be happy to reheat your food."

I slide it back, a smirk playing at the corner of my lips. "I want you to do it." I shove the plate a little farther until it meets her waist. "And quickly. I'm tired of waiting."

I realize about two seconds too late, as my delicious steak and potatoes slide down my shirt, that I was right. Those eyes did have some fight in them.

"Oops," she says, feigning shock. "I'm so sorry. I will have Tucker order you another." Her eyes go hard as she backs away from the table. "I'll even have him order it warm."

Rowan shoots up from the table about to teach our little waitress a lesson.

"It's fine," I assure him, knocking the remnants of food onto the floor before lifting my gaze to the hotheaded waitress. "I appreciate that"—I read her name tag and say with a low warning—"Ainsley."

Her throat works. She's not so big now.

"Look, I'm—"

I cut her off. "Going to tell my waiter to bring my food now before I call Sam personally."

She agrees, nodding up and down. "Yes, sir—I mean, of course. Right away. Again, I'm so sorry."

Once Ainsley has disappeared into the back, I manage to get most of the food off my shirt before—"I told you we should have gone to Gigi's."

Chapter Five

Ainsley

Rumor has it she's banging an old dude.

"You threw food on him?"

The horror in Boss's eyes doesn't give me the warm and fuzzies. I'd just about had myself convinced in the car that it was no big deal, accidents with plates happen all the time. For all the hot guy knew, I was a new waitress with butterfingers.

I look down at Bostic's feet, his black combat-style boots, shiny and clean, unlike my scuffed ballet flats. "Technically, I didn't throw it," I say hesitantly, raising my gaze to meet his. It's not as aghast as it was a few seconds ago. Maybe the killer cup of sweet tea I made is helping.

"So, it was an accident, then?" The one arched brow he raises dares me to lie.

"Uhh . . . I wouldn't say an accident. More like . . . his fault."

The other eyebrow rises just a fraction. "His fault?" I'm starting to believe that coming back to the firehouse after my shift was a bad idea.

I blow out a breath that makes my lips vibrate with a funny noise. "Fine, okay. I did it on purpose." Hair falls across my shoulder, blocking Bostic's and Luke's—who's pretending not to listen as he stirs the pot of spaghetti noodles for the ten thousandth time—view of my reddened cheeks.

"Did he do something to upset you?"

Yes! This is precisely the question Bostic should be asking. Except, how can I admit the truth without sounding like a hateful ass that needs to be shamed? I bite my lip and flash a look of help to Luke, who quickly turns back around and stirs. Traitor.

"He did." I nod several times, hoping Bostic will jump in with another question. Spoiler alert: he doesn't.

Okay.

No big deal. Women lose their shit all the time. If they didn't, men would act like they ran the world. A little bit of crazy never hurt anyone.

Except for the dick-ish dude's shirt—that's for sure ruined. He can kiss wearing that sexy as sin, dark button-down goodbye.

"What did he do to deserve his dinner on his lap?"

Okay, now Boss's tone seems like he's trying to make me feel bad. It's working.

I stand from the table, grab his empty tea glass, and go to the refrigerator and pour him some more. He's going to need it after this story.

"Taylor was giving me a hard time," I admit with a soft shrug. "She had Tucker take all the good tipping tables and left me with the high school kids and some of the frat guys. You know those guys never leave a tip."

Luke flashes me a sad look, but Bostic's stare never wavers.

"I know that wasn't a good reason to take out my frustrations on a customer." It was supposed to be my table, but Tucker changed my zone at the last minute. "But Tucker had warned me off their tables, and I had enough drama already, but the guy kept insisting I take his food back and heat it."

If I hadn't been in such a pissy mood, I would have stopped to appreciate his glacier blue eyes—and I'm not talking about the pretty, light, icy color like you find above the water's surface, warning you of impending doom. No. I'm talking about the dark menacing glacier that sits just below the surface, waiting to destroy the next unsuspecting victim. He was frighteningly beautiful, the slight twitch of his lips luring you in as his next breath destroyed you. And I fell epically for his bait.

"Why couldn't you have just taken his food and heated it? Would it have been that bad?"

I finish pouring Bostic's tea and make my way back to the table, setting it down harder than necessary. "Don't start making sense, Boss. I can't take it." I suck in a deep breath and take a seat. "All I'm saying is I didn't want any more trouble. I simply wanted to get Tucker, but he started doing this thing with his mouth."

Luke makes a noise, turning around. "What kind of thing? Like something kinky?"

It's the first time I've smiled all night. I turn, touching my finger to the corner of my lip. "No. It was like this twitch. Like he was mocking me or something." I think back to the man with the thick head of hair that looked mussed and wild as if he got out of the shower and dried it with a towel and didn't bother taking a comb to it. Right. His lip thing. "It was as if he was trying to get a reaction out of me."

Luke cocks his head to the side. "Like he wanted to piss you off?"

I nod. "Yes. Exactly. I'm telling you, he wanted me to be mean to him."

The groan that comes out of Bostic is low enough that I can ignore. "I'm sure that wasn't the case."

I shrug. "You weren't there. You didn't see this guy. He wanted a reaction, so I gave it to him."

"What did Tucker say afterward?"

Eh. That's where the night went even more downhill.

"He screamed that I had lost my mind, and I had no idea who I was fucking with." I shrug. "Apparently, the guy is someone Tucker likes to kiss ass to because he comped their meal and spent a while talking to them before they left."

"Did the guy look upset when he left?" This was from nosy Luke.

"Not really. His friend passed Tucker a card as they were leaving." I shrug. "He didn't even eat his new steak." Not that I can blame him, but why not take it home?

"Are you going to lose your job?"

I make a face. "I hope not. All Tucker said when he returned was that I better be grateful he still cared about me."

I pretend to gag.

My no-nonsense fire-savior doesn't let me down. "So, you aren't fired?"

"No, Boss." I smile. "Not yet. Your girl will get to see another payday."

"What do you think he meant by—"

I can't discuss this anymore. "I don't know, Boss Hog, but let's just call it a win and move on."

He frowns at my new nickname. "Were you able to find anywhere to stay tonight?"

Lie. Just lie. It's for his own good.

"Ye—"

Those dark, beady eyes narrow at my fidgeting hands. "Yeeeaaah," I drawl. "That would be a negative, Captain. I tried really hard, but no one had any available space." And they are all twattastic, but I don't need to tell Bostic that. He probably already knows, being the closest fire station to the college.

"You'll stay here tonight. You'll take my room," he says, sounding all hero-y.

"You have a room?" Do all firehouses have rooms?

"Yes. The others share sleeping quarters."

I feel a grin slide onto my face as I cut Luke a look that clearly shows my amusement with this whole firemen hierarchy.

"But, where will you sleep?"

Boss nods to Luke. "In one of the other beds."

Luke looks like he tasted something gross. Guess nothing sucks worse than sleeping with your boss. I make myself laugh, thinking of the two huge dudes tucked into their twin-sized beds while one probably nods off promptly at 9:00 p.m. while the other probably has ample amounts of phone sex until he passes out from exhaustion.

"One night," says Luke, draining the noodles and giving me the side-eye. "One night is all you get. The captain snores."

I'm sure that's the issue, but nevertheless, their kindness is unnecessary. "Look, you guys are so sweet with feeding me and not reporting me to the authorities, but really, my car is quite comfortable."

"No."

"You didn't let me finish," I say to the angry-looking man. "All I need is possibly a pillow, and the floodlight left on. Simple." I dust my hands off like my solution is done. "No one needs to give up their bed. Besides, I bet you'd be breaking like a ton of rules."

Bostic grunts. "You'll stay here. End of discussion."

"Come on, Boss H—"

His chair scrapes along the floor as his big body folds out. "I'm going to take a shower."

He walks off, leaving me with my mouth hanging open. "Did he just cut me off?"

Luke grins, mixing the noodles with the sauce. "You don't argue with Cap. His word is law around here."

"I wasn't arguing." Okay, I was, but really, they don't need to break any more rules for me. "I was just suggesting you be like a Motel 6 and leave the light on for me."

Luke snorts. "I think that slogan means they will leave the interior lights on for you. Not toss you a pillow and flip on the bug light."

"The floodlights, not the bug light. I wouldn't be able to sleep if that thing was zapping poor little bugs all night."

Luke and I both laugh.

"Fine," I say after a minute. "But I want to slide down the fire pole before bed."

The thing about sleeping in a firehouse is that you don't really sleep. It's more like that movie *Groundhog Day*, where you repeat the same day over and over. Except instead of repeating the same day, you repeat the same fifteen minutes of sleep before the fire alarm thingy goes off. It was worse than sleeping in my car. I assured Boss that I would find somewhere to crash from here on out. I appreciate their kindness, but there is no way I will make it another night in the firehouse. Sliding down the pole was cool, though.

"I don't know, Mom," I mumble into the phone, scanning the corkboard outside of Westminster Hall. "Maybe he was removing the stick up her vagina and fell in."

My mom, who had been ready to drive up here and cut a bitch

when I finally told her about Tucker and Taylor, laughs on the phone. The sound is soothing and almost convinces me to take her offer of coming home this weekend. I could use a hug and someone stuffing me full of food and doing all my laundry.

"I just don't know what happened to that boy. He's always adored you."

He adored me all right. He loved me and the spare key to my apartment so he could fuck my roommate. I know, I know. Jesus take the wheel and all that. But it burns, right down to my little heartbroken soul. These couple of days have not lessened the burn. Tucker and I had plans. Legit plans of being a family and traveling the country. How am I just supposed to move on from those plans?

Hell, I don't even know if those were my plans or his plans. Is that still what I want? Why is all of this so confusing?

"Well, baby, think of it this way, you have your whole life ahead of you with a clear and unobstructed path. It's a fresh start. Now you can figure out what you want and do it. Tucker won't be there to weigh in with his opinions."

She's right. I know she is. And honestly, I've told myself that, but I still want to nut punch him a few times.

"I know, Mama. And I will. I think I just need a little time to grieve the loss of us, you know?"

She sighs into the phone.

She knows. If anyone on this planet can relate to this situation, it's my mother. When she was my age, she fell madly in love and whoops, got pregnant. Her beau, we never speak his name, disappeared, transferring schools and leaving her with an unfinished degree and an infant. She dropped out of school, moved back home, and became a waitress. She never married and ended up being a jam up manager at the local diner called Mae's.

No, she isn't Mae. But Mae taught her everything she knows, and now Mae's is opening another store in Atlanta. Mom's proud to have been such an integral part of this expansion. So is Grandma, but she would never admit it.

All this to say, my mom is not a proponent of men. The only

man in her life is the cutest dog ever, Opie. Together, they live a single, happy life.

"Loss, any kind of loss, is hard. Take all the time you need. Find yourself, Ainsley. The world is a vast place, and there's no need in limiting yourself over one prick with a saggy ass."

"Mom!" I can't help the snort that escapes.

"You're going to hell for saying such things."

But it's true. Ten billion squats could not help Tucker's ass. It's flat as a pancake. So flat that you can't even see the curve in his underwear. But when you love someone, you love them for all their faults and imperfections.

"Well, if I'm going to hell, then I'll sit by your father, so I can torture him forever."

I smile, noting all the *in search of* flyers. There's several, but they are all out of my price range.

"I think that's the perfect punishment he deserves."

I try not to encourage her online stalking of my father. It's been twenty years, but I guess when you've been burned as she has, you want to know what someone has that you didn't. I've never met or spoken to my father. He's been a ghost in our lives, and that's just fine with me. My grandfather was the father in my life. I never wanted for love or attention, so there was no need to seek out my sperm donor. I'd rather not know if he's equal to or less than my thoughts of him after all these years.

I can feel my mom's smile through the phone. I miss her crazy ass. "Are you looking for somewhere else to stay?"

I nod at the bulletin board. "Yep. I'm looking as we speak. Not much is listed that I can afford."

The line goes silent, and I know what she's doing. "No, you aren't taking another loan on your retirement account. I'll be fine. I'm sure there are rooms I can afford somewhere. I've only hit one board so far. There's like a bazillion here, not to mention the ones posted online. I got this."

She exhales a worried breath. I'm only lying a little bit. This isn't the first board I checked. It's about the eighth, but she doesn't need to know that. The woman is a fixer. She'd auction off her soul if she thought I needed something.

"I can ask your grandmother for some money," she says, her voice strained.

"We're not that desperate," I respond.

That gets a laugh out of her.

"I promise I'm fine. I can make this work. I just need to find the right person." And she has to be here somewhere on one of these boards. All I have to do is keep searching.

"Okay, sweetheart, if you're sure. You promise to let me know if you can't, though, right?"

I nod again and realize she can't see me some eighty miles away through the phone. "I promise." Opie, the one and only man in her life, whines in the background. "It sounds like Opie is ready for his afternoon walk."

She baby-talks to him, and I miss what she says, but he stops whining, so she must have assured him they were heading out soon. "Call me tonight?" she asks, as shuffling crackles over the speaker.

"I promise."

I'm sure I'll need some comforting when I'm sleeping in my car again. I won't even be able to sleep at the fire station because I assured Boss I would secure a place tonight. And the whole alarm thing was awful. I just can't do it another night.

Mom and I hang up, and I stuff my phone back into my bag. There has to be something here. I'm not picky. If I could find another part-time job, I could afford the steeper rents posted. Either way, I have options. It's just a little slim today.

Scanning, I find listings from everything from turtle sitting (which doesn't sound too awful) to tutoring to sharing a one-bed-room, one mattress apartment. Yeah, like that's going to happen, Clint, whoever you are. That's not a real listing. Our fine Clint is looking for a hook-up. You have to be careful with ads. I've seen *Single White Female*, and if that movie didn't teach me enough about stranger dan-ger, then the last two years at Havemeyer and these bulletin boards sealed the horror.

Rumor has it these boards are mostly hook-up ads. Any guy

looking for a roommate is a no-go. I would never want a guy for a roommate anyway. After sleeping over at Tucker's apartment, I feel pretty damn sure that guy roommates are basically code for a free, live-in maid. I'm not about that life. I want a quiet roommate who enjoys studying and contributing to her share of groceries and cooking. Picking up after herself and a Netflix subscription is also a plus. But I'm not going to be picky. For now, I'll settle for a roof over my head and running air conditioner.

This board scavenge has been a waste. There's nothing here I can afford or that I want to tempt fate with and have some kind of Ted Bundy roommate. I don't mean that to sound like this is some kind of war zone around here. It isn't. Havemeyer is a bustling university. The problem is it's a rumor mill of epic proportions. Half the time, I can't distinguish the rumors from the truth. So, in instances that I'm unsure between fact and fiction, I err on the side of caution.

I'm not down to become some captive or frat girl being passed around between the guys. I just want to do my time, get my degree, and move on with my life sans Tucker and his horrific morning breath.

I check my watch and realize I don't have enough time to check out the board outside of Morgan Hall. That one will have to wait until after I endure a two-hour Behavioral Psychology class where I can spend the whole time self-analyzing what happened between Tucker's and my relationship. Then, once I realize it's merely a case of it's not me, it's you, I can move onto self-discovery. Who am I without Tucker? What the hell am I going to do after I graduate? Clearly, I'm not buying a house with him and making wedding plans. Do I go home? Stay in Atlanta and find a job? Who knows? All I know is that I made the fatal mistake my mother always warned me about.

In loving Tucker, I lost sight of me.

Women should never lose sight of their hopes and dreams. They should be individuals that are amplified by their mates—she for real used the term mate. Women should always be independent because the older you get (her lecture, not mine), the more you forget who that woman is. I'm pretty sure she's speaking from experience, and at the time she gave me that sound piece of advice, I was already in love with Tucker. My relationship was going to be different from hers and my dad's. We were different.

Until we weren't.

But I can't change what happened.

People make their own choices. Tucker made his by slipping his dick into my roommate while I slept, and he supposedly couldn't. It's not my fault he's a whore. It's not Taylor's fault that she's a conniving little cunt.

We are who we are. Ugliness and all.

Hustling, I make it to the lecture with mere seconds to spare. This breakup has shaken me. I've never *just made it*. I'm always in my seat with at least ten minutes to spare. Tucker thought it was annoying that I was always on time, but I thought it was respectful. Why set a time if you don't intend to be there at said time?

But we've already established Tucker is a dick, so I need to move on. He's already invaded my thoughts for far too long this morning. I take a seat toward the back and pull out my laptop—thank you, Boss—and boot it up. I'm not a heavy note-taker, but occasionally Dr. Mathis will say something note-worthy.

And I'm in desperate need to play Who Wants to Be a Millionaire.

Don't judge me. Since I've basically been a nomad, I haven't had much time to dedicate to my quest of millionaire-dom. I know that's not a word, but you knew exactly what I meant.

The game is my security blanket. My home away from home. And seeing how I no longer have a home, I'm more than a tad bit needy.

My finger hovers over the trackpad. Do I have enough time for one game? Eh—"No, dude. He's never here. I heard he was locked up for the weekend."

The male voice startles me, and I click open a new document instead of my game. Guess that's a sign—no games until after class. Wait, no games until after I find a roommate.

"That's why he's looking for a roommate. The last one moved out. Rumor has it he couldn't deal with the cops knocking on the door all the time."

Great. Rumors. In my head, I clear my throat like I'm a WWE announcer. "This morning, wearing the distressed jeans, weighing in at 200 pounds of bullshit is Stan! His competitor and partner in the spread of inaccurate and stupid information, weighing in at 235 pounds of bullshit, is Booker! Hold your tits, ladies. You'll be liable to lose your bras over this malarkey."

"I don't know about you, but I'd kill for a peek inside Maverick's apartment."

Stan, I think, makes this giddy noise. "I heard there is a plethora of women in and out of there at all times of the day. Can you imagine?"

I snort. I can imagine it being annoying that you'd never get any sleep with all that commotion. And cops? Yeah, I'll pass. I'd like for my first background check to come back clean.

"Pussy would be aplenty. If I weren't locked into my lease, I would gladly take his empty room."

Booker scoffs. "No, you wouldn't. Last time you saw Maverick Lexington, you ran, and all he did was shuffle the cards in his hands."

"You know what those cards do!" Stan whisper hisses. "Paul in my Econ class won't even speak to me since he took one of those cards."

I don't know who Paul is, and I've only ever heard of—well, I do know who Maverick is. I don't know him, know him, but I've heard of him. Maverick Lexington is well-known around this campus for the deck of playing cards that he keeps tucked in his back pocket. Rumor is, if you need a favor, you can go to him, and he will grant it. On one condition. You will owe him a favor. He's like our own magic genie. Or so I've heard. He could be some geek behind an iPad for all I know. I'm just saying, I've heard of him.

And, no. It's a stupid idea.

I'm not that desperate.

Chapter Six

Ainsley

Rumor has it she was caught stalking her ex.

Okay, I am that desperate.

One hundred and twenty-five percent that desperate.

After I endured the longest bitchfest ever, by two grown-ass men, I hightailed it out of class and across to the bulletin board outside of Morgan Hall.

If you need used sheets and cat toys, they have you covered.

If you're like me and need a room, the board was fresh out. Just like my options.

I have no choice.

We all witnessed this, right?

Frank is a no-go.

The firehouse is a big nightmare, not to mention they could get into big trouble allowing me to crash there.

Then there's my car—loyal but not very comfy, but still an option. I just might have to find a better parking spot—aka hide from Boss. He won't go for me sleeping there for the rest of the semester.

And then there's Maverick Lexington—granter of all the things. Or so I've heard. If the rumor is real, and he really needs a roommate, I might be able to solve my problem quickly. If the rumor is untrue, I'll ask for a favor. Heaven knows I could use one—or five—right about now.

I mean, how bad could it be?

He probably just wants someone to do his homework or wash his car.

I'm not proud. I could totally handle that.

I put my car in park and stare at the white-washed building.

Typical and basic.

Those are the words that come to mind when I take in my potential home. Surprisingly, with all the rumors that have circulated around Maverick, I feel like it should look something more like Elsa's castle—frozen and cut off from the outside world. Not a decent, mid-scale apartment complex. It could use a little color and some shrubbery, but it looks clean and well maintained. And really, that's all I need—clean sheets in a dick-bag free zone.

I get out and check the text, verifying that I am at the right place. How awkward would that be? I'd probably be banned from this complex if I knocked on a stranger's door, begging for a favor. I think most places frown on scaring their residents.

But that's what the text from Maverick says. At least, I think it's Maverick. Considering I didn't know where he lived, I did what most sane people would and stalked him on social media. Which, in all honestly, was relatively disappointing. His social media profile consisted of a picture of a playing card and his phone number. No cute selfies or photos of his dog graced his page—just that one single picture and his first name. Maverick is a man of few words, apparently.

I grab my bag and debate if I should text him that I'm here. He didn't seem very responsive when I asked if I could talk to him with a little heart emoji. The text was cute and friendly, but it was returned with an address—nothing more. Not even an emoji.

So I'm going with not texting and just showing up. Hopefully, he's here. It never crossed my mind that I could be walking into a different Maverick's apartment. Surely there isn't another one with a playing card as his trademark. That would be insane.

But then again, I never thought Taylor would have banged Tucker on my good throw—people surprise you.

I stride up the pathway and up the stairs to the apartment listed on the text. I don't know what I expected to find—maybe a dropbox for your soul? Certainly not the underwhelmingly plain door. Perhaps

I have the wrong apartment? However, the nerves in my belly warn me that looks can be deceiving. It's his apartment. The stale quiet of the empty hallway gives it away. Most complexes who rent to students are lively and loud. But not this one. This one gives off a secretive vibe. Like you need a code word to enter the real complex that lurks behind plain doors.

Or maybe, the quietness can contribute to the level of fear that living with the rumored devil is, plus a thousand. They could be scared to death to make a peep. A few months back, I heard about this one guy who had made a deal with Maverick and had to quit the football team to become Maverick's security due to the flurry of death threats he received from family members.

I can't remember his name, but I bet with a little snooping online, I could find it.

The point is, deals with Maverick have been rumored to ruin lives and destroy families. But the way I see it, I don't have anything left for him to ruin. My mom is the only family I have, and she would never let us be torn apart. She will most certainly be upset with the decision I'm making, but she's my mother. She'll have to forgive me.

Besides, I've never paid much mind to rumors anyway. They aren't true ninety-nine percent of the time—at least about me. So I doubt all the rumors about Maverick are either. Though, I imagine some rumors hold a kernel of truth. For example, I'm not a pyro, nor did I try to set my apartment complex on fire. But I did set the curtains on fire. So see, some truths are hidden in the rumors—which does not make me feel better standing at Maverick's door. If the rumors have any truth to them, then he's not a nice guy.

Deep breath. You can do this, Ainsley. All you have to do is knock on the door.

I eye the intimidating door once more, noting at closer inspection streaks through stained handprints just below the handle. Are they the tears of his victims? Were they begging for their lives? Their friends' lives?

It's perfectly sane that I'm here, right? It's sane that I'm desperate enough to offer up anything Maverick chooses, just for a place to stay. Crazy people don't know they're crazy when they do things. I do. So this can't be crazy.

Granted, I haven't thought about the possibility of Maverick turning me down. It's not like there is a rule book or something. I tried to find out more online, but we all know how that went. And asking his victims—I mean, his clients—wouldn't have gotten me the truth. If there has ever been one consistent rumor, it's been that no one talks about Maverick Lexington's favors. You thought I was going to say Fight Club, didn't you?

Either way, there's a really good chance I'm wrong, and Maverick will call the cops or vanquish me straight to hell with his other minions. Worse, he could invite me in for a drink and a blow job. I'm pretty sure he wouldn't grant my favor after seeing the horrific sight of me gagging around his dick like I had food poisoning. Sucking dick is not my forte. I never got good at it, and Tucker never really cared. So it's not on my sexual résumé. It's one of those things I would need an online class for.

Sleeping with him, though—even if he's a geek behind an iPad—might not be too horrible. Not like I'm a whore or anything, but I'm just saying that might not be the worst thing in the world for a woman scorned. It'd be like a nice little fuck you to Tucker with an orgasm on top, but that's beside the point. The point is, there are so many rumors surrounding Maverick that I could be walking into an ambush.

I have no idea who is going to answer this door or what they will say. What if this whole card thing is a scam? I mean, what if it's some old geezer who gets his rocks off making up rumors on the online campus forum? It could happen. This could be a whole catfish scam for all I know, but I'm desperate, and Bostic is not going to allow me to keep sleeping in my car and lying. Besides, I'm not a person who lies on the regular. The fact that I've probably told more lies now than I ever have before is not doing good things for my soul.

Truthfully, the two guys who mentioned Maverick was looking for a roommate could be full of shit. But I'm going to knock anyway. Even if it is some old dude behind this door, I'm going to offer up my soul, or whatever it's going to take, and I'm going to beg. Even if I have to get down on my knees and do it. I need a place to stay. I can't go home. I'm not willing to admit defeat to Tucker and Taylor. They do not get to dictate my future at this university. This is my life, and I have control.

I am in control.

I curl my fingers into a fist and contemplate just pounding on the door like some guy would do, but I don't because he may come out ready to fight, and then things would only get awkward. I'm just going to be a girl and rap a few dainty times. Maybe he'll have a little compassion seeing as I'm a lowly desperate girl.

Lightly, I rap on the door and then pause. Dammit. I didn't knock hard enough. Should I knock one more time or leave it? Great, now I'm obsessing. I should have knocked like I was the police. Fine, I'll just give it another minute and put my ear to the door like most sane humans. You know it's not that crazy of an idea. If I hear footsteps, I'll know my knocking was loud enough. If I hear nothing in the next sixty seconds, I'll knock again but harder.

With my ear to the door, I strain to hear. Nothing clatters, nothing groans, it's just silent. And right when I pull back to knock again, the deadbolt clicks. Oh shit. Oh shit. Oh shit. He's unlocking the door— or someone is unlocking the door.

I step back just as the door swings open with force, and a rock-hard body fills up the empty space. My gaze starts at the top, noting the firm grip he has on the molding. The muscles strain against his taut skin, flexing as he leans forward, cocking his head to the side. His face—

Oh shit.

This is bad—really, really bad.

"Oh no."

His scowl curves up into a lazy grin.

"Waitress," he purrs. His voice has this melody of a luring song— one meant to pull you in and destroy your heart in a matter of seconds.

It doesn't affect me, though.

"Dick at table forty-three, the princess who needed his steak warmed."

Slap me with a stupid sticker because I have lost my damn mind. Why did I just say that? Yes, he was the rude-ass who insisted I warm his food up, and yes, he's the one I dumped said food on, but that was yesterday, and I have moved on. Hopefully, so has he.

"Dick, huh?" He drops one of his massive arms and rubs a spot just above—ah damn, his nipple is pierced. Not to mention the whole right side of his ribs are covered in a massive tribal tattoo. Even on his left, a smaller tattoo wraps from his back and ends on his stomach, teasing me to gaze longingly at the ridiculous set of six-pack abs between them.

Why is life not fair?

I drag in a deep breath and try to let any animosity of yesterday go. "Can we start over?"

That lazy grin of his falls in an instant. "No."

No. Okay. Well, that's not good.

Sighing, I watch as his body goes rigid, and his arm goes back to the top of the doorframe, blocking any view behind him. His icy blue eyes stare back at me unyielding and hard, not the same guy who grinned when he first saw me. "I'm sorry about last night." Hopefully, my sincerity will soften him.

"What can I do for you?"

Okay, so we're going with a hard no on being softened.

With no hint of emotion, other than the apparent tone of boredom, one can surmise that Maverick will not be bought with sweetness and apologies. I'm going with plan B, which I'm making up as I go.

"Are you Maverick?" I could have said that a little stronger and without the slight tremor.

He drops his hands and reaches into his back pocket, producing a handful of playing cards. Oh no. I'm not prepared for it to get real this fast. What if those two idiots in class were right? What if I'm never the same after this?

"How much is it worth to you?" He drawls, producing a marker.

I swallow and straighten, plastering a snide grin on my face. "Nothing. Just producing the cards tells me I have the right person."

He nods, seemingly pleased with my answer. "I would say you're a smart girl, but the fact you're standing at my door speaks otherwise."

This ass.

"I need a favor."

Yes, girl. Be bold. Don't let him intimidate you.

His brows arch and the smirk he flashes pisses me off.

"You do grant favors, don't you? Or are they just rumors to get you laid?"

My snippy words only add to his amusement as his lazy gaze moves from my flip-flop covered feet to my tank top.

"I don't think you have anything I want, waitress."

Oh no, he did not just refer to me as the waitress again.

"I'm sure you can find something you can take."

He makes an amused humming noise in his throat as he shuffles the playing cards in between his fingers, never meeting my gaze. "What is it that you think you need?"

The menace in his condescending words knots my hands together. What do I *think* I need? I think I need a new job and a new parking lot—one that Bostic won't find.

"I-I-I need a place to stay"—okay, so the stutter is new—"and I heard you were looking for a roommate."

The laugh that erupts from his chest is enough to send a lesser woman home with broken confidence. But not me. I stand tall, waiting for him to wipe the smile off his face as if my being here has been the highlight of his day.

"Tell you what, the rumors never disappoint me." He shakes his head and steps back, about to shut the door in my face.

"Wait!"

I shove through the small space, wedging my body between the door and throwing away my last shred of dignity. "Look, even if you aren't looking for a roommate, maybe you know someone who is. Please." My eyes plead with everything I am. "Please help me. I'm begging you. You're my last hope."

Too much to disclose? Probably. But again, I'm that desperate.

Desperate enough not to comment on the substantial annoying sigh he lets out as if giving me two more seconds of his time is painful.

"Fine," he clips just before bringing the marker to his mouth and biting the cap off. He spits it out at my feet, and I refrain from staring at his tongue snaking out and wetting the spot the cap just left. "Hold your hand out," he demands.

His voice might be a little scary, and I might be a little scared, but I hold my hand out, as crazy as that is. I wonder if Bostic would be proud or if he would be tempted to kick my ass? I guess we'll find out eventually—like later tonight at dinner.

Slowly, I stretch my hand out in the small space between us. If Maverick notices the trembling, he doesn't comment. Instead, he presses the playing card into my palm with his left hand, holding the card flush as his other fingers wrap around me as if he's making sure I don't move.

"I assume you know the rules," he drawls quietly.

I nod and then decide to be honest. "Sort of."

He scoffs. "You sort of found me, came all the way here to ask for a favor that you don't know the price of?"

Well, now that he says it like that, it seems as if I was a little hasty.

"I know enough." I lift my chin just in time to see him smirk.

"Doubtful."

But he begins scribbling out the first letter—I—on the card. "You will give me your phone and I will write down your number."

Oh. Well, that's totally fine.

He rounds out the O on the card. "When I cash in my favor, I will call you and give you a time and a place with instructions. You will not ask questions, and you will do as I ask. There are no refunds for my favors."

I swallow. That sounds a little dramatic and mob-like.

I nod my consent slowly as he finishes writing the U on the card.

"You will never mention me or my favors, nor will you disclose what favors we trade. I am a ghost to you."

Or a genie. I think a genie is way less scary.

"Do we have a deal?"

"Ainsley. My name is Ainsley James."

I felt like it's important he knows my name.

"Do we have a deal?"

It's like he purposely didn't use my name, so this deal sounded less personal. Whatever. I don't need him to be a friend. I just need a favor.

"We have a deal." I want to add devil at the end of my statement, but I'm not that crazy.

At my acceptance, Maverick steps back, his masculine scent of an expensive smelling cologne pulling away and dissipating into the new space around us.

"Come in," he murmurs, holding the door open like a gentleman.

It's not like I rush in. Maybe I hustle a bit, but I try to seem cool and not like his hard glare on the card in my hand concerns me. Surely he won't change his mind before I can adequately grovel.

The door slams behind me and sue me, I jump. It's a little freaking scary. Sure, Maverick's apartment is light and airy with a touch of modern college decor—meaning he isn't using storage containers as coffee tables, but he definitely doesn't give a shit if he has fresh flowers on the table. He doesn't even have a table. Well, he does, but it's got a green felt top on it. He definitely doesn't eat at it.

The couch looks comfy as I head to it for a test sit, that's all that matters. I need something softer than Jane Honda's back seat.

"Go ahead, make yourself at home."

He pops the top off a bottle of beer, and I sink back into the cushions. "Oh, wow. This is a really nice sofa." The back is made out of these big pillows that just swallow my body. "It's like it's giving me a hug." And I really need a hug right now.

I'm basking in the snuggliest sofa ever—eyes closed and everything—when a low growling type noise has me popping one eye open. "Oh. My bad." Seriously, I got lost for a second.

"Your favor," he prods, rolling the bottom edge of his beer against the kitchen counter.

Dammit. Farewell, best sofa ever. I wonder if Maverick will let me come back to nap on it. Nah. It'll probably cost me a favor. I shift, scooting onto the edge—which is soft too. Maybe a favor is worth it.

"Right," I tell him, shaking off the haze of relaxation that came over me. Maverick's modern college vibe works for me, I think. I haven't felt this comfortable since living with Mom. "So, I'm looking for a roommate."

Maverick—the dick—rolls his eyes. "I caught that much."

"Well, isn't that where you come in?" I mean, really? What good is a genie if you have to do all the work?

He snorts. "It'll take some time. I don't keep a running list of vacancies."

My heart skips a beat. "I don't have time. I need a place tonight."

Maverick's dark brows arch perfectly up his forehead. "Tonight?"

I bet he has that listening problem Tucker had. Mom says all men have it. Maybe she's right.

"Yes, tonight. I told you I am desperate."

His mouth goes tight. "Don't tell people you're desperate."

"Whoa, okay. You don't have to get all bossy. I'm just telling you the truth. I don't have time to play games."

His mouth relaxes a fraction. "Why can't you stay with friends?"

Grr! "Do you ask everyone this many questions when they ask for a favor?" I think not.

Before I can even apologize for my outburst, he slams his beer down and has the door opened. "Out."

Pleadingly, I hold out my palms. "I got thrown out of my apartment! I'm sorry!" I can see the flinch in his cheek. "Please help me. I don't have any friends who will let me room with them. Trust me. I've tried."

He pushes the door closed slowly like he's trying to convince himself not to drag me out. "Why won't they let you stay with them?"

I shrug. "I might have started a small fire in my apartment."

Dammit, I've scared him. His eyes have gone from narrowed suspicion to holy-shit-I've-let-in-a-psycho wide.

"What's a small fire?" His words are smooth and unhurried, like I didn't just make him nervous.

"Like a small curtain fire that ended with the fire department and a ban from the complex owner."

Yeah, that did it. Now he's scared.

Chapter Seven

Maverick

Rumor has it she has to do his laundry for a year.

"You were banned? From a college apartment complex?"

Just when I think I've heard it all. I don't know if I should be impressed or fucking terrified.

Her cheek twitches just before she shrugs, the strap of her tank top sliding off her shoulder in the process. "Not officially. It wasn't like he made me sign anything. He just said he didn't want to see me on his property *ever* again." She adjusts the changeable strap, slipping her bra strap underneath so I can't see the clashing color. "I read between the lines."

She read between the lines.

I shake my head.

She seems so normal. Sure, she's gorgeous, most of the crazy ones are too, but Ainsley has this genuine quality to her. Like what you see is what you get. She doesn't hide who she is, nor does she waste time doing those fancy knots with her hair. She opts to keep it simple, allowing her long waves to drape over one shoulder, the sheen glistening in my overhead lighting. Even if she's taller than most girls, she doesn't lack curves. Her body is lean, and her hips prominent. That doesn't even take into account her tight ass shoved into those jean shorts. If I were interested, I'd note that she's stunning in a girl next door type of way, but I'm not. I'm just pointing out how normal she appears to be on the surface.

She's obviously a handful, but is she really crazy enough to get banned for causing a fire? I find that hard to believe. Do you know all the shit college students do in their apartments? Students make up the majority of renters around here. Owners are used to a certain level of stupidity and "accidents." But she gets banned for a curtain fire? What am I missing here?

"So that's why your friends won't let you stay? Because they think you will set the place on fire?"

She has the audacity to look meek. It pisses me off. "That and I don't have that many friends. I came here with a boyfriend, and since the rumor will eventually make it to you, you should know he was banging my roommate when I came home that night. I threw a candle. One thing led to another and—"

"You set the place on fire," I finish for her.

"I wasn't trying to kill them."

I almost laugh at that one. To think this hundred-and-thirty-pound, hot mess of a girl is worried I might think she was trying to hurt someone. Please.

"So you need a place with working sprinklers," I suggest.

She nods, appearing a little more deflated than a few minutes ago when she nearly passed out on my couch.

Goddammit. Don't do it, Mav.

"I'll have to make some calls."

Her head drops a little farther. Argh! "But you can stay here." I point to the couch. "I don't have an empty room—but you can crash on my couch until I find something for you."

A slow smile tugs at her cheeks. "I can crash with you?"

No.

"One night. Twelve hours. However long it takes me to find you a roommate that has flame retardant tapestry."

"Haha. You're hilarious but thank you."

Don't thank me just yet.

"So, we have a deal?"

She jumps up and down. "We have a deal."

It's way too fucking easy.

I slip my hand into my back pocket and pull out a card. What the hell did I do with my marker? I spot it on the counter and eat up the distance in a couple of strides. Now, where was I?

Oh right. "Turn around," I bark, my voice gruff and edgy with an absurd amount of frustration.

"What? Why?" She notices the playing card in my hand. "I only asked for one favor," she starts to argue.

Rookie mistake.

"No. You asked for two." I take a few steps closer, coming toe to toe. I don't need her to turn around after all. I can be flexible.

I hold the card in front of her face. "The first favor you asked was to help you, which got you through the door." I push the card against her lips, cutting off any argument. "The second is for finding you an apartment. Don't get it confused. I offer no freebies. Everything with me is quid pro quo."

I take the marker and scrawl the letters IOU, taking my sweet ass time. I want her to know I'm the one in charge here. No pouty mouth and tight body is going to make me forget who I am. I'm not doing this out of charity. It's a deal just like any other. A favor bought and housed in reserve.

When I'm satisfied she understands the shit she's now in, I release my hold on the card and let it fall to the floor, her shocked expression morphing into something else entirely. Something incredibly sexy. Something incredibly pissed.

"You lied!"

I cock my head to the side, a silent warning to watch her fucking mouth. "I didn't lie. You didn't know the rules. Not my problem."

Sure, I could have warned her, but where would be the fun in that?

"You could have been a little more thorough," she says, her bottom lip quivering just a bit. She doesn't beg me to take it back, and I admire that she's accepting the terms and dealing with them, even if she doesn't agree.

"Do I get a key?"

I bark out a laugh. "No."

She shrugs, unaffected. "Whatever. Don't blame me when you have to crawl out of bed at 11:30 to let me in. That's when I get home from work."

Don't blame me when your ass sleeps out in the hallway with that smart mouth.

"I'll be up," I assure her, going back to my beer.

She takes a deep breath and nods. "I need to take a shower before work."

Motherf—"Fine."

Now she needs a bathroom. Next thing I know, she'll want something to eat.

The smile she flashes me makes my dick jump.

This is a bad idea—a terrible idea, Maverick. The worst you've ever had.

"Great! I'll just be a second. I need to grab a couple of bags from my car, so don't lock me out, okay?"

I clench my jaw and try to seem hospitable. "Sure."

"Eep! You're so not as awful as people said." And there lies the problem. She's too observant, and I'm breaking all the rules. This is what happens when you only sleep two hours fulfilling a fucking favor you should have never had to do in the first place. Never again.

"Your phone," I demand, holding out my hand. At the tone of my order, the smile falls from her face, and she reaches into her back pocket, pulling out her phone, pausing only a second to unlock it. That's better. That's the fear I need to see from her.

"Just ignore the screen saver. It was a dare, and I don't know how to change it back," she mutters, her nose pinking just a little on the tip as she places it in my palm. She's embarrassed. Huh.

I lower my gaze to her phone, and a picture of a sea lion stares back at me. I almost grin. Bullshit, she doesn't know how to change it. This picture is edited with a filter, and if I'm not mistaken, it's not from the internet. The background has our local aquarium's logo behind the smiling sea animal.

"Cute," I muse, scrolling through her pictures, noting hundreds of images of her and a guy. Must be the ex-boyfriend. I click on one of her and him pushed together in the bed. Wait. "This was our waiter last night." God, what was his name? Thomas?

"Yeah. He's Taylor's and my boss."

"Who the fuck is Taylor?" Why are there so many T names in her life?

She fidgets with a tweed bracelet on her wrist. "My ex-room-mate." She says it like a question. "It's why I was in such a bad mood when, you know . . ."

When she tossed food in my lap.

"Ah. Will you be looking for a new job too?" The patrons need one of them to quit. Had I been someone else, I would have had her fired.

"I mean, I would like to, but there aren't many openings around here, and I refuse to be a stripper, not that I'm judging the women who are. I just don't have that kind of confidence in my body."

Good Lord. I take it back. She has eight hours and then she's out of here.

"It'll be fine," she says, waving off my doubt. "Things will blow over, and I'll be fine. It isn't like I'm heartbroken over it."

Famous last words.

It's midnight, and I've read the same set of numbers four times now, and I'm no closer to digesting what they mean to Braylon's portfolio than I was fifteen minutes ago. The same fifteen minutes before she came home from work and threw herself down on the sofa face first. I hadn't even cared at the time. It wasn't my business to ask how her day was or to offer her a nightcap. I simply nodded, locked the door behind her, and went to my room.

But then the sniffling started.

"Ahh!" I hear her muted cry through the closed door.

I don't know who she thinks she's fooling, but she's not masking that horrific squall of pain. It sounds like a coyote screeching into my throw pillows while attempting to guzzle a beer. Exactly, it's not pleasant.

Another whimper.

Fuck!

I'm not getting involved. I'm merely fulfilling a favor by letting her have a place to stay tonight. And possibly tomorrow. So far, my attempts to find her a roommate have failed. For some reason, this girl has pissed some people off. Enough people that I'll have to use a favor just to get her out of my apartment and off my sofa. Granted, I'm intrigued. I admire someone who can ruffle a few feathers at this university, but I am not for all this crying. I don't do nursing someone's mental well-being.

I'm not her friend.

This is a deal.

It's as simple as that.

"Do it, Ainsley. Do it! Press the button!"

Oh, God. Is she talking to the remote? I have neighbors, for God's sake—ones that I want to keep fearing me. I can't have them thinking I'm running a slumber party over here.

Sighing, I pluck the unlit cigarette from my lips and set it down. I need something to drink anyway. On my way to the kitchen, I will pass by and give her a once-over. If she's drunk, and indeed talking to the remote, I will come back, turn on some music for my nosy neighbors, and put my headphones on to drown out the rest of this crazy night.

I can do that.

It's not like I'm really checking on her. I'm just ensuring she won't destroy the remote or lash out at any of my shit. I'm protecting my assets and my lease agreement. The deposit wasn't that much, but I'd prefer not to lose it.

I throw on a shirt and head out into the hall, where the whimpering becomes more apparent. She's not just sniffling now. She's holding back some massive sobs.

This isn't my thing. I don't do crying women.

The last time I witnessed a woman cry was when my mother found out she had MS. Her sobs are still burned in my memory. I wasn't equipped to deal with it back then, and I certainly am not equipped to deal with it now. Crying girls are not in my wheelhouse.

"Press the button! Remember what he did!"

What the fuck? Is she giving herself a pep talk? And what button is so damn important that she needs to press it? Dammit. Now I have to know. Call it fucking curiosity. Maybe she really is crazy and just hides it well. Sebastian always says the prettiest ones have the craziest personalities.

I pad down the hall, careful not to interrupt her sobs, and come to a stop a few feet in front of the sofa. There, hugging the spare pillow from my bed—I'm not a complete shit of a host—sits the brave girl I admired earlier today. The one who begged me to hear her out. This time, though, instead of a strong jaw and a smart mouth, she sits curled over her knees with swollen eyes glaring down at her phone, a grip so tight it's turning her knuckles white.

"Should I pull out the fire extinguisher?"

Shitty thing to lead with, I know, but again, crying women are not my thing.

She pulls her murderous glare from her phone and aims it straight at me. I'll be honest. It unnerves me a little. Not enough to deter me, though. I've seen better.

"Are you going to need to raid my freezer too?" I head to the kitchen, ignoring the heated glare I can feel on my back. Please, God, don't let her have one of my kitchen knives stashed in the cushions. "Full disclosure, it'll cost you another favor." I'm lying, don't go all girl power on me. Someone needs to pull her out of this spell, and I'm all she has at the moment. Poor girl.

"Do you have a girlfriend, Maverick?"

I roll my eyes. Here we go. Why must they all ask this question? Shouldn't the rumors squash this question? "No, but let me warn you that girl talk and boy bashing will cost you another favor. Choose your questions and comments carefully." I pour myself a glass of water from a jug I keep in the refrigerator, and before I put it up, I take out another glass and pour her one too. For free. Because I'm feeling charitable at the moment, and I'm not so sure she isn't armed.

"So you don't know what it feels like to have your heart ripped out of your chest, do you? A pain so violent that you can't bear to delete the memories of your past."

Whoa. Is that what she's trying to do? Delete pictures of her and what's-his-name? I thought she said this would blow over, and she wasn't heartbroken over it?

Without looking directly at her—she looks a little wild—I take a sip of water and decide for once in my life to answer honestly. The poor girl looks like she can't take many more lies. "I've never had my heart ripped out by a girlfriend, but I do know the pain of losing the most important woman in my life." Let her piece that statement together if she wants.

"Oh," she says softly. "I'm sorry. I shouldn't have brought it up." She hiccups, but the comment seems to have settled her.

"It's okay. It was a long time ago." I take her the glass of water and hand it over.

"Will this cost me a favor?"

I deserve that. Honestly, it makes me smile. I like a client who learns quickly.

"It's on the house."

"I thought you didn't do freebies?"

See what I mean? She remembers too much. She has to go.

"I also don't do guests, but here you are."

She bites her lip and mumbles, "Here I am."

I take a seat on the coffee table, directly in front of her. She seems calmer, and the air feels a little safer. "What'd she do tonight?" I'm referring to the Tessa or Tonya girl she used to live with. She gave her a hard time last night if I remember correctly.

"He moved in with her."

"Who? Your ex-boyfriend?" No, I'm not stupid, but with women, you never know what upsets them. Not that I have a whole lot of experience, but Sebastian has made more than a few cry and run to me for help. Never mind. I just need to be sure we are talking about the ex and not a stepdad or something.

"Yes. Tucker, my cheating asshole boss and former boyfriend, moved in with my cheating ass roommate and coworker."

Now she's just being a smartass.

"And this upsets you?"

"Yes! Would it not upset you if your girlfriend moved your roommate in with her?"

I want to answer honestly and tell her no because that would never happen with me. I don't allow people to become that valuable to me—to have enough power to control my emotions. Everything is a deal in my life. Nothing is organic or free. Except for Sebastian and Rowan, but even then, I think I could write them off with a minimal headache if they were to betray me.

"I would move on. You shouldn't mourn the loss of a lie."

Wrong thing to say.

"Tucker and I weren't a lie! He loved me!"

Okay, therapy time is over. It's time to remind her why she's in this situation—some tough love or the truth. "He bent your friend over your pink sheets and fucked her so hard that she bit the fabric and screamed out his name."

She rears back, her plump lips forming an O. "Shut up! He did not!"

Maybe not on her pink sheets. They could be blue or some shit, but rest assured the bastard more than likely fucked her on Ainsley's bed. She needs to let this dick go and get some sleep—hell, so we can both get some sleep. I need the girl from earlier. "While you were making him the perfect dinner, she was riding his cock in the back seat of her car."

"Stop!"

I'm not going to stop. She needs to hate him or delete the fucking pictures, whatever the end game is here.

"While you were texting him that you couldn't wait to see him, he was texting Tiffany with all the things he would to do to her as soon as he got away from you."

"No!"

The sobs that shake her entire body almost get me to stop, but the finger she moves to the screen, hovering over the picture, keeps me firm. "Press the button, Ainsley."

"He loved me." Her voice sounds defeated. I should feel better that she's doing what I want—that she's letting go, but instead of turning back, I ignore the pain that throbs behind my ribs. In the morning, if I have to search all day, I am finding her an apartment. I'm not doing this again.

"He might have loved you once, but he doesn't anymore. He used you, Ainsley. He threw you away like last season's Christmas sweater."

I watch her chin quiver, and like a bastard, I keep going. "Press the button." God, forgive me.

With one last scream of anguish, she jams her finger to the screen and deletes the picture. And then another one. And another. She's so consumed with cursing her screen, she doesn't even notice when I get up and leave.

Chapter Eight

Maverick

Rumor has it he took all her belongings as collateral.

"Where's all your shit?"

When I get back from lunch, Ainsley is sprawled across the sofa with a blanket and a stuffed—is that a sea lion? What the fuck is she doing with a stuffed sea lion?

It doesn't matter. What matters is that she's been lying on the couch for the past three hours watching some aquarium reality show when she should be unpacking. See, my ass could not find her a fucking apartment, and to make matters worse, the favor I pulled only got me a "Dude, my dad said that girl is banned from nearly all the complexes around campus. It will take some time." It was not the answer I was looking for, and that particular favor cost Mike, my mechanic and classmate, another goddamned IOU.

So I came home, ground out the news, told her to move in her shit, and then proceeded to toss my poker table and all my shit from the spare room into the living room where Ainsley has stayed, unmoving and grating on my last nerve.

"In my room," she responds, never looking away from the TV.

I narrow my eyes, my cheek twitching in frustration. "There's only three bags in your room."

I know because I just looked while she did absolutely nothing. "I'm talking about your furniture. Where's your bed?"

Logically, I know she didn't move it in the past two hours, but shouldn't she be making plans, or does her plan include sleeping on the floor? Honestly, at this point, I don't care either way.

She presses pause on the TV like my questions are disrupting the riveting penguin walk currently transpiring on my fifty-five-inch screen. "I'm going out later to buy an air mattress." She presses a button on the remote, and her program resumes.

Don't get involved, Maverick. Who cares if she sleeps on an air mattress or the floor? Her favor is a place to stay, and it doesn't include a feather top and box springs.

"What happened to your old bed? The one you slept on at your other apartment?" I briefly wonder if my mention of her ex fucking her roommate on it turned her off. Again, it doesn't matter. She's only staying long enough until Mike's dad, a realtor, finds me what I need.

She pauses the show again, but this time she sits up and faces me. "I didn't realize there would be an interview about what I sleep on. I thought our deal was for the room, not the shit in it."

Her words are harsh and biting.

My dick twitches.

I contain a smile, scrubbing a hand over my mouth, and nod firmly. "True. Our deal is for a room that you don't have the money for. 'Yet.'" I quoted her words when I told her she would stay here for a few days. She was scared she would owe me another favor when she couldn't pay half of the rent. I didn't even mention rent. Our deal didn't include money, just the place to stay, but since she was offering, I was willing to let it play out. Who am I to tell her not to be a decent person? Again, I make a living off fear, and that's precisely what Ainsley needs right now.

I let the mask of The Maverick Lexington harden on my face just as my smile turns into a sharp line, my gaze holding her in a greedy headlock. "The way I see it, Ms. James, your only luxury here is my mercy. You'll answer my questions, or you'll find yourself on the doorstep of a safe haven. Tell me, do you prefer the church or a fire station?"

She swallows thickly, her eyes darting around the room before they find their way back to mine—the fight in her wilting away.

Shame. I like her venom.

"I don't need to go back for my bed. It's just a bed."

I stay quiet, holding her eyes, making the silence awkward so she'll keep explaining.

"It's a long story, but don't worry. I'll round up some friends and get it soon. The air mattress is only temporary."

"So, it's a matter of muscle?" I finally ask, relieved to know it isn't because she doesn't have one.

Her nod is slow, like she isn't sure if that's the answer I'm looking for. "Great. Call them." I tip my chin to her phone on the coffee table, insinuating she do it now.

A sound, almost like a laugh and cry mix, bubble out of her throat. "They're all at work. I'll call them tomorrow. Promise." She makes this crossing motion over her heart and flashes me a pleading smile.

I've encountered better attempts at persuasion. Sadly, I don't win over that easily.

I shrug, tip my chin, and head back into the kitchen where I hear the sigh of relief before she lies back and presses play, resuming her ridiculous show once again.

Usually, I'm not one to get involved. I find it rather exhausting taking on other people's problems, but for some reason, I can't get those goddamned tears out of my head. I'm doing this for me. I lose enough sleep with my own problems. I don't need one more thing to keep my head spinning.

With my back against the counter, I scroll through the numeric contact names based on status, favor, and initials of first and last names. I'm looking for someone in particular. Someone with a truck and more brawn than brains. Someone I paid off a gambling debt for

. . .

I press his contact name, and it rings once, twice—"Maverick."

I spare Logan no pleasantries. This is not a social call. He's not my friend, and since he's already paid me for the loan, he's only one favor short of being paid in full. "Meet me at FallsPoint Apartment complex. Bring your truck and some friends." I hang up before he can blubber out a response and text one more person. Rowan.

Me: Meet me at FallsPoint Apartments in 15.

PIF-owehim-RM (Aka Rowan): Need to bring anything?

Me: No.

He doesn't text me back, and I don't expect him to. Rowan will be there—he and Sebastian are the only loyal friends in my life.

I slide my phone in my pocket, walking over to Ainsley, who has resumed her fetal position and vacant stare at the TV.

"Give me your hand," I bark out, startling her.

She messes with the blanket, pulling it up to her chin as if it were a shield between us.

I almost smile. Nothing will protect this girl from me now.

"I thought you were in the kitchen." Her shocked expression is cute.

"Tsk, tsk." I admonish her. "You should always be aware of your surroundings."

She narrows her eyes, a small crease forming in the corner. "But I'm at home."

Exactly.

I snatch the throw from her chest and toss it to the ground, getting my first glimpse of her bare legs. "You should always be aware. Especially at *home*."

I'm the shark, and she's the unsuspecting sea lion floating lazily in the ocean.

Eyeing her bare feet, I let my gaze travel slowly up her body, hesitating at the tight clench of her thighs.

"What are you doing? Give that back!" she shrieks, sitting up and kicking at my legs in anger. Spoiler alert: I like it.

Grabbing her knees, I hold them still, leveling her with a stern look and trying like hell not to think about the smoothness under my palms. "Are you finished?"

She swallows. "Yes."

I let her knees go and straighten, towering over her. "Give me your hand."

She does as I ask, albeit shakily, and extends her arm toward me. I hesitate, waiting for more yelling, kicks, or tears. When all she does is hold her chin higher and her arm out taut, I smother my approval and take her wrist. Silently, I reach with my free hand into my back pocket and produce an eight of spades and a Sharpie.

"I didn't ask for another favor!" Her eyes are wide and sharp—the braveness dissipating.

She may not have asked me for a favor, but she's getting one anyway. I ignore her and take her hand, flipping it palm up. "It doesn't matter. You can't live here and sleep on the floor. I won't have people thinking you're a fucking captive."

She cringes. "Look, I promise. I will call my friends and get my furniture tomorrow."

Too late. I place a card in her hand, sliding my hand along her wrist and then to her forearm, holding her still. "We'll do it today."

Her voice cracks. "We'll?"

I take my time scrawling out the three simple letters that will leave her indebted to me even more. "Yes. Put some clothes on." I close her fingers around the edge of the card and release her arm. "You have five minutes." And then I walk the fuck away.

"So . . . I wasn't completely honest with you earlier."

The past few silent minutes have been blissfully appreciated while we head in the direction of her apartment. "About the friends or the furniture?"

She chews the inside of her cheek, creating something almost like a dimple. "The friends?"

"Are you not sure?"

She sighs and looks out the window. "I don't have any friends to help me move, but even if I did, I wouldn't have gone back for my furniture."

"Why not?"

She shrugs, clearly nervous about telling me. "I don't want to see them right now."

"The exes?"

I take a sharp left turn, not bothering with a blinker. The motion wrenches Ainsley off the window, grasping the console for support.

"Yes," she says, giving me a side-eye. "Do you think you can get us there in one piece?"

I like this spunk from her. It's the most fun I've had in a long time. No one gives me this much backtalk or stands up to me anymore. But this girl . . . This girl flips switches I didn't know I had.

"Tell me the truth. You wanted to kill them, didn't you? At least singe some hair." I've seen scorned women. Trust me, Sebastian has evaded quite a few murder plots in his time at Havemeyer.

She sends me a glare. "I didn't try to kill them—don't arch your brow at me like you don't believe me. You weren't there! If I wanted to kill them, I would have used the gas from Taylor's car and Tucker's Vegas commemorative matches to burn the place down." See? She thought about it.

I fight a smile at her descriptiveness. "So you were, what? Clumsy with the candle?"

Mike told me all about the rumors. Ainsley James, the psycho pyro who almost killed her boyfriend and roommate just because he was there waiting for her to get off from work.

"You had no idea they were having an affair right under your nose?" I probe for no other reason than to see that spark of fury again. She needs to be tough when she sees them. I don't want any of those annoying tears when we're moving her shit out.

She snaps around to face me. "No! If I knew they were having an affair, I wouldn't have walked in on them fucking!"

Women only go crazy for two reasons: a sale and a man, but Ainsley . . . I think she's just being herself. Not crazy, just extremely passionate.

"They were even using the condoms from my room." She leans back with a huff just as we pull into the complex, and I spot Logan's truck parked in one of the visitor spaces.

Parking, I turn the car off and stuff the key fob in my pocket. "He's a piece of shit. Now, come on."

Her eyes go wide. "But they're home," she argues. "Tucker's car is right there." She points to an old BMW sedan.

"Get out." My tone holds no room for negotiations. This Tucker asshole is making my days hell just by breathing.

I get out, and a few seconds later, I hear the passenger door close. "What floor?"

"Second." The fire is gone from her words.

Grunting, I slam my door and round the car, walking toward Logan and the ten guys he brought with him. I give the parking lot a bored gaze before I find who I'm looking for. Rowan. He's perched on the steps with one knee bent and a lit joint hanging from his lips.

"Come here," I snap, aiming my words at Ainsley but my glare at Logan. "Apartment number. . ." I look at Ainsley to fill in the number.

She mumbles out, "It's 201."

Good enough. I focus on Rowan, who takes one last drag and tosses the blunt on the sidewalk, smashing the lit end with the toe of his boot.

"Follow me," I say, brushing past him and leading them all up the steps. I offer no opportunity for questions. Instead, I take the stairs as if I have nothing better to do. I do, and that only adds to my annoyance. This Tucker bitch better steer clear. My mood is not to be fucked with.

The corridor's walkway is short and narrow, and if I were the one moving the furniture, I would have groaned at the sight. It's going to take some maneuvering to get the pieces out and down the stairs without a back injury.

"Do you have a key?" I ask Ainsley, who is lurking behind one of Logan's roided-up friends.

"Uh—"

I bang on the door with my fist until the door is yanked open and I'm face to face with angry eyes. "Who the fuck are—"

I shove past the girl who I'm assuming is Taylor and tip my head as an instruction to the idiots behind me to follow.

"Ah! What are you doing? This is my apartment!"

I pluck the phone from her hand and hand it back to Rowan. "Ainsley," I yell. "Show me to your room."

I don't bother looking back at Ainsley. My focus in on the aghast tart in front of me. "She doesn't live here anymore!" she screams. "Tucker!"

And . . . I've had enough. I only have so much tolerance for bullshit, and I've reached my limit. "Scream again, and you'll be the one banned from this complex." It's not a threat. It's a fucking promise. I may not know the owner of this particular complex, but I have a contact list full of eager clients ready to pay up. It won't take me long to find who I need.

Taylor's annoying whine is silenced when Tucker comes into view, quickly realizing who's at his front door.

"This is the guy from Studs and Spuds," Rowan whispers. I know who he is and what favor he asked for, but still, I find it amusing to pretend I can't remember his name.

I nod, acknowledging Rowan, and hold my hand out, looking at Ainsley. "Do I need to repeat the instructions?" It's a total dick move, but we're in public, and I am in front of clients. She gets the public Maverick today.

My comment seems to snap her gaze away from Tucker, and she starts walking forward. I follow, right behind her, leaving Rowan standing guard.

Her room is light and airy with a lot of blues and yellows. And sea lions. I need to ask her about that. Who still has stuffed animals on their bed?

"I don't have any boxes," she says softly.

I smother a groan. Why must this be so fucking difficult? "It doesn't matter. They will carry it piece by piece until it's all out." Or I lose my patience and decide to leave it. It's truly a gamble at this point.

I wave Logan in, who hovers at the door. "Start taking it all out. Every piece you lose or damage is another favor." I don't have time for incompetence.

He nods curtly. "Understood."

Thank fuck. Now to deal with Ainsley, who's just standing, staring at a picture frame on her dresser. Not again. I take the frame and smash the glass and rip out the photo and shove it in my pocket. "Get your shit, and I'll let you burn this when we get home."

She grins, and something in my chest deflates even though the word home tastes sour coming from my mouth.

It takes almost three hours before we have all of Ainsley's shit packed up and moved into my apartment. Tucker and Taylor had sense enough not to speak as we proceeded to clean out anything that Ainsley thought she paid for. We even took the bread from the pantry.

I thought it was a bit excessive, but it seemed to make Ainsley happy and therefore, would make my night a little less awful.

"You want a sandwich?" she calls from the kitchen.

I look at the time on my computer screen. "It's seven o'clock."

She drops the butter knife onto the counter, the clanging sound pulling my gaze from the work I desperately need to get done.

"Are you too good to eat a sandwich for dinner?" Ah, the fire is back. I was wondering how long it would take.

I shut my laptop. "No, I'm not too good, but I don't typically eat after six."

Her nose scrunches. "Why? Are you afraid you might get fat?"

Who can I fucking call? Hugh? Would he know how to bribe someone into letting her stay with them?

"I get indigestion if I eat too late, if you must know." Why? Why am I telling her this? I don't owe her an explanation. She's a guest.

"But it's only seven."

I let out a deep sigh.

"A sandwich is fine."

She smiles casually as if she won some internal argument. "Okay. I'll leave the stuff out for you."

Chapter Nine

Ainsley

Rumor has it she tried to burn his apartment down too!

"How's it going with the new roommate? What did you say her name was again?"

Would it be awful if I didn't tell Bostic Maverick's name? Would it be sparing him stress if I said Maverick's name was Mavis? Right. No more lies.

"*His* name is Maverick," I admit.

Why am I so tense? It's not like Boss is my mom, who would be very wary of me moving in with a complete stranger who's known around the campus as a scary mofo. I'm a grown woman—at times—but definitely not the last few days. Honestly, with the way I've been acting—crying and eating all the carbs from Mav's cabinets—I'm scared he's going to renege on our deal before he finds me an apartment. He says his guy is "working on it," and I should not get too comfortable, but then he asks why I haven't unpacked my shit. He's a weird one.

Boss hums a non-answer. Does that mean he's okay with me living with a stranger? If you ask me—which no one is—it's better to live with a stranger than live in a parking lot.

"Is he a good guy?" he finally asks.

Why is he asking hard questions this morning? I shovel in a forkfull of pancake. "Uh-huh."

That's the semi-truth. He hasn't been entirely awful—at least to me. As for others, I can't say with certainty.

"Do you have your own room?"

Yes! A question I can answer honestly. "Yes, I do. It's nice. There's no puke stains or barred up windows."

It's actually really clean with relatively fresh paint, but I haven't been sleeping in it. Each night, when Maverick finally turns his light out at like two in the freaking morning, I sneak into the living room and curl up on the couch and tiptoe back into my room when the sun peeks through the balcony doors. I know Maverick did a lot for me to have my own bed, but I don't want it. He was right. Tucker probably did fuck Taylor on it. And even if he didn't, he probably lay awake at night, next to me, and thought about her.

I know it's stupid.

I know.

But ever since the survival instinct left me, and I found myself safe with a man everyone fears, the tears flooded my soul, and pain invaded every inch of my heart. I can't stop it. It's like waves and waves of memories hit at the worst moments. Moments when I should be showing Maverick that I'm grateful, and I appreciate him leaving a clean towel on the bathroom sink when he finishes showering. It's like he's the most hateful, considerate host ever. I don't want him to think I'm a mess of a person. I might be a mess now, but I haven't always been.

"So he's being good to you? You're okay, I mean?"

Look at Boss being all paternal.

I flash him a confident grin. "I'm fine, and I won't be there too much longer. Maverick's friend is looking for a place for me to stay. Me staying at his apartment is only temporary."

I don't know why I added that last bit, but I felt like I needed to justify what we're doing. It's not like I'm banging him, but if I were a dad, that would be the first place my mind went.

That big head of his tips just a little before he nods. "You'll let me know if you have any problems with anyone." It's not a question. My fire-savior is my very own Thor—protector of my Universe. I'm legit living a Disney movie. I have a genie and an Avenger.

"Will do, Boss. Now, I gotta run. I have a class to get to."

I stand to leave and look at Kyle, who is already reaching for my plate. "Sorry," I mouth. He waves me off, and Bostic grunts like I'm ridiculous by feeling sorry for the trainee.

"I'll see you guys later," I say, reaching for my bag and pointing from my eyes to Luke's, letting him know I'm watching him. The shit has been on the phone the entire time I've been here. I didn't even get to speak to him.

Next time.

Right now, I need to get through this next class, and then I'm going to go home and make my magical genie a surprise dinner to show him that I'm not the worthless slug I seem.

Have I mentioned I have zero cooking skills? Like below awful. Once, my mom tried teaching me how to bake cookies, and I mixed up the measurements for salt and sugar. Why do you put salt in cookies anyway? Isn't the whole point to make them sweet?

Anyway, my cooking Maverick dinner before he gets back from wherever he goes every day—hell maybe—is going epically bad. So bad that when he finally does come home, I'm standing on the kitchen/poker table, waving a dishrag in the air trying to get the smoke detector to shut the hell up before someone calls the fire department.

"Everything is okay," I assure him.

A hint of a smile plays on his lips. "Looks like it."

Such a smartass. "Who changes the batteries in these things anyway?" I'm out of breath, and my arms feel like noodles.

"The person who's living with a pyro," he says smugly, going over to the stove and turning off the switch, which, in hindsight, I should have done before I ran to the smoke detector. Still, given my recent experience, I didn't want to get Maverick or myself kicked out of this apartment.

"What the hell were you cooking?" His nose scrunches up, and he grasps the pot handle with a dishtowel, leaning it to the left so he can look at the contents.

Oh no. Not now. Not again.

The burn starts at the bottom of my eyelids. *Don't do it, Ainsley. Don't you dare cry.*

"I'm so sorry." Sniff. "I was trying to show you that I'm grateful for the room and"—hiccup. Fan the blasted smoke detector—"that I'm not such a mess all the time. But—"

He dumps the contents of the pot in the sink, ignoring my emotional outburst and the wailing alarm.

"Is that macaroni?" He sounds shocked. "Were you trying to make mac and cheese?"

A tear streaks down my face just before the proverbial dam breaks. "I can't even make boxed macaroni and cheese," I wail. "I truly am worthless." And throwing the world's greatest pity party. I have stooped to new lows. "I wanted to make you dinner, but I'm not much of a cook."

He flips the switch for the garbage disposal and fights an eye roll. "Get down."

Oh shit. Now he's mad. Instead of him coming home to a hot bowl of mac and cheese—that I wanted—he's angry.

"I'm so sorry."

The words would sound so much clearer if I could stop sobbing. What is with me? Is this the five stages of grief? Could I be—"Ahh!" My legs are yanked out from under me, and I brace for the impact that never comes.

"What are you doing?" I choke back the fear. At least the tears are gone, and Maverick's shoulders are . . . amazeballs. Like these things are boulders shoved under his shirt. When does he work out?

His answer never comes. Instead, he sets me down and snatches the rag from my hands. "Go get dressed."

"Oh, no. Are you throwing me out because I really was just trying to say thank—" I stop at the glare he's giving me.

"Would you like me to repeat myself?"

Uh, no. I don't think so.

"I'll be just a minute then." I try not to sound defeated when I click the door closed, and the smoke alarm quiets. But when I hear the dishes rattle and him cleaning up my mess, I succumb to the ache. Why had I never learned to cook? Why did I rely on Pat, our cook at

Studs and Spuds, to leave me a plate every night? Would it have been that difficult for me to YouTube some kind of class?

It doesn't matter. What's done is done. At least spring break is coming up in the next couple of weeks. I can go home and see my mom and eat about a billion calories. I can sleep in my own bed that hasn't been tainted with bad memories and affairs.

"You have five minutes," comes the low voice at my door.

Great, looks like we're headed back to the fire station. Bostic will not be happy. He'll for sure think it's me this time.

I hurry and throw on some leggings and a sweatshirt—no sense in looking fancy while being tossed out of your second apartment in a week.

It's whatever, though. This too shall pass. I will be stronger than I was before all this happened. I hope.

A few minutes later, I'm packed and standing in an empty living room. "Maverick? I'm ready to go. I'll come back tomorrow for the rest of my things."

When he doesn't clap or answer, I take a look around, noting the clean kitchen and the balcony door cracked. Ahh.

I walk over and peer outside into the dark, noting his tense form sitting in a chair. Rapping softly on the glass, I tell him, "I'm packed and ready. I'll need to come back tomorrow for my things."

At first, I think he intends to ignore me, but then I see his arm extend—is that a beer?—and pour the contents of the bottle on the porch.

"Eek!" I hear someone cry from below and then a "Shh," before the door closes.

See? Even the neighbors know when he's in a bad mood.

When the bottle is empty, he rises unhurriedly and almost lazily. He takes a sweep of my clothes. "You're ready?"

I look down at my comfy attire. "Yeah, these are my eviction clothes."

No smile. No laugh. Not even a comment that I now have designated clothes for evictions. He just brushes past me, tosses his beer in the trash, and grabs his keys. "Come on."

"Do you really need to escort me out? I promise I will leave. I won't even camp out in the parking lot. I'll pick another."

"Stop talking."

Oh. Okay. This is serious.

I nod and let a little, tiny, baby sigh go. I think I'm going to miss his couch the most.

"Leave your bag."

Devil say what? "Uh, I need my bag. I can't drive without my license, and I need my wallet to get gas so I can sleep—"

"Ainsley!"

I drop my bag. I don't need it tonight anyway. I can ride on fumes for a while.

"Let's go."

Without further objections, I follow Maverick out the door and—

"Get in."

Is he planning to kill me? Did I really find a new age Ted Bundy? For the love of all that is holy.

A deep sigh bursts from Maverick's chest while he holds open the passenger door of his car.

"Are you planning to drop me off somewhere deserted where no one can find me?"

You never know. A lot of rumors float around about Maverick. One can never be too careful.

"I might if you don't get in and hush."

Hush. That's better than shut up or "Hey, down this drink and let me secure this gag in your mouth."

"Where are we going?"

Maverick rubs his forehead like I'm giving him a headache. "To get something to eat. You're hungry, yes?"

I told you he was an angel, and people just talk shit about him.

I grin really big and do a little bounce on the balls of my feet. "Damn straight I'm hungry!" I streak past him and burrow into his black leather seats. Gah, why must everything of his feel so comfortable? "Besides, you owe me. You scared my blood sugar low." Seriously. Sitting in this seat, I'm suddenly exhausted and starving—all his fault.

He slams the door, ignoring my comment, and walks around the front of the car, shaking his head. Must be the headache.

In what seems to be an hour, Maverick pulls up to a little pizza place and throws the car in park. "Do you like pizza? I know it's not mac and cheese but—"

"Don't even start," I interrupt. "I've had a stressful night, and I could use a little less of your sarcasm right now, okay?"

Yes, it was a bold thing to say, but when he's sarcastic, he seems to be in a little better mood.

One of his eyebrows arches in a way that could be playful or threatening. I'm going with playful. "I want plain cheese."

That gets a better reaction out of him. "Just cheese? What kind of person are you?"

I cock my own damn eyebrow. "A plain one."

He chuckles, getting out of the car. "There's nothing about you that's plain."

"What's that supposed to mean?" I ask, following behind him as he pauses to lock the car. "Are you saying I'm complicated?"

I guess that would be true. I have my issues like everyone else.

"What do you want to drink?"

Great, he's ignoring me. "Why are you asking me about my order in the parking lot and not inside?"

He holds the door open. "Because you started ordering in the car. I thought that might be your thing."

"I thought I asked you to tone down the sarcasm?"

"I thought I asked you to hush?"

Touché.

I grin, knowing he doesn't really mean it, and walk inside. The restaurant is small and quaint. Dare I say it's even cozy. It's exactly my thing, and I'm in love with it.

We follow the nice woman to a booth in the corner. It seems like she knows Maverick, but she never addresses him by name. After taking our drink orders, she leaves, and of course, I must be nosy. "Do you know her?"

He's mid-sip into his water. Yes, you heard that correctly. He's drinking water with his pizza. Who drinks water with their pizza? Everyone knows you need carbonation with pizza.

"Why do you think I know her?"

I watch for any signs of nervousness. None. "She smiled at you," I note.

"I imagine that would fare well for her with tips."

He's impossible.

"I mean, is she one of your clients? Like me?"

He makes an amused noise. "Like you?"

I nod. "A client?"

A sinister grin forms, and he leans on the table like he's trying to get closer to tell me a secret. "Remember what I told you the rules are for being my client?"

Ew. I think this is a tricky question. "Can I admit that I may have forgotten a few minor details?" I was pretty worked up that day. I can't even remember what I was wearing and if I had eaten. Those few days blur together.

"Let me remind you then," he says all sultry and—

"What? No! Why are you giving me another card? I didn't ask for a favor."

He slides the ace of hearts across the table, clenching the cap of the marker in between his teeth just like last time, and scribbles out IOU before placing the cap back. "You never talk about me or my favors, remember?"

I do now.

"But I was just talking to you about it," I argue.

"Never in public."

But that doesn't make sense. "Don't you do business in public?"

He puts the marker back into his pocket. "Sometimes."

"And . . ."

He doesn't smile. "My rules."

"So that's just it. You can make up the rules, and I'm just supposed to do whatever you say and be indebted up to my earrings?"

"Sounds about right."

It sounds unfair to me.

"Why were you cooking for me tonight?"

He's changing the subject, and I'm not sure I want to. Sure, I don't want to end up with yet another IOU, but didn't I already try to explain this, and he cut me off?

I let out a deep sigh; talking to Maverick is exhausting.

"I just wanted to do something nice for you. I know it hasn't been easy living with me for the past couple of days. I've been crying and just a total disaster. I wanted to tell you that I'm sorry and that I appreciate you helping me get my stuff from the apartment. I know it was a deal and all that—" I wave the comment away in case he tries explaining the rules again. "But I appreciate your kindness nonetheless."

"So, you thought cooking boxed mac and cheese would be thanks enough?"

"Are you making fun of me?" Seriously. Is that a smile on his face? I think it is!

"I'm not."

"You are. You're laughing."

"I'm not laughing."

Yes, he is, and it's cute. Really, really cute.

"I'm not that great of a cook, and well, Tucker was always the one who cooked in our relationship, and I noticed you mainly just have a bunch of fruits and vegetables in the refrigerator, so I thought I would cook something warm and yummy for you."

"Warm and yummy," he repeats but in a way that makes me think he's thinking of something else or mocking me.

"Clearly, I'm still perfecting the recipe," I say, interrupting his lazy smirk.

"Clearly."

Now I'm sure he's mocking me.

"I'm going to learn how to cook when I get my own place. There's so much I didn't do when I was with Tucker."

He stirs his water with the straw, only glancing up at me briefly. "Like what?"

I pause, thinking hard about all the crazy things floating around in my head the past couple of days. "Like—"

Our waitress places the plain cheese pizza in the center of the table, breaking our connection.

"I thought you didn't want cheese."

He pulls off a slice and slaps it on my plate. "I never said that."

"You asked what kind of person I am for wanting plain cheese," I remind him.

He puts two slices on his plate. "And? Where did you hear that I wouldn't or couldn't eat plain cheese?"

He's freaking infuriating!

"Fine. You win," I say, taking a bite of the cheesiest, most delicious pizza I've ever tasted. "Oh, wow. This is really good." I moan with each bite. "You're going to need to carry me out of here. I plan on eating way more than this one piece."

He snorts. "That's why we ordered the whole pie."

"I'm just saying," I continue, slapping another piece of pizza on my plate. "I'm not one of those girls who won't eat in front of a man. I honestly don't care what men think of me anymore."

Maybe I shouldn't have said that last part since I'm not being honest. The fact is, I do care what he thinks of me—sometimes. I wish I didn't, though. I wish I could give zero fucks and not care what anyone thought, but I do.

I shrug when he only stares at me like I'm a mystery or weird. "Anyway, that's what I want to work on. Me. Who I am and what I enjoy. I don't know where the old Ainsley went, but I'm going to set out to find her. This time, I'm doing me."

Chapter Ten

Maverick

Rumor has it he did her in a kiddie pool.

I asked her for one thing.

One fucking thing!

"You have nine minutes! I have no qualms about throwing your ass out naked."

And she can't bother obeying my one rule. Okay, so it isn't one rule, but it's the main rule.

She can't be here for Wednesday night's poker game.

"Eight minutes!"

It might be easier to explain why I broke the bathroom door down than it would be to keep fucking counting.

I rub the ache behind my ribs, my heart rate increasing with the dwindling timeline.

One meal.

One mistake.

Showing her I cared that she didn't starve was the worst thing I could have done. It didn't matter that I pushed an IOU across the table last night and barked out orders for her to remain scarce tonight. She's not scared. Maybe she is a little; she did hustle out of the kitchen when I was yelling at Rowan on the phone earlier.

But the air has shifted. Ainsley James realizes that I'm not as scary as the rumors make me out to be.

Which. Is. A. Fucking. Problem.

I need those rumors. I need fear. My life depends on them.

"Six fucking minutes!"

I know she can hear me over that deranged singing she's doing.

My watch buzzes. I know, I know. I need to walk away and calm my ass down.

I march through the living room and jerk open the balcony door. Yes, this is precisely what I need—fresh air. A beer would be nice too, but I'll open one of those later when the guys get here.

I set the timer on my watch for five minutes and take the chance to call Pops.

"Yell-O."

His old Southern greeting puts a smile on my face. When I was growing up, he didn't speak this way, he was always so professional on the phone, but since his stroke, words have been harder for him to form—hence the Southern slang he adopted.

"Old man," I return smoothly.

"Maverick! How you doing, my boy?"

My boy. My father never called me his boy or his son. Only Maverick. "I'm good."

"School going well?" I wouldn't know. I haven't been in a few weeks. "Getting good grades?" I better be, or someone will pay the price.

"Yep. All good up here."

I can hear the question in his voice before he says it. "Have you been sleeping? You sound tired."

I take a seat in one of the plastic chairs, pulling the deck of cards from my pocket along with a marker. Checking my watch, I note Ainsley has three minutes. I think that deserves three IOUs just for pushing her luck.

I begin scribbling the letters on the cards with the phone pinched between my shoulder and cheek. "You don't sound so chipper your-self, old man."

He grunts. "You didn't answer my question."

I shuffle to the next card. "I'm sleeping fine. I just had a late-night studying." Is it exam time? Maybe I should ask Rowan. I like to take those exams myself.

"Uh-huh," he says in a tone that tells me he knows I'm lying.

"You know it kills me that even after a massive stroke, you still think you know better than everyone." I walk back into the house and shove the three cards under the door, feeling better already.

"I do know better than everyone, boy. Especially you and your sneaky brother."

Oh hell. What did he do this time?

Walking back to the sofa, I plop down, landing on something hard. I dig through the cushions and find not one, but two, stuffed sea lions. Seriously, Ainsley? The least she can do is adequately cover her tracks by stowing her walruses or sea lions—whatever—in her room if she wants to keep pretending she sleeps in there every night.

"He thinks I don't know what he's doing when those girls come over for tutoring. They don't bring books! You need books to study."

I grin, rolling one of the sea lions over, and spot writing on the tag. Lawrence. She named him? This girl never ceases to shock me.

"I told you, Pops, everything is online. The schools use online books now. As long as the students have a phone or a tablet, they can study."

True, but not in Cooper's case. He's fucking those girls or at least the one, Melissa. His girlfriend. The others probably are there to study for a little while.

"Uh-huh."

My watch vibrates, letting me know Ainsley's time is up. "I gotta go, Pops. Lay off the sodas, yeah?"

"I told you I just have one after supper!"

"Yeah, yeah. Now who's lying?"

"Get some sleep, Maverick." His voice turns serious. "I mean it. I *will* come up there."

Yes, he will, and no one needs to see my pops knock me down a few pegs. "Yes, sir." My mother didn't raise a disrespectful shit.

"Call your brother later," he says just before hanging up on me. He probably didn't mean to. His fine motor skills aren't what they used to be.

I stride back down the hallway, the warm breeze from the balcony invigorating me with excitement. Nah. It's not the breeze. It's fucking with Ainsley.

"Time's up!" I raise my hand to beat one last time when it wrenches open, and I'm met with stunning blue eyes and a wet head.

"Something is wrong with you," she says, brushing past me and not gently.

I feel a smile tugging at my mouth. "I will shove you off the balcony, Ainsley," I call after her, the door to her room slamming before I can finish. "You will be out of here before the guys get here."

I don't care if she's upset at having to clear out. Any other day, she can veg out on my couch and consume the Wi-Fi, but not tonight. Tonight is poker night, and no girls—or distractions—are allowed. And the whole keeping her a secret thing . . . Let's just agree that I have more than one reason to need her gone. I need some privacy, like yesterday.

Knowing she ignored me, I open the bathroom door and let enough steam out to power a train. She must have had the water that hot. I'm surprised she doesn't have third-degree burns.

Not your problem, Maverick.

Wiping off the mirror, I snag the stupid amount of hair ties and scrunchies on the counter and stuff them in my pocket. Why does she need so many—something floats in the toilet, catching my eye.

Squatting, I lean over for a closer look and see that it's the three IOUs I slid under the door, each one with the letters FU written in what looks to be lipstick.

And . . . my dick is getting hard.

Why must her fight turn me on?

I snap a picture—it was funny and brave—before flushing the cards and yanking open the shower curtain. There I round up the eight almost-empty bottles of shampoos and conditioners and—her fucking toothbrush? Who brushes their teeth in the shower? Never mind. Of course she brushes her teeth in the shower. Opening the hall closet, I shake my head and dump all her shit in before slamming it closed.

Do I care if they spill or she can't find them later? No, because she didn't bother to hide the shit like I had asked her.

Maybe it's about time I follow through with my threat to Mike.

He needs an IOU for every day Ainsley stays here and not in her apartment. It's not enough that I don't have any privacy, but it's getting harder every day to hide my secrets. I'm tired of living in my bedroom. I want my space back.

Finally, the door slams, and I look up to see Ainsley standing in a bikini—a very tiny bikini.

"Where the hell are you going?"

She puts a hand on her hip, cocking it out just enough to draw my eyes lower than they need to go. "Since you're banning me from your little sleepover, I'm going to hang out by the pool."

The hell she is.

"Not the pool here, people will notice you. Go somewhere else to soak up the sun."

She narrows her eyes. "Fine. I thought you were finding me a forever home. I'm tired of living here."

The feeling is mutual.

"Why did you say it like you are one of those abused dogs they try to guilt people into adopting with sad music?"

"I'd just like to have a place where I'm not kicked out every Wednesday so my roommate can throw down a spade and belch out a victory jingle."

She's in a mood today.

I like it.

"That's not how it works. We—"

She waves me off, clipping my remark.

"I don't care, Maverick. I'm not going to let you get to me today. I'm just going to take my boxed wine to the gym and drink it in the car."

I rear back. "Why the gym?"

"Why not?"

I have no fucking clue how to respond to that, so I go with "I'm not bailing you out of jail," and walk away.

I need a fucking shower—a cold one.

Sebastian breezes through my door like he lives here, heading straight for the balcony and hanging over the ledge as if he's looking for something. "Dude, did you know there's a chick floating in our beer pool?"

I sigh, closing my laptop, and rub my temples. I knew I shouldn't have left her alone. When I came out of the shower, she was gone. I assumed she heeded my warning. Evidently, not.

"Where?"

He doesn't look at me. "On the sidewalk. Her feet are propped up on the hood of your car, and I'm pretty sure she's chugging wine from a box."

I'm going to kill her.

"A brunette?" My tone borders on indifferent, but I'm anything but. I want to be damn sure who I plan on killing.

"Hell yeah. All that silky hair is piled up into this sloppy bun that just begs to be yanked." Told you it was notable. "Want me to shoo her off?"

I bet he would like that. He'd shoo her off with his number programmed into her phone and then he'd leave the game early to celebrate his loss, balls deep. Too bad that won't be happening. Ever. My new roommate is off-limits and still very much a secret to Sebastian. Guess that's about to end.

Let the rumor mill flourish with this new information.

"No, I'll take care of it. Get the table set up while I'm gone."

"Maybe you should wait a minute, push the game back an hour or so?"

"What the fuck for? Just because you lose money, doesn't mean the rest of us want to delay our payday."

Sebastian turns his head, speaking to someone outside before facing me. "Because we all want to enjoy the show a little longer."

We all?

You've got to be shitting me. I walk the few steps to my balcony and look out. Half of the terraces are occupied with men staring down, directly in front of my parking space. A front-row parking space I've had since I moved in. Renters want it, but no one dares park in it. But leave it to my disobedient roommate to indeed be floating in two feet of water in the plastic pool we use for chilling beer, propping her damn feet up on my car.

When I told her to go soak up some sun, I meant for her to go to a sorority house or a club or something. Not drag the pool down to the parking lot and use my hood for a fucking footrest.

I take the steps two at a time, ignoring the audience on their balconies, until I come face first with the biggest pain in my ass. Ainsley is sprawled out with only the scraps of fabric covering her breasts. Never mind the straw connected to her reddened lips as she slurps at what I assume to be more wine in her tumbler.

"What the fuck are you doing?" I drawl lazily as if her oiled skin glistening in the sun is doing nothing to my dick.

"Can you move a little to the left?" Her voice is bored and slurred. "You're blocking my sun."

I'm going to block something else of hers if she doesn't get her ass upstairs in the next 2.3 seconds.

I stay rooted to the ground, never moving. After a few awkward seconds tick by, Ainsley raises her ridiculously round shades and sighs. "Can I help you, Maverick? Did I leave the toilet seat down or something?"

God, help me. It takes all my patience not to snatch all one hundred and so pounds of her out of the pool and push her inside. "I told you to make yourself scarce." I take a slow look around as if it isn't obvious that the parking lot of the complex is not scarce.

She takes a long pull from her straw. "I am scarce."

An incredulous snort escapes my lips. "The sidewalk is still in the complex."

"You didn't specify the parameters. You only said I needed to be out of the apartment." She grins as if she's won this debate and swipes a hand through the water before letting the droplets drip into her navel. "It looks to me like I'm outside of the apartment."

My teeth grind, and the muscles in my jaw work to keep me from shouting at her. "You're drawing a crowd," I grit, enunciating each syllable.

"Am I?" She feigns concern, and my patience lowers to negative seven. "Well, we certainly can't have that." The water sloshes as she pulls herself up, her tits bouncing with the waves, and tosses the tumbler at my feet. My pants are doused with water. It's not amusing. But then, she extends her hand, and like a fool, I take it, allowing her to pull me closer, nose to nose. "Tell me something, Maverick." I hum out a nonanswer, trying to keep my eyes from drifting lower. "Look closely. Do you see two shits or a fuck anywhere in my eyes?"

I rear back at her words. Did she—

"I don't give a shit that I'm drawing a crowd," she lashes out, shoving me away. "This is my apartment"—she eyes the vacant spot next to my car—"and my complex. I am not moving just because your little friends can't focus on their game of Go Fish."

She wobbles on her float, and I realize she's drunk. And not only that, she's a mean drunk. "How much have you had to drink?"

I snatch my hand from hers and grab the now empty box of wine. No wonder she tossed the tumbler—she was out.

"Get up," I growl.

Her pupils are wide, but her glare is firm. "No."

This cannot be happening.

"Get up. I won't ask you again." I'm not known for my hospitality.

She laughs, a throaty sound that shoots straight to my dick. *Now is not the time, dude.* "You don't scare me, Maverick. You men can't hurt me anymore. I won't let you!"

I'm going to carve my initials into Tucker's skin until the only thing he sees in the mirror is the horror of my name.

"Is that what this is all about? Fucking Tucker?"

I can feel the weight of the stares on my back.

"Are you honestly drinking yourself into a stupor because cocksucker Tucker upset you? Again. What did he do this time?"

Her eyes turn glassy, and her lip begins to quiver.

"Don't you fucking cry over that asshole," I demand. "He's not worth it." And frankly, I can't take much more crying. Never in my life have I lost so much sleep worrying over someone. And she's only my roommate.

"He proposed to her," she finally mumbles out through tears.

I release a harsh breath and run my fingers through my hair. The game is about to start.

"Get out of the pool, Ainsley."

At my stern tone, she snaps out of her crying and levels me with a look. "No."

I can't very well leave her out here drunk and in a bikini. God only knows what would happen. College guys are creatures of convenience. A pretty girl, wet and crying? Yeah, she's like a bloody heart tossed into a den of wolves. "I'm not going to ask you again."

She turns her face away and slides her glasses back over her eyes. "Leave me alone, Maverick. Go back to your game."

I hear chuckles above me.

That's it. Fuck it. I asked her nicely and look at where that got me—pissed off.

I crack the bones in my neck and take a deep breath right before I stomp on the edge of the plastic pool, sending the water rushing through my legs.

"Are you fucking crazy?" Ainsley shrieks, trying to stop her float—and her body—from going with the current and right into my clenching hands.

"Am I crazy?" I mock. "I'm not the one shitfaced, floating on an innertube in two feet of water out in the goddamned parking lot."

"It's the sidewalk," she screams, grabbing onto my pants leg and trying to stand. She wobbles and takes two steps back before I've had enough and grab her arm and haul her over my shoulder.

"Put me down!" Her screams don't come close to masking the laughter from the balconies. "I'm serious, Maverick!"

Ignoring her, I make the weighted steps through the front lobby and punch the button to the elevator. I refuse to carry her kicking and screaming up the stairs.

"I'll scream," she threatens.

"You already screamed, but be my guest and do it one more time for the people who haven't seen your ass cheeks yet."

Her wiggling stops. "Is my ass really hanging out?" It's the first time since I found her that she's sounded sober.

I debate lying to her but decide I'd rather she learn this lesson the hard way. "Yes."

She sucks in a breath and pounds a weak fist into my back. "Put me down!"

"No."

I'm not letting her down. She is coming inside the apartment and sobering the fuck up.

"I'm sorry, okay?" Her voice is strained. Battered. Not the badass it was a few minutes ago when she asked me to look and see if I saw two shits or a fuck in her eyes—something in my chest clenches.

"I'm sorry I took it out on you."

I figured she would be eventually. She doesn't like to be mean.

"Apology accepted, but you're still not getting down until you're inside and clothed."

I feel her stomach concave over my shoulder as if she's accepting defeat, and I relax a little.

"Fine. Will you at least fix my bathing suit? I don't want your friends seeing my butt cheeks."

That's one thing we agree on.

I nod, clearing my throat. "Fine."

But it's anything but fine when my finger skims up the side of her leg, over the wet and scalding flesh. She's silent, and not even her breathing can be heard when I slip a finger under the elastic of her bathing suit bottom. Slowly, I pull the material from the middle, my knuckles grazing the soft and supple skin, before letting go.

Her hands relax against me, and she strokes down my back. "Thank you."

I don't acknowledge her. I'm seconds from slamming her against the wall and seeing what the rest of her feels like.

Finally, the elevator dings and opens. I readjust Ainsley and open the door to our—my apartment.

"Get out," I bark at a wide-eyed, grinning Sebastian. He throws his hands up in a placating manner. "I was on my way out anyway."

He attempts to pass by, and I grab his shirt, forcing his eyes from Ainsley's ass to meet mine. "Tonight's game is canceled. Let everyone know. I don't want any visitors."

Sebastian's tongue snakes out over his smirk and wets his lips. "I'm sure you don't."

A noise rumbles through my chest, and it isn't until Ainsley says, "Bye," that I realize I still have a fistful of his shirt. I shove him away, and he laughs.

"See you tomorrow." He winks. "Goodbye, *waitress*."

Fuck. He knows.

Fuck. Fuck. Fuck!

I sigh.

So much for keeping her a secret. Now that Sebastian knows, it won't be long before the others find out. I need a plan, and I need one like yesterday. Everyone knows I don't do girls or roommates. This goes against all the rumors. Dammit.

"Can you set me down now?" Ainsley asks quietly. Even she knows now is not the time to press me.

Giving in, I plant her on her feet, holding on to her arms so she doesn't fall.

"Are you steady?"

She takes a minute, shifting her weight from side to side before nodding. "I think so."

"Good. Go shower and change. I'll make you something to eat."

Are you serious, Maverick? Are you going to tuck her in tonight too?

A hint of a smile plays on Ainsley's lips, but she never lets it loose. "Okay."

Yes, okay. Go. For the love of God, go and take that fucking bathing suit off.

When she finally manages to shuffle to her room, and out of sight, I take a deep, cleansing breath.

What the fuck am I doing?

I never show my cards.

Chapter Eleven

Ainsley

Rumor has it she's pregnant with his baby.

is shampoo smells like him—of mint and cedar but with way less attitude. I like it, and it's a good thing too since none of my stuff is in the bathroom. I knew throwing those IOUs in the toilet was a bad idea.

But I was pissed.

At the time, I loathed anything with a penis—Maverick included. Even if he has been a decent roommate so far. Sure, his moods swing more than mine, but in those calm moments, when he's not trying to scare me away, he's a nice guy. I'd go as far as to say he's been sweet to me.

He keeps his distance, that's for sure, but I understand that I'm not a welcome guest and my being here is disrupting his life. I get it, I do. And I don't want to be a burden to him. I really am appreciative of his kindness and efforts to find me another apartment.

But today I couldn't keep my hatred from spewing out at anyone in my path. Freaking Tucker proposed to Taylor—on social media! Live! I watched him get down on one knee while Taylor's friends oohed and aahed behind her.

I'm devastated.

I know I shouldn't have kept following both of them on social media, but sometimes I do crazy things I'm not proud of, okay? I trusted them both, and their betrayal ran deeper than I thought. Sure,

Maverick convinced me to delete a few pictures, but it didn't delete the love I had buried behind my smile.

Trust me, I want to move on. I want to forget both Tucker and Taylor like a bad blind date.

I don't want to remember how he smelled or how he kissed my forehead before class. I don't want to remember any of it, but I do.

"Ainsley." A fist bangs on the door. "You're not drowning, are you?"

It's cute the way he acts like he doesn't give a shit, but yet, he's checking on me. Of course, his voice strains, like he had to force the words out, but the point is, the big bad wolf cares, even if he would love for me to believe he doesn't.

"I'm fine. I'll be out in a moment." Turning the water off, the bathroom is quiet, save for the steady drips from my body.

"Mav?"

Is he still at the door?

"Your food is on the counter," he says, his voice clipped. I know he leaves after that because my chest feels lighter like his massive presence made it harder to breathe.

Quickly—as quick as a drunk girl can—I dry off and make a mad dash to my room where I toss on a romper and brush through the massive amount of tangles.

I didn't look when I passed the kitchen, so I don't know if Maverick was there or if he retreated to his room like usual. I mean, I think we had a moment just now—at least I did. Those strong fingers that slipped under the elastic of my bathing suit sent crazy tingles throughout my body—no, it wasn't just the alcohol talking either. Granted, Maverick was the whole reason my butt was showing in the first place, but he could have left it for his friend to see. But he didn't. He cared.

I take one last look in the mirror. I don't look great, but I don't look that awful either. It'll have to do; besides, Maverick doesn't care what I look like. He might be nice occasionally and have chivalrous moments, but he isn't interested in me and I'm not looking for a guy. I've had my fill of those for a while.

With my head bowed—I so need a pedicure—I walk into the kitchen like a dog caught unraveling the last toilet paper roll.

"Don't ask me to warm it up," he mutters.

At his comment, I pull my head up and see his tall frame leaning against the counter with a bowl of—

"Did you make mac and cheese?" I'm way too excited over this discovery. I've dreamed of this delicious, calorie-filled delicacy for the past three nights.

I rush over to the counter and snag the remaining bowl. "You made this?"

I don't know why it seems shocking that he cooked. Maybe it's because he doesn't do it much. He mostly lives off beer and raw vegetables. However, he does have ice cream in the freezer so . . . "Your eating habits are like a pregnant lady," I note, tilting my head at his beer, sitting full on the counter.

He lifts a brow. "Pregnant ladies drink beer?"

I shovel a non-ladylike bite of cheesy noodles down my throat. "Mmm," I moan, my knees going weak at the cheesy goodness. "This is divine."

I ignore the scoff and eye roll he gives me. "It's not a filet."

Mumbling around another bite, I agree. "No, it's much better than a filet."

"You're ridiculous."

"You're"—I stop mid-sentence because I need another bite—"ridiculous. Don't judge me. I don't judge you when you waste your beer every night."

Fact. Every afternoon, Maverick comes home from taking souls or stealing firstborns, grabs a beer, twists the cap off, and rolls it through his fingers before carrying it around dutifully, as if it's his phone.

He rears back at my words. "I don't waste beer. I've drunk some of this one."

He does waste them, even the one sitting next to him. The question is, why? Why waste them if you don't like them? Why not just drink tea or milk? What does it matter if people see him with a beer or a Capri Sun just as long as he drinks it?

"Sure, you don't. The one next to you is so fresh that it's no longer sweating."

"I like it room temp," he argues, picking it up like he might drink it.

"That's why you keep it in the refrigerator." I nod like his explanation makes perfect sense when it doesn't at all.

"Eat your food," he snips.

"Drink your beer."

The playful look he had earlier drops in a matter of seconds. Here comes the "cold" Maverick. Not the one who lives here. My theory is the real Maverick Lexington is buried somewhere beneath all the lies and rumors but coaxing him out will take the right hand and one amazing bluff.

"I have work to do." He snatches his beer and tries to walk past me.

Not happening. I might not be as drunk as I was earlier, but I still have enough of a buzz to make me brave.

"I thought you were taking the night off for poker?"

He cocks a brow, keeping his distance like he's scared to touch me. "I was, but then someone decided to put on a show for the neighbors, and well, here we are."

"You didn't need to cancel. I would have stayed in my room."

He snorts out a sound of amusement. "Please. You've never followed one rule I've given you."

True. "I don't do well with many rules. It makes me antsy. Why do you want to keep my living here a secret anyway?"

I eye the almost full bottle in his hand. "Aren't you going to take a drink? I've been told that I drive people to drink with my conversations."

It's true, I have been told I'm nauseating at times, but really, I just want to see him take a swig of the beer he always carries around but never drinks.

"It's no one's business what I do at my own home."

See? He doesn't address the beer situation. He only gives me a morsel of the truth.

"Agreed. But you still haven't drunk any of your beer, and from the stress lines in your forehead, you could probably use it."

Come on, tell me the truth. Show me the real Maverick.

"You need to sleep. You're sounding belligerent."

"And you are sounding like a little faker."

"Who says I haven't drunk any? You were in the shower when I opened it."

Why am I doing this? Why am I trying to corner Maverick into admitting he doesn't drink beer? Honestly, I don't know. I think I would like to see that he doesn't have it all together, as he would love for you to believe. I want him to show me some of his truth like I've bared mine.

"I know you haven't drunk any. You never do."

He lets out a big sigh and rakes a hand through his hair.

Fine. I'll let it go. For now.

"Did you have a good day?" I change the topic.

That's neutral, roomie type conversation, right? I mean, it's not like I'm asking whose soul he took this afternoon.

His eyes snap to me and narrow. It's taking all he has not to shake me or chain me up in my room, but the chivalrous Maverick wins out. "It was fine."

His voice sounded pained.

"Like every other day," he adds when I just stare at him, waiting for details.

"I'm guessing that every day to you is like living your best life for most people."

Everything is at his fingertips. People want to be him. They want freaking tours of his apartment, for goodness' sake. I can't understand it, though. From what I've seen of Maverick Lexington, he's quite the bore except when he's making or enforcing deals. He's quite sexy and alpha-y and scary when he does those things.

But here?

Here he retires to his room early except for Wednesday poker night. He doesn't watch TV, and he doesn't go out much at night. I mean, he goes places, I suppose. He doesn't invite me along, so I can't say for sure what he's doing. He could be going to the library or the hospital to read to children. All I know is that he's here—a lot—always working away on his laptop.

At some point, though, he maintains that body. No way is he naturally blessed with muscle on top of muscle. I've never even seen him do a push-up or a P90X DVD or anything, though. However, I wouldn't be opposed if he decided to do either of those after dinner.

"Don't be ridiculous. My life is not someone's best life. My life is exhausting."

And complicated. And probably full of more rumors than truth, but we'll let him go with exhausting.

"Did you procure any new favors then? Is that why you're in such a good mood?" Blame it on Boxed Wine Ainsley. She wanted to know more about all this favor business.

His eyes roll dramatically.

"What have I told you about asking questions about the favors?"

He reaches into his pocket and pulls out a playing card. It doesn't scare me anymore. I have so many now that Maverick will die before I can repay them all.

Well, that's not true, but let's just say I owe him more than a handful at this point. What's one more?

"I just noticed your back pocket looked a little thin this afternoon."

All right, fine. I was looking at his ass. It's quite the firm masterpiece. Round and curved up into the perfect half-moon. Sue me. A girl can look.

He steps forward and sticks the card into my empty bowl of mac and cheese. I hope he made more.

Like he read my mind, his mouth quirks, and he nods to the stove. "I made extra."

The extra IOU was worth it for another bowl.

I grin and playfully punch him in the arm, nodding to his beer. "I hope you don't get dehydrated."

"I hope you don't get another IOU for getting on my nerves."

His threat has no bite to it, and again, he knows these IOUs are just another maxed-out credit card in my wallet—a debt that will one day be paid, but not today.

I grin and toss the card he put in my bowl on the counter. "So, did you go to class today? I hear the professors don't know what you look like. The guy in my Econ class said you were a redhead from Britain." That comment earns me another eye roll.

"People are stupid. I go to class."

Ehh. I'm going with a lie on that one. I never see Maverick around campus. Never. Had I seen him, I would have known who he was at Studs and Spuds.

"So, what did you do after class?"

Since I'm no longer blocking his path to freedom, he shakes his head and moves to the living room, plopping down on the couch.

Huh. That's shocking. I felt sure he would go to his room and slam the door and not come out until I was sound asleep.

"What is this, an interrogation? Am I being accused of something, or did you try to burn another apartment down and need to know if I can be your alibi?"

I fake a laugh, doubling over but careful not to spill my cheesy goodness. "Funny. Maybe I just want to get to know you better."

His scowl is back. "You're better off in the dark."

So that's a little mafia-like. "Fine." I move toward the sofa and sit on the coffee table—hopefully it's good quality and doesn't break beneath my weight. "I won't ask about what you do every day, but you gotta do one thing for me."

He laughs out loud, a deep rumbling sound that vibrates in his chest. "I do, do I? I thought I was already doing something for you."

I wave that away. "Me living here is a favor. This favor I want comes with a roommate discount."

He leans back, a big grin on his face. "I'm listening."

That's progress, right? At least he didn't laugh in my face and tell me no. Well, he did laugh in my face, but he didn't—never mind. You know what I mean. He also didn't squash the roommate discount proposal.

I set my bowl down on the table and ready myself for his reaction. *Stay with me alcohol, I'm going to need it after this.*

"I want to smell your breath."

Give it a second. One, two—there it is—Maverick doubles over laughing, the beer in his hand spilling a little on my precious couch.

"How much wine did you drink?" He finally manages to get out between laughs.

Okay, so it came out a little weird, but I stand by my favor.

"You say I didn't see you drink your beer since I was in the shower. Prove it to me. Let me smell your breath."

Shh. I am a little tipsy, but still, I want to know. I need to know some of his truth.

"What are you doing, Ainsley?" His tone turns serious.

"I want to know if you're lying."

His eyes narrow and his jaw clenches, the prominent muscle in his cheek flexing, making his bone structure look even more chiseled—if that's even possible.

"I didn't realize I had to prove I drink my own beverages to guests in my house."

I was prepared for him to get mean.

Still don't care.

"You don't," I tell him, a light tone to my voice. "But I'd like to know that I can trust you."

"You can't trust me."

His jaw is still tight, and he seems serious.

"I think I can."

"I think you're drunk."

And here we go again.

"I think you like people to believe you're this big bad, beer-drinking, poker-playing god. But really, you're just a water drinking nerd."

His head rears back like I slapped him.

Maybe I went too far this time? I need to know, though. "Are you plastic like everyone else?"

Plastic. Imposter. Fake. It doesn't matter what word I use. The question still means the same.

"I want to know the truth."

It takes him a second, digesting my words, but then he relaxes and settles back into the couch, lifting one hip and fishing out those damn cards. Ugh. Have we not been over this? These don't scare me anymore. I mean, they do, but they don't. They are future Ainsley's problem.

"Okay, Ainsley. I'll play," he says finally. "You want to see me drink this beer?"

I nod, ever so softly. "Yes."

"You think I'm fake?" His voice has taken on a hard edge, and I'm not sure I want to keep playing this game. It's taken a trip down the serious hill. But still, I'm a sucker for the truth.

"I do."

"You think I'm not drinking the beers I keep buying at the store every week?"

He says it all sarcastically, like I should feel stupid for thinking such things. Trust me; I don't. I feel pretty confident I'm right on this one.

"Again, I do."

He smirks and settles back into the couch.

"All right. Let's see how much it's worth to you." He flips the playing cards between his fingers, like a threat.

"I thought we were doing the roommate discount?"

I already know the answer to my question.

"You forget, I don't do freebies."

I didn't forget. I was just hoping I had grown on him a little, enough for him not to consider everything with me a deal.

Whatever. I didn't grow boobs overnight. Maverick needs a little more time.

"How about we up the ante?" I offer like a complete fool. "Make it like a poker game? If I'm right, you have to take back one of my cards and owe me a favor. If I'm wrong, I'll owe you two favors."

"That's not how this works." That's what his voice says, but his eyes say something else. At the mention of a bet, those midnight irises go hungry.

"Are you scared I might win?" I tease. "Come on, it'll be like a twofer, right?"

He licks his lips.

Come on, take the bet.

"The big bad Maverick isn't nervous, is he?"

He shakes his head after a moment of just staring at me as if this has been the most ridiculous afternoon he's ever had. Which, I'll admit, this probably ranks pretty high up there for me too.

"I mean, if you're scared, then don't worry about it." I shrug. "I know I'm right anyway."

That gets him. You never threaten a poker player with being scared. Maverick watches me intently for a few more seconds before saying, "Deal," and leans back on the couch, allowing his knees to fall open.

"All right, Ainsley. Come smell my breath."

He pats his leg with his free hand.

Shit. I really did not think this through. Too late now, though. I inch slowly, heart in my throat at what could possibly be severe indigestion, and swallow past the nerves.

"Closer." He coaxes. "Can't smell my breath from there."

Ugh. "You can lean forward more," I whine.

It's not like he doesn't look all sexy and snuggly, but I'm starting to have doubts now that he is allowing me to follow through with this crazy bet.

I inch in further with my hands braced along his muscular thighs, until we're nose to nose, staring into each other's eyes, a silent challenge hanging between us. I'm usually not that competitive of a person, but Maverick Lexington brings out the challenger in me.

"Breathe on me," I tell him. We're close enough that I don't need to get any closer.

A smile forms on his face before it turns into something more sinister.

Ah hell. He's going to kill me, isn't he?

He opens his mouth and, with his free hand, grabs the back of my neck, holding me close. I'm tense, holding still and waiting on his breath to hit my nose, but instead, a cold liquid splashes my cheek, dripping down into my mouth as he takes a big drink between us.

"Hey!" I cry. "You cheated!" I try to pull away and wipe my face—what the fuck?—but Maverick shoves me backward, my back hitting the table, and my legs pinned between his. A crash sounds outside, and a quick look shows he tossed the bottle out on the patio. The glass shatters, and there's no time to scold him.

Before I know it, his face pushes against mine, his nose angled just so. His chest is heaving, pounding against my own. Stormy eyes, filled with fury lock onto mine before he presses his lips to mine, his hands spanning my jaw to the back of my head, tilting me back and opening my mouth. Bitter and warm, the beer floods my mouth, and I have no other option but to swallow it. It glides down my throat, lighting my body up with heat as Maverick replaces it with his tongue. My hands are at his head, pushing? Pulling?

I don't know what I'm doing. I can't tell if I'm so mad that I'm turned on or if his crazy speaks to my crazy, and I want to fuck him out of my system. Is this what losing it feels like? My hands are in his hair, pulling and kneading, taking everything he won't say as he licks and sucks my bottom lip, exploring my mouth as if he could do it all day without tiring.

And then it's over, just like that. Maverick pulls away and licks the remaining beer off my cheek before swiping his tongue along his lips.

I don't miss a beat.

"You still cheated."

He leans back casually like we just didn't devour each other's faces.

"You didn't say I couldn't *continue* to drink my beer. You only asked to smell my breath."

"Which you didn't let me do," I add.

He leans in and breathes on my face. "Happy?"

Have you freaking ever? This man.

"Now, if you're done doing cavity searches, I'll be in my room."

He stands, righting me by the shoulders so I don't topple over, and grabs the marker and a couple of cards. He does his thing with them and tosses them onto the sofa. "Nice playing with you, James. Next time, know your opponent better."

Then he strides to his room and closes his door.

Are you freaking kidding me?

I want to yell that he still cheated, and this doesn't count, and these cards are just wasted on me. I do not plan on fulfilling these favors. Let him do with me what he wishes. I sweep the cards off the couch and head to the kitchen for the broom. Someone has to clean the glass up from the patio. I rather enjoy sitting and watching the sun come up, and I prefer not to need stitches when I forget there's glass on the floor. Better to clean it up now since clearly Maverick's ass isn't going to.

Frustrated, I drag the broom over the chunks of glass and get as much up as I can. I reach for the bin Maverick keeps out here just for his empty beer bottles and stop.

"Are you fucking serious?" I say to no one.

A fire extinguisher awaits on the small table next to the chair Maverick usually sits on. He has some nerve. I pick it up and notice it's full. The label lists that it's a Class A extinguisher, which will smother fires containing cloth, wood, rubber, paper, and plastics.

Such a thoughtful smartass my roomie is.

I'm shaking my head, containing a stupid grin when a rolled piece of paper falls out of the handle.

Unrolling it, I read it aloud. "Some people are meant to burn, and others are meant to rise from their ashes."

What? What does that mean?

I look at the table again and spot it.

There, lying face up in an ashtray is the picture of Tucker and me that Maverick caught me looking at when we were moving me out of my apartment. At the time, he smashed the frame and took the picture, stuffing it into his pocket. I hadn't thought about it since.

But he did.

He held onto it until today.

I re-read the note and pick up the picture, a lighter hiding underneath.

Some people are meant to burn, and others are meant to rise from their ashes.

And then I set that bitch on fire.

Chapter Twelve

Maverick

Rumor has it the neighbors heard screams coming from his room.

"Is he okay?"

A familiar tingling in my hands has me standing up to pace around my bedroom.

"Yeah, just a TIA," my brother says, sounding amused and slightly distracted.

Good, I can handle brief stroke symptoms. "Are they concerned about another stroke?" I rub at the pain in my chest. "Are they going to keep him overnight at least?"

"I'm talking to Mav, old man. Mind your business and eat your Jell-O," he says, talking to Pops instead of me.

"Maverick? Why is he up at two in the morning?"

I sigh into the phone. I already know what's coming.

"I called him," my brother returns, exasperated. "You're the one making our young bodies lose sleep."

"You weren't losing sleep, you little shit. You had to give that poor girl cab money so we could leave."

Their arguing has me craving a visit home. I miss both of them.

"It's called Uber, Pops, and she was lost. I was looking up hotels for her when you called out that the Reaper was here to take you."

"Maverick!" Pops hollers, most certainly disrupting other patients at the hospital. "Go to bed! I'm fine."

My brother quickly jumps in. "Funny how you had no concern in waking me up! Where's the concern for my sleep deprivation?"

"You weren't asleep!"

I snort. "Sounds like he's just fine," I tell my brother.

"I told you he was fine in my text."

Thunder rattles the window. "I know, but I needed to hear it from you."

"You mean, you needed to make sure I wasn't lying?" He's not offended; he knows how I am.

"Exactly." No sense in lying about it. I needed to hear my brother's voice to make sure he didn't sound bleak or stressed. With text, he and Pops could say whatever to ensure I did not come home.

"Sure you don't want me to come down and help?"

It's an excuse to see them, but I really do want to help more. Apart from what Pops thinks, I won't drop out of school and work at the QuickMart. Sure, I've considered moving home and helping out more, but Pops has been downright vicious in keeping my ass firmly planted at Havemeyer. It's always been important to him that we boys go to college. Cooper can beg Pops all he wants about joining the MLB, but he will go to college if Pops has anything to say about it.

"No, Mav. We don't need your bossy ass coming down and telling us what to do, right, Pops? We got it. Stay there, get some sleep and pus—"

"Boy!"

I grin at Pops jumping in. They are like two old men arguing over a chess game.

"I was just telling him to have a Push Pop, old man. Why is your mind always in the gutter? Is that a side effect from the stroke or—"

"I will get out of this bed, Cooper Lexington."

I laugh. "Don't make him get out of the bed, Coop."

"The doctor says he needs to move around more," Coop argues, but it's a joke. The fact is, Pops and Coop have a great relationship, one that I miss having with them.

"Stop gossiping to your brother and go home. You and him both should have been in bed hours ago."

Cooper laughs into the phone. "Oh, I'm going back to bed. Don't you worry, Pops."

"I swear on your mother, Coop. You are not too old for me to tear that ass up with my belt."

Pops is so full of shit. He's never spanked nor laid a hand on Cooper or me, but it gets a laugh out of us, just as I'm sure he intended.

"All right, Pops, you scared us. Maverick is already tucked in, and I'm heading out. Behave yourself. I don't want to have to sacrifice my virginity to convince these nurses to let your hateful ass stay here."

Good Lord. "Bye, Coop. Bye, Pops."

Cooper and Pops laugh. "Good night, Maverick."

I toss the phone on my nightstand and stare out at the black skies, watching as the rain pummels the earth with its soothing ointment.

The fire extinguisher I left Ainsley is gone from the patio. Not that I can see it but because I watched her take it in, right after she set the picture of her and that fucker on fire. I might have smiled as she watched it go up in flames and flip it off, yelling something I'm sure sounded crazy to the neighbors.

But she was healing, and for that, I was proud to help with.

I don't have experience with breakups, but I can't take watching her cry. This T-named fucker has tarnished enough of her free spirit.

The thunder rumbles again, and I'm positive I won't be going back to sleep anytime soon. With the news about Pops and all the work still sitting open on my laptop, I may as well get something to drink and burn off this restlessness. Maybe I can finish a few things, and the ache in my chest will dwindle to something milder. Knocking out files always makes me feel better.

The kitchen light is on when I crack open the door, and a few steps later, I know why. Ainsley is perched in one of the kitchen chairs, her knee bent with her iPad in her hands.

She doesn't look up when I approach, and it annoys me to the point of grinning. No one is comfortable in my presence. The rumors make sure of that, but not Ainsley, she sees through the mask.

"Couldn't sleep?" I ask her.

She shrugs, still not fucking looking at me. "The storm woke me, and I couldn't go back to sleep."

I nod even though she doesn't see me do it.

"Do you want anything to drink?" I'm already snagging an extra cup from the cabinet. This whole routine feels domesticated.

"Yes, please."

The air around us doesn't feel awkward, but I don't think it ever has. From the moment I found her begging at my doorstep, it wasn't awkward. The banter comes easy, and the give and take between us feels genuine. It feels normal, and for some reason, that worries me. When have I ever felt comfortable in the past few years?

I pour water for both of us and set it on the table.

"What are you playing?" I can already guess it's a game. She's addicted to them. At least that's what her weekly screen time suggests. Yes, I snooped. Call it a background check.

"Who Wants to Be a Millionaire," she answers, glancing up at me with a faint smile. "It's my favorite."

Another surprise. She's playing trivia and not something mindless. "Are you winning?"

Just because she plays doesn't mean she's any good at it.

She shrugs. "I'm at two hundred and fifty k."

"Not too shabby." I pull out a chair and wedge in beside her, looking over at her screen.

"Uh . . . What are you doing?"

I hit the button for the next question. "I'm helping you win."

She sweeps my hand off the tablet. "I don't need your help. I can win it on my own."

Don't care. I want to play now.

"Well, you better hurry then."

She gasps and hurries to read the question. "Which of the following phrases describes a close association with someone?"

I smirk when she mumbles out the answers, seemingly confused.

"Maverick! Help me!"

"I thought you could win on your own?"

The timer is ticking down, five, four—"I can't! Please help me. I've never come this close before."

That'll work.

"C. Hand in glove."

She scrambles to press the button, not questioning if I'm sure. The button lights up green.

"How did you know that?" Her forehead wrinkles.

"I told you I go to class."

"No, you don't. I've never seen you on campus."

Ah. This is what I needed. My chest is already feeling lighter, my pulse slowing with every sentence. "I've never seen you on campus either. Does that mean you don't attend class as well?"

The lips I kissed mere hours ago purse, drawing my eyes to their fullness.

"Why do you never like to answer questions about yourself?"

I cock a brow. "Why do you always ask so many questions?"

I love getting under her skin. It's better than poker.

"Ugh. You're impossible."

That I am.

"And you're about to lose."

"Shit!"

She hurries and presses the button for the next question. "Which of the following phrases begins a professional dart match? Game on, fire away, or drink up?"

She has no clue. The wide-eyed expression confirms it.

"That's an easy one," I muse.

"Well then, help me!"

"How much is it worth to you?"

She narrows her eyes, her cheek indenting. The look is violent. "I will cut you, Maverick Lexington. Do not come between me and this game."

She's so cute when she's attempting to be tough.

I close my mouth, pressing my lips together as if I'm not budging until she gives me what I want: a debt.

"Fine! Slide a damn card in my trash can later. Happy?"

"Very."

Too happy. This has been the most fun I've had in months.

"Game on," I answer.

She clicks the answer and gives a little squeal of delight when it turns green.

"You want to know what I think, Maverick?"

I snort out a laugh. "No, I don't."

"You're getting it anyway."

I always do, and secretly, I enjoy it.

"I think you keep these scary rumors going on around you, so no one will find out you're really a water drinking trivia nerd."

See? Observant little thing.

"Are you making fun of me for being smart?"

Redirect her, Maverick.

"I didn't say that. I'm impressed you're smart. I just don't understand why you try to hide it. "

"Who says I hide it? I've never denied I was smart."

She pauses a moment, and then waves away her comment. "Okay, I take that back. Maybe you don't necessarily hide it, but you keep people from finding out the real you." She grins. "The super-duper smart you."

I nod, rather impressed. "Maybe you're right—"

"I know I am."

I ignore her comment and finish my sentence from before she interrupted me with her bragging. "Maybe you're right, but how many people know the *real* you? The you that sleeps with stuffed sea lions and watches aquarium reality shows."

That smug smile of hers drops.

Not so confident now, are we?

"How many people at Havemeyer know you spend your late nights up playing trivia games?" I add, just to drive my point home.

She's quick to snap back. "You're playing too! And you're up just as late!"

I shrug and press the button for the million-dollar question. "Guess you know some of the real me then."

It's all I can share with her right now. As much as she's growing on me, eventually, I will find her an apartment, and she will leave, taking the real me with her.

Her face relaxes at my comment, and she takes a breath, nodding like I've made her happy admitting that *some* of her observations of me are correct. "Last question. You ready?"

"Ready." Excitedly, she shifts in her seat, pushing up against my hip. "Can you see?"

I swallow. "I can see." Right down her tank top where the soft swell of her breasts rises with each intake of breath. If that weren't torture enough, the smell of my shampoo coming from her hair is enough for me to want to stake a claim.

"All right, here we go. What can be both a resinous substance obtained from turpentine and part of a cricket field?"

I worry my lip with my fingertip, making her fear that I don't know the answer, but really, I'm just taking a few extra breaths to settle down my rock-hard dick. Must she be this close?

"Please tell me you know because I'm seriously thinking about Googling the answer, Maverick!"

I grin. I like her calling out my name all desperate like.

"I'll take another IOU. Please!" she begs.

I would have done it for free.

Clearing my throat, I answer quickly. "The pitch."

"Are you sure? It's for a million dollars . . ."

I cock a brow.

"A fake million," she clarifies, "but still. It's the principle of the matter." Her eyes dart to the screen, watching the clock count down. She's waiting on my confirmation.

"I'm positive," I say, feeling the anxiousness from her body.

"Okay. Water drinking nerd for the win," she drawls out loudly, ignoring the bored look I give her and finally pressing the button.

Images of confetti and balloons explode on the screen right before she tackles me in a bruising hug. "We did it!"

Holding her close, I try to hold on as she bounces up and down, her braless tits torturing me through my shirt.

"Be still." I press her down.

"What? Why? Why can't we celebrate? We won a virtual million dollars!"

For the love of God, she's still moving.

"Ainsley." My voice is a growl and stops her mid-air, where she realizes what she's doing to me.

"Oh," she says, very amused. "I didn't realize you were that excited about winning."

What a smartass.

"Yeah, it's been quite the revelation."

She eases down to my lap, careful not to impale herself on my dick straining to get through my pajama pants. "Thank you," she whispers, her breath fanning across my lips. Her words hold sincerity. She's not just thanking me for helping her win the game.

"Who knew you could be so poetic?" She inches closer, and with each word, her lips drag against mine.

So much for calming my dick down.

"I don't know what you mean," I lie.

It's verbal foreplay with enough sexual tension to drive me mad. How badly I want to hoist her up and slam her against the table.

She presses her lips harder. "I'm calling your bluff, Maverick Lexington."

Haven't I told her to know her opponent before she plays the game?

I snatch her by the hips and yank her lower half forward so my hard cock meets her softness. "Are you sure you want to do that? Remember last time how that game played out for you." I'm referring to all the IOUs she racked up.

Her hips rock and heaven help me, I enjoy the feel of her against me for just a moment before I stop her, and she moves her lips over mine. "I remember, and I'm willing to go all in. You left me that note. Why?"

Fuuuck. Why did she have to say it so confidently—so challenging?

Now I have to play, but I have the losing hand. It's not that I don't want to admit to Ainsley that I left the fire extinguisher and the note, because clearly, she knows it was me. But forcing me to admit that I care about her well-being is out of the roommate zone and into something else that I can't handle just yet.

"I was merely protecting my apartment from future fires," is what I go with instead.

I can feel her smile press against my frown. "Hmm . . . I suppose that is partly the truth."

Yes, yes, it is.

"Well," she says after a moment, "nevertheless, I appreciate the thoughtfulness. It's been a long time since I've had a friend who cared."

A friend who cared.

Is that what I am? A friend? My dick sure disagrees. Sure, I'd like for her to stop trampling on my personal space and sure, I'd like my sofa back sans the stuffed sea animals, but I'm not that much of a dick. I don't like to see any woman cry, especially over someone so undeserving—someone like my father who put his image and business above his wife and kids.

That's all this is between Ainsley and me—a contract. I owe her a place to stay until I can find her something permanent. It's in my neighbor's and my best interest to keep the crying and the crazy down to a minimum.

It is a contract, Maverick. Don't forget.

Her lips press against me again, and this time, my mouth opens and allows her full access. Soothingly, her tongue sweeps in, leisurely exploring as her hands find my hair and sink in.

God, it feels so good.

Her touching me anywhere feels so fucking good. How long has it been since I've felt a woman's touch? Months? I can't even remember. All I know is that it has been way too fucking long. And if I could trust myself not to flip her over onto this table, I would let go of her hips and tangle my fist in all those messy curls and enjoy the feel of the silky strands that smell like me.

I won't, though.

Taking this any further breaks all my rules.

I can't afford any more of a distraction than I already have.

I put these rules in place to keep me motivated, to keep me focused, but I'm already fucking it up by having her living here.

She needs to go.

I need to stop.

I grip her hard, moving her hips over mine one last time. And one more time and—*Great, Maverick. Good job convincing yourself to let her go.*

The friction between us is so magnetic that I can't physically let go.

"Mmm . . ." she moans in my ear.

Let her go, Mav. She just ended a long relationship. She's vulnerable and needs comforting. You can't give her what she needs.

But I could comfort her, for the night anyway.

My subconscious kicks in, chasing the horny advice away.

Ainsley needs stability and real love; neither of those things I'm nailing right now. I live a lie—a very exhausting lie, and I can't stop. I'm in too deep. It doesn't matter if I enjoy Ainsley's company. I need to finish what I started.

"Wait," she says, pulling back. Her lips are swollen and glossy, her face flushed with heat.

I almost groan at the cold air that hits my neck, but I don't.

This is good.

No, this sucks.

"What's wrong?" I force myself to ask. Any other time the fake Maverick would be mean and just stand up and walk away, but the real Maverick actually wants to know what's wrong and possibly high five her for being the bigger person and breaking the connection. I sure as fuck couldn't.

"I'm so sorry," she says, breathing the words along my lips.

A little farther back would be nice.

"I don't want to use you."

I grin. Her use me? Ha!

She's serious, though, so I don't comment. "You've been so nice to me that I don't want to mess things up between us. All I've done is mess up with my decisions—"

Remind her that what we have is a contract, not a friendship.

"I don't want to make our relationship one of those."

Remind her!

I kiss her on the nose instead. "Good night, Ainsley. I expect half of my fake million tomorrow morning, payable in IOUs."

Chapter Thirteen

Ainsley

Rumor has it she poisoned him.

"This is so awkward—just stop. You've given me too much information as it is."

My ears are bleeding and I'm seriously concerned about all the times my mom said the moans coming from her room at night were really from eating Truffles.

"You asked for my opinion!"

"No, I didn't!"

I sort of did, but she's the one who took it to Inappropriateville.

"Yes, you did. You asked me how I handled being alone. I merely said books and rechargeable batteries."

"Ahh! Don't say it again. I just meant like what do you do when the toilet is clogged and the trash needs taking out."

Maverick asked me this morning how I would feel about renting a house versus an apartment. His friend said we might have more luck with a private home versus an apartment complex. I don't really want a house at this point in my life, but Maverick wasn't in the hearing-me-out mood. His glare suggested this wasn't a multiple-choice question but rather him letting me know, in a non-shitty way, this is what I would be doing.

It wasn't the time to tell him that even if I could afford the rent on my own, I wouldn't know what to do with a house. Apartments have idiot-proof chutes to dump your trash and a maintenance man who lives in the building who will unclog your drains as long as your roommate wears a crop top short enough to show underboob.

I don't know much about renting houses, but since I have no desirable underboob to flaunt, I need to learn what to do with trash and toilets if this is going to be my new way of living—hence the reason I called my mom—a big mistake, by the way.

"Well, you need to be more specific, dear. I thought you meant something else entirely. Either way, sweetie, books and rechargeable batteries are great to have on hand during a power outage."

Give me freaking strength.

"Also, there is nothing wrong with a woman who knows how to please herself. How can you expect a man to know what you like if you don't?"

A whole bunch of ick is spewed in those few sentences, but when I think about it, she's right. Last night, Maverick had my body tingling in places I didn't know existed. And when I went to my room—just kidding, it was still the sofa—I tried to bring those tingles back and finish the job. I couldn't, if you're wondering. Part of me was a little scared Maverick would come back out and catch me, and the other part of me wished he would volunteer to rekindle those blessed tingles.

Maybe I was tired or just too excited that I had finally won a fake million dollars, which I wrote an IOU for and slipped under Maverick's door. It wasn't fancy, and I didn't waste five hundred thousand cards like he probably expected. Instead, I emptied a box of mac and cheese—that I hope he will cook before I get back—and flattened the box, writing: *IOU too many favors to count—consider my life yours. Do with me as you wish.*

I thought it was pretty funny, but when Maverick emerged, all devil-like and sweating, I knew he didn't appreciate my humor first thing in the morning. But it could be he's just in a bad mood or suffering from a severe case of blue balls. Clearly, he was just as affected as I was. Maybe he too had problems finishing the job last night.

"Ainsley, did I kill you? Mumble if I need to call an ambulance."

I shake off this morning's encounter with Maverick. "I'm here. What kind of books are you referring to?" May as well be thoroughly grossed out and satisfied. "Like Kama Sutra type stuff?"

My mom hesitates for a moment. She's probably shocked I asked her to clarify. "Yeah, those and other instructional type books. The internet works well too."

"Mom!"

"You asked!"

I take in a deep breath. "You're right, I did. So do I just go to a sex shop for one of these books?"

She's quick to respond. "Personally, I like the brick and mortar bookstores. They have the best selections."

Later, I'll worry about whether she stumbled upon this discovery or if she asked someone to show her the sex section—I know it's probably called something a little cuter like Women's Fantasy.

"Noted. I'll have to check it out on my way home," I tell her, already thinking about which store I want to stop at.

"Are you off tomorrow?"

I take off my work shoes and throw on a pair of flip-flops to drive in. "Nope. Tucker gave me more hours this week."

She hums in the background like she could say something nasty about him but keeps her mouth shut. "Is that cunt still giving you a hard time?"

I snort. "Mom!"

I don't care if she calls Taylor a cunt. She is.

"A little. Tucker stepped in a few times, so it hasn't been too bad."

"Don't let that weasel make you think he's helping you. He's the reason you're in this mess in the first place!"

My mom, the no bullshitter in my life. "I'm not, Mama. I'm just trying to get through the shift so I can pay Mav—Mavis some rent and save for this new house I could possibly be renting when she kicks me out."

Don't judge me. She did not need to hear I was living with another guy after just breaking up with a liar. Remember, she's not a man's biggest fan.

"How much is Mavis charging you? Maybe I can help."

I slip off my pantyhose while cranking the car. "She won't say. Every time I ask her, she just ignores me."

"Maybe she's just a really sweet girl."

I smother a snort.

"Too bad you can't stay with her through the rest of the semester."

I nod, grinning big as my mom goes on about Maverick being a sweet girl. "She likes her space, Mama. You can understand that." Seeing how she's always lived alone.

My mama sighs a deep and disappointed sigh. "I suppose. Maybe give her what you can in rent, and perhaps she'll change her mind and let you stay."

Or she'll throw a hellacious packing party so that I'm out in a matter of minutes.

"Maybe," I agree. "Kiss Opie for me. I'll call you later. Love you!"

"Love you too, sweetie. I'll send you some author names of these books and you can look them up later."

God, no. "It's okay. I'm sure I can find something on my own."

Find one I did. This two-hundred-and-ninety-five-page instructional manual on pleasuring my vajayjay embarrassed the utter shit out of me when I bought it. The dude behind the register said it was really informative, though, so I let the embarrassment go. I'm going to do me. Literally.

I knock on the door of our—Maverick's apartment. He still hasn't given me a key, and that's fine. It's a good reminder that our arrangement is temporary. Often, I find myself getting too comfortable with our shared space and his lips.

I bang again, placing my ear to the door like the first time I stood behind it. "Maverick! Open the door. I swear I won't use your deodorant again. It was only one time!"

Gah, he's such a sourpuss about his stuff.

A blaring alarm sounds just as I raise my hand to knock again.

Wait. I know that sound. It's the smoke detector.

"Maverick!"

Oh shit. He's going to burn to death.

I look around the hallway. Empty. "Help—"

My cry is cut off by a door opening and a hand covering my mouth. "Don't you dare," he says all breathily, pulling me in and locking the door behind us.

"What's going on?"

I notice a pot on the stove—my precious macaroni noodles overflowing and burning on the stovetop. He was making it for me but why is—

"Help me shut this fucking thing up." He shoves a towel in my hand. For a moment, I just stand there, taking in his wet shirt and pale skin, shaking as he fans the smoke with enough force to barely move a feather.

I tug on his shirt. "Let me fan. I have more experience with fires than you do."

I expect an argumentative comment or at least a laugh, not a grim nod and acceptance. Moving a chair, I step up and take his place, fanning as hard as I can while Maverick turns off the stove and tosses the pot into the sink. After a few seconds, I have the alarm quieted, and notice Maverick is leaning against the counter, looking like death.

"Are you okay?"

I push the chair back under the table and take a few steps until he stops me by holding his hand up. "I'm fine, just tired. Can you just order pizza or something tonight?"

His voice sounds weird. Is this what tired Maverick sounds like? I don't think so. It sounds like he's sick.

"Sure. No problem. Can I get you anything?"

He really does look like death.

He shakes his head. "I'm just going to lie down."

I agree. "I think that's a good idea."

Hopefully, it helps.

He nods and brushes past me without so much as another word. Once the door closes, I begin cleaning up the apartment. It's not too bad, but I don't want Maverick waking up and finding a pile of dishes and burnt—is this water? Can you burn water?—on the stove.

One less bra and a lot of elbow grease later, I'm praying I won't be beheaded as I stack the poker chips on the table in neat, color-coordinated piles. I've noticed he likes to mess around with the chips when he's thinking, so they never stay organized until Wednesday when he has game night. He has instructed me not to call it that—game night. Per him, it's called poker night, and apparently, he gets all bent out of shape if you make fun of his little get-togethers with his boys.

I'm almost finished cleaning when his laptop dings with a notification. He never leaves it open. Walking to the coffee table, I lean over and take a peek. One look won't hurt. I simply want to know if I can swipe it away and let him rest.

From the way he looked, he could really use it. I've never seen Maverick sick or even less than one hundred percent. He keeps that part of himself hidden away along with his laptop. So him leaving it lying around where I can see it is a big deal.

I rub the touchpad, and his lock screen comes up, but part of the notification still remains.

I'll take your advice and not sell. Keep the 30% in my Roth IRA and the additional 20% we spoke about in mutual funds. I—

The preview ends, and no matter how much clicking I do, I can't get in without the password.

What in the fresh hell?

Does this guy have the wrong email address? What would Maverick have to do with mutual funds and IRA accounts? I don't even know what exactly those are. I mean, I do, but not much. I've heard of them, though.

A clattering sound echoes down the hall.

Jerking up, I close the laptop. "Maverick? Are you okay?"

My voice carries down the hallway before I follow, placing my hand on the door handle. A million questions race through my head—ones like: What if he's fine and just rolled off the bed? What if he sleepwalked into the nightstand? Will he be upset if I go into his room?

I've never gone into his room. It's like willingly walking into the abyss. I don't know what's behind that door, but I know it won't be good for me if I cross the threshold.

But what if he's hurt?

He didn't look good.

"Maverick? Just yell that you're fucking fine, and I'll leave you alone."

I add the word *fucking* because that's how he would say it. Not that he was fine but that he was *fucking fine* and to go away. I'm being realistic here.

"Ains—" My name sounds strained from behind the door and much like *come in and check on me*. Don't you think?

Twisting the knob, I ease it open. "Maverick," I warn. "I just want to check—Oh my God!"

I sprint to Maverick's side, finding him on the floor, half propped up against the footboard of his bed. His face is ghostly white and sweat soaks his clothes.

"I'm fine." He tries to wave me off, but he can't even lift his hand.

"Sure, and I'm a supermodel," I agree, lifting my hand and placing it on his forehead. "You're not running a fever. What's wrong?" This is the craziest thing I've ever seen. "Should I call an ambulance?"

He grunts out a firm, "No."

I should have known. "Tell me how to help you," I plead. I'm scared he might die right in front of me.

He shifts and casts me a worried look.

I glare. "Now is not the time to worry about your fucking image! I won't say anything, I swear. Please let me help you."

Maverick's eyes close, and I put my hand in his. I'm just about to shake him when he says, "Breathe with me."

"What?"

His face pinches. "I need to hold my breath, but I need you to count the beats, so I know when to stop."

He places his hand on his chest.

"Is it your heart?" I ask, more afraid than I was thirty seconds ago when I thought he had a cold or something.

"Please stop asking questions." He groans.

"Fine," I agree, willing to do anything at this point to help. "Do you need me to just breathe normally? You don't want me to do the pregnant-labor-y type breathing?"

For just a moment, he tries to be the Maverick I know. "Do you know how to do 'labor-y' breathing?"

"Well, no, but I could look it up if that's what you need."

The internet has everything.

His slow head shake is pitiful. "No. It isn't what I need, but I appreciate your willingness to do what it takes." It's not a thank you for helping or talking or getting in his way, but it is an acknowledgment. He appreciates me and loathes asking for my help.

"Okay." I take a deep breath, not for his sake but for mine. I need one relaxing breath before I start. "Ready?" I ask him.

I don't wait for his nod. I'm already pulling in a breath and exhaling, hoping I'm doing it at the pace I normally would and not faster since I'm nervous.

Maverick watches me for a few seconds, and then I see his chest rising with mine, but it's too fast. He can't pace his breathing with mine.

"I need to hold my breath," he grates out. "Count for me?"

I nod hesitantly. "Maybe we should go to the hospital instead?"

"No."

Okay, so he's going to die on the floor. Check.

"What do I need to count to?"

His chest is rising and falling rapidly. "Ten."

I can do that.

I start counting and watch in horror as Mav holds his breath, clenching his fist as if he's bearing down. Finally, he lets go and exhales a burst of air. "I can't get it to convert."

For the first time since knowing Maverick, he looks afraid.

"I don't know what you mean about converting," I add, "but I think we need to call for help, Mav."

"Don't call me that," he barks between short pants.

I scrunch my nose. "Why?"

He manages, "Only my friends call me Mav."

I *almost* smile. We are friends. He can fight it all he wants, but friends don't let friends lose a game of Millionaire.

"Okay. I'll rephrase. I think we need to call for help, *Dummy*."

In the midst of dying, he manages to roll his eyes before his head falls back against the footboard. "We can't call anyone."

"Why?" I mean, what the hell? "The apartment is clean, and I can stash whatever you want to hide in my room. Please let me call someone." I want to add *dummy* again onto the end of my plea, but I refrain. I am serious—this is serious. We need help.

"I'll go to the hospital if you will take me," he says with horror-stricken eyes like he can't believe he suggested such a thing. "Just you, though. You can't tell anyone."

Of course. Whatever. "I'll take the fact that you do actually have a heart to the grave," I return, crossing my heart.

I stand to get my bag and keys. "But, Mav . . ." I don't care that he doesn't want me to call him that. I don't have time to say his whole name.

His eyes are heavy, and he looks exhausted. "Yeah?"

"You promise you aren't going to die on me?"

He's still shaking, but he stares at me, locking eyes. "I promise I won't die on you."

With that, I race off and grab my keys and bag, snagging a pair of Mav's sweats that ended up in my laundry—fine, I stole them—and one of my larger T-shirts, shoving them in my bag. When I get back to Mav, he's standing, looking like a sick mess.

"Lean on me," I tell him, wedging myself under his arm. He looks at me like he'd rather fall down the steps and die before using me for help, but I grab his arm anyway and force him forward. He eventually goes with it, and it's not that terrible. We hustle as much as one dying man can hustle, taking the steps excruciatingly slow until we reach the bottom and my car.

I open the door to the passenger side. "Get in," I order him.

The frown I'm used to seeing makes its appearance.

He doesn't move.

"Fine." I put my hands up. "Be a stubborn ass."

I trot around the front end of the car and watch as Mr. I-don't-need-your-help slams his door shut and opens it back up himself.

I smile. He's so ridiculous.

When he's finally in and settled, I speed off to the nearest hospital, trying to ignore his shitty remarks. "I would have been better off dying in the apartment. At least then, my family would have a body to bury. The way you're driving, and your history with fire, we're sure to end up a pile of ash."

"You were better off calling an ambulance about an hour ago, smartass. Why did you wait so long?"

He doesn't look so smug now. "I can usually convert the rhythm on my own."

I glance over, catching his sweat-soaked face still strained.

"This happens a lot?" I ask.

"Occasionally."

He would never admit exactly how often.

"Do you take medicine for it?" Clearly, he knows what he's supposed to do when this happens.

"No."

"Why not? Do they not have medicine to treat"—I wave my hand between us—"whatever this is?"

"I treat it conservatively."

My eyes narrow in his direction.

He mimics me but adds, "I should have put you up in a hotel. What was I thinking?"

He was thinking I was pretty fucking awesome, and he would eventually need my help.

"All right, Maverick. We're going to stop your heart for just a moment. You might feel a little weird, but everything is going to be fine."

Okay, so maybe I'm not much help to him. I might pass out.

When we arrived at the hospital, Maverick was rushed into a room, his shirt cut from his body, and wires upon wires were stuck to his beautiful chest. I followed along in a daze, not sure what I was supposed to do.

"Can we try the techniques again?" Maverick asks. His voice shakes with exhaustion.

They've been doing different things like asking him to blow on his thumb and bear down, but nothing has worked. His heart is still beating too fast. The doctor called it supraventricular tachycardia. I don't know precisely what all that means other than a spelling nightmare, but I gather it's a faster than normal heart rate for us non-medical people.

"How long has he been this way?" The doctor who seems to know Maverick looks at me.

"You're asking me?"

He nods, pointing at Maverick. "This one only gives me half the truth."

I want to grin so bad. He nailed Maverick perfectly. But instead, I cast a wary look at Mav. He's where my loyalty lies. He's my genie in the apartment and . . . my friend.

The corner of his lip twitches and his eyes beg me to keep quiet. "I can't lie," I whisper. "This is your life we're talking about."

His eyes squeeze shut. Maybe they shut from acceptance or maybe they shut because he's plotting my death. The world may never know.

"At least half an hour," I answer the doc.

He frowns, nodding simultaneously. "I'm sorry, Maverick. It's been too long."

Maverick doesn't answer him. No one does. Instead, the doctor starts calling out orders, and everyone moves, including me. I edge closer to the door as the nurse draws up the medication. I'm not sure if Maverick wants me in here, especially since I ratted him out to the doctor.

Maybe I should wait in the lobby. I think that's a good idea.

"Ains." Maverick's raspy voice stops me.

I turn, expecting him to pull a card from his pocket. "Yeah?"

He twists his head away, and I almost think he didn't mean to call me, when I see his hand. Outstretched from the mattress, his palm lies face up, inviting me to him.

Of course, I go.

When my genie needs me, I'm going to be there for him like he was for me.

Interlocking our fingers, he turns his face, holding my gaze. And then, I hang on, gripping the hand of the man who pretends not to be my friend until his heart stops.

Chapter Fourteen

Maverick

Rumor has it he likes wearing women's clothes.

"This is escalating, Maverick. I thought the last time we spoke you had everything under control?"

I watch as Ainsley paces the small ER room, on the phone with Fuckface. He had an extra shift open and knew she needed the money. She doesn't, but I felt like I couldn't interrupt since Dr. Kallay has been in my damn face for the past ten minutes.

"Maverick?"

This is all such a mess.

"Everything is under control," I promise, noting and discarding the disbelieving gaze of my cardiologist.

"So this was random? You haven't had any stress or lifestyle changes here recently?"

I almost bark out a laugh and ask him to see Exhibit A pacing my hospital room animatedly. "No."

"So, what do you think triggered the tachycardia if not from your usual stressors?"

Uh, let's see.

I had a great time with a girl last night playing a stupid fucking game that wasn't poker. I might have been pissed off that I allowed her to see the real me. Then, I might have been so mad that I reacted and told Mike just to find her somewhere to stay ASAP, agreeing I would cover the additional rent just as long as she was gone sooner rather than later.

But then she had to slide that fucking five hundred thousand IOU under my door. Fuck, what did it say again? Oh yeah, *IOU too many favors to count—consider my life yours. Do with me as you wish.*

I read that damn IOU fifteen times before I finally realized the pressure in my chest was mounting. Not even a run after she left soothed it. Not that she caused the tachycardia. I'd been battling it for a few days now, but after last night—the night I realized I wanted Ainsley James and not just for the semester but for longer—that's when all hell broke loose. For the first time since all this happened, I wanted to be selfish.

"Have you continued working?"

My gaze snaps to my doctor. Speaking about work is a no-go zone. "N—"

"Yes, he has," Ainsley interrupts, apparently finished with her call. "All the time. He's on his laptop *all* the time."

My dick twitches, and this is so not the time.

Is she seriously ratting me out again?

I'm fucking speechless and not that it matters because I can always squash what she thinks with a few well-placed rumors, but how? How does she know? Better yet, what does she know? I've never given her an opportunity to see the truth of what I was doing. Granted, she's seen me on my laptop, but I could have been fucking around on the internet. How does she know I've been working?

The monitor I'm connected to starts beeping faster.

Dr. Kallay frowns. "I thought you were going to tell your grandfather about it. We discuss—"

"I know," I cut him off. "He had a setback. I promise I'll tell him."

Like when I graduate, and it no longer matters.

"Maverick, listen, I know you're trying to protect him, but you're killing yourself. He wouldn't want you to do this."

A quick look at Ainsley shows she's listening to every word Dr. Kallay is vomiting out. She's not even trying to hide it.

Fuck. Fuck. Fuck.

I sigh, a deep, weighted type of sigh.

Dr. Kallay gets the hint. "Get some rest. I'll be back later, and we'll finish this conversation."

Can't wait.

I nod tightly, considering leaving against medical advice as soon as he leaves.

When the door closes, I make it a point not to look at Ainsley. The ceiling is good. It's nice and plain and not gorgeous or concerned about me.

"How are you feeling?" The bed shifts under her weight. So much for ignoring her. "Can I get you anything?"

"No." The answer is rude considering all she's done for me today, but I feel exposed, and that's not a place I like to be. I mean, why now? Why did she come into my life now instead of two years from now? I'd have my shit together by then.

"How do you know about my job?" I probe, redirecting the conversation to something more productive than my health.

She stands, folding her arms, and shrugs. "You left your laptop open in the living room."

Bullshit. No way does she know enough from me leaving it open. It's locked. Who told her? Sebastian? But he wouldn't dare speak to her outside of my presence. He's crazy but not stupid. I cock a brow for her to continue.

"No, sir," she scolds, appearing quite cute with a dainty scowl on her face. "You are in no position to demand. We'll negotiate."

I scoff, but she ignores it.

"For every one of the answers I give you, I get one in return."

No is right on the tip of my tongue, but so are other words like thank you and come—"Fine. What's your question?"

"Were you scared earlier when they gave you the medicine?" She looks down at her hands, wringing them tightly. "The one that stopped your heart for a moment . . ."

It was a weak moment on my part and exactly why I stay with contracts and IOUs. I don't do owing people anything, especially explanations. And especially explanations to Ainsley.

"Yes."

I'm not explaining. She was there. I reached for her hand, for fuck's sake. No way am I talking my way around that one. I was fucked-up when they gave it to me. "It was the first time they've ever had to convert my rhythm with medicine." Hence the reason I'm here for longer and not already back home, pouring beer through the deck of the balcony.

"How did you know about my job?" I ask again.

She grins smugly. "I didn't. But I tried to silence your notification earlier, and I may"—she drags the words out like she's proud of herself and finally has something on me—"have read the preview of an email you received about IRAs, CEOs, and such. Are you like *The Wolf of Wall Street* guy?"

I let out a sigh of relief. Good. She doesn't know everything.

"Is that your question? Am I like *The Wolf of Wall Street*?" I want to laugh so bad, but I hold it in, maintaining her seriousness.

She nods, never moving her arms. Weird.

"No, I'm not. I'm not a stock trader. My grandfather owns an investment company that I help out with from time to time. You could say I'm a part-time broker."

Partial truth and her eyes narrowing to slits tell me she knows it.

"My turn." I can already feel my mouth twitching at the corner. "What's going on with—" I tip my chin in the direction of her folded arms.

"With my arms?" she suggests.

Yep, that's exactly what I mean. Let's get off the topic of me. "Yeah, your arms. You cold?"

A faint puff escapes her lips.

She won't give me the satisfaction of admitting why she's standing there, suddenly stiff and awkward when she had no problem bossing me around earlier.

"I'm fine," she lies.

I nod, feeling a tiny, baby grin tugging at the corner of my mouth. "You can turn the air up if you're cold. The thermostat is on the wall."

She won't, though, because then she will have to drop her arms.

"Thanks, but that's not necessary. I'm fine."

My eyes never leave hers. "Did you hurt your arm fanning the smoke detector earlier?"

She can't contain the eye roll. "Funny. But no. I just happen to find this position comfortable."

She shrugs, but it's forced and still blocked with her folded arms.

"Really?" I challenge, the monitors going off again.

Settle down, Maverick. No one needs to come in here and realize the reason the monitors are going off is because your roommate is turning you on.

She cranes her neck to look at them. "Are you okay?"

"Fine. Answer my question."

Now isn't the time to admit that bantering with her excites me.

"I did. I told you it's a comfortable position. You should try it. You might find it's more comfortable than keeping that scowl on your face all day."

A hearty chuckle bursts from me. "Is that so?"

She nods. "Yep. It must be hard forcing a frown all day."

"How do you know it's forced?"

She shrugs one shoulder. "Science. It's been proven you use more muscles in your face frowning than you do smiling. You would know that if you went to class."

Again with the class attendance. "I go to class."

She nails me with an annoyed look that makes me laugh.

"Sometimes," I amend. "Happy? I go to class *sometimes*."

"How do you get away with that?"

Easy.

"Maverick shows up."

It's not actually that hard. Most professors do not care what body calls out "here."

Her mouth drops open in an O. "Who would voluntarily go to class for you?"

I arch a brow. We're wading into forbidden territory. "Who says they volunteer?"

She gasps and covers her mouth with her palm, leaving her chest in plain view.

"I knew it! That's what you use the IOUs for! So you can work during the day but still attend classes!"

Fuck her and her astute reasoning.

"Is crossing your arms as comfortable as me holding a frown?" I bring her attention back to her chest and off my life.

"Oh my God!"

She will never learn.

"Fine!" she admits almost shamefully. "I don't have a bra on and"—she takes a breath—"I thought you were sleeping and didn't think I would be going out tonight."

Suddenly, being trapped here, vulnerable in her presence, feels much better.

I drag a finger lazily around my lips. "I see. So you came home and took off your bra?" I just want her to elaborate.

"You were supposed to be sleeping! I thought you were sick!"

My oh my. How this day has perked up, literally.

"And here we are. Me shirtless and you braless. Oh, the rumors that will be spread tomorrow."

Not that I care. I just want her to know that whatever rumors are created around me will now include her. Yes, she and I have a contract, but I'm not sure I have enough IOUs to keep her quiet about all of this.

I've never had this happen.

Sebastian and Rowan know the truth about the favors, but they profit from my deals by collecting interest. I don't need the money. I just want the IOU. But Ainsley won't profit. There's nothing to stop her from getting mad at me and spilling everything she knows about my IOU operation.

She stands a little taller. "I don't care what people think of me or the lies they will tell after this."

And that's what I adore about her. She is who she is. Take her or leave her—she conforms to no one. Not even me.

"I'll use one of your IOUs as payment for bringing me to the hospital," I tell her. It's not a thank you but a contract. I need all of this to stay as a contract.

She flops down on the bed, not caring if she jostles me, and grabs the remote. "Shut up."

I chuckle. "I'm serious. I appreciate your help. Let me take one of your million IOUs away."

She scrolls through the channels.

"They have limited channels in here," I say after realizing she intends to ignore me. "You won't find that sea otter shit you're looking for."

"They're sea lions, not otters," she corrects, settling on the National Geographic channel and lying back, pushing me over in the process.

We sit quietly for a moment, watching rhinos bumble around when she whispers, "I didn't help you because I felt like I owed you."

Ahh. Always the giver. "You should."

"You don't scare me, Maverick Lexington."

I shake my head. "You don't want to be my friend, Ainsley James."

I catch her lips tip up in an almost smile. "You're right. I don't want to be your friend. I want to be your roomie."

After a miserable few hours in the hospital, Dr. Kallay finally agrees to release me but not before stressing that I need to tell Pops about what I've been doing to his company. I don't plan on fulfilling that request anytime soon. What Pops doesn't know won't hurt him.

"You want anything to eat?" Ainsley calls out from the kitchen.

I shake my head. "No, thanks."

I just need a shower and maybe a fucking nap. Every time I'm tachycardic, I sleep for hours afterward. It's like the world's worst workout.

Fingering the snug and ridiculous shirt of a penguin eating ice cream, I snatch it off and toss it in the hamper. Ainsley was so proud of herself when she pulled that damn thing from her bag and handed it over.

"Here," she had said. "I grabbed a change of clothes for you."

I thought she had meant my clothes.

"I'm not wearing this," I told her, handing it back over.

She had looked so smug. "Then you'll walk out in a hospital gown. Your choice."

I was so done and so turned on that I yanked that stupid shirt over my head, grabbed her hand, and pulled her out of the building in 2.5 seconds flat.

Today went to utter shit—almost comically so.

Yesterday, I was leaving her a picture to burn and hoping she would move on, and today, I'm holding her hand and wearing her fucking penguin shirt.

Sebastian would get such a thrill out of seeing me like this. Confused. Pissed. Happy. I'm like a hormonal teenage girl.

I guess it doesn't matter, though. Soon, Ainsley will be gone—thanks to Mike and his dad and my generous donation to her housing fund—and she'll take all these fucking feelings with her.

Quickly, I hop in the shower before shutting myself in my bedroom for a while, chewing on the end of an unlit cigarette, and shuffling a deck of cards.

I need some fucking Zen. I need a poker game.

There's just one problem.

"I made you something to eat," Ainsley says, bursting through the door without knocking.

Please note Exhibit A—her bursting into my room without permission. She's too comfortable around me now. She knows my secret and knows I'm not the big bad bully she once thought.

"Don't you need to go to work?" I ask, hoping for a little privacy and some time to think.

Her face scrunches up. "No. I told Tucker my *friend* needed me." She says the word friend like she knows it gets on my nerves.

I groan. "We're not friends. I'll be fine. Go to work."

She turns to leave, ignoring me. "Your food is on the kitchen counter."

My food is on the fucking counter.

I shake my head, watching her ass sway down the hallway.

My stomach growls, and my dick twitches. Apparently, we want everything this girl has to offer.

Tossing the cigarette, I shuffle down the hall, following her to the kitchen, where a plate of raw vegetables and a glass of water sit.

"This is mine?" I point to the food. I felt sure I was walking in for a bowl of macaroni and cheese.

"Yep," she manages between bites of—

"Is that pizza?"

She nods. "A frozen one, but yes."

I look around the kitchen for the rest of it.

"Don't look around like I'm some kind of greedy pig, eating all the food in here. It was a single serving size. You, with your heart issues, clearly did not need to eat it."

"But it was mine," I argue, plucking a carrot from the tray and biting down hard enough the crunch echoes between us.

"Did you not just get discharged from the hospital?"

"Did you not just root through my freezer and eat my pizza? What if I was saving it for a special day?"

Total bullshit. I don't really care, but I like to give her a hard time. It helps with the awkwardness I feel at her taking care of me.

"You weren't."

The TV is on and playing her aquarium show.

I moan. "Can we please watch something else tonight?"

Her lips flatten, and she gives me the side-eye like how dare I request to watch something on my own TV.

"Maverick, I need calm right now. You scared the shit out of me, and only a sea lion can fix it. Sit down and eat."

This bossy thing she has going is . . . refreshing.

"You would think you were the one who almost died," I mumble, sitting alongside her.

I didn't almost die, but since she's being all dramatic, I figure I will too.

"What's with all this sea lion stuff anyway?" I point with my carrot to the stuffed sea lion that now basically lives on my couch.

"What's with all the poker stuff?" She points with the slice of pizza in her hand mockingly.

"It's a business," I respond. "I make a living off playing the game."

She swallows a huge bite. "Liar. You make a living out of doing all the IRA-y type stuff for your grandfather."

"Pops," I correct her. "I call him Pops."

She smiles, and I shove a stalk of broccoli down my throat to shut myself up.

"Did your pops raise you?"

She already knows my mother died.

"Yes, you could say that."

"What about your dad? Is he still alive?"

I snatch the remote and turn the volume up on the TV. I don't want to share pasts with her right now. I've already shared too much as it stands.

"I've never met my father," she volunteers. "My mom raised me all by herself." Her gaze is fixed on the television. "My grandma helped out a lot too. So I never had a traditional upbringing either."

Don't answer. "Does anyone?" Sebastian is the only one out of my friends who was raised with a mother and father. Rowan and I had pieced-together families.

She snorts. "Probably not."

"Is that why you play Who Wants to Be a Millionaire? Because of your grandma?"

I catch her grin. "Yep. What about you? Does the poker stuff come from your pops?"

I snort. "No, the making money part does, though."

He really is going to kick my ass when he learns what I've been doing to his company.

A sea lion barks on the screen, and I watch as Ainsley completely forgets about me, her face lighting up with something like pure happiness.

"You never answered my question," I probe.

"Shh! Hush for just a minute."

Just a minute turned out to be until the sea lion went off, and a commercial came on.

"Now, what were you saying?" she asks me, totally serious.

She really just shushed me so she could finish watching her precious sea lions do nothing but bark and flop around on a fake rock.

"I was asking, again, what's with you and these sea lions?" I point to the stuffed one she now has clutched in her lap.

"I like them," she answers vaguely.

I cock a brow. "More like you're obsessed with them."

"I like them a lot, okay?"

Not okay. She is not going to weasel personal information out of me and think she can get away unscathed.

"Why do you like this aquarium show so much?" I try again. "It's rather boring."

"You're rather bor—" She sighs, stopping herself. "When I was little, I wanted to be a marine biologist and work with the sea lions. They've always been my favorite animal."

I assumed.

"You don't now? Want to work with sea lions, I mean."

She turns her body to face me. "It's too late. I'm a psychology major now."

She says it like it's a death sentence and not something she's excited to embark on in another couple of years as a career.

"You can change your major." I don't see the problem here.

She scoffs like I'm a complete fool. "Do you know how hard it is to get into the marine biology program at Havemeyer?"

I shrug. "I'm guessing hard when you don't know the right people." Or have them owe you favors.

"It's *really*, really hard."

I sit my plate down on the coffee table, exhaustion creeping up on me. "So what, your grades weren't good enough to get you in?"

She bows her head. "My grades were perfect. I even had a scholarship at another school."

I feel my eyes widen, fighting the fatigue. "And . . ."

"And Tucker got into pre-med here where there were no openings."

I shift. "You're telling me that you gave up your dreams so he could pursue his?" I leave off the part about "with another woman" because, obviously, she knows that.

"No!" She stands, her face red and eyes watery. "I was realistic and cared about him. You wouldn't understand since you care about no one!"

At that, she throws the remote at my chest and storms off, slamming her bedroom door.

Wow. That went sideways fast. I didn't expect her major to be such a sore spot, but I didn't know she gave it up for Fuckface.

Shaking my head, I turn the TV off and leave my half-eaten plate and her empty one on the counter before making my way to my room, pausing briefly at the hall closet.

"Ugh," I moan.

Leave it alone, Maverick. Stop the proverbial bleeding. Let this girl go. You don't have the time, and she doesn't have the space. Fuckface did too much damage.

I can't help it, though. I grab a pillow and blanket, taking it back to the couch and laying it down. And for shits and giggles, I tuck the damn sea lion under it before walking away.

Something—or someone—is hovering above me.

Again.

For the sixth time tonight.

"Stop checking on me." I groan, snagging the hand on my chest and tugging her entire body across me so she's wedged into my side before I place her hand back on my heart.

"Now, go to sleep," I order.

And we do.

Together.

Side by side, making a mess of our contract.

Chapter Fifteen

Ainsley

Rumor has it she beat him with a bat.

"I'm not calling you Murphy."

I jump up from the table, eyeing the smile on Luke's face. "I'm serious, Boss! I almost gave the man a heart attack. They legit had to stop his heart so he wouldn't die right there in front of me." I've been arguing with Boss that my mother should have named me Murphy since I literally define Murphy's law.

"Tachycardia doesn't develop from annoyance," Boss adds all seriously. Which, he really isn't ever silly, so what did I expect? "It was probably stress or an underlying condition."

I shrug and sit back down, needing some coffee after waking up in bed with Maverick. Who, by the way, looked absolutely delectable all curled up with the three inches of sheet I shared with him. All the hard lines and angles looked softer in the morning light. It was as if he was at peace for once in his tense life.

"Maybe," I agree. "He did mention something along those lines, but you have to admit, I have the worst luck with roommates lately."

I say lately, but I've only ever had two roommates. One is a boyfriend-stealing, wannabe social influencer, and the other is a crabby, water drinking nerd who likes to scare the shit out of me on weekdays.

My chest clenches with the thought of moving out and away from Maverick. I really do like living with the scrooge. He shares most of his stuff with me—even the things he doesn't know about—and he tucks in stuffed sea lions even when the owner of said sea lion is an asshole to him.

I felt so damn guilty when I crept back into the living room and saw Lawrence resting in my spot under a soft blanket, all I could think after that was what if he dies in this room? What if I lie here all night and my only friend's heart stops, and I'm not there to help him?

I couldn't let the last thing I said to him be nasty.

So I checked on him a few times.

And what do you know? His bed was way comfier than the sofa.

Sleeping hugged up next to Maverick was the best sleep I've had in months. Not to mention his arms are crazy strong, and his body puts out a massive amount of body heat.

"I bet it's stress-related."

My gaze snaps to Luke.

"My heart does crazy shit too when I get all pent-up," he adds with a stupid smile on his face.

I start to laugh, but then Boss makes a low noise, and Luke's chair moves back violently from the table as if someone kicked it.

"I'm serious." He laughs, aiming his words at me and not Boss, who is still glaring holes in the guy. "Men's bodies aren't equipped to handle such stress. Didn't you say he works a lot?"

"You think it's blue balls causing all of this?" I've never thought of blue balls causing such physical reactions. I thought it was just a mental irritation.

"No," Boss barks, startling me for a moment. "Luke is just messing with you."

I narrow my eyes at Luke and sigh. "Is there anything I can do to help his condition, you think? Other than moving out?"

Boss watches me closely. "Did he ask you to stay?"

A short burst of a laugh barrels out of me. "No, but I'd like not to shorten his lifespan if I can help it. He's been a pretty decent friend."

Yeah, I said friend. Maverick wasn't here to stop me.

"Just be yourself, kid," is all Boss recommends, which is completely unhelpful.

Good thing I'm a problem solver.

When I get back home, the door is unlocked, and Maverick is awake, sitting on the sofa with Lawrence tucked away in the opposite corner. "You're up," I say lightly. "Feeling better?"

I head straight for the refrigerator. Kyle's omelets were not great this morning, and I need to wash the taste out of my mouth with something other than his equally bad coffee.

"Tell me something," he says as I root through more fresh produce than one college student should have. "Did you really pay $20.99 for this shit?" His tone borders on amused and horrified, and that causes me to snap up so fast that I bang my head on the top of the fridge.

Oh no.

Oh no.

"Where did you get that book?"

How did I not notice he had my book in his hand? You know the one I bought yesterday after my mom gave me that horrific lecture about knowing how to please yourself before expecting a man to know. How did I not remember to hide it? Oh, that's right, because he was dying!

"Well," he drawls, a stupid grin on his face. "I was looking for my laptop—"

Eww. Yeah, I hid that before I left. He needed to rest, that's what the doctor told him. I knew he wouldn't do it, so I took matters into my own hands and helped.

"And found this." His eyes dance with curiosity. "Do you read these types of books regularly?"

I grab a stupid apple and close the fridge. Might as well be honest. Maverick has seen me at some pretty low points in my life, just add this one to the list. "No, but ever since I broke up with Tucker, I've decided that I was going to do me."

Dammit.

"Literally, huh?" He grins.

"That's not what I meant! I just meant that I'm going to find the woman I once was. The one before Tucker."

"And finding your G-spot helps you with that?"

I stand taller, fighting a grin. I love all this push and pull we have. "Learning to scream out my own name helps, yes."

That wipes the smug smile off his face.

He swallows and places the book on the table like it burned him.

"Where's my laptop?" he asks, suddenly serious.

I take a bite of the apple. Maverick Lexington does not scare me. "It's safe."

How exciting is this? I'm nearly shaking with anticipation. Bantering with Maverick has always been fun, but now, seeing the fire burn in his eyes . . . this is fun.

"I'll only ask you once. Where is it?"

His steps are calculated and strong. Gone is the weak man from last night. This man is formidable as he forces me against the counter.

"Give it to me. Now."

His breath is on my face, fresh and minty like it hasn't been long since he brushed his teeth.

Standing firm, I smile, forcing out a, "Later. And only if you're a good boy."

He shoves me slightly, taking my shoulders in his hands, his mouth going to my neck as my hair drapes around his face like a shield. I can feel his watch vibrating with notifications.

"You better slow your heart down," I tease, forcing out a breath. Yep, that's my lady bits throbbing this early in the morning.

He takes a deep breath, and I feel it all the way to my toes.

"Don't play with me."

I scoff, grinning triumphantly. "That's exactly what I plan to do." I lean my head into his face, forcing his lips to my neck. "I know my opponent now."

Maverick's hands clench against me once more before he pulls back, his hot body leaving mine cool in its wake.

His eyes burn with anticipation. "All right, James. I'll see your bet and raise."

"This is stupid. I'm not doing it. I thought you meant a game of Millionaire or poker to help with the stress, not this."

Maverick really is cute when he's being all awkward, looking around like he's scared someone will recognize him at Crush It, a place where you can literally smash anything. The internet claims it's all the rage and is known to alleviate stress. Yes, I took Luke's advice, somewhat. I'm fairly certain Luke was insinuating that Maverick needed to get laid, but relief is relief, right? Either way, at Crush It, Maverick can release some tension and still let loose some testosterone should he need it.

"Shut up and choose your weapon," I tease, offering up a baseball bat with a few playful swings. "Unless you're scared."

He casts a dark predatory gaze at me. "I'm not scared."

Sure.

"You know what?" I chirp.

He groans. "No. I don't want to know."

Too bad. "I think you're scared you might actually enjoy it."

Maverick likes to go around being the cool kid. Asking him to step outside his comfort zone and join us mortals is a scary place.

He scoffs. "It's just breaking shit. We could have gone over to Sebastian's and done the same thing. He would have loved to have new footage."

The guy who checked us in hands over two helmets, vests, and face masks.

"I'm not wearing this shit," says the sourpuss in the room.

I offer the Crush It guy a smile and take the safety equipment. "Thank you. We appreciate it."

The guy looks warily at Maverick, who stands there with a perpetual scowl on his face and his arms crossed at his chest. "Press the button when you're ready to start," he tells us.

"Will do," I say excitedly before he turns—eyeing Maverick one more time—and leaves.

"Come on, Mav. You signed acknowledging the rules."

Another scoff. "Fuck the rules. I signed a waiver too. If I get hurt, it's on me. And don't call me Mav."

"Wouldn't you rather not get hurt?" I argue. I'm not addressing the Mav thing. I will call him what I want. It's time he crawls out of the denial hole.

"I'm willing to risk it. I'm not wearing a face mask like some kind of pussy."

Whatever. Everyone sees I tried, right? If he loses an eye, he loses an eye.

"Fine." I sigh, setting the vest and helmet he refuses to wear on the floor.

I slip on my mask. "Okay. But don't be mad when I accidentally miss and you get a nut shot."

That comment gives him pause. "What do you mean, 'When you miss'? Is there a chance you're going to miss?"

Men. They'll lose an eye, but heaven forbid the jewels take a hit.

I cut him a look. "I'm just saying I don't have that great of an aim." I shrug like he should know this. I did miss hitting Tucker with a candle and almost set my previous apartment on fire.

He eyes me suspiciously.

I grin. "I could ask the guy for a cup."

His lip quirks before he shakes his head. "You won't miss."

"How do you know?"

He rounds one of the tables and approaches me, placing his hand on the bat at my side. "Because that's not a debt you'll want to repay." His voice is low, and the warmth of his breath tickles the hair at the back of my neck.

"Got it," I manage to choke out not because I'm scared but because I'm kind of excited. I'm indebted to Maverick up to my eyeballs, including this little outing—three IOUs if you must know—but the way that particular threat sounded, seemed like it was on a whole different payment scale.

"Good," he clips when I just stand there gawking. "Now press the fucking button and let's do this before I change my mind."

I do.

Not only do I press the button on the wall, signaling to the staff that we're ready to go, but I pick "Legend" by The Score to play over the loudspeakers. It's a catchy and kick-ass kind of tune that you can destroy stuff to.

"I'm surprised," says Maverick, his fingers grazing over one of the aluminum bats. "I felt sure we'd be listening to Beyoncé or some kind of girl power song."

My heart flutters just thinking he would be willing to endure girl power music if I wanted.

"Nope," I say with a smile. "This trip is all for you."

And me. Sort of.

I've wanted to try this place for a while, and well, now was the perfect opportunity. Maverick and I both have demons we need to work out of our system.

"How thoughtful," he muses right before rearing back and leveling an old fax machine on the table. Pieces of plastic and metal fly everywhere, sliding along the concrete floor.

"You're right," he says, rolling his shoulders with a stupid grin on his face. "This feels incredible."

He takes another swing at a glass vase, shattering it with a victory yell that pops a silly smile on my face.

Then he takes another swing. And another.

I'm watching in awe as the uptight man I know lets loose and enjoys himself like a big kid gone rogue in a toy store.

His swings are strong, and his form is impeccable, but that just might be me. I don't think I've ever really sat back and enjoyed the view that is Maverick.

Sure, I've noticed sexy qualities here and there. Especially his dark, messy hair and tattoos. But he always has a shield up. That shield keeps you from enjoying the hottest things about him, like his smile. His quick-witted personality. And his beautiful broken heart.

I think even if Maverick were on the lower end of the hot spectrum, I would still want to stare at him for hours because I know that underneath all the rumors and masks is a good guy with a caring heart.

"Ainsley, stop standing there and hit something!" he yells between panting breaths.

I grin. "I'm not sure you're going to leave me anything to destroy."

Those broad shoulders stop mid-swing before turning and leveling me with a look that says *I will* break some shit before we leave.

"Come here. Now."

Yep, that tone he just used tingled below my belt line.

I clench the bat and walk over to where Maverick waits impatiently, one hand tucked halfway into his pocket. "Look at this old TV and tell me what you see."

I cock my head to the side, looking for a hidden image or something.

"Uh . . ."

I can hear his sigh over the music.

"Ahh!"

He snags me around the waist and places me in front of him roughly, his bat clattering to the floor. Warm and strong, his hands grip my hips. "You want to know what I think you see?"

Gah, his breath tickles along my neck. I should not have put my hair up. This outing is destined for a mistake.

"I think you see the woman Fuckface and his wannabe girlfriend kicked out of her apartment."

It's like he threw an ice-cold bucket of water over me. I try wrenching out of his hold, but he keeps going. "Look at the TV, Ainsley. Tell me what *you* see."

I swallow. "I don't want to do this anymore."

Why did he have to bring up Tucker when we were having such a good time?

"You will do this," he growls. "Look, Ainsley. Look at the TV. Tell me what *you* see."

Fine. If it will shut him up, I'll look.

Hesitantly, I pull my gaze from the floor and find the screen of the TV. Huh. The reflection is me and Maverick, locked together, his hands on my hips, proving strong and imposing.

"I see me," I tell him softly.

"And?" His voice is approving.

"And I see you."

"Want to know what I see?" he asks, his voice warmer as his head bows to my ears and speaks the words directly to my heart. "I see a survivor—a force to be reckoned with."

Chills break along my skin.

"I see a strong and independent woman. One who forgives no

matter what she's been through. The woman in that TV reflection is brave, bold, and full of life."

His fingers wrap around mine before he repeats the process.

"She's caring and kind."

He brings my left hand across my body and places it on the bat.

"Beautiful and funny."

He turns us to the side, and I stare at our image. His penetrating gaze peering at me through the reflection.

"She cowers to no man."

His head leans into mine like he can't get close enough. "She takes what she wants."

The bat is lifted.

"She's fucking invincible."

And then we swing together. Glass and hardware go in all different directions.

"Ahh! You're right!" I do this little jump in his arms. "This does feel great! Fuck Tucker! And Twatface!"

I turn and face him, and immediately his arms go to my waist. I feel small tucked into his imposing body.

"Thank you for saying all those nice things about me."

A groan vibrates in his chest. "Shut up."

"I mean it. It was really sweet."

He's just a big old scary teddy bear.

"You deserve to be happy," he finally says after a moment.

"I am happy." The words came out before I realized it. "I—" I start to apologize but think better of it. "You know what? I won't apologize. I am happy. I'm glad Tucker cheated on me. I'm glad he forced me out of my apartment. I'm a better person because of it."

I hesitate with my last declaration because as scary as Maverick is, I think he gets spooked with too many emotional words. "I'm happy because of *you*. Thank you for being my friend, even if you didn't want to be." He rolls his eyes. "And thank you for letting me crash on your couch, eat your food, and pretend to be your roomie even if it's only temporary, and I owe you like a million firstborns and souls."

I pull back and flash him a megawatt smile. "You truly are my genie in a bottle."

"What?" His brows furrow.

I wave off his concern. "Don't worry about it. I'm just saying you're not such a bad guy after all, Maverick Lexington."

I stand on my toes and kiss his cheek. "And I'm going to miss you when I move out."

Those stormy eyes flash with an intensity I've never seen from Maverick. At least when he's not been pissed.

His hands graze up my waist and over my shoulders until they rest at my cheeks. His jaw ticks as he watches me watching him. Gah, he really is stunning.

And then he growls out, "Fuck it," before smashing his lips to mine.

Chapter Sixteen

Ainsley

Rumor has it she mugged him at the grocery store.

"I'm ready to leave."

Why is he talking?

Pulling his face closer, I smother any other words he attempts saying. Currently, my legs are wrapped around his waist, my back against the wall of the Crush It room that we've completely abandoned. Maverick and I both silently agreed that grinding against the wall with his tongue down my throat was way better at releasing tension than smashing old electronics.

"Ainsley." He tries prying me off and setting me on my feet.

I have no shame. "Nooooo."

His chest rumbles with laughter. "Not here. Let's go home."

Home.

Yes, home sounds good.

Releasing my legs from their vice grip, I allow Maverick to place me on my feet, which honestly, are a little wobbly, but they manage to keep me upright and that's all I'm asking at this point.

"You good?" he asks, tucking away his massive boner.

It's tacky if I ask if he wants to disappear into a bathroom stall, right? "Not really, but I'll manage until we get home," I answer honestly.

I exhale a breath of pent-up frustration. No sense in lying. I want this man. I've wanted him since I used his shampoo and slept on his amazingly comfortable sofa. I don't even care that this may be a one-time thing. I can live with that.

"Let's go. We need food first," he clips out.

I groan out something that sounds a lot like blatant disappointment. "I'm good without food," I add just in case he is too.

He pulls us out of the room. "We'll pick up a frozen mac and cheese for afterward then, yeah?"

He's my spirit animal.

Well, not my animal. He's my spirit human and I might just have to stay indebted to him so he can never get rid of me.

A million and three years later we arrive home. Maverick has been quiet and I wonder if he's come to his senses. Let's be honest, I'm a mess fresh off the breakup boat. I'm not key banging material.

Keys are shoved into my hand as he shuffles the bags on his arms. "You want me to unlock the door?" I ask. Am I a little shocked? Yes. He's never let me unlock the door or even have a key.

"Do you want to hold these bags of macaroni and cheese while I do it?" he asks sarcastically.

Right. His hands are full, which is totally his fault. He said to get whatever I wanted at the store. What I wanted was ice cream and dick with a side of mac and cheese. So here we are.

"You should have paced yourself with the junk food. I read you should be eating a heart healthy diet," I tease. I really did go overboard. What can I say? Destroying things had my appetite through the roof.

He chuckles, shaking his head. "Open the door, smartass."

I fumble with the lock and I feel his body press against my back like a warning. His breaths fan along my neck as he leans his head down, the motion angling my head to the side so he can get to the sensitive spot behind my ear. Oh hell. He's going to make me come against the soul-stained door.

A teasing comment about such plays on my lips, but I swallow it down when he pushes his erection against my ass. No, now is not the time to kill the mood with comedic commentary. His dick, like me, is hungry, and we need to get inside before I let him ravage me on the cheap linoleum.

Somehow I manage to put the key in the hole and twist just before Maverick shoves me inside, drops the bags of frozen mac and cheese on the floor, and pins me against the wall.

His watch beeps like crazy, but he never looks down. Instead, all his attention is focused on me. This is it. We are so doing this.

A ball of nerves sits in my throat. I swallow to work it down. "I need you to promise me something."

He doesn't even give me a second to finish. "No."

"You don't even know what I was going to ask."

"The answer is still no. You know what to do if you want a promise."

Ugh. "Fine. Give me a card."

I'm not even shocked.

The corner of his lip twitches. "I'm afraid my hands are otherwise engaged. You want a promise, you know what to do."

I eye his hands at my face, caging me in. Mmm. I kind of like feeling caught.

"Fine." I will get my own IOU in his back pocket, right over his firm ass. Really, I probably could live without the promise, but I don't want to take that risk. Not yet, at least.

Deep breath. You totally can do this, Ainsley. Tucker may not have had an ass like this, but they all feel the same.

My fingertips graze along the sides of his body. I can see his shirt indent with his quick intake of breath. "I think maybe this should come off," I suggest, tugging at his shirt. "It's the most effective way for me to get to your pocket." Not really, but I want to see all of him. Sue me.

I'm prepared for a cocky smile or even a laugh, but one never comes. Instead, Maverick drops his hand, trailing his finger along my cheek and down my body until he's able to reach the hem of his T-shirt. He bunches a handful of fabric in his fist and drags it to where my hands rest at his ribs.

"Go ahead, take it off."

Swallowing, I take a look at the tribal tattoos peeking out from underneath. Yes, this is definitely the best way to his pocket.

Painstakingly slow, I lift his shirt over his head. He even leans down to help and that makes me feel short for the first time in my life.

"Okay, so"—I clear my throat—"now that we have that out of the way."

Gah, I just need time to stare at the exquisiteness of Maverick. He's all muscle and tats like a good boy wrapped in a really edgy package.

"The cards are in my pocket in case you forgot," he teases.

"I knew that. I was just giving your heart time to pace itself." Total lie and he probably knows it.

He chuckles. "My heart can handle you, I promise."

I almost tell him that's a free promise he just made me, but I don't because I really liked hearing the words. I'm scared if I bring it up he might back out of this whole situation and honestly, I think that will devastate me.

Hiding a smile, I reach around his back and let my cheek rest against his pecs. Almost lazily, I slide my fingertips down the planes of his back until the smooth skin stops and the denim begins.

"You said your pocket, right?" I ask for no other reason than to keep my hands on his ass.

"Uh-huh." His voice is strained and when his head lies on top of mine, I know it's just as torturous for him as it is for me.

I reach into his back pocket and find the marker and the cards while grazing—possibly squeezing—the firmest ass cheek I've ever felt.

All butts definitely do not feel the same.

"I might need two favors," I mutter against his chest.

"What's the first one?" He pulls back and I push the cards between us.

Swallowing, I uncap the marker and place a card to his chest. "First, if this is a terrible idea—which it probably is—I need you to not kick me out if I suck, or you don't want to see my face again. At least not until your guy secures me another place."

After a moment, I look up to see his nod and notice his jaw clenching hard enough he may crack a tooth.

"Maverick?"

"Fine," he grits out like it pained him to agree, which is weird. But whatever, Maverick is an odd one. Maybe that's why I like him so much.

I write the letters IOU, attempting to mimic his serial killer handwriting, and then toss it behind him, hoping it lands somewhere proper, like the trash.

"And the other favor?" he prompts.

"Oh, yeah."

I meet his gaze and grin. Maybe he'll lighten up. The moment has become pretty tense.

"You can't grab my ass."

He rears back.

"Yeah, after feeling yours I'm a little ashamed. Clearly those few squats I do every year have not done me any favors."

"No," he snaps, a tiny, baby hint of a grin forming. "I won't honor that favor."

Fine, but I warned him. If he's disappointed, he's disappointed.

With that game-ending remark, he plucks the cards from my hand and tosses them behind him where they scatter along the floor. I'll put them in the trash later.

"Do we need to put up the grocer—" His mouth seals over mine and his tongue pushes in without warning, consuming me in his tight hold.

What was I saying? Right. I don't care.

Maverick hoists my body up and my legs go around his waist like second nature. We're on the move, wasting no time finding a solid surface. "Wait!" I cry out. "Not in here! Not on my bed."

He pauses for just a moment, but then he turns around and heads toward the living room and to the best sofa ever. "We are burning your mattress," he mutters, setting me down carefully and then yanking my knees apart so he can kneel between them.

Ooh. I kind of like Mr. Lexington on his knees—feels all queen like.

"I want you to show me what you learned from your book," he drawls all cute and curious while tugging at my skinny jeans.

I'm full-on smiling at his effort to get my jeans off—I plan to pretend like he didn't mention the whole book thing. "You might need to put some force behind those pulls. These jeans are a little snug." I'll admit, I had to jump a few times just to get them on.

With a firm tug, Maverick has my jeans around my ankles in a matter of seconds. "Wow. You're seriously good at that. Maybe I need a standing favor for when I've moved out. I could come over, you could yank off my jeans, and we could eat mac and cheese before I go back home." I shrug. "It'll work out for everyone."

A muscle flexes in his jaw.

Wait. Is he mad? I meant it as a joke. "You know, because you'll get your privacy back soon when I move and—"

"Shut up." His words are biting and a tad bit growly. Whoa. What did I say?

"Gotcha," I try soothing his irritation. "I'm sorry." I take a deep breath. "And nervous. I'm totally ruining the moment."

It's the truth. I've only ever been with Tucker and since he cheated on me, I can't help but to live with a nagging doubt that I wasn't good enough somehow.

Finally, a hint of emotion—other than aggravation—flashes on his face. "Since you seem so into talking, why don't you tell me what you learned from your book since this is the second time I'm asking." He nods to my open bedroom door where I stashed that blessed book.

"I didn't read it," I admit.

He cocks a brow like I'm lying.

"I haven't had time!" My voice rises and I squeeze him in between my legs. "You were too busy dying all over the place since I got it." I huff. How romantic this excursion is turning out to be.

"Besides, I doubt I'll ever read it. I have neither the time nor the privacy to experiment with such things. It was a stupid idea." Thanks, Mom.

Amusement flickers in his eyes for just a moment before it turns into something more feral. "Maybe I can give you the CliffsNotes version of some of my books." His hands skim up my legs and come to rest against my thighs.

Oh, man. Is his thumb pressing on my thigh supposed to feel so good? Is that normal that he's turning me on just by staring up at me between my legs?

I swallow. "I don't know if you're the best person to teach since you make a habit of never going to class."

My breath leaves me in a swoosh as my body is yanked down the cushion and his face aligns with my center.

"Mmm . . ." he hums above me, his chin dragging along my seam. "You're right. Maybe I need a refresher."

Smug. That's all I can think of to describe the look on his face when he places a kiss to my soaked panties.

"Then again, you seem to be really responsive to my tutoring so far."

Smartass.

He's not wrong, though.

"Positive reinforcement is better for mental—"

He nips at my inner thigh and my heart flutters, creating this quickening sensation. It could be because of his teeth on my skin or the way he's hovered above me bare-chested, either way the man is turning me on.

"Your soaked pussy," he drawls, dragging a finger over my wet panties, "is all the reinforcement I need."

Sounds good to me considering I'm shaking as his fingers graze over me, smearing my arousal around, the only barrier a thin piece of cotton. Holding my eyes, Maverick silently asks for my permission.

I nod. "Yes. Please, take them off." Why has it taken him this long?

Sure hands grasp the edge of the cotton material before he tugs ever so lightly, pushing my knees to my chest to get them off.

Oh shit. The cool air hits my center just as my panties are slipped off my ankles. He places a kiss to one foot, lifting it before sliding it over his shoulder and rendering me completely bare to him. "Orgasms are better when you're swollen," he coos, placing my other foot flat against the cushion.

Swollen? Does he mean . . . ?

He swipes a finger through my slit and my head falls back. "I don't even care what you're talking about," I moan.

His finger presses against me. "Are you swollen for me, Ainsley?" He breathes along my center and my legs clench around his head. I'm guessing yes.

"Tsk, tsk," he scolds, readjusting so he can pull my legs back and keep them pinned within the crease of his elbow. "Stay still. I want to make sure you're absorbing my lecture."

He says it like he's a professor, but we all know I'm not learning shit here. All I know is that my body is feeling crazy good under his skillful hands.

"Ainsley. You still with me?"

Underneath all the sexual prowess he's exuding lies amusement.

I shake off the cloud of euphoria of his firm grip, holding me open. "I'm absorbing everything very, very well, Mr. Lexington."

His lips do a little half tip before he leans down and licks up my slit. "Ahh!" My back arches and he has to force my hips back down.

"Some would argue you aren't absorbing much at all," he says with his lips against my clit. "Some would say you're dripping."

I don't even care if he's trying to be all smart and cute with this word play.

"And some would say that you better be careful or I will burn the apartment down if you don't stop being a nerd and keep your mouth on me."

He is the one who brought up the whole book thing. I was fine with just fucking and not talking. He's the one trying to be all clever and slow.

"A nerd, huh?"

A glimmer of mischief dances in his eyes before it disappears. "Lift your shirt. Now."

Shit. I'm going to come on his face. Seriously, I'm not even going to get to see his dick before I come.

I lift the fabric over my chest. "Do you want it all the way off?"

His gaze roams all over my chest. "No. Now your bra."

You know, any other day I would have worn my comfy bra. The one I probably should toss since the wire is almost poking through the fabric, but I didn't today. Maybe because taking Maverick to Crush It seemed a little date-like. Either way, the front clasp bra I have on is super cute and supportive.

I finger the clasp watching as his left hand traces up my thigh and over my stomach, just waiting for me to free them. When I don't do it fast enough for his liking, he flips the clasp himself and my breasts spill out. "Do the CliffsNotes say to suck a woman's nipple because I wouldn't be opposed to that," I offer.

He grins. "Is that so? You want me to put my mouth on your tits, Ainsley?"

Why does his voice have to sound so seductive?

I tip my chin and pull away the rest of my bra. His eyes dart from left to right, taking in each breast as if they were a work of art worthy of being memorialized.

He pushes up, one knee on the cushion, lifting his body enough to fold over me. "Tell me what you want me to do, Ainsley. How do you want me to get you off?"

I can feel the length of him hard against the soft of my stomach.

"I really didn't need to know how to get myself off. You're doing a great job, though," I admit. That is the last time I listen to my mother. I should have known I didn't need a book to orgasm.

I just needed an apartment genie.

"Oh no, I think it's important you know what you like. Tell me. Tell me what you want me to do to you."

Great. Just freaking great. I mean, really, it is great, but I wish he would let the whole book thing go and just fuck my brains out. It would save us all some trouble.

"Touch them," I mumble, a little sour.

He doesn't move. "Touch you where? Here?" He pushes two fingers against my clit and I nearly come apart.

"There's good." I pant.

"Are you sure?" he teases. "What about here?" His hand moves along my breast and around the swell of the curve, to the middle, stopping on the nipple.

"Put your mouth on them," I tell him, not even concerned that my face is probably pinker than my nipples themselves.

His tongue is hot and firm. So much that I arch from the pressure he applies with each suckle. "Oh shit. Oh shit," I cry. I didn't think a mouth could bring forth these sensations. My toes curl into the sofa and my legs instinctively close around his jean-clad waist, but they don't get the pressure they're looking for.

"Keep moving your hands," I pant, instructing Mav to caress and squeeze while his mouth works greedily at my nipple. Clearly, I've jumped on board with this game.

Maverick moves to the other breast, doing just as instructed, but this time he makes this sound of contentment like pleasuring me is just as pleasurable for him.

"Tell me what to do next," he pants between licks and the occasional nip.

My mind is so cluttered at the moment that I don't know what I want him to do other than strip and shove his dick so far in me that I can't breathe from the pressure.

"Pressure. I need more pressure. Your fingers," I pant. "I want them inside of me."

A groan vibrates deep in his chest as he places a wet, open-mouthed kiss on my lips before he slides down, spreading me open even further with his big body, his index finger trailing down my center at a snail's pace.

I don't know that I'm prepared. I don't know that I'm going to recover from this night with Maverick. But I do know that I'm going to come like a freaking superstar. Fuck that damn book, they never had a Maverick to show them how to feel good. If they did, they wouldn't have needed to write a book about how to pleasure yourself. I never knew my body could feel this alive.

Slowly, as if he's milking every ounce of anticipation from me, Maverick drags the pad of his index finger over my outer folds, circling the soft skin like a warm-up before the main event.

"Now, Mav. I need you now," I whine, completely out of patience.

I don't bother looking up to see if he's smirking. Something tells me he's just as consumed with this moment as I am. His hand touches the inside of my knee as he holds it down and ever so torturously, slides his index finger inside me. I bear down immediately, clenching as if I can keep his finger inside me for the rest of our lives. But he's stronger—of course—and pushes forward, deeper into my center, stealing my breath and any thoughts from my head.

His hand squeezes my knee and that too feels amazing. It's like he's using some kind of grounding mechanism to keep himself from going in with both hands. "Now what?" he prompts all gravelly.

He knows what's next, but we're both too freaking turned on to quit now. And, at this point, neither of us cares.

"Now, move it in and out," I tell him between shallow breaths. He tips his chin but holds my gaze . . . Then he moves his finger in and out. The fullness. The rhythm. His freaking eyes on me. It's too much. It's all too much.

"I need more," I cry out, arching, moving as I try to build more friction between us.

"One more finger?" he asks quietly—thoughtfully.

My body is feverish, wet with sweat. I'm going to freaking explode. "I don't care if you shove your whole fist inside me! I just want more!"

Sorry not sorry. The man is driving me to oblivion.

I hear a soft chuckle and then Maverick leans over me, kissing me while that damn finger maintains its steady rhythm. "How about we start with one more finger? We'll save the fist for another day."

I think I say okay. It could have been just a mumble of unintelligible words. Either way, the next thing I know I'm being stretched, filled with blissful pressure as he adds another finger, pushing into my core over and over again.

"Oh, God. Yeah, you're doing great. This is exactly what I think the book would have said to do," I praise. I'm a freaking mess under his hands. A mess. I can't control the quaking and the shivers that take over as I try grinding into his hand for more.

"You sure? We can try something else."

He says it teasingly, yet his voice is calm and collected, not like he's torturing me by dangling the best orgasm of my life right between my legs.

"Hush and put your mouth back on me," I beg with absolutely no shame. If this is the best sex I'm ever going to have then I'm going all out. Maverick Lexington is a god. A god I tell you!

"You want my mouth where? Show me."

I groan. He's also annoying. But I do as I'm told and drag my hand over my stomach and to the bundle of nerves that are craving Maverick's attention. "Here. I want you to put your mouth here."

I don't get all the words out before my hand is knocked away and his hot, wet mouth is on my clit, sucking, nipping, and—"Oh shit! I'm going to come. I don't want to come yet."

Cold air hits me as Maverick comes up for air, removing his blessed mouth from me.

"I didn't tell you to stop!" I cry.

He looks confused. "You said you didn't want to come yet."

I motion for him to lower back down. "Yeah, but—" I have no idea what I'm saying. All I know is that I'm on the cusp of a mind-blowing orgasm. "Just ignore what I'm saying. I want to come, Maverick. Like yesterday."

He tips his head, waiting on further clarification, and like any well-mannered woman, I give it to him straight. "On your face. I want to come on your face, Maverick. Right now. Don't stop again."

I'll regret those comments later. Right now, all I can think about is his mouth on my clit and his fingers inside of me.

With what is pretty much a smile for Maverick, he nods an okay, kisses my lips softly, and then yanks my hips to the edge of the sofa. "Keep your legs open and your eyes on me. Got it?"

I'm not going to comment that I'm supposed to be the one giving all the orders because honestly, I don't give two single shits. I'd do anything Maverick tells me right now.

I nod eagerly and then watch as two tanned fingers disappear between my folds. And then for the last time, I let myself get lost in the depths of his eyes before his head bows, and his eyes close, and his mouth clamps down on my clit and works me into a frenzy.

"Fuck!" My body arches and all I want to do is fight against the strength of the sensations. His hand—God bless it—keeps my right leg pinned to the cushions while his fingers pick up speed and his tongue swirls the sensitive bundle of nerves in a pattern until sweat drips from my forehead and the pressure builds so high that I scream out, "Squeeze! Squeeze my boob, Maverick!"

Without so much as a hesitation, Maverick's free hand snakes out and instead of squeezing my breast like I instructed, he pinches my nipple and I explode in a tangle of "Holy shits and oh my Gods."

It takes a full minute—really, who's counting—for the ringing in my ears to stop. It probably takes another minute for my legs to stop convulsing and relax from around his head.

"I think we should really return that book when the feeling returns to my hands," I mutter out.

Maverick raises his head and wipes his mouth against the back of his hand. "I agree. It wasn't very informative."

Chapter Seventeen

Maverick

Rumor has it they eloped.

"Did she like the place?"

I pace alongside the edge of the complex. I needed some air and privacy when Mike called about Ainsley's new house.

"She'd prefer something updated in this century," I clip. Truth is, it's a cute house just on the outskirts of the city. Ainsley would love it—if I told her about it.

"Come on, Maverick. You need to convince her that this place is perfect. It's a ten-minute drive to campus and comes fully furnished. My dad can even get the security deposit waived. The elderly couple just needs someone to rent it until they return in six months."

Mike said the owners are moving in with their daughter in Wisconsin. She's having twins and since they've retired, they offered to help out with the babies for a while. It's the perfect solution for their family and for Ainsley. It'll give her a place to herself, away from the drama of Havemeyer's rumors. But . . .

"I'll talk to her, Mike," I lie. "But she's already demanded an open concept with modern decor."

Ainsley would never say that, but Mike doesn't need to know that.

He lets out a deep sigh. "She does realize she's a college student, doesn't she? There aren't many options in her price range given her history as a renter."

"She's not desperate." She was before, not now. "Her cash is as good as anyone else's."

Why am I snapping at Mike for doing what I've been begging him to do all along?

"Fuck!" I growl. "Just find something else!"

Mike makes an exasperated noise. I don't blame him. I'm being a complete pain in the ass today.

"Whatever you want, Maverick. I'll ask my father to keep looking."

I grunt out something close to a "thanks" and hang up. I'm in a terrible fucking mood.

You would think my mood would be as euphoric as the first drag of a cigarette.

Maybe it was last night after I tasted Ainsley and felt a rush of feelings that were not supposed to be there. But that's when it all went to shit too.

I didn't just please her, I worshipped her body like it was the last item on my bucket list. I honored her. I begged to please her.

And I voided my contract.

Everything is so messed up.

I'm messed up.

I vowed to always be an honest businessman and I blew it. I allowed business to mix with pleasure.

Last night was . . . eye-opening.

I care for her.

God, I think I might be in fucking love with her.

And eventually she will find out the truth and I'll lose her. Maybe I should just let her go. I could call Mike back, accept the house, and help her move. That's what she expects from me—a favor.

But that's not what I'm doing, am I? I'm sending Mike on a wild hunt for a place that will never be good enough. I know this. Yet, I still fight it. Ending our relationship now would save us both pain at the end of the day.

She'll never trust me once she finds out the truth. She'll think I did all this because—my phone rings in my hand.

I swipe the screen. "Pops? You all right?"

"Get—your—ass—down here! Right now!"

My heart sinks. He knows.

"I can explain," I hurry out.

Pops takes a breath that I'm sure is forced so that he doesn't swear at me. "Yes, you will. Tonight, Maverick. Don't make me come get you."

He hangs up and I'm left staring at the blank screen, my stomach churning.

How did he find out?

Fuck! Not now! Not yet.

All I needed was a few more months until I graduated.

My steps are labored when I drag myself back to the apartment, finding Ainsley bent over a textbook, one of my playing cards in her hand. I tip my chin at it. "What are you using the card for?"

A conniving grin spreads along her face, plumping her lips. The same lips I kissed last night before leaving her spent on the sofa. I wanted to give her space in case it was too soon and she was going to freak out. I didn't want her feeling used or like she had to return the favor.

Walking away was one of the hardest things I've ever had to do.

And this morning, when she woke, I expected tears or a pool full of ice cream; but nope, she was up, ready for class and had Cheerios sitting out on the counter, hinting it was my breakfast. "Heart healthy and all that," she had said before kissing my lips and pinching my ass before she rushed out the door.

It was like what happened between us yesterday was natural—expected even—like the pieces just fell into place and we could finally be ourselves with each other. Granted, today's ass grabbing and kiss was a great bonus.

"Funny story," she starts, flipping the card between her fingers like I usually do. "I ran out of index cards and I realized I had all these IOUs lying around."

I smother a grin, already knowing where she's going with this.

"It would be such a waste not to use all the space on them, don't you think?" She shrugs one shoulder. "And since I have more than I'll ever pay back in a lifetime, I figured they should be put to use somehow."

She's right. I haven't stopped sliding them under her door, sticking a couple in her bag, leaving one in the shower when she uses my shampoo. Any trivial thing she does, she gets an IOU. No, she'll never pay them all back and honestly, I don't expect her to. It's just a game between us at this point. Once I surpassed the limit where I knew she would never escape me, I started writing them just for the fuck of it.

"Want to come with me to meet my pops?"

The random question stops her cold. Believe me, it stopped me too.

"Your pops?" Her hair falls in her face. "Like your *pops* pops?"

I run my finger across my lips nervously. "That would be the one."

"Uh, sure." She doesn't look sure.

"You don't have to, I just thought—"

She cuts me off. "No, I want to. I just thought . . ."

That I'm a bastard and have drilled into her head that we're only a contract and she would never know the real me.

I can see the hesitation in her, but people change, right? And since my life will probably go to shit the minute Pops gets me in his sights, I figure what the hell?

"It doesn't matter." She waves me off with a smile that lights up her whole face. "I'd like to meet him. Just let me change first."

"Whatever you do, stay in front of me."

Ainsley gasps. "Oh my God, Maverick! Do you really have a boner right now?"

I shake my head, exasperated, and position her by my side, locking our hands together. "Please. I got rid of my boner when you fell asleep with your mouth open and let the drool run down to your shoulder." I grin. "Sexiest fucking thing I've ever seen. I had to pull over I was so horny."

"Haha. You're hilarious," she says, side-eyeing her shoulder just in case I wasn't joking. I'm not, by the way. She did fall asleep and she did get me hard, but she didn't drool and I didn't pull over. Although,

I probably should have. Then, maybe, I would be a lot calmer standing in front of my childhood home.

"I'm teasing. I'm using you as a shield in case Pops wants to smack me. He won't with you in front of me."

Those big blue eyes go wide.

"I'm joking," I tell her. "He won't smack me. He'll wait until you're distracted to whisper yell in my ear."

Pops isn't a violent man, but his disapproval is worse than a hit. I dread hearing his lecture about honesty and responsibility. All I wanted to do was help.

Ainsley turns in my arms. "Don't worry, I'll protect—"

"Thank God you're here!" my brother yells, flinging open the front door, a grin the size of my car on his face.

"What did you do?" I accuse, not sparing him with a simple hello.

He waves me off. "Nothing nearly as bad as what you did." He holds out his fist for a bump. "Couldn't have come at a better time, bro."

I roll my eyes as his lock on Ainsley. "Well, hello. You must be the reason I haven't been getting any cuddle calls lately from my big bro."

Ainsley turns again and mouths cuddle calls.

"Ainsley, this asshole is Cooper, my little brother."

Her face brightens. "Hi, Cooper, it's nice to—"

Cooper wrenches Ainsley from my arms and wraps his arms around her. "We're a hugging family," he explains over her head, making this face of ecstasy to me.

"We're also a violent family," I drawl, pulling Ainsley back to my side. I know Cooper hugged her just to be an aggravating shit.

I shove him out of the way and he laughs, clapping me on the shoulder while following me in.

"Is he in a good mood?" I ask, referring to Pops.

Cooper scoffs. "You mean since he found out he was going to tear you a new asshole?"

I don't respond.

"Sure is. Perked him right up."

I should have just fled the country.

"I'm happy to know your mood has perked up too. How's the team? Any scout activity?" Baseball season is almost up.

"Uh." His tone sobers. "Not yet."

I nod, taking a deep breath. This isn't what I needed today. "I might know someone who can help. Give me a couple of days?" If I wasn't desperate to help my brother achieve his and my mother's dream, I would never even consider asking *her*. The person I know is not a person you want to get involved with. Making negotiations with *her* doesn't come without consequences.

Coop nods, a half-smile tugging on his face. "Sure. Thanks, Mav." He tips his chin to the front room. "Come on and let Pops yell at you so we can eat. I'll entertain Ainsley while you're gone."

I tighten my grip on Ainsley's hand and Coop notices. "Or maybe not. I'm impressed, big brother. I never thought you'd grow a soul."

Ainsley chuckles. I'm sure she finds his comment hilarious. Isn't that what she says I do, take souls in return for favors?

"Fuck y—"

"Maverick! Get in here!"

I groan at Pops's voice.

Coop wiggles his brows and makes the sign of the cross. "I promise to take good care of your car when you're gone. Ainsley, too, if she needs me."

Clearly, Cooper needs another sibling to annoy.

I flip him off and inhale. "Come on," I say to Ainsley. "Let me introduce you to my pops."

In the front room, Pops is sitting at his desk, his head bent over a large stack of papers.

"Hey, Pops."

His head rises slowly and meets my eyes.

"Seventy-two percent," he says, holding up a single sheet of paper.

I let out the breath I've been holding. "Yes, sir," I confirm.

Pops's gray hair doesn't move when he shakes his head and motions to the chairs in front of him. "Have a seat, boy, and don't be rude, introduce your friend."

I tug Ainsley behind me and we both sit. "Pops, this is Ainsley, my . . ." I look at Ainsley, watching the curious expression on her face. Dammit. Fine. "My friend and roommate."

There, that's all the truth I can force out for now.

Ainsley's mouth ticks up into a big ass grin. I finally admitted we are friends—friends who like the taste of each other.

"It's nice to meet you, Ainsley," Pops says, bringing the focus back to my dire situation. "I'd like to say Maverick has told me all about you, but I've recently found out he likes keeping things from me."

Ugh. That stings.

"I planned to tell you." I sigh, raking a hand through my hair.

"When?" He probes, all seriously. "After you graduated and took over my company?"

I can feel my explanations dying a slow death. "You've been recovering." It's not a good excuse, but it is the truth. "I was just trying to help. Laraunt quit out of nowhere and you were losing money."

The old man's mouth quirks. "Apparently. Tell me, boy, how did you find out about Laraunt's departure anyhow?"

I bite my lip—damn, I wish I had a cigarette to chew on. "I might have gotten ahold of the password to your files, including your email." I cringe. *Please don't ask me why. I was a different person back then.*

"Why didn't you just ask me for them?"

Fuck. I breathe out a heavy sigh. "I lost some money a couple of years back . . ." I don't need to add that it was playing poker. He knows. You don't become good unless you experience every aspect of the game, including losing everything. "I borrowed a little money." I hold my hands out pleading. "And I paid it back with interest."

A smirk is still on Pops's face. What the hell? "How much interest?"

I rear back, confused. "Five percent."

Pops huffs. "I would have made you pay eight."

I shift in my seat. "Eight was too much given the fair market value at the time," I retort, a little snippy. I didn't shortchange him, except, maybe, borrowing the money without his permission.

"Anyway," I add, redirecting. "I had been depositing the money"—I don't add that I slowly put the money back over time, while forging the records. I feel like that's not relevant at the moment. The point is, the money was repaid in full from a new client (aka me)—"and I saw the email Laraunt sent to you, resigning." I shrug a shoulder. "At the time, you were in the rehab hospital and I didn't want to worry you."

He nods. "So you just decided to keep running my company on your own as Laraunt?"

"It sounds a little shady when you say it like that," I agree. "But I only had our family's best interest at heart. I swear."

Pops grins and hands me the piece of paper he was looking at. "Did you know that in the past year, since Laraunt quit, my company has grown seventy-two percent?"

I look at the graph and nod. "Yes, sir. I know."

"Did you also know it's the most growth this company has seen in one year since before you boys moved in with me?"

I can feel Ainsley's eyes on me.

"No, sir. I didn't know that. I just wanted to do a good job." He couldn't afford to lose any money. He and my brother needed it. Not to mention the faith his clients had in him.

He motions for the graph back. "You did more than just a good job, son. You did magnificently well. Although I could wring your neck for keeping this from me, I'm very proud of you."

I swallow thickly. I didn't expect his praise.

"Just one thing, though," he adds. "How have you managed to run this company and go to class?"

I toss the entire deck of cards into the passenger seat. "Find a marker and start writing on them."

Ainsley cocks her head to the side. "All of them?"

I buckle my seat belt and start the car. "All of them. That's the third time you've ratted me out. I don't take being tattled on lightly."

She rolls her eyes and swipes the cards off onto the floorboard and buckles in. "Please. Your pops was going to find out eventually about the ER visit. You're still on his insurance," she argues.

"I was handling it. I didn't file it on his health insurance." I don't have all these favors for the fuck of it.

She shrugs, grinning at me as if she enjoyed the lashing I received about the ER visit and the heart issues. She and Cooper disappeared into the kitchen, supposedly making everyone food—though I didn't get any—while Pops made me sign in to my healthcare portal and show him my medical records. He then proceeded to growl out a lot of, "I should kick your ass," comments before finally telling me that this will not happen again.

My heart sank when he informed me that he will be hiring someone to replace me within the company.

"Whatever, he was just concerned about you. I don't know why you're in such a shitty mood anyway." She messes with the radio, knowing it will get on my nerves. "Didn't you walk out of there a CEO?" Her brows arch, daring me to deny it.

"When I graduate," I correct her.

"Which is in, like, two months."

She's bouncy and all excited over the news. Don't get me wrong, I am too, but until I graduate, Pops is hiring someone to help me out so I can stop ditching classes and actually finish on my own. I was half excited at the accolades and the support to take over the company upon graduation and half disappointed that he was requiring me to finish. It seems pointless to have a framed piece of stock paper when I've already proven I can handle the company without a degree.

I get it, though, it's important to my pops for his kids to graduate. So, I swallowed the argument and thanked him for not kicking my ass like he probably wanted to.

"Either way, it's soon," she adds. "Now you'll have time to focus on school and playing poker if you want. You don't have to go around capturing all those souls."

I reach over and try grabbing for the tanned skin exposed from her shorts. "There you go again with all that soul stealing. I've told you, I don't need to steal them." I grin. "They beg"—I pitch my voice like she did when she first stood at my door—"for me to take them."

"Haha. You think you're so funny."

I cut her a disproving look. I *know* I'm funny.

"Whatever," she waves me off. "I'll agree you're a little bit funny. You've had a bad day—no reason to kick you while you're down."

This girl.

"So do you want to stop at Crush It on our way home and work out some of that tension?"

I scoff. The only tension I plan on working out with her involves her naked body. "I thought we could try something different."

"Oh my God. Oh my God. Oh! My! God!"

I can't stop the smile that comes over me. She's so excited. "Maverick!"

I scrub a hand over my lips. "It's sea lions you love, right?"

She swats me on the arm as her eyes water. "Why are you the sweetest asshole ever?"

I shake my head at the confused trainer. Through Sebastian, and a mutual favor, I was able to secure Ainsley a behind the scenes tour at our local aquarium. The animal she's seeing . . . you guessed it. Her beloved sea lions.

"You ready to go in?"

She nods, swiping the tears away. "Am I really going to get to pet one?" Her gaze volleys from me to Matt, the sea lion trainer.

"You can pet them all if you would like," Matt says, holding the door open.

Ainsley sucks in a breath and looks at me. Her face is flushed and full of anticipation. "I don't care how many IOUs this will cost me, this is the best day ever!" She wraps her arms around me and squeezes. "Thank you."

I welcome the heat of her body and hold her tight, breaking all my fucking rules today. "This isn't a favor."

She pulls her head back, shocked. "Then what is it?"

I shrug in her arms. I'm not any good at being myself. It feels off. But she deserves the truth, even if it embarrasses me. "A gift. I wanted to make you happy."

Chapter Eighteen

Maverick

Rumor has it Tucker begged for his life.

The sea lion excursion left Ainsley and me exhausted, but we still managed to stop for ice cream before going home. I couldn't leave that off. If my goal was to make her happy today, it most definitely had to include ice cream and mac and cheese—but we'll save that for tomorrow.

"I'm going to take a shower," she says, lifting my chin from looking at my phone. "Maybe you want to join me?" Her smile is honest and real and so damn sexy before it flattens. "Like in a minute. Give me time to shave and condition my hair so I look sexy and not like a prickly raccoon."

A laugh burst out of me. "I think I can do that," I manage out.

If there's one thing I love about this girl, it's that she's wholly herself.

"Good," she manages a little shyly. "Give me about ten minutes."

I nod when she lets go and watch her dart down the hall and into the bathroom. Ten bucks says she uses my razor.

Back to my phone, I'm answering Pops's emails about potential candidates to assist me. Although I'm happy he isn't cutting me off entirely, I'm not so sure about bringing in a stranger to work on my accounts with me. I'm a little territorial. Okay, I'm a lot territorial.

My fingers fly across the screen. Paul is a hard no. I don't care if he did graduate from Harvard and has been running an independent brokerage for eight years. He looks like he farts in paper bags for fun.

I decide to text Pops instead of finishing the email.

Me: Are you sure I can't keep managing alone? We only have two months.

I get an immediate response.

Pops: Pops said stop texting him because he doesn't do this texting thing and therefore has to get me to help him, which ticks him off—his words not mine—because I'm a nosy little shit and get all into his business. He said be happy you got off as easy as you did and pick someone. Coop.

I grin. I had missed them, more than I knew. I start to text back when a knock on the door stops me.

Who the fuck dares to disturb me this late at night?

I yank open the door and there stands the asshole of my eye.

"Uh . . . hi. Is Ainsley here?"

Is Ainsley here? Is he fucking kidding me?

I hold Tucker's gaze as I push the door closed without acknowledging him at all. This prick has done enough damage to Ainsley.

"Wait!" He shoves his foot in the door, stopping it from closing.

I look down at his expensive loafers and shorts that rest at the thigh. What a prick.

"What the fuck do you want?" I block his view so he can't peer around and catch a glimpse of Ainsley or the apartment.

"I would like to see Ainsley," he says after taking a breath and standing taller.

"I don't know an Ainsley," I say flatly. "Try next door."

I go to shut the door once again when he stops me cold. "Come on, Maverick. Let's not play this game. Let me see my girlfriend."

I snort. "Your girlfriend?" I arch my brows at his boldness. "Don't forget our arrangement, Tucker. You don't want to get in over your head." I sneer. "At least any more than you already are."

Reminding him of the debt he owes me seems to shake some sense into him.

"I'm sorry. I just need to talk to her for a minute. I promise I'll leave after."

Not going to fucking happen.

My expression bored and unreadable, I ask, "And what would you like to discuss with your *ex*-girlfriend? Are you here to ask her to be your best man or Tonya's maid of honor? I'm sure she'll be thrilled." I purposefully get his girlfriend's name wrong. I don't want him thinking they matter in the least.

He bows his head almost remorsefully.

"No. I'm not here to hurt her. I just want to talk to her."

Don't care. "I'm sure you do. Unfortunately, I can't allow that to happen."

She's finally moved on from this prick. He isn't coming back into her life. Not now. Not ever. She's fucking mine.

"Please. I only need a minute of her time."

"Her time is expensive."

He narrows his eyes. "Are you implying that in order to speak to her, I have to go through you?"

See? He finally caught on.

I tap the doorframe. "I knew you had to be smarter than you looked."

"You can't keep me from her. This is her apartment too!"

Aww. Look at him trying to stand up to me.

"You get through this door just like anyone else," I tell him firmly.

"A favor?" He makes a scoffing noise like he isn't making that mistake again.

I offer him a malicious grin. "Please. You have nothing I want anymore."

He swallows, his throat working as his eyes dart around, attempting to peer around me, because that's just the type of person he is. A loser. Pussy. Now he realizes why he should have never gotten involved with me. I never play fair.

I reach into my back pocket for a card and a Sharpie, twirling the card between my fingers and drawing his eyes to my hands. "But maybe I can make an exception. Maybe you do still have something I can take."

Guys like Tucker aren't the type of guys to owe me favors. It's important to them to never get their hands dirty. However, he did it once. Maybe he'll do it again before he goes off to med school, buys a house in the Hamptons, marries a debutante, and has a couple kids with his mistress. Guys like Tucker are dirty in their own way. Too bad I'm not interested in anything else he has to offer. I already have her. And now, he knows it. "Time's a ticking, Tucker. How bad do you want to come in?"

He sighs and steps back, darting his gaze to the ceiling. "You're a real piece of work, Lexington."

I don't move, I simply continue to flip the card over in my hand. It is what it is. Ainsley is under my roof and she is mine now. Tucker has nothing to say that she needs to hear. He had his chance and he fucked it up.

I don't plan on giving him the opportunity to make it right.

Regrettably, Ainsley could use the closure, but what happens if that closure comes at a price to me? They were together for years. She and I aren't officially together because I've continued to remind her that we are simply a contract. Sure, today was different, but I don't know if one sea lion encounter makes up for years of memories with Fuckface.

Call me a coward, but I can't risk her talking to him. She might forgive him and . . . it doesn't matter. Turning Tucker away is for her own good.

"Whatever," Tucker says, scoffing. "Enjoy my leftovers."

I slam the door in his face and step back into the kitchen, fighting the rage that tries to consume me.

"Who was at the door?"

Ainsley is wrapped in a towel, this beehive sort of thing wrapped around her head. She looks like a badly wrapped Christmas present.

I step into her. "Another desperate soul. I took care of it." I touch the softness of her cheek.

"I got tired of waiting," she says, sliding her hands underneath my shirt.

Her skin is slick, damp, and red against mine.

"It's a good thing you got out when you did," I tease, eyeing the pink skin on her shoulders. "Otherwise you might have had third degree burns." Tugging at the white knot at her chest, I expose her tits. "How hot did you have the shower?"

"It's not that hot," she argues. "I just turn red very easily." That's for sure, except normally it's her cheeks and not her whole body.

"Hmm," I hum. "Maybe you should cool off." I wrench the towel away, exposing her fully.

"Maverick!" she teases, but she sounds excited. She invited me to shower with her for a reason. She wanted to taunt me with her nakedness.

"I'm pretty sure I'll be fine. With the temperature you keep the air set on, I'll be sure to cool off in no time." She crosses her legs and each of her hands attempts to cover her tits.

Honestly, I don't give a fuck about cooling her off. All I see is pink skin that reminds me of pussy. Call it horny. Call it an excuse to fuck her. One way or another, though, I don't plan to deny myself anymore. Tucker had it wrong. She was never his. She's always been mine; she just didn't know it yet.

"I disagree." I fight the urge to bum rush her like a juiced-up football player. A little tussling on the floor is great foreplay. "Move your hands." They're blocking my damn view.

Her palms move over her weighted tits voluntarily, like the heat of my stare on her naked chest has her aching for my touch. I take a step forward, pushing against her damp body. The wetness is cool against my shirt, but it does nothing to cool the heated skin underneath.

She swallows. "I want . . ."

Her eyes follow the movement of my hands reaching out to skim across the goose bumped flesh along her forearms until they reach their destination—her hands. "You want what?" I whisper, the head of my dick stretching against the fabric of my jeans.

A flush creeps up her neck and I follow it with my gaze. Pink. More fucking pink. She's killing me.

"I want to see you this time," she admits softly. "I want all of you."

I groan, holding her gaze, watching as her eyes volley between my fingers curled around her hands to my eyes.

"Granted," I whisper softly, teasing at her referring to me as a genie. "Now, let me see all of you."

So many meanings are tied up in those eight words. I want everything from Ainsley James. Every second of crazy. Every angry word. I want it all. Every inch she's willing to let me see.

She exhales, her minty breath fanning across my lips. My eyes never leave hers as she drops her hands, taking mine down with them. I take a minute to revel in the fact that she's trusting me to make her feel good—allowing me to worship her perfection.

My fingers smooth along the sides of her thigh and up over the curve of her hip. "Where should I start this time?" I droll.

Her intake of breath is shaky when she places her hand over mine and moves my hand to cup the bottom of her tit. The air is thick with our breathing. I still haven't looked down and she hasn't either. "Here," she says, moving my hand so the pads of my fingertips drag along the skin on the underside of her breast, where it meets her chest.

"Mmm. Here is good." I confirm.

She nods as I drop my hand and kneel at her feet, my head at the perfect level. And before she can say anything, I mumble, "Gorgeous," before tracing the bottom of her tit with my tongue. Her head falls back against the support beam.

"You're so good at this," she says as I wrap my arms around her hips and suck the pink nipple into my mouth. It's cold against my tongue and I work hard warming it up to my body temperature before popping off and going to her other tit.

My right hand crests along her back and over the curve of her ass, following the exceptional lines of her thighs until it comes to rest on the inside of her thighs. I push through and nudge her legs open. I want to see all of her. Dragging my fingers along her bare legs, I stop when I can feel heat coming from her core.

She exhales loudly, her legs quivering against me.

"I must not be that good if you're still talking," I suggest, breathing the words along her tits, my lips dragging against the soft skin of her nipple before I slip a finger inside her. She whimpers against me, the sound of her surrender my undoing. Biting softly, I hold her firmly against me. No way is she moving away. I want her to feel everything.

Her fingers tangle in my hair. "Ignore me." Her voice is gravelly—unhinged.

I add another finger, plunging into her heat with fervor. If I don't get inside her soon, I'll be an angry asshole. "Are you sure?" I tease her, curling my fingers and stroking the rippled flesh inside her. "We can wait until I render you speechless."

She moans. "Shut up, Maverick. You've made your point."

Damn right I have. I grin and give her nipple a soft kiss before trailing kisses along her stomach and down to her bare pussy. I press a kiss to her center, the smell of her arousal drawing me lower. "I need to taste you," I mumble.

"Oh, God. Please."

Her face is flushed and the towel that was on her head falls to one side. I love that she doesn't move it. She doesn't worry about looking perfect. She's just living in the moment, taking everything I'm giving.

My dick jumps eagerly in my jeans.

I bow my head and pull her forward by her ass, elevating her hips so I can drag my tongue through her slit.

"Maverick," she says pleadingly. It does all kinds of things to my heart. My watch is vibrating, alerting me that my heart rate is elevated. I don't care, though. Seeing Ainsley come apart with the flood light shining through the open patio door, and her wet, tangled hair a mess along her shoulder, is exhilarating, erotic, and all fucking mine.

Fuck Tucker. He'll never get a chance to tell her he's a douche.

Ainsley James is mine and there's no way I'll ever let her go.

My tongue and teeth battle to get closer, to crawl inside of her and eat her from the inside out. Her fingers are tight in my hair. Her back is arched against the pillar and her moans encourage me to go deeper, harder.

"I need you to stop," she chants between breaths. "I want to feel you inside me."

My lips quirk as I pull back and say, "Trust me, I'm inside you."

She cuts me a look that I'm sure she thinks is stern. "Smartass. I want your . . ." Her boldness trails off with her words.

I cock a brow. "You want my what?"

I want her to say it. I want her to tell me she wants my dick.

"I want all of you," is all she says.

Leaning back on my heels, I put space between us, allowing the cool air to hit her center. She shivers. "Please, Maverick," she begs, attempting to tug me closer.

"You're going to need to be more specific." I tsk.

A guttural moan escapes her. "I want your dick. I want it inside me now."

"That's my girl. Tell me what you need."

With a growl, I stand, clasping her hip and walking her backward toward the sofa, watching the excitement in the depths of her ocean blue eyes. When the backs of her legs hit the arm of the couch, I flip her around and shove her over the armrest, her perky, glorious ass high in the air.

I groan and follow the curve of her spine with my fingers, coating her with her own arousal. "You're so goddamned beautiful."

She places her hands on the cushions. I can see her body rise and fall with each inhale and exhale. "Maverick."

Maverick is freaking right.

"Say it again," I demand, fumbling with my zipper like some kind of teenager, all excited and shit.

"Maverick," she says, and I can just hear the smile in her voice. She likes that I want to hear her say my name. She likes knowing she gets to me—likes knowing she can break through my cold and rough exterior.

Finally, I get my fucking zipper down and my dick literally jumps free from my boxers. I grip it hard, coming closer and kicking her legs out wider so I can stand between them.

"I love you like this," I tell her, stroking my dick in a bruising hold.

"Like what?" Her words are labored and breathy.

I let the tip of my dick leak arousal over her stunning ass cheeks, marking my territory. It does something crazy to my chest. When have I ever felt the need to mark a woman? Claim her for myself. When have I ever cared enough?

It's a goddamned mystery. One I don't think I'll be able to solve just yet.

I reach into my back pocket, finding the cards and the sharpie, and toss them onto the floor where they scatter. Ainsley's head follows the noise, but I don't bother explaining. All I can do is focus so I don't jack off and come all over her pretty back. She wants me inside her, not all over her.

Finally, I find my wallet and the condom I keep for emergencies. I pluck it from the leather and toss it onto the floor as well. I'm sheathed in mere seconds and lined up with her entrance. I don't warn her. I don't think I can—the wait is too much.

The first push in sends a hiss through me. "So fucking perfect," I mumble, almost incoherently. She's tight burning flesh around me. A glove a size too small. I pull back and ease back into her, watching for any signs of discomfort. It's a lesson in patience.

"Are you okay?" I barely get out through clenched teeth.

"Yes," she moans. "More than okay." Her fingers grip the cushions beneath her. "Please move."

I can do that. I can *fucking* do that. I slam into her with an intensity, I'm ashamed to say, I haven't ever seen from myself. What is it about this girl that gets to me?

I'm slamming into her over and over again, the sofa inching up with the impact of my thrusts. I'm a fucking monster attempting to bury myself entirely inside her. I reach around, trying to slow my ass down and find her clit.

"Oh, God. Ainsley!"

I pause. "Did you just call out your own name?" I ask her.

She chuckles. "I figured you wouldn't mind. The tagline of the book said: 'Learn how to scream out your own name.' It was the one sentence I read."

That fucking book.

I shake my head and slam into her. "You better hold on," I tell her through clenched teeth—dammit she feels amazing. "You won't remember your name by the time I'm finished."

The deep groan that bursts out is felt deep inside her. Harder, I thrust so aggressively into her that my finger can't stay on her clit. It's messy, sloppy, and unbridled. Skin slapping skin, grunts and gasps the only noise around us, I push into Ainsley until my dick and I are satisfied that we've explored and ruined every inch of her pussy.

"I'm close," she chants excitedly, like this is a new concept to her. I'm sure Fuckface didn't care enough to demolish her insides. But I'm nothing if not thorough. I slow my thrusts and pinch her clit.

"Ahh!"

Her body shivers in my arms and I pick up the pace, chasing the only time I've ever wanted to come with a woman at the same time. Her muscles grip me, holding me closer to her, milking everything from me, one thrust at a time. Sweat is dripping down my chest, plunging onto her butt cheeks, which bounce every time she absorbs a brutal thrust.

"Come with me, Mav," she begs, stretching her hand back.

I stare at her hand reaching out for me for a second, a million things running through my head.

Fuck it.

I'm all in.

I lace my fingers with hers and pull them across her back and thrust one last time before collapsing on top of her.

Chapter Nineteen

Ainsley

Rumor has it she nailed Bennett!

He killed me.

Or at least paralyzed me for a while.

I drag my fingers along the ridges and dips of his abs as if it were a maze—an ab maze. He's been drifting in and out of sleep this morning while I watch *The Aquarium* naked, tucked neatly to his side as if I were small and delicate.

There's no reason to move or to even be up this early on a Wednesday, but I couldn't sleep. All these thoughts kept running through my head.

Could I be in love with Maverick?

I think so. I mean, surely you don't feel this way about a rebound.

Does one normally want to ease their rebound's blanket down just to gaze at the penis that made you come harder than you ever thought possible?

Does a rebound make you crazy with worry with every erratic beat of his heart?

What about wanting to hug him, like all the time? Those can't be normal thoughts you have of a rebound.

Hell, I don't know if they were even thoughts I had about Tucker. Sure, I cared for Tucker and I stupidly gave up my goals and followed him here, but I don't remember feeling this wholly consumed.

I literally wake up and wonder how many IOUs I can rack up from Maverick in a day. Like, what can I do to make him laugh or piss him off so he does that whole growly thing in his chest? I'm constantly Googling all the newest stress relief activities and I've even been watching Rachael Ray when he isn't home so I can cook him better dinners.

My mama always said you know you love a man when you don't want to poison his food.

I *so* don't want to poison Maverick's food.

I might want to eat half of it, but not poison it.

Scary Maverick Lexington has become more than just my roommate. He's become something far more permanent. Maverick makes me feel like my crazy is perfect and adorable . . . I've never felt so adored.

I wasn't supposed to fall in love with him.

I said I would spend my last years at college focusing on me.

"Stop thinking," he says sleepily, leaning down and placing a kiss to the top of my head.

See? See how fucking hard he's making this?

"How do you know I'm thinking?"

He makes this rumbling sound. "You're still."

I'm still?

"Are you saying I only sit still when I'm thinking?"

I look up just in time to see him roll his eyes and yawn. Gah, his teeth really are perfect. So white and straight. I wonder if my teeth will be that white if I keep using his toothpaste?

"That's exactly what I'm saying. The only time you ever sit still is when you're deep in thought."

I watch his jaw settle back into his signature frown.

"That's awfully observant of you," I note.

He shrugs. "It's what I do."

How could I forget?

"Uh-huh." He shifts and lifts me so I'm straddling him, my bare breasts on display only for him. "Do you want to go out tonight?" he asks hesitantly. "Grab something to eat maybe?"

I watch him carefully. "Are you not going to Gigi's with Sebastian?"

He's canceled all the poker games here since I moved in. Apparently, he and his friends have been meeting up at some place called Gigi's to play instead. I didn't care since it's such a pain for me to leave and find something else to do while they are here.

"I don't have to go," he says, a yawn clipping the last word.

He has to love me, right? Before, he would have never missed a game to hang out with me. And he wouldn't have spent an obscene amount of time sitting on a hard bench while I cooed and hugged as many sea lions as the aquarium staff would allow. I even forced Maverick to take pictures with me and the "sea otters" as he likes to call them.

Someone who didn't love you back wouldn't make arrangements for you to spend hours with your favorite animal right after you met his family, right? I don't think so.

Which begs the question. "Did your friend ever find me a house to rent?"

His body tenses under my fingers. "No. Why? Did you find a place?"

I laugh. "Uh, no. I'm just wondering since the last time you mentioned it, it sounded like a done deal."

He clears his throat. "The rental fell through."

"Too bad," I say, not meaning it at all. "I guess you're stuck with me for a little while longer."

I'm not eager to move out of Maverick's apartment, but if he's still looking for a place for me to stay then my theory could be wrong about him loving me. Then again, he could still love me but want his privacy. Who knows?

He makes a low noise in his throat. "I've gotten used to it."

That wasn't a "Don't worry, we'll find you a place soon" answer.

That means . . . "I've kind of gotten used to you too."

He rolls his eyes and I grin just before someone bangs on the door.

Maverick jumps, pushing me off him, and stands. "Put some clothes on."

I nod at his back as he sprints off to his room, throws on some clothes, and tosses me a pair of his sweats and a T-shirt.

Well then, guess he isn't waiting for me to do it myself. I pull on his clothes and watch as he stomps to the door, looking back to make sure I'm dressed before he yanks it open, seemingly ready to blast whoever is on the other side. Except, he never does. Because when the door gives way and he gets a good look at the stunning blonde, he sucks in a breath, taking a step back.

Quickly, I move to his side, getting an up close and personal look at the girl in the doorway. She is stunning with her long blonde hair and her navy stained eyes.

"Aspen," he drawls, looking past her size zero body toward the stairs. "Are you alone?"

I rear back. *Is she alone?* Is he expecting an army? Granted, the way she holds herself does look a bit regal even if she is dressed in workout gear.

She grins at Maverick. "I'm alone," she answers, clearly amused.

Mav nods but doesn't step back to let her in. "I don't want any problems with Jameson," he adds.

Who the hell is Jameson? Is that another one of his poker buddies I've yet to meet?

Aspen smiles and levels me with a curious look. "You must be Ainsley," she says, extending her hand out. I glance at Mav, a silent question transferring between us. Is she a friend? He nods and I turn back to the blonde bombshell and shake her hand.

"It's nice to meet you," I add, even though Maverick has never mentioned her.

"I have to say, I'm impressed. I wasn't sure that any girl could break Lexington."

Is she validating all the wild and crazy thoughts I've been having this morning? I think she is.

Mav snorts and seems to relax a little. "Yeah, yeah. What are you doing here, Von Bremen? You were supposed to call, not show."

Is she indebted to him like I am? Is this a deal going on? Wait, is Maverick calling in a favor?

Aspen turns her attention back to Mav, pausing only to give me a little wink. I'm not sure who this girl is, but I think I kind of like her.

"Always the charmer, Lexington." She fishes a card out of her pocket, handing it over with a smug look. "I assume you have a marker."

The muscle in Mav's cheek twitches, but he doesn't react until she raises her brows.

"What's it going to be, Lexington?"

After a moment, Maverick runs his hand through his hair and sighs, dropping his chin to his chest. "I assume you can make good on your part of the deal?" he asks, slowly pulling out the marker from his back pocket.

She nods. "I already did."

The tension in Maverick seems to relax as he passes her the marker. What the hell is going on here? Is he—

"Turn around, Lexington. I want to enjoy this."

I feel my jaw go slack. I've never seen anyone not fear Maverick and—is he really turning around and giving her his back?

"I don't envy Jameson for a minute." He laughs, shaking his head and turning around so she can press the card to his shirt. At this point, I have no doubt as to what she's doing. Maverick Lexington is owing someone a favor. I've seen him take favors and call in favors, but I've never seen him go as far as to owe someone else a favor where the terms aren't by his own making.

It takes Aspen only a second to scrawl out the letters and hand the card over to Maverick. "Make sure your brother is playing in Sunday's game. He gets one shot and one shot only to impress him."

Mav nods, fighting back his emotions, but I can tell her favor pleases him.

Aspen Von Bremen just did him and his brother a favor. One that Maverick couldn't do himself. The question is, what?

"I'll make sure of it. Thank you, Aspen." He tips his chin at the girl. "I mean it."

Everything to Maverick is a business deal. Nothing is ever personal, but this—this favor—this is personal for him and he appreciates it. "Now get the fuck out of here. I don't want any issues with Jameson."

Who the hell is Jameson? And since when has Mav cared who has a beef with him? Typically, he doesn't give a shit what anyone thinks about him. He's the almighty at Havemeyer.

Aspen chuckles as her phone rings in her bag. "You let me handle

Jameson." She looks at the screen and holds up a finger, signaling for Mav to wait or hush, I'm not sure which.

"Where the fuck are you?"

A deep voice roars through the phone and I look at Maverick, who just shakes his head. But it seems not to faze Aspen since an even bigger smile tugs on her face.

"What do you mean, where am I? I'm right where you told me to be," she lies, setting her shoulders as if she's readying for a verbal sparring.

Another growl sounds through the phone, but I can't make out his words. I can only assume they were not sweet. Again, though, this doesn't upset Aspen. "Bennett, for the love of God, I am waving at you. How do you not see me?"

I feel a grin slipping onto my face when Maverick shakes his head as if me encouraging her is not the thing to do at the moment.

"I swear, when we get home, we're having your eyes checked. Just stay there. I'll come to you."

The angered voice interrupts her laugh, but I can still make out the sentence, "When I get to you."

Maverick worries the card in his hand while the voice on the other end of the phone continues yelling at Aspen until she puts the phone on mute and addresses Mav once again.

"I'll be back to collect my debt. That is how this works, yes?"

Maverick sighs, no doubt rethinking his deal with Aspen and whoever this Jameson guy is. "Yes, that's how it works."

Aspen smiles at me, her phone still on mute. I wonder if she's in any trouble. Why is this guy so mad at her? "It's nice meeting you, Ainsley."

"It's nice to meet you—" Stomping sounds behind Aspen and she grins, never looking back at the massive body filling the stairwell with a scowl that would scare off armies. His phone is clutched in his hand as if any minute he will shatter it to pieces with one squeeze.

"I told you I was right here, Bennett. Geeze."

A man the size of an MMA fighter doesn't move, he only has eyes for Maverick. "Lexington," he drawls, eyeing Aspen and the three or so feet between her and Maverick.

Maverick clips out a gruff, "Jameson," and a chin tip that seems respectful.

He doesn't seem scared of this Jameson guy, just like maybe getting involved with Aspen is a headache he doesn't need right now. Which, after everything these past few months, is true. The less stress the better for him and his heart.

Jameson, as Maverick calls him, returns his chin tip like some kind of brotherly handshake, and then he turns his glare to Aspen. "Let's go."

It's not a suggestion.

Still, Aspen doesn't turn to leave. Instead, she smiles down at Maverick's fingers, reaching for me. "Be careful, Mav. You're showing your hand."

I know she doesn't mean literally. It's a poker reference. She means that Maverick is showing that I'm valuable to him, and his whole I-don't-care-about-anything-but-a-deal persona is failing him.

I'm giving him a tell and I don't know if that makes me happy or guilty that I might be messing up his scary reputation that he's worked so hard to build.

When Maverick doesn't respond, Aspen laughs, pocketing her phone. "Nice doing business with you, Lexington."

Jameson takes a step forward, looking like he's ready to toss this girl over his shoulder and throw her into his car. Finally, though, she does as he wishes and walks toward him. "You know, Bennett, you don't follow directions for shit."

The hulk of a guy doesn't look amused at her comment, but when she's close enough, she stands on her tiptoes and kisses his cheek, and that seems to settle him down, or at least erase the harsh scowl on his face to something more like a frown. "Fenn and Drew are out front waiting," he says, pulling her to him and tucking her into his side as if he were her human shield.

She catches me still watching and winks, giving me a little wave as her grumpy man tugs her down the stairs behind him.

I turn to Mav. "So . . . uh . . . he's intense."

Maverick pulls me inside and shuts the door, locking the deadbolt. "He's a nightmare is what he is. Him and his brother."

He pulls us back to our spot on the couch, snagging the blanket off the armrest. I snuggle into the crook of his arm and pull the blanket over us.

"Do you not like him?"

I feel his shoulder shrug underneath my head. "He's fine. The problem is Aspen."

I'm confused. "What's wrong with her? She seemed nice to me."

He laughs, the rumbling of his chest tickling my cheek. "You're right. She is nice. She's just . . ."

I wait as he processes his thoughts and exhales. "Aspen Von Bremen is like a rare unicorn. She's never seen alone. Not without the Jameson brothers or her brother, Fenn."

A memory stirs. "The Jameson brothers? Is that . . ." I had never seen them, but I've heard about the Jameson twins before.

"The one and only Bennett Jameson. Destined for the NFL and madly territorial about his childhood love, Aspen Von Bremen."

"That's not what I heard," I tell him. "I heard both the Jameson twins were single, or at least that's what the rumors were a couple years ago."

Maverick scoffs. "Drew might be single, but Bennett has never been single."

"But I've never heard that Bennett was in love with Aspen. Why would that be such a secret?" At a university known for its rumors, you would think word would have spread if they were together. Aspen is beautiful and I've heard girls talk about trying to nail the Jameson twins. If they knew Aspen had him on lockdown, they would go after her or at least attempt to be friends with her to get closer to the twins, right?

Maverick makes a noise low in his throat. "Aspen Von Bremen is a well-guarded asset. I took a risk asking her for a favor, but I was desperate. Aspen's father and uncle are baseball scouts. Since Coop's high school is not known for their baseball athletics, I needed to get eyes on him. If I don't, he'll never get into a college and on a good team. His hope to ever play for a major league team will be over. I needed Aspen's help. I needed her father to give Coop a chance to prove himself. Dealing with Bennett and Drew, and her brother, Fenn, is a risk I had to take."

"Why do they make you nervous?"

Shifting, Maverick moves so my ass is against his dick. "They don't make me nervous. They give me a headache. I don't want Bennett thinking Aspen owes me a favor or that she's indebted to me in any way. The Von Bremen and Jameson families have a lot of pull at this university. The last thing I want to do is end up on their bad side."

I nod. I get it. "So you want to keep them as an ally," I supply.

"Yes. I need them as allies. But Bennett isn't the friendliest person and even less so when you deal with Aspen. I used to think his tight hold on her was excessive. But now"—he squeezes me, nudging his hard length into my backside—"now I understand."

Does that mean he loves me? Or does that mean he understands why Bennett loves Aspen?

"I won't let anyone come between us," he murmurs, moving the hair off my neck and placing a soft kiss against my heated skin. "It's not about staking a claim, but about protecting a future."

I'm beginning to like where this is going.

"Bennett might not be able to be with Aspen yet, but he sure as fuck can make sure he protects a possible future with her for when the day finally comes."

It sounds complicated and a little heartbreaking. She seems really nice and well, Bennett seems a lot grumpy. Maybe that's because he's frustrated by not getting what he wants. I'm not sure what the story between Aspen and Bennett is, but I hope it works out for both of them.

And I hope all these subtle words and sentences mean that Maverick is not a rebound but loves me just as much as I love him.

Chapter Twenty

Ainsley

Rumor has it she was only a pawn in his game.

"I did it. I applied!"

My voice is loud enough that Maverick winces, but I don't care. After waking up in Maverick's bed, Lawrence snuggled in between us, I realized it was time to take my life back. I finally had a man—or a really amazing friend—we haven't labeled it yet—who gives me extreme orgasms and never minds sleeping with a stuffed sea lion in his bed.

It was Maverick who inspired me to chase my dreams. Lying there in his arms while he talked passionately to a guy about his retirement, not only turned me on, but convinced me I wanted that passion again.

So I decided to take my life back. Never again will I miss out on doing me. If someone can't stand behind my dreams, then they don't deserve to be in my life.

"Thank you for pushing me to fill out the application this morning."

Maverick squeezes me in his brawny arms and I take a moment to soak him all in. Has he always smelled this good? Wait, that's me. He smells like me, which is even better.

"I didn't push you," he says smugly. "I simply agreed that you needed to apply during your passionate girl-power-women's-rights speech you gave me after we watched *GI Jane* last night." Oh yeah, that movie inspired me too. I had forgotten about that. It happens when Maverick scrambles your brain with morning sex.

"It was a good movie." I grin, snuggling in deeper. "Either way, this has been the best day ever, and I think we need to celebrate by getting lunch together after class, since it's your first day and all."

Can you believe it? He actually came to class. Ever since he had that talk with his pops, he's seemed lighter. He is still working since he and Pops haven't settled on an applicant yet. Honestly, I think Maverick is trying to drag it out, so he won't have to hire anyone. I get it. He's territorial. But from the arguments transpiring between him and Pops, they will be hiring help. Apparently, Maverick has grown the company so big that even if he wasn't trying to finish school, they would still need help with all the accounts he has.

Pops threatens him regularly about his heart and even makes him send a snapshot of his watch readings, which haven't been too bad recently. Probably because we're having crazy amounts of sex. Luke was right, it really is the best way to reduce stress.

Either way, things have been different. Maverick and I have been spending a lot more time together and now we are doing couple-y things like eating lunch after class in honor of his first day.

"I'd rather eat at home," he says in a gravelly voice, dragging his finger along the inside of my jeans.

"Mmm . . . That sounds like a great idea," I agree. "But I'm afraid I won't make it back in time for my afternoon class."

"Skip it."

The mere suggestion sends a smile to my face. Gah, I'd love to be a bad girl and crawl in bed with this undercover nerd and veg out, but who are we kidding? We might bang each other's brains out, but once we recovered, Maverick would be back at his laptop and I would hurry off to class.

Reaching up, I trail my hand along his jaw. "Tomorrow, when I don't have an afternoon class." I can feel the muscles clench underneath. "Besides, you have an afternoon class too."

He frowns like he just remembered he's been reduced to a mere college student and not a finance mogul. Is that even a thing?

"Fine." He groans, stepping back and putting distance between us. "Run before I change my mind."

It's cute how he says it so seriously, like he's really tempted to grab me and run away. "Don't worry. You'll be fine. First days are hard on everyone."

He rolls his eyes. "Funny. I'll meet you here after class. Don't be late." He says the last part firmly and I have to stifle a grin.

I get it. He isn't used to being on campus or even out in the public. My closet water-drinking-nerd is used to sitting up in his kingdom and ordering people around via email. When he does get out, it's always at night and always with his crew. Him going to class all alone is really out of his element.

Standing on my tiptoes, I place a chaste kiss to his lips. "I promise. I'll be waiting."

For the first time in months, I don't mind the titters and whispers going on while I sit at a picnic table waiting for Maverick. Had it not been for the rumors about Maverick, and my history with fire, I wouldn't have ended up at Maverick's door. I wouldn't have struck a deal and become his roommate and he damn sure wouldn't have found me so irresistible that he let me stay with him.

So bring on the freaking rumors, I welcome them.

I text Maverick. I'm freaking starving.

Me: I'm going to eat your food. You better hurry.

He's only five minutes late but still. I may be able to handle all the rumors, but it doesn't mean I want to sit out here all alone. Luckily, he responds quickly.

Water drinking nerd: I had to grant a favor. #genielife Be there soon.

I grin at the screen, giving everyone something to lie about when another text comes through.

Water drinking nerd: And don't eat my food!

I pocket my phone and consider eating Mav's chips. He doesn't know I bought him anything but a sandwich, and really, his heart doesn't need fattening chips anyway. Maybe I will eat them.

Opening the bag, I grab my sandwich and unwrap it. I'm about to take the biggest bite ever when I hear, "Ainsley."

Slowly, as if Ted Bundy himself is behind me, I turn and meet the eyes of the man who shattered my heart and stomped all over it while he moved his shit into my apartment.

"Tucker," I grit, giving him a hello eye roll. "What do you want?"

With some nerve, he eases down into the bench across from me. "Can we talk?"

I take a bite of my sandwich, channeling my inner Maverick, and shrug like I don't give a fuck if he even breathes.

"Okay," he says after a moment, watching as I chew. "Look." He pauses, clearly nervous, and swipes a hand through his hair. It's gotten longer since the last time I saw him. "I just wanted to tell you I'm sorry about how things went down between us."

Ha! So he's not sorry that he cheated, but he's sorry about how "things went down"? What the fuck does that even mean?

"Aww, you're so sweet, Tucker. How did things not work out between us?"

Tucker picks up on my sarcasm.

"Look, Ainsley. I never meant to hurt you, but you knew things between us had been rocky for a while."

I rear back. "How were they rocky? I came here with you—for you!"

"Exactly!" His voice rises and his fists clench. "You were so clingy. Coming to Havemeyer was supposed to be the time of my life. Instead, I was just as tied down as I was in high school. You were supposed to go to Florida!"

I can feel my face heat and my eyes swell with unshed tears. "Get the fuck out of my face, Thomas."

Tucker cocks his head to the side like he isn't sure if I called him Thomas. I did. I took a page out of Mav's book and called him something random. I don't want him thinking he just ripped my heart out again. I'm stronger now, though. Now I'm able to tell him to get the hell out of my face and move his sorry, disgusting soul from my table.

I'm done with him.

Screw him and the "time of his fucking life." They can eat shit for all I care.

"All I'm saying, Ainsley, is we should have spent some time apart. Couples do long-distance relationships all the time."

What he really means to say is he wanted to fuck all the sorority sisters in peace and when he was good and spent, he would come home to me on the holidays and we would pose for his parents' Christmas card.

I am so done with being treated as a pawn in his game.

"Goodbye, Tucker. Catch an STD and live the good life." I wave my hand like I'm sweeping his disgusting ass away from me while I take another bite of my sandwich. I'm definitely eating Mav's chips after this. I deserve them. Maverick will agree after he hears this shit.

"Look, I just came over here to apologize and ask you for a favor."

Ha! I stare at him all wide-eyed. "Why would I ever do you a favor?"

"Because you once cared about me," he bites back.

I sneer. "*Once* being the operative word."

"Come on, Ainsley. Don't be like me. You're better than that."

See how freaking manipulative he is? He wants me to feel bad for being mean to him. Honestly, it's working. Being mean is not in my nature.

"What favor do you want?"

I have to admit, I'm curious. Tucker's family is wealthier than mine. What could he possibly want that he can't get himself?

He scrubs a hand through his hair and looks around. "You know Sebastian, the internet guy?"

I arch a brow. "Maverick's friend?"

He nods. "Are you friends with him?"

"No . . ." I drawl, still confused as ever. "Why? What do you want with him?"

Tucker blows out a breath and looks at the sky before slowly lowering his head to meet my eyes. "I need him to stop posting clips of Taylor on his MyView videos. It's making her look bad."

My heart fucking sinks. "You came to me for a favor to help

Taylor?" I take a big breath and laugh. "I can't believe you. After all these years."

I'm not hungry anymore. I roll the sandwich up and put it in the bag with Maverick's. "Enjoy your life, Tucker."

I stand to leave when his next sentence stops me cold. "Maverick and I had a deal!"

"What did you say?" The wind blows a lock of hair in my face. "When did you make a deal with Maverick?"

His eyes stare down at the ground and then it hits me. "That day I dumped food in his lap . . . You weren't comping his meal because of me; you were negotiating for your little girlfriend." This is unbelievable. "Tell me, Tucker. Did you ever care about me or was I just someone to pass the time with?"

Why I even asked, I'll never know. The point is, it doesn't matter—lesson freaking learned.

"I did care about you, Ainsley. But you were never supposed to turn down that scholarship and come with me."

Stupid, betraying tears trail down my face. Bastards.

"What the fuck are you doing here, Thomas?" a familiar voice growls. If I wasn't so hurt at the moment, I would have high-fived Maverick for using the same name I did.

I feel his big body dwarf mine as he slides in behind me and secures an arm around my waist. Immediately, I relax into his hold.

Now let Tucker talk some shit about Maverick's friend.

Tucker stands, giving me one last fleeting look before focusing on Maverick. "I needed to talk to you," he lies.

"Ha! You said you needed to ask me for a favor!"

Tucker narrows his eyes and Maverick's body goes tense behind me. "Is that so, Thomas? Are you asking my girl for favors?"

I can't help but enjoy the tingling in my nipples as he calls me his girl.

"You know better than that," Maverick scolds, his grip on me tightening.

Tucker inhales and puts his hands up in a peaceful gesture. "I need you to talk to your friend Sebastian. He's destroying Taylor's reputation on social media." He nods in the direction of someone behind Maverick.

"I heard she was getting more followers than ever," Maverick says, a light laugh mixing with his words.

"He posted clips of her and her friend arguing." Tucker's face is red, and I want to laugh. He's very passionate about his girlfriend's social media page. "That was a private moment!"

Maverick's eyes narrow. "The way I heard it, your girlfriend had been fat shaming her *friend* and teammate. Sebastian simply covered the story."

"That wasn't our deal!"

Maverick's chest vibrates with a chuckle. "Correct me if I'm wrong, Tommy, but I believe your favor was, and I quote, 'to help your girl-friend become internet famous.'"

Maverick's arms go up like he shrugged behind me. "I believe I did that. Our deal never included how I got her internet famous."

Know your opponent he once told me. Tucker definitely did not know his opponent when he struck a deal with Maverick.

I grin. Both of them deserve it. "I guess next time you should know who you're dealing with," I add with a smug look.

Tucker shakes his head and scoffs. "Like you? Do you know who you're dealing with, Ainsley? Who you're sleeping with?"

A knot forms in my stomach as an unsettling sensation spreads across my skin. "I know my opponent," I tell him, relishing the strength of Maverick's tight squeeze around me.

A smug smile tugs along Tucker's cheating face. "Does she, Maverick? Does she know the only reason you let her stay with you is because you were forced to?"

Gah, Tucker is a moron. "Of course he was forced, stupid. I asked him for a favor and like a good businessman, he honored it."

Tucker doubles over, his eyes alight with laughter. "She has no idea, does she?"

Suddenly, Maverick's arm around me doesn't feel like he's offering me support, more like he's keeping me from running. I tug his arm and turn. "What is he talking about?"

I'll never forget the pain I see cemented in Maverick's eyes. He swallows, his Adam's apple working. "I was going to tell you—"

Tucker's vicious laugh cuts him off. "Sure you were. Allow me, it's the least I can do."

Shivers trail down my spine. Part of me wants to run from this whole ordeal, but the other part of me wants to know the truth. I deserve the damn truth! I've been tossed around like garbage by Tucker. The least Maverick could do is show me his true colors before we get in too deep.

I'm lying to myself. I'm already in too deep. Whatever Tucker plans to tell me is going to hurt worse than me finding him ass up, plowing into Taylor.

I shove away from Maverick where he can't touch me. I don't want to be near either one of them right now.

Tucker grins at the movement, seemingly pleased with destroying me. "You weren't the first person who asked him to take you in."

"What?" I whip around and look for the denial in Maverick's eyes. There isn't any. His head hangs like he lost a million-dollar poker game.

"I'm sorry," he says, reaching out for my hand.

I take a step back. "Who asked you to take me in, Maverick?"

My voice is hard, but my mind is racing a thousand miles per hour. Who knew I was kicked out of my apartment? Well, not that question. Everyone heard about me getting kicked out. But who would have asked Maverick for a favor to take me in? Who would do that?

"Tell me!" I shout when he just stands there, worrying his lip.

"I can't do that." His words are resigned.

I huff. "Because you're an honest businessman? Is that it? Tell me, Maverick, do honest businessmen get paid twice for the same favor?"

"It wasn't like that," he hurries out. "I owed him a favor. He received nothing in return."

You have got to be shitting me. "I guess that makes it okay then?" I throw my hands up before deciding it's not good enough. I rush him and shove the man who made me whole only to cut me in half. "I loved you!" Tears fall down my face. "I trusted you!" A sob bursts from my lips. "And this whole time you've been lying to me."

"I wasn't lying." He tries to grab for me, but I sidestep him.

"Lying by omission is the same thing."

I'm so done.

I toss his fucking sandwich at his feet and then dig a couple of IOUs out of my pocket that I had planned to sneak back into his pocket as a joke and toss them at his feet. "Consider my debts paid in full."

I take a few steps backward and ignore the twitching in Maverick's cheek. "Don't come for me," I tell him. "You have no idea what I'm capable of right now." Hashtag, I am a freaking psycho at the moment. I will burn all their shit in their cars.

"I hate you."

I look at Tucker, who looks on like the smug bastard he is. "I hate you more and hope you get diarrhea. Maybe you'll shit out some of the ugly inside."

And with that, I flip them off with both hands, big, fat tears streaming down my face.

"Ainsley, wait!" Maverick takes a few steps and stops.

"I will set your laptop on fire, Maverick. I'm not even playing."

The guy I thought I loved rocks back onto his heels. He's no fool. "I'm so sorry," he whispers. I nod. "I'm sorry too. I thought I had finally gotten it right this time." I shrug like I missed my Uber and can order another one. "Guess not."

I don't want to see the pain in his face any longer. I'm sure he is sorry and maybe later when I don't feel like I want to cut him, I can actually hear him out. But not now. Not when he won't even tell me who asked for the favor. His loyalty should lie with me, not his business.

With my head down, surrounded by titters and whispers, I walk away, ignoring the "You're dead" roaring out of Maverick and the distinct sound of a bone breaking.

Fuck 'em both.

Chapter Twenty-One

Maverick

Rumor has it he died for her.

"Calm down," Sebastian barks as Rowan pins my arms behind me.

All I can see is her face. Confused. Shocked. Defeated. I betrayed her. I chose anonymity over the person I loved and trusted. I should have told her the truth about the favor, but it wasn't any of that fucker's business. No way did Tucker know the truth or the circumstances surrounding Ainsley's and my arrangement. He simply spat out one of the circulating rumors which, unfortunately, held an ounce of truth to it.

Growling, I fight against Rowan's hold.

"Maverick. Stop fighting us and calm your ass down."

"I am calm," I grit out to Sebastian, tugging at Rowan's grip just in case he eased up and I can break free and get one more hit on Fuckface. He needs more than just a broken nose. And he would have had more if I hadn't walked up to Ainsley's table with Sebastian and Rowan behind me. We had just made a deal and I needed to get back to Ainsley. They were being pains in my ass and wanted to be introduced to her. They are such girls.

But then I saw Tucker perched at the same table as my girl. Rage powered through me faster than my legs carried me to the table. I knew Tucker wanted to speak with her. I assumed things hadn't worked out with him and the ex-roommate, but I had no idea he was so upset over what we did to Taylor's social media presence.

Honestly, I don't see the point in him being upset. His girlfriend is a narcissistic bully. We simply showed the true her. She wanted to be famous. Now she is, just not for the reason she—or he—would like. I'm sure her bad rep wouldn't look good to his fancy parents or his med school application.

But that's what they both deserve.

Ainsley might have taken the high road and not sought revenge on her roommate and ex, but I did. Burning curtains wasn't enough for what they did to her.

They both deserved to suffer like she did over the past few months. I wanted Taylor to shed tears like Ainsley had all those nights, and Tucker, well, I just wanted to ruin him. He never deserved the loyalty Ainsley gave him. He didn't deserve either of the girls. What he deserved was to be alone with his expensive shoes and bad haircut.

Granted, I didn't join Ainsley's crusade on honest terms. That evening when she dumped food on my lap, I had gone to Studs and Spuds to check out this new girl I was supposed to help. I knew she had been kicked out of her apartment and suffered a breakup in the process. I was supposed to find her a place to stay. I wasn't supposed to offer her my apartment, but when I saw how Taylor treated her and the way they fucked around with her tables, I knew her situation was as dire as he claimed it was. I balked at the idea of taking her in. The last thing I needed was some heartbroken woman crying to Adele songs in my apartment for a month until I could find her a place to rent.

But then she threw the plate of food in my lap.

I knew then she wasn't going to sing some sappy breakup song. This girl was going to fight. This girl had no idea who I was, only that I was making a shitty day worse for her. I was intrigued. And when Tucker came to me a little while later for a favor, I decided I wanted to see how this played out between them.

Seeking revenge on her behalf came later. Ainsley became a constant in my life. I looked forward to going home and seeing what ridiculous shit she had done, and when I couldn't stop the inevitable tears, I took matters into my own hands. Everyone needs their dreams to come true and given my deemed genie status, I decided to grant Taylor's wish to become internet famous.

Not to say that makes me the good guy in this situation. I should have told Ainsley about the favor. Honestly, I planned on it, but when she went with me to the hospital, and I wanted her to meet my family, I chickened out. I didn't want to fuck up what we had by admitting the truth. It was easier to keep it from her, at least for a little bit longer until the newness wore off.

Rowan scoffs, "Punching the pussy is not calm behavior, Mav. We need to go before security shows up."

Fuck security.

"Your watch is going crazy, dude," Sebastian tries to rationalize with me. "Take a breath. You don't want to end up in the ER right alongside your friend, do you?" He points at Tucker, and for a fleeting moment, I consider the idea. I could use one more hit to make myself feel better. The look on Ainsley's face . . . She was devastated.

My heartbeat pounds in my ears. "He's not my goddamned friend, asshole, and neither are you," I lie, which just causes Sebastian to laugh.

"Holy shit. You're right, Row. He does love her."

I attempt to shrug out of Rowan's hold. "Shut the fuck up. I'm fine. Let me go. I need to find her."

There's no need in denying that I love her. I can fool the entire campus, but I can't fool these two idiots, they know me too well.

Rowan's grip tightens around me. "We're going with you."

Of fucking course. They can't let me lick my damn wounds in private. I knew coming back to campus was a bad idea. All I needed to do was lie low for another couple months. Fucking Pops and his demands.

"I need my hands," I tell Row. "I need to text someone."

I see Sebastian nod like he's giving Rowan his nod of approval. If I wasn't so anxious to get to Ainsley's ass, I would send an elbow straight into Rowan's ribs for even asking for Sebastian's approval. No one runs me, especially not Sebastian's crazy ass.

After a second, Rowan eases off me and I dig out my phone, nodding over my shoulder for Rowan and Sebastian to follow me. "Drive," I bark at Sebastian, tossing him my keys.

I jump in the passenger side and unlock my phone and fire off a text to the person who started this whole mess in the first place.

Me: Is she with you?

IOH-MB: Yes. Give me a few minutes with her. She's very upset.

The hell he's getting a few minutes with her. He's getting the few minutes until I get there. After that, I'm dragging her ass back to the apartment and locking her in until she agrees to listen to me.

Me: I'm on my way.

IOH-MB: You need to calm down before you get here. You'll just make things worse.

Why does everyone think I'm not calm? I'm calm, dammit!

Me: Don't let her leave.

IOH-MB: Maverick. . .

Me: Mitchell. . .

IOH-MB: You're both giving me indigestion.

Totally Ainsley's fault. If she had just listened to me and not run off, we could have sorted this out at home, naked. I would have even begged while she hugged her sea lion and I poured beer off the balcony and onto the neighbors. We both would have had our vices. Now I'm running around campus with blood on my knuckles like some kind of a psycho.

A few minutes later we pull up to Fire Station 764, and no sooner than we park, Sebastian shouts, "Oh shit! Look out!"

I look up just in time to see a fire extinguisher come down on the hood of my car. "Why didn't you tell me Boss put you up to this?" Ainsley screams.

I jump out of the car and attempt to snatch the fire extinguisher out of her hand, but Mitchell "Boss" beats me to it. "Why aren't you mad at *him*?" I yell back, taking a step closer as she takes one step back. "Hit the fucking firetruck, not my car! He's the one who started all of this!"

"You both should have told me," she cries, tears streaking down her cheeks and dropping onto her shirt. Her face is flushed and her hands are shaking. All I want to do is wrap her in my arms. I never meant for any of this to happen. The last thing I ever wanted was to cause her any more pain.

"And told you what exactly?" I answer for both Bostic and me. "That Bostic gave a fuck about you and didn't want to see you sleeping in your car anymore?"

She sniffles.

"Or that he asked me to find you a place to stay and one look at you had my crazy ass offering you my poker room instead? I could have easily secured you an apartment if I had asked Sebastian's mom. She's the best realtor in Atlanta!" I take a breath, trying to calm down. "But I didn't, Ainsley. You want to know why?"

Bostic puts his hands on her shoulders and pulls her to his front. It pisses me off. She should be with me.

"Because I liked living with you."

She swallows and a small sniffle squeaks out before she turns in Bostic's arms, hugging him like *he* was the one who just admitted that he broke all his rules for her.

I take a step back and yell "Fuck" into the open air, grabbing my hair and tugging. I want to feel pain. I *need* to get rid of this feeling in my chest.

"I love you, okay? Is that what you want to goddamn hear? I've been in love with you since you called me out on the beer."

I think back to the time when she asked me to breathe on her to prove I drank the beers I carried around all the time.

"You figured me out in a matter of days. No one has ever had the nerve to question me."

Sebastian lets out a scoffing noise that I don't bother addressing. I mean someone other than him. He didn't need to figure me out because he knew me before the rumors created me.

"You want to know the reason I don't smoke those cigarettes I tuck behind my ear when I'm thinking, or drink the beer I carry around to feel normal?"

Ainsley's tears lessen and she quiets.

"Tell her, Mitchell. Go ahead and fucking tell her why I owed you a fucking favor in the first place."

At least the nasty look she gives is not aimed at me this time.

"Boss?" She turns and steps out of his hold. Fucking finally! She folds her arms over her chest and settles her shoulders as if she's preparing to self soothe.

Mitchell flashes me a glare and then clears his throat. "A year ago, we got a nine-one-one call."

My watch starts beeping and Ainsley and Mitchell both stop to look at me. I wave my hand that I'm fine.

"To my apartment, to be exact," I add when they both just continue to watch me and not speak.

"Maverick had been pulling all-nighters, working and playing poker, trying to get his grandfather's business back up and running," Mitchell explains. "He had developed the heart condition and didn't know how to control it, so he began drinking and smoking more. It dulled the effects of the fast rhythm until one day it didn't."

Ainsley gasps and makes a move like she wants to come to me but stops herself.

Bostic continues, keeping his gaze on me, his eyes flicking to my watch occasionally. "I was the first one on the scene."

I remember the night when I answered the door, sweating and terrified. I wouldn't let anyone else in. I knew I needed help, but I didn't want anyone to find out and call my grandfather. He was in the rehab hospital, learning to walk again after the stroke. My brother was a junior, running the house and spending his evenings at the rehab center, annoying the old man. They did not need another thing to worry about. I was supposed to be working hard and getting my degree, not being found in my apartment drunk and having a heart attack.

"After a little coaxing, Maverick allowed me inside and I put him on the monitors. After a lot of drunk arguing, he finally agreed to do some breathing exercises."

I was such an ass that night. Even if I was scared, I would have rather died than gone to the hospital.

Ainsley interrupts, "You taught him how to convert the rhythm."

Bostic nods. "He refused to go to the ER, though."

Ainsley looks at me as if she could beat my ass.

I shrug. She should know this about me. "It was a year ago," I add.

Is she going to be pissed off at me forever?

"So, when his rhythm converted and he refused to go to the ER, I made him something to eat and then I left."

I narrow my eyes. "But he came back," I tell her, filling in the missing information. "Just like he did with you. Your 'Boss' over here is a nosy bastard."

I chance a look at Mitchell, who only grins at me. "He talked me into going to the ER and getting checked out," I add. He also swore he wouldn't tell anyone. "Then he drove me home and I felt obligated to return the favor. So I offered him a game of poker, which he lost epically." I point at him. "I did learn something, though," I admit. "His tells."

I offer the man who's been like a father to me this past year a grin. "As time went on and we began playing poker regularly, I noticed he would always bring a case of beer and a pack of cigarettes. But he never drank or smoked. Ever." I shake my head and smile. "I had the worst time figuring out the purpose behind it. One night, about six games in, I finally asked him why and he said, 'Everyone has a vice. I've found that I don't need to drink or smoke to feel the comforts of its effect. There's power in restraint.'"

I flash Boss an exasperated look. "I had no idea what that meant until the day I was out on my balcony, and the neighbors below me were fighting. It was an exceptionally stressful day and all I needed was a minute of quiet and here they were in a screaming fight. The beer was doing nothing to calm me down, so I poured it out. Coincidentally, it hit my fussing neighbors and they screamed, moving their fight inside. It was the first time I smiled all day."

Ainsley grins and my chest feels lighter.

"I realized what he meant after that. I could take matters into my own hands. I didn't need beer or nicotine to calm me, I could do that in other ways. Me keeping those two things around is a reminder that I am not dependent on anything but myself. I, too, have power in my restraint." I shrug. "And it throws off the poker players when I leave a bottle sitting full on the table or a cigarette unsmoked. They are so busy trying to figure out if that means I have a good hand or a bad one that they give away their own tells."

Greatest thing Bostic ever taught me, except for how to convert my rhythm obviously.

"Anyway, I cleaned up after all that and took better care of myself thanks to Mitchell over here, who seriously needs a woman to occupy all his hero time."

I don't mean it. Mitchell has been a really great friend to me. I don't think I would have made it this past year without his guidance.

Ainsley throws her arms around Bostic. "I knew you were a superhero!"

He barks out a hearty sounding laugh. "Not quite. But I've taken solace in helping kids like you over the years."

I can see Ainsley's shoulders shaking as she clings to Bostic for dear life. "Thank you for helping me," she mumbles.

Fury courses through me. "What about me?" I ask her. "Don't I get a thank you?"

Those dark tresses swing like a whip. "No. You don't!"

That's it. I'm done. Ainsley James will hear me out if I have to force her. I did not break all my rules for nothing.

I take a menacing step toward her and Bostic. "Why not?"

"You lied," she snaps, still holding on to Bostic like a life raft.

My watch starts beeping again and her eyes go wide as she strains to see the numbers.

Fuck it. If she must be stubborn. . .

I fall to the ground and clutch my heart.

A car door slams and Bostic yells out for someone to grab the AED, but it's Ainsley who reaches me first, which is exactly what I hoped.

"Breathe with me," she barks all authoritatively, dropping to her knees and slipping her hands under my head. Grimacing, I try turning my head away from her. "Stop being so stubborn, Maverick, and breathe with me!" she scolds.

Ha! Me stubborn. That's rich.

When she's bent over me, vulnerable and unprepared, I wrap my arms around her and roll, pinning her beneath me.

"Ahh," she screams, smacking softly at my arms. "You're an asshole! You tricked me."

I can't deny it. I did what I had to do.

"You wouldn't listen to me any other way," I tell her, hearing Bostic swear and call off the firefighters behind him.

"I'm sorry," I say earnestly. "I should have told you about Bostic and his fucking favor, but I didn't know we would become friends." It was a shock to me too. "I thought I would let you stay a couple nights and then you'd be gone." But then she had to ask me to look into her eyes and see if I saw two shits or a fuck. "I didn't know I would fall in love with you."

Her face softens as she takes my head in her hands. My watch beeps and she tips her chin so I will show it to her.

I huff like it really annoys me, but I show her.

My rhythm is still fast. Which I think we can all agree is her fault.

"Breathe with me," she whispers softly.

"Promise you'll stay and hear me out?" I'm not opposed to dying on top of her.

She tilts her chin and agrees. "Breathe with me and I'll listen to you."

I roll my eyes. "Fine."

I take a few deep breaths in rhythm with hers until my watch stops hollering. "Happy?"

She nods, looking less like Angry Ainsley and more like Maverick's Ainsley.

"Mike, the guy I know," I begin, "found you a place to rent last week."

She sucks in a breath and I hold her tighter, not giving two shits that we're lying out in the parking lot of the fire station with Sebastian, who is probably filming this whole shitshow.

"I found myself making excuses as to why the place wasn't right for you." Here goes nothing. "But the truth is, Ains, it wasn't right for you because *I* wouldn't be with you. I like living with you." I correct myself. "I love living with you."

I test moving one of my hands up her arm. "I love buying

toothpaste once a month because you use all mine. I love waking up to you in my bed and burning macaroni and cheese on the stove."

A tear rolls down her cheek. I swipe it away and replace it with my hand. "I love watching your stupid walrus show."

That gets a laugh out of her. "They are sea lions, don't act like you don't know the difference."

My heart aches at the teary strain in her voice. "You were the best thing to ever happen to me," I admit. "I don't care that you love Lawrence more than me, I'll settle for being second best in your life."

Her grin rivals the largest pot I've ever won at poker. "How do you know I love you?"

I shrug one shoulder and grin. "Sebastian recorded it when you screamed it at me earlier."

"He did not!"

I let my other hand go and caress her face with both hands. "You're right, he didn't, but he probably is now. We're probably making him millions."

Her eyes go wide and she tries pulling up, but I don't let her. "I'm willing to owe you a favor for as long as it takes for you to believe that I love you."

"Really?" She knows I would never willingly owe someone an open favor.

"Really," I promise.

She leans closer. "You promise to never keep things from me again?"

I nod. "I promise."

And then I yank her body up to mine and seal it with a kiss.

Rumor has it . . . no one fucking cares. We're out.

"It's normal, right? It's normal to want to strangle the breath out of them. I mean, it's not like we haven't had a good run. Six years is a long time to be with someone."

I look at Sam. Her deep brown eyes stare back at me curiously, or is that fearfully?

I wave my hand in the air. "Fine, it's crazy all right? I know it is and honestly, I don't want to kill him. Maybe I want to smack him around a little, but not kill him. But he canceled, Sam! Canceled! What kind of boyfriend does that? I'm thinking one who wants to die, don't you?"

Sam, my sea lion coworker, nods up and down. "See? I knew you would agree. We women have to stick together."

Maverick better thank his lucky stars that I have Sam to confide in, otherwise I'd be driving to his office with a stack of playing cards and a fire extinguisher.

Okay, maybe not the cards. That's his thing. I'll just take the extinguisher and smash his computer. Yes, it's a little crazy but kind of not.

Ever since that time in college when we went to Crush It, Maverick and I have kept up the routine and now have a standing reservation to alleviate our stress. So really, taking an extinguisher to his laptop wouldn't be all that shocking to him.

What was shocking to me was that he canceled our dinner date. We never cancel and I had news, dammit!

I kiss Sam on the nose. "Come on." I nod, giving her the signal to follow. "Mama needs to go home and straighten out her man." Sam barks and I give her a little pat on the head. She knows men need a woman to handle them. She has a time with Barker, the only male sea lion in her habitat.

I knew when I got accepted as an intern with the aquarium that Sam was my spirit sister. No, not spirit animal, even though she is that too. Sea lions have always been my spirit animal, but Sam, in particular, is the best sea lion a girl could ever ask for.

I cried for two solid days when I was promoted to be her trainer. I had worked so hard to prove myself. I cleaned whatever I needed to clean, I studied, I observed. I did everything to get a trainer position. It was a dream come true and I did it all on my own.

Sure, Maverick bought me a season pass to do all the extracurricular sea lion petting I wanted, but I was the one who wowed the staff with her incredible sea lion wooing skills and grades. After Maverick and I hashed out our differences in the fire department's parking lot, we went back home.

We went to class.

We witnessed Tucker getting arrested for bribing a professor who flunked his ass. His girlfriend, Taylor, well, she changed schools. Come to find out, students hate bullies.

The rumors still spread around Maverick and me, and that was fine. We knew who we were, and we spent our time together, drinking water and playing Who Wants to be a Millionaire until we graduated.

Now we have a house close to our families. Maverick's pops is doing well, living in an assisted living facility—he refused to live with us—since Cooper was drafted to the minor leagues straight out of high school, thanks to Aspen's dad. He didn't attend college like Maverick and Pops wanted, but they are happy for him regardless. Cooper, like his big brother, lives by his own code. He wasn't about to let Pops's and Mav's dreams for him get in the way of his own.

I lock Sam in her habitat and kiss her nose. "See you tomorrow, chica. I'll let you know if we need to plan a funeral. Sam nods like she understands. Maverick is sexy and all, but sometimes even the sexy ones have to die.

Leaving Sam to her own devices, I find my jacket and purse, and pull out my phone. A text flashes on the screen.

Mom: Should I wear the green dress or the gold one?

I grin, so excited that my mom is finally dating.

Me: He's a firefighter, Mom. You always wear red!

You guessed it. My superhero, Devon Sawa, guardian angel, aka Boss, is dating my mom. You can thank me for hooking them up. I might have set them up on a blind date by asking them to lunch with me. Except, I didn't stay. I rushed out the quick story about how Boss looked out for me and then kissed my mom on the cheek and waved goodbye.

They hit it off by bonding over how kids were such a pain in the ass. I didn't care, though, because I knew they were talking about Maverick.

Mom: Are you sure?

I fire off a text, getting into my car.

Me: Positive. Don't be late! It's his only night off this week.

Of course I keep up with Boss's schedule. He's all lonely since Mav and I have moved away, but rest assured, I keep him visiting so much that he's actually looking to move and commute to work. I'm not even sorry. I may not have known my real father, but I have adopted Boss and he's better than that sperm donor.

When I'm sure my mom is settled and not going to text me anymore, I head home, not bothering to call my pain in the ass boyfriend and warn him. He's been acting odd all week. At first I thought maybe it was his heart acting up, but when I checked his watch history, everything seemed okay.

We live about five minutes from the aquarium. On really pretty days, Maverick will walk with me to work, but today he didn't, deciding to head to his office early. Mr. CEO has not slowed down one little bit. Just this past fall, he opened a new branch in Atlanta where he has to be chained to the bed to keep from trying to take over that branch too. He hired an extremely knowledgeable branch manager and the company is thriving. One thing about my man is he knows how to run a company.

His problem is following up on our plans.

Parking, I pull out the keys and dash up the walkway, finding our front door unlocked, which isn't all that odd. Maverick still has the personality that no one would dare come in his house unannounced, but I still lock the door because hello, we live in a crazy world.

Pushing open the door, I find the living room empty just the way I left it. A blanket is thrown over the edge of the sofa where Maverick ate his breakfast and settled his heart down with my body. It's been mutually beneficial for both of us to relieve stress.

"Maverick," I call out. "Are you here?"

I take the stairs to the basement where he still holds his Wednesday night poker games with Sebastian and Rowan.

I knock softly. "Maverick?"

When he doesn't answer, I crack open the door and find him sitting at the table, his head in his hands and a pile of cards in front of him.

"Are you okay?" I ask softly into the darkened room. "How long have you been in here?"

He turns at the sound of my voice. "You're late."

I feel my brows pull together. "I'm late? I'm not the one who canceled our date." I never said I wouldn't be bitter.

His lean body straightens slowly, a dark look in his eyes. "Come here." His voice is low and dangerous and I'm not sure copping an attitude was a good idea.

I take a step farther into the open space toward the poker table. Maverick watches each step, his finger drawing lazily across his lips. I guess he isn't going to comment on the whole date cancelation thing. That's fine. He will.

I walk toward him, watching as his eyes drink me in, and when I'm within his reach, he pulls me to him. I make a soft noise at the sudden jerk and stabilize myself by throwing my arms around his neck.

"What are you doing in here?" I try again. It's not Wednesday. It's not like anyone is coming over to play poker.

He nuzzles my side with his scruffy face.

"I was just analyzing all this debt we have."

I rear back. "What? I thought you said the only debt we have is the house!"

A sly grin tugs along his face as he directs his gaze to the poker table. There, scattered all over the green felt, looks like all the IOUs he's written me over the past six years.

"The way I see it, you'll never pay off all of this debt. It would take you a lifetime." He rubs the scruff on his face, pulling me closer. "So, a lifetime is what I will take." He pushes me back so he can stand and then . . . kneels while digging into his pocket and pulling out a black velvet box. "Ainsley James. I'm full of total shit."

I burst out laughing at his vulgar beginning.

"You owe me nothing and everything. I'm a man who played his odds. The over-under for a woman as incredible as you ever being with a man like me was ridiculous. I knew I didn't deserve you and I never will. You see me. You got to know me when no one else did. You make me a better man. Marry me—"

He doesn't phrase it like a question.

"And let me be indebted to you for a lifetime."

I can feel tears welling in my eyes.

"I can't," I admit softly.

He rears back, that stunning face of his falling. "Wh-why?"

I run my fingers through his hair and smooth the clenching muscle along his jaw. "Because I come as a package deal."

He rolls his eyes. "I've dealt with Lawrence this long, what's a lifetime?"

I grin at his sweetness. He has dealt with Lawrence and has bought Lawrence a friend every year on our anniversary.

"I'm not talking about Lawrence."

He still looks confused and it's freaking precious.

"Let me show you," I suggest, removing my shirt, leaving me only in my leggings. "I wanted to surprise you tonight."

He looks me all over, trying to find a clue on my body. "For a man who reads people, you sure are dense tonight." I laugh, grabbing his hand and plucking the box from it. "I'll hold this." I grin and then I place his hand on my belly. A belly that just this week cannot squeeze into a pair of jeans.

His hand trembles along my skin and the meaning of my words sink in. "I come with a free gift," I tell him. "It's not just me you're committing to for a lifetime."

His jaw ticks and his eyes turn glassy. "Are you saying—"

I nod. "We're having a baby."

The man who scared an entire university bows his head and places a kiss to my stomach before pulling up and leveling me with a look of resonation. "Let me try again?"

My entire world rests in this man's eyes.

I nod, handing over the box.

With trembling fingers, he opens the box and takes out the most exquisite aquamarine diamond set in a platinum band.

"Ainsley James." He clears his throat. "I love you more than life itself. Let me owe you a lifetime. Let me attempt to be the man and the father"—he kisses my stomach again—"you both deserve. Marry me."

I nod. "Yes, I'll marry you." Tears stream down my face as he slides the ring on my finger where it will never come off.

"One more thing." He holds up a finger and reaches around, finding a marker on the table. Uncapping it, he places another kiss on my stomach before writing out the letters IOU on my skin. When he's done, we both stand there staring at the words on my body.

"So what do you want, Maverick? What do I owe you?"

Those long fingers drag across his lips thoughtfully while his eyes rake down my body lazily.

"We," he corrects. "You *both* owe me everything."

He stands and pulls me closer, the distinct smell of Maverick wrapping around us like a warm blanket.

"You owe me every smile."

His hand cups my face, his thumb dragging the corner of my lip down.

"Every laugh."

I don't smile but instead I watch the intensity flash across his face. This is the man people fear when he collects a debt, yet all I feel is safe and revered as he states his demands.

"You owe me every tear."

A soft kiss is placed to the corner of my mouth, his strong hands tilting my head so he can nuzzle in close.

"Every second you breathe . . . is mine. I want it all, Ainsley James. Every. Single. Part."

It's a hefty price to pay, but someone has to do it.

"What if I say no?" I'm completely full of shit. I love the hell out of this man.

His chest rumbles and his breath tickles the fine hair on the back of my neck.

"All right, I'll play," he says, pulling back, his poker face in play.

I eye the man who showed me that one bad apple doesn't ruin the whole bunch. That some men are good with good intentions and good hearts. They might be standoffish and gruff, but deep down there is a gooey center.

"What will it take?" His voice is clear, but his mouth twitches.

"Your soul," I tell him with a grin.

The twitching stops and a boyish grin forms. Gah, he's adorable when he wants to be.

"I'll take your soul and raise you—"

"Mav!"

This negotiating ass . . .

His arms go around me before I can get the rest out.

"We have a deal, Ms. Lexington. A soul for a soul."

Acknowledgements

Ahh! My readers! Why must I love all your asses so much? I know! Because you are amazeballs. I'm not just blowing smoke up your ass either. I mean it. I'm so very grateful for all that you've done and continue to do for me every single day. You inspire me, you make me laugh, and you make me want to write all the books for you. You are my spirit humans! Let's be clingy and never leave each other.

Whether you loved or hated *IOU*, I would be forever grateful if you left a review as one more "Fuck you," to Tucker. Ainsley and I think that would really show him how much you loved and/or hated her story but secretly, she hopes you loved it.

Laura, Laura, Laura. Why can't you move to the US so we can laugh at all these night owls who are losing all the good sleep time before ten. Thank you for always having my back and making teasers and graphics since clearly, I would have a blank Facebook page without you.

Jaime! I'm not sure why you're still my friend when I legit send you material at all hours of the day and then proceed to chat and bullshit so you can't work on it. Thanks for managing my writing schedule and editing random things on short notice. And talking me off a ledge. And—let's not document all my flaws and how much I drive you crazy just yet. I'll text you.

Sarah P., thank you for always making me look like I can write, and tolerating my last-minute requests. I swear, one day I will get my shit together and stay with a deadline.

My street team. Why are you all so freaking amazing? Thank you for pimping me out every single time without fail. Your dedication and excitement for these stories inspire me every single day. Love your faces!

Jessica, six books! Can you believe it? Where has the time gone? Thanks for sticking with me since my very first word was written. You may never leave.

Sarah S. I'm not even sorry for being clingy. It should serve as a lesson that you shouldn't be so awesome. Thank you for alleviating all the stress of teasers and graphics. I'm sorry I threw you to the wolves, but you came out the wolf whisperer. Own that shit. One day I will have my shit together and give you more notice. Fingers crossed.

To my betas who are always my biggest cheerleaders and toughest critics. You make me a better writer, especially with your gifs in the group chat.

Autumn. Can you believe our marriage has lasted a year? I think that's a good sign since you haven't killed or divorced me yet. Thank you for always giving it to me straight and ignoring my bullshit. We all know I wouldn't ever publish a book if you didn't make me.

Emily of Lawrence Editing, So. . . I am a little psycho at editing time. I'll own that. This time, though, I swear the kids drove me to level ten thousand. Thank you for having so much patience and working with my tight as shit deadline. You are a superstar!

Letitia, you are my hero! I know I tell you that all the time, but I really mean it. You take these clusterfuck of ideas from me and somehow make magic with it. Thank you for being a mind reader. You are stuck with me so don't even try escaping.

Stacy, of Champagne Formats, thank you for always being so flexible and literally making my words a work of art. One day, I shall come hug you!

Bex, thank you for always keeping my website looking professional and like I'm a real author. You are the master!

A special thank you to the best reader group ever established: Kristy's Commanders. You guys are my safe haven.

And a huge fuck you to the COVID-19 virus that turned my whole schedule upside down while I was trying to write *IOU* with three kids at home. You suck and I hope you die.

The Pretender

For my middle child.

(Proof that you do get individual attention sometimes.)

I know you'd rather shave off your eyebrows than read a book, but one day, you'll be able to tell my grandchildren I wrote a cringy romance story and dedicated it to you.

Don't worry, every high schooler needs one embarrassing parent story… this is yours.

#staceysmomaintgotnothingonme

#iknowyoudontknowwhothatisbutitmakesyourdadandilaughreallyhard

Valentina: I was thinking we should use an original quote, you know? Something that relates to our story…

Sebastian: Done. See below.

Women are complicated and crazy. It takes booze and chocolate to live happily ever after. The end.

Valentina: Seriously?

Sebastian: You wanted something true, yes?

Valentina: One day someone is going to hit you with a car.

Valentina: On purpose.

Sebastian: So you're saying you don't like the quote?

Valentina: Sebastian!

Sebastian: Fine. See next page.

Some are born great, some achieve greatness, and some have greatness thrust upon 'em.
William Shakespeare, The Twelfth Night

Based on a true fake story.

The
Pretender

"What in the mother of all fucks?" My mouth falls open. "Have I been roofied?

Was someone stupid enough to actually slip something in my drink?

I scrub a hand down my face and over the dusting of hair already growing back from this morning's shave.

"Am I foaming at the mouth?" I ask Vee, looking around at the empty townhouse. Trash and empty beer cans are scattered on the counters—a fucking mess that someone, who is not me, will clean up later. "Where's my phone? I need a mirror. If I'm about to die of poisoning, I prefer not to go out looking like I frenched a Saint Bernard."

"Sebastian… I'm sorry," she explains, her voice lighter than before. "I didn't mean for—"

Oh, yeah, she meant for this to happen. Don't let that pouty mouth fool you. I've had this shit coming, and she served her revenge up frosty with a side of fries. The camera won't lie when she airs this video. All of her followers will see me go down like a little bitch—all red-faced and wide-eyed. Hell, I'd have been less shocked if I stuck my dick to an antenna during a lightning storm. She fucked me up good, and I have to give credit where credit is due.

"Shh… now, now," I say, holding myself upright. "Don't go getting all soft on me." I mean to hold my finger to her lips, but I'm drunk as fuck, and end up shushing her with my thumb instead.

"You won fair and square. Never apologize for winning." Gravity—or the alcohol—pulls me closer to her body. "You hear me?"

The unique gold flecks swirl lazily in the depths of her chocolate eyes as she stares up at me, a frown line creasing her flawless skin. She probably expected a different reaction. One where I yell and throw shit around while downing the last two beers sitting on the coffee table. But that would be too satisfying for her. What Valentina Lambros needs is what we've always had together. War.

"Sebastian—"

"Tsk, tsk." I chide, shushing her.

I want to force my thumb into her lying mouth and feel the warmth of her lips wrap around it and ease the ache. Instead, I swipe away a tear and drag my disappointed thumb through the layers of makeup, revealing her bare face inch by inch.

Grasping her chin between my fingers, I tilt her head to the side, allowing my breath to flutter over her ear. "You may have won the battle, Valentina. But I promise you this—I will win the war."

CHAPTER ONE

Valentina

University CamFlix Competition Submission
Entry Number: 75
Sebastian and Valentina
First Interview, also known as day one with the fake demon boyfriend

The clapperboard snaps in front of our face. I can't believe I agreed to this. And with Sebastian of all people. Apparently, I like to torture myself for fun. Wait, no, for money.

"Why don't you start from the beginning? Tell our producers why we should consider you for this competition."

I glance at Sebastian, who has a stupid grin on his face. "Go ahead, tell them, sweets." His voice is like satin: smooth, cool, and silky enough to slip off his bed of bullshit.

I'd like nothing more than to junk punch him and watch his eyes water, but I made the bastard a promise—act like I love him until we win. Trust me, it's not as easy as it sounds. The boy might have abs for days and a face you could see yourself doing those, "see what your future baby would look like" apps, but it doesn't help me in this situation. You see, Sebastian has a personality that makes me a little… stabby. Amongst other, violent things.

Inhaling, I level Sebastian with the fakest smile I can manage. "Sure, honey." The words are bitter and taste a lot like hatred. "You see, Tom—" I clear my throat and smile at the camera, "—It all started with a war."

Two months after the incident Sebastian and I agreed to never discuss again.

"You do realize this is breaking and entering, right?"

My sister from another mister, also known as my roommate, Aspen, actually looks like a real—and very hot—burglar in her all-black attire. Me? Not so much. I didn't bother changing out of the worn, flannel shirt—courtesy of my brother—and the denim cut-offs I wore to class this morning. I had other things on my mind. Things like stalking my neighbor so I can break into his house, uninterrupted.

I turn from the door lock where I'm squatted. "No, it isn't. He gave us a key." I hold up the two lock picks as evidence of said key and blow a wayward strand of hair from my face. "Besides, it's only B&E if we break something when we enter."

I know that's not true. I'm not an idiot. But I need my roommate to not chicken out, since someone has to hold the flashlight while I pick this lock.

"Sebastian—" who I like to call 'Bash-hole'— "practically begged me to break into his house this morning when he stole my chair, Aspen. We can't let him get away with it, it'll set a bad precedence for the other neighbors."

Aspen chokes on a laugh. "You mean to tell me that we're only doing this to set an example?"

I don't even care that it sounds ridiculous. "Yes, exactly. An eye for an eye and all that." I wave away her silly grin. I'm doing this. I don't care how crazy it makes me look. Sebastian Carrington will not get away with stealing my chair and then acting like I was high this afternoon when I asked him about it.

Those frosty blue eyes were cold enough to chill a drink when he narrowed them in my direction and laughed. "Good afternoon to you, too, Valentina. You're looking rather handsome today."

Of course I didn't hit him, but I really wanted to. Instead I flipped him off and asked, "Where's my chair?"

"Why would I have your rickety old chair?"

I popped a hip and tried really hard not to let my eyes wander down the length of his body. "Uhh, I don't know, because you hate me?"

That stupid dimple, the one that makes smart girls take a trip down regret lane, pops when he grins down at me. "That's one way to describe it." He touches the bow of my lips with his finger. "Have a good one, neighbor." And then he slammed the door in my face.

Now, I don't know about you, but no one slams the door in my face, especially not my nemesis. Sebastian Carrington may be the face of MyView, the social media site made specifically for amateur reality stars, but to me, he's just the shitty neighbor next door who I may or may not have kissed a couple months ago.

Everyone has those *shoulda, woulda, coulda* stories.

Sebastian is mine.

I *shoulda* told him the truth and not played that last prank.

It *woulda* changed everything between us.

If I *coulda* done it over… well, I still probably would have played the prank. If I hadn't, we would have never become friends—even if it was short-lived.

The point is, Sebastian wants me to break into his house because that's what we do to each other. Sure, he hasn't played a prank on me since I won the last one, but it was only a matter of time. I knew he would come around and start the prank battles up again. He might have pouted about losing, but there's no way he'd let me be the winner for long. His pride wasn't *that* wounded.

"Earth to Vee." Aspen's voice is a harsh whisper that pulls me out of my head. "Hurry up before we're caught."

I ease the picks back in. "We're not going to get caught. Besides, I've never known you to be scared of breaking the rules."

Aspen fidgets next to me. "I'm not, but I'm on thin ice with my dad right now, so if we get caught, we'll need to call Aunt Bianca. She won't ask questions."

I nod, still focused on the lock in front of me. "Agreed." I'm not on thin ice with my parents, but something tells me they wouldn't be very happy if they had to bail me out of jail in the middle of the night.

Twisting the metal, I hear something click. "I almost have it," I tell Aspen.

"Good, just hurry. Sebastian's neighbor just turned on her porch light."

I'm literally going as fast as I can. The last thing I want is for Bash-hole to come home and catch me pilfering through his shit like some kind of broke pirate.

"That's just Pam. She's harmless," I assure Aspen. She's also a stripper, but I keep that tidbit to myself. "She's just getting ready for work."

"How do you know this?" I don't know why Aspen seems so shocked that I actually know things about our neighbors. Well, never mind, I do know. I'm not a people person nor as outgoing as Aspen. Quite frankly, I prefer dogs over humans.

"Hold the flashlight steady," I demand, ignoring her question and moving the picks around. My tongue is sticking out, but I don't care. Aspen knows this is how I concentrate.

"I thought you and Sebastian were done messing with each other anyway?"

I almost groan and tell her to hush. My history with Sebastian is not something I like talking about. Okay, fine. I'll admit, I might have a teensy, itty bitty, minuscule amount of guilt that I'd rather no one know about. Questions about our history will lead to answers, and answers will lead to his and my embarrassment.

Hence the reason it will always be referred to as the incident we never discuss.

I lean my head to the side, swiping the sweat from my forehead. "We were. It's been two months since our last prank." She's my best friend. I may not be able to tell her the whole truth, but I can throw her some crumbs to satisfy my guilt and curb her curiosity. "I don't know what triggered him to steal our chair this morning. He was probably drunk." Now that I think about it, that's probably the case.

"Have you considered Sebastian might not have been the one who took it?"

Ha! She has no idea the crap Sebastian and I will do to get one over on each other.

"He stole it, Asp. I have no doubt."

The question is, why?

"If you say so."

She starts scanning her phone, and for a minute, fear creeps in. "You're not posting this are you?"

Aspen looks at me as if I'm that crazy girl that posts videos of her birds picking food out of her teeth. "Of course not. I'm not Miss Social Media Celebrity. I'm asking Fenn if they cooked dinner. All this criminal activity is making me hungry."

Whew. She's just texting her brother, who lives across from us. I don't know why I even worried about her posting. It's not like I don't post every day, but I'm on a reality cleanse right now. Instead of posting clips of the pranks Sebastian and I play on each other, like I used to, I've gone back to my roots and only post 'how-to' videos for special effects makeup.

If someone were to post me pranking or having anything to do with Sebastian right now, it would go viral and then we'd be forced back together and that could get really awkward since the last time I saw him, he declared war. Yeah, we didn't end our relationship with a high-five and a smile.

I shrug, pulling my focus back to the lock. "Oh good. I could eat too."

"We'll go over there when we're finished. I'm sure Drew cooked up something good." Mmm… I bet he did. Drew and his brother,

Bennett, are Aspen's brother's roommates. We all grew up together in the same neighborhood. Our parents are such close friends that we refer to Drew and Bennett's mom and dad as our aunt and uncle.

"Got it!" I almost jump up and down when the lock finally turns to Bash-hole's townhouse.

"Took you long enough," Aspen says, pushing me forward and through Sebastian's back door.

"You're just used to me picking the door to our townhouse," I murmur. "It's easier than his." We forget our keys a lot. My dad keeps threatening to have one of those electronic keypads installed, but then I wouldn't have the practice of picking locks. I think we can all say that particular skill came in quite handy just now.

Aspen flips a switch and Sebastian's sin pad comes to life. "We're looking for that wicker chair you sit in and watch those horror movies, right?"

"Yep, that's the one." I head for Sebastian's bedroom. I know, it's not on my bucket list to see either, but at a quick glance, I don't see my chair in his living room. He had to have stashed it somewhere more hidden. "You check in here. I'll check the hazardous rooms."

Aspen doesn't need to suffer for my mistakes. This is my war, and if anyone is going to have a limb rot off by catching something in this cesspool, it's going to be me.

I dart off, eager to get the hell out of here and back to my room where a low budget horror film awaits me. I know, sounds like a great time for a college freshman, but when you pair it with butter and a side of popcorn, it's not too shabby for a Friday night.

I'm not one of those college girls who need constant attention or even a date night every weekend. I'm the girl who would rather spend her evenings at the K9 shelter with the rescued service dogs and making "tough guys" cry at the pool hall.

You can imagine how proud my mother is. I take that back, she's proud. She'd just like it if I, occasionally, wore something other than flannel shirts and Doc Martens boots to holiday gatherings. But I'm not interested in shoes that make my ass look bigger for a man's viewing pleasure.

I close my eyes and hold my breath because, let's be real, this is

Sebastian we're dealing with. I'm liable to be scarred for a lifetime. Slowly, I open the door to Sebastian's bedroom. Believe it or not, I've been in here before, but it's been a while and things could have changed. Sebastian used to keep his room tidy—I know, shocked me too—but apparently, not anymore. His film books and journals are scattered across the floor next to the bed, which doesn't make sense because he normally keeps them in the bookcase.

I snag one of the balled-up pieces of notebook paper, unfolding it slowly, in case something springs out of it. (I've watched a lot of horror movies, okay?) On the paper is a bunch of stats for his MyView page—the page we both became stars on. His follows and likes have taken a dramatic hit these past two months, since we haven't been pulling pranks on each other.

My stomach clenches as the guilt gnaws at me.

He told me not to be sorry for besting him, and I have to hope that he truly meant what he said.

Tossing the first piece back onto the floor, I grab another, this one is about the campus contest, UniCamFlix. The producers of the hottest reality show on MyView are hosting an open call for all future filmmakers, actors, producers, etc. I entered last week, hoping that my special effects makeup videos will be considered. The flyer says anyone in the film industry is eligible, but sometimes, they don't post the fine print.

But I didn't know that Sebastian was entering too. I mean, I should have guessed, since he's all about that reality life, but he's been quiet since our last encounter, so I figured he settled down a bit. I know his parents are pushing business school, which he's passing, but hates.

I toss the loose-leaf paper down and get back to what I came here for—my chair. I glance around the room and don't see the pretty white wicker lounger my dad bought when I moved in with Aspen.

"Asp?" I holler out. "You find it?"

I hear paper crinkling. "No. But his refrigerator is stupid stocked."

Oh my gosh. Why is she a bottomless pit all the time? "Are you seriously eating his food?"

"He has those fruit bars I love. Would it be shitty if I grabbed one?"

Ugh. "Yes, Asp. It would. Don't eat his food." It might be poisoned or as delicious as I remember. "I'm going to check the bathroom. If I can't find my chair there, we'll have to come back another time."

His poker games usually last a few hours, but lately, he's been coming home earlier than usual.

"Okay," Aspen hollers, but she sounds sad.

High-stepping around a couple of shirts on the floor, I push open the bathroom door and flip on the light. And, like he knew I was coming, my chair sits in the tub with a pink bow on the backrest.

"Douche," I mumble to myself, but I can feel myself smiling. I might want to drown this man but that doesn't mean I don't appreciate a good prank. Believe it or not, I've missed figuring out ways to piss him off these past couple of months.

"Aspen! It's in here. Come help me move it."

I hear her footsteps before I see her. "Huh. I don't know why I thought it would feel like I needed to bathe in bleach after walking into Bash-hole's bedroom, but it's really not that bad," she muses.

"Yeah," I agree. "I was shocked at first too."

Her brows furrow. "What? You've been in his house before?"

Oops. "No. I mean, when we first broke in. Come on, hurry so we can get out of here."

Aspen accepts my somewhat truthful response and comes to stand halfway in the tub. "On three, we'll lift and walk it out."

I nod, not even bothering to argue with her plan. One, it's a solid plan, and two, Aspen is not only the older one of the two of us but also the bossy one.

"One. Two. Three." We get the chair all of two feet off the porcelain before we meet resistance.

"What the hell?" Aspen says, putting the chair back down. "Where is it stuck?"

Something like defeat churns and settles in my stomach. Of

course he wouldn't make it this easy. Easing to my knees, I lean down and notice that not only is my chair chained to the exposed pipe in his tub, but it's secured with a combination pad lock.

"Dammit!"

I exhale and try to calm myself when Aspen points in the tub. "Look, there's a note."

I snatch it up and read it aloud.

I'm guessing a combination lock is harder than my front door.
Be a good neighbor and fold the clothes in the dryer while you're here.

Bash

I glance at Aspen, who is hiding a grin behind her hand.

"I hate him," I say with a straight face.

She nods, schooling her amusement. "Do you think you can pick this lock too?"

I scoff. "Who do you think I am? A career criminal? I don't know how to figure out the combination."

I crumble the note in my hand and toss it in his sink. Sebastian won this round; there's no way I am getting my chair out of here tonight.

"Want me to get Fenn and Bennett to come over?" Aspens suggests. "Maybe they can find something to break the lock."

I shake my head. "No. This is between me and dick face. I'll handle it."

Aspen rises from her squat and gives me a slight squeeze. "We'll get it back, Vee. In the meantime, you can pull the chair from my room to sit outside."

It's a sweet offer. "Thank you, but I'll be okay for a couple of nights without it. I think it's supposed to rain anyway."

I don't know if it is or not, but I think it makes us both feel better.

"Let's go before he gets home." Sebastian and I might play these games with each other but that doesn't mean he won't report a break-in, just for shits and giggles.

Aspen nods and heads out. "I'll make sure the coast is clear."

I barely muster a smile. "Thanks. I'll be right behind you."

When Aspen is gone, I take one final look at my chair. "I will come back for you," I tell it. "I'll negotiate with the terrorist. He'll wish he had never taken you."

It's the truth; I feel nothing but pure determination when I march out of the bathroom and back into Sebastian's bedroom, where I pounce on his bed and snag the pillow I know the diva can't sleep without.

Yeah, he's weird and has the sleep habits of an eighty-year-old retiree. I stuff the memory foam under my arm and make my way to Aspen but then I spot his tripod. Since Sebastian lost his cameraman, he's been filming his videos himself. Yes, they look terrible, but you can't blame someone for not wanting to work with Bash-hole. He might act like a lazy housecat, but when he has an idea, he'll film all night until he gets the perfect shot. Just ask his neighbors.

Stuffing his tripod under his bed, between several plastic storage containers, I hurry back to the bathroom and retrieve the note he left for me. I scratch out his shitty comments and write below:

You're right. I'll have to come back with my bolt cutters. Sweet dreams, bro.

Vee

Short and simple, just what Sebastian needs in order to understand my message. Having his most prized possession in my hand, I sprint from his room where I find Aspen chest deep in his fridge. "You ready to go?"

She pulls her head out and closes the refrigerator. "I'm ready."

Her gaze focuses on Sebastian's *precious pillow* under my arm. "Was that the best you could steal? His pillow?"

I shrug. "I was in a hurry. Besides, I need something to bargain with."

Her eyes narrow. I'm not sure if she's suspicious or tired. "And you think he'll negotiate for a pillow?"

I grin. I know he will.

CHAPTER TWO

Valentina

University CamFlix Competition Submission
Entry Number: 75
Sebastian and Valentina
First Interview Continued, or also known as that fifteen minutes that I didn't vomit in Sebastian's lap

"So this war… Who started it?"

I fight a glare at Sebastian and smile sweetly at Tom. "Sebastian did." I rub the jerk's knee in faux affection. He's sitting so close I feel claustrophobic. "At the time, I didn't know that crashing my video was his subtle way of flirting." I grin and revel in watching Sebastian's smile fall into a frown. "It was so immature it was cute."

I should have known he wouldn't take that comment without adding a little payback.

"Oh, Tom," Sebastian interrupts, pulling me to his chest, squeezing my hip in a silent threat. "Don't let her fool you. Interrupting her video was a public service. No one should have been subjected—Ow!"

I smile at Tom, sliding my hand out of Sebastian's shirt, where I'm sure I left a mark on his side. "What he means is that my videos haven't always been about makeup."

"Tsk. Tsk. Those rippled hills of ab muscles won't save you, my little friend."

I watch as the drop of water trails the length of Sebastian's chest, dripping down to his belly button. "Ah shit, wrong turn. Now, you'll die a slow death in those stupid yellow shorts of his."

The drop of water absorbs into the fabric of his waistband and disappears from sight. "Farewell, my friend. Hell might be hard, tanned and smell like sunscreen and moonshine, but its demonic ruler is quite the dickhead."

I'm over-caffeinated and hangry as I watch the chair thief, through the window, slip a t-shirt over his head and fill a glass of water straight from the tap, pausing long enough to pop what looks to be painkillers. It appears our neighborhood hoebag had a rough night and an even rougher morning, considering he pretty much crawled to the kitchen.

A pot of coffee brews while he leans both hips against the counter, waiting while he smashes his temples between his palms. Poor baby. It's hard staying pretty when you're trashed and sleep deprived, but somehow, he manages, which is really a shame.

The last time I was hungover I looked like an actual troll, hissing at Aspen when she offered to wash the dirt and leaves out of my hair before I crawled into bed.

I frown at the window, at his perfectly coifed hair and celebrity housewife complexion. He might look like he's put together on the outside but underneath those ugly shorts is a mess of a man with the personality of a house cat.

Sebastian's hand drops slowly from his temple and hovers in the air. He's staring directly at me when he lowers all his fingers but the middle one.

Good morning to you too, jerk.

Being the more mature one, I don't return the juvenile gesture. I simply put down the binoculars and trade them out for the foreign gray pillow I commandeered last night. Sliding the window up, I hold Sebastian's precious pillow and dangle it out the window like Michael Jackson did to his baby that one time.

Relax, I'm not really going to drop it. At least not while he still has my chair.

That perfect jawline of his falls in an instant, taking his rude hand gesture with it. I can feel a triumphant grin emerge, but then the bedroom door clicks behind me, startling me and sending the pillow out of my hand and clear across the room, where it lands gracefully in front of my roommate's pink-painted toes.

"Were you just dangling Bash-hole's pillow out the window?" Aspen's knowing gaze volleys between the pillow at her feet and my crouched position by the window sill.

The situation looks bad.

I know this.

But really, how much can Aspen prove with just a brief look? Maybe I slept on the floor? Maybe I was looking for a sock. Maybe—I clear my throat and straighten my spine. "No, of course not. That would be a shitty thing to do." I cock my head to the side, my eyes wide, feigning hurt. "How could you think such a thing, Asp? I simply dropped my contact and used the pillow as a cushion while I searched for it."

Lying is not normally my default in stressful situations. I promise. Consider me the girl not taking the high road today. What can I say? Sebastian always brings out my worst qualities.

Aspen nods, her mouth curling into a grin. "I hate when that happens." Dammit, she knows I'm lying. "Here," she squats down for the pillow, "let me help you find it."

"That's okay." I wave her off, then stand as she comes closer to the window where our hungover neighbor awaits. "Really, I got it. I'll just grab a new pair."

She ignores me and pushes forward to the window. It's okay, though, I'm not panicked. The demon next door has probably gone to do the Devil's bidding by now—fingers crossed—and Aspen won't see anything when she looks out the window.

"Why is Bash-hole naked?" Her gasp pulls me from my thoughts in an instant. "And who gave him that hickey on his ass cheek?"

Two things go through my head in a matter of a millisecond.

One, did he finally change those awful shorts? Two, have women really resorted to sucking on ass cheeks now?

"What?" I try shoving her out of the way, but she stands firm.

"Is ass sucking a new thing?" Aspen continues, her feet planted on the floor. "I mean, I've never done it before, have you?"

I roll my eyes. "You're distracting me. What do you really want?"

Clearly, I need something to do since I've resorted to getting my kicks out of knowing Sebastian slept terribly without his pillow last night.

Aspen turns her back to the window, blocking my view. "You're supposed to be getting ready for the party. Have you been watching Bash-hole this whole time?"

Surely, she doesn't need an answer. I think the evidence is clear. I've been watching the ever-loving shit out of our neighbor for hours. He didn't get up until two, dammit. I couldn't leave my room and miss him waking up with a stiff neck and a bad attitude. That would have ruined my whole day.

"Of course you have, why am I even asking?"

Told ya. She knew I was being ridiculous.

"Anyway," she says on a breath, "I came to make sure you aren't wearing a t-shirt to Bennett and Drew's birthday party. I know how you don't like to show off the girls."

Okay, so let me explain. It's not that I mind showing off my boobs or "the girls" as Aspen calls them, but I find that they attract the attention of the stupidest males. Frankly, I don't have the time or the patience to try and talk to someone while they constantly stare at my tits.

"I plan to wear a swimsuit," I tell her. "Drew already told me it was a water-themed party." Technically, it's slip and slide kickball themed, which is so ridiculous only Drew would think of it.

"Which swimsuit?" Aspen probes, still blocking the window and my view of Bash-hole.

I shrug. "I don't know. The blue one maybe?"

Aspen's mouth drops open. "The one that looks like athletic wear?"

My lips flatten in return. "It's a sporty swim top and shorts. There is nothing wrong with it. Especially since I'll have to run to play kickball."

My girls aren't huge, but they have some bounce to them. Forgive me for not wanting an epic nip slip wearing those triangle tops that are only held together with string.

Aspen glances down at my—you guessed it—flannel pajamas. "You can wear one of mine. I invited Vance to the party and I thought… you know…. You two could…" She does this stupid face where her eyes blink fast and her mouth opens on one side.

"If you mean we could have a seizure together then I'll pass."

She really does need to work on her facial expressions.

Her laugh is light and bubbly. "That's not at all what I meant. I thought you guys could talk. You've been at Havemeyer for almost a year and you've yet to go on a date. You need to mingle, Vee. Let someone take you out for a change—actually watch a movie on something *other* than your iPad for goodness sakes. We have theaters, you know."

Look at her projecting her single girl problems on me.

I take the opportunity and shove her to the side, chancing a glance out the window, where I find Sebastian's kitchen empty. Sighing, I rake a hand through my hair. I was interested in someone at Havemeyer once, it just didn't work out.

Turning, I face Aspen and grimace. "Fine. But only this once."

"Yay!" Her stupid clap forces a smile from me. "Vance will be all growly when he sees you in the bikini I have picked out."

I don't kill her joy by falling face first onto the bed. Instead, I let her dash out of the room with the promise of letting her fix my hair.

When she's out of sight, no longer all up in my business, I slide down the window until my butt hits the floor. Today is going to hell in a designer handbag. I mean, I knew it would be, considering I tossed and turned once I got home from seeking revenge on the neighbor.

Without my horror movie and popcorn under the stars, I was left to my own devices, which were as follows:

A shower.

A popsicle.

A quick scroll through my old videos, which resulted in me watching the last clip that I shot with a body cam—the one that never aired.

I lost hours of sleep replaying the video, watching helplessly as my lips pressed against his. His blonde hair had tumbled over his eyes when he pulled back, staring at me in complete and utter shock. And then it all clicked. It was as if I could see him putting the pieces together as he swiped through the layers of makeup on my face. It was a gut punch that left me with stupid girly tingles I've only ever felt around him.

I hate I was sucked into his vortex of charm. That stupid personality of his completely messed up my game. I would have aired that damn video if my guilt and feelings for him didn't get in the way. But they did, and I lost a crap ton of sponsored ads because of it.

But I just couldn't do it to him.

Sebastian might be a weasel, but he's my weasel and, really, him knowing I beat him in our epic war of pranks is payment enough. At least it will be until I can't make my car payment and end up begging my brother to wire me some money.

The K9 shelter I work for pays minimum wage, and honestly, that's fine; I don't do it for the money. Caring for retired service dogs who lost their handlers in battle is what gets me through the week. I would help out for free, but Mason, my dad's Marine friend and owner of the facility, insists on paying me, so I don't argue. I do need the money. My dad pays for a lot, but he insisted that his kids know the value of hard work. So my brother and I have always had a job. It's a great escape from classes and social media. Which, obviously, I need since social media is what got me in this war with Sebastian in the first place.

"Vee!" Aspen shouts through the door. "How do you feel about a thong?"

"I feel like my butt is full from breakfast," I return.

She chuckles. She knew my answer would be no. "Never hurts to try. One day, I'll talk you into it."

Please, she may own a thong, but she'd have to vacation alone in another country to wear it.

With a groan and Aspen's retreating footsteps, I stand and walk over to the bed and flop down face first like I wanted to earlier. If Drew and Bennett weren't my best friends and like brothers to me, I'd blow off their party and spend the evening googling how to crack a combination lock.

But alas, such is not the case. Drew would drag me out of the house and Bennett would cut me that disapproving frown of his, ruining my night. So I'm going to this party whether I feel like it or not. Don't get me wrong, I love Drew and Bennett, but knowing that I might have to go one more day without my nightly movie in my ratty chair, sends a level of anxiety through me that I only get with my waxer.

Do not side-eye me. I might wear flannel but that does not mean I have to rock a bush. I'm girly in all the right places, trust me. I just find flannel a little more comfortable than spandex or camisoles. Where do you keep your phone in those outfits? I'm certainly not stuffing it in my bra or carrying around a purse.

I have a backpack and that's the extent of my accessories which— my phone dings and I roll onto my side and snag it. Huge mistake.

Apparently, his coffee and aspirin have kicked in.

Demon Douche: Quick! Do I have something on my face?

Ugh! I squish my head into the mattress and muffle a scream. If I text him back, he'll like it. How do I know he'll like it? Because I would like it and Sebastian is just as warped as I am with our back and forth.

Demon Douche: Hurry, T! I need to make a good impression.

Demon Douche: I mean V. Stupid Autocorrect.

Autocorrect…my ass. This man needs an ankle monitor and a muzzle. I swipe the text away and hit the red button to delete. I'm not playing his game today. Sure, I want to—badly—but I'm not, because

I'm better than that. And, unless he's texting a drop point for the exchange of my chair for his pillow, I'm not interested.

Demon Douche: I was thinking the yellow shorts looked better than the red ones.

I grit my teeth and clutch the phone in my hand. He knows those shorts are ridiculous.

Don't do it, Vee.

You know better. You'll just be egging him on. Don't let him bait you.

Fuck it. I ease down to the floor and crawl to the window for one tiny look-see. Sure enough, the bane of my college existence is turning his head side to side in the window, as if he were directly in front of me, and I was his personal mirror.

Demon Douche: I'm serious, V. You might as well give me your opinion. What's the range on those binoculars anyway?

If only I had a paintball gun, I would… do nothing because then I'd be scared that I'd shoot the annoying idiot in the eye and spend the rest of my life groveling for his forgiveness or—gasp—taking care of him. Not to mention he would retaliate, and I'd end up being the eighty-year-old woman still playing pranks with a single, immature old man. Yeah, no one is marrying that. A big dick ain't everything. Not that I know if Sebastian's dick is big, but something has to be going for him to keep women in his bed. I'm just saying that *if*—and that's a big if—Sebastian manages to keep a woman, I'll admit I was wrong in my assessment. But I'm not wrong because this is Sebastian we're talking about. He's no prince.

And, apparently, I'm no angel because my fingers betray me, and I swipe up to reply to his message before my conscience can change my mind.

Me: Those shorts look like you sat in baby shit.

It's like I can feel the smile that forms on his face. Why do we love to do this to each other?

Demon Douche: It's mustard colored. Very trendy. You wouldn't know since you never wear anything but hand-me-down dish towels.

Really? Dish towels? Please.

Me: If I recall, you enjoyed the feel of my flannel.

His reply comes quickly.

Demon Douche: Fuck you.

I'll admit his response makes me smile, but then that stupid guilt creeps into my belly and I change the subject before we take this playful banter into asshole territory.

Me: Who are you trying to NOT impress?

Demon Douche: Now, now. That's not how this game works anymore. Thanks for the chair, V. I don't owe you one.

Not how this game works *anymore…* my stomach drops. His text hits me right in the guilt. He's right; the game has changed. Because, once upon a time, he would have told me who he was *not* dressing up for.

Because, once upon a time, he told me everything.

CHAPTER THREE
Sebastian

University CamFlix Competition Submission
Entry Number: 75
Sebastian and Valentina
*First Interview Continued, or otherwise known as the fifteen minutes
I didn't shove Vee off the sofa*

"How did Sebastian sabotage your video to start the war between you two?"

That's the question everyone wants to know, but not one she likes talking about.

I can't stop the snort that comes out of me. "Should I tell it, sweetie, or would you prefer to do the honors?" This entire interview has been a delight. I love fucking with her while she can't do anything about it.

Her cheeks puff with a fake-ass smile. "I'll tell it. I'd hate for your fans to think you were a camera hog."

She intends for that comment to sting. It doesn't. It's no secret I enjoy being in front of the camera but seeing her squirm, while trying to spin this story into something less embarrassing, makes my fucking year. I nod, forcing down a shit-eating grin and extend my hand to the camera. "By all means, spill the tea, sweets."

Not even rubbing it eases the stiffness. No, not my dick—although that maintained a decent pudge earlier—but my neck. This particular stiffy is brought on by sleeping on a flat pillow. The other stiffy was brought on by my delightful neighbor.

That I hate.

Most days.

Okay, probably around six out of the seven days of the week, if I'm being honest.

She puts the bat in batshit crazy, and for some reason, that gets me rock fucking hard.

My dick is a traitorous bastard.

"Sebastian." Maverick, my friend, snaps his fingers in front of my face, effectively pulling my gaze from the window. "Focus. I don't have time to sit here all day and play matchmaker. I have shit to do."

He has time; he's nowhere near as popular as he thinks he is. I level him with a flat look. "Playing *Who Wants to Be a Millionaire* on the iPad is not having shit to do, Mav. It's called being a boring motherfucker."

Once deemed the best of my friends, Maverick has gone and abandoned me for a girl. His entire life now revolves around date nights and endless texts about what's for dinner. It's disgusting. You'll never catch me abandoning my guys and poker nights in favor of cuddling with a certain someone. If I'm cuddling, you bet your ass it's going to be because she was mind-blowing amazing in bed, and I want to make sure she stays put for round two.

"I'm answering emails, dick. Not playing a game. Not that it matters to you since you're only half-ass giving Brad, here, your attention."

He motions to the film student in front of us who, I'll admit, I almost forgot was here for an interview. The neighbor's window and this pounding headache have been quite the distraction this afternoon.

"My name is Brick," the potential cameraman says, correcting Mav, who is already focused back on his phone screen.

"He doesn't care," I return, glancing one more time at the window. "All Maverick cares about these days is stupid sea lions and macaroni and cheese."

Maverick's head pops up at my comment, but he doesn't bother denying my observations. Which really aren't observations at all—more like facts. "Brian," Mav addresses the guy, but keeps his gaze on me, "do you have a problem with being the voice of reason? How 'bout being the designated driver because that's really the job you're interviewing for. Sebastian needs more of a nanny than a cameraman. I'm not sure why the flyer says otherwise."

See what I mean? Having a girl has made him soft. Before Ainsley, he would have dropped at least a couple of F bombs in that spiel. I couldn't be more disappointed.

"I'm not sure I understand the question," Brick answers slowly, his eyes widening.

I wave off Brick's concern and kick the wicker chair under Mav—the one I dragged from my neighbor's patio—and hold up my middle finger. "Ignore him. He takes joy in other people's misfortunes."

Maverick rolls his eyes but says nothing. Which is good because, the truth is, I don't need a D.D. or a voice of reason. I'm not self-destructing. Well, not as much, anyway. I've done better lately, like since yesterday, when I stole Valentina's favorite patio chair. Her cute little ass didn't sit outside last night and munch on ten pounds of popcorn as she gasped and jumped at the worst 90's horror movies.

I did the neighborhood a solid.

And myself.

Because I really do feel much better knowing we both suffered.

"Sebastian." Maverick punches my arm.

Shit. Right.

Focus, Bash.

"Why do you want to be my cameraman anyway?" I ask, trying

to, somewhat, adult. It lasts for all of a second because I catch movement in my peripheral. *Did she close the curtains?*

"Goddammit. Sebastian!"

Ugh. *Another time, neighbor.*

I straighten and smile at Brick like a boss would because that's what I am when I feel like it. "From your resume, it seems like you've done well in the film industry. Being a cameraman for a MyView page can't be all that fulfilling, considering you've been filming a three-year documentary."

Brick really is talented and well-known around campus. I should be more impressed. *Should* being the operative word.

Brick nods and swallows. "Subscription media is on the rise. If I want to pitch to the likes of Netflix and Hulu one day, I'll need the experience. I thought this job would be the best route."

Smart.

So far Mr. Potential New Cameraman has aced this interview. At least he did when I was paying attention. He's given me all the right answers and even spat out a few 'Yo Mama' jokes earlier that made me laugh. Basically, he's exhibited all the traits I admire in a good cameraman. But since my last one quit, I'm gun-shy to jump at the next person with a shitty sense of humor and a great eye for angles. Brick here, will need to provide me with a little thing called proof.

"He's the best you've seen out of fifty applicants," Maverick mumbles next to me. "Hire him and let's move on with our lives."

I ignore Maverick, and the word "best" that just left his mouth. I already had the best cameraman. This guy in front of me, clutching his expensive fucking Nikon, is merely a wannabe cameraman, not the best I've ever seen.

He's right, though. Brick is the best I've seen *so far*. It's been months since I lost Tweener, my last cameraman. My ratings are dropping like a drunk mountain biker. I can't afford to keep filming selfie-style or on a tripod; that's a rookie move.

My videos are becoming basic, and at this point, I can't afford to lose any more subscribers or advertisers than I already have. I need the money. Having steady income is the only way out of Georgia and away from a past that haunts me each and every day.

"One last question, Brick."

What kind of name is Brick anyway?

I suppose a film one. Maybe I should come up with something short like G-Easy or Eminem. Not that I'm a rapper, but maybe that's the rebranding I need in on social media. I loathe the fact my name coincides with hers. If I get asked one more time, "Where's Vee?" someone is getting punched. Apparently, my fame was born from her and, obviously, my fame has died with her, which only adds to my warm and sarcastic personality. The one thing I thought I succeeded in, she snatched away from me, reminding me that I've yet to really succeed at anything on my own.

Brick sits taller, clearing his throat. "Hit me." His voice is deep and edgy with a hint of a southern accent. Good—if I never hear a southern Latina accent ever again, it'll be too soon.

"If I offer you this job—and I'm not saying I am—but if I do…" I draw out the words with a cringe and fight the urge to look out the fucking window. "Would you be able to provide a copy of your birth certificate?"

Brick may think that's a strange fucking question but so is his name. Dealing with my cynicism comes with the job.

"Uh…" His eyes go left to right in rapid sequence, before finally landing on the pussy-whipped asshole beside me. Maverick—the scary, unhelpful paperweight.

I snap my fingers, drawing Brick's attention back to the proper asshole. Me. "He's not the one hiring. I am."

A muscle in Brick's throat works as he swallows and averts his eyes to the prerequisite questionnaire I had him fill out a few minutes earlier. I'm nothing if not a thorough employer.

"Let it go, Bash," Maverick mutters, not looking up from his damn phone. "Your interview questions are escalating with each applicant." Maverick's voice is laced with amusement. Almost as if he's refraining from laughing. "Soon, you'll be asking them to pull up their shirts, so you can check for wires and nipple hair." I watch as he grins into his phone, one last time, before I snatch it from his hand and toss it on the sofa out of his reach.

His blinks are slow as he eyes me seriously. "Don't deflect because you're uncomfortable. Stop this charade. You don't need any more drama and rumors floating around about you."

Tingling races up my forearms at his mention of drama and rumors. It isn't the drama I'm scared of. I'm used to rumors. The anger is what I can't get over.

I was played.

And that both turns me on and pisses me the fuck off.

Granted, I deserved the payback and even instigated the war between us, but that's beside the point. The point is: one moment—one real moment—changed who I was altogether. I hate this version of myself—the version that doesn't bed new women every night or drink and smoke the night away. This version of Sebastian Carrington is confused, vulnerable, and downright mad at the fucking world. No, not the world. Just *her*.

Why did she have to come into my life and make me see myself differently? Why couldn't she have left me alone, wallowing in my own insecurities, self-deprecating until I lashed out and drowned my sorrows in moonshine?

I've never loved something more than I loved the prank wars I did on MyView. I was the king of clickbait, and she took it all away from me in one night.

"You know, Maverick," I say, narrowing my eyes in the asshole's direction. "You've been as much help as a crocheted condom during these interviews."

"I offered to send Rowan—" he says, pulling out the iconic deck of cards he keeps in his back pocket, "—or anyone other than me, for that matter." The cards make a swishing noise as he shuffles them, and it causes Brick's shoulders to snap to attention. "It's been two long-ass months, Sebastian. Frankly, Rowan and I are sick of babysitting your self-destructive ass. Hire Bill and move the fuck on with your life."

I grit my teeth. "I have moved on."

I have dammit, and I'll prove it.

"You're hired," I fling at Brick rather vengefully. Fuck Maverick. I am so over her; I can taste my ratings skyrocketing. "Be here tomorrow at seven a.m. I don't want to hear you overslept or need a water and an aspirin when you get here. I'm not a CVS or your girlfriend." I don't practice what I preach, obviously. "I don't do hungover employees."

Maverick scoffs and I add, "Anymore. I don't do hungover employees anymore."

I fight the urge to look back at the window.

Why does fucking with Valentina float my demented boat?

Yes, we're enemies and I'd very much like to never speak to her again after what she did.

But yet, I sat at my window downing moonshine shots after moonshine shots while I watched her snuggle into her ratty old chair in her stupid flannel pajamas and mismatched socks.

I could see all the lies as I looked at her all peaceful and cozy. Meanwhile, I was stalking her like some loser. The drunker I became, the more ridiculous my thoughts were.

I didn't miss her.

I didn't care what movie she was watching.

I was fine without her.

It's not like I won't graduate in another year and move clear across the country. I don't need Valentina in my life, not for views and especially not for my own entertainment.

So I removed part of the equation. If she couldn't sit in her chair, then she couldn't pique my interest and suck away my entire night.

Except, it didn't quite pan out that way.

"Great. Now that we've found you a new friend, I'm going home." Slowly, I pull my gaze forward and find that Maverick has stood and grabbed his phone from the sofa, texting someone—probably Ainsley.

"Gigi's tonight?" I ask, refraining from demanding it like I want to.

He sighs a long and exaggerated breath. "Sure. I'll meet you there at ten."

Fucking finally. We haven't been to Gigi's in months.

I nod, hiding my excitement, and walk to the door, hoping Brick takes the hint and follows Maverick out. "Sounds good. Tell Ainsley I'll answer her text later." I take a look around my townhouse, noting the dirty clothes, I think I might have been wearing last night, laid haphazardly over the trash can. "I need to do a couple things first."

Maverick doesn't take the bait about Ainsley. He knows no one is stupid enough to text his girl. "Come on, Brett, I'll show you out," he says instead, forcing a grin from me.

He's a really good friend, even if he is lame.

I nod to Brick and flip off Mav. "Don't cancel on me, bitch, or I'll bring Monopoly, and we can all sit around and be a family."

It's an empty threat. I don't own a game of Monopoly, but even if I did, I wouldn't crash on Maverick's time with his girl. I'm not that shitty of a friend.

Maverick ignores me—like usual—shoving Brick forward and out of my life for the next fifteen hours. I release a big breath. I finally hired a cameraman. That's one obstacle down and one step in recovering my views and sponsored ads on MyView.

My self-destruction is ending.

I've found the motherfucking light at the end of the tunnel.

Fuck the hot neighbor and her sweet smile. They both can kiss my ass. Literally, if she wants to. I'm not selfish. Giving of myself is my best attribute.

I swipe the shirt from the trashcan, take a jump shot, and ring the hamper, following it up by bagging up the trash. Several jars clang together and I cringe. I really need to lay off the moonshine Rowan distills in his spare room. I don't know what he puts in the brew, but the shit knocks me on my ass. Not to mention, I feel like I'm on an episode of *Moonshiners* when I go over and grab an armful.

I'm pretty sure his neighbors know what he's doing simply from the smell, but no one is crazy enough to complain. Rowan is like an angry version of Vin Diesel, which serves Maverick well, since Rowan is his game enforcer on Wednesday night poker. For me, though, he's just a big ol' grouchy teddy bear that I like to text *The Fast and the Furious* memes to.

Opening the door, the heat stops me in my tracks. Fuck. You'd think it was midsummer rather than late spring. The shorts were definitely a good idea. Taking the back steps barefoot, because I can't be bothered with shoes, I stuff the bag inside the rolling trash can and let the lid slam shut. Trash pickup is tomorrow. I can't miss it again.

I chance a glance over at my neighbor's front stoop. Her trash can isn't out yet, but I bet it will be by morning, along with separate cans with her recycling.

I shake my head remembering the lectures she used to give me about throwing all my shit in one can. *"This is plastic! Do you know how long it takes for it to decompose in a landfill?"* I didn't know at the time, but a few weeks later, I bought another stupid trash can. I don't use it now, since she shit all over our friendship, but I still have it, and, occasionally, I consider throwing a milk jug in there just to spite myself.

Turning back, a bright light catches my eye, stopping me. Shielding my eyes, I ease my head down and notice a set of keys dangling from Vee's front door.

Don't do it, Sebastian. She has your pillow.

I nod to myself, fidgeting with my bottom lip.

She does have my pillow, and while I thought she would beg me for the return of her chair this morning, she didn't. Which, I'll admit is slightly disappointing.

What Valentina Lambros needs is a little more incentive, and maybe a lesson in self-preservation. Just because we live in a decent neighborhood, we can't assume we have decent neighbors.

See exhibit A, me stealing her chair and exhibit B, her stealing my pillow.

But that's sort of what neighbors do, right? Loan each other sugar or some shit?

That's all this is. A little bit of borrowing with a little bit of menace behind it.

With a quick look around, I sprint across the hot as fuck sidewalk, ignoring the first degree burns on the bottom of my feet and swipe the keys from her front door, slipping them into my pocket smoothly and quickly then leaping onto the grass between our houses. Vee's side is professionally landscaped, which I'm sure her daddy paid for; whereas, mine is overgrown with a few random weeds that have sprouted flowers.

I used to pay a guy to come and cut the grass, but since my sponsored ads reduced drastically, I don't have the kind of money I used to. I meant to buy a push mower. Instead, I was impulsive and bought a wakeboard that I've yet to use because I don't have a boat. I'm a dude. We do stupid shit sometimes.

Laughing bubbles from Vee's back door, and I hurry to my back patio, only swearing twice when I step on something prickly.

"Are you sure we don't need the duct tape?"

I recognize that voice. Aspen Von Bremen, my nemesis' roommate and childhood bestie. She's the reason our neighborhood get-togethers are tense and awkward. Her brother's roommate, Bennett, is like her personal bodyguard or party pooper. I can't quite figure out which. All I know is Aspen is fun and Bennett is…not so much.

"I'm not duct taping my boobs, Asp. If this game gets that out of hand, I'm quitting. I'm not flashing the neighbors."

The word, "flashing," grabs my attention as I reach into my pocket and pull out my phone, staring at a blank screen. I don't want the traitor thinking I want to see her boobs or even imagine her wrapping tape around them, plumping them into round globes—What the fuck kind of game are they playing anyway?

"You can't quit!" Aspen laughs. "I made a bet with my brother. If we lose, I have to clean his bathroom. Don't ask me to take on that torture."

"You shouldn't have a made a bet in the first place! You know I suck at most sports."

A grin tugs along my lips. She does suck at sports. A lot.

"Shit. I don't have the keys to lock the deadbolt, do you?"

And that's my cue to leave.

CHAPTER FOUR

Valentina

University CamFlix Competition Submission
Entry Number: 75
Sebastian and Valentina
First Interview Continued, or that few minutes I wanted to poison
Sebastian's water

"So you were a singer?" The producer asks, looking confused. The sofa Sebastian and I are sitting on shakes. The bastard is attempting to hold in his laughter, but the stupid pig snort he smothers with his hand only makes it feel like I'm sitting right next to Old McDonald's idiot pig.

I narrow my eyes at Sebastian. "No, I wasn't a singer. I—" Sebastian actually snorts, and I swear to God, I am going to key the shit out of his Jeep the minute we leave this studio. "I was practicing a song for my uncle's birthday party. He owns a karaoke bar."

I'm not giving him all the details. All he needs to know is that I wasn't labeling myself as a singer. I was simply trying to practice. My family is musically inclined and well, I can't carry a tune in a bucket. It's a little defeating to be the only one who can't sing or play a musical instrument. And it's that defeat that led me to this moment right here, playing freaking Bash-hole's loving (gag) girlfriend.

I'm naked.

Well, not really. Let's just say this bikini Aspen picked out leaves little to the imagination.

"You look fine. Stop messing with it."

I level Aspen with a flat look. "I swear I will never forgive you if my tit pops out of this thing."

I'm being dramatic. My boobs are secured, but they have never been on this much of a display.

"Your girls are nice and secure. Stop worrying about it."

Easy for her to say. Aspen never worries about anything. She's a make-life-decisions-over-beers kind of girl. I'm the more reserved one. I would rather know what I'm walking into. "I just don't think a strapless top is the right choice given the fact that I will have to run when I kick the ball."

A loud snort interrupts our walk across the courtyard. "Since when have you ever gotten on base in any of the games we've played?"

Dressed like a Hollywood celebrity in his Ray-Ban aviators, Fenn Von Bremen, star pitcher of Havemeyer University, shoots me a shit-eating grin.

"Don't be a shit this early in the afternoon, Fenn. We just ate." Aspen pretends to gag just as Bennett walks up behind him.

Oh shit.

I nudge Aspen in the side as Bennett's eyes narrow into slits, seemingly right at Aspen's top. "I think you forgot the rest of your swimsuit," he drawls, his voice simmering with barely controlled rage.

Aspen shrugs a shoulder and snatches the vinyl sheets from Fenn. "Where do you want these set up?"

A low growl rumbles in Bennett's chest, making Fenn drop his head to his shoulders. "I swear I will lock you in the trunk of my car if you piss him off again, Asp. I'm tired of living with Bruce Banner."

I chance a look at Bennett. He's still staring daggers at Aspen's body. "I think I'll go check on Drew while you guys get things sorted out."

Fenn flips me off, but Aspen grins and waves. "Bring me a drink when you come back out."

I nod, inching around Bennett before hightailing it across the lawn with my sights on a familiar black door.

Midtown Heights, the townhome complex where we live, lines two parallel streets with green space in the middle. Basically, all the backyards face each other. The complex has done a good job with creating shrubbery walls for privacy and adding gardens and fountains so you can walk your dogs, but it's still as private as an outdoor shower.

When I get to the guys' back door, I don't even bother knocking. I just barge right in.

"Drusilla!" I call. "Are you making me a drink, biotch?"

A rumbly laughter comes from the kitchen and I follow the sound until I'm greeted with a pair of board shorts with the word LIFEGUARD down the side and a grin that makes all the freshmen girls swoon. "Your bubba is about to yell at Aspen. I figured I'd come help you where it's safe and quiet." I look at the counter full of liquor bottles and wince. "Are you planning on celebrating your birthday with alcohol poisoning?"

He cocks a brow, those mint green eyes alight with amusement. "My *bubba*, huh?" He gives me a thorough once-over. "Did my *bubba* also yell at you?" The replica of Bennett narrows his eyes at my bathing suit but with much less anger. "You left half your swimsuit at home."

The Jameson bothers are hotheaded, but fortunately for me, Drew is the easier one to sweet talk.

"It was Aspen's idea. I opted for a t-shirt and shorts."

Drew makes a face like he can't decide if my t-shirt would be better or worse than this bikini. "I bet it was. Let me guess, her bathing suit is worse than yours?"

Honestly, neither of our bathing suits are that revealing. Sure, mine shows a lot more skin than I'm used to, but if I were to rate it from fully covered to a cheek hanging out, I'd say it was a solid, appropriate, college two-piece.

"Aspen's bathing suit is fine. You both are being ridiculous. You don't see Fenn making a big deal about it."

Drew raises a brow, and I quickly wave him off.

"Never mind. Forget what I said."

Fenn is a little different; half the time he doesn't give two shits about anyone and the other half, he's a downright asshole. It probably doesn't bother him because he knows no one will say anything in front him about me or his sister, without him ending the evening with an assault charge.

Drew chuckles, probably thinking the same thing as me. "Here," he pats the countertop, "come put the ice in the blender for me. I assume you want something where you can't taste the alcohol."

Eh, not really, but I'm not going to correct him. Truth is, over the past few months, I've learned how to shoot tequila and drink moonshine, without gagging or throwing up. Fruity drinks are no longer in my repertoire of alcoholic beverages. Nevertheless, I hop up on the counter and begin scooping ice from the bag in the sink, dropping it into the blender. "So, who all did you invite to this little shindig?"

Drew eyes me funny while he pours way too much Jäger into his own glass. "Any one person you're particularly interested in?"

Yeah, the damn neighbor. If Sebastian graces this party with his presence, then his house would be unattended, and he'd be a whole lot of distracted.

"I was just curious if you invited some of the neighbors. Like the girl who lives next to what's his name…" I point to Sebastian's house. There's no reason for Drew to get any ideas about my and Sebastian's issues.

"You mean, Pam?"

I grin. "Yep, that's the one."

Drew nods and presses the button on the blender. "Yeah, we invited her and the rest of the neighbors. Bennett thought it'd be easier to head off the noise complaints if we invited everyone."

Of course, Bennett would be logical about his birthday party.

"That's really sweet of you two." I rub his shoulder. "So, am I supposed to slide on my stomach or butt with this whole waterslide kickball thing?"

Drew turns and grabs his drink, taking a big gulp. "Oh, you won't be running in that thing." He eyes my bikini up and down. "I'll be your pinch runner."

"Pinch runner is a baseball term," I correct him.

He winks. "No one knows the real term because kickball isn't a sport."

This ridiculous human. "So why did you pick it to play for your birthday? Why not bikini baseball?" He is the university's star catcher after all.

"Dammit, Vee! Why didn't you offer up that idea earlier?"

"I didn't know you were looking for wet sporting events; otherwise, I would have suggested swimming or a lake party."

Drew shrugs. "The 'rents are at the lake house this weekend. There's no way I was scoring with my Dad breathing down my neck."

"Are my parents there too?" My mom didn't mention it when I talked to her a few days ago but maybe she forgot.

"Nah. Just Dad and Uncle Theo." He shrugs. "Yearly fishing trip."

"Ah. Well, we can always go another weekend when they aren't there." I love the lake house. Aspen's parents own it, but we all have a key and can use it any time. It's about an hour from the University, but it feels like it's miles away from everything. I miss it.

"Asp and I were talking about maybe taking a road trip to see your brother in Cali. Since it's Asp's last year and all."

I open my mouth, and Drew holds up one finger. "Hold that thought." The blender whirls to life, and after a few seconds, he hands me a strawberry daiquiri. "Do I not get a Jäger bomb?" I nod to the drink next to him.

"Hell no," he laughs. "Jäger makes the undies drop. Yours are staying put tonight. Mine, however, are not."

I take the drink and shrug. My panties weren't coming off anyway, but it's nice to know I have back up in case Vance takes this invite as a code word for hookup. "So, we're taking a road trip soon?"

Drew shrugs a shoulder. "Bennett isn't on board yet. I'm working on it."

I nod. Bennett is always a tough sell. Why he's so grouchy and responsible, we'll never know. "Well, I'm sure if anyone can sell him, you can."

He does this stupid little wink that makes me laugh. "Did you see that competition Malcolm is bragging about?"

I fake a gag. If there was ever someone who I loved to hate more than Sebastian, it's Malcolm Desantis. "I try to stay clear of anything Malcolm says."

Drew's forehead scrunches. "But it's a million dollars. How have you not heard about it? Isn't the internet like your personal playground?"

"Yeah, but…"

I don't want to tell him I already entered. For some reason, I don't want him to know quite yet.

"But?" Drew prompts me.

"But I don't follow Malcolm. He's a vulture." He never plays by the rules. Copying others and spoofing their videos is his go-to technique. He lacks originality.

Drew takes a sip of his drink and nods. "I agree, but it's still a million dollars, Vee. You'll be seen by millions of viewers. Who knows? Some studio or production company could be in the market for a makeup artist. It's a big opportunity."

I know and I'm on board three thousand percent, but the thing is, the rules weren't exactly clear.

Drew grabs his phone and shoves it in my face. He's like a little boy all excited to show me what he found. "This is what I'm talking about." I take his phone and grin; this boy has always been my biggest fan. Scrolling through Malcolm's page, I act like this is the first time I've seen the announcement. I haven't seen Malcolm's entry, so I snoop through his hashtags, clicking on the one #unicamflixcompetition. There I find the ad for the upcoming reality show.

I read aloud to Drew, "Looking for the next rising MyView star. Producers, actors, cameramen, and writers are all welcome. Use hashtag #unicamflixcompetition on your daily videos as entries. The top two accounts with the most subscribers will face off with a final fan vote. The winner will be awarded one million dollars and a one-year MyView reality series."

I finally look up and meet Drew's glassy eyes. I snatch the drink from his hand and toss a piece of ice at him. "Pace yourself, Drusilla. I'm not dragging you to your room again. I sprained my ankle last time."

Drew catches the ice easily and tosses it into the blender, mixing another drink. "The competition is cool, huh?"

"Yeah, it's cool. I just don't know if my videos will qualify." I'm not sure it's a skill they are looking for.

"Message them and ask," he says and shrugs. Nothing is ever a big deal to Drew. That's one of the reasons I love his crazy ass.

"I hate that Malcolm is participating, though," I say to myself. "He'll be a nightmare to deal with."

Drew takes another drink and cocks a brow. "Why is that?"

"About a month ago, this one guy claimed Malcolm copied his videos before he posted them. I don't know exactly how it happened, but I don't put it past Malcolm to cheat."

I'm pretty sure Drew hasn't heard a word I've said since something on his phone snagged his attention four sentences ago. "You got this, Vee-Dog," he mumbles, giving me a thumbs up.

"Ugh." I jump from the counter.

"Where the hell do you think you're going?" His head jerks up quickly.

"Outside. I was going to see if Bennett and Fenn needed any help since you seem to have this managed." Really, I just want to see if Bennett and Aspen are still arguing, and if not, maybe I can use the excuse to separate them and go back home and plot ways to get my chair back.

Okay fine, I really just want to stalk Sebastian. He didn't wear those ugly shorts for no one. And the fact that he won't tell me who only ramps up my curiosity.

"Alright but be careful out there." He eyes my swimsuit one more time. "I'd hate for you to get dirty helping me bury a body tonight."

This crazy fool.

I stand on my tiptoes, and he leans down, so I can kiss him on the cheek. "Will do. Happy birthday, Big Dog."

Outside, Aspen is setting up the waterslide lanes with Fenn. Bennett, however, isn't helping. "Happy Birthday," I tell him, wrapping my arms around him and giving him a squeeze.

I know he's pissed off at Aspen, but honestly, when is he not? Rarely does Aspen do as she's told. She's not one to take orders. She'd rather suffer the consequences than take the advice of others. If she wants to wear the cute bikini, then by God, she's going to wear the cute bikini. The only way she's changing it is if Bennett rips it off her body. And he would never do that. He's a gentleman. An angry gentleman, but still a gentleman, nonetheless.

"Thanks, Vee," he finally returns, squeezing me back, but still glaring at Aspen.

"You know," I say, pointing at the Von Bremen siblings who are in a standoff with each other. "Yelling at her only feeds her desire to break that promise of yours."

Bennett's head whips around and down at me. I shrug. "We're best friends. She tells me almost everything."

At Bennett's death stare, I hurry out. "Your father will forgive you," I assure him. "It's okay to let him down sometimes."

Heaven only knows I've experimented with that aspect of my life.

"It's non-negotiable," he grits out. "And something that will never be discussed again, got it?"

I hold my palms up in a defensive gesture. "Whatever you want, big guy."

I did my best friend duty. I tried to talk some sense into Bennett, and it went exactly how I thought it would. Terrible.

"Okay," I say, forcing a smile and taking a step away from Bennett and toward the safety of Fenn and Aspen. "I'm going to break those two up before she makes him cry."

I've never seen Fenn cry. Most days, I have a hard time believing he even has a heart, but I need an excuse to get away from Bennett and his pissed-off state. It's no way to spend his birthday, but apparently, he doesn't care.

Approaching Aspen and Fenn, I grin and put my hands on my

hips. "Are we playing kickball or mud wrestling because you moving those slides eight million times is only getting them dirty."

Aspen snatches the vinyl slide from Fenn's hands and grins. "Boys are as efficient as waxing with masking tape."

I grin, just as Fenn snatches the slide back and slings it down on the ground and kicks it away from us. "And girls are petty as fuck." He gives the slide one more farewell kick and takes a deep breath. "Stop fucking torturing him and go change, Aspen. Staying out here and 'helping' me is just making this party tense as fuck."

I shrug when Aspen looks at me and rolls her eyes. Fenn is right; Aspen and Bennett arguing or not speaking makes everything and everyone around them stressed. But I get her side too. She should be able to wear what she wants to wear.

"Let's just drop it," I tell them. "It's his birthday. Let's get this all set up before people start arriving."

The birthday comment seems to sober the siblings, and they both nod, Aspen's gaze flicking back to Bennett, just once, before she leans down and picks up the slide and begins straightening it out.

I grab an end when Drew comes to the back door and shouts, "Vee! Your phone is buzzing."

"Who's Demon Douche?"

I feel my cheeks go hot.

Fuck.

I dart over and snatch the phone from Drew's hand and smile. "Lab partner," I lie. "A real jerk."

Drew shrugs and goes back inside, without asking anymore questions, which is good.

Exhaling, I swipe the screen and read the text.

Demon Douche: Will they just fuck already? Even I have blue balls from watching them.

I lift my gaze just in time to see Mr. Ugly Shorts lounging on his back patio with a drink in his hand.

Me: Some of us have something called morals. You should google it sometime.

I see a grin creep onto his face. He loves getting to me.

Demon Douche: You of all people should not be surfing the morality board, Ms. I Lie On The Daily.

It's a shot to the heart. One I deserve, but nevertheless, it still stings for all of about 2.5 seconds when I realize what he's sitting in.

Me: That's my chair, asshole!

This man is seriously sitting in my patio chair with me right here. The nerve!

Demon Douche: What? You're seeing things. Pam let me borrow this—

He sends the rolling its eyes emoji.

Demon Douche: —last Sunday. Stop trying to cause neighborhood drama, Valentina.

I swear to G—My fingers fly over the keyboard.

Me: You're the liar, Sebastian Carrington!

He eases back into my wicker chair.

Demon Douche: Sucks, doesn't it, bro?

Don't scream. If you scream, Fenn and Bennett will demand to know what's going on and that can never happen.

No one can ever know what went down between Sebastian and me.

Me: I hate you.

It's sort of the truth. I do hate him, sometimes, but this one time—never mind. Those days are over. All that matters is the here and now. Sebastian and I are enemies. I turn back to Aspen and Fenn, not able to help them at all because my damn phone dings again, and I swear on all things holy that I really do try not to read it.

Demon Douche: Knock 'em dead, Tiger. I won't be rooting for you.

I flip the idiot off.
Fuck being a good neighbor.

CHAPTER FIVE
Valentina

University CamFlix Competition Submission
Entry Number: 75
Sebastian and Valentina
First Interview Continued, also known as those precious few minutes
I will never get back

"What exactly did Sebastian do to sabotage your video?"

Had I known the producers would be so damn nosy in these interviews, I might have negotiated with Bash-hole for a sixty-forty split instead of fifty-fifty. This is awful.

"Have you ever seen the movie, *Titanic*?" I ask the producer.

He nods. "Great film."

I narrow my eyes. "Yes. It also has an iconic scene where Jack and Rose are at the bow of the ship and they are 'flying.'"

Tom, the producer nods, and scoots to the edge of his chair, captivated by my story. "Well, you see, I was singing that song, and I might have been standing, singing with my eyes closed and my arms out wide, just as Rose did, when Sebastian stumbled upon me."

The party is in full swing, complete with girls in way less clothing than me and Aspen, who, by the way, is now wearing Bennett's t-shirt. She finally gave in and felt bad that she was causing him stress on his birthday. I, on the other hand, am still in my bathing suit, sans any sort of cover up. I wanted to go across the courtyard and grab something from the house, but then people started arriving and I had to help Drew with drinks.

We're two hours in to this shindig and people are still arriving. I don't know what Fenn did to convince the complex manager to let us have the party in the courtyard, but I'm impressed. Tony usually never allows parties of any kind. Which, let's be realistic, Fenn and Drew violate that rule all the time, but they usually don't do it outside. Generally, they are more discreet about it.

"Gross." I narrow my eyes at the guy walking in with a girl I don't know. "Who invited that weasel?"

I nudge Aspen, who seems to be cracking the plastic cup in her hand. "Huh?" She asks with a frown. I follow the path where she was looking and see a girl from my chem class talking to Bennett. Well, she isn't talking to him, just standing close in case he wants to pass out or something.

"Malcolm," I redirect her by pointing to the sniveling waste of space several feet from us. "Did Drew invite him?" There's excitement in my voice as I ask this question. If there was ever a time I wanted Drew to throw someone out on their ass, now was it. No way did Drew invite Malcolm to his party.

Malcolm Desantis is like the high school bully of MyView.

I know, it's the internet. Pretty much every other person is a bully, but Malcolm… Malcolm is their king—a wretched and wicked ruler. If he was a character in a horror movie, I would want him to be the first victim who was gutted in the kitchen while he screamed for help in an empty house. But alas, Malcolm isn't. He's the psycho who you have to kill eight million times before he dies, and even that might not be enough.

Yeah, he's that guy. And sadly, since the wars between Sebastian and me have stopped, he's been the reigning MyView star of Havemeyer.

"Uh…maybe?" she says, still looking at the girl next to Bennett.

I huff. Aspen is useless when it comes to obtaining info. "I bet he bribed one of the baseball guys." Drew and Fenn's friends aren't the best influences.

"Probably," Aspen agrees, only half listening.

She's upset. I can feel it. The queen bee of our group isn't always as strong or as confident as she'd like everyone to think she is. Sometimes she's just a girl in love with a boy that we can't nut punch for being a loyal idiot.

"Come on," I say, pulling her away. "Let's go play. Kicking the guys' asses always cheers us up." It's true. Nothing excites Aspen more than winning and well, nothing excites me more than being away from Malcolm and the nosy neighbor eyeing me from my own chair.

Aspen nods, and we make our way to the circle of insanity, also known as the kickball field. Think of a baseball field, but instead of dirt-lined base paths, they're lined with vinyl slides with an inflatable kiddie pool as the base.

"You want to be on our team?" Baylor, a third baseman I recognize from Drew and Fenn's baseball team, holds his hand out like he means for Aspen to take it and cross over to the dark side or something.

I smack it away. "Thanks, but we'll take the other team." The one without the baseball players with a death sentence. Had Bennett saw Baylor offer his hand to Asp, he would have been drinking his meals through a straw for the next two months.

Baylor eyes me with a look of disgust. "I wasn't asking you," he says with a sneer.

Really? How many times do I have to watch this rerun? Guys like him think they really hit girls like me where it hurts by insulting us with comments like we're somehow not as hot as the woman beside us. Well, let me give all the men in the world a little tidbit. Women come in all shapes, sizes, and attitudes. Just because we don't look like Malibu Barbie or dress like Gigi Hadid does not make us any less likely to get a man. Not only can we get a man, but we can keep that man until the mood strikes for us to let him go. I don't need an asshole like Baylor in my panties, and I certainly don't need him in my damn face.

I open my mouth to tell Baylor where he can take his chauvinist ass when an unfamiliar voice stops me. "I'm sad to see that black eye Jameson gave you last semester didn't teach you a lesson, Baylor."

"Vance!" Aspen jumps up and down and wraps her arms around the guy who is almost as tall as Drew. "I'm so glad you could make it!"

"Anything for you," he says, placing her down gently.

Aspen nods and sends me a wink that she does not disguise at all.

"This is Vee, my best friend and roommate. She just moved in with me this year."

Vance's eyes are the darkest green I think I've ever seen. "Hi," I say, extending my hand and proving Baylor right that I'm not much of a lady. But what else was I supposed to do? Curtsy? I think not. Vance might be tall, dark, and pretty damn fine, but a king he is not.

A deep rumbling of laughter explodes from his chest as he takes my hand, giving it a firm shake. "It's nice to meet you, Vee. Any friend of Aspen's is a friend of mine."

I'm sure it is. You'll excuse my jaded opinion. I've heard this line many, many times and it goes down like this: they are my friends when Aspen is around. When she isn't around, neither are they. This includes girls, too.

But it doesn't bother me. One, I'm new here, considering I'm just a freshman and two, I don't have the time to maintain many friendships given my after-school activities of annoying my neighbor and keeping up my MyView videos.

"It's nice to meet you," I return, pulling my hand back and tucking my hair behind my ear. Why? I have no idea. I guess just feeling Sebastian's eyes on me as he watches from my chair is making me seriously nervous. What the hell is he doing over there anyway?

I fight the urge to glance in his direction and instead give Vance my best smile. I'm sure he didn't really care if he met me, but he's being decent, so I will be too. Even if I would love to turn around and see what the demon next door is up to.

"Vee is also into all that, right, Vee?"

Wait, what?

"Uh…" I hesitate and wince, making Vance laugh.

"That's alright, Valentina. You wouldn't be the first woman I bored with my talks of conservation efforts."

Dammit, Vee. Look at what you did. Here's a nice guy who isn't stealing your shit and you can't even bother not zoning out when he speaks to you.

"Oh, no. That's not it at all," I apologize. "I am into conservation." I shrug. "Well, more like recycling. I haven't had a whole lot of time with much else, but I try to help out where I can."

"Awesome," Vance replies. "If you're interested, I run the Stay Green program at Havemeyer, we're always looking for more volunteers."

As cute as he is and as much I love the cause, it sounds like way too much peopling for me. "Oh, wow. How often do you meet?"

Maybe I can squeeze in a session or two. I mean, it's for a good cause, even if I have to suffer through a few conversations with people I don't know.

"Three times a week." Vance flashes me a boyish smile that I don't hate. "You should come."

At least the view would be good, right?

"Yea—"

"Valentina."

The voice that makes me gag every time I hear it sends a cringy shiver down my spine when he says my name.

"Malcolm." I turn and smile with a fake friendliness. "So awful to see you. Are you here to clean up?"

I look at my wrist like I have a watch. "The party won't be over for another few hours. Maybe you should go wait across town. We'll call you."

Aspen chuckles next to me while Malcolm holds his stomach in a fake laugh. "It's so nice to see you in the daylight, Valentina. I was worried you might have transferred schools in the past two months."

He snaps his fingers. "Oh wait. Let me guess? You've been in mourning since you and your neighborhood crush called it quits." Malcolm pokes his bottom lip out into a fake pout that makes Vance shuffle awkwardly.

He's not completely wrong with his assessment. Sure, I'm not Miss Social Butterfly, but I have been staying in more since my fallout with Sebastian.

"Did he break your little manly heart?"

"That's enough," Vance says, just as Aspen takes a threatening step directly in Malcolm's face.

It only serves to amuse Malcolm more.

He peers around Aspen, still taunting me. "Aww. Did I hit a nerve?"

I've never needed anyone to stand up for me, and I especially don't now. Malcolm doesn't know what he's talking about. He has no idea why Sebastian and I stopped pranking each other. "You don't know sh—"

A hint of moonshine wafts through the air like minion droplets, introducing their leader before he arrives. I would know that smell anywhere. It took me months to get it out of my clothes after we stopped speaking.

"Valentina," Sebastian grits out, like each syllable was painful for him to say.

"Dick," I return without hesitation.

His glare is volleying between Vance and Malcolm, like I purposely wanted to be over here between them.

"Are you hurting these poor boys' feelings again? We've talked about this. You can't afford another restraining order."

My smile is forced as I try to cover up the exasperated sound trying to erupt. "So nice of you to walk over uninvited, Sebastian. But we're fine here."

I don't need him trying to come over here and be some sort of hero.

"Unlike you, Aspen was sweet enough to invite me."

Aspen was sweet enough to stir my ongoing pot of drama with

the neighbor is what she was. She needs something to do other than meddle. I knew she had a reason for inviting Vance.

"You two are adorable," chides Malcolm. "Too bad your fans don't support your solo careers." He sneers at Sebastian. "At least Vee's video entry had substance. She doesn't qualify to enter, but even her worst videos are better than your best ones."

My stomach churns just as Sebastian takes a step forward, crowding Malcolm. "I'd watch your mouth if I were you."

I know Malcolm is being a douche, but if Sebastian and I ever had an Achilles heel, it's being nothing without the other. I figured my videos might not qualify for the contest but is Sebastian's video really not doing well? I need to check it out. Surely Malcolm is just talking out his ass, per usual.

Vance steps between Sebastian and Malcolm and places a hand on Sebastian's chest, playing the peacemaker. I think they know each other, but I'm not sure. "Come on, man. He isn't worth the police report."

I look at Sebastian's heaving chest, his jaw working as his fists open and close by his side.

See? I told you Malcolm is hated on MyView.

Malcolm flashes me a smirk, taking a step back from Sebastian, the explosive. It's been a while since I've seen him red-faced and—well, I guess it hasn't been that long. Last time he was this enraged was with me.

"See you around, Valentina. I'll be sure to say hi to your subscribers for you."

I roll my eyes as Malcolm turns and leaves. He couldn't win over my subscribers if he grew a vagina and burped rainbows. Women know a weasel when we see one.

The air around me eases, but then Sebastian has to go and mess it up.

"What the fuck are you wearing, Valentina?" His voice is low and threatening. I'm so not in the mood for it.

"What the fuck are you wearing, Sebastian?" I say his name all growly like he said mine. "I told you those shorts looked like you sat in shit. Why do you still have them on?"

He mumbles out something that I don't understand, but I do catch Vance's words. "Settle down."

Oh no. Sebastian is not coming over here in a bad mood and taking it out on me. "Go home, Sebastian. You need a nap." And a swift kick in the ass, but I leave that part out. I don't need more drama from the diva next door.

He rears back, and I know that Malcolm's taunting got to him. I don't know who I hate more right now. "I need a nap?" he says aghast, like he can't believe I would suggest such a thing. "You need some fucking clothes! What is this?" He waves down at my body, and I hear Aspen snicker.

"Uh, a bathing suit?" I say for the man who isn't thinking clearly. "You saw me in it earlier," I remind him. When he was texting me. Why wasn't he upset then?

"Uh oh," Aspen chides, tugging me away from a red-faced Sebastian. "Looks like you might need to find a t-shirt too."

She pulls us away from the guys and sends them a little wave. "Have a drink, boys, and settle down. We'll be back."

When we're inside and tucked away in Drew's room, Aspen pulls out a shirt from his dresser. "Here," she says handing it over.

I grab it and eye the mischievous look in her eye. "You knew this would happen," I accuse her.

"That Malcolm would crash the party and spew his drama?"

I cock my head to the side. "You know what I'm talking about." I finger my top. "The bathing suit…"

She puts her hand to her chest in mock innocence. "How would I know that Sebastian would come over all growly and jealous?"

True, but…

"He likes you," she says out of the blue, digging through Drew's top drawer where he keeps all the condoms and begins stacking them.

"Who?" I ask, slipping Drew's oversized t-shirt over my head. "Vance?"

She turns and catches my eye. "The neighbor."

I scoff. "How much have you had to drink?"

Shutting the drawer, she jumps on the bed next to me. "I think you have a secret."

I laugh and push my arms through the shirt. "Trust me, I don't have a secret."

"You have a secret," she challenges. "I just don't understand why you won't tell me." Her voice is soft and a little sad. It makes me feel like complete dog shit.

"Come on, Asp. Don't force me to tell you."

Aspen has been my big sister all my life. I can't stand to withhold something from her, but I just can't tell her about me and Sebastian. She thinks we were secretly dating, but we weren't. He didn't get mad at my bathing suit because he was jealous. He was lashing out at me because of what Malcolm said about his video. Sebastian hates me. I'm the reason his videos aren't doing well. Granted, I never aired the last prank, so no one really knows why we stopped pranking each other, but we became internet famous together because of those pranks. We lived our fifteen minutes of fame and now it's over. He just hasn't accepted it yet.

Aspen sighs, and after a moment, lies back on the bed and stares up at the ceiling. I follow suit. "Do you think we'll ever be able to move on?" she says softly.

"From what?" I roll over and face her. She's still looking at the ceiling.

"Loving them."

Oh.

I roll back over and join her in staring at the ceiling. "I don't love Sebastian," I admit. "Our situation isn't the same as yours and Bennett's."

We're quiet for a moment as the party rages on outside. And then finally, she whispers, "Maintaining the denial is the hardest part."

CHAPTER SIX

Sebastian

University CamFlix Competition Submission
Entry Number: 75
Sebastian and Valentina
First Interview Continued, also known as another fifteen minutes of torture

"So you what? Sang with her?"

Poor Tom is so confused. It's okay, Vee was too until her comments started blowing up while she was live-streaming her video. The weirdo actually thought only a handful of people would see her belting out that heart going on song. Newsflash, it's the internet, where privacy is nonexistent and public humiliation is gold.

I scrunch my face and level Tom with a bored look. "Hell no, I didn't sing with her."

I nudge Vee in the side. She's stiff and tense, so I pull her close and give her a fake boyfriend squeeze before adding, "I stood behind her and put my arms out like the guy did in the movie and mouthed "watermelon" until she realized I was behind her. Which took a while. Had the comments from people laughing not started chiming, we probably could have gotten through the whole song."

Two things I wanted out of my college experience: fame and more fame.

This clusterfuck of a conversation is neither of those things.

"All I'm saying is, it wasn't that funny."

I eye Rowan with something like disbelief. Or is that malice?

"It was just lame pick-up lines."

The playing cards clenched in my hands bend inward. "They weren't just pick-up lines," I argue. "They were the best of the best in cheesy lines."

Rowan shrugs, and my voice rises with my poor judgment in friends. "I used them to hit on my chem teacher!"

You had to be there.

"I didn't think it was funny."

Is he serious? "Let me show you," I offer, settling into my chair and leaning forward.

As if Rowan were my chemistry teacher, I lick my lips like I did to her and say, "If I was an enzyme, I'd be DNA helicase so I could unzip your genes." I grin and give him one more. "You must be calcium bicarbonate, because if you let me get you wet, then the reaction will be explosive."

"Dude." Maverick chuckles. "That's so lame."

And Ms. Harp agreed, ushering me to the campus counselor and giving me the crisis hotline number as if my pick-up lines were a cry for help.

I slouch back onto the metal chair. "It's not lame, it's clever."

Needless to say, yesterday was rough. Hence the reason for my hangover this morning. Something had to wash away the looks of pity.

"I'm just saying it wasn't your best stuff," Rowan adds, his gaze on the pot of chips in the center of the table.

Wasn't my best stuff… I shake my head. "This coming from a guy who thinks *The Fast and the Furious* deserved an Oscar."

Rowan's head snaps up from his hand of cards. "Don't even start with the Vin Diesel jokes tonight. All I'm saying is, since you and Vee stopped your prank war, your feed has been inconsistent. You need to find your niche. You can't just keep posting random videos. Your audience needs to know what they can expect from each clip."

They can expect me to kick Rowan's ass soon.

My lips flatten, and I feel the muscle in my cheek twitch. "Thanks, Mark Zuckerberg. I'll keep that in mind the next time I ask for your fucking opinion."

Maverick sighs like the old man he is. "I raise." He's trying to get us to focus back on the game and not continue to argue about how my last video performed. The one that Malcolm referred to as lacking substance tonight. Never have I wanted to kick someone's ass as much as I did Malcolm's. If it wasn't for Vance shoving me back toward my house, I think I might have stalked over and beat the shit out of him, just because I had to stare at Valentina's cleavage the entire time I endured talking to him.

All I wanted to do is sit out on the back patio in Vee's chair and watch her fall while she attempted to kick the ball, but then Vance showed up and was talking to the little liar, distracting me from my entertainment for the evening. So by the time Malcolm monopolized even more of my shitty night, I was done.

I don't even care that my UniCamFlix entry video yielded less than optimal results. I have eight weeks to submit more. With my new cameraman, I plan on stepping up my game on the next one.

Rowan takes his turn and stays his hand. "Forget the singing chick, dude. Malcolm is your newest competition. Watch his videos. He's hilarious and consistently finds fresh new material to use. Here—" Rowan thrusts his phone in my face. For a second, I worry I might crack a tooth from how hard my jaw is clenched, "—watch. It's the funniest shit I've seen."

I push his phone away. I don't need to see how sucktastic Malcolm's material is. He's never been a threat to me.

"Please." I scoff. "Malcolm couldn't get views unless he offered a hand job with each watch. The only reason he has sponsors is because he bought most of those subscribers with Mommy and Daddy's money." Malcolm's videos suck just as much as his 90's haircut. I'm not worried about his ridiculous spoofing videos.

"You're in a shitty mood," notes Mav, shuffling the cards in his hands. "I thought you wanted to come to Gigi's tonight." He eyes my hand and the stupid small bets I've been tossing in the pot.

I sigh. I did—I mean I wanted to come to Gigi's. I could certainly use the distraction, but instead of poker distracting me, it's the image of Vee in that fucking bikini smiling up at Vance's stupid ass with his talk of recycling. Please. I could smell the lame from all the way in my backyard.

"The neighbor piss you off again?" asks Rowan, putting his phone away and pulling his cards toward his chest. No one is looking at his fucking cards. He's going to lose regardless. I can already tell Mav has a good hand. That damn cigarette hangs from his mouth carelessly and relaxed.

I shake off my mood. I need to focus on the game. Not my video and definitely not Vee. I mean, I don't give two shits that she had been hit on by several fuckwits by the time I'd left for Gigi's. She's a big girl and can take a man down without warning. But shouldn't Drew or Bennett be looking out for her? Isn't that what they do in between classes and games? Stalk the ever-loving shit out of my neighbors… No one gets close to Vee and Aspen. And here Vee was… For God's sake, I could see every one of her curves, the swell of her tits, the soft edges of her hips—

"So you entered the competition?"

I force myself to unlock my hands from clenched fists. "Of course. No one dominates the internet like I do."

"Except for Malcolm," Rowan adds, getting a laugh out of Maverick who adds, "And Vee."

They both can eat shit.

"I didn't realize you both were so interested in my film career," I snap.

A light chuckle goes through Maverick. "We aren't. We're interested in when this pouty bitch phase is coming to an end. The competition will be good for you. It'll give you something to focus on instead of—" He shrugs, not wanting to say her name. Which is good because her name evokes powerful emotions like rage and lust and I don't have room for that right now. I only have room for ambition. I'm getting out of Georgia, no matter what.

"We came here to play poker, didn't we?"

Maverick grins, knowing when to leave me alone. "Yes, we did. So don't cry when you're two grand lighter tonight."

I'm not fucking losing. Not while I'm in this mood. I push all my chips to the middle. "I'm all in."

"Sebastian!"

Fuck, I did it again.

I roll out of bed with a groan and fall to the floor. The wood floors are cool against my skin. I could sleep a few more hours before class starts, if the banging would stop.

"It's Brick! Your new cameraman. You know, the one you hired yesterday."

The name sounds vaguely familiar. And then it hits me.

Last night.

I pull my hands close to my face and focus. The permanent marker is still there. A grin, the size of something really huge—I'm hungover, don't judge me—tugs across my face as I remember bits and pieces of last night.

Her keys.

My failure of a video.

Her stupid bird feeder that she just had to hang in the tree that I park next to.

Her 'Save the World' attitude.

Her stupid texts.

All of it came to an explosion that ended up with another drunken idea.

"Sebastian?"

I spring from the floor, ignoring the pounding in my head, and wrench open the door to find my shiny new cameraman. He's sober and has two coffees clutched in his hand.

I tip my head. "Hurry. Get your camera." I literally pull him through the door and slam it shut.

"Hurry. She gets up at 7:30," I bark, snagging one of the coffees and chugging.

"Who?"

I find a shirt on the sofa and pull it on. "Vee. My neighbor. Are you rolling yet?"

He fumbles with his camera bag, and I rush to the window, prepared to pull out my phone, just in case.

"I'm rolling. I'm rolling," Brick says, out of breath and really flustered for a guy who seems like he has his life together. "Do you want to livestream this?"

I shake my head. "No. I want to go back and edit it later." I can feel the warmth of the coffee making its way down to my stomach and staving off the hangover. Why does messing with Valentina bring such joy to my miserable soul?

"Where do you want me to set up?"

My last cameraman didn't need this much instruction.

I push up the window above the kitchen sink. "Here." I tap the sink.

Brick's eyes widen before he cocks a brow. "You want me to set up next to the sink?"

I ignore him and hop up on the counter, excitement coursing through my veins. "No, not *next* to the sink." I toss last night's dishes onto the counter and rest my feet in the stainless steel bowl, a clear indication where I'd like his delaying ass to set up.

Getting low, I peer out the window and into the courtyard, not bothering to see if Brick takes the hint. If he wants a job, he'll get his ass up here quickly. "Did you know *National Geographic* photographer, Krystle Wright, dangled off the side of a Tasmanian cliff to get a perfect shot?" I ask him.

My mood has really improved in the last few minutes. "I think if she can put on her man pants and hang from a cliff, you can squat in the sink for a few minutes."

I don't look back to see if I might have hurt his feelings. If I did and he leaves, then I'm better off. I don't need a chickenshit cameraman on my payroll.

A few seconds and a sigh later, his camera is plopped on the counter on the opposite side and then his body follows. My eyes never leave the courtyard.

"Remind me what I'm shooting," Brick says, a little edge of attitude seeping out.

"Did I hire you to film or ask an annoying amount of questions?" Seriously. I realize this isn't his expertise, but if I'm staring out the window, and I ask you to roll, I mean for you to shoot wherever the hell I say.

"But there's nothing in the courtyard," he adds, continuing to grate on my nerves.

"It's almost time," I say, watching the back door of Vee's townhouse like it's a stripper pole. "She's coming. Just make sure you stay on her the whole way. Don't veer off and film her friend. Stay on her."

I think Brick nods, but he may have taken a sip of coffee. I won't ever know for sure because Vee opens the back door and all my attention goes to the trash bag in her hand.

A stupid and completely unwarranted grin pulls onto my face. I shouldn't get this excited. Vee is the enemy. She should not be eliciting these types of feelings.

"You want me to film her picking up the party trash?" Brick's words are nearly a whisper, but I don't miss the disgusted shock buried in them.

I nod, the stupid grin still going strong. "That's exactly what I want you to do."

I don't much care if Brick thinks I'm this crazy, drugged-up college student. Mine and Vee's prank battles run so deep that he'll never grasp the lengths we go to get one up on each other—or at least we used to.

But looks like old habits die hard.

Literally.

I turn from Brick, hoping he doesn't see my sweatpants tenting in the center. Watching my neighbor bend down and begin picking up trash is like watching the opening commercials to the Victoria's Secret Fashion Show. Anticipation that you're sure to see the tightest of bodies with the bitchiest of looks.

If Brick didn't think I was weird before, he'll for sure think it now. "Stay on her," I mumble. It's annoying how hyper I am at seven-thirty in the morning.

"I got her, don't worry," he reassures me.

Finally, someone sounds like he's taking his job seriously. Fine, okay, it was me who wasn't taking this job seriously.

"Are you awake?" Vee asks into her phone, bending over and picking up a plastic cup and tossing it into the bag. "It's a half past seven." She pauses, grabbing a beach ball and popping the air tube.

My heart feels like it spasms a bit. What the fuck is wrong with me?

"I'm already out here… I don't care if they are asleep! Wake them up, Asp. I'm not cleaning all of this up by myself."

She's frustrated, and I'm going to take a not so wild guess and say it's from being the only one in her crew awake this early with a huge mess in front of her.

"Okay, bye." Vee hangs up her phone and stuffs it into the front pocket of the shorts she's wearing.

I do a silent drumroll to myself, seconds away from sneaking outside and getting a front row seat to her soon-to-be fury. A quick glance at Brick confirms he is, indeed, recording.

"I got her," he mumbles, with what will soon be our company motto.

I nod, refusing to acknowledge aloud that I'm being a little psycho about all of this. But fucking with Valentina brings way too much joy to my life. Don't judge me.

The beauty, who is very much a beast in everything she does, leans down and picks up the first slide. It's muddy and grass clippings stick to it. But in true Vee fashion, she doesn't fuss over her nails or the dirt getting onto her hands. Instead, something catches her eye, and she cocks her head to the side, her eyes narrowing.

God, I hope Brick doesn't look over here and see the dumbest grin on my face.

Slowly, as if something was lurking within the folds of the vinyl, Vee drops the trash bag and grasps the slide with both hands, flipping it over for a better view of the writing on the back.

It's the highlight of my shitty week when her face falls into a frown, and her gaze snaps up to my townhouse. A few seconds later, her phone is in her hands, and mine is buzzing with a notification.

I'll be honest. I can't wait to read it.

DO NOT TEXT THIS NUMBER: Really?

I admire my contact name for her, one that I clearly ignored yesterday morning, and grin.

Me: Good morning to you too, Valentina. I'm fine. Thanks for asking. You're looking fresh-faced and full of deceit this morning.

I watch as her head falls back, and she looks at the clouds as if she is praying.

DO NOT TEXT THIS NUMBER: Did you know that there is a break-in every 13 seconds? Really?

I grin. I couldn't remember what exactly I wrote on the bottom of several of the slides. It was late and I was drunk, but it still makes me laugh.

Me: Okay. Thanks, Sherlock Holmes. I'll keep that under advisement.

DO NOT TEXT THIS NUMBER: I know you wrote this. I can tell by the second-grade penmanship.

Don't worry, I'm not offended. On a good day, my handwriting looks awful. On a drunk day, I'm sure it's even worse. I think she's being generous with the second-grade assessment.

Me: If I were you, I would do a little less accusing and a lot more hurrying. Tony will be coming out for his morning paper soon.

Her gaze snaps up to our complex owner's door. Her friend may have offered him game tickets for the party, but that doesn't mean he won't fine the shit out of them for the mess. This isn't a frat house. There are strict rules to living in this complex, and I'm pretty sure a littered courtyard is in the fine print somewhere.

Vee pockets her phone and takes my advice, hurrying to clean the mess.

"Is that it?" Brick asks beside me.

I feel my mouth pull tight. "Have you ever heard of delayed gratification, Brick?"

Seriously. A good video needs click bait—a mystery you have to keep watching in order to figure out the story.

"Yeah, but now her friends are out there," he notes.

Even better. Now she'll be worried about what else I wrote on the slides.

"Just keep filming. Keep the camera on her."

Brick grunts out his understanding or frustration. I can't tell which. It really doesn't matter as long as he catches every second of Valentina Lambros going down.

Vee scrambles outside, barking orders at her friends, giving them each a job. She does a pretty good job of making it out like she's worried Tony will come out and catch the mess versus them finding all my secret notes to her.

She hurries over to the courtyard, picking up all the slides, reading covertly as she finds more than a handful of notes on the bottom of the slides. When she and her crew have all the trash and slides bagged up, they all retreat back inside.

"Can I stop recording now?" Brick asks.

I lick my lips, the taste of victory sweet on my lips. "Take thirty."

His brow raises. "What happens in thirty minutes?"

Was it really a good idea to hire Brick? I'm thinking no. "You'll see. Just keep the camera on standby."

It takes exactly thirty-one minutes before Brick is able to press record again.

CHAPTER SEVEN

Valentina

University CamFlix Competition Submission
Entry Number: 75
Sebastian and Valentina
First Interview Continued, or that time I thought about how long I
could hold my breath until I passed out

Tom coughs, attempting to mask his laughter. "So, Sebastian acting the scene out behind you was the start of the wars?"

Why must he ask me to repeat it? "Yes. He humiliated me on camera."

Sebastian, unable to mask his laugh, adds sweetly. "Oh, come on, baby. I think you were doing a jam up job of that on your own. I was merely your funny sidekick." He kisses me on the cheek, and I manage not to vomit. "Your fans loved it."

They loved it all right. They loved it all the way to his page.

"You're a dick."

The asshole neighbor of mine grins and slides his hand down his bare stomach, lingering dangerously close to the button on his jeans. "Mmm… Don't pull out that southern Latina accent of yours. You know what it does to me."

His words say it like it sounds sexy; yet, the look on his face his nothing but pure distaste.

"Where are they?" I push through the space between his hard body and the door frame. I don't ask if I can come in. Once upon a time, I was over here more than my own apartment.

"Where is what?"

Deep breaths, Vee. I know you want to throat punch him, but you can't. You need to get what you came for first.

"My keys. Where are they?"

I notice a guy who I haven't seen before rounding the kitchen counter with a camera pointed right at me. "Cute," I tell Sebastian. "You managed to blackmail a decent human to document your misdemeanors."

Sebastian flinches as if my comment stings, but he schools his features quickly. "Smile for the camera, Valentina. Show all that hostility to our loyal fans. You know they love when mommy and daddy fight."

If my father wouldn't be sorely disappointed in me, I'd headbutt this fool in front of me. Instead, I go with, "If that camera gets anywhere near me, I will shove it so far down your throat, you'll be your own personal nightlight."

My comment brings a smile to Bash-hole's face. "Violence isn't very ladylike, but then again, you've never been much of a lady."

He's not wrong there. When your father is a Marine and all your friends are boys with Marine fathers as well, you learn to hold your own. Before I could talk, I could perform a chokehold. Such is the norm in my life, and it's served me well.

"I want my keys, Sebastian."

He leans against the wall, smug and annoying as shit. "Not until you tell me what you learned."

And… his cameraman is about to witness a murder.

"I've learned that my neighbor is one misdemeanor away from being a serial thief," I spit.

"And?" he prompts flatly, as if my comment did nothing to deter him.

"And one day I will see his face on one of those missing person boards when someone finally offs him for being a complete pain in the ass."

He grins. "Oh, come on. Not a complete pain. I could only dream of being a complete pain in the ass. Right now, I think my status is one of a minor pain or just a twinge, but not a complete pain in the ass."

"Sebastian!" I pop a hip and blow out a breath. "Give me my keys. I have places to be. I don't have time for this shit."

He rubs his jaw casually, as if he has all day to grate on my nerves. "All you have to do is tell me what you learned."

It's finally reached the point of loathing.

Sighing, I pray for patience and look up at the ceiling, before leveling him with a look. As bored as I can manage, I state the stupid facts that I'm impressed he spelled correctly when he wrote them. "There are two million burglaries a year which translates to a burglary once every thirteen seconds." I roll my eyes. "Happy now?"

He pushes off the wall and leans into my personal space, forcing me to endure that organic smell of cedar. "Wrong. It was two point five million break-ins a year. And you, sweetheart, need to be more mindful of that. Just because Daddy pays for your posh little townhouse doesn't mean your neighbors are decent."

"Clearly," I mutter. "Now, hand them over."

When the smuggest grin emerges on his face, I know this little shitshow of torture isn't over.

"I'll offer you an exchange," he says, his eyes dancing with delight. He loves torturing me.

I sigh. I'm not getting out of this. No matter what I say or do to him, he will continue to taunt me until he gets his way. "Your keys…" He dangles the words out as bait.

"I'm listening."

"For my pillow and eight weeks of playing my girlfriend."

I choke on a gasp.

"Are you high?"

"Sober as a nun."

"Why the hell would I want to pretend to be your girlfriend? And why in the fresh hell would I subject myself to it for eight weeks, even if I was stupid enough to agree?"

Sebastian pulls his phone out between us and opens the MyView app.

"I don't have time for this, Sebastian. Give me my keys and we can negotiate the pillow and chair later." I add my chair to the mix because he's giving that back, even if I have to pry it from his cold, dead hands. "I don't need to be subjected to your MyView escapades."

Really, I have been tortured enough the past couple of days.

I fold my arms and then I hear it. My voice. "What the hell are you watching?"

Sebastian holds the phone out of my reach and starts rattling off random comments. "Holy shit! They're back! I've missed seeing their videos."

I scrunch my face. "What video?" I wasn't shooting a video at the party and neither was he. I'm not allowed since Drew and Fenn can't seem to behave. Fenn is one more suspension away from expulsion from the baseball team. He doesn't need any more bad publicity than he already has.

"Aww! He's jealous! That's so sweet. I want a man who gets pissed if I wear a bikini. OMG! Are they together? It looks like he was about to kick that guy's ass! Swoon alert."

I jump for his phone, and he holds it out of my reach and says, "Apparently, someone at the party shot this video of us and posted it. Now there's a rumor floating around that we might be an item." He grins. "Or at least a couple who are currently fighting."

I pretend to gag, and he ignores me. "You don't have to believe me. Just look at your subscribers. I got a thousand overnight."

Don't do it, Vee. It's a trick, an elaborate prank, just so he can get back at you.

"It doesn't matter what the internet thinks. We aren't an item, nor will we ever be."

He's quick to respond. "Agreed but seeing how your video is disqualified and mine needs…" he grimaces, "—help. Neither of us is going to win the competition. Stupid Malcolm with his copied ideas is going to beat us in our own house."

I level Sebastian with a flat look. "The internet isn't our house."

"Yes, it is. Our videos ruled the top ten page of MyView's best videos for an entire semester. Are we really going to let Malcolm take that from us?"

I throw my hands in the air, so done with all of this. "Sebastian, I'm tired, and honestly, I don't care about the contest or Malcolm or you. All I want is my keys and my chair that you stole."

It was a bad morning. Aspen's words at the party kept me tossing and turning all night. She doesn't understand what this is right here. This drama and constant back and forth. This isn't love. It's a friendship that went bad.

Sebastian sighs and pockets his phone. "Look, I know this isn't what either of us want. I would much rather film alone and I'm certain you would prefer to continue creating your makeup videos, but the cold hard truth is that we won't win. I know you want to get noticed by a studio."

I narrow my eyes. He's making sense and that's unlike him.

He takes my silence as my acquiescence and continues, "You won't get noticed without the views. You know that, and I know that. This is a good opportunity for both of us."

I chew the inside of my cheek. The demon is right. Neither of us will get the views we'll need to win the competition.

"It'll be like old times," he adds.

"Ugh." He knew that would get me. I remember the time he's mentioning. We had to make up this elaborate story in order to get backstage into a concert. It went sideways, of course, and we were caught, but I had the time of my life. He did too, but he'll never admit it.

"Please, Vee. We'll split the money fifty-fifty."

"Of course we'd split the money equally." I scoff. "Did you really consider offering me less?"

I don't know why this shocks me. One minute he's begging and the next he's saying some dumb shit that makes me want to walk straight out the door.

His face looks appalled, but I know him better than that. "Of course not."

Sure he wouldn't.

He holds out his hand. "Deal?"

This is so incredibly stupid, but then so is stealing each other's shit. I guess Sebastian and I aren't known to make the best decisions around each other. Sighing, I slip my hand in his. "Deal. Now give me my keys then we'll discuss details."

That smug smile of his reemerges. "Sure." He nods to his front pocket. "They're all yours."

Oh hell no. "You really are sleep deprived if you think I am sticking my hand in your pocket." Give me a break. I might be a moron for signing up to play this idiot's girlfriend, but I draw the line at reaching into his pocket.

"No?" He asks, his voice carrying a hidden challenge. "My girlfriend should have no problem reaching into my pocket to get her keys." He flashes me a wink. "Some might even call it sexy."

Some might call it nauseating.

But he's right and his cameraman behind us is probably still filming. A girlfriend would have no qualms about digging into his pocket. I guess it's better to just rip off the proverbial Band-Aid. If Sebastian and I are really going to trick the campus and the producers of the UniCamFlix competition, then we better start behaving more like lovers and less like enemies.

"Fine," I agree. "But I swear if your dick touches my hand—even through the fabric—then all of this is over. Do not even try to mess with me." I take a breath. "Matter of fact, let's go ahead and shake on a truce." I look him in the eyes, so he knows I'm serious. "No pranks while we do this."

With a terse nod, he sticks his hand out. "Agreed."

A huge weight feels like it lifts off my shoulders in that moment of shaking his hand. Maybe it's a truce from the months of war between us, or maybe it's because I'm relieved to finally get my friend back. I guess we'll never know because the ass opens his mouth and ruins the euphoric feeling in an instant.

"Go ahead, sugar. Get your keys."

"We're not using pet names either," I add, already making a mental rulebook that I plan on writing down the minute I get home. It's not like Sebastian will follow them, but at least I can point to them in writing when I yell at him. Regardless, we have to have rules because last time we didn't and look what happened.

"We're using pet names, babe," he argues. "Any girlfriend of mine would expect such things from me."

Gag me.

"Fine, but no stupid ones."

He cocks his head to the side. "Define stupid."

Heaven help me. This is worse than that time I thought it would be cute to have curtain bangs.

"We'll define them later," I tell him, taking a deep breath and looking to the ceiling. I don't know what I think I'll find there, but I'm hoping it's patience or at least some top-shelf alcohol. Either would work at this point.

"Sounds good. Now, would you like me to sit or stand for the shot of you getting your keys. I think we'll caption it: 'Girlfriend leaves keys hanging in the door. Boyfriend saves the day.'" He does this stupid little wink that a girlfriend would find swoon-worthy. But as his enemy, I simply find it annoyingly hard to ignore.

"That's a terrible caption. No one will click on that video."

He shrugs. "They will if the picture is of my abs and your hand in my pocket."

Ugh. He's right. Anything that remotely looks sexy or risqué will have our viewers clicking on the video.

"I think I'm going to need a scalding shower after this," I mutter, wiping my hands on my shirt. They're sweaty, okay? It's not like I have experience sticking my hand in guys' pants. I mean, I'm not a virgin, so I have been close to a man's dick before, but this is Bash-hole we're talking about. The closest I've ever gotten with him is feeling his lips on mine, which was short-lived. Instances where we have to be close and have our hands on each other will be new for me. For him, only having one person this close at a time will be a new experience.

"Vee," he says, pulling my attention back to him and that stupid pocket.

I wave him off and glance back at his cameraman. "Are you rolling?"

He nods, and I take a step into Sebastian's body. I can already feel the heat from his bare chest warning me away. It's a safety mechanism meant to alert girls like me away from boys like him. But like all women, I need to feel the burn before I back off.

Swallowing, I reach up and cup his jaw. He tenses at my touch, and it makes me feel slightly better. Sebastian might act like he's at ease and has no problem with me being close to him, but this deal of ours will torture him just as much as it will me.

"Thanks for locking up this morning after you left," I say sweetly, completely pulling the words out of my ass. I had to have some reason that he would have my keys. Well, he could have just locked the door from the inside, but our viewers won't care. We'll just chalk it to him wanting to make sure I was safe by locking the deadbolt behind him. That sounds like something a sweet boyfriend—not Sebastian—would do.

"No problem," he says, his voice raspy and thick. I don't know if he's trying to make it sound sexy or if he needs to clear his throat.

I trail a finger along his jaw, pausing long enough to let it linger in that damn dimple that makes girls stupid. His cheek clenches, and I feel a grin emerge. I think I might like this little deal with Bash-hole. Being able to torture him on a daily basis feels pretty good right now.

With slow strokes, I let my fingers drift down his neck and over his chest. His head comes forward almost as if we're magnets pulling together. My arms go around his neck and his to my waist. There isn't but a few inches between us.

"I hope you slept like dog shit," I whisper in his ear.

Sebastian's cameraman moves to the side, capturing the moment of two new lovers whispering in each other's ear.

"I hope the dumpster is fresh out of chairs," he returns, gripping my hair in his hand and tugging. "Because you're never getting yours back."

To the fans, it'll look like we're having a hard time not mauling each other. That's the truth, just not in the sense they are thinking.

My hands drift down his stomach, and I smile. What I wouldn't give to be able to sucker punch him right now. But alas, I can't because I made a deal with a demon.

With a warning look to Sebastian, I trace the edge of his waistband with my fingers, before walking them down to his pocket where my keys are waiting. His grip tightens on my hips, and he folds over me, burying his head in my hair. For a moment, I wait for a shitty comment, but then I realize, he doesn't intend to make one.

Slipping my fingers into his pocket, I'm met with warmth and a whispered groan. I don't know if he's doing it for the camera or if he's groaning that I'm too close to him. Either way, I don't care. I just need these keys, and his breath on my neck is making it hard to remember exactly what we're doing this for.

Finally, I loop the key ring with my finger and pull my hand out of his pocket, without any sort of dick touching.

"See you later," I tell him with a fake smile.

He nods and swallows before he aims a glare at his cameraman. "We're not using all that footage," he barks.

"What's your name again?" I ask the cameraman. I think it's classier if I pretend that Sebastian was decent enough to tell me his name before I came over here.

"Brick," he says, adjusting the camera. He has a nice smile, and if I was into the Ed Sheeran look, I might consider chatting Brick up, but instead, as usual, Sebastian ruins it by taking my arm and manhandling me to the door.

"I'll pick you up at seven for our date. Wear something less—" he eyes my current outfit of shorts and a flannel, "—you."

I flip him off just as he slams the door in my face.

We might have a truce, but we certainly didn't negotiate the hate. That little caveat still seems to be a standing rule.

CHAPTER EIGHT

Sebastian

University CamFlix Competition Submission
Entry Number: 75
Sebastian and Valentina
First Interview Continued, also known as that time she threatened to kill me in a public bathroom

"I'm assuming you retaliated after he ruined your video?"

I look at Valentina and grin. "She tried…but—" Vee clamps her hand over my mouth. Her eyes carry a threat to not say another word. The air around us feels thick, but Tom doesn't notice, since he was scribbling something on his clipboard.

"What do you mean by *tried*?" he asks, clueless to Vee's glacial look and our subsequent stare down. "Do you mean she was never successful at pranking you?"

I scoff and Vee snaps her fingers in front of Tom and the camera crew. "Can we have a smoke break?"

My brows pinch. "You want a smoke? Since when do you smoke?"

She pushes my hand off her thigh and then remembers we have an audience and grabs for my hand, interlocking our fingers. "Since now, Pookie. Come with me?"

I frown at the nickname, but I stand anyway, knowing she wants to ream me out, which is fine. I get off on that kind of pillow talk. "Sure, honey. Whatever you want."

Why are girls such pains in the ass?

Me: Are you ready? It's 6:30…

Pretend Like You Like Her: Almost. I needed Aspen and she's at Bennett's. Pick me up there.

Normally, this wouldn't bother me, but today, after the video and rumors of Vee and I dating… I'm not exactly eager to face the Jameson twins and their irrational protection of Vee and Aspen.

I don't know much about Bennett Jameson, but what I do know doesn't give me the warm fuzzies. He's the football team's quarterback and rumored to be the NFL's number one draft pick this year. I wouldn't know, though, because I don't watch football.

Drew, on the other hand, seems okay. He's never been a dick to me, but I've also never "dated" his childhood friend. For all I know, he's in love with her and is too much of a pussy to tell her.

Rolling my shoulders, I crack my neck and rap on the door. I hear muffled whispers and then… heavy stomps that end at the door. And as it flies open with a pained creak, I'm met with a human shield.

It's Drew.

He doesn't say anything, only eyes me up and down with blatant disdain. Looks like he isn't happy to see me.

"Vee," he calls behind him, "I'm not fucking playing with you. You're not leaving until you find something else to wear."

He never looks back, just assumes she'll do as she's told.

I, not so quietly, smother a laugh—he must not know Vee like I do. She never does as she's told.

"Can I help you?" He clips out at the sight of my amusement.

I'll forgive his dickish behavior. Valentina brings out the asshole in me too. "The girl with improper attire," I drawl, "she asked me to pick her up here."

Drew eyes the phone in my hand. "Your camera better be off. We're not fans of your little shitshow."

I hold my phone up and show him the black screen. "Tonight is off the record." I almost cross my heart, just to be an asshole, but think better of it. I'm here for Vee, not a war with one of the Jameson brothers.

"Drew!" A female voice shouts from behind him. "Don't be such an asshole. Let him in while he waits on Vee; she might be a minute."

Drew's lip curls like he'd rather drown kittens than let me come in.

"It's alright, I'm good out here," I reassure him.

He inhales and rolls his shoulders. "The lady of the house dis-agrees." He steps aside and opens the door wider for me to enter, which I do, albeit slowly.

I don't want Drew Jameson thinking I give two shits about his permission to enter. Clearly, he has as much authority as the 'lady of the house' allows him.

Bennett hovers in the kitchen and snaps at the blonde by the stove when the door closes behind me. "You go put some fucking clothes on too. I don't understand why you both had to confiscate my bath-room to do your makeup." He glares at Aspen. "You aren't leaving."

Wow. Bennett so needs a blow job and a beer. Dude is wound tight.

I tip my chin at Bennett as a simple hello and ignore the 'lady of the house,' Aspen.

"Hi, Bash!"

Fuck.

I tip my chin. "Aspen."

Swear to God, Bennett growls.

"How's Maverick and Ainsley?" she continues.

For a second, I think about texting Vee to hurry the hell up, but then I realize I'm ignoring Aspen and that can be just as lethal as talking to her.

"They're good." I tuck my hands in my pockets.

"Good," she returns all too chipper. "Do you want a beer?"

"No, he doesn't," Bennett answers for me, before turning to his brother and barking, "Go see what's taking Valentina so long. She needs pants and a long-sleeved shirt. It's doesn't take that fucking long to throw them on."

It's April and an easy eighty degrees out. I think the long-sleeved shirt is a bit overkill. But I get it, I have a sister too. Not that Bennett and Drew are Vee's brothers, but from what I know about their crew, they were all raised as family. Their parents are best friends, so essentially, they act as siblings. Except for Bennett and Aspen. The way they look at each other is anything but familial.

When Drew lumbers off in search of Vee, Fenn, Aspen's brother, comes barreling down the hall with his pants undone. "Asp, give me your purse."

Aspen scoffs. "I'm not giving you money, Fenn. You'll have to call Dad."

Fenn finally realizes he has a guest and tips his chin, as if this is just like any other night. "I don't need cash, I need condoms. I'm out."

Aspen's wit rivals her brother's. "How do you know I'm not out?"

A low rumble comes from Bennett's direction that makes Fenn grin. "Because of that. Now cough 'em up. You're not using them anytime soon as long as Chastity's Child over there keeps up the good little soldier act."

I feel my eyes widen and Bennett doesn't miss it. He snags a purse—presumably Aspen's—and hurls it into Fenn's chest. "I'm tired of guests, Von Bremen." He eyes me in particular.

Fenn bounces on the balls of his feet. "Don't worry, I won't let mine stay long, big guy. Have an apple and gaze longingly at my sister. That'll make—"

Bennett shoves him, cutting off whatever teasing word he was about to say.

I clear my throat. "I...uh...I'm going to wait outside."

Bennett's voice is thick with authority. "I think that's a good—"

"Wait! Sebastian!" I freeze and turn around to see Valentina Lambros, who's not in a long-sleeved shirt and pants or a flannel;

instead, she's in a summer tank dress that I've never seen. "I'm so sorry. I needed Aspen to do my hair. And well…"

She was over here like usual.

"It looks great," I tell her, noticing it's in loose curls that fall over her shoulder, ending nearly at her elbows. Her look is simple, understated, and my damn dick likes what he's seeing.

"Thanks," she says, knotting her hands together like the compliment makes her feel awkward.

"Be back by ten," Drew grits out, glaring at me.

Vee laughs and shakes her head as she stands on her tiptoes to kiss him on his cheek. Turning, she looks at Aspen, "Will I see you tonight?"

Aspen grins but looks at Bennett who simply folds his arms and glares. "Depends."

Yeah, depends on if she can get away from him. I don't know that I've ever seen a college dude so possessive about a girl. I thought Mav was being all weird with Ainsley, but Bennett acts like Aspen is the Hope Diamond and he's the one entrusted to its care. The dude has the entire campus scared to even look at Aspen.

"Okay. Just text me so I know to lock the door if you're not coming home."

Wait, what? Is that why she leaves her keys in the door all the time? Because she doesn't bother locking the door?

Bennett's head whips to Vee, but he's looking over her shoulder at me when he says, "You better handle that."

I nod. I assume he means making sure she locks the door when I drop her off. I can do that. I tug Vee to the door and step outside when we hear Bennett growl out, "Are you fucking serious? Do you sleep with the door unlocked?"

Vee cringes, and we pull the door closed, leaving Aspen to fight her own battles. I exhale in the evening air as we walk back across the courtyard and to my Jeep. "You…uh…look." I can't even finish my sentence. Valentina Lambros looks… different.

"Shut up," she barks, but it lacks her usual bite. She's nervous.

"Beautiful. You look beautiful," I add, when I can get my tongue to work correctly. "No flannel today?"

She tugs at the waist of her dress and grimaces. "I thought if we were really going to sell this thing, I needed to look the part." She pulls her eyes from the ground and stops, facing me. "You would never be seen with someone in flannel."

I nod, but I only do it because she expects me to. Truth is, I'm known for always being seen with the girl in the flannel shirt. It didn't bother me then and it certainly doesn't bother me now. "I'm okay if you want to keep the look. I think our viewers are used to your style."

I don't want her to change for me or this competition.

"It's okay," she says, walking forward, "We can try it and see. If the views are higher, I'll take one for the team. If they're lower, I'll bring out the trusty flannel again."

She's hasn't changed at all. Not that I expected her to act like a different person, but with our history, I wasn't so sure.

Valentina Lambros is unpredictable.

The rumor around campus is no one is bold enough to date her. You would think it's because of Bennett and Drew, but that's not the case. The truth is, Valentina Lambros is too much for one man to handle. To date her, you need a good sense of humor and a hefty life insurance policy.

"Why are you staring at me?"

I flick my eyes to hers. "Was I staring?"

She nods and glances down at her chest. "Yeah, you were. Keep your eyes up top, playboy."

I chuckle at her scolding. I wasn't checking out her boobs since I already did that way back when she first became my neighbor. She may have worn flannel over the top of her tank tops, but nothing masked the curve of her tits. I know what she's working with. I'm a dude. We know how to admire tits under layers.

"Okay, so where are we eating?" I push the start button and allow the rumble of the engine to relax me.

She shrugs. "Tacos?"

I nod my agreement. "Tacos sound good. Any place in particular?"

She grins and points to the street on the right. "Turn there. I know just the place."

I ease off of the curb and follow her directions for a few minutes, until the silence becomes awkward.

"So…uh. Nice roommates you have."

She cuts me a look that says she doesn't approve of my sarcasm. "It was a bad day for Bennett. He usually isn't *that* bad."

"What happened?"

I don't really care about Bennett's issues. I think it's pretty evident he needs to bang the shit out of Aspen and loosen the fuck up.

Vee shrugs, adjusting her seatbelt. "I don't know. Something about spring break."

I cock a brow. "Trouble in paradise?"

She shakes her head. "No, just typical Bennett and Aspen drama."

See? Told you. They need to bang.

"So your parents are really close friends too, right?" I mean, I know Aspen and Vee grew up together.

Vee chews on her lip, watching the road intently. "My dad used to be homeless. Aspen's mom took him in when no one else would."

Oh.

"I didn't mean to pry—I didn't realize…" *Way to go, Sebastian. Bring up something super sensitive for her.*

She shrugs. "I'm not ashamed of my dad. People think we're all close because we all lived on the same street, but the truth is, we're family."

It's definitely not your basic family history. "Do you ever feel smothered with all the attention?"

She grins. "I assume you mean by the guys?"

That's exactly what I mean. Drew, Bennett, and Fenn watch her and Aspen like I watch Ramen noodles boil in the microwave. Well, when I can sneak them in. My sister refuses to buy them for me.

I nod.

"They can get a little bossy, but I don't let it stop me. I was raised around six Marines. Von Bremen and the twins aren't shit compared to my dad and uncles."

My heart sinks. "Your dad is a Marine?"

"Yeah."

Well, this conversation just took a turn. Who knew her history with Aspen and the guys was so intricately connected?

I can feel her eyes on me when I turn onto the next street she points to. "So," she drawls, changing the subject and easing the tension. "Do you have plans for spring break?"

The lines in my forehead crease. "I don't know. Maybe. Most of the time I go with Mav to see his Pops." I shrug it off. "My parents travel a lot," I lie.

Vee nods. "Mine do too, they travel to California a lot to see my brother."

"He's in the movies, right?"

I know a little bit about Vee's brother, simply by the pictures of him on the walls at Havemeyer. He's apparently a musical legend around these parts.

"Yeah, he writes scores for movies. My parents are super proud, so they try and see him as much as they can."

Something in her voice tells me she's not all that excited about her famous brother.

"Is that why you went into film? Because of your brother?"

She lets out this scoffing noise like that's the most ridiculous thing she's ever heard. "No. I went into film because of my uncle Felipe." She smiles like she's remembering something. "He's always loved the theater, so I grew up watching him apply a mean eyeliner while singing Céline Dion."

Her eyes narrow, and her voice turns hard. "But you knew that."

The comment is a reminder that this isn't like old times. It sobers us quickly and casts an uncomfortable quiet over the rest of the drive. That is, until I put the Jeep in park and eye the monstrosity in front of me. "You wanted tacos out of a food truck?"

She gets out of the car and cuts me a look through the window. "Is the diva too good to eat from a taco truck?"

I hate when she says shit like this. "Ugh, no. But I figured since Brick is filming this 'date,' you might like something a little classier than a food truck." I hop over the door of the Jeep—it was too nice out to leave the top on. "I thought you'd want all your fans to swoon over something romantic."

Vee points to the lights hanging in the trees over the parking lot. "This isn't romantic enough for you?" She pulls her iPad out of her purse. "I even brought a movie."

Dammit. I feel myself smiling at this ridiculousness. "I'm not watching one of those low budget horror movies of yours. We're discussing the rules of this arrangement."

She shrugs. "We can do both since this 'date' is interrupting my movie time."

I level her with a bored look. "We'll see. Let's eat first."

She shoves the iPad back into her purse and nods. "Fine, but you're buying since that's what guys do on dates."

I'm not even going to argue because, one, this was my idea, and two, she's right. Guys typically pay on dates, and if this date goes smoothly then my bank account will have no problem losing five bucks on the cheapest meal I think I'll probably ever spend on a girl.

Vee addresses the guy behind the truck by name. "Do you know him?" I say, when she finishes ordering two fish tacos. "Yeah, that's Juan."

I arch a brow. "Do you know Juan… personally?"

No, I'm not jealous. I simply want to know if I'll have to worry about Juan blowing our cover as we film bits and pieces of this date. Speaking of which, where the fuck is Brick? I thought I was clear when I told him seven.

"Are you asking if I've slept with Juan?"

I pull out my phone and scoff. "Uh, no. I'm just wondering if Juan will need convincing that we're a real couple. I would imagine that your friends would find it strange that you're, all of a sudden, dating the enemy."

I know Maverick spit out his water when I told him I was taking my neighbor out for dinner and I wouldn't be able to meet him at Gigi's. I'm pretty sure he knows something is up, but he won't ask me because, he too, likes his secrets.

We have a 'don't ask, don't tell' type of friendship.

"Juan isn't my bestie." She laughs. "I just eat here a lot."

Somehow this bothers me. In all the stalking and prank plotting, I feel like I would have discovered this about her.

"I don't ever remember you coming to eat here when we were—you know—friends." It's awkward saying the f word. I try not to remind myself that we were once friends, but sometimes, it just comes up, and I can't help it.

"I just started," she says softly. "It was after, you know."

Our friendship ended.

"What do you want?" she asks me, motioning to the menu above Juan's head, blessedly changing the subject. She always knows when the conversation starts heading into tense territory.

"I'll take what you're having."

I don't want to waste any more time looking at the menu. I allowed myself two hours to film this date and discuss the rules. I'm hoping that Vee and I, being the professionals that we are—insert sarcasm here—can do it in half the time. Less time ordering food will contribute to that rushed timeline.

Juan puts two baskets on the counter, and I hand him a twenty and tell him to keep the rest. Again, this isn't a nice gesture on my part. This is me speeding this date up as fast as I possibly can because being around Vee is hard on my liver. Just ask my trash guys who side-eye each other when they hear nothing but clanging bottles in my bags.

Juan tips his chin and I grab the baskets, following behind Vee like a dutiful boyfriend bitch. Where the fuck is Brick? He should be here filming. This is primo boyfriend material and his ass is missing it. I don't plan on repeating it for the sake of getting it on film.

I set the baskets of food on the table and take a seat next to Vee, leaving the bench on the other side of the picnic table open because cuddling up on the same bench is what a good boyfriend would do, right? He would sit next to her in case she couldn't eat all her food. Waste not, want not, and all that.

"So," I say, snagging one of Juan's tacos and taking a huge bite.

"So," she repeats, waiting for me to finish chewing.

Huh. Juan's tacos aren't half bad.

When I've swallowed, I wipe my mouth with the paper napkin Vee hands me. "So, I was thinking we should be seen together around campus and at each other's houses. It'll be easier convincing our friends that this relationship is the real deal."

Vee nods her head but looks pensive. "You don't think they will believe the video?"

Her lips tip at the corner, just as her head cocks to the side.

"I think it will be easier to convince them this relationship is real if they see us together without a camera."

Vee waves me off. "I know. I'm not saying we shouldn't be seen together." She shrugs. "I just think the video shot at the party was pretty convincing on its own."

"You watched it?"

She huffs. "Of course. I had to see what the hell you were all excited about."

"I wasn't excited," I correct. "I was merely pointing out the business opportunity that presented itself to us."

"Look at you sounding all professional. Those business classes are paying off."

And we're done.

I take another bite of my taco and try to find the patience to get through this date that is definitely not going to end well.

"Are we in agreement to try and be seen together?" I wipe my hands. "You think Aspen will believe it?"

Vee keeping something from Aspen is my biggest concern. Best friends tend to share everything, at least girls do. Maverick and I like our secrets.

"Yeah." She sighs. "Unfortunately, I think she'll believe it."

I want to prod as to why she added unfortunately, but then I remember my timeline and let it go.

"Can I ask a favor, though?"

She's asking for a favor and not demanding? That's new. "Sure."

"Can we do some of the filming ourselves?"

"What's wrong with Brick?" Other than the fact he isn't here filming when he should be.

She shrugs. "Nothing. I don't really know him. I think I just prefer shooting some of the more—" she covers a cough, "—intimate shots ourselves."

The word intimate shoots straight to my dick, and he rejoices at the mere thought of doing any kind of intimate related things with the enemy. I never said he made sense. "Are you not worried about using the tripod?"

I know she doesn't like to use them.

"I think between the two of us we can manage," she says.

I nod. "Agreed. We'll use Brick for the public shots, and we'll film the raunchier ones ourselves."

I feel a grin emerge before she says anything.

"At no point will we be doing anything raunchy together."

I shrug. "Whatever you say. Just remember when you suggest our next date be at a hot dog truck in an abandoned alley, you'll have to add the time for us to stop and have a quickie while we're running for our lives."

Her face scrunches up, and I can't hold my laughter in.

"That makes zero sense," she finally says when I take a breath.

"I agree. But the characters in your crappy horror movies seem to think sex is the best way to go out, even if they hated each other the entire movie."

CHAPTER NINE

Valentina

University CamFlix Competition Submission
Entry Number: 75
Sebastian and Valentina
First Interview Continued, also known as those five seconds I didn't hate Sebastian

"Back from your break?" I nod to the producer. "Yes. I'm much more relaxed now."

"Good." Tom nods, looking eager to get back to the love story of Sebastian and Valentina. "Do you want to pick up where you left off?"

I eye Sebastian who just shrugs. "Up to you."

He's no help. Sighing, I twist my fingers together. Here goes nothing. "Sebastian is right, I did try to prank him, but he always caught on to my antics and ended up spoiling my videos instead."

For some reason, when I look at Sebastian, he doesn't seem as smug as I thought he would.

"You were close a couple of times, though," he adds, trying to make me feel better. And it does, a little, because I know it doesn't matter how many failed attempts I had; when it matter most, I nailed the prank of all time.

"He's still not up," I mumble to myself, fishing out my phone and checking it for the two thousandth time.

After spending more time than I intended at the taco truck, Sebastian and I parted ways with a smile and a promise to meet for lunch to discuss scenes and strategy for the competition.

But by two o'clock, lunch had come and gone with no word from the shitty neighbor. I'm thinking he either had a change of heart or overslept at someone's house, because my trusty binoculars and I have yet to see him emerge from hell.

Breaking into his house would be like checking on him. And checking on him would be a business decision. Right? I mean, we have a deal and although no pillow or chair was exchanged last night, it doesn't mean we didn't shake on it.

Shaking on it is like law in my house. You don't go back on your word and if that's what Sebastian is doing then I'm going to steal way more than his pillow. Maybe I'll take those car keys of his and make him dig them out of *my* pocket.

Wait! His Jeep.

I rush out of my room and onto the front stoop. If Sebastian is home, his car would be here. And wouldn't you know it, there it is. All shiny and yellow, taking up two parking spaces.

I swear if he's pulling this stunt, claiming that he didn't sleep well without his pillow, then I am going to smother him with it.

I snatch my hoodie from the chair and slip it on, slamming the front door and finding myself at Sebastian's back door. It's locked, of course, so I pull out my trusty set of keys—aka my lock picking tools—and let myself in.

I'm sure I'll be sorry if I walk in on him and a lady friend, but

I'm willing to take the chance and witness someone slapping that stupid dimple on his face. "Honey, I'm home!" I yell, hoping if there is a girl in his bed, she'll realize he is a cheating scumbag. "Good news! I'm pregnant!" When no one screams and runs past me in tears, I close the door and pocket my lock pick set.

"Sebastian? Are you dead? Did someone finally murder your ass? I told you those jokes you make up are so not funny."

Nothing. Nada. Not even an argument that he is funny—which he isn't.

The living room is eh. It's not messy, but it's not necessarily picked up. There's a hoodie and a glass on the coffee table and one sock on the floor. Why just one? I have no idea, but it doesn't surprise me.

"Sebastian?" I call out. "Are you here?"

I could have missed him. It's possible he woke up earlier than me and went out. With Sebastian, there is no telling. He's irresponsible and sporadic.

A groan that sounds a lot like "Vee" comes from his bathroom.

I take a few hesitant steps down the hall. "You missed our lunch meeting, dickface. You better not be hungover." I am not nursing this man back to health. I came over here out of curiosity.

"Go away," he rasps out between groans.

I pause. "Why does it sound like you're dying? I do not want to perform CPR. Heaven only knows where your mouth has been."

"Agreed," he calls, sounding pitiful and seriously sick. "I'd rather die than have you save me."

At least we're in agreement.

"What's wrong with you anyway?" I'm at his bathroom door with my hand on the knob.

"Go away! It's your fault."

What? "How is this my fault?" I inhale, not waiting for him to answer and open the door. If he's naked, he's naked. We all have to have scars. Seeing Sebastian naked will just have to be mine.

"No!" His raspy voice stops me. There, on the bathroom tile, is a man who looks a lot like my asshole neighbor, but instead of a smug grin and tanned skin, he lays on the floor, sweaty and pale, with a grimace and a pair of boxers that cling to his ass like a second skin.

"Oh my gosh!" I rush to his side and drop to my knees, putting my hand to his forehead.

"Go away," he moans, trying to swat my hand away.

I roll my eyes and ignore his pitiful attempts to stop me. "You aren't running a fever."

He tries to push up from the floor but stops when he realizes he can't lift his own body weight.

"Tell me what's going on," I try again.

His head rolls to the side, and his red-tinged eyes stare up at me hatefully. "What's going on is that you had Juan poison my food."

I burst out laughing. "No, I didn't." This man is delirious. Funny, but delirious.

"You did." His eyes are hard. He really thinks I tried to poison him.

"Sebastian, I ate the same thing you did. You grabbed both plates, remember? You probably tried to poison me and switched our plates by accident." Honestly, that sounds like something Bash-hole would do. He has the attention span of a gnat.

He groans and rolls away from me. "Just let me die in peace."

I smother a laugh. "Since when have I ever let you do anything in peace?"

Please. He should know better.

He shivers, and his words come out broken. "Come on, Vee. Show a little mercy."

What does he think I'm going to do to him? Force him up and make him recite the alphabet backwards?

"I am showing you mercy, dick. Come on, sit up." Gah, here I am thinking I'm going to come over here and catch the douche in bed with another woman and end up helping the ass.

"Have you been able to keep anything down?" I pull him into a sitting position.

His head falls back onto my shoulder. "Nothing."

Eww. That's not good. I remember one time when I had this

virus, I ended up having to suck on ice chips just to get something into my stomach.

"You think you can shower?"

His chest rises with a sarcastic scoff. "Yeah, sure. I just slept in the bathroom all night because it was comfortable."

At least his sarcasm is still strong.

"You never know with you," I say, untangling myself from behind him, and stand. I reach for his hands. "Will you puke on me if I help you up?"

He gives me a flat look. "I haven't thrown up since around three this morning."

Good to know. "Come on." I shake my hands and after staring at them angrily, he finally takes them and lets me pull him up. It's not easy. I almost fall backwards, but I don't.

"Brace yourself against the cabinets," I tell him, before turning to the tub and seeing my chair. "What's the combination?"

His eyes harden. "No. Just leave it in the tub. It needs a good rinse."

And he needs a good punch in the dick.

"Sebastian."

"Valentina."

"I swear I will drown you in the toilet. Give me the combination."

We have a stare off for a few seconds but then he finally gives in. "22, 18, 24."

I turn the dial clockwise, then counterclockwise, before turning the final number clockwise and popping the lock. I don't get excited to finally have my chair free, even though I really, really want to. Instead, I lift it out of tub, only struggling a little before setting it down.

I turn back to the tub and twist the knob on the shower, feeling the spray until it warms. "Have you not showered since you stole my chair?" I ask him. What's it been? Like two days?

He makes a noise that sounds amused. "Of course I have. I take it out during the day, so I can pile dirty laundry on it. At night, it goes back to the time-out tub."

I should have had Juan poison him.

"Ha. Ha. You're hilarious. Take a shower and try not to drown. I don't want to have to cover your dick when I call 911." I shiver like the thought is disgusting.

He waves me off. "Glad you broke in to check on me," he says. "You can go home now and tell Juan your plot fell through."

I side-eye him and open the closet, grabbing a towel and setting it on the counter. "Get in the shower, Bash."

I go with Bash. Not Sebastian but Bash. The name I used to call him when we were friends. He swallows and stares at me for a beat but then pushes off the counter. "Are you going to watch me get naked?" he asks, pulling back the curtain and giving me a smirk that usually annoys the fuck out of me. But it doesn't today. I guess it's because I think he had to force it. If I didn't know any better, I would think he seemed almost shy. But we're both feeling a whole lot of awkward right now, so maybe that is it.

Friends don't let friends see their ding dongs.

I grin. "I'll spare my eyes, thank you."

I close the bathroom door behind me and let my head fall back onto the door.

Don't do this, Vee. He wouldn't do it for you. Would he?

I think Sebastian would have taken care of me—at least at one point in time. It's also what a girlfriend would do, even a fake one.

Ugh. This is such a bad idea.

I push off the door and head back through the living room and hall, leaving the front door unlocked while I dart across the greenspace between our houses. I grab my bookbag and a tote, filling it with crackers, Gatorade, and popsicles—all stuff Aspen and I raided from the guys' house the other day when we had forgotten to go to the store. Lastly, I snatch Sebastian's pillow that currently has a yellow pillowcase on it. Yes, I've slept on it while I'm holding it hostage. Sebastian is not wrong. I sleep great with it.

Hightailing it back to Sebastian's, I slip through the door and unload the groceries onto his counter. When I have everything put away, I snag a blanket from his hall closet and lay it on the sofa with his precious pillow.

"Sebastian?" I knock on the bathroom door. "You okay in there?"

The door opens before I can knock again. His hair is dripping wet and the towel I put out for him is around his waist. "I need pants."

I grin and step aside. "By all means, get pants."

He grunts out something I can't make out and brushes past me. I leave him in his room to dress and head back out to the kitchen. I pull a glass from the cabinet and fill it with ice and pour the Gatorade over top.

"Are you trying to finish off Juan's piss-poor job of poisoning me?"

I grin, not bothering to turn around quite yet. "Not today."

Sebastian approaches and I finally get a good look at him post shower. He looks rumpled and clean in a pair of plaid pajama pants and a white t-shirt that somehow manages to brighten up his pale coloring. He takes a seat at the island and lays his head on the bar top. He looks exhausted and plain pitiful.

My chest clenches. I might like to aggravate him, but I don't like seeing him miserable and in pain. "You want to try drinking something?"

He shakes his head, not bothering to lift it. "Not really."

I set the cup down and sigh. "What about a popsicle? Think you can suck on one of those?"

Slowly, that head of sandy blonde hair rises until I can see his grin. "What kind?"

I look at the ceiling, fighting my own grin. "Strawberry."

His face scrunches.

"Fine, I have lime, your favorite."

We've always fought over the lime popsicles. You can't find many in lime flavor, but when I did, this ass would eat them all.

"I'll take it."

Of course he will.

I open his freezer where I stashed the popsicles and pull out a green one, unwrap it, and hand it over. He gives it a once over and then pushes it between his lips. His real girlfriend would think it was a shame that he looks so hot eating a popsicle when he's sick as shit. His fake girlfriend would tend to agree with her.

"I brought your pillow back," I tell him, tipping my chin to the sofa. "But it's only a supervised visit. It goes back when I go back."

I'm not that nice. If he doesn't want to give me my chair, then he certainly isn't getting his pillow.

"How generous of you," he teases, getting up and heading to the couch. He doesn't even bother with the blanket. He just flops down, stomach first, and tucks his pillow under his head the best he can with one hand.

I bite my cheek. "Let me help you." I tug the blanket out from under him and lay it over his body. He makes a contented sound. "Eat the popsicle, Bash. You need some kind of fluids."

He brings the popsicle to his mouth and sucks, all the while watching me. "Were you using your binoculars this morning?"

And he's good now.

I fold my arms. "No. I was using my watch when you didn't show for lunch."

He nods and, this time, takes a small bite of the popsicle. "I haven't had one of these in forever." He moans.

And I know why. They remind him of me and that's something he tries hard not to do.

"You want to watch something or get some sleep?"

I set the remote next to him and he rolls over. "Are you leaving?"

I really should. "Umm…"

"Don't."

It's not a request or a demand. It's simply a plea that guts me straight to the core. "Okay."

I tip my chin to his room. "I'll go straighten up while you eat and rest." I make the sign of the cross on my chest. "I promise not to snoop, steal, or poison anything while I'm in there."

Sebastian grins but doesn't comment. His color is looking better and with his pillow back, he looks like a happy Bash-hole.

I walk off and proceed to straighten up his bathroom and change the sheets on his bed. Heaven only knows when the last time he changed those. When I'm finished, I turn and almost run into a hard body. "You scared me," I say, putting my hand to my chest.

"You watch too many scary movies."

I shake my head. "Not lately. Someone has my chair."

He nods to the bathroom. "You can use it while you're here. Consider it a thank you for hiring incompetent people to kill me."

I send him a glare that has no bite behind it. "How sweet of you," I lie.

He shrugs. "I try."

I notice the popsicle stick in his hand. "You want another one?"

He grimaces. "No, thank you."

"Are you still feeling nauseous?"

He wiggles his hand, the universal sign for "so-so."

I take the stick from him and motion to the bed. "Why don't you try sleeping some?"

He eyes the bed longingly and I know he wants to. "I'll come back later and check on you."

His cheek twitches. "Or you could stay and watch a movie in your chair?"

Ugh. The man makes a good point. "You don't think I will stab you in your sleep?"

He grins. "Nah, you only strike when it's dark."

His grin falls in an instant, and I know he's thinking about all those times I tried to prank him.

"I'll just go," I say. "You won't rest with me here."

Frankly, neither will I. I'll probably stare at him the whole time instead of my movie.

"Go get your stupid chair. You know you aren't leaving." He lumbers over to the bed and climbs in. I watch as he burrows down in his sheets, his eyes closing instantly.

For a man who is a whiny bitch about his pillow, he sure forgets it a lot.

I walk out to the living room and grab his drink and pillow, taking them back to the bedroom. I set the Gatorade on the bedside table and he stirs.

"Do you want your pillow?"

He nods, and I slide it under his head. "Try drinking just a sip of this Gatorade," I encourage, and when he doesn't shut me down, I grab the cup and ease it to his lips, but he stops me. "Don't."

"Don't what?"

He falls back onto the pillow. "Don't help me anymore. Don't remind me…"

He doesn't finish his statement. He doesn't need to. I know exactly what he doesn't want me to remind him of.

We've been in this situation before. Back when we were friends.

"Don't start. I'm not letting this kill you before I can." I know a little case of food poisoning won't kill him, but I had to say something to steer the conversation back into new friend territory.

That makes him crack a smile. "I knew you cared."

He's had to know I've always cared. That was the reason I blew the prank in the first place.

"Here." I push the glass into his hand and wrap his fingers around it. "You got it?"

He nods, the icy frost of his blue eyes watching me as I pull the blankets up to his chest before he stops me with his hand, his fingers stroking down my face. "How did I not know?" he mumbles to himself, while the back of his hand grazes my cheekbone, stopping just before my lips.

I swallow a couple times, but my voice doesn't make a sound.

Sebastian Carrington has always been the biggest pain in my ass, but he's the only one who's ever really known me. He may hate me for what I did to him, but he has to know we have history that no one can ever erase. We have something few people ever get to experience. No amount of time, hate, or separation will ever change that.

We'll be forever haunted with the memories of each other.

His eyes close, as if he forced them to stop staring at me. "Go watch your movie, Vee."

I nod and pull away, making my way to the bathroom as fast as I can. I drag my chair out into his bedroom and sit, pulling my knees up under me. It occurs to me that I don't have my iPad, and while I have my phone, it's just not the same. So I decide to sit quietly until

Sebastian falls asleep. Then I can go back to my house and check in on him later.

It's what we both need.

"You know where my iPad is," he says sleepily. "Use my login if you want to. You should still be able to remember all the passwords—you created them."

I fight the stupid flurries in my stomach. They have no place in there right now.

"Don't be stubborn, Valentina."

I chuckle and stand, going to the trunk that he uses to lock up his expensive shit at parties. I lift the heavy lid and there I find, not only his iPad, but the pajamas I gave him for his birthday.

"You kept them," I whisper.

He grunts. "They make for good packing material."

CHAPTER TEN
Sebastian

University CamFlix Competition Submission
Entry Number: 75
Sebastian and Valentina
Second Interview, or those three minutes that I was glad I applied extra deodorant

"Thanks for coming in, guys," Tom says, ushering us into his office. "We wanted to touch base with all of our competitors since the contest started."

I lean back on the plush sofa and tug Vee's tense ass down with me. "No problem. What can we answer for you today?" I hope it's not something that will send Vee off into a bitching fit. I can't take another one of those wonderful car rides home.

"I thought you could answer some fan questions. You two have garnered quite the fanbase so far."

I nod slowly, dreading what questions we might be tasked with answering. "Sure. Hit us with what you've got."

I knock my knee into Vee's and she knocks mine back harder than is necessary.

"Sarah from MyView asked, 'When did you know you loved Valentina?'"

I smile at the camera trained on Vee and me. "Hmm… Well, probably when she asked me for some Vaseline. Her thighs were chafed, you see—"

"I'm not doing that."

I nudge Valentina's hip with mine. After a nice nap with my pillow, I'm feeling much better. So much so that my energy has returned and I'm using every bit of it to convince Vee to do one of the popular MyView dances.

"Don't tell me you suck at dancing too?" I tease.

I guess it's possible that someone sucks at dancing and singing, but I'm thinking Vee's hesitation is more shyness than lack of moves. But that's just a guess. I could be totally wrong about her, like I have been many times before.

"I don't suck at dancing, thank you very much." Her lips purse and she sends me a glare that I'm pretty sure relays that I can eat shit. "I just think those dances are silly."

I tilt my head to the side, looking for the real reason she doesn't want to dance with me. "Is it because you feel bad that you paid your friend, Juan, to poison my food?" I shake my head and give her a quick pat on the back. "I told you, it's fine. I know you meant to. I'm just happy you had a change of heart and came over here to nurse me back to health."

I knew that last comment would get to her.

Her mouth drops open, and she finally faces me. "That's not at all what happened. First of all, I did not come over to nurse you back to health."

Didn't she?

"Second of all, I can't help it that you have a weak stomach and can't digest anything but your organic rice bars."

I belt out a laugh. "Why do you hate on my organic food? I can't help what's on sale at the grocery store."

I also can't help what my sister buys and shoves in my fridge. All I know is that I didn't have to go to the store, and, most days, I don't have to worry about not having anything to eat. Although, for the most part, I can't eat the majority of it, but I would never tell my sister that. It makes her feel better knowing she's taking care of me, so I let her do what she wants.

"I'm not hating on your food," she finally says. "I just…"

"You just what? Thought I didn't eat because I'm a demon?"

She narrows her eyes. "I know you eat, dummy. I used to eat with you, remember?"

I feel myself tense. We're creeping into the no-go zone again.

"I'm just saying it doesn't fit with your personality."

"Maybe that's because you don't know everything about me like you think you do." I push up from the sofa. "I think I'll go lie down again and spend the last few minutes with my pillow before you leave."

I think we've had enough time together. Any more and we're liable to start full-out arguing for the rest of the day.

"Sebastian," she says, exasperated. "Come back."

She's always been the one to feel guilty when she acts shitty. It's a terrible trait to have.

"I'm good. We'll reschedule our strategy meeting for tomorrow."

I just want her to go—far, far away. At least until tomorrow.

With an exasperated sigh, she mumbles something I can't quite catch.

"Did you say something?" I prod.

Her mouth purses and she gives me a flat look. "I said, fine. I'll do that stupid dance with you."

Valentina's guilt is a dangerous tool to use against her, but since I love to see her uncomfortable, I'm going to use it for my own selfish desires. Consider it payback for ordering the salmonella fish tacos. I push off the doorframe and shrug. "If you must. I think I can muster up enough energy for one dance."

She rolls her eyes, and it sends a stupid amount of excitement through me.

I hope she sucks. I hope she has the rhythm of a newborn.

Fishing my phone from my pocket, I nod to her. "Go get my tripod." I act like I know where she hid it, but in full disclosure, I've yet to find the damn thing. This way, I'll get both things I want from Valentina.

She grumbles to herself but gets up and pushes past me to head to my room. I follow her and see her get on her knees. My dick twitches, and I cough. "Hurry," I tell her, "I'm getting tired." And hard. The last thing I need to explain to my enemy is that seeing her kneel at the side of my bed makes my dick a throbbing missile in my pants.

"Would you shut up and just go sit down? If you didn't hoard all those old movie mementos under your bed, I wouldn't have to pull a muscle trying to get the tripod out."

"Who hid the tripod under the bed?" I argue. "Lay off my memorabilia. One day it will hang in my studio office."

Ugh. I cringe as soon as I say it. Those words were what the old Sebastian would say to the old Valentina.

"It's still a bunch of shit to comb through in the meantime. No wonder you need an entire townhouse to yourself. You have way too much shit."

And a guilty sister with a doctor husband. She wanted a place she could check up on me and traipsing through the dorms was where she drew the line.

"I keep hearing a lot of talking but no tripod," I chide. "I'll meet you in the living room when you finally manage to retrieve it."

Really, I just want to get out of here since she's slid partly under the bed, and her ass is sticking up and although it's partially covered by her hoodie, I can still see the curve of her cheek, peeking out from underneath the fray of her jean shorts.

Yes, another room is good. And cold water. And visions of grandma.

"Thank goodness," she returns, her voice muffled from under the bed. "You're getting on my nerves."

Ditto.

I turn from the door, leaving Valentina in her search for my shit and flop down on the couch, staring up at the ceiling. My dick is calmer without her ass all perky in front of us, but he's longing for another peek, even though we both know it would be terrible for our sanity. Her pretending to be my girlfriend for eight weeks will fuck me up. Looking at her ass for longer than necessary might irrevocably damage the desire to ever look at another ass that isn't hers.

It's best my dick and I stay put right out here.

"Found it!" she hollers from the bedroom.

I grin. She hid the damn thing pretty well. I would have never found it on my own.

"'Bout time!"

"Shut up. Why do you always have to be such a dick?" Her voice is close, and I jerk my head to the side and see her standing right above me.

"What are you? A ninja? Make noise and whine like most girls," I say, glaring at my dusty tripod in her hand.

"I think you do enough whining for the both of us," she pops back, blowing a dust ball off the tripod before extending the legs and setting it up. "Where do you want to do this lame dance?"

This is why I'm going to hell.

"On the back patio." I grin.

"No." Her voice is firm, and I knew that would be her response. In fact, I was counting on it.

I sigh, running my hand through my hair. It's mussed because I was too busy keeping myself upright in the shower to give a fuck about combing it when I got out. "We'll just have to do it in my bedroom." Where I wanted all along.

"Why?" Her voice raises, making my dick hard again. "Why can't we do it right here in the living room?"

I stand and adjust my crotch. "Because I don't have a full-length mirror in here and I need to see what I'm doing." I give her body a cursory glance. "I can't post a video when we aren't in sync."

Frankly, I just want to watch her.

"I also think it'd be a perfect video to post showcasing our new relationship." I flash her a smirk that I know gets on her nerves. "Don't you think?"

I have zero ideas about how this plan of mine is supposed to work. All I know is that our fans go crazy when they see us together. So while there were only rumors of us from the party, I solidified them last night after Vee and I had Juan take a picture of us sitting together under the Edison lights in the parking lot, sharing a romantic (insert eye roll here) dinner in the parking lot before the salmonella kicked in.

Afterward, Vee came over and we drank a little moonshine until we were both tipsy enough to edit the picture and post it. As you can imagine, the photo went viral, and when I woke up this morning, I had several emails regarding potential new ads and sponsorships on my page.

So, while I might not have a plan for how to go about winning this contest, I do know that the 'non-plan' is working. Vee and I are dominating the internet again. And although the picture we posted was not part of the contest, it ramped up our followers so that when we do post our entry as a team, we'll bring both of our fan bases along with us and kick Malcolm's ass out of the running.

Vee looks up to the ceiling, something she does when she's thinking. "Yeah, you're right."

My stomach dips. "Did you just say—"

She doesn't let me finish. "Shut up and do not say another word." She shakes her head. "What I'm saying is that I agree that keeping our fanbases happy will not only increase the believability of us as a couple, but it would also help our numbers when we post our entry video."

See? I told you I was right. If your fans love you as a couple, they will support anything you do, and if we have a bad 'breakup' then, hopefully, they pick sides and stay with me to nurse my 'broken heart.'

But instead of offering Vee a high five for thinking as brilliantly as I do, I shrug like there's a small possibility that she's onto something. "Probably. We won't know for sure until we try."

It'll work; I have zero doubts at this point. Taking pictures and picking at each other comes naturally to us. It's the kissing and cuddling part we'll have to work the hardest at.

I clap my hands together. "Alright, let's move this little disaster to my bedroom."

I jump up with a lot more pep in my step than earlier. My plan is finally coming together. "Are you coming?" I ask, brushing past Vee.

She eyes me for just a second, staring.

"What?" I look down at my clothes. "Is there something on my face?"

When she doesn't answer, I add, "Do you need a drink to get through one dance with me?"

I meant it as a joke, but my stomach churns (probably from the salmonella) waiting for her response.

Finally, she shakes her head and grabs the tripod. "No, I'm fine. Come on."

A little anticlimactic but whatever, she didn't leave or slap me, so I'm calling that a win.

Nodding, I lead the way to my room where the bed has clean sheets, thanks to Vee and her guilt and, sometimes, sweet heart. I move her chair away from the mirror where she had watched her dumbass horror movie. In my dreams people were screaming, but it wasn't because they were dying.

Vee side-eyes me and frowns.

"You got to sit in it for two hours," I say. "Don't act like you're already going through withdrawals."

She doesn't answer me; instead, she flips me off and begins setting up the tripod. I take the few minutes to re-watch the videos that show the dance steps, so I'm not the one fumbling around while we try this.

"I think I should be in pajamas when we do this," she randomly says.

"Okay." I shrug. "Doesn't matter to me what you wear."

She hangs her head and pauses her adjustments to the camera. "I'm just saying if I wear one of your shirts or some of *your* pajamas, it'll look like I spent the night with you."

Oh.

Oh.

"Uhhhh. Okay. Sure."

My mind has literally been stunned into only producing simple words. She needs to wear my shirt or my pajamas. This is a big step for me. One, I don't let women sleep over and two, I never give them a memento to take home with them. They come in with clothes; they can certainly leave with them. The last thing I want to do is buy a bunch of nice shit that walks out with my one-nighters. I'd be a broke man. And besides, I haven't had a woman even see the inside of my bedroom since Vee's conniving ass dropped that prank on me two months ago.

"I know it's weird, considering—" she motions between us, "—our history, but you can give me something old and burn it after I take it off. Just a t-shirt will be fine. It should cover most of my legs."

This is not going down at all like I planned. Is it too much to ask for a win today? All I wanted was to see Vee's shitty dance moves and make her feel just an ounce of the awkwardness that I've felt since she's been here taking care of me. Which is her fault since she just had to have Juan's toilet bowl tacos.

I rake a hand through my hair. "I don't think a t-shirt will work," I muse, my hand moving to my lips, worrying the bottom one while she's bent over the tripod, finding the best angle.

"It'll be fine," she says, dismissing my concerns without so much as a glance. "I'll keep my shorts on."

That still won't help. My dick agrees. When a man sees a woman in his clothes, it sparks this sort of territorial feeling. Now, I don't know this personally, since I refuse to try it, but recently Maverick did, and he said the saying is unequivocally true. I'm not for feeling territorial and all alpha crazy over a female, especially Vee, the frog saving, horror movie junkie with the mouth of a teenage boy.

"Do you not have a t-shirt under your hoodie?"

Vee lifts her head slowly and catches my gaze in the mirror. "It's not long enough. Do you want me to wear underwear and a shirt that hits at my hips in the video or your t-shirt?"

An evil grin pulls onto her face, and she adds, "Or I can go back to my place and pull out my flannel pajamas."

My lip curls.

"I'm sure your fans would be shocked to see your girlfriend all decked out in her winter wear alongside her boo in his flannel bottoms."

She's hilarious but knows me well.

"Fine," I nearly growl out. "I'll find you something."

Without waiting to see her grin in victory, I stalk over to my dresser and start rummaging through the drawers. I find several shirts I think would match my clothes, but with each one, I find a reason for her not to wear it. I like it. I don't want to burn it. She might look too good in this one. You know, the basics.

Finally, in the drawer I never use. The one with the sweaters my mom sends for Christmas, and the stupid pajama sets my sister makes us take pictures in, I pull out a flannel top. One that belongs to the pants I'm currently wearing. I've only worn it once in a stupid Christmas card photo that I refuse to look at, but, for some reason, I've never thrown it out.

Considering Vee loves flannel, it'll be perfect. I won't mind tossing it when she's finished. And besides, flannel will kill any boner I might get by seeing her in it.

"Here." I toss her the shirt, and she catches it in midair.

"You want your 'girlfriend' to wear a flannel shirt in a video?"

I shrug. "It matches my pants. It'll look totally 'Gram worthy.'"

I don't add that the baggy flannel will also make me and my dick less likely to poke her in the back. I feel like she might not take that comment well.

"Okay. Can you finish setting up while I change?"

I groan just thinking about her changing in my bathroom.

"Are you feeling sick again?" she asks, and dammit if her concern doesn't make my stomach feel weird.

"I'll be fine," I lie.

No need to tell her the truth. She'll think I'm being a typical horny dude, and I am, but it's different when it comes to Valentina. Our history complicates things, and it's not a territory I want to inch back into. That ship of ours has sunk to the bottom of the ocean where pirates and a Megalodon shark have ravaged it into nothing but pieces. We're incapable of being put back together.

"Okay." Vee gives me one more once over before she heads into the bathroom and closes the door. When I hear the lock click in place, I finally take a breath.

Why does this girl make everything around me so damn complicated? Even breathing seems hard when she's near.

My phone buzzes in my hand. It's been going off all morning and, just like the last fifteen times, I send it to voicemail. I have been busy dying, so I haven't had the strength to deal with my mom or my sister. They are just going to have to give me a fucking second to call them back and chat for an hour about when I can come home and visit them.

I don't like visiting my parents. At all. My sister, I see more often, but that's because she forces herself into my life and, since she pays for my house, she also will pay for a locksmith to let her in if I 'pretend' I'm not here. She's pretty relentless when she wants to be.

"Sebastian?"

"Yeah," I return through the door.

"Will you bring me my bookbag?" Her voice sounds close to the door, as if she's speaking through the crack. "It's by the door."

"Why?" I return. What the hell does she need from her bag in order to change her shirt?

"Sebastian!"

"Fine." Whatever. I lumber into the living room and down the hall to the foyer and see her bag on the floor. It has a dog hair on the front, so I dust it off and take it to the bathroom. "Here," I say, "Open the door so I can hand it to you."

She does and mutters a quick, "thanks," before snatching it out of my hand and closing the door in my face. When she re-locks the door, I mutter, "Okay."

Women are the strangest creatures. I've never understood them and I doubt I'll ever truly figure them out completely.

I plop down in Vee's chair. It's surprisingly comfortable. It might look like it's in need of a new home in a good dumpster, but it does have this comforting quality about it. I sit back and rest my head against the wicker. I feel tired but not tired enough to sleep more. Luckily, I will perk up with new energy as soon as Vee does whatever the fuck she's doing and comes out of the bathroom. Watching her dance, albeit in my shirt, should be very entertaining.

My phone buzzes once. It's a text and not a call. I texted Maverick earlier today and he never responded. I swipe the screen and see the text is not from Maverick, but from my sister. Again.

Mom #2: Do you want me to leave the Hamptons to come kick your ass? Answer your phone.

I grin. My sister might live in this fancy house and vacation in the Hamptons but uppity, she will never be.

Me: Don't feel good. I'm alive though so let me watch porn in peace and heal.

Her response is nearly instantaneous.

Mom #2: I'm calling you and you better fucking answer.

Ugh. See? This is why I can't tell her shit. She's worse than our mom. My phone rings a few seconds later and I know I can't ignore it. I answer with a loud sigh, so she knows I'm not in the mood to have this chat.

"Do you think I give a shit that you don't want to talk to me, little boy?"

I grin. "Oh, I'm well aware that you don't care that you're disrupting my college sinning."

She ignores the sinning comment and gets to the point. "What's wrong? Why are you sick?"

"Uh…" I chuckle. "Because apart from what most women say, gods can fall to mortal illness every now and again."

I love giving my sister a hard time. It makes it easier to deal with her guilt too.

"Shut up. Tell me what's going on."

There's no point in lying. She really will come down here and see for herself. "Bad fish tacos last night," I tell her. "But I'm fine and before you ask, I'm hydrated and I'm not running a fever. Looks like I'll make it another day to worry you."

She's quiet for a moment and I worry that I might have upset her. "Cal?"

"I'm here." She exhales a breath and then, "Bash, are you sure you're okay? I'm worried about you."

I fight the urge to pop off with something shitty. This is my sister and no matter how much she gets on my nerves, I know it comes from a good place.

"I'm fine, I promise. You have nothing to worry about."

She isn't talking about today. Calista knows I want to leave Georgia like yesterday, but I think now that I'm getting closer to leaving, she worries I might actually follow through with it. Then she won't be able to force her quality time on me like she does once a month. I'm not saying I don't love my family but like everything in my life, it's complicated.

"Okay," she responds, sounding unsure. "If you promise. Do you need me to send you some Gatorade or electrolyte drinks?"

I laugh. "No. I'm capable of going to the store." And Vee already brought some, but even if she hadn't, I wouldn't go to the store. Maverick's apartment is closer and cheaper.

"Okay. Well, I'll stop by next week when I get back, okay? I'll bring Emmy too. She's been asking about you."

Emmy is my one and only niece. She's much cooler than my sister, so I don't mind hanging out with her.

"Sounds good," I return. "Tell her I want a rematch in cup pong."

We play online, and for a seven-year-old, she's much better at it than I am.

"Okay. Love you."

"I love you, too."

When we've finally hung up, I'm tense and ready to alleviate some tension by torturing the neighbor.

"Vee! You better not be stealing anything!"

I pound on the door until I hear, "Fuck you."

CHAPTER ELEVEN
Sebastian

University CamFlix Competition Submission
Entry Number: 75
Sebastian and Valentina
Second Interview Continued, also known as that time I genuinely smiled

"Her thighs were chafed?" Tom looks shocked as I pry Vee's hand from my mouth.

"Yeah, we'd been running and it was hot—"

"Shut up, Sebastian. I swear to God I will smack you on camera."

I grin. "There's nothing to be ashamed of, sweetie. It was a hot day and those baggy pants you had on were not the best at wicking away the moisture."

I can see the redness spread across her cheeks. I shouldn't fuck with her like this, because she won't hesitate to return the favor and share one of my embarrassing stories, but I can't help myself. "All I'm saying is I knew I loved her when she wasn't embarrassed to tell me she needed a hot shower and a big tub of Vaseline."

I've grown a beard in the amount of time I wait for Vee to *not* open the door.

"Valentina!"

I bang on the door with my fist. "Do I need to call the crisis hotline?"

I might have struggled coughing up a shirt for her to wear, but it looks like she's struggling to actually wear said shirt.

"I'll be out in a minute!" she yells back.

"You said that half an hour ago. It's going to be dark by the time you come out of there."

Is it sad that I've sat here by the door, waiting? Why didn't I watch TV or at least scroll through MyView? Maybe it's because I didn't think I would be waiting a million and eight years.

I raise my hand to bang on the door again when the lock flips.

I try the handle and it turns.

"I'm feeling like this might be a trap," I say, easing the door open. "Those shitty horror movies you watch usually start with some idiot checking out a room."

I shove the door all the way open and find Vee sitting on top of my counter amongst a plethora of makeup. "Did Cover Girl take a shit on my counter?" I can feel my eyes widening as I take in all the containers and tubes.

Vee makes a scoffing noise and rolls her eyes. "Do women really like that crass mouth of yours?"

A muscle in my cheek twitches. "They do, actually." I push off the door frame and take a step forward, invading her space and forcing her legs apart. "As a matter of fact, the crasser I get—"

She slaps her hand over my mouth. "It was a rhetorical question. I did not mean for you to think I really cared."

It's cute when she tries to act unaffected, but the faint blush on her cheeks is not from the makeup.

Deciding not to push my luck, I change the subject, nodding to the two tubes of lipstick in her hand. "Can't decide which color to wear with your outfit?"

I have an older sister; I know what a—insert sarcasm— 'struggle' this can be.

Vee looks down at her hands and then back at me. "Actually, I can't decide what color would look best with *your* outfit."

"Come again?" I take a step back, but her legs lock around my waist and pull me forward until my hips hit the counter. "I'm not following." And if I'm being honest, I'm a little nervous with the way she's chewing on her lip. "I don't see how my outfit has anything to do with your choice of lipstick shades."

Her gaze drifts to my chest.

"You're making me nervous," I ramble, checking for a camera she might have set up somewhere. "We have a truce," I remind her.

That finally snaps her out of it. "You're so paranoid." She shakes her head like this surprises her.

"I can't imagine why," I add with a glare.

The girl who fucked me up so badly that I haven't been able to date since 'the incident' lets out a long sigh. "It's not a trick. Can you just trust me?"

I want to be a shit and say no. I don't trust her. But deep down—very, very deep down—my gut tells me I can trust her. She might have tricked me for months, but she didn't do anything with the information. She didn't expose me like she could have. I exhale and roll my shoulders back, looking to the ceiling. I don't want to make eye contact with her. "I trust you." Sometimes. Occasionally. When I've had enough alcohol to make me forget everything. "I trust you more often than not." There, that's more truthful.

I lower my head and see her pained smile. "I deserve that."

She does. I'm not even going to lie and say she doesn't. But she only deserves it this one time. I'm man enough to give second chances.

"It's the last time I'll bring it up," I promise. "I said we could start over and I meant it."

I hold my hand out for her to shake. She switches the lipstick tubes into her other hand and we shake on it.

"To a do-over. For real this time," she promises, and for some reason, it really does feel like a do-over. This isn't a fake shake-my-hand-because-I'll-say-anything-to-get-you-to-agree-to-my-terms-so-I-can-win-this-money. This is a real handshake—a real promise.

"For real this time," I agree.

We lock gazes for a moment before Vee breaks it with, "Okay. Since you're back on the trust wagon, can I show you what I mean about the lipstick decision? I sort of need your help anyway. If I keep us too much longer, we'll lose the good light."

I promised a do-over. I promised I would trust her.

"I'm listening."

My stomach does this weird thing like I'm hungry.

"Okay," Vee says softly, bringing my attention back to her and not my empty stomach. "If you insist on wearing that shirt—"

"What's wrong with my shirt?" I pull the bottom of my shirt out, so I can see it better. "Is it wrinkled or something?"

The corner of Vee's mouth crinkles. "No, no it's not wrinkled. It's just—"

She looks up at the ceiling for just a moment. It tends to be our go-to move when things get awkward. "Let me show you," she finally says, scooting closer, the warm core of her body pushing into the front of my pajama pants.

I want to step back. Wait, no. That's a lie. I don't want to do anything of the sort, but I feel like that's the gentlemanly thing to do.

But what the fuck am I thinking? I'm no gentleman.

Vee pops off the lid to one of the lipsticks and, with a shaky hand, applies it blindly to her lips.

"Impressive," I muse, trying and failing not to stare at the fullness of her lips. They are more than impressive. I know. I felt them once and all hell broke loose afterward.

She presses her lips together, and I mask a groan with something like a growl. "I'm getting a cramp. Can we hurry this along?"

So, so shitty, Sebastian.

But my dick… fuck. My dick doesn't give two shits about what happened between me and Valentina Lambros. He wants to feel those lips again. He wants them around us like a tight, wet vise— "What are you doing?"

I startle back when her hand wraps around the back of my neck. Surely I didn't say all those things about my dick out loud? Did I? That would be weird and—

"I thought you said you trusted me?" Her grip is firm, and, I'll admit, I'm so hard I could be the guy who pops the holes in dough-nuts. I know. That's not a real job, but it should be.

I swallow all the teenage-like nerves and let the cool camera-ready Bash slide over my expression. "Do your worst."

I don't mean it though. Her worst could be my demise.

Valentina shakes her head like she knows I'm full of an epic amount of shit, but she pulls me closer until her lips are on my neck and her breath is warm against my jaw. "Be still," she whispers.

My balls ache and my dick is rabid. I don't nod—I'm afraid to move any closer to her face. Instead, I grunt out a word that doesn't exist in the English language. Vee doesn't stop to question it or even poke fun. I think she, too, is worried about accidentally letting my dick poke her center.

I should step back.

She should toss the lipstick back on the counter.

But we're not quitters.

In the mirror, I watch as my nemesis slides the collar of my shirt to the side.

"Ah, fuck."

Her lips press down on my neck, just below my jaw. My heart is pounding. My stomach is doing that ridiculous tingling thing again and now my dick is on the verge of leaking jizz.

The asshole part of me wants to ask her just what the fuck she's doing, but when she leans back, her hand goes to my jaw and all thoughts of saying anything are smothered by pure lust.

"See," she says, trailing a finger down my jaw, just like I did to her the night we became mortal enemies. "If I go with the wrong shade, it won't show up well on camera."

Her thumb swipes through the perfect outline of her lips,

smearing it down the side of my neck before looking up and meeting my eyes. "It's not enough just to have a smear. The mark has to pop on the screen."

I have no idea what the fuck she's talking about. All I care about is the fact that she's now applying the other shade of lipstick to her lips.

"You have to do it again?" My voice sounds pained and hopeful, at the same time. I'm a fucking mess. My body yearns for this girl, but my mind is like, "Eh. Slow down, champ. This is the chick we hate, right?"

"I need to decide," she says, already pulling me close with her hand around the back of my neck. "You promised to help me."

Did I? Did I promise to help her or to trust her? God, who the fuck cares Sebastian? This is the first time you've had anyone this close to your mouth in months. Chill the fuck out and enjoy kissing the enemy. Well, not kissing, but you know.

"I did," I admit softly, swallowing down a golf-ball sized knot in my throat. My head is guided to the side and her fingers slide under my collar, once again, before her lips touch the heated skin of my neck.

It feels like she lingers there for a solid half-hour, but I know, in reality, it's probably only a matter of seconds. "See the difference?" she asks quietly, pulling back and letting her finger drag through the mark.

I don't see.

In fact, I think I'm blinded by lust.

"Sebastian?"

I shake off the feelings of wanting to ravage the girl in front of me. It's a challenge. It wouldn't take much for me to shove her back onto the sink, yank both our pants down in seconds and fuck all the hate out of our systems in one blessed go. Maybe then we would really be able to start over.

"Sebastian?"

She shakes my shoulders and my brain finally sends a signal to my dick to calm the hell down.

"Yeah."

It's not a great answer, but it's something.

"See?"

My patience is gone or maybe I'm so damn sexually frustrated that all I want to do is beat the hell out of something.

"Yeah, I see," I lie, removing her legs from around my waist and stepping back. "The one on the right looks better against my shirt—" Okay, so after a few seconds, I see what she means, but it was a painful test, "—which I'm not wearing."

In a dick move that will forever haunt me, I yank off the shirt and use it to wipe both marks off and toss it to the floor. "I'm not in the mood to do this anymore."

I thought I could, but I was so fucking wrong.

"You *will* fucking do this," she says, grabbing my arm. "We made a deal and you're not going to let your PMS get in the way of our success. Tuck your bitchiness away and let's do this dance that you just *had* to do with me."

Her bossing me around is less than ideal, but for some reason, my dick digs the attitude.

I clench my jaw, trying like hell not to break my teeth. "Fine." I yank her down and pull her behind me. I don't care if she's been nice and cleaned up my house or that she's taken care of me all day. All I can think is that her Good Samaritan time is up. She needs to be gone, only to return when I've calmed the fuck down.

I pull us in front of the mirror. The hem of my shirt hangs just past the curve of Vee's ass. It's painful to look at.

"Do you need to watch the dance?" I ask her, pressing play and holding my phone out in front of her. I know she needs to watch it. I can't imagine Valentina knowing any of the trendy dances. She might be popular on MyView, but it isn't because she spends her time learning all the trendy dances. She probably only knows the "Thriller" dance, given her specific viewing tastes.

"Yeah. Can you play it once more?"

I don't want to. Not because I don't want her to learn it but because I'm uncomfortable from standing so far back. Apparently, the flannel is sexier than I thought it would be. The last thing I need is for Valentina to see this raging boner tucked into my pants.

I let the video play a couple of times and ignore her hand over mine when she pulls my phone closer for another look.

"I think I have it now," she says.

Thank fuck.

Clearing my throat, I tip my chin and step back. I secure my phone into the tripod and motion for her to come over. "See if it's good."

Vee walks over and avoids my eyes, which is good, because my shirt on her is distracting the fuck out of me.

"It's good," she says, after a moment of looking through the additional lens I use on my phone. "I think all we need is a little more light."

I'm certainly not going to object, considering I still look a little peaked, and she looks a lot fuckable.

I flip the switch on the wall, and Vee looks through the lens once more. "Perfect."

Yeah, a little too perfect. "Should we do a couple of test shots?"

I nod. Any MyViewer worth their popularity knows you always do test shots. Apart from what viewers might think, nothing is on the fly. Everything is scripted and staged.

Vee presses record and rushes to the mirror to stand in front of me before the music starts. The beat is slow and hypnotic with this Latin feel that Vee's hips naturally find the groove to. Her arms go up over her head as her hips sway against my front, my dick hardening with each motion. My shirt rises up her thighs and stops dangerously close to her pussy.

"Why aren't you dancing?"

I shake off the haze and meet her gaze in the mirror.

"I was giving you time to practice," I lie.

Those honey brown eyes of hers narrow into slits. "How considerate of you. Now go restart the video. I don't want to be here all day."

But she already has been, hasn't she?

"You think I'm enjoying this?" I spit, rounding the tripod and resetting the video. "I had shit to do too."

Vee scoffs. "Please, I know what you do on the first weekend of every quarter, Sebastian. It literally takes you all of an hour."

When the video is reset, I stand up and glare over the top of the camera. "Don't act like you know me, Valentina." I say her name for the simple fact that she said mine like she had some kind of dirt on me. "A lot changes in two months."

She shrugs. "Maybe. But I bet you still do it regularly."

I roll my eyes. She isn't wrong but that doesn't mean I will admit she actually knows one of the few secrets I keep all to myself.

"Let's do this shit for real," I say, coming to stand behind her. "You've worn out your welcome."

Her lips flatten. "Agreed. Let's get this over with so I can go home and scald myself in hot water."

Ditto but I'll start with a cold shower first.

The music starts again and when Vee's arms go up above her head, mine meet them and trail down the length of her body until they stop at her hips. My gaze meets hers in the mirror. We're rumpled and sexy as our hips move in sync with each other. My head lowers to her neck, and I nip the soft skin there, amping up the thrill for our fans. My hands inch Valentina's shirt up just far enough that you can see the milky soft skin of her upper thighs.

My dick loses all restraint and digs into her back as the tempo picks up and her arm goes around my neck. She flashes the camera a sleepy, mischievous grin that indicates that this dance is only a precursor to what happens next. She's a natural, flirting with the camera, and all I can think is the man behind her looks as if he's in pain and in love at the same time.

The music stops and I take a step back, knocking the tripod over. Right now, I could throw my phone and the attached tripod out the window and not give a single fuck, just as long as Valentina leaves with it.

"Fun's over. You weren't half bad, bro."

Calling her bro feels better than calling her Valentina. It changes the dynamics of the room, reminding me that we are enemies and not a real couple.

"Agreed," she says, heading into the bathroom. "I'll text you."

I nod, the hurt and angry asshole in me coming out and putting her back into the enemy bucket where she belongs. "Don't forget to take my pillow because you're not getting your fucking chair back."

CHAPTER TWELVE
Sebastian

University CamFlix Competition Submission
Entry Number: 75
Sebastian and Valentina
Second Interview Continued, also the time Vee couldn't
keep a fucking secret

"Wow. Okay. Interesting story." Tom looks to Vee. "How about you, Valentina? When did you know you loved Sebastian?"

I can see the evil grin stretch across Vee's face. "Well, Tom. I think I knew he was the man of my dreams when he was shit-faced drunk, and I had to drag him to the car after he puked on the courthouse lawn."

Tom's brows raise. "The courthouse? Why the courthouse?"

Vee shrugs, and I groan. I know where this dreaded story is going. "You see, Tom. We had been at a party, and well, Sebastian, here, had wanted to see the stars and he insisted you could see them best on the courthouse lawn in the square."

I interrupt. "I was really, really drunk. I wasn't making any sense and I find it hard to believe that I gave a shit about some stars."

"Oh but you did, honey. In fact, you told me when you were a little boy you would lay out in your yard, in awe, because that same star could be seen from all over the world."

I've been up since five and jerked off twice in the shower before I decided that I needed something more physical to burn off the tension raging through my veins. Instead of going to the gym and reminiscing about the times Vee and I worked out together, I headed to the hardware store. A few hundred bucks later, I'm shirtless and sweating from the eighty-five-degree weather, but my grass is starting to look somewhat kept.

"And I thought the only thing you knew how to run was your mouth."

I'd know that snark anywhere, even yelling over the motor of a lawnmower. I flip the switch and turn slowly, eyeing my neighbor who's back in her own flannel shirt with a tight tank top underneath. Her shorts are high on her thighs and her boots look like they could use replacing.

"You're trespassing," I tell her, making sure I give her a look of boredom.

"And you're an asshole, but let's not get technical." She shrugs. "I'm just stopping by to let you know that I won't be able to meet for lunch. I have a thing."

After the awfulness of the dance, Vee left, and we didn't speak again until around midnight, two hours after I posted the video of us dancing and the thousands of comments that came in. The competitor in me kicked in, and I decided that with enough jerking off,

I could handle being Vee's fake boyfriend. At least until the contest was over. So I texted her.

Me: Lunch? Strategy? I promise to take my Midol.

She made me sweat for a couple of hours, but she eventually texted back.

Pretend To Like Her: Fine. You pick the place, Princess. I'd hate for us to spend it in the bathroom again.

I didn't respond.

"What 'thing' do you have to do that would be more important than strategizing?" I try to keep the frustration and curiosity out of my voice.

She smirks. "Now, now. This isn't how this game is played anymore." She turns, intent on leaving me with the same comment I once said to her when she inquired what I was doing.

I grab her by the elbow and haul her into my sweaty chest. "Where the fuck do you think you're going? You better not be going on some 'save the tree frogs and their plastic ecosystems' expedition with fucking Vance. We had an agreement."

She pushes her palm against my chest and frowns. "Slow down, Major Douche. I'm just going to work. You know those places where broke people go to earn money?"

I narrow my eyes. "I know what a job is. The question is, why are you working? Don't you make enough in sponsorships?"

I know I do. Seems like she would too.

"I do, but believe it or not, sometimes I like helping more than just tree frogs."

I narrow my eyes, and she sighs. "I work with rescue dogs."

"Dogs?" How did I not know she had a job before now? "You work at the pound or something?"

She hitches her bag up her shoulder. "No, not the pound. It's a rescue shelter for military dogs that have lost their owners. Some don't adjust without their owners and fall into a depression. My uncle runs it."

She rolls her eyes. "When I get back, maybe you can pop another Midol, and we can talk strategy on the phone."

I'm not so sure about that. Talking to her is worse than seeing her. Hell, everything that deals with Valentina sucks.

"What kind of dogs are they?"

I've always wanted a dog, but due to my sister's condition, the only time I ever got to pet one was when they would bring the therapy dogs, so she could pet them. My mom said she couldn't take care of me, my sister, and a puppy too.

"Different kinds. Mostly German Shepherds but there are few others. Why?" Vee is suspicious and rightfully so.

I shrug and put my hands in my pockets. "I'm just thinking maybe it would be cool if we did a shot of you and the dogs. Everyone loves dogs, right?" It's true. "Animal videos go viral just as much as human ones. Who's to say that we wouldn't knock it out of the park with a dog video?"

"These aren't puppies."

"I know that," I argue, "but they are rescues, which is even better. Who doesn't like a couple doing charitable work with dogs?"

What could go wrong? Famous last words.

"So, what do you think? Want to try a video there? If it's terrible, we don't have to use it, and besides, it'll be good publicity for your uncle's charity, right?"

Vee still doesn't look convinced, but I can tell she's going to say yes. Even if she would like to junk punch me, she won't, because, like me, she wants to win.

"I'll call Brick. He can meet us there," I say, pushing my new mower onto the patio because I have no idea what I'll do with it until next week.

"Us?" Her voice is amused. "We aren't riding together."

I open the back door and nod for her to follow. "Why not? Aren't you all about conserving fuel and shit?"

Her head tips to the sky, and she exhales loudly.

"I need five minutes to shower," I promise. "You can have a popsicle while you wait."

The last bit gets her, and she drops her head and follows me in.

The shelter Vee works at is a small outfit deep in the country. All rolling hills and wheat fields. "You make this drive every day?" I ask her.

"Not every day. Just a few days a week. My uncle doesn't want me too distracted from my studies and sometimes I think he just likes being out here by himself with the dogs."

"Oh," I mumble. "Was he like your dad?"

I know she told me her father was once homeless and Aspen and Fenn's mom helped him out.

"Yeah," she says, but I can tell she doesn't want to say much. "He's better now, though."

I nod. I'm not one to pry, even though her family history intrigues me.

The driveway is gravel and about a mile long when we pull in. It's quaint and doesn't look like a shelter at all. "Wait," I say, throwing my Jeep in park. "Is this where your uncle lives too?"

She opens her door and gets out. "Yeah. He keeps the dogs here."

Oh. Okay. Well, that changes things.

"Why do you look like you're about to be sick?"

I roll my eyes. "I'm not about to be sick. I just didn't realize your uncle would be here. You just said he owned it."

Her brows furrow as she looks at me, blinking several times. "Did you think he was never here?"

I wave her comment away and get out too. "I just thought he owned it. I didn't know he'd be here and I'd like—" I'd have to meet him. "Never mind. It's fine. Just took me off guard for a moment." I reach into the back. "I'll grab our stuff."

Vee nods slowly. "Okay. I'll let him know we're here."

I grab the bags and follow her up the front porch steps of an old farmhouse. She raps on the screen door, which I can see straight through.

"Uncle Mason!" She yells with no answer. She turns to me and tips her chin. "He's probably around back. Come on."

My heart beats erratically. "Don't you think you should call him first before we just go around the back?"

Is this not how her horror movies start?

"Don't be silly. He doesn't mind."

I find it hard to believe that a Marine doesn't mind if his niece, or whatever she is to him, traipses through his house with a strange guy in tow. Yeah, cue the credits because this movie is going to be over before it begins.

Vee opens the screen door and motions for me to follow. "Did you text Brick the address?"

"Yeah. He's on his way." My focus is everywhere but on the conversation.

Vee's uncle's place is spacious and rustic, much like you'd think a cabin in the woods would be. But where you would think it would have deer heads hung on the wall, there's black and white framed pictures with who I assume is her uncle and a blonde-haired woman. In most of the pictures, they have this German Shepherd dog with them that's always staring up at the woman like, he too, loves her.

"That's Killer," Vee says, noticing me staring at the photos. "She was my Uncle Mason's service dog. She died a few years after I was born."

"I'm sorry to hear that."

Vee smiles. "She was the reason my uncle opened this place. Her death was devastating for him."

"I can only imagine," I tell her, taking once last look at the photo. "I've never had a pet before. My sister was—"

"Allergic?"

I nod. "Something like that."

Vee doesn't pry, and I'm grateful. She already knows more than I would like her to know about my past.

"Come on. Let me introduce you to the dogs." She's excited. The pep in her voice gives it away.

"Alright." I motion for her to lead the way and then I wipe my palms on my jeans. For some reason, I feel fucking nervous. It could be that we aren't at a pet store and these aren't puppies like Vee makes them out to be. Or it could be that Vee and I, out on a semi-adventure, feels a lot like old times. Either way, my anxiety is high.

Once out of her uncle's house, I relax. Maybe it wasn't the dogs or the adventure. Maybe my ass didn't want to get thrown to the ground in a choke hold. Vee leads us out to a barn where barking starts the minute we get close.

"They know we're out here," she says with a smile.

"Super."

I hope they don't attack strangers or men with Vee. She tends to bring the crazy out in people.

"Who's excited to see fresh meat?" she calls out as she punches the keypad.

"What?"

I feel the blood drain from my face.

"Relax, you big sissy. They won't hurt you."

I flash her a bored look, so she knows I'm not amused with her shitty jokes.

"I'm serious," she tells me. "Here, hold my hand. I'll protect you."

She thinks she's being fucking cute by making fun of me, but honestly, her hand feels nice, so I'll play her game for a few minutes. At least until I can get a better read on the dogs and their temperament.

The door slides open, and I'm hit with cool air and a view of a huge open space with obstacles and dog toys strewn all around. "The barn has air?"

Vee nods. "Yeah. Do you like to work out in the heat?"

I go to answer her, but the minute the door is opened far enough, something barrels into Vee, which sends both of us to the ground.

"Whoa! Hey, girl," Vee says, after taking a second to catch her breath. The giant dog gives her a few licks and then moves to me, but instead of licking me, she sniffs as if she's trying to determine, just by my smell, if I'm cool to enter her playground.

"Dogs are a great judge of character," Vee says, as I lay stock still, not even breathing. "Scarlett, here, once took out an entire house of terrorists. She was shot taking down the leader who had her partner at gunpoint."

"Scarlett sounds like a badass," I whisper, hoping my speaking doesn't trigger her to attack. If what Vee says is true and Scarlett is a good judge of character, she might eat my face.

"She is a badass, and she's secretly my favorite."

Scarlett finally puts me out of my misery and licks my face in one slippery lick.

Vee hums. "Maybe she isn't such a great judge of character after all."

I sit up and rub the furry head in front of me. "Or maybe she is."

Vee smiles. "Maybe."

Scarlett flops down and pins me to the ground with one of her massive paws.

"I'll give you two some space and check on the other dogs."

Scarlett swipes a slobbery kiss over my cheek, and I laugh. "Alright. I hope they all aren't as brutal as this one."

Vee stands and grins down at me. "She usually isn't this friendly with strangers."

I look at the beast lying on top of me. She looks calm, like she's never seen war a day in her life. I scratch behind her ears and shrug. "Maybe she's just having an off day or—" I roll my eyes dramatically, "—maybe my Midol threw her off?"

Vee belts out a laugh that isn't very dainty. "I bet that's it."

"Of course," I agree.

Two hours into Vee's shift, and Scarlett and I decided to let her continue running around and entertaining the other dogs—seven in total.

"Are you sure you don't want to put the suit on again?" she teases, tossing a frisbee for one of the dogs who darts after it.

"I'm sure," I return. "I may never get the feeling back in my arm after the last time."

It was Vee's idea to put me in the K9 tactical bite suit. I knew it was her payback for me acting like such a dick last night after our dance video. So I took my punishment like the good team player I am. Besides, I don't want to piss her off too much. Otherwise, she might decide she doesn't give a fuck about this competition and go save the frogs with Vance.

Vance and I are friends, somewhat. We don't hang out or anything, but he's connected to the mayor, therefore Maverick likes to keep him in his pocket, meaning I can't be too much of an asshole and scare him off.

But I can tell you that Vance cannot handle the likes of Valentina Lambros. She has way too much personality for him. Vance seems like he could use a soft-spoken woman who will rub his shoulders after a long day and then finish him off with a delicate hand job.

Valentina will push a shot of moonshine across the island and force you to down a couple, before tagging along while you blackmail a guy for Maverick and sneak into the girl's locker room to get the footage you needed to do it. I don't know if she would have offered me a hand job because we didn't get that far, but I'm thinking she would have been a lot more exciting than Vance's hope for a sweet, under the cover tug.

"Have you heard from Brick?" she calls, tugging the frisbee from the same dog's mouth. I forgot his name. Seems like she said it was something like Turner, but maybe that's the tan one.

"Yeah," I tell her, stroking Scarlett's back. "He's in the driveway. I told him to stay put until we're ready for him." The fucker can sit in the heat with his piece of shit car that broke down a couple of days ago when he was supposed to be filming mine and Vee's date.

She cocks her head to the side. "Why wouldn't you just let him come on back?"

Uh, because I didn't want him to think he needed to have a seat and talk or interrupt my time with Scarlett. Okay, and with Vee, but more so Scarlett. And bad employees deserve to be punished.

"He's fine."

She levels me with a look. "Text him to come back."

Ugh. Reluctantly, I pull out my phone. Scarlett looks at me with half-open eyes.

"I know," I tell her. "He's going to make things awkward." And annoying.

"No, he won't." Vee laughs, coming to sit with me and Scarlett on the grass. "We need to shoot anyway. My uncle said he and his wife would be home in a couple of hours. They were meeting a new dog."

I rub Scarlett again and her eyes close. "The dogs seem really happy here," I muse.

"They are."

Vee nuzzles one of the dogs who comes up and flops down in her lap. "It's good therapy, right?"

I cock my head to the side. "Therapy?"

"Yeah." She kisses the top of the dog's head. "When my mind is messed up and all chaotic, I can come here and somehow everything just becomes so still."

She looks up and her mouth tips down into a frown. "After… you know, what happened between us, this was the only place I felt… welcome."

Her eyes flick up at me, and I feel this ache in my chest that spreads out, weaving its pain around my ribs.

"I didn't mean to make you feel like you didn't belong at your own home," I admit.

"You didn't," she clarifies. "I mean, sure, the hateful looks you gave me when I passed you in the parking lot were tense, but I did it to myself. I think I was ashamed."

She was ashamed.

Wow.

"Why would you feel ashamed? We were playing a game." I shrug like her last prank was no big deal. "We had a prank war. You won. There's no reason to feel ashamed."

She lowers her gaze back to the dog in her lap. "I took it too far."

Heaven help me. "I deserved it."

It's the truth. I did deserve it. I forced her into one-upping me over and over again. I challenged her wits every day until she showed me just how brilliant she was. Even if she pissed me off and shit all over our entire relationship, she has no reason to be ashamed.

"You did deserve it," she finally agrees with a grin. "But I still shouldn't have done that to you. It was wrong."

I shrug. I don't know that I would classify what she did as wrong. Maybe a little devious, but that's how you win a prank war.

"Oh look, there's Brick," she says, moving the dog and standing, still holding its collar. "Hold Scarlett while I get the others."

I look down at Scarlett as she cracks an eyelid. "Brick's an easy target," I tell her. "You won't have any trouble getting him down should he get on your nerves."

Scarlett acts like she understands me and closes her eyes, ignoring the six other barking dogs. I knew she was the cool one. She isn't threatened at all by the Ed Sheeran looking filmmaker.

"I'm going to give Brick a tour around the grounds," Vee says. "You going to be okay here?"

I nod, and then glare at Brick. "But I'm getting hungry so try not to shoot the grass and the tubs of dog food."

Vee rolls her eyes. "Your Midol wore off I see."

I could argue and say Brick puts me in a shitty ass mood, but I don't, because that would show spending the day with Vee didn't put me in a shitty mood and that's a big fucking problem.

CHAPTER THIRTEEN

Sebastian

University CamFlix Competition Submission
Entry Number: 75
Sebastian and Valentina
Second Interview Continued, or that time I counted the gray
hairs on Tom's head

"Sweetie, I think you aren't remembering correctly. I think I was trying to give you a science lesson and you clearly misunderstood me."

Vee smiles and shakes her head. "I feel pretty certain you told me you loved me that night when I changed your clothes and tucked you into bed."

Okay. So I vaguely remember saying that part but, again, I was completely and utterly trashed. I offer Tom a tense grin. "As you can see, Vee and I go way back. It's actually kind of hard to determine when exactly we realized we were in love."

"It still doesn't look right," she whines, moving the pillow under my head. "It looks staged."

I grunt when she snatches the pillow—the one she still hasn't given back. My head falls against the mattress. "It looks like it's staged because it is." I lean up enough to see her eye roll.

"I think you're just stalling. It doesn't matter if we're up against the wall or in a bed, our fans just want to see us kiss."

Last night when Vee came over to watch a movie in her chair on my back patio, we scrolled through the comments of the video at the dog rescue her uncle owns. Brick managed to get a clip of me arguing with Vee that Scarlett was nothing but a lap dog at this point. To prove it, I scooped up a squealing Vee, pretending to kidnap her, while Scarlett watched on, unamused. It was all fun and games until Turner (I was right. He was the tan one) caught up to me and took me and Vee down with one well-placed jump.

Vee was on the ground. I was laughing, hovered above her, while we both tried to calm Turner down. It was a mess, but apparently, our viewers went crazy and commented with the likes of: "Kiss her already!" "I wish he would kidnap me." "Some guys have all the luck." "Kiss her!" "Kiss her!"

"Kiss her already!"

You get the point. Our viewers had spoken, and if we want to keep them voting by liking our videos, we have to give them what they want. And what they want is for me to suck Vee's face.

"I'm not stalling," she says, huffing so hard that a piece of hair flutters over her face.

"I disagree. When you've set this pillow up eight different ways, only to make me move to the sofa and back again, I'd say you're stalling."

I can see the determination set in when she narrows her gaze on my face.

"I promise, I've brushed my teeth."

"Shut up." She sits down on the bed and hands me the remote to her camera, which is set up on the tripod. We opted not to let Brick film this one since it would be difficult for the two of us to relax enough to kiss. Clearly, that was a good decision.

"Let's just do it really quick."

She leans in and purses her lips like a kid would do, all while squeezing her eyes shut as if it's painful to get this close to me.

"You're going to have to kiss me," I tell her. "Sitting here acting like you're about to vomit is just slowing us down." I blew off a night of poker at Gigi's for this. Not that I expected a big payout, but it's extra money, nonetheless.

Vee throws her head back, her dark, satin hair falling off her shoulders like a curtain. "Gah! I wish we could find some stock videos to insert into this clip."

I don't let her lack of excitement dampen my mood. Really, just seeing her suffer perks me up more than shoving my tongue down her throat again. The last time I was too pissed to enjoy her discomfort.

"Such a shame, but the last time I checked, the angry tomboy clips were all sold out." I shrug, back to being a shit. "They probably make around one a year. I think that look died in the 90's."

"I will stab you," she threatens, easing her head up and leveling me with a look that I think might be a real threat.

"I hope you'll at least film it when you do. My mother would like to be proud of me one day, even if it's just seeing my corpse on Dateline."

My cheek twitches as my comment hits a little too close to the truth.

"You're sick," she says, twisting her hair up and piling it on top of her head before letting it go. "Why is it so hot in here?" she groans.

I refrain from stating the obvious cliché. I think she might actually hit me, and I get turned on by a slap just as much as the next man but not today. I'd rather we get this torture over with quickly so she can take her sweet-smelling self next door and give me some damn space. Being with her every day this past week has not been the highlight of my college experience. I mean, sure, she's hot, but she's argumentative and the enemy. I haven't forgotten that part.

"We could open a window," I suggest for the both of us. It'll keep my room from smelling like her. It probably won't cool her down with the high humidity, but the breeze might help a little.

She eyes my window, where I watch her seven days out of the week, and tips her chin. "Fine. It's gotta be better than sweating my butt off while we do this."

She gags once more and I roll my eyes. Really. She's not that great of an actress. She's not disgusted by me. I know because we've kissed before, and she was the one who initiated it.

I get up and go to the window and push it up halfway, before walking back to the bed and flopping down next to her.

I nod to the remote in her hand. "No more bullshit. Let's get this over with."

With an extreme sigh that our other neighbors can probably hear, Vee nods and presses the record button. I almost forget what I'm supposed to do, but then she leans forward and her hand comes to my cheek.

I don't know if it's instinct, lust, or plain old want, but my hand goes to the back of her head, my fingers knotting in her soft tresses, and I yank. She yips but doesn't speak. Last time we did this, she surprised me by pressing her lips to mine. This time, I'm the one in charge.

I angle her head back, admiring the smooth, tanned skin at her jaw. Unlike that night, her face is bare of any makeup and her lips glisten with a gloss I plan on smearing all over her face. Wrapping my hand around her neck, I pull her down, nuzzling under her ear, and inhaling the scent of something floral. I nudge the soft skin at her hairline before I nip the bottom of her ear with my teeth.

Her hands go to my shoulders. Whether they are holding me to her or pushing me away, I'll never know, because I pull her close and press my lips to hers. Unlike the first time, our lips don't come together softly. My lips meet hers, hard and unyielding. Our teeth clash and her hands grip the sides of my face. She's trying to control the kiss, but she forgets one thing.

She didn't surprise me this time.

She isn't getting that Sebastian. She's getting the real me. The me who wants to consume her *and* hate her.

I grunt when she bites my bottom lip, but with one tug of her hair and a small whimper from her compliant little body, I'm back in control, slipping my tongue into the warmth of the mouth that has lied, deceived, and made me horny, all in the span of half an hour.

My tongue eases in and out, exploring every inch of her mouth. For a moment, I forget we're on camera or that we're supposed to be just filming a sweet kiss, not an intro into a porno, but there's no way I can stop. We'll just have to redo the shot later.

Like when we get ourselves together and calm the fuck down.

"Sebastian," she mumbles, when I move to her neck, kissing down the side. "I think we got the shot."

Fuck. I think I'm addicted. "One more, just in case," I say, breathily and slightly growly.

"Okay," she agrees.

And this moment right here is where we went wrong. Again. For the second time in our relationship.

"Tell me again why girls think this is—" I frown, drawing a blank. "What's that stupid phrase you use?"

I should have been able to predict the hard shove to my chest, but for some reason, I'm off my game, and it sends me a step back.

"What did I say?"

One thing I've learned from hanging out these past three weeks with Vee is that women expect you to know how they are feeling at all times. Granted, Vee is so much more low maintenance than most girls, but I still find myself wondering what I've said when she walks off and flips me the bird. Case in point, right now.

Valentina spears me with a sharp and deadly look. It's meant to make me nervous. It doesn't. All it makes me want to do is shove her ass down on the sofa and show her exactly where she can put those lips. Trust me, it's not somewhere tasteful.

"I don't use the phrase," she scolds me. "I simply said #couple-goals is the internet trend and all couples, who are anyone online, try to create pictures and videos that make the single girls swoon with hope that there are men out there for them and it makes the girls in relationships tell their boyfriends to do better."

My brows furrow. "But it's all fake. Seems like they would know that. I mean, what dude actually wants to play video games with his girlfriend on his lap?"

I flop down on the sofa and grab the controller as to demonstrate. On the edge of the sofa with my elbows resting on my knees, I grasp the controller and stare straight ahead at the TV. "See, when I want to win, the last thing I'm doing is lying back in my bed or reclining on the sofa with my arms around my girl, pressing the buttons."

I wave a hand over my body's position. "This is how I play. I have room to jump up, drop some F bombs, and get right up to the TV to make sure I beat my competitor."

This whole 'pretend we're playing video games together' thing is ridiculous and totally Vee's idea. When we actually managed to strategize, it was her saying, "Can we just agree to let me do all the planning? I don't think you have any idea what our viewers want to see."

I didn't argue because, honestly, I didn't know what the hell they wanted. All I know is that everything we've been posting has been blowing up. We're the number one favorite in the UniCamFlix Competition. So if Vee's crazy ideas get us there, then great. Winning and getting the fuck out of Georgia is my end goal.

Vee looks up from the camera, making sure the angle is right on the tripod. "Don't be ridiculous. Girls know that you don't play seriously with them on your lap. The point is you allow them to enjoy something you enjoy."

I think about her words for a minute. "Really? You all want to play video games with us?"

This time, she shakes her head and flops down beside me, jostling us both. "Please, bitch, I plan on kicking your ass after we shoot this video."

She sounds so serious that I throw my head back and laugh. "I should have remembered. You're not a typical girl."

She nods, examining the controls on the handset. "Don't you forget it either."

Her comment sends a jolt of memories through me and my grip

on the controller tightens. She notices, but she doesn't say anything and that's good because we somehow need to get through this shoot without arguing.

"Okay," Vee says, then exhales, as if preparing herself for this conversation. "In order for it to look super 'coupl-y' you need to change into those gray sweatpants you have and leave off the shirt."

I can feel my eyes go wide. "What in the hell do sweatpants have to do with playing video games?"

She rolls her eyes. "Think about it, Bash. Do you think couples snuggle with a lot of clothes on?"

"We have to snuggle?" I am one hundred percent sure she did not mention that earlier when she was pitching the idea to me. "You didn't mention any snuggling."

Why is this an issue for me? I don't know. I mean, on average, I'm not a cuddler, but with Valentina, I'm *really* not up for a cuddle session.

"Stop being a baby," she says and rips off her shirt.

"Oh my God! What the fuck are you doing?" I toss the controller down and stand. "Put your shirt back on."

Well, maybe wait a minute. No. No, she definitely needs to put it back on. Seeing her in a sports bra that dips dangerously low, showing two rounded hills of smooth skin that look like two ass cheeks squished together… I can't be trusted with a bra like that.

It's painful—literally painful, as my dick stands at attention. We're not used to seeing Valentina Lambros in any other way than as a friend and the annoying neighbor. The bra and— "Why are you taking off your pants?"

She walks away, her panties on full display as she ignores me, pulling something out of her bag and slipping them on.

"Why are you changing into those shorts?"

Fuck me. These shorts are pink and girly and sit high on her thigh. I rake a hand through my hair. I can't do this.

"We can shoot the scene without our faces," I try to negotiate. "We can get Pam next door to do it."

Vee isn't having it, though, and comes to stand in front of me. "Shut up and strip. If you want to win the prize money, then you have to do what it takes." She motions to her bra and bare stomach. "This is what it takes, Bash. Are you pussying out?"

I glare at her. "Don't challenge me, Vee. You know I'll rise to the occasion."

Which she knows and that's exactly why she said it. I snatch off my shirt and toss it somewhere toward the kitchen then stalk to my bedroom where I find those fucking sweatpants she was talking about and pull them on. When I'm done, I walk back into the living area to find that she has pushed the coffee table closer to the sofa and it looks cozy and date-like.

I hate it already.

"See? Was that so hard?" she asks, eyeing my bare chest before going back to the pillows she's arranging.

"I need something to drink," is all I respond with. Clearly my mood has plummeted into asshole territory. I've never been one to deprive myself or suffer, so I'm not eager for my neighbor's half-dressed body to be pressed up against me while we shoot half an hour of footage that we'll only use three minutes of.

"No alcohol," she tells me, and it stops my steps to the kitchen.

"Why the hell not?" Alcohol is the only thing that is going to get me through this torture.

She doesn't even spare me eye contact when she returns. "I don't want you getting sloppy and debating stupid shit with me on camera. I know how you can get."

Where is something I can throw?

I growl out something that sounds more like a muted scream. She does know how I get, and she's also fallen prey to such arguments when we both were tipsy.

I take the last few steps to the kitchen and yank open the fridge and grab a fucking water because, apparently, this is going to suck epically. I down half of it in one go, before setting it on the counter and taking a deep breath.

One million dollars, dude. Los Angeles. A fresh start.

This will all be worth it. All you need to do is suffer through half an hour and then she can go home, back to her own space, and you can spray Lysol and attempt to get rid of her sweet smell in the house.

My pep talk does little to comfort me. I don't own a can of Lysol and burning the place down would be in bad taste. I'll just have to open the windows and possibly go to Rowan's. Although, I'd prefer not to see him or Maverick right now and have them ask a million questions and give me shit, thinking I finally hooked up with my neighbor.

I gave Maverick so much shit when he started dating Ainsley. He'd, no doubt, jump at the opportunity to return the favor.

"Let's get this over with," I tell her in a shitty voice, one I'll probably regret later once I've settled down. But Vee doesn't seem to mind. Maybe this sucks just as much for her.

"Alright. You sit down first."

I take a deep breath and follow her directions for the first time and sit amongst the pillows and blankets on my sofa.

"Okay, now lie back. Put your head on the pillow behind you."

I feel awkward and exposed as she watches my every movement, judging the angles and the way my body is posed for the greatest sex appeal.

"Good," she praises. "Now put your leg on the coffee table. Keep the other one on the ground and scooch down so your chest is wider."

I arch a brow. "Scooch?"

She grins. "Don't act like you don't know what I'm talking about. Scooch."

I do know what she means. It's just been a long time since I've heard her say it.

When I'm down and looking exactly like she wants me to, she walks over. "Now I'm going to join you, alright?"

My hands flinch as I stare up at her flat and smooth stomach. This is way worse than the kiss. Her chest is flushed and is the only giveaway that she's nervous too.

"Don't say it like you're warning me," I tell her.

She huffs. "I'm just preparing you."

"I'm prepared," I lie. "I knew what I was signing up for." I also knew I wouldn't like it, or I'd like it too much, which is even worse.

Valentina sits delicately between my legs and lies back so that her back touches my chest. Her feet follow as she lays them over mine.

I swallow thickly. The position we are in is definitely not one for gaming or one for not getting hard. Each time she takes a breath, I can feel it on my chest as if I'm the one breathing. Her hips are cradled between my legs and my dick does not miss the weight of her body bearing down on us.

"You okay?" she asks after a minute.

I want to shove her off, but I also want to dry hump the shit out of her, so I just stick with "Yeah."

"Okay. I'm going to hit record now if you'll start the game. Remember this isn't about the game, it's about making playing the game look sexy."

I nod. Trust me, in this position, there is no way I'll actually be able to focus on playing. Not with the warmth of her body burning me from the inside out.

Focusing, I turn on the game. I don't play many video games, but I keep Call of Duty because Rowan likes to play when he comes over. The bastard is too cheap to pay for WIFI, so he comes over here when the silence gets to be too much and he needs a little socialization.

So, seeing how I don't own many games and Call of Duty is already in the console, I boot it up and turn it on. Vee grabs her controller.

"Do you need me to go over anything with you?" I ask. I mean, I don't think she will need me to but sometimes she surprises me.

"Nah, I know how to play. Drew and Fenn play this all the time."

Of course they do, and I'm willing to bet she knows how to play well.

Fuck.

"You're going to have to put your arms around me," she says, lying back in my arms.

I take one—no, two—deep breaths and wrap my arms around her with the controller securing my hands in her lap .

I groan.

I'm not going to make it half an hour without doing something shitty. I can already feel it.

"We're recording." She tilts her head back and catches my eyes. "Remember to act like you love me."

I swallow before rolling my eyes. "Worry about acting your own part," I tell her, which only makes her laugh.

She knows I'm struggling. Fuck her.

Fifteen minutes later and I'm sweating. I grab her hips as she yells "Suck on that, Bash-hole."

"Stop fucking moving," I grate out. Yes, I'm losing epically, but what's more concerning than losing to a girl is that my dick is having trouble keeping his head from bruising Vee's back.

"Don't get all pouty," she says, laughing as her silky legs move along mine.

I throw my head back and toss my controller to the floor. I am so fucking done. In the last two weeks, I've slept like shit, been taken down by a rescue dog, felt Valentina's hands tangled in my hair, and had her tongue tangled with mine. And if that wasn't enough, all the talking, nightly movie watching, and stupid dances have absolutely tortured the living fuck out of me. A man can only take so much.

Today, is that day.

"What are you doing?" She follows the controller landing on the floor. "Are you really that much of a spoilsport?"

Sure am.

I grab her hips, and I grind my rock-hard dick into her ass cheeks.

"This," I grit. "All this celebratory movement…" I grind into her hard, and she gasps. "Yeah. This is why these videos are bullshit. It's not possible to actually play while you're sliding up and down my dick, taunting me."

"Oh," she whispers.

I grind into her once more. "Oh is right, Valentina. This is torture."

I can feel her heavy breaths against my chest and then her hips start to move. I clamp down on her hips tighter. "What are you doing?"

She doesn't stop, instead, she drops the controller and turns off the camera. "Do it," she tells me. "You don't have to look at me."

I cock my head to the side. "I—"

She starts moving her hips, and my head falls back on its own. I groan. "This wasn't part of the deal," I mutter, but I don't mean it. Truth be told, ever since I laid eyes on Valentina Lambros, I've wanted her. Sure, she pissed me off worse than anyone else in my life but, some-how, I'm okay with it because if our roles were reversed, and I would have thought of the prank she did, I would have played it with a fucking smile on my face.

She outsmarted me, and I hate that it turns me on.

My neighbor, my nemesis, turns her head back so as not to look at me and I can't do it. I don't want her to think I can't stand the sight of her. It's quite the opposite.

"Face me," I demand, my voice raspy and thick with want.

She hesitates but eases up and untangles her feet from mine. I shift on the sofa so that my entire body is on it as Vee straddles me and lowers herself down. My hands go to her hips and I swallow. We're crossing a line, but I guess we're both up for making terrible decisions today.

Vee's head falls back the minute I press her down on my dick, which is not at all impressed with dry humping and would much rather be set free into something hot, wet, and full of fire.

I move her body back and forth once and I can't even keep my head up. The pressure, the friction feels so damn good. I moan and I can feel the muscles in my neck tighten. This will not last long. Valentina Lambros is grinding down on my cock. It's a nightmare that dreams are made of.

I hate that I love the feel of her body and I especially hate that I love coming to the view of her on top of me, riding me like she has it mastered.

I push and pull her faster and faster until her hands come down and reach for my chest, hanging on as I pull her to a stop and come in my fucking pants like a fucking teenager.

We stay there, still and panting, as we come down from our high.

"I'm going to shower," she says, easing off. The missing weight of her body feels wrong.

"Okay," I tell her, as she disappears down the hall.

CHAPTER FOURTEEN
Sebastian

University CamFlix Competition Submission
Entry Number: 75
Sebastian and Valentina
Second Interview Continued, also the time Vee admitted she gets off on the sight of my dimple

Tom writes something on a piece of paper and passes it off to his assistant. "Okay. How about we take another question?"

Vee and I both tense up. "Sure."

"Vee, this question is for you. Brittany asks, 'What is your favorite feature of Sebastian's?'"

I shift in my seat and look over at Vee. Finally some decent questions. I was tired of all the love shit.

Vee clears her throat and offers the camera a soft smile. "Probably his dimple."

The shower has been off for five minutes now. Vee opted to shower here. She says it's because she didn't feel like going home, but I know she only wants to use my organic soap. I see the way she ogles it, so I know the reason I've been able to change, grab a snack and stare at my phone while my sister blasted me with several hateful text messages is because she is enjoying the hell out of the frog-free ecosystem friendly lather.

Mom #2: I'm on my way to beat your ass. Mom said you weren't coming home for spring break.

Mom #2: Why the fuck not?

Mom #2: Sebastian!

Mom #2: I will call Maverick. Do not test me.

Her last text sends a groan through me. I open the message thread and quickly tap out a reply.

Me: Calm down, Cujo. I happen to have plans that don't include sitting around Mom's house and getting drilled with a million questions.

I take a breath then tap out one more message, just in case my last text hurts her feelings.

Me: If I'm going to get drilled, it's going to be by someone a little less chatty and will help me pass my chemistry final.

My sister, considered the no bullshitter in our family, quickly catches on.

Mom #2: What's her name?

I feel my blood pressure rising as my head falls back against the sofa.

Me: Come on, Cal. Let a man live a little.

It's a cheap shot. Playing on Calista's guilt is a low blow, but I need her to let this whole visiting for spring break thing go.

Mom #2: I think you're avoiding us again.

Me: Not true. I miss you all. Especially, Little Bit. I miss her more than all of you put together.

Bringing Emmy, my niece, into the mix is always the way to my sister's heart.

Mom #2: Promise you aren't just avoiding us?

I can't lie to my sister.

Me: I'll come see you soon. Promise.

"What's wrong?"

My head pops up at Vee's soft voice.

I shake my head and give her a once-over. She's in another one of my shirts. This time, it isn't flannel. Not that it isn't sexy on her, but flannel is her trademark.

"Nothing," I lie. "Why?"

She shrugs and comes to sit down beside me. "You just look sad."

"I'm definitely not sad," I assure her with a grin. Although, that might not be the case for my sister.

Vee nods at my phone. "Someone bothering you?"

I forget how well Vee knows me from before this whole fake girlfriend thing. "My sister is disappointed I'm not coming home for spring break."

I don't know why I tell her. Maybe I wanted to feel better about breaking my mom and sister's hearts. Or maybe I just wanted to talk to Vee and see where her head is after I came in my pants while dry humping her.

"Oh," she says, "I'm not going home either."

I'm pretty sure she isn't avoiding her family like I am mine. "Any particular reason?"

She tips her chin and takes a sip of my water, like we're a real couple and share things like clothes and drinks. "They're doing some fundraiser this week. A car wash or something for the school my dad works for."

"Oh" is all I say, watching as she takes another sip. "And you don't want to go?"

She shakes her head and tries not to grin. "Nah, it's their thing. I don't like to be there when it's time to clean up."

I arch a brow. "Why? What happens?"

"You don't want to know."

I chuckle. "Okay. So you didn't make plans with Aspen?"

She chews on the inside of her cheek. "Last I heard, they were thinking of going to the beach, but hadn't decided for sure."

The beach sounds nice. "A trip sounds like the way to go," I agree.

Vee nods to the untouched wakeboard propped up against the wall where it has been since I bought it. "You like to wakeboard?"

I take my drink from her and down the rest of it. "Yeah. I don't get much of a chance to use it though."

Vee fidgets for a second, and we're both quiet, staring at the wall. "We could go to Aspen's parents' lake house if you want," she finally says. "I mean, you don't have to, but I can check and see if anyone is there for the weekend. I have to work some next week, but I could manage a long weekend." She shrugs and takes a deep breath, her cheeks flushed. "You could wakeboard. Aspen's parents have a boat."

I sit there, not responding, like a total idiot, when she adds, "I mean we could use the footage for the competition."

She puts her hands in the air, imitating a billboard. "We could say: Spring Break Getaway, Couple Style."

Her smile wavers for a moment, and it's in that moment I know I am completely and utterly fucked with this girl. It doesn't matter what she did in the past, there's not enough hate in the universe to keep me away from her now.

I tuck a wet strand of hair behind her ear. "I think that's the best idea you've had yet."

"Wait. We're bringing real food?"

Vee cuts me a bored look. "As opposed to fake food we can't eat?"

Ugh. Why does that sarcasm shoot straight to my dick?

I narrow my eyes and refrain from snatching the bag of groceries from her hand, slamming her body on the hood, and putting that mouth of hers to better use. Ever since I came in my pants to the feel of her body against mine, I haven't been able to chase away the images. I find myself wanting more and more time with her every day. I can't get enough of her company, and I'm pretty sure that's a bad sign.

"I'm merely pointing out that I don't know how to cook," I say. "So unless you know how to—" I nod to the bag of charcoal in the back, "—use that, then this little 'romantic weekend' will turn into a 'bathroom getaway' again."

Vee stuffs the remaining bag into the back of my Jeep, which looks like we robbed Costco every day for a week. "We'll google it. Besides—" she shrugs, "how hard can it be?"

I'm thinking pretty fucking complicated, but I'd never admit it.

"Whatever," I clip, slamming the hatch and giving her a shove around to the passenger side. "At least the video will look authentic if we fuck it up."

Vee's eyes go wide. "Yes! Now you're thinking! Did you see Malcolm teasing his viewers with a surprise in his last video?"

I nod. "Yeah."

There are rumors about Malcolm and his video ideas. I honestly don't know if the rumors are true about him stealing other MyViewer's material, but something in my gut tells me they probably are, given Malcolm's creepy personality.

"I wonder who he'll rip off this time?"

I shrug. "Does it matter? We're beating him by a landslide."

Vee climbs into the passenger side and buckles in. "Do you think we have a shot at really winning this thing?"

I walk around the front of the Jeep and get in. "Absolutely. After this weekend, nothing we post will cause us to lose our spot. Malcolm doesn't have a chance in hell of winning."

"Stay on the road!"

I ease back to the middle of the road and cut Vee a pained look. "I'm sorry. It was like my hands knew the only way to peace was to run us into a ditch."

I smother a laugh when her eyes narrow. "I swear to all that is holy I will cut your pillow to shreds and use it as dog bedding if you make one more joke about my singing."

I shrug, not promising I won't make another joke about her horrific singing. "I'm kind of used to sleeping without it now. Do with it what you wish."

I focus back on the road but then tell her, "I'm still not giving your chair back though."

She scoffs. "You think that concerns me? I'll just continue to come watch my movies at your house. All your future girlfriends will have to learn to adapt to your nightly houseguest."

The words, 'future girlfriends,' send a chill through the warm air. It reminds me that whatever this is with Vee isn't real nor will it last until 'future girlfriends.' Once we win, I'm leaving. I don't plan to stay and finish school. Instead of Vee watching her stupid movies on my patio while I pretend to watch something else, she'll be watching them back on *her* patio like before. Alone.

Vee's chuckle dies when she notices that I didn't contribute to the laughter. I could have faked one, but I don't see the point. The contest will be over soon, and I think it's best we both remember that. It'll make things easier.

"So…" She clears her throat, turning the radio off. "I was looking on the map and there's a town coming up."

"Do you need a bathroom break again?" I roll my eyes. I swear she needs to stop to pee every fifteen miles.

"No, jerk face. I don't have to pee, but I know there's a Red Cross there." She looks down at her hands. "It's not out of the way and since you were sick on the week you normally go, I thought you might want to make up for it."

I sigh. I hate that I took her with me that one time. "Are you going to faint this time when they stick me?"

She grins. "Maybe."

"Maybe?" I repeat, my lips tipping up at the corners into a grin. "Maybe you should wait in the Jeep?"

She waves me off. "I'll be fine. Second time's a charm."

I scoff. I highly doubt it, but I guess we'll see.

"Alright, you can come in, but if you faint, you can't sing for the rest of the ride."

I don't mean it, but it feels good changing the subject.

"You're a dick." She side-eyes me, but she's smiling.

"And?"

She turns the radio up, the wind blowing in her hair. She doesn't care that it's tangled. I like that she's not a diva about her appearance. "And you have a deal. If I faint, you can sing the rest of the trip."

About fifteen minutes later, we pull up to the donation center. The parking lot is sparse and almost looks abandoned.

"Do you want to put the top up on the Jeep?" Vee asks.

I shake my head. "Nah. It'll be fine. We'll just take the camera bags in. If someone steals our clothes and food, it'll just make for a more entertaining video."

I don't really hope someone steals our shit for the sake of likes; I'm just too lazy to put the top up and then back down an hour later when we leave.

Vee shrugs one shoulder. "Whatever you want."

Grabbing the bags, we head into the blood donation center, and I sign all the paperwork. Vee follows behind me and the tech without a word.

"Sure you're not going to faint again?" I toss behind me, which Vee responds with a middle finger salute.

"Have a seat right here, Mr. Carrington." The tech pats the recliner. "And your girlfriend can sit in this empty one next to you."

The girlfriend term stops Vee in her tracks, but she recovers quickly and hurries to sit.

I slide into the leather chair and prop my arm up on the armrest, while the tech busies herself with prepping my arm and asking me to make a fist while she finds the vein. I glance over at Vee, who is seriously pale. I knew her weak ass stomach couldn't handle the sight of blood. She might be able to shoot whiskey and moonshine like a dude, but a little bit of blood will send her eyes rolling into the back of her head. I groan and put my hand on the tech. "Hang on just a minute."

I then look at Vee. "Come here. I'm not dealing with having to carry you to the car and stopping by a diseased taco truck to get your strength back after you faint."

Sliding to the side of the recliner, I pat the few inches of space next to me. The tech cuts me a disapproving look that I ignore. Vee will either squeeze her little ass in or she'll faint on the floor. I'm guessing the tech would rather see two grown ass people squeeze into a recliner than to deal with the paperwork of writing up an incident report.

Vee eyes the needle in the tech's hand and then the spot beside me.

I already know what her decision will be, but she needs time to prepare herself. I get it.

With a groan, Vee leaves the bags in her recliner and puts a knee on my seat cushion then hesitates.

"She's about to stick me so make a decision," I add.

"Promise you won't tease me about this?" She's so serious that I can't help but laugh.

"No. Definitely not."

"Then I'll just faint and you can stop at the next taco truck."

For fuck's sake. "Fine. I promise. This one doesn't count."

At my assurance, she slides in on her side, so she can fit, putting her arm over my chest and burying her face in my shoulder.

"Okay. Tell her to stick you now."

I chuckle and nod to the tech who looks like this is the craziest shit she's ever seen during a blood donation. But she does it, and before long, I'm bleeding into a bag with my neighbor's face shoved into my shoulder hard enough that it'll probably bruise.

"Sebastian," she says, her voice muffled.

My eyes are closed, opting not to watch TV while I donate. "Yeah?"

"Are you ever going to tell me why you do this?"

I turn my head and admire her dark hair while her fingers grip my t-shirt like she's scared someone is going to force her to pull her head up and see all the blood. I trail my fingers down her back, watching as she visibly relaxes her grip.

"Maybe one day," I whisper.

It's not a no, but it isn't a yes.

"Does it have to do with your sister's illness when you were little?"

My fingers stop. "How do you know about that?"

She tries to pull her head up to face me but then thinks better of it. "When we were friends you told me that your sister had been sick when you were little."

I try relaxing when the tech comes by to check on the progress. "I forgot I told you."

She tightens her grip when she hears the tech placing a bottled water on the table. "You used to not mind sharing," she manages to get out.

"You used to make it easy to talk to you," I admit.

She pulls her face up and levels me with so much sincerity in those big brown eyes. "I don't now?"

I touch her hair and let my fingers trail along to the bow of her lips. "No. Now, it's definitely harder."

She watches me for a second, both of us locked in a heated stare laced with months of lies and friendship, before she notices the blood and slams her face back down onto my shoulder. "I'm still the same person, you know?"

I wrap my arm back around her and make sweeping strokes with my fingers along her back. "I know," I finally whisper.

"Aspen's family owns this place?" I tip my shades forward, so I can get a better view of the three-story lake house. Stone nestles the wooden accent beams across the deck. "This is…"

She cuts me off with a wave of her hand. "Lavish, I know. But it's home. I can remember spending many summers here."

After we finished with the blood donation, we stopped by a taco place for lunch—a chain restaurant this time—and had lunch, which fueled her vocal cords, so she could sing to me the rest of the way to the lake house.

I've never been so happy to get out of the car.

Vee smiles and flashes me a playful wink. "Come on, playboy. Get out of the car. We have an audience to impress and we aren't leaving until we make this look like one hell of a romantic getaway."

I straighten and get out of the Jeep, piling a couple bags on my arm from the back. "You're sure Aspen said we can use the boat?" If I were Aspen's parents, I wouldn't trust two college kids with my boat and million-dollar house for the weekend. I wouldn't care how close my friends and I were. No one would fuck around with my expensive toys.

Vee shoves me aside and grabs the board. "I'm sure. Come on, we're losing the good light."

Right.

The contest.

A half a million dollars and a new life away from Georgia.

Focus, Bash.

We take the steps up to the front door, and Vee pulls out a key.

"I'm surprised you actually have a key," I tell her.

I had my doubts since I never see her with any.

She turns back and grins. "I only break into my neighbor's house."

I shake my head and follow behind her as she pushes the door open into the grandeur of her summer home.

"Wow," I tell her. "Not a bad way to spend the summers."

She smiles. "It wasn't summer camp, but it was fun." She points to the sofa that is stark white and plush with red, white, and blue throw pillows. "Just set the bags over there. We can put everything away when we get back."

She shoves the bags of groceries in one of the two refrigerators, leaving the cooler we brought on the floor.

"I don't think all that needed refrigeration," I tell her.

She waves me off. "It's fine. Come on. Get changed and let's take the boat out. That's what we came here for, right?"

I nod and gaze out through the back of the open living space. The back wall is made of glass where you can see the view of the lake at every angle.

"You can use the bathroom on this floor to change if you want.

I'll change in the one downstairs." She points to a door down the hall that, I assume, is the bathroom, before taking the circular staircase and disappearing out of sight.

It only takes me a few seconds to throw on board shorts, but it takes Vee a little longer. When she finally comes back upstairs, I'm on the sofa, scrolling through my phone.

"You ready?"

I lift my head and admire the same bikini she wore at Drew's birthday party. I hated the sight of her in it while Vance stole glances of her tits. But now, I think it'll be the perfect scenery as the boat bounces along the water.

I'm a dude. Any type of titty bounce makes for a good day.

The word 'boat' seems like an insignificant term when we finally make it down the hill and to the boathouse. "Are you sure you know how to drive this thing?" I have my doubts. This boat is massive. If I didn't know any better, I'd say this looks more yacht-like than ski boat.

She throws off the boat cover and levels me with a look of contempt. "Are you saying since I'm a girl, I wouldn't know how to drive a boat this big?"

Fuck. Way to walk into this pile of shit, Sebastian.

I match her stare. "Why you always gotta bring gender into this? Did I say girls couldn't drive boats?"

"That's what you implied." She flips me off.

"I did not imply you couldn't drive it because you're a girl. I was implying that you couldn't drive it because you can't drive a car for shit. I'm simply assuming driving anything with a motor isn't your forte."

"Suck a dick, Sebastian. I drive fine. Just because I might have cruised through a couple stop signs that one time when I was your designated driver does not mean I didn't see them. Relax. I can drive the fucking boat." She tosses a life vest at my head. Clearly, I was staring at her boobs and not her face. "Just like I can drive a car. You're already getting on my nerves. I don't know that we'll end up with any useable footage from today."

Oh, we're getting footage. I did not drive all this way, listening to her ridiculous 90's bitch bands and playing a sign game that I still don't completely understand, for nothing.

"We'll get the footage. Don't you worry your pretty little head." I step over the ledge and set our cooler down on the leather seats. It's good there, right? "Should we put it on the floor or something more stable?"

Vee's eyes go to the sky. "It's a cooler, not a baby. It doesn't need a car seat. I'm sure it can handle a little wind."

Okay damn. I just didn't want it to go flying when Vee's crazy ass driving sends it airborne.

"I'm just checking. It wouldn't be the first time you lost something while you were driving." I'm referring to the time we drove overnight to attend a concert in Tennessee. You know, before, when we were friends.

Her eyes narrow to slits. "You were the one who lost the tickets!"

I hop over and lounge on the plush back seat, letting my legs fall open. "I told you to drive straight." And she didn't. She ran off the road because she was too busy critiquing my camera angle. One curve led to me grabbing the "Oh shit" handles and our backstage tickets went flying out the window and into the road dust.

"That wasn't my fault," she argues, starting the boat.

"I beg to differ."

As the engine purrs, my excitement mounts. Whether it's from arguing with Vee or knowing I'm about to be on a board that I haven't been on in years, one will never know.

"I'm the one who found the tickets!"

She's still arguing about her driving.

"I think it was fitting since you technically lost them."

"I swear, I'll drown you out here, Sebastian. The lake monsters will enjoy a little bitchy snack."

I grab my side and pretend it hurts from fake laughter. "You're so funny, Vee. Why don't you have more followers with this material?"

She flips me off and then, without another word, pulls out into the open water and throws the throttle down, sending the cooler sliding into my thigh.

See? I told you.

CHAPTER FIFTEEN

Valentina

University CamFlix Competition Submission
Entry Number: 75
Sebastian and Valentina
Second Interview Continued, also that time the demon sort of
complimented me

"Sebastian, next question is from Maureen. 'What is it like loving your best friend?'"

Eww. I cringe at the question. I'm glad Sebastian has to answer it. It'll be one he would rather chop off a finger before answering, but since we're on camera, he'll have to do it with a smile. Not that he won't lie, but still, he has to answer with a non-shitty answer.

"It's uh…" he looks at me and shakes his head with a grin, "always interesting. She's always surprising me."

Watching Sebastian wakeboarding is like curling up in my comfy chair and turning on a movie. It's relaxing. It holds my attention. And I know watching it one time won't be enough.

I keep the boat straight and glance back once more, watching as the asshole next door's muscles flex with each impact. Initially, I was hoping he would get out on the board and suck majorly, face planting the first go, but such was not the case.

We've been on the water for an hour now, filming Sebastian skimming across the water's surface. He's yet to tire of wakeboarding. I guess he really does love it. When we were friends before, he never had a board, so I thought this newfound sport was something he might have wanted to do but didn't necessarily know how to. But, as usual, Sebastian isn't what he seems to be.

For example, the blood donation. I knew he went every few months because, as he pointed out, I went with him and fainted. But that's not the point. The point is that it's such a selfless act, and to this day, I don't know why he consistently does it. Sure, I think it's because of his sister, but I don't know why. He's never said what happened to her. He keeps his relationship with his family to himself.

But I guess we all do to some extent. I don't go around telling everyone I know that my dad was once homeless, so it makes sense that he wouldn't go around exposing the skeletons in his family's closet.

I turn back and make sure Sebastian is still on the board when I hear a loud horn blare just to the left of me. "Shit!"

The noise startles me, and I jerk the steering wheel to the right before I realize it's just a party boat full of morons. I flip them off and turn back to check on Sebastian.

"Oh no!" He's not on his board. "Sebastian!"

I circle back around and notice he still hasn't come up. The idiot refused to wear a life vest, even though it's the law.

Surely, he can swim. Right? I mean, that seems like something you would know how to do before you go wakeboarding and refusing a vest.

"Sebastian!" I yell one more time.

His board floats up, and my heart stops. No!

I tie my hair up before I take a breath and dive into the cloudy water. I didn't even think to bring the life ring with me. I just reacted. I swim around, slashing my arms through the water as if he's floating just beneath the surface.

Why isn't he kicking or flailing?

Did he hit his head? Did he pass out?

My stomach churns with the thoughts of Bash-hole drowning and me just above him.

"Bash!"

I'm in tears, searching and slashing frantically in the water when I'm suddenly yanked under. I take a quick inhale, but I don't have time to prepare and end up swallowing a crap ton of water.

I kick for the surface as hard as I can and then something helps me up and I'm through the water, choking to the sounds of Bash-hole's laughter.

"You're a dick," I scream out between coughing fits.

Next to me is my annoyingly fine fake boyfriend, laughing as if he didn't have a care in the world.

I slap his chest. "I hate you."

He rubs the spot on his chest and tries to pull me in for a hug. "Aww. Come on. I thought you wanted to drown me."

I turn and start swimming back to the boat. "I'd certainly like to now."

He catches up to me easily. "Were you trying to save me, Valentina?"

I don't look at the stupid grin I know is on his face. "No. I was looking for the end of the rope. I didn't want it getting caught in the motor when I left your ass here."

Sebastian laughs, and I clamp my mouth shut, so I don't let my own laugh slip out. But then he snags my foot and pulls me toward him. We're both treading water while we face each other. I'm looking at him like I could really dunk his ass under and not feel bad about it and he's looking at me like it's taking all he has not to laugh more.

"It wasn't funny." I'm so over this whole outing.

He holds his fingers up, his thumb and forefinger spaced only an inch or so apart. "It was a little funny. Admit it."

I'm not going to admit it.

"You're going to hell," I tell him.

He grabs my chin and leans in close. "I'll save you the spot next to me."

And then he kisses me.

Whether it's for the camera still rolling in the boat or because he wants to, I'll never know, but, just in case, I channel all the fear and frustration into this one kiss.

I bite his lip, and he growls, yanking me to his bare chest. "You drive me mad," he growls out between nips, as I leave a trail of marks from my grip on his shoulders.

"Ditto."

Our mouths are vessels of hate as we devour each other's faces in the middle of the lake. Boaters pass us and several honk their horns, but no one stops and asks if we're okay. The only thing to finally tear us apart is when I feel something brush against my leg.

"Ahh!"

I climb onto Sebastian, and he immediately wraps his arms around me. "What? Did something bite you?"

Here's the thing. For the most part, I am rough and tough. I don't need a man to kill a bug or take my trash out. It's nice for them to do it, but I'm not for having to sleep with them to get such perks, but snakes… those bastards are on a whole other level.

"Something touched my leg." Even I cringe when I say it.

Sebastian grins.

"Shut up," I tell him, though he hasn't said a word yet. "I know it sounds stupid, but I'm deathly afraid of snakes, and growing up, I've seen several water moccasins in these waters."

For a second, I think Sebastian looks concerned, but then he tosses me off him. I go under the water and pop up quickly and see him swimming for the boat. "Are you fucking kidding me?" I shout, but I keep swimming, eyeing the water around me. "Are you really racing me to the boat?"

"Who says I'm not scared of snakes too?" The bastard says between laughs.

"You're unbelievable. I cannot believe I was going to rescue you. Next time I will let your ass drown."

Suddenly I'm met with a solid wall of asshole. When did he stop swimming? "I call bullshit," he says, his voice hard with a hint of something else.

"Get out of my way." I try to shove him, but he catches my arm and pulls it over his shoulder. "What are you doing?"

Heaven help me, he is putting me on his back.

"I'm making sure the big, bad snakes don't get you."

He needs to drown or at least experience a few minutes of waterboarding.

"Oh, wow," I say with heavy sarcasm. "My hero."

"Damn right," he says, just as he grasps the ladder and hoists both me and him up and out of the water.

I'd like to say I'm not impressed with his show of manliness and delicious arm muscles, but I can't. My damn vagina tingles. The demon has charmed me yet again.

"I'm impressed," I say, taking a bite of my burger. "It's not as bad as I thought it would be."

Sebastian gives me a bored look. "It doesn't take a genius to grill."

I raise my brows. It may not, but, for a while, he had a flame taller than me he was trying to contain, so I had a valid reason to worry about the fate of my burger. "All I'm saying is I had doubts. Consider me pleasantly surprised."

After the near snake encounter—that was probably a fish—Sebastian and I decided it was a good time to head back to the house and eat.

An hour and three MyView tutorial videos later, we have food.

And a blanket.

And bugs galore.

"Ugh!" I swat at another yellow jacket. "Why are there so many bugs?"

Sebastian leans around the perimeter of the blanket, unhurried and unconcerned that a violent winged creature is going to sting the bejesus out of him at any moment. In all actuality, they probably pick up the asshole vibe he gives off and steer clear. Me, on the other hand, they seem to enjoy taunting.

"I don't see anything," he says, his voice careful.

My eyes narrow. "I am not making this up. I promise they keep flying around my head."

Again, he looks around, as if proving there is no flying insects and I'm merely being paranoid.

"Fine," I say after a minute when, coincidentally, the yellow jackets disappear. "I swear they were there," I add, pointing my finger around the blanket. He can make fun of me all he wants, but I know what I saw.

"I'm not arguing with you." He shrugs, taking a bite of his own burger.

"I think you are," I argue, sitting back down on my side of the blanket. The camera is still rolling from earlier when we documented Sebastian's almost grill fiasco.

With his mouth full, he mumbles something I don't catch, but then swallows and tries again. "Why would I argue about there being yellow jackets? If you say they are swarming around you, then I believe you. Stop trying to start a fight."

He says 'start a fight' like we're this married couple that gets bored and stirs up some drama just to bring back the spark in the relationship.

"Because you like to argue with me." And clearly, I like to argue with him, because we're basically having an argument over arguing.

A stupid grin, that should not be allowed, pulls onto Sebastian's face. "If memory serves correctly, you are the one who enjoys heated debates. Wasn't it me who had to step in front of you and that guy who was protesting recycling on the quad?"

Oh, wow.

He went there. He went back to that time that we promised never to discuss again. I shift and sit cross-legged on the blanket. "That dipshit was trying to get on the five o'clock news and you know it. There was absolutely no reason he couldn't throw his plastic water bottle into a different trash can, which was sitting right next to the one he threw it in. He wanted a lashing."

Sebastian chuckles. "And a lashing you gave him, right up until he shoved you and I had to step in between you two.

My lips quirk. "I could have taken him," I say, only frowning slightly.

"I had concerns back then that you weren't even tall enough to look him in the eye, much less land a punch. Knowing you now, I understand my instincts were right. He would have kicked your ass."

We both know Sebastian would have never let that happen. Not then and especially not now that I'm his fake girlfriend.

"It was like little David and Goliath." His rumbling laughter is not at all cute. Full transparency, it is really cute and I'm glad the camera is rolling, catching this rare show of Sebastian letting go.

"I was not David," I mutter, in between his gasps for air. Have mercy. "It's not that funny, dick. Stop laughing."

But he doesn't. Instead, he falls back onto the grass, holding his stomach. "If I would have known then…" Another bout of laughter. "I might have…" Seriously, this is getting ridiculous. "Just to see what he would have done."

"Great." I stand up, interrupting Sebastian's good time and glare down at the hyena. "I'm going to put the food—AhhOww!"

I dart around the blanket, a stinging on the inside of my leg like I've never felt before. "Oh my gosh!" I'm swatting at an invisible attacker as my leg starts to burn.

"What's the matter?"

Sebastian's laughter comes to an abrupt halt as he stands, looking around for the threat. Which, he probably thinks is me, but I don't have time to explain. Something is biting, stinging, tearing me from the inside out mighty close to my—

"Valentina!"

His voice is a roar, and it halts me midjump.

"What is wrong?"

I think it's pretty obvious, but sometimes I can get a little antsy, so maybe Sebastian needs me to confirm if there's a real issue or if I'm just being a spaz.

I shoot him a clear look of, 'I told you so.' "Something is sting-ing me!"

Or stung me. My whole leg is throbbing at this point, so for all I know, the little bastard could still be chomping away, and I wouldn't be able to tell new pain from the initial sting.

"Where?" Sebastian says, his hand coming to rest on my back.

Oh wow. He moved fast.

I shoo him off and take a step toward the house. "My shorts—oh my gosh! Is it still in there?"

I was wrong; I can still feel the sting. Oh my gosh. Watch this thing be in my panties. That's all I need— "What the hell are you doing?"

Before I can react and smack his hands away, Sebastian has my shorts down and pooled at my feet. "I'm making sure it's not in your clothes."

He tries to keep his gaze on my face and not on the movie reel panties I'm currently wearing. They aren't awful, but they aren't the lacy kind that Aspen wears that literally only cover half of her butt cheeks. I kind of like my cheeks secured and not hanging out like half-wrapped Moon Pies.

"I'm going to make sure it's gone, okay?"

He holds his hands up as though he's coming in peace and not planning on copping a feel. His throat works and I'm mesmerized by the action of a strong man kneeling at my feet.

"Okay?" He prompts me again.

I nod, fighting the urge to fidget as his eyes hold mine and drift lower going from my face, to my chest, and then losing my gaze and examining the skin below my hips.

I can feel goosebumps rise as his fingers lead the hunt for the devil bug, moving gently across my heated flesh and around my hip. I can feel his breath against my skin, and I can't tell if it's cooling me down or setting me on fire.

"I don't see anything," he notes softly at my hip, his fingers dangerously close to the edge of the only fabric covering me.

I swallow and avoid his concerned eyes and look up to the sky. It's blue. The clouds look like soft pillows. Like the one Sebastian *used to* sleep on when his pouty lips were at rest, all boyish and cute and—*oh no. No, no, Vee. We are not doing this again. We promised not to fall for Sebastian again.*

I focus and lean my head down and meet his eyes. "It's not at my hip."

I cringe, and Sebastian nods like this is a fight he can handle, even if neither of us want to.

"Where exactly?"

Yeah, he's definitely just as nervous as I am. This is uncharted territory. We might have been friends before this competition, but we've never been this close to one another. I can feel his breath at my center and his hand, still on my hip, is trembling.

This will not turn out well.

"My," I swallow, "—inner thigh."

Yeah, he winced, but I'm not mad. I understand. If our roles were reversed, I would act the same way.

He takes a deep breath and nods like a good little Boy Scout and lets his fingers slide over my hip bone, cresting toward the middle until they stop, reaching the split of my legs. I highly doubt the yellow jacket is still lurking on my skin or in my panties or shorts, but I feel like now is not the time to add that little tidbit and distract Sebastian.

Sure, I said this would probably end badly, and I still stand by that bet, but I've never been known to make good decisions when it comes to Sebastian. I've always just let rationality fall to the wayside and indulged my spontaneous and wild side when it came to him.

This evening is no different.

The pad of Sebastian's finger is soft and warm as it slides over my skin and hesitates before he looks up at me and swallows.

Oh yeah, I'm not the only one who thinks this is an epically terrible idea.

I nod, giving my consent to this shitstorm, when Sebastian eases my thighs apart, his gaze heating me to a boil. I can feel my knees trying to kneel on the grass for support, but I don't give in. That would be ridiculous and send the wrong sign that Bash-hole's touch made me weak and jelly-like.

And that's totally the truth, but I'm not ready to admit it.

Sebastian clears his throat. "Put your foot on my shoulder."

Come again?

He must pick up on my sheer panic because he clarifies. "The inside of your thigh is welted up. I need to see where the actual sting is."

My eyes feel as big as saucers. "You're not planning to pee on me or anything, are you?"

Sebastian rolls his eyes. "That's jellyfish stings and, last I checked, we weren't oceanside."

I knew that. I did, but I panicked.

"I think you put tobacco on wasp stings and such but since I'm fresh out—" He cocks a brow that does something tingly throughout my entire body. "I think I'll just check and make sure the stinger isn't still there."

"Can that happen? I mean, do the stingers just break off and stay lodged into skin and keep stinging?"

It does kind of feel like I'm repeatedly getting stung.

"I think it does with some insects, but I don't think it's true for yellow jackets, but since you can't distinguish a jellyfish from a bug, I'll check to make sure. For all I know, it could have been a bee."

He's so funny.

Not.

"It wasn't a bee," I say, my voice flat and annoyed. "I'm positive it was a yellow jacket."

He shrugs like he still doesn't believe me. It pisses me off to the point I just hike my leg up and onto his shoulder for proof. "Go ahead. See that I know what the hell a yellow jacket looks like."

It was a really stupid move.

Want to know how I know?

The breeze.

The angle.

My center directly in his face.

His grip on my thigh.

Something happens. I don't know what it is, but someone, who I had no idea existed within me, whispers, "Do it."

CHAPTER SIXTEEN

Valentina

University CamFlix Competition Submission
Entry Number: 75
Sebastian and Valentina
Second Interview Continued, also known as phase two of torture

"Sebastian, can you expand on what you mean by Valentina always keeping things interesting? What has surprised you about her?"

Tom is relentless in this interview. I know Sebastian won't tell the truth because that would expose the lies about our story and that's the last thing we would want to do right now while we're in the lead.

Sebastian fidgets next to me, but then he takes a deep breath and settles before he says, "I thought I knew who Valentina was just from our prank wars but the more we hung out, the more I got to know her."

Tom butts in. "And getting to know her proved you were wrong about who she was as a person?"

Sebastian looks me in the eyes. "Yeah. She was so much more than I thought."

Sebastian stares, his body coiled tighter than the time my mom braided my hair so tight my eyes went squinty.

"Sebastian?"

"Shut up," he clips, his fingers flexing against me.

Ugh. I try and move my leg down. Clearly he's uncomfortable. Maybe I misread his body language. Maybe he's just trying to be a good friend and make sure I don't die from an adverse reaction. It's possible all this tension is not because he's as turned on as I am.

"Be still," he barks. "I just need a minute."

I sigh. "I'm fine." I try to move my leg from his shoulder, and he grips it, holding it still.

"I said, I need a minute."

I feel my eyes go squinty. "I heard you." I try pulling away, but his hold is stronger than my pull. "But I'm fine. I'll just go shower and see if we have any cream in the medicine cabinet. I'm sure it's gone."

Honestly, I could call Aunt Anniston, Aspen's mom. She's a doctor and could easily tell me what to do. Sebastian and I don't have to pretend to truly care about each other.

"Shut up."

Oh hell no. "Why are you growling at me? I told you when we set this blanket down that yellow jackets were buzzing around. If anyone should be getting pissed off, it should be me. I told you I was going to get—"

Warmth.

Weakness.

That's all I can think when a million tingles shoot through my core as his mouth closes over the center of my panties, right over my clit. My hands tangle in his hair, and I fold over his body, groaning.

His fingers take advantage of my lack of verbal skills and slip under the edge of my panties.

I think we can all agree that we're no longer looking for a stinger or a yellow jacket. We have just crossed over to giving into something primal, something we've—well, at least I have—wanted to do for so long.

"Sebas—"

"Don't speak," he says, his words muffled against the fabric of my underwear. "Don't ruin this by speaking."

I should be offended, but I'm not. Instead, another moan rips from me, and I give the thick locks of blonde hair in my hands an aggressive tug. Why his asshole personality speaks to me, I will never know…

The warmth of his breath as he presses a kiss to the inside of my leg, as if he's kissing my boo boo before going back to his real mission of making me a mess underneath his hands, is sweet and caring.

And then he shifts, moving my leg off his shoulder.

"What—" His finger goes to my lips.

"No talking, remember?"

I nod, moving his finger with the motion as he bends and puts his arms around my backside and hoists me up and over his shoulder, fireman style.

I yip, and then remember the diva requires pure silence while we make bad decisions, and hush. With more athleticism than I gave him credit for, Sebastian navigates the back deck's steps easily and even manages the door, without so much as jostling me.

The cool air from the house is what I notice first. The second thing I notice is Sebastian bypassing the living room and carrying me down the hall like I'm some value-sized bag of dog food.

Finally, he stops at the bathroom door, hesitating.

"What are we doing?"

For a minute I think he isn't going to answer me but then, as if he makes up his mind, he backs out of the bathroom and heads to the guest bedroom where he's staying.

His hand goes to my back as he lays me down on the bed like I weigh nothing. "Don't move," he says, pointing at me like I'm one of the rescue dogs I train.

I nod and go against saying anything. I'm curious where all this is going and I don't want to ruin it by speaking, since he seems to be heavily opposed to it.

After a second of just raking his eyes up and down my body, he nods and then stands and walks out of the room. Finally, I relax and let the muscles I didn't know I was tensing, relax. Really, what are you doing Valentina Lambros? This is Bash-hole, and yes, we once thought he was a really decent friend with a body that we found incredibly distracting, but it's all just for a few more weeks. Once this competition is over, Sebastian will take his winnings and disappear. He won't finish college because he's always wanted to be in Hollywood. Unlike my parents, his don't support that dream, and he won't get their blessing or financial support unless he finishes his degree—one that he loathes.

My point is, this is so temporary that it doesn't deserve a memory that will haunt me forever. I doubt Sebastian will even think of me or these wars once he gets to LA. He'll live the life he wants with a new cutie on his arm and money in his pocket and a camera in his face. He won't wonder how I'm doing with classes or if I figured out how to make a bloody gash using makeup.

"Stop thinking," he tells me, as if he knows me well enough to know I'm worrying about everything that could go wrong.

"I'm not thinking," I lie, simply because I don't want him thinking he's right. His horn doesn't need tooting any more than it already does.

The smirk he gives me pops his dimple, and I swear those damn tingles start up again. "Liar."

I shrug. He'll never know for sure because I'll never tell him.

"What are doing with that—"

The rest of my words are cut off when he grabs my ankles and drags me across the sheets so that my legs go around his imposing body.

He tosses something next to me that I don't bother seeing what it is. Frankly, it could be a spider or a stick of gum and I wouldn't give a shit. The only thoughts running through my head is how fucking low his pants hang off his hips and if I could push them down the rest of the way with my feet.

Before I can try, though, Sebastian's big body leans over me and lets his stubbly jaw scratch up the side of my leg that's laying helplessly at his side. He takes the one he just grazed with his pretty face and places it on one of his broad shoulders and then he repeats the same motion with my other leg.

Dammit.

He's ruined me. At the very least, he's set a precedent for all the other fake boyfriends that may follow him. The scruff makes the lady bits purr in compliance. When both of my legs are resting—wobbling—on his shoulders, he licks his lips and reaches between my legs.

My eyes close, and I prepare to smother a moan and terribly smutty thoughts, but his touch never comes. Instead, my eyes flash open, as something cold hits my inner thigh.

I suck in a breath and ignore the stupid smirk on his stupid face. He meant to tease me.

"The sting doesn't look too bad," he says through a grin, as he wipes what I now realize is a wet cloth against my welted skin. "I don't see a stinger either."

Is he really going to remain calm and collected while my legs are on his shoulders, spread apart for his viewing, while he rubs dangerously close to where I want him to be?

Here's a hint: Fuck the sting.

At this point, I don't care if I die of shock or my leg rots off. All I want is for that smartass mouth of his to be smothered in my vajayjay.

Yeah, I said it.

I'm not going to act like I'm some kind of reserved person. My lady bits haven't seen a man in over a year. And even when they experienced a man for the first time, he did not look like Sebastian or make me want to punch him and then make it better.

No, my first time was with Thomas, a guy from the high school band. He played the trumpet and he acted like the sight of my vagina scared him.

It wasn't a magical or even much of a memorable night, except for the fact that I realized that I had no idea what all the girls were talking about. The D was not that good.

But feeling Sebastian's scruff against my sensitive skin, the heat from his kiss searing through the cotton of my panties… I'm willing to bet this is the D that I've been missing. I bet Sebastian has never played the trumpet, but I'm willing to bet he's going to be able to blow my horn.

When the cloth is tossed behind Sebastian's head and his eyes hood with something like torment and want, I finally speak. "If you fucking stop again, I will punch you in the face."

My comment catches him off guard, and he pauses.

Shit. He's going to stop and more than likely leave and go home, leaving me stranded until I can get Aspen or Drew to come get me.

After what seems like a few tense minutes, Sebastian finally throws his head back and laughs this big hearty chuckle.

I grin, relieved that he didn't toss my legs off his shoulders and tell me where I can take my violent self.

But then his laughter suddenly stops, and his gaze drops to mine.

Oh shit. Not good, Vee. This is the part where he leaves.

His hands go to my hips as he leans over me, my knees going to my chest with his movement. "Cute," he muses, burying his face in my hair, right under my ear. "Here you are, legs spread, and under the weight of my body and you think you're in the position to demand anything from me."

Oh.

Well.

That's a little dominating.

I think I like it.

A bite of pain sends a shudder and a gasp through me as Sebastian nips the skin of my neck, replacing the burn with a soft kiss.

"I've wanted you like this for so long…"

I don't know if he's talking to me or himself, but I want to hear more. So long you say?

"Every day—" Another bite. "—watching you—" A kiss to ease the sting. "Hating you."

Oh, well, this is not the direction I imagined this going.

"How did I miss it?"

His kisses are becoming erratic and sloppy, but they're moving down my body, and right now—yep—that one was on the nipple.

"I'm going to rip this fucking shirt off your body." He's gone from sexy neighbor to growly neighbor in mere seconds. You would think that would turn me off. It so doesn't.

I simply help him tear *this fucking shirt* from my body. It doesn't rip because, really, this isn't a movie and it hasn't been precut to do so, but he eases it up, snatching it off of me and tossing it where I hope I can find it later.

He takes his time on my bra, though, pushing me back down and giving me a thorough once over. "I figured it would be flannel," he notes, smoothing his hand over the black satin, cupping my breast in his palm.

I close my eyes, letting the flannel comment go, mainly since his hand is on my breast. I repeat, his hand is on one of my girls. No man has ever touched my boobs before. Ever. Thomas didn't even bother taking my shirt off when he nearly hyperventilated, while shoving his dick in.

"I hate you." I moan. "Do the other one now."

Okay, so I didn't let the flannel comment slide and I know he went all Hulk-like earlier when I demanded he not stop again, but, this time, he actually does as I ask, somewhat. Instead of moving to the other side, he pulls the cup down and replaces his hand with his mouth and really, I vote this is where his mouth stays forever.

My eyes pinch shut, and I suck in a breath, my stomach concaving from the sensation overload. "Oh my gosh, why didn't you tell me you were so good at this?" I mumble. "I think this should be the kind of things friends share with each other instead of rumors and subscriber stats."

Something like a snort comes from above me before he grows tense under my hands and says seriously, "Amongst other secrets friends should share."

I slide my hand up and down the expanse of his back as a silent apology. I can't change the past. What I can do is let him love on me until we both feel better about those secrets.

After several blessed minutes of lavish attention to one boob, Sebastian finds his way to the other, only pausing to readjust my legs twice when they slip off his shoulders.

"I want to touch you," I say into his hair, noting the soft, damp strands against my face.

"No," he clips out, adjusting his grip and adding more weight, just in case I get the bright idea to do it anyway. He knows.

"I—"

His finger slips inside my panties, and every thought I had about touching his chest leaves me.

"Are you wet for the enemy, Valentina?"

Heaven help me, I am, and I'm not even mad about it.

His finger grazes my slit and I gasp.

"Don't let your legs fall," he barks.

The angry, bossy thing is really affecting my comebacks. It's not, however, calming my horny self down. I attempt to channel all my effort into keeping my legs on his shoulders, but when his finger breaches my slit and slides inside me, I let them fall.

He groans and I fight off the feeling that I'm on the brink of an orgasm induced coma but then he adds another finger and I'm pretty positive the delicious stretch is the only thing keeping me conscious.

"I'm going to take these off," he says, pulling his fingers out, the wetness coating my skin as he tugs on my panties. "You're not going to move or speak."

I can do that.

He pulls back and slips off the barrier between us. I'm exposed, my heated flesh cool from the ceiling fan above us. I thought I would want to cover myself or would be nervous or scared that this is happening, but I'm not. Even with his gaze all over my body, I feel quite comfortable with what's happening right now.

"I—"

He shushes me with a finger to my lips and, I'll be honest, I almost bite it. I want to see him, dammit, and with the smirk on his face, I think he knows it. He likes depriving me. He always has.

He waits until he thinks I'm not going to speak before he removes his finger. I stay quiet, even though it pains me to do so. With a strength that is pretty freaking awesome from a MyView star, Sebastian slips under my legs, spreading me open and letting my legs fall to the crease of his elbows. Oh, this is much better than his shoulders. He's literally doing all the work.

And then he leans down, his mouth finding my center and his tongue slipping into my opening. I'm pretty sure I'll never be able to look at him again without seeing those frosty blue eyes gaze out from between my legs, hating, lusting, and finally surrendering.

My fingers knot in his hair, and I try not to smother him. No one needs to call an ambulance, forcing me to explain the reason he isn't breathing is because I smothered his pretty face with my vagina.

Yeah, that would not look good.

Sebastian's tongue does things inside me that no one will ever know about because, frankly, that kind of mastery of a clit should be a well-guarded secret.

"Bash," I whisper, my back arching against the bed, the weight of his body pressing me back down.

"I'm sorry," I tell him. I don't know why I decided that in the middle of the best oral—the only oral—I've ever received, I'd try mending fences, but weird things happen when someone's face is between your legs. I just wanted to clear things up if this weekend is going to continue in this direction.

"I never meant to deceive—oh, shit."

His teeth scrape down the sensitive bundle of nerves and, you know what, fuck it. I already said I'm sorry and he isn't torturing me or popping up to tell me to shut up, so I'm just going to let the shit go. What's done is done and— "I'm coming. Holy shit, I think I'm coming!"

I don't know why I felt like shouting it or that it would have been nice for him to at least give me a thumbs up as he finished me off, but when shivers and muscle spasms locked up my entire body, I was grateful for his sweet kisses as he held me until they stopped.

This sweet, shitty neighbor of mine just made me come like a rock star and I'm so screwed.

CHAPTER SEVENTEEN
Sebastian

University CamFlix Competition Submission
Entry Number: 75
Sebastian and Valentina
Second Interview Continued, also known as that time Tom made stupid shit go through my head

"Okay, last question," Tom promises.

I nod. I just want this to be over. I feel more exposed than ever.

"If you win, do you and Valentina plan on moving in together?"

I sit up on the sofa and look over at Vee. "Wow, Tom. You sure know how to put a guy on the spot." I rake a hand through my hair. "Vee and I haven't talked about it, really. I think, right now, we're just taking it day by day."

It's the second round of brushing my teeth after a three-hour nap. I still can't get the flavor of her off my tongue. It's fucking torture and heaven and a goddamned kick in the gut all at the same time. A damn yellow jacket was the catalyst to my destruction.

I want to say I hated it and the noises Vee made turned me off but that would be a big fat lie. Fact of the matter is, I want more. So much fucking more and that's a problem.

My phone buzzes on the dresser, and I walk over to grab it. It's my sister.

Mom #2: I went by your house and stocked your kitchen. What's with the patio chair in your bedroom? Do you want me to buy you a real sitting chair?

I grin. I'll give up that chair never. Valentina might as well shop for a new one.

Me: What? You don't like it? I think it gives the room a raggedy edge.

Mom #2: You're ridiculous. Where are you? Emmy and I thought we could have lunch with you.

This is the time that I wish I wasn't a mess. My sister means well and my niece, well, she's an innocent bystander in all of this.

Me: I'm at the lake with friends. Next time?

It takes my sister longer than usual to respond.

Me: I promise, Cal. Okay?

She finally responds.

Mom #2: Okay. I'll talk to you later. Have fun.

I don't text her back because I know my sister, and anytime she tells me to have fun, it means she's mad and I need to give her time to calm down and regroup.

It's not her fault I'm like this. It's not any of their faults. I simply can't help but feel out of place in my own family. It's not like they didn't allow me on family trips or made me wear a scarlet letter; I just feel like I don't belong. Like I was a last-minute plus-one to their family.

I love them, and I will always be grateful for the life I was given, but I'd like to get away from my past and start somewhere new.

I shove my phone in my pocket and exhale. Why is everything so fucking complicated? First my family and then Vee, my enemy, my friend, back to my enemy, and now my fake girlfriend that I just made come on my tongue.

Oh, the tangled web I have weaved.

I make my way to the living room and look outside. It's after ten and Vee is surrounded by the cover of darkness on the dock, only the light of the moon and her iPad giving her position away.

Instead of disappointing two women in my life today, I decide, for once, to do the right thing and at least make peace with one of them. I brew a pot of coffee and pour it into two mugs, adding the cream and sugar like Vee likes, and then head out the back door to the dock.

I don't turn the lights on because I know she likes to stay in the moment and scare the shit out of herself, so I try to make as little noise as possible when I walk along the dock to where she is bundled in a blanket.

"I brought you some coffee—"

In a blur of movement, the light from the iPad soars through the air in a mixture of "Ahhs!" and "Oh shits!" before it splashes into the lake.

I stand there, wide-eyed, as I listen to Vee's erratic breathing. "Sebastian?" she finally asks.

I make sure my voice is smooth and non-threatening. "Yeah."

She releases a breath, and I add, "I brought you some coffee. I'm sorry. I didn't mean to scare you."

I really didn't, although a stupid grin still tugs onto my face.

"Sure you didn't," she says, pushing past me.

"Wait!" I put the mugs down on the dock and catch up to her easily, grabbing her around the arm. "Calm down. I really didn't mean to scare you."

I can't see her features clearly in the dark, but I can only imagine the glare she's giving me.

"I really was just bringing you some coffee."

She doesn't try to pull away this time and I take that as a good sign.

"My iPad is at the bottom of the lake," she notes with a tremble in her voice, and it does something to my stomach.

"I'm sorry. I know how much you love it. Maybe we can stop on the way home and pick up another one?"

Our sponsorships have been picking up with our new videos. I'm sure she can afford it.

"My treat," I add, when she doesn't say anything. "Since I'm the one who made you toss it in the first place."

I want to add that if she watched her horror movies on a TV, inside the house, like a normal person, this wouldn't happen, but since she doesn't, this is what it's come down to. Her scaring herself out here in the dark and losing her precious iPad.

"That's sweet of you," she returns, touching the top of my hand with hers. "But that's not necessary. I was the one out here on the dock." She pulls out of my grasp. "I didn't think you would come out here."

Her comment sends regret swirling around in my gut. She's right. Most of the time when I'm aggravated or upset with her, I retreat and not speak to her for a while. Hence the two-month silence after her final prank.

"I'm sorry," I tell her. "I shouldn't have been such a dick to you after the last prank."

We're in the dark. I don't have to look at her face when I say this.

"I was so angry at you."

I tuck my hands in my pocket. "I had no right to be, but I still lashed out at you. You were only playing the game I started."

"I didn't mean to let it go on as long as it did," she says, and I shake my head.

"I just didn't—"

I stop, catching my breath.

"What I'm trying to say is that I don't normally connect to anyone like that."

"But you and Maverick are friends," she adds, "and Rowan."

I nod. "It wasn't the same."

I confided in her. I told her about my dreams, and we both shared in the excitement of making it in our respective fields.

"I'm sorry," she says for probably the hundredth time.

I reach out for her hand and like she knows it's there, she takes it, threading her fingers through mine.

"I have my phone," I offer. "It's not your iPad, but you can at least finish your movie." I reach into my back pocket and pull out my phone, the screen brightening the space around us.

She smiles. "Is this your way of accepting my apology?"

She knows me well.

I tip my chin, fighting the urge to say something shitty and ruin the connection. I push the phone toward her. "Take it."

She places her fingers around the edges, but doesn't take it. "Will you watch it with me?"

"Yeah."

The word comes out before I can stop it. I mean, I do want to watch it with her, but then again, I'm drifting into territory that I won't be able to recover from. Once I win this money, I plan on leaving. Valentina plans on staying here and finishing school. It'll be like losing her all over again.

But I don't voice any of this. I simply let her lead me back to her bed of blankets along the edge.

She kneels first and then tugs my hand and I follow while she slides the throw pillow to the center. "Here," she offers, patting the pillow. "You can take it."

I ease down and lie on my side. Then, in the most natural way, I tug her down with me. She curls onto her side, sliding her back to my front. Her head rests on my arm while my free arm goes around her, holding the phone. She takes it from me, clicking the streaming app and finding the point she was at in her movie before I disrupted her.

The screen flickers to life and the girl on the screen runs with her boyfriend right behind her. A deranged man is chasing them and when the guy realizes they won't be able to outrun the killer, he stops.

My grip tightens on Vee as the guy tells his onscreen girlfriend that he loves her and to run and not look back. He's sacrificing himself to keep his girlfriend safe. And while I would have balked at such a cliché move in the past, right now, with the only girl who's ever been able to crack through my bullshit exterior, I feel different. I feel protective. I feel loved.

As the girl on the screen cries and kisses her boyfriend, I feel Vee's hand drift lower, rubbing the flannel of my pajama bottoms.

I don't need to see her to know she's smiling. "These are nice," she says.

I nuzzle her hair. "I thought you might appreciate them."

She smothers a laugh.

"Why do you like these movies?" I ask her, as the guy gets stabbed for the final time. "Are they not depressing?"

Her shoulders shrug against my arm. "I don't know. I think I like the fact that there's always a survivor. That even when the circumstances seem bleak, your instinct and faith in yourself will always get you through."

"What if the main character dies though?" I've seen some movies that don't end in happily ever afters.

"I guess they can, but at least they go down with a fight."

"Like you did when I bombed your video?"

She definitely fought back. Not as fast as I expected, but she did, and in the end, she survived me. The problem was, I didn't survive her.

"No one had ever told me the truth," she says softly.

I grunt. "I was an asshole," I admit. "That wasn't telling you the truth. That was making fun of you. I'm sorry."

Now that I think back on it, I was a massive dick and deserved everything I had coming to me.

Her body shakes in my arms. "You were right, though. I couldn't sing."

"Yeah, but I shouldn't have said anything."

"You didn't. You just started acting out the scene behind me."

I'll admit it was not my best moment. Some things you just can't take back.

"Why were you singing that song from *Titanic* anyway?" I ask her.

"My uncle Pe's birthday was the following month. He owns a nightclub, and every year for his birthday, he hosts a Céline Dion karaoke night with family and friends. I wanted to practice."

"So you thought singing online was the best way to go about that practice?"

She has bigger balls than I do.

"I knew the internet would be honest, unlike my family. I'd know for sure if I should get up on stage."

"And did you, sing on stage?"

I can feel her exhale. "No. I didn't."

And now I feel like the biggest asshole on the planet. "I'm sorry. I never meant for that to happen."

She waves her hand in front of the screen. "Don't worry about it. I was glad that someone finally told me the truth. My entire family is musically inclined, except for me. For some reason, I felt like in order to fit in with them, I had to be musical too. In your own stupid way, you taught me that I didn't have to."

"What do you mean?"

I appreciate her trying to make me feel better, but honestly, I can't see how me mouthing 'watermelon' and pretending to be Jack from *Titanic* helped her in any other way than getting us subscribers and sponsors.

"I figured if I couldn't sing like Céline then I'd look like her. I learned how to do makeup and my uncle Pe had the best time taking selfies with me."

I smile into the darkness. "So that's where the wig idea came from?"

She wiggles in my arms. "Yep. You brought it on yourself. You created the monster."

I take a second and absorb everything. This fiery neighbor literally turns everything in her life around. She's the 'make lemonade out of lemons' person.

"I can't say I regret it," I whisper.

I don't care one bit that I created the so-called monster because, somehow, I've fallen for the monster in my arms.

Vee leans back and tips her head up. I meet her in the middle and kiss her lips. "You're crazy."

"Ditto," she returns.

We lay in silence for a little while, watching the girl on the screen navigate the woods and avoid getting stabbed to death, when Vee finally breaks the silence.

"Bash?"

"Yeah."

"Can I ask you something?"

I already know I'm not going to like what she's going to ask me. Any time you start off a question with a question, you know it's going to go badly. But I owe her that much.

"Yeah."

She doesn't even hesitate. "What's up with you and your family? Before—you know—"

Before the prank she means. "You would always avoid your mom's calls. Why don't you ever want to see your family?"

Only Maverick knows this answer, and to be honest, I almost told Vee, but then she kissed me and ruined everything. But she shared an insecurity with me, so I guess opening up even more than I already have with her wouldn't be that terrible.

"You said your family is all musically talented," I start. "Well, mine are all successful."

She turns to face me. "Are you saying you aren't successful?"

I don't ever discuss this. Ever. "I'm only good at one thing. Making people laugh."

Vee's brows dip. "You're good at a lot of things."

I match her stare. "Oh yeah? Name them."

"Poker."

"I rarely win."

She looks to the sky. "Okay, school."

"Maverick tutors me every Wednesday after poker."

I can keep going with this all night.

"You're still successful, though," she adds, "just because you have to work harder than others doesn't mean you aren't successful."

I try to move my arm, but she catches it and secures it to her side. "Talk to me like you used to."

I used to not feel like I was baring my soul to someone.

"I have mommy issues. Is that what you wanted to hear?"

It's shitty and I'd like to say I'm better than that, but it's a sore spot in my life.

"What kind of mommy issues?"

Ugh. "I don't want to talk about it," I say after a long pause.

"Okay," she says, patting my hand patiently and turning the volume up on the movie.

The girl in the movie finally makes it to the road and has her hand up trying to hitch a ride to safety when I finally decide to just blurt it out. "I'm a disappointment to my family. In your story, you still added value and fun to the party. I do neither. My sister, whom I love dearly, is the star of my family. She can do anything. She was the Valedictorian in high school. Captain of the cheerleading team. Went to college on a scholarship. I could go on, but it's nauseating. The point is my parents pay out the ass for my tuition because I can't maintain a high enough GPA to keep a scholarship. I didn't go to a college in California because I couldn't get into one. Both of my parents are successful real estate agents in my hometown. They are the 'it couple' with the precious daughter and then there's me."

Vee chimes in, "You, who has over a million subscribers and doesn't have to work a day job to support himself because he has such a successful MyView page."

She just doesn't get it.

"My sister is ten years older than me." I take a breath. "When she was nine, she got cancer. The doctors tried everything. Nothing worked. The last possibility was a stem cell transplant from a sibling."

Vee's arm grabs onto mine like a mini hug. "I was born to save her."

"Sebastian," she scolds. "You were born to be her hero."

Not quite. "Her body rejected the cells. A stranger matched and ended up being her hero."

"Is that why you give blood every month? So you can be someone's hero?"

I grunt. "No. That's not why I do it."

Vee squeezes me and I know she's smiling when she says, "It's okay. You don't have to admit it. I know you're a hero."

CHAPTER EIGHTEEN

Valentina

University CamFlix Competition Submission
Entry Number: 75
Sebastian and Valentina
Second Interview Continued, also known as the time Tom became
suspicious for good reason

"Day by day," Tom muses with a stupid grin on his face. "I get it. I was young once."

I have a hard time believing Tom was once young. The collared shirt and khakis make me think before he was Tom, the annoying interview guy, he was Jake from State Farm.

I pat Sebastian's leg and lean in, avoiding smelling that distinct smell of organic palm oil free soap he uses, but acts like he doesn't know anything about. He knows he buys it because I spent a solid half hour bitching about how it was destroying the rainforests. "Sebastian and I just want to enjoy our new relationship." Also known as the time we didn't totally hate each other.

Tom nods. "Sure. Sure. I get that." He writes something on his clipboard. When he looks up, he smiles, and it feels wrong. "But I can't help but think that you guys aren't being completely honest with me."

Well, Tom, we aren't. We're liars.

"What's the matter?"

His voice is muffled and raspy from sleep. His legs are thrown over the blankets and his shirt is off.

When I don't answer, he calls out softly, "Vee?"

I tuck a wayward piece of hair behind my ear. Let's be honest, there's more than likely several wayward pieces. I'm not one of those women who can wake up with silky strands all in place.

"Valentina. You're making me nervous. Are you here to kill me?"

His words are soft, but there's an edge to them that finally makes me laugh. "Not tonight," I tell him, climbing onto the bed and onto the other side where I slide under the covers.

Sebastian lays back down and I roll toward him, easing my arm onto his chest. "Can we just pretend not to pretend for a moment?"

I'm not going to spell it out for him. We've been *not pretending* for most of the weekend. I know that makes him nervous since he doesn't want to like me. He wants to keep that line drawn between us so that we never have to address our confusing past or our fake present.

I love him.

I always have. Well, not always, but love comes on in strange ways. Sometimes it's those butterflies when they stare deep into your eyes and then there is my kind of love like when he spoiled your video and stole your chair, the butterflies flutter. The truth is, we love to hate each other.

But with all this, the only thing I've pretended is that I don't love him.

His hand is warm as it intertwines with mine. "Agreed," he answers, before rolling over and sliding me closer to his body.

This time we are face to face, no cameras, no barriers, and all

I see is the broken boy who has always been the man everyone expected him to be. Sure, he took several wrong turns but, deep down, Sebastian is loyal to his friends and family.

He may think he was only a DNA donor to his family, but I see the way his family checks in on him. They love him and while they may have their own expectations and ideals of what he should be, he will always be Bash-hole to me. Strong willed, free-spirited, and full of life. He was meant for more than just being a donor, and one day, I hope he will see that too.

"What are you thinking?" he whispers softly. His breath isn't even bad after having been asleep.

"That you're a beautiful soul."

It's not as hard saying the words in the dark.

"Ugh."

He tries to roll over, but I lock my legs around him, preventing him from leaving.

"Why do we fight?" I ask him.

I can feel him shrug into the mattress. "I don't know, maybe because we're bored."

"Are you sure?" I don't feel like I'm bored.

He sighs heavily. "Because it's fun."

I smile. It is fun.

"Because," he adds out of nowhere, "you get feisty when you're mad."

"I'm half Latina. We're always feisty."

At least that's what my dad says.

"It's not the same when you fight back." He rolls over and traces my forehead. "There's this little line that forms and—"

I kiss him.

Out of nowhere and I don't feel an ounce of regret for it.

I suck his bottom lip into my mouth and moan before he gets on board and takes over. His hands grasp my hips in a bruising hold and he rolls over me, pinning me beneath him. I can see his swollen lips in the glow of the moonlight, streaming in from the window.

His chest is heaving when he says, "No more games after this."

I nod, swallowing down the knot of fleeting panic. "Except when we're bored." Who are we kidding? Pranking each other is our thing. I'm sure we will grow out of it one day but that doesn't mean we have to completely give it up.

He grins and agrees. "Except when we're bored."

I place my hands on his face, the atmosphere turning thick with seriousness. I smooth my thumb over the spot on his cheek where my favorite dimple appears and press my lips to his.

A tortured sound rumbles from his chest as he pushes me down with the weight of his body, heavy and perfect.

I take a breath and turn my head to the side. "Bash?"

I can feel him tense above me. "Yeah?"

I want to know if he forgives me or if we will go back to being only neighbors once the contest is over, but I don't. "Never mind."

Some things you just don't need to ruin with a reality check. I know what I signed up for when I agreed to do this contest with Sebastian and having sex with him is probably a huge mistake, but it's one I want to make. I've never made good decisions where Sebastian is concerned, and I don't plan on starting now, even if it does make things messier between us.

"Are you sure?" He probes suspiciously.

"Yeah, I'm sure. No going back, right?"

"Right."

His hands move under my shirt and graze up my ribs. My back arches and I suck in a breath. Sebastian's hands have always felt good on my body, even when he didn't know I was enjoying the feel of his touch. A simple pat on the back. A high five. I wanted to be repulsed. I wanted to hate the warmth of his touch, but I didn't. I couldn't. Ever since playing his fake girlfriend, feeling his hands willingly roam the expanse of my body… I've not only welcomed his touch, I've craved more.

"Can I take this off?" His fingers tug the hem of my shirt, lifting it ever so slightly.

I nod. "Please."

His chest smells of soap and the heat of his skin begs me to come closer. I press a kiss between his pecs, and he flinches as if it burned. I lift up and allow him to pull my shirt all the way off. The air is cool against my skin, but only for a second, before he wraps me in his arms and his heat, warming me instantly.

Deep in his embrace, I feel small, cherished, and revered. I pull my hand through our bodies and place it at his throat, feeling him swallow.

"You're more beautiful than I ever imagined," he whispers in the moonlight, removing my hand and kissing the palm.

"You were expecting something different?" I joke.

He grins, lowering himself down, his weight a reminder of what we're doing. "I think you're done talking," he says, pushing his thumb into my mouth. I don't wait for him to tell me to suck. I know what Sebastian Carrington needs. Control. A redo of that night.

Sebastian buries his face in my shoulder and moans as I let his finger slip from my mouth. "Look at me, Bash," I demand. I want to see his face. I want him to know that it's me making him feel this way. Not the girl he hates or the one he used to prank, but the friend he used to spend his days with.

Slowly, he raises his head, pushing up on his forearms, and swallows. His frosty blue eyes lock onto mine and, for the first time since we've known each other, I feel like he's seeing the real me. "I see you, Valentina." His voice is a soft whisper while his fingers stroke down my cheek, lingering on my lips. "I've always seen you."

My stomach dips as I absorb his words. *He sees me.* Just me. Not anyone else. That may not seem like a big deal to most people, but to me, it's everything.

I lean my face into his hand and close my eyes. This man has seen me at my worst. He's elicited the most immature actions I wish I could take back, but right now, in this moment, feeling his eyes on my face, all I can think is: it's all been worth it. Had it not been for those wars or insane actions, it would have never led me to this moment. This one singular moment of love.

"Vee?"

I blink up at my best friend hovered above me. "Yeah?"

A boyish grin plays at the corner of his mouth. "Are you going to take my dick out or just keep rubbing it through my pants?"

Oh. *Oh.* I release his pants and grin. "I didn't realize I was…you know."

He lifts a brow. "Jerking me off?"

"I was not jerking you off!" I shrug. "It was more like a dick massage."

His eyes harden. "Put your mouth on me."

He doesn't mean a kiss on the cheek.

I swallow and he rolls onto his back, leaving my bare breasts exposed. Pushing up, I throw my leg over his and curl my fingers over the waistband of his pants. "I like bossy, Sebastian," I say, grinning.

He scoffs. "I don't know why. You never listen to him."

I shrug, inching his pants down slowly, drawing out the torture for both of us. "That's because he's typically never right, but since you're almost naked, I'll make an exception."

"Is that all it takes then? Me being naked when I ask you to do something?"

Uh. I'm thinking yes. "I'm just saying it's a better motivator."

He grins. "I'll keep that in mind."

"You do that," I tell him, yanking his pants down just enough to free his cock. It springs up toward his stomach, and I wrap my hand around the thickness.

A groan rips from his chest, and he grabs my free hand, placing my palm over his heart. It's intimate, feeling his heart pounding against my hand while his dick pulses in the other, leaking his need onto my fingertips.

"You do this to me," he bites out, his eyes going to the hand on his chest.

His jaw is clenched and the muscles in his neck strain. "Do what?" I whisper. "Make you angry?"

His eyes close as if my statement isn't what he wanted to hear but then he sits up, suddenly tangling my hair in his hands. My body is pulled forward so that we're nose to nose. "You make me…" he says softly and a little growly. He kisses the corner of my mouth. "You make me come undone."

"Is that a good thing?" I swallow, gazing down at the head of his dick, peeking out of the top of my hand. I swipe the pad of my finger through the bead of liquid. He groans, untangling himself and easing back down on the mattress, his breaths heavy and pained. "No, this is not a good thing at all," he finally answers, but his words are resigned. If he doesn't think this is a good idea, he's still going to go through with it.

As am I.

Because we're done fighting whatever this is between us.

I scoot down, holding his eyes as I lower my head, opening my mouth and slipping him between my lips. He feels like soft velvet when I close my lips around him.

"Oh, fuck." He moans, grasping my hand that has slid down his stomach.

I bob my head up and down, tasting the saltiness on my tongue. His hand squeezes mine and I circle the head with my lips, paying special attention to the soft skin underneath. I pull up with his dick still inside my mouth and hold his gaze.

"No more," he grits out, sounding as if he's unhinged, pulling me up and forward, already aligning our centers.

"Wait." I stop him with a hand on his chest.

His eyes are heavy and lidded with want. "What?" It's as if he's out of breath.

I smile nervously. "Condom."

Like the thought had never occurred to him, his eyes go wide and he nods. "My jeans. Find my wallet."

It's cute that he can't even form complete sentences.

I grin and ease off his body; his hand still grips mine like he's scared I might bolt for the door. Grabbing his jeans off the floor, I toss them onto the bed where he finally lets my hand go and uses his finger to skim the center of my eyes.

"Take them off," he says, his gaze focused on my center.

I nod slowly and swallow the knot in my throat. My hands shake as I slip my fingers under the waistband and pull them down.

Sebastian's gaze never wavers, the only way I know he's still breathing is the twitch of his hand, begging to touch me again. Without looking down, I reach into his jean's pocket and pull out the leather wallet and take out the foil wrapper.

"May I?" I ask him, the same way he did when he was removing my shirt.

He nods and I put a knee on the bed, climbing up so I'm straddling his legs again. I whisper, "No take backs."

His voice is raspy. "No take backs."

He palms my bare ass as I open the wrapper and roll the latex over his length.

His throat works as his eyes stay locked on my hands inching over his cock. "I can't fucking wait to feel you wrapped around me," he says, pushing down on my hands as if I'm taking too long to roll the condom on.

"Wh—"

I gasp when he pushes in, stealing my breath and my snarky comment.

"It's just like I imagined," he admits, his face tight and his dimple gone. "I knew it was going to fuck me up."

I don't know who he's talking to but I feel like I should add that my vajayjay and I feel the same way as we stretch around him, his cock barreling in and out at a torturously slow pace. I may be on top, but clearly, I'm not the one in control here as he pushes my hips up and down exactly how he wants.

"Look at me," he barks out, startling my eyes off his chest. "When my dick is inside you, you keep your eyes on me."

I nod as a shiver races up my spine. He seems pleased by my lack of retort and pushes my hips up, driving me back down. My head falls back, and I remember his demand. I look down and find his eyes. His lips tip at the corners, offering me just a hint of a smile before he moves his hand and drags his finger down my lips. I nip at him, but he moves to my breasts and all thoughts go out the window.

"Ride me, Vee."

His body relaxes into the mattress and both of his hands cup my breasts, massaging them before his fingers toy with my nipples until they're peaked buds. "You still with me, Valentina?" I used to hate it when he called me Valentina. But now, hearing him say it all concerned and tortured, it's my new favorite word.

My head drops forward, and I find his eyes. "I'm still with you."

And then I show him how much by moving my hips backward and forward, until the muscles in his neck tighten and his breathing is shallow pants. His hands find my hips as I brace mine against his chest.

"I'm so close," I tell him between gulps of air.

He picks up the pace and I don't have time to brace myself as he swells inside me and I fold over his body, an orgasm ripping through me like a freight train. He grips my hips and holds me to him, not letting any space between us as he empties himself inside me.

We're both sweaty as we lay there, dragging in as much air as we can.

"Come here," he finally says, rolling me over and tucking me into his arm.

"Do you need a hug?" I tease.

He barks out a laugh. "I think I might, Vee. I think I might."

CHAPTER NINETEEN

Valentina

University CamFlix Competition Submission
Entry Number: 75
Sebastian and Valentina
Final Interview, also known as the time this shitshow came to an end

"Where's Sebastian?"

I look at Tom and fake a smile. "He had something come up. He'll be here though."

Tom doesn't look like he believes a word out of my mouth. "Are you sure?"

No. "Yeah, I'm sure. This contest is important to him. He would never not show up."

I don't really know though.

"I'm sure you're aware of the video that surfaced of you two?"

Tom looks like he needs a Snickers and maybe a cigarette.

"Yes, sir," I say, attempting to keep my voice even.

Tom nods. "Then why don't you start from the beginning and

tell me why I shouldn't disqualify you for that video. I knew you two were hiding something."

Disqualify us? "I'll be happy to start from the beginning, Tom, because I owe our fans an explanation but unless you can point me to the section in the rules that defines what Sebastian and I did was grounds for disqualification then I suggest you sit back and let me entertain you with our real story, because that's what your viewers pay for."

"Fuck!"

I should have known nothing good ever comes out of the word fuck. Not even fucking because up until now, any time that I've slept with a man, which has just been twice, it's ended badly.

"What's wrong?"

I wipe the sleep from my eyes, but they are still having a hard time focusing. What I can manage to make out is a furious Sebastian pacing in front of the mirror.

"It's over," he yells, slinging his phone against the wall.

I scramble up in bed and tuck the blankets so they cover my breasts. "What's over?"

I know it's stupid that my heart is racing at the mere thought that our fake relationship is ending; I feel like my heart won't be able to take it again.

"The contest," he says loudly, his hands going to his head and pressing. "We lost, Vee. Malcolm posted a video and ruined us. How could I be so stupid? Everything—" He drops his head against the glass. "—Everything is gone. No half a million. No California. No nothing. It's all over."

His body is visibly shaking, so I pull the sheet off the bed and stand, but he stops me. "I don't want your pity."

"It's not pity," I offer. "The contest isn't over. We haven't lost yet. All we need to do is post another video from this weekend."

Sebastian scoffs and shakes his head. "Watch the video, Vee. It's over. I'm going to pack up. Be ready to go in thirty."

My partner-in-crime walks out of the guest bedroom and leaves me standing with only a sheet holding me together. Last night, the intimacy, the falling asleep in each other's arms… It's all over. I knew the contest was important to Sebastian, but I guess as it went on, it became more about fun and spending time with my old friend. I had forgotten why it was so important to Sebastian. He needed the money. He wants to pursue his dreams and I'm not part of those long-term plans.

I grab my phone from the nightstand and sit on the edge of the bed. I pull up MyView and find Malcolm's page. There, on the front page as click bait, is me staring up at Sebastian, my hand against his bare chest when he offered to be partners for the UniCamFlix contest.

"No," I say to myself as I watch the video, "He wouldn't." The footage that plays was only witnessed by three people: me, Sebastian, and Brick. "It can't be him."

Why? Why would he do something like that?

I mean, I don't know Brick personally, but what I do know is that he's a respected cameraman around campus. Why would he feed our footage to Malcolm? Unless… Could he be how Malcolm ripped off other filmmakers? If Brick has been stealing footage and ideas for Malcolm for over a year, it's no wonder Brick wanted to work with Sebastian. I bet he planned all along to take Sebastian down, but then when we joined forces, we gave him more dirt than he ever dreamed. We gave him the power to destroy both of us.

Our fans will never forgive us.

Tears roll down my face as I watch the raw, unedited footage Brick shot of us that day play the entire scene where we negotiated our deal to be a fake couple. I can't bear to watch anymore and turn it off.

I climb out of bed and pull on my tank top and pajama shorts. I can only think of one person I want right now, and it isn't the asshole in the kitchen.

Me: You home from the beach?

I get a response almost instantly.

Aspen: No. We decided to stay through the week. Why? You

need me? I can get Bennett to drive us home. We're out for our run, but we can go back.

I bet she's kicking Bennett's ass. If there's one thing Aspen excels at, it's running. Bennett might be a whole lot of muscle, but he never beats her.

Me: That's okay. I'm good. See you this weekend?

For some reason, I really want her to say yes. I need my friend.

Aspen: Of course. Are you okay?

I look at the girl staring back at me in the bedroom mirror. Her makeup is smudged, and she looks like she's been rocking in a corner. Her eyeliner would make her uncle Pe proud, though. Even through that sweaty, fantastic as shit sex, her eyeliner held up.

I force a smile to the mirror and text her back.

Me: I'm fine. Just miss your face.

I pick up Sebastian's phone from where he threw it and leave it on the bed, before hurrying to my room. I need to get the hell out of here. My heart is acting like it's breaking, and my head is feeling guilty. How did I not know Brick was an assmonkey? I need—I need a damn hug and maybe a shower.

Me: You promise you won't be mad?

Dad: I promise I won't kill anyone. Will that work?

I smile. My dad is ridiculous.

Me: You promise not to tell Mom?

Dad: You're asking a lot of me, kiddo.

Me: Please.

I know he'll agree eventually. He always does.

Dad: Deal, but if she finds out, I will throw you under the bus.

Me: Deal. Can you come pick me up?

His response is almost instant.

Dad: Where are you?

Ugh. Why couldn't Aspen and the guys have been home?

Me: At the lake house.

Dad: Alone?

I bite my lip and say a little prayer. My dad is a calm man, but sometimes, he loses his shit. I can only hope this isn't one of those times.

Me: I am now.

Dad: Thankfully, you have an hour and a half to pray I cool down before I get to you.

Me: Maybe bring Uncle Mason as a witness?

Uncle Mason won't let my dad go all Hulk-like when he gets here and finds out I spent the weekend with a boy. I might be nineteen and a grown woman, but my dad gives zero shits about my age. To him, I will always be his little girl.

Dad: Don't you move until I get there.

As scary as my Dad is when he's mad, for some reason, it's a lot better than riding home with Sebastian, who basically just told me it was all over and to pack my shit, so we can go home and go back to being enemies.

No thank you. I'd rather my dad yell at me and then hug me before he feels bad and takes me out for tacos and ice cream. My mother broke him in well.

"Vee! Let's go!"

At Sebastian's angry roar, I come out of my room and hover in the doorway of the guest room. "I think I'm going to stay here for a while."

Sebastian's hair is a mess, like he's been raking his hands in it. "You want to stay?"

I nod. "I think you might need time to cool off."

I think that may not have been what he wanted to hear since he shakes his head and huffs. "Fine. I'll see you around." He shoves the rest of his clothes in his bag and pushes past me.

I try not to take it personally. Winning this competition was his way out. This was his fresh start away from his family, where he wasn't the failed son and stem cell supplier. I don't believe his family truly feels that way about him, but he does, and I know it's harder to believe others when you don't believe it yourself.

The front door slams, and I know it's the last time I'll see my friend.

The car ride was… awkward, but I did get my hug and really, that's all that mattered.

"Go ahead, Dr. Parker. Ask me all the embarrassing questions."

My dad smiles, when I mention his friend, Dr. Parker, who is, in fact, an audiologist who got my dad through some hard times in his life. Apparently, they became good friends and now my mom and Dr. Parker work together and run a community outreach program for the deaf in my hometown. But unlike the real Dr. Parker, my dad likes to play dirty.

"How long are you going to hold my tacos hostage?" Yeah, the man pulled into my favorite restaurant, ordered my favorite combo and then refused to hand them over. He's not even ashamed about it. What can I say? The man knows the way to my secrets.

"Is this about that boy at school?" He motions to his phone in the cup holder. "The one you have those wars with?"

I look at the man who let me put his hair in a bow and who swung me around like I was weightless more times than I can count. "How do you know about the wars? Please don't tell me you and Mom have been watching them." I'm not sure I want to know the answer. Some of those videos were pretty racy. My father may hug me, but my mom will kill me. She's the real crazy in our house. We love her anyway, though.

My dad grins. "Just because you aren't down the hall anymore doesn't mean I don't know what's going on with my daughter. It's my job to protect you. My contract didn't end when you turned eighteen."

I narrow my eyes. I smell a rat. "You paid Drew to spy on me, didn't you?" That little shithead.

He chuckles low in his throat, the same sound I remember when

I would lay in the crook of his arm when he sang me to sleep. "Please, I didn't have to bribe Drew. He watches you for free. In full disclosure, though, I know about the wars because your uncle Pe likes to over-share." He shakes his head. "MyView, apparently, is one of his favorite sites. All I asked him is if you were behaving."

Eww. I hope Uncle Pe wasn't truthful.

I wait for my dad to scold me, to give me that disappointed look. When he doesn't, I offer the truth. "I've been behaving. I mostly do makeup tutorials but this war…" I swallow, thinking about how much I actually want to disclose. "The wars with Sebastian just happened and then," I look down at my hands, knotting them together, "and then it just grew into something more. When the competition came along, I entered, but I wasn't eligible. Joining forces with Sebastian was the only chance I had at winning and getting noticed by possible studios."

I don't know why I feel like I'm justifying why I entered some silly contest. "It was stupid, I know. And now, here I am, having essentially lost, and wasted valuable time when I could have been doing more tutorials and getting noticed the right way."

My dad shifts in the seat and leans back, handing me one chip as a reward for playing nice. "And what would have been the right way?"

"I don't know." I shrug. "Keeping my head down and in my studies?"

He raises a brow. "Are you failing?"

"No."

"Have you dropped any classes or fallen behind?"

"No. Nothing like that."

He seems to relax, and I shove the whole chip in my mouth and try to look hungry. "Well, it seems like not only have you kept your head down and stayed up with school, but you've gained the atten-tion of producers in the process. I don't understand, Valentina. Why are you making it seem as if you're a failure?"

Because that's how I feel.

I feel the heat rush to my cheeks. "I don't like failing."

"Is that what you think you've done?" His voice is soft and com-forting as he hands me the bag of chips. He's such a softy.

"Yes? No. I don't know. I just feel like I let Sebastian down by not winning and not picking up that Brick was reporting back to Malcolm." I stare out the window, admiring others enjoying the best tacos ever.

"What's this really about, sweetheart? Because there is no way you could have known this Brick guy—Is his name really Brick?"

I double over laughing. "Yeah, that's his name."

My dad hands over my bag of three delicious tacos.

"All I'm saying, Vee, is that I've never known you to be a quitter. Why would you let this guy win?"

I shrug, taking a bite of my taco and moaning. "This is so worth enduring this session, Dr. Parker." I wink, and my dad chuckles.

"I'll be sure to tell him you said hi."

We sit in silence for a few minutes and then I decide to be brave. I don't ever want to think I'm not as valued as my brother, like Sebastian feels. "Are you disappointed in me for doing makeup tutorials and not going into music like you and Oliver?" I don't add my mom, though she is a talented singer as well.

"What?" His face falls. "Is that what you think? That because you didn't do something in music that I'm somehow disappointed in you?"

Okay, so it does sound a little silly when he says it like that. "I mean, no. I don't know. I just see how proud you and Mom are of Oliver's success and I don't know. I guess, I feel like doing MyView videos seems a little less than impressive."

A small grin tugs on his face. "Less than impressive? When Oliver was in college, do you know how often he called me for money?"

I feel myself smiling already as I shake my head. Oliver is such a loser. I say that in the sweetest, sisterly way.

"That boy called me every week. He'd either forget to pay his rent or overspend on a new piece of equipment for his board. He was a dreamer with his head in the clouds. Sure, he spent twenty hours of each day playing music and immersing himself in his craft, but you know what he didn't do?"

I blink, knowing he doesn't really need me to answer.

"He wasn't self-sufficient. He didn't make his own money and pay his own rent. He didn't make himself dinner. He didn't do his own laundry. Your mother and I called him so much because we were afraid he wouldn't eat or he'd fall asleep on the street or something."

He takes a breath and sits up, so he's in my face. "Guess how often you have called me for money?"

This answer I know. "Not very often."

He nods. "Three times."

Not too shabby. I really thought I called him more.

"Valentina, my love. You're just like your mother, fiercely independent, determined, and full of fire. You've never needed us. Since you were little, the youngest of the kids. You fought your way into the Von Bremen and Jameson's lives. You wouldn't let them ignore you or say you were too little to hang out with them. You showed them you were their equal. You, my girl, are a brilliant and beautiful light."

He takes a breath. "So no, I don't ever feel any sort of disappointment when it comes to you. You are more than I could have ever asked for. I'd actually love for you to need me, but you don't—" He smiles. "At least not that often."

I feel tears stinging the back of my eyes. "You mean that?"

The same brown eyes as mine stare back at me. "With all my heart. You are never a disappointment, my angel."

At least not to him.

"And you're not a disappointment in this competition. Win or lose, I know you will have fought and scratched your way to the finish line. It doesn't matter if you come in first, Valentina. All that matters is you finish the race."

My dad is right. Malcolm hasn't won yet. And once I finish these tacos, I'll prove it.

"Are you sure you want to do this again?" Uncle Pe's lipstick shimmers in his vanity lights as he pulls my hair back with a tie from his wrist. "Didn't you tell me this was the worst mistake you had ever made and that I was to stop you from ever doing something so insane ever again?"

He makes a point. I did say that.

"Things are different now." Doing this may not make things right, but what choice do I have? If I don't, Sebastian won't win the money. Malcolm knows our secret, thanks to shit-tastic Brick. Malcolm played my game, and he played it well. But what he doesn't know is I've been the master of spying for longer than his butt hairs.

I have one more card to play.

Sebastian and I can still win this.

We have a secret no one knows. One that I've kept under lock and key. It could ruin me for the next three years of my college career, long after Sebastian graduates, but I think at this point, it'll be worth it. I'll be five hundred thousand dollars richer, and Sebastian will fulfill his dream and move to California.

My stomach clenches with the thought.

Am I seriously thinking I am going to miss the demon next door?

I nod in the mirror. I really am. I am going to miss his ass. How did this happen?

I sigh. I lost him once; I can lose him again. "Do, it, bro."

CHAPTER TWENTY

Valentina

University CamFlix Competition Submission
Entry Number: 75
Sebastian and Valentina
*Final Interview Continued, otherwise known as the day this shit
finally ends*

"What?" Tom, the producer, doubles over in laughter. "Really?"

Sebastian, having finally shown up an hour late, narrows his eyes at me as if to say, "Now look at what you've done."

All I can do is shrug. He should have been here earlier instead of brooding over potentially losing the competition.

Tom's laughter only amplifies as the video of our final submission plays in the background. "You mean to tell me—" His pig snort interrupts his ramblings. "—that you were—" Another snort. "—this whole time?"

I nod, feeling my cheeks heat with embarrassment. "This is what you both never spoke about?"

Clearly, we were correct in keeping it a secret, since Tom is struggling to breathe through his laughter.

"Yes." My answer is almost a sigh. "You don't have to air the submission videos, right?"

Tom leans back in his chair, funneling his laughter into something more manageable. "Oh, no. This is better than the original show we had planned. This," he taps the screen, just as I remove the wig on camera, "is gold."

"What are you guys doing here?"

My hands go to my face on instinct, and Aspen slaps them down. "Your dad called me," she says with a grin. "He wasn't sure what was going down, but he thought you might need your crew."

My daddy, my hero.

I can already feel my eyes stinging with gratitude as Aspen wraps me in her arms. "We always have your back, Vee. Forever."

I'm going to miss the shit out of this girl next year, which only brings on another bout of tears that I was attempting to hold back. "I love you, Asp."

"I love you too, Vee-Boo." A heavy arm wraps around me and Aspen, shoving us against each other so hard I can barely breathe.

"I love you too, Drusilla," I squeak out.

A groan interrupts our declarations of love with a quick hug to my shoulders. "You know I sometimes love you, too," claims Fenn. "Even if I end up suspended from school after this shitshow."

Fenn's words are sobering. I might be throwing myself to the rumor trolls with this stunt, but now, with my friends at my side, they will be at their mercy too.

"Look, I really appreciate you guys coming with me, but this is my battle. There's no reason for you to go down with me."

Bennett scoffs and unfolds his arms. "Your battles are our battles. If this is what you want to do, we'll stand beside you."

Why does he have to be the most lovable grouch ever?

"Yeah," Aspen speaks up. "If Sebastian is important to you, then he is important to us."

"I wouldn't go that far."

Aspen pulls back and cuts Fenn a look. "I'm just saying this—" she waves her hand at my attire, "is important to her, so it's important to us."

Fenn doesn't look convinced, but he's going to do it anyway; I can already see him putting on his game face.

"Fine. I just want you both to know that if I end up in a holding cell, someone will have to give a heartfelt speech—with tears—to Mom. She will kick my ass if I miss another game from another friendly brawl."

I cringe. Maybe this isn't such a good idea.

"Shut up, Fenn. If you weren't getting suspended every other Tuesday, this wouldn't be an issue. Stop making excuses for your behavior."

Aspen has never been gentle with her brother, but then again, Fenn is never gentle with any of us.

"We got you, Vee. Let's do this." I lay my head against Drew's chest. His words are reassuring and strong, implying that, together, we can take on the world.

"Okay," I say, exhaling a deep breath. "Let's do this."

The quad is the most populated area at Havemeyer. It also happens to be Malcolm's favorite hangout. Here, he can scam and con his nasty little heart out. If shit is about to go down, it goes down at the quad. It's the place you can get a diet soda with a side of extra dirty drama.

I feel my steps slow as I reach the center of the green space. Surrounded by big oak trees and shaded picnic tables, I scan the area for The Wicked Bitch of the West.

"Did you call in your marker?" I ask, turning to face Aspen. Apparently, Maverick, Sebastian's best friend, owed her a favor. She really didn't need anything from him, but since Maverick is all about that favor life, she enjoyed fucking with him by beating the master at his own game.

"I did," she grins, seemingly pleased she wiggled a favor out of Maverick. "He said he would be here, and Maverick always pays his debts."

Good. I don't know a whole lot about Maverick Lexington and his favors, but I do know Aspen, and if she says he will have Sebastian here, then he'll be here.

"Okay," I say, taking a deep breath and scanning the crowd. As usual, Malcolm is sitting on his throne, aka, a wooden picnic table with his troop of jesters entertaining him with, what is very likely, promises of fame since Sebastian and I haven't posted another video. The traitor and subpar cameraman, Brick, is also standing next to him with his hands in his pockets and a scowl that will soon be a frown when I get through with him.

Bro thinks he has this in the bag. Bro don't know shit.

Sebastian and I have a much bigger secret than just being a fake couple: before we were a fake couple, we were true friends under fake pretenses.

And I'm about to expose our secret scandal.

I'm about to lose my reputation at Havemeyer in the process, but, hopefully, our fans will take this spin on the real story and see it for what it truly is.

Love.

Apparently, I have always been willing to do whatever it takes to get Sebastian Carrington, whether that be to score a point on his competitive ass or to make a complete fool of myself, so he can win this competition and move far away from me. But no matter my intentions, my love for him has always been there, buried underneath excuses, pranks, and fake dates.

I loved him the first time my lips touched his and now…

My stomach knots.

And now, I'll love him even when he leaves for California, after winning his half of the prize money. There is no doubt we will win this competition. Our secret is what movies are made of.

"I need my camera," I say to Aspen, nodding my head to myself.

This is it. I'm doing it. I'm doing this insane stunt, so my asshole amigo, the bro to my bromance, and my own personal neighborhood demon can win this competition.

"Here you go." She sets the camera in my palm. "Just set it up and tell me what button to push, and I'll capture everything."

Somehow, her words aren't reassuring.

It takes me a minute, fumbling around with the settings, until I get them just right. "When I walk away, push this button." I point to the one with the red dot in the middle—the one that will end me for the next three years. "Don't stop until I come back."

This all feels so death sentence-y. But I guess if I'm walking the green mile down dicks and divas' alley, I might as well go out as the superstar I am.

"Got it," Aspen says, her tone perking up quite a bit in the last few minutes. "There's Maverick with Sebastian." She points to a table where Maverick is getting food settled for Ainsley.

"He looks so sad," notes Aspen.

I nod. "He won't for long."

I hand her back the camera. "Don't stop recording," I remind her one more time. "No matter what happens."

Aspen grins. "I wouldn't in a million years."

Ugh.

"Now, go get your man!"

The smack to my ass startles me forward and my friends' muffled laughter keeps me from looking back. My friends might laugh, but they won't let anything happen to me—at least physically. Mentally— only my future therapist knows.

The walk to Malcolm's table of shitheads is long and filled with so many deep breaths that, instead of feeling calmer, I feel a little light-headed. Gah! That's all I need, to pass out in front of his table and have the paramedics come. That would ruin everything.

Okay, no more breaths. Focus. You did this for months. Today is no different.

"Yo!" I holler, my voice sounding rough and gritty. "Are you Brock?"

Brick's head snaps up, and he follows the sound of my voice. I know what he sees: dark cropped hair, sideburns, and pasted on eyebrows that should be banned.

"Uhh…" Brick scans the quad, hoping someone will come to his rescue, but they won't, because if there's one thing this campus loves, it's good old-fashioned drama.

"Yeah, I'm talking to you, bitch." My strides are stronger and more aggressive as I get closer to his table. "You think you can take my job without my permission?"

I can feel Sebastian's eyes on me, but I don't dare turn around and face him.

"Uh…" Brick stumbles out. "I don't know what you're talking about."

I scoff and try to make it sound like I'm hocking a loogie, but it ends up sounding more like a cough.

"Don't you lie to me!" I yell, balling my fists like I'm getting ready to swing at the fool.

Clearly, I'm not, but that's what dudes do. They fight for no damn reason other than to show who has the bigger dick.

Well, here I am, boys. See how big my peen is. Not really, because I don't have a peen, but that's the vibe I'm trying to pull off here.

"Where the fuck is Sebastian?" I spin around, knowing good and damn well where he is, but I need him to come into this shot or my plan won't work. "Sebastian Carrington! Come out and face me, you liar!"

Whispers and awkward coughs sound to my left as the crowd pushes forward and I turn, finally finding my demon douche with eyes as wide as Fenn's sunglasses.

I crook my finger, yelling across the space between us. "You think you can replace me, bro?"

Even from this far away, I can see a muscle tick in Sebastian's jaw, which is quite sexy, even when his expression went from disbelief to pure, unadulterated rage with one sentence. But that's okay. The anger will bring him to me.

"You have nothing to say?" I'm baiting the shit out of him. "I tell you I need a couple months to handle some family business and you think you can enter this competition without me?" I stomp my foot and cringe. "You think you can replace me?" My words are sharp and challenging and that's all he needs to eat up the space between us and grab my arm, hauling me to him.

"What the fuck do you think you're doing?"

Gah, he really is so predictable.

I push him off and take a step back, pointing to Brick who stares on, confused as to who the hell I am.

"Why am I here?" I spit and grab at my non-existent balls, which sends Sebastian's ticking jaw into overdrive.

"Don't do this," he grits, but it's too late. I've already done it.

"Do what?" I yell for the camera. "Expose you?"

My words are biting, and everything nightmares are made of. Well, Sebastian's nightmares at least. "I'm just wondering why you hired this asshole," I point to Brick, "when you knew I was coming back."

Sebastian shakes his head, and I take a few steps back, closing the space between me and Brick. "You're a liar and a cheat, but you know what, Brock?" I push at his shoulder and, like the pussy he is, he stumbles. "All the lying and conniving was never going to win Malcolm the competition."

I turn back and give Sebastian a look that clearly says, brace yourself. "You know why, Bruce?"

Brick wipes his mouth and glares. "Because no matter how sneaky you thought you were, you will never be able to play with the big dogs."

And with those parting words and nausea in my throat, I rip off the wig and let my long hair drop, ripping off the eyebrows and sideburns and tossing them at Brick's feet.

"You," I say in my own voice through the gasps and OMGs, "will never replace me."

At which point I turn around, leaving Malcolm's mouth hanging open, and face my naughty neighbor. "And you... should always know we'll win. MyView is our house."

Then I launch my ass at the man who once confided in me that he thought beer tasted like an old sock and even lent me his Desitin when I lied and said I had ball chaffing. This man was my bro, my bestie, and my asshole amigo, whether it be when I'm wearing a bra or pretending I have a dick.

This is my human.

Sebastian catches me with an oomph, and I go in for a kiss. I don't care that everyone is putting it together that I am Tweener, Sebastian's elite cameraman, and the one who abandoned him only to be right back in his life, playing his fake girlfriend. What can I say? We like to keep our relationship interesting.

Our mouths collide, and Sebastian's groan fuels my wanting.

I might be crazy.

And I might have embarrassed the shit out of him.

But he still wants me and that's all that matters.

Well, that and winning this money. There's no way we won't at least give Malcolm a run for the prize money with this video.

When I pull back from our kiss, I immediately bury my face in his neck. "I'm sorry I went rogue on you, but I couldn't let you lose. This is your dream, dude."

Those big hands that have stolen more shit than is acceptable, palm my ass, ignoring the fact that I have on my uncle Pe's jeans and boots, and shift me farther up his hips. "I've missed your crazy ass, bro."

Our laughter is met with others, and for the first time since I got here, I allow myself to look around. Amongst the drama hogs, our friends are standing around us: Aspen with a camera; Bennett on guard, looking around like someone is going to snipe us at any minute; Fenn on his phone, so over me being dressed like a boy; and Drew, chatting up one of the girls who looks like she'd be happy to take a ride on Big D. Then there's Maverick, ready to go, with a tight grip on Ainsley, who I don't know, but by the way she's clapping and whooping, I already like her.

"I cannot believe this is what you were doing for two months," Aspen muses. "How did I miss my bestie dressing up as a guy and living this whole double life?"

I shrug. "I waited until you would sneak over to Bennett's at night." I slap my hand over my mouth. "I mean, fell asleep."

Aspen waves off my comment. "It's fine. It's not like Fenn doesn't know I come over. I always end up using his razor."

Fenn makes a noise low in his throat. I'm sure he's used to sharing with his sister and I highly doubt he cares if she is sneaking over to see his friend. "I knew you were into some weird shit, Vee."

I shrug. "It isn't weird. Winners do whatever it takes."

I look back to Sebastian whose face has lost its smile. My heart sinks to my toes. Surely he's happy we, more than likely, blew up the internet with this crazy show.

"You alright?" I ask him.

He nods and sets me down. "Yeah. I'm fine." He touches my cheek with his thumb, and it feels final, like this is our goodbye.

I swallow and force a smile on my face. I knew this would happen. I was prepared that if this went well, it would only lead to one of two outcomes. Winning the contest and Sebastian leaving Georgia *or* exposing our story and embarrassing us both so much that he's forced to leave Georgia to save face.

"Want a lift home?" he offers.

I look at Aspen who stares back at me. She's probably wondering the same thing I am. Should I take him up on his offer and endure the 'what the fuck were you thinking exposing us' lecture, or should I avoid his goodbye at all costs?

Avoiding sounds pretty good at the moment, but I'm not a coward. "Sure." I cut Aspen a small smile. "Will you bring my stuff home?"

She nods, and Sebastian gives me his hand, which I take, and follow him toward the parking lot, away from the cacophony of laughter and what was probably an epic exit by Malcolm and Brick.

When we're in the quiet of Sebastian's Jeep with the doors locked, Sebastian drums on the steering wheel for a moment. "Just say what you want to say," I tell him. "I embarrassed us both, I know, but I didn't know what else to do. I didn't want you to lose out on your dream."

He doesn't answer me, only sits there chewing the inside of his cheek.

"Yell at me or something," I tell him. "I've never known you to be so quiet. Are you scarred for life?"

Finally, he laughs a deep rumbling sound that sends shivers across my skin. "What am I supposed to do with you, huh?"

I shrug. "Text me occasionally when you're all famous."

His smile drops, and he puts the car in gear, pulling away from the curb. I try not to look like my heart is fracturing into a million little pieces on the backroad to our house, when he finally clears his throat and promises, "Always."

We don't speak after that. I guess there's nothing really to say. We had a deal to win this competition, and although we don't know that we've actually won yet, I think we can agree that we have a good shot at it. Sebastian will see the west coast, and I will stay here, save my money, and finish school. Then, I can decide what to do after that.

We pull up to our complex, and Sebastian jumps out, before I can say anything else like goodbye or thanks for the best year of my life sans the two months you weren't speaking to me.

"Okay," I say to myself, as he hustles around the front of the car. "Have a great day. Thanks for saving my ass."

My door is suddenly wrenched open. "What did you say?"

My eyes meet his, and I suddenly have the urge to kiss him. I open my mouth. "I love you."

Yeah, that wasn't supposed to happen.

CHAPTER TWENTY-ONE

Sebastian

She played her ace, and wouldn't you know, her crazy prank won us the competition.

There's just one thing that keeps me from celebrating.

She said she loved me and then slapped her hand over her mouth and ran into her house without another word, which is where she stayed the rest of the evening.

"So, Vee was Tweener all along?"

I'm two beers down after a shot of moonshine. My body is buzzing, and today's trauma seems a little more catastrophic than it did earlier.

"Yep." I let the 'p' pop as I stare out into the night. Maverick's apartment doesn't have that great of a view, but tonight, it's better than mine and my incessant staring out the window.

Maverick chuckles and shakes his head. "And I thought Ainsley was crazy." He pours a little of his beer out and kicks my foot. "How long was she your cameraman?"

I mumble out the answer. "Two months."

"Two months! Dude, and you never picked up that she was a girl?"

I shoot him a glare. "I mean, sure," I start, defending my actions. "She did some things that I questioned, but, you know, everyone has their quirks." I arch a brow. "Look at you and Ainsley."

If quirks were a sport, they would come in first every time.

"I'm just saying, any time I would have doubts, she would slam down a shot of moonshine and burp and grab at her junk. It wasn't as obvious as you think it would be."

Maverick still doesn't look convinced. "What about her tits?"

"What about them? Did you notice them at the poker game I brought her to?"

Maverick pauses, more than likely thinking about that night I brought her to the game. Maverick wasn't impressed, but, like me, he had no idea we were both being played. "Wonder how she hid them?"

I sigh. "That night, right after she revealed herself, I had a few too many drinks and googled all the movies I could find where girls pretended to be guys."

"You watched them? All of them?"

"Come on." I huff. "Don't look so disgusted. I was doing exactly what you were doing. I was asking myself how I didn't know. I pride myself in noticing beautiful women and I had one sleeping over and spending nine hours a day filming with me. And I fucking missed it. I had to see how she managed to get one over on me."

"And did the movies tell you?"

I shrug. "They were all different, but the one consistent trick used was bandage wraps to strap down their tits."

Maverick releases this loud and hearty belly laugh. "Dude, I'm impressed. I've never known anyone to get one over on you, much less me."

It was impressive. I've always been able to acknowledge that much but what gnawed at me was the fact I *truly* believed she was Tweener, my friend and someone I desperately missed once he was gone.

"So why are you over here and not at home?"

I stare out at the parking lot. "Can't I just have a beer with my friend?" I'm not in the mood to tell him about Vee saying she loved me.

Maverick scoffs. "Sure, but I've never known you to turn down stalking your neighbor for having a beer with me." Maverick doesn't drink, but he likes to sit on his balcony and pour out his beers. It's weird. I can't explain it, other than to say it was one of those quirks I was talking about.

I exhale a deep breath. "I'm leaving. What am I supposed to do?"

Maverick picks at the label of his beer. "What do you want to do?"

Any other time I would talk to Tweener, or T as I called her, about my conundrum, but not tonight. Tonight is different.

"Our video has over two million views in the past twelve hours," I state. "The producers already called me. We won."

"I'm not seeing how that's a bad thing."

"It's not. It's just—" It doesn't feel like a win. A win should have been celebrated with Vee and shots of moonshine. Instead, she's not speaking to me.

"I'm proud of you, dude," Maverick says. "This is something you've wanted for a long time. I'm just wondering why you don't seem more excited. Perhaps it has something to do with a former cameraman."

I'll never admit that I love her to Maverick. I'll never admit that I'm contemplating staying and finishing my degree just to see where things take us, since she's no longer pretending to be my cameraman or girlfriend.

"Maybe I'm just in shock" is all I say.

"Yeah, and maybe you're in love."

My bags are packed, and I've sent Vee a couple of congratulatory texts which she promptly replied with a thumbs up. Maybe her ignoring me is for the best. If she didn't mean what she said, then there's no reason for me to stay. We'll still be friends, even with two thousand miles between us. I struggled with walking next door and telling her I loved her too, but she never turned on her light, and I took that as a sign. But I couldn't leave without saying goodbye.

So there, on her back patio, sits her chair with a fucked-up bow on the top. I didn't know how to tie one and MyView, although help-ful, could not teach me any bow tying techniques.

"You want me to drive you to the airport?"

I don't answer Rowan immediately. Instead, I look down at the contents of my duffle bag. It's minimal, only clothes and the flannel top Vee once wore when we did that stupid dance. All my stuff—in-cluding my film memorabilia—is packed away in a storage facility, so my sister can rent this place out to the next college kid who wants to take on a thieving neighbor.

I swallow, feeling a bout of panic flare up. It feels like I'm aban-doning my entire life, and I guess I am, but this is what I wanted, right? This was the whole point of entering the contest in the first place. To get away? To start over? To do what I wanted? But now, it doesn't re-ally feel like something I want. I'm sure once I leave, it'll be fine. I just need to do it. Rip off the Band-Aid.

"Nah. Thanks, though," I tell him with a pat on the shoulder. "I think I'll just take an Uber. I need to handle a couple of things first." Like watching Vee for a few more minutes before I leave her forever.

"Are you sure? I don't mind."

I look at my *Fast and the Furious* friend and shake my head. "Yeah, I'm good."

Not that I think Rowan will cry or ask to hug me, but I don't know what to say to my friend of four years. I'm leaving, and I won't be grad-uating with him in a couple more months. Stupid, I know, but I've never been one to make great decisions. I don't care that I'm close to graduating with a business degree. Business can go fuck itself. I don't want a desk job and a monotonous future. I want to see the world. I want to live the life I've always dreamed about.

"Alright, man." He holds his hand out for me to shake. "I'll see you around."

We both know that's a lie, but I nod anyway. "Yeah. Behave your-self. Don't let Mav take all your money."

Fucker knows he sucks at poker.

He grins and shakes his head. "Take care of yourself, man."

His voice turns serious, and I know this is the last time I'll see him. If everything works out, I'll never come back to Georgia, at least while Rowan is still in school.

I swallow. "You too."

And that's it. That's how dudes say their goodbyes. Rowan turns and walks away while I'm left with a bag and pair of binoculars I stole specifically for this occasion. I walk to the window and raise them to my eyes, peering out for the last time at the girl who taught me that friendship comes in many forms. Sometimes it's disguised as hate and sometimes as a fake girlfriend. Either way, as I watch her pacing her bedroom, I know that she deserves better than me. She deserves a real boyfriend. Someone who will be with her the next three years of her college life.

She deserves someone better.

I just hope that Vance isn't that someone.

I know it's selfish but leaving isn't easy. It should be, because that's what I want, at least I think it is.

My phone buzzes in my pocket. I look down, hoping to see it's Vee saying goodbye or at least giving me hell about watching her with binoculars, but I'm disappointed.

Maverick: You have one minute to get in the fucking car.

I smile. I knew he would show. He might have called me and said he didn't do goodbyes, but I knew he would. Deep down, Maverick Lexington is a softy.

Me: Aww. You did miss me.

Maverick: I owed you a favor and since you won't be here to claim it, I'm taking you to the airport. I always pay my debts.

He doesn't owe me any kind of favor, but this is who he is.

Me: If you say so. Let me grab my shit.

Maverick: I don't have all day.

I pocket my phone and take one last look at the girl next door. She's gone from the window, and my heart sinks. I should go over there, at least give her a high-five, but for some reason, I can't bring myself to make it final.

Grabbing my bag, I sling it over my shoulder and walk to the front door. I turn and give everything one more look before I close the door and lock it, leaving everything behind.

"Took you long enough," Maverick says, as soon as I open the passenger door and chuck my bag into the back seat. His eyes follow its landing, and he frowns.

"Thanks for taking care of the Jeep while I'm gone," I tell him, ignoring the sour look he still has. His leather is fine. It's not like my bag was made of jagged metal.

"Yeah," he mumbles, pulling away from the curb and gunning it down the road, not even giving me the opportunity to look back.

"Fuck. Seriously? You told them?"

My friend is the devil.

Maverick shrugs, not bothering to look up from his phone. "Ainsley made me. I told her you didn't want to see them." He flashes me an apologetic look. "She didn't care."

I shake my head. "Tell her I'll miss her sensitive self."

I swear, she's worse than Vee about saving the world and shit.

"Get out of the car and text me the address when you land." Maverick sounds a lot like my father instead of my friend, but I wouldn't have it any other way.

I nod. "I'll see you soon." It's not a question with Maverick. He keeps up with his family and I have no doubt he won't allow me to disappear out west and never speak to him again.

With one last fist bump, I get out of the car and open the back door to retrieve my bag and then turn to face my mom, dad, and sister.

"Maverick told us what time your flight was leaving. We wanted to say goodbye." My mom wraps her arms around me, her body shaking.

I loop my arms around her, exhaling.

"We are so proud of you," she says between sobs.

I snap to attention. "You are?" You can't fault me for having doubts. All my parents have ever wanted for me to do is go to school and get a good job. I think I always felt like they just wanted me out of their house. Once my sister married and moved out, I was the last hurdle in their way to freedom.

"Of course we are, sweetie. Why would you think we weren't?" My mom pulls back from my arms and wipes her eyes. "I don't know what you're looking for, Sebastian, but all we've ever wanted for you is to be happy. If that happiness is in California, making movies, then we hope you take California by storm and live the life you've always dreamed of." She smooths her hand over my cheek. "You deserve it."

It's like a dam of tension breaks in my soul. My mother didn't declare that I wasn't a failed stem cell donor, but she admitted that all she ever wanted was for me to be happy and, honestly, just feeling seen by the most influential people in my life is all I could ask for. It doesn't fix all the years of insecurities I've brought onto myself, but it's a start, and right now, that's all I need.

"Thank you," I tell her, kissing her on the cheek and giving her one last hug.

My sister steps up next and grabs me by the shirt and squeezes me. There are no tears in her eyes, only a threat. "You will tell me where you are staying and you will not avoid me when I come to visit you. Do you understand me, little boy?"

It's cute when she tries to threaten me, even though she's a foot shorter than I am. "I understand," I tell her, grinning and feeling a lot lighter than I did before.

When she finally lets me go, I turn and look at my dad. He nods and then pulls me by the shoulder and hugs me. "You take care of yourself, Son."

I nod. "I will. Take care of them for me." I tip my chin to my mom and sister, who are now hugging each other like I'm dying instead of moving.

"You better go so you don't miss your flight," he mutters.

I don't tell him that I changed my flight three times since I bought the ticket. I kept finding shit I needed to take care of before I left. What was an afternoon flight ended up as a red-eye flight. But the airport will have some good footage I can shoot and it's not at my house where I will be tempted to watch a particular neighbor until it's time to leave.

With another round of hugs and promises to call as soon as I land, I make my way to security. "Ticket," the TSA agent demands.

I unzip the front pocket of my bag and pull out my ticket and hand it over.

"Don't play with me, boy," the agent says, handing the ticket back. "You need a real ticket to get through."

"What?" I take the ticket from him and flip it over. There, instead of my flight information, is a note in handwriting I will never forget.

Yeah, I said it. I love you and I know deep down in that demon soul of yours, you love me too. I couldn't let you leave without one more prank. If you want to get on the plane, you know where to meet me for the ticket.

Tweener

Aka your bestie

Aka Vee

Aka yours

No one needs to see the ridiculous smile I'm sporting right now. I pull out my phone and text Maverick.

Me: Can you turn around?

His response is immediate.

Maverick: Never left the parking lot.

I turn and walk back to the parking lot, apologizing to the TSA agent for the mix-up.

Me: She got to you, didn't she?

Maverick: She needed a favor.

And Maverick is the granter of all things.

Me: You just couldn't leave it alone.

Maverick: Don't take it personally. Ainsley is a sucker for happy endings.

Honestly, just knowing Vee wants to see me makes me stupidly happy. And bringing my friends in on this prank… solidifies my decision.

Maverick drops me off at my house, and I don't bother with getting my keys. The door is already unlocked.

"You know," I say, setting my bag down and striding to the kitchen, where the girl who dressed up as a guy for two months sits at my counter with two shots of moonshine in front of her. She has that fucking wig on, and I can't help the grin that emerges.

"I'm beginning to think you're a serial burglar. This makes, what, four times you picked my locks? I'm assuming you broke in and stole my ticket?"

She smiles and it's all teeth. "Actually, Rowan stole the ticket. So, technically, I only broke in three times."

I take a seat next to her, and she slides the shot in front of me. "One last drink between friends."

I take the shot glass and we turn them up at the same time. "Another?" I say, licking the last of the liquor off my lips. She cocks her head to the side, wondering what I'm up to. "But maybe we drink to the first of many between lovers."

Her mouth drops open, and I grab her bar stool and slide her toward me so that she's in between my legs. "Because I love you too and I'm not going fucking anywhere."

With absolutely no restraint, I let every bit of anxiety I've experienced over leaving her channel into the feeling of pressing my lips to hers, giving her everything I never thought I would feel for a woman. I steal her breath, crushing her face to mine until she pulls back, her dark eyes meeting mine. She smiles, running her hands through my hair. "I'd love that, bro."

EPILOGUE
Valentina

One year later and that time I won the prank war. You're welcome.

"Rowan will probably bring moonshine if you want that instead of beer."

I scrunch my nose. Moonshine fucks me up. I can drink beer and can even shoot liquor and stay sober, but moonshine… knocks me on my ass. The last time I drank it, I passed out on the back stoop of the guys' house and Aspen had to drag me across the courtyard, without the guys knowing and asking where the fuck I had been. Drew would have not been pleased but that's okay because Drew is not the boss of me.

"Cool," I tell him. "But Maverick will have beer, right?"

Sebastian cuts me a look of disgust. "Yeah, but it tastes like old socks."

"Of course," I add, cocking a hip out and dropping my shoulder. "I was just wondering. I like to chase my moonshine with beer."

Be cool, Vee. Remember who you are.

Sebastian looks impressed. "Whatever you want, dude."

"So, uh, how many honeys are going to be here? I could use some of that Gorilla Grip cooch. My dick has been hella dry lately." I shake the crotch of my baggy jeans and watch as Sebastian's eyes widen, before pocketing his wallet.

"Uh, no girls are invited to Wednesday night poker, but we could always go out and celebrate later."

Is that what I'm asking? To celebrate later with a bunch of girls?

"We can find chicks for you to, you know—" he waves his hand at me. "—to handle that."

Oh my gosh. How in the hell am I going to get through this night? Uncle Pe only taught me the basics and watching Teen Wolf wasn't very helpful, since I just found myself staring at the sharp teeth and hard bodies. Not only am I going to sit through an exclusive poker game, but now we're going to celebrate with a bunch of girls who think I have a dick.

"Good," I say, clearing my throat. "We might need to bounce out a little early then."

Sebastian's eyes narrow.

Fuck. He knows. There's no way he doesn't know. He's going to out me in front of everyone at this game. What the hell was I thinking? I'm so done at this school. I am so stupid!

"Don't bail on me, T. First, we win some money and then we'll celebrate. Got it?"

I breathe a huge sigh of relief. I don't know if he's just playing a game with me or if he truly doesn't know.

"You know I got your back, brother."

"You're either in, or you're out, Tweener. Make a decision or go giggle with the girls next door."

I glance up at Rowan, who is beyond serious about this so-called friendly game of poker. At least that's what Sebastian called it when he convinced me that I would have a great time, making a couple extra grand at the Wednesday night poker game. But as I sit here, not knowing what in the hell I'm looking at, I'm thinking Sebastian downplayed, not only the complexity of the game, but the fact this was, in fact, not a friendly game.

"Relax. Tweener is new."

I tip my chin at Maverick like I've seen Sebastian do in the past. Out of all the guys, Maverick looks the least relaxed, but I guess I shouldn't look a gift horse in the mouth. If he hasn't thrown me out yet, maybe he won't. I doubt Sebastian will have much sympathy if they figure out my game.

I'm not here to play poker. I'm only here to keep up the ruse. Sebastian Carrington, my nemesis, expects his friend to click with his other friends. So here I am, in a wig that my uncle lent me and a makeup job that I'm proud of. I might not have the best eyeliner or the prettiest highlights on my cheeks, but it's simple, underplayed, and looks very manly, if I do say so myself.

Not knowing what card I should lay down, I look up at Sebastian who has this stupid grin on his face. Ugh. Why must the demon look like an angel?

"You might want to wipe that fucking smile off your face," says Maverick, his expression stern and no longer hospitable. "Because if he goes belly up, you're not leaving here until you cover his debt."

I cringe. Sebastian covered the two thousand dollar buy-in too. I might not want the shithead to win next week's subscriber war, but that doesn't mean I want Maverick to shank him in a dark alley. Out of all Sebastian's friends, Maverick looks the most unstable. Rumor has it he will grant any favor asked of him, but in return, you will owe him a favor that he will claim at a later date. It all sounds really sketchy, so as much as I want to ruin Sebastian, I don't want him to go out when he's doing something sweet for a change.

"You know what you need, Mav?"

Oh hell. I know that look. Any time Sebastian's head cocks to the side and that ridiculous damn dimple pops, he's up to no good.

"What you need is a bad fuck or a mediocre blow job. Wait, no, I got it!" He shuffles in his chair excitedly and winks at me. It's hard to keep a straight face. "A sloppy rim job! That would loosen you up."

Maverick doesn't look up from his cards, and Sebastian takes that as his cue to keep talking. "See, you don't need a good dick sucking, just a simple, mediocre, wet the tip and fondle the balls until you're so frustrated you come, just so you can send the pretty little thing home. You need to loosen up, Mav. Accept that people aren't perfect and need to learn."

Sebastian takes a breath and pauses, waiting on Maverick to comment, but he only lifts a brow in warning which, clearly, doesn't concern him. "I'm telling you, man. You haven't lived until you've came to the worst fuck ever."

My stomach churns, but it's short-lived when Maverick taps out a cigarette and says, "Sebastian, if your friend doesn't check or bet, I'm going to shove this beer bottle up your goddamn ass and see how you enjoy a sloppy rim job."

Sebastian spews his beer all over the cards. "And here I thought you were in a bad mood today." His chuckle is annoyingly cute and it takes a serious amount of effort not to grin at his ridiculousness.

"Dammit, Bash. You got the cards wet." Rowan wipes off his cards and aims a growl in my direction. "Check or bet. Now!"

His deep baritone voice and heavy fist slamming on the table make me jump in my seat. I'm frozen amongst men that could lift me with one hand and toss my fake ass out in one breath.

"I swear to God," Mav threatens. "I will—"

"Check. I check," I rumble out quickly, doing my best to make my voice deeper and less frightened. I don't know what check means, but that's one of the only two options he offered me.

Maverick nods. "Row?"

Rowan looks at Sebastian and then at Maverick, narrowing his eyes. I don't know what he sees in their expressions, but whatever it is, he doesn't like it. "Fuck you both," he says finally, slamming his cards down. "I fold."

The rest of the conversation is a blur as Sebastian pokes at Maverick, raising the pot by pushing more chips in, but then Maverick mentions a straight on the river or something like that and we all show our cards. I had a bunch of numbers, which meant absolutely nothing to me, but apparently, it was a losing hand since Sebastian pushes back in his chair and mumbles, "Fuck."

We lost.

I expected it, but I think Sebastian was hoping I was better at poker than I was. I wasn't his wing man like he wanted. Honestly, though, I'm just impressed that they didn't realize I was a girl the minute I walked in.

"Let me win my money back?" Sebastian teases.

Maverick gives him a look that reminds me of a killer about to attack. "No."

Sebastian chuckles, not even giving a shit about pissing Maverick off. "I guess that's my cue to go."

Maverick walks out to his patio, and I stand from the metal chair and give a goodbye nod to Rowan who returns it, surprisingly. Sebastian says something that I don't catch, but I follow him out, relieved to be leaving the worst game of friendly poker I've ever seen.

"You did pretty good in there," Sebastian notes, as soon as we're in the parking lot.

I scoff. "No, I didn't but I had a good time. It's been a long time since I've played poker." Like never.

"You'll get better the more you play and learn everyone's tells." He starts the engine to the car and I buckle my seat belt.

"Absolutely. I appreciate the invite."

Sebastian grins and squeals out of the parking lot, heading to his house, where he says we're going to invite a few people over. Honestly, I'm exhausted, but I can't bow out now. He's liable to film tomorrow's video or at least give me the plans on where to film it. Tomorrow is the day. The day that Sebastian Carrington finally loses. This prank war has been one-sided since it started, but not now. Now, I have the upper hand, and I plan on uploading this entire body cam footage and for once, giving Sebastian exactly what he deserves.

It's four in the morning and everyone has finally left. I'm tired and my boobs hurt like a bitch from this wrap. All I want to do is cozy up in my flannel and let the girls breathe.

"I think this is the last of the moonshine. Let's finish it up." Sebastian hands me the glass of moonshine that I honestly want to vomit at the sight of.

I smile. "Damn straight." I try to make it sound like I'm excited to get even drunker than I already am. But the reality is that keeping up with a dude's lifestyle is exhausting, and in Sebastian's case, a constant state of tipsy.

He raises his glass and I follow, throwing it back and fighting the gag reflex. I can't afford for him to catch onto me now. I'm almost done. This is for the win.

Sebastian sighs and puts his glass on the counter. "You want to watch the footage from yesterday?"

I really don't, but something won't let me leave him for the night. I shrug. "Sure. I got a little time before I need to meet up with my side piece."

I cringe but mask it quickly when Sebastian just shakes his head. "Alright." He moves to the sofa, plugs in the camera, turns it on, and hits play, but instead of yesterday's footage, it's a video of me. Well, me as a girl.

"Wait, wrong thing. Hang on." He tries to skip it, but it's just more and more footage of me out on the patio watching a movie on my iPad.

I nudge his leg. "Looks like this is more than prank footage."

Sebastian rakes a hand through his hair, hitting the fast forward button before he quits and unplugs the whole thing. "It's not what it looks like," he says, leaning back onto the sofa. "I admire her."

Tingles rush through my stomach and I'm sure it isn't the moonshine.

"I thought you hated her."

Keeping his eyes closed, he presses his palms to his head and sits up. "It's weird. It's like I hate to love her and I have no idea why.

Maybe it's because she's smart and so goddamned sexy. She's every man's dream, but yet, she can't stand the sight of me." He scoffs. "It's the first time I've ever wanted a woman and she hasn't wanted me."

Suddenly my lips are pressed to his. They're warm and soft and—

"What are you doing?" Sebastian jumps up from the sofa, and I stand, holding my palms up and forgetting I'm supposed to be a man when I apologize. "I'm so sorry."

His eyes widen and narrow to my head. Shit. I reach up and find my wig has shifted. "Guess the secret is out, huh?" With an apologetic grin, I pull the rest of my wig off, letting my dark hair fall around my shoulders.

"What in the mother of all fucks?" Sebastian's mouth falls open. I've shocked him. That's understandable. It's quite the difference. "Have I been roofied?" He scrubs a hand down his face over the dusting of hair.

"Am I foaming at the mouth?" He asks me seriously. "Where's my phone? I need a mirror. If I'm about to die from being poisoned, I prefer not to go out looking like I frenched a Saint Bernard."

"Sebastian… I'm sorry," I explain, "I didn't mean for—"

"Hell yes you did, you liar!" He slams me against the wall as the camera crew starts laughing. "And now you're going to make up for it with your mouth." He nudges his face in my shoulder, nipping at my neck. "I want a blow job for every time you pissed me off."

This idiot.

I smile, gripping his shirt and tugging him to me as fast as possible. It's been a long day of pretending I hate him. I'm ready to feel his lips on mine, the warmth of his body pressed against me. This is my demon—my ridiculous, crazy man. Whether I'm his bro or his hoe, I'm still his.

"Cut! That's a wrap for today. Take the rest of the night off. We'll start again in the morning."

Sebastian pulls up from where his head is in my neck and grins. "Works every time. I am so tired of not seeing you naked."

I giggle into his shirt, inhaling the sweet scent of moonshine he specifically drank for this scene as the film crew shuffles about, cleaning up their equipment in a staged townhouse that isn't the real one this all went down in.

"Thank fuck." Sebastian rises, lying to the camera crew with, "Vee was molesting me under the table that entire scene. I was either about to file a complaint or fuck her on the table." He winks down at me and then looks up at the director who just shakes his head. I bet he will be so happy to see this movie finished.

I shake my head and try to push the big goof off, but he only wraps his arms around me. "No, ma'am. Where do you think you're going?"

I arch my back, trying to maneuver out from under him to at least touch him, but all it does is send a pained groan through him. "Keep arching, T, and we'll end up with a bonus scene fit only for the dark web."

This man hasn't changed much since the day I first met him as he mimicked the scene from the movie, *Titanic*, mouthing, "watermelon" as I sang (awfully, per him) for the internet and started this whole war. He's still rambunctious and never gives two shits about telling me like it is. But probably the most noticeable difference about Sebastian is he seems genuinely happy.

No longer does he avoid his family and tense up at the sight of a wig on my head. He calls me T whenever he wants to be a shit or just remind me how far we've come. But most of all, he stayed in Georgia and finally made it his home.

After changing his major to film, he spoke with his parents and they agreed he should chase his dreams and be happy. It took only a few days to see the result of a happier Bash-hole who is enjoying being the star of a soon-to-be major motion picture.

Yep, you heard me correctly. Not only did we win the UniCamFlix competition, but merely days after our story aired on the UniCamFlix, a major film network, Ustream, offered us a deal. They wanted to tell our story—the full story, not the fake one.

They wanted to tell the story of how Sebastian and Valentina really fell in love. The name of the movie… *Subscriber Wars*.

ALTERNATE ENDING
Also known as Sebastian's Epilogue

Six years later

"You see all of this out here?"

I pinch Vee's nipple between my fingers, which sends a moan through her tight body as she drops her head onto the wooden railing of our balcony, panting and spreading her legs wider.

Yep, you heard that correctly. Legs spread, her head on *our* railing.

Vee and I bought a house.

Together.

On. The. Lake.

And we celebrate by pounding one out on every solid surface we can manage, without offending our neighbors.

Buying our lake house was a dream come true for both of us.

Just like having her bent over the railing and fucking her brains out to the sounds of boaters on a Sunday morning. I didn't care that she was sitting out here, enjoying her coffee and answering emails as the sun rose. All I saw, when I rolled over in an empty bed, was her delightful ass just outside the French doors, donned in nothing but that flannel shirt. Bam. My dick was rock fucking solid in a matter of two seconds.

"See what?"

I pound into her, the wet, slapping skin, drowning out her breathy words. I don't need her to answer. Although a moan, scream, or a dear God help me would put a smile on my face.

I pull out slowly and rock back into her, drawing out the torture of where she wants me the most.

"Bash," she whines.

I sink in deeper, fighting my own need to drive into her unbridled, but this is how we like it: torturous. Her muscles clench around me, trying to keep me in deep. "Huh uh," I whisper.

She shivers against my chest. "Please."

I groan. She knows what a well-placed please does to me. "Not until you tell me what you see."

I honestly don't give two fucks about what she sees. The fact is I ask her this question every single time I strip her down on our property. It's a game at this point. She knows what to say, but she won't because she likes withholding from me, and I like pretending I don't love it.

"I don't know," she lies. I can hear a smile in her voice.

I start to pull out. "No, no, no." Her hands reach behind her, pushing at my pajama pants that I didn't bother to pull down but a few inches.

"Look at all of this," I remind her, pointing to our lakefront backyard, complete with a boat dock and jet skis. "It's all ours."

"Mmm…"

It's not the answer I was looking for, but then again, she knows this. I pinch her nipple, making her yelp. "Let's try that again, shall we?" I roll her nipple between my fingers, before dropping my hand, and listening to her whimper.

"You're not playing fair today." I ignore the impossibly cute whine she's giving me.

"And you're not giving me what I want, Valentina. You know how to play this game."

She pushes back against me and I let her. For one, I'm selfish, and two, I like to see her needy. "It's all ours," she finally relents with a whimper.

I look over the curve of her ass to the messy hair on her head, damp with sweat. She's stunning amongst the scenery of our two-story lake house that not only has plenty of space for our families to visit, but two studios in the basement. One for me and my movie memorabilia (told you I'd have a space for it) and one for Vee to continue her makeup tutorials, even though she has a job with a studio.

Our studio.

After our movie, *Subscriber Wars*, made headlines, we signed a contract for two more. But after the third film, Vee wanted to retire from the big screen as her passion has always been behind the camera. I didn't like being away from her, so I started producing, and together, we released two blockbuster hits.

With both hands on Vee's hips, I pull her close and kiss her neck, absorbing every moan and clench of her body. "You smell so good," I whisper. "Like lake water and mine."

She chuckles and tries to reach back and smack me. "I do not smell like lake water."

I push into her again, this time rolling my hips, so I hit that spot deep inside her that sends her folding over the railing. "Not yet." I reach my hand under her shirt and find her clit, rubbing in a circular motion. I've tortured us both long enough, especially when her knees go weak. "You gotta stay upright," I tell her. "And then we will get this shirt out of the way and take a dip in the water."

She's clenching around me so hard that I almost lose my footing and send us both toppling to the ground. "You're going to come all over my dick," I tell her. "All you have to do is let go."

She groans and pushes back against me, grinding her hips up and down as I drive ruthlessly into her, from the back.

"Keep going," she mutters. "Don't stop." Her body tenses and then she trembles in my arms, her pussy clenching around me like a vise.

I thrust in deeper, harder, obeying her just this once and hoping I don't cause her to get a splinter. "Tell me you love me," I pant. "Hurry, so it sounds sexy."

She turns, her deep mahogany eyes fighting to stay open as she comes. "I love you, Sebastian."

And that does it, I pull out and come all over her ass. Don't gasp that I didn't grab a condom. There wasn't time, and besides, Vee is on birth control and that shit is the bomb. Coming all over her is my new favorite thing. Who says relationships grow stale over time?

Laying my head on her back, we both catch our breath. "That was better than coffee," I admit. "Definitely the better way to wake up in the morning. I would go as far to say—"

"Vee? Honey? Your dad wants Sebastian to come and help him unload all the groceries."

"Fuck." I hiss. "What is it with your family and locks?"

Vee chuckles, her back shaking with laughter under me. "I'll remind my mom that her key is only for emergencies."

"Sebastian!"

"Ugh." I look at Vee. Her Uncle Theo's voice is one I recognize after being with Vee for seven years. Why the fuck are they all here?

"Get your ass down here and unload all this shit, boy."

"They're here early." I groan and it's not a happy sound. "They were supposed to come for dinner."

Vee shrugs. "They're morning people."

I cut her a flat look. "But they were supposed to come *tomorrow* for dinner."

She pats me on the back and smiles. "I'll be down after I clean up. Take a breath and then go help them." She cringes. "Otherwise they might come and check on us."

I nod, scrubbing a hand over my face. "That would not be good."

She grins and shakes her head. "No, it wouldn't. I kind of like you alive."

Right. Her dad is downstairs and I'm standing here with my dick hanging out ogling his daughter's legs.

"Sebastian!"

"I'm coming!" I yell to my father who is also here early and decided that if Vee's family is going to yell at me then so is he. Throwing on some jeans and a t-shirt, I take the stairs and meet Vee's entirely too large family in the kitchen.

"The food is in the cars," the guy with dark hair says, pointing to the open front door.

"Good to see you too, Uncle Theo," I say, simply because I know me calling him uncle gets on his nerves.

"Yell when the food is ready," he says, snatching a fishing pole from Vee's Uncle Cade, who is Drew and Bennett's father, and nodding to my back door. "Jameson and I will be out on the dock."

So much for a goodnight balcony romp.

I nod as Theo passes by me, leaving Cade lingering behind. "Thanks for having us," he says, as he claps me on the shoulder.

"We're happy to have our families together."

I refrain from reminding him that I offered to have them tomorrow evening but then he says, "There is a ton of food that needs unloading."

I shake my head. "So I've heard. I'm on it."

Heading outside, I find my mom with her purse and bag. "Hey, sweetie!" My mom wraps me in her arms as my very pregnant sister walks up.

"It took us a million years to get here."

I shrug. "We like the solitude." Especially since our new-found fandom. We might like to be on camera most days, but we certainly like our privacy.

My sister rolls her eyes but then kisses me on the cheek as she heads inside.

"Where's Emmy?" I ask.

Calista nods to Vee's father who has Emmy's sleeping body over his shoulder while he grabs the bags his wife is trying to bring in.

"I got it," I tell him, making my way over and taking the bags from him. He gives me a terse nod of approval.

"You are too sweet!"

I smile at Vee's mom. If it weren't for the height and the eyes, they could be twins. She gives me a squeeze. "And you wanted to kill him when he moved our little girl away from us," she says to Tim, Vee's dad.

I chuckle and let her go. I'm used to Milah's ribbing and Vee's father's threatening stares. I've never done anything to piss him off. Except for the reason he's here, but he gave me his blessing and that's the only thing that matters to me. The fact is both of Vee's parents have been good to me. Actually, Vee's mom was an integral part of me rebuilding my relationship with my family. She referred me to this great therapist, where my parents join me on occasion, as I work through some of my issues. I don't have to go very often anymore, but it's still nice to know I have support when those demons try and worm their way back into my life.

Once all the family is out of their cars, Vee is a gracious host and gives everyone a tour, leaving me and my dad to put away enough groceries to feed a small country.

"I'm proud of you, Son," he finally says when we get everything unloaded. I know he doesn't mean he's proud of me putting away the groceries.

He's proud of what I'm doing tonight and why they are all here. To celebrate.

"Come on," I tell Vee. "I already have your iPad and blanket setup outside."

She tugs on my hoodie and whispers, "What about our parents?"

I wave her off. "They're all asleep. Don't worry about it." But I am worried about it. This isn't exactly how I wanted things to go down. But alas, it's out of my control. I'm just rolling with it.

Pulling Vee down the hall, we slip out the back door and I move one of the patio chairs in front of it, just in case someone decides to come out for a front row seat. We race through the evening air, holding in our laughter, until we get to the dock.

"Oh my gosh. I never thought I would be sneaking out of my own house at twenty-six," she says through heaving bouts of laughter.

I take her hand and lead her to where we once laid and

watched a scary movie on her phone. This time, it isn't her Uncle Theo's dock, but ours, and that makes this all the more special.

Vee gets to the blanket first and drops to her knees. "What are we watching? Did you decide?"

I've resorted to watching horror movies with her. They aren't terrible and if I can cop a feel while she watches them… yeah, I definitely don't mind the nightly movies.

"I thought we could watch *The Ring*," I tell her, watching as she shines her phone's light over to the iPad and stops.

I can just barely make out the quick intake of breath. "Sebastian."

I kneel on one knee. "Open it."

She picks the black box off the iPad, setting her phone down so the light shines around her. She hesitates. "I promise nothing is going to jump out at you."

She grins and then looks at me on one knee and starts crying. "Is this why our families are here?"

I nod. "They were supposed to come tomorrow and celebrate with a dinner. At least Aspen and the guys followed directions."

"Oh, Sebastian," she says, crawling over to me and taking my hand. "You are the best thing that's ever happened to me."

This woman.

"I think I'm supposed to say that," I correct her.

She grins. "We both wear the pants in this relationship, bro."

I grab the ring from her playfully and put my finger to my lips. "Shh. For once, just listen."

She nods and the cool night air around us turns serious. "Valentina Lambros, aka Jacob 'Tweener' Whoever. You have the worst singing voice—" she play punches my shoulder, but I don't stop, "—that I want to listen to for the rest of my life."

A sob tears through her throat.

"You're my best friend, my best dude, and the best fake and real girlfriend I could ever want. Marry me and spend the rest of our lives teaching me how to love you as much as you deserve."

I crack open the little black box and wipe her tears with my thumb.

"Marry me, T? Make me a happy man?"

The woman, who occasionally still puts on that dreaded wig and waits for me to come to bed, pushes up on her knees and takes the ring from the box and slips it on her finger where it will never come off. "Yes," she cries, kissing me on the mouth. "I'll marry you, Bash-hole, and sing to you forever and ever."

I wrap her in my arms and kiss her forehead just as our balcony lights come on, and we hear, "You want me to stab him, Lambros, or do you want to do the honors?"

Acknowledgments

It's always a privilege to write to those who read my stories. I don't take for granted that you have plenty of options to spend your hard-earned money and downtime on. It's always my goal to give you a story you can fall in love with.

The Pretender had been a plot I've had for years, and when I wrote *IOU*, I knew this was Sebastian's story. It was wild and ridiculous and oh so fun. I hope you loved it. I hope you got to this page and wished there was one more epilogue or excerpt.

There isn't, (insert sad face) but I will tell you Aspen and Bennett are next, so make sure you sign up for my newsletter and see when I finally decide to drop this moody boy's and crazy girl's book.

If you loved Tweener and Demon Douche, I'd love it if you would leave a review and share your love. Reviews mean the world to me.

Now, to the nitty-gritty of what really happened with the birth of this book.

I honestly didn't think this book was going to make it to see a publish day. Whether it was a house full of kids (the husband counts too) or being a new homeschool teacher or slumming it braless for four months, I honestly couldn't get my shit together to make this book turn out the way I wanted. Then in those last few weeks, the story hit me, and I was literally sending my editors new content days before arcs went out.

It was a shitshow, but hey, at least my boobs were happy, right?

In no particular order, these are my heroes.

Jaime, good freaking heavens, I am so happy I finally got to meet you and hug your ass. Otherwise, I think you might have run screaming after dealing with me throughout this process. Why are you so good to me? Why is Dansby so fine? And why in the fresh hell do we live so far apart? You are my GIRL. Forever. And freaking ever. Thank you for being my shoulder to cry on and reading this book so many times that you could vomit out the words verbatim. You are a genuine soul that I hate sharing with your man. I love you like I love baseball. I'm also looking for you a house across the street. You know, just in case you're feeling spontaneous.

Rebecca, I bet you think you should have just kept scrolling and have never read IOU. This is what you get when hop on the crazy train with me. Thank you for pushing me to be a better writer and then checking up on me when I completely fell apart and told you to delete everything. I'd like to promise I'll do better next time, but let's be honest, it's not really my thing. All I can promise is to be timely, so we can let the crazy run its course without interrupting our timeline. But thank you for rolling with it and enduring. You indeed are a gem.

Sarah P.! Did I ever tell you that you're my hero? Thank you for telling me Vee and Bash were shit so I would start over. I'm kidding—nobody sends her hate mail. You totally didn't say that, but you know I'm crazy, and I took your comments and turned *The Pretender* into something I could be proud of. Thank you for checking up on me and being so flexible and fast! You are spectacular, and I love you bunches!

Sarah S. Choo Choo! The hot mess train is pulling out, and we are the conductors. Thank you for always sending me the pretties and rolling with my lack of attention to dates and self-promotion. You are the shiz-nit, ma'am! I can't wait to make more magic together.

Peanut butter, aka Jessica, I can't remember if I'm jelly or you are. That should tell you how close we are. We've merged into that mixed shit in a jar. Thank you for being my external brain and my partner in everything. Without you, I wouldn't remember even to post that I write books. You make me a better person and a better friend. I think I owe your ass a call now, right?

Autumn, can I just say that I love it when I have these epic meltdowns, and I start texting you saying, "This is garbage and we need to push the release back," and then you text me with: "Shut up and go to bed." I live for those texts because you know how to roll with my writing process. Thank you for enduring all my personality quirks and keeping me focused and organized. Another book down and endless more to go!

To my betas, we were a little unorthodox with this one, but I promise that Aspen and Bennett will be back to normal, God willing. Thank you for checking on me and being my sweetest critics and best supporters. I'm honored to call you my crew.

Bex, thank you for always keeping my website looking professional and like I'm a real author. You are the master!

Laura, you my boo and I love that you're keeping our relationship spicy. Love you forever and I promise I'm stocking up on mint M&M's to send you as soon as the borders open back up.

Letitia, of RBA designs! I think we can all say you are the cover wizard. You also have the patience of a saint. Thank you for not blocking me and still letting me hop onto your calendar with stupid ideas and crazy drawings. Oh, and also for letting me send you like eight thousand images only to say, Nah. Let's find someone else. You are my one and only, and I cannot wait to annoy the shit out of you for these next three covers.

Stacey, of Champagne Formats, why are you always so unique and creative and so damn flexible? You bring my work to life, and I will always be eternally grateful for your art.

To the most remarkable reader group ever established: Kristy's Commanders. You guys inspire me every day and keep me motivated to always give you the best storylines I can dream up. YOU. ARE. THE. REAL. DEAL.

And last, but certainly not least, to you, who's reading this page. You are the reason I do this. Thank you for reading my words and purchasing this book. I owe you everything.

The CLOSER

For my husband.
Every love story I write starts with you.

Proverbs 31:11 NIV
Her husband has full confidence in her and lacks nothing of value.

The CLOSER

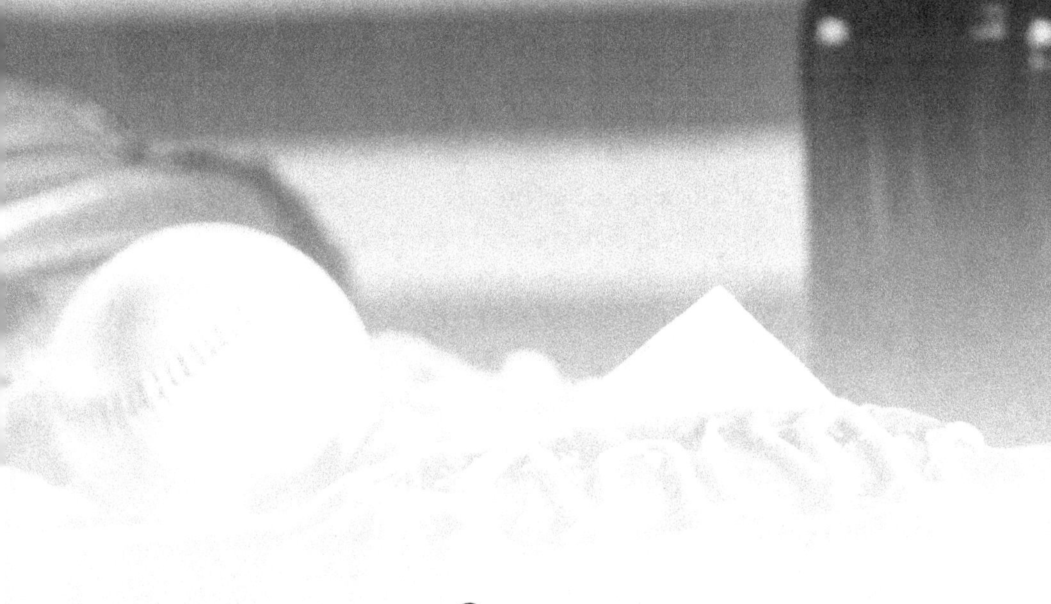

Chapter
ONE

McKinley

Once upon a time, in a not so far away land, lived a girl who… was three seconds away from shoving a sign up this jerk's ass.

"Swear to God, McKinley, if you don't get back in the truck, I'm calling the cops."

Glaring at the offensive sign in Griffin's yard, I slide my gaze to the asshole standing behind it, a cell phone clutched in his hand as a warning. "Go ahead, call them."

The bastard needn't think I fear a little overnighter. Been there. Done that.

"McKinley, be reasonable." Chris, aka, the man who is about to taste dirt, sighs. "Do you think Griffin would want you behaving like this?"

I think Griffin would be proud I contemplated killing his brother and didn't. It shows an epic amount of restraint I once lacked.

"Don't act like you knew him," I snap. "You abandoned him when he needed you the most!" When *we* needed him the most.

Calm the rage, Mac. Calm. The. Rage. Chris isn't worth the tears.

"You're right. I should have visited." At least he has the balls to look ashamed. "But that doesn't change the circumstances. Griffin is dead."

His point? Dead people don't need houses, and the small ranch-style home that took Griffin two years to purchase is no longer my concern. "Can't you just fix it up? Rent it out for a little while?" I can feel the sting in the back of my eyes, threatening to turn into tears.

"No."

Just no. Not *I'm sorry, but I can't afford the upkeep*, or *it's too much work between my family and job*. Just no.

"Please." I try a softer tactic. "Just wait a little while longer." Until it doesn't hurt as bad. "This was his home." And I drove him away.

The moon shines down on the weathered roof, and I watch as Chris's jaw hardens, all the issues he had with his little brother bubbling up in one hateful breath. "That's right, *his* home! Not yours! You were merely a guest, on occasion, and a drain on my brother's life. This is my house now, and I will do with it as I damn well please. Now get off my fucking property. We're done here."

I don't know if it was his tone or the actual words that shattered the last of my sanity, but I don't hold back the battle cry when I charge the *For Sale* sign and kick it with all my might. Immediately, I fall to the ground with a face full of grass, reaching for my toe with a cry. "Ow. Ow. Ow!"

Later, I'll realize kicking anything while wearing flip-flops is a terrible idea.

"Always a pleasure seeing you, Mac." Chris turns away, fighting a grin. "See that you find your way out of the subdivision before you wake the neighbors. I'd hate for you to embarrass yourself further."

I won't cry. Not in front of this prick.

I've already cried enough these past few weeks. Losing my best friend has been difficult. Losing him after we had a heated argument has proven more than I can bear. But I refuse to let *Dick Jagger* here stop me from taking what's rightfully mine. Griffin and I might not have been blood-related, but he was family. And like with any family, you develop memories. Memories I refuse to leave behind.

Ignoring the throbbing in my toe, I stand and hobble toward the back fence. "I'm not leaving without my tree."

As if in slow motion, Chris turns, holding up his phone. "Whatever. You have until the cops get here."

That's fine.

"Let the cops know I'll be in the garden shed."

Fucker.

The cops can pull me from that rickety old building with spiders the size of chipmunks. It won't be me screaming. Unlike Chris, Griffin and I were always hiding out in dark, dilapidated buildings. Spiders were the first thing I learned to get over.

Chris shakes his head, a nasty sneer helping his face look more human and less asshole-robot. "I hope this is the last time I ever see you, McKinley."

I try to say something shittier, but my mouth fails. All I can do is watch as the boy I knew, who I secretly admired, closes the door, shutting me out of his life forever.

You won't cry. It doesn't matter if your toe is swelling and it feels like it's splitting in half. You're going to walk to that garden shed, find a shovel in the dark, and dig up your palm tree. Because that's all you have left of Griffin and the stitched-together family you once had.

Nightmare of the Living Brother didn't call the cops. I guess he had a heart after all. Just not one big enough to help me dig up. Psalms, the small palm tree Griffin gifted me on my last birthday.

But you know what? Screw him.

I have pain reliever at home and half a bottle of rum I snagged from the garden shed when Griffin asked me to hide the alcohol when he was doing one of those trendy cleanses.

Me and my toe will be fine as soon as Lu and I make it home, which isn't but twenty miles from Griffin's. The problem is Lu, my 1950s truck, is a stubborn, old bird and thinks coasting to a stop in the middle of the exit ramp is a fun way to spend Friday night.

"You know, Lu?" I muse, tapping my fingers on the steering wheel, trying the engine again. "A little more to the right and we could've parked on the shoulder. You know, where broken-down vehicles are supposed to stop. It's a place where owners don't get slammed into from behind."

Lu doesn't answer because, well, she's a truck, and this isn't a Pixar film, and what would she even say? *You're welcome? Or that's what you get for driving a truck Griffin used to kick and hit with the same wrench in your purse on a daily basis.*

Lu should have retired several years ago when I spent an entire month's salary on her suspension. Griffin told me to buy something newer, but I couldn't; Lu had been on many adventures with Griffin and me. We all had our issues, but we were a family. A family that dissolved into tears and accusations, leaving me alone, with no closure from my best friend.

"All right, Lu," I say aloud. "Have it your way."

Grabbing the metal wrench, I eye the flip-flops in the passenger seat. I could slip them over my swollen toe—help ensure I don't add another injury to my list of pains, but the thought of even touching the now black and blue toe sends shock waves of pain through my spine.

"I better not step on a nail, Lu," I threaten the inanimate object. "If I do, I'm jamming it through your tire." Which would be a stupid thing to do, but after the past two weeks, I don't care. I'll walk to work if I have to. I'm so over everything in my life going to shit. If slashing Lu's tires makes me feel better, then that's exactly what I'll do.

Therapy comes in many forms. Personally, I enjoy taking my frustration out physically. Griffin called it crazy; I call it exercise. But it's not like I run around wielding the wrench from my purse like a weapon. I don't. Mostly, I'm a patient person. It takes a lot to ruffle me, but with Griffin dying like an asshole and Chris *being* an asshole, and my job being a *pain* in my ass, well… it's all just been building toward one epic asshole-palooza that is my life.

Sliding out of Lu, my toes touch the asphalt, and I let out the mother of all hisses. I'll be the first to admit kicking that sign wasn't my finest moment.

Gingerly, I apply more weight on the likely broken toe. *It doesn't hurt. It's just uncomfortable.*

And I'm completely lying…

Currently, my big toe throbs like a penis at a porn convention, but finally, after a lot of weight shifting, I'm standing on both feet, nodding like I didn't just use six different variations of the F-word.

But that's beside the point. The point is I *only* swore and didn't beat Lu's fender with the wrench tucked into the waistband of my shorts like I wanted.

Lu better be grateful for my self-control and optimism.

And optimism, at the moment, is me moving Lu on my own to the emergency lane. A foot (or five) from where she's currently parked. Easy peasy.

Turning back to Lu, I knock the gear into neutral and pray the tires don't roll while I hobble to the back and place my palms on the tailgate, which looks amazing with the contrasting dirt under my fingernails. Again, it doesn't matter. All that matters is I got what I came for. Psalms. (Smacking Chris was on my list for a hot minute, but I'll save it for another time, like his birthday.)

Channeling all my hate, pain, and aggravation from tonight, I shove against Lu's scratched tailgate.

She moves all of a centimeter.

"Come on, Lu. Show some mercy." I drop my head, allowing the slight sting of the metal to clear the tears threatening to fall.

Breathe, just breathe and move. You're fine.

I nod, chanting to myself that I can breathe. I can move on—alone, without the person who mattered most.

I can do it.

I can totally move this truck when my toe feels like it's on fire.

Lifting my head, I drag in one last breath before giving Lu another firm shove, this time with more force and a battle cry (because that helped last time). "Move, you stubborn bat!"

Lu's tires roll. "That's a girl, Lu. Keep going. Keep—"

But then sudden flashes of light and screeching tires silence my cheers as I brace for impact.

Chapter
TWO

Cooper

"*An intervention? Really?*"

At some point, my brother thought it'd be nice to utilize his spare key and take a shit on the remaining hours of my day by camping out on my couch and annoying me with a lecture.

"You weren't answering our calls." The statement rolls off his tongue casually, like he just walked next door and didn't board a plane, flying across the country with his pregnant wife and my agent in tow.

"I was busy. I didn't think a few missed calls would cause you to get all up in your feelings."

A sinister smirk meant to cower lesser men crosses Maverick's face while rolling up his sleeves, as if readying for a fight. He isn't, though. My older brother is simply getting comfortable on my fucking couch, enjoying the verbal sparring.

"Come on, Coop." Aspen, my agent since high school, sighs. "This is a safe space."

"No," I correct, "this is an ambush."

Snorting comes from the sofa. "We could have saved ourselves the jet lag if you'd just returned our texts, calls, emails—Should I go on?"

I'd like very much for him to "go on" back to his home in Georgia, but since his posture screams he won't settle for anything less than a long conversation and a hug, I fear that may not happen as quickly as I would like.

With the grace of my seventy-six-year-old grandfather, I fall into the chair, stretching my legs out in front. "Say what you need so you can catch the next flight out."

On a good day, I'm not so much of an asshole and more antisocial, but getting a lecture from my older brother and agent at twenty-three years old would put anyone in a pissy mood.

"Great." My brother is apparently going first in the circle of bullshit. "What were you thinking?"

This question would bring out the immaturity in anyone. Luckily for my brother, I refrain from speaking, instead, reaching over and snatching the straw from Aspen's cup. "What are you doing?"

The metal save-the-turtle straw rolls between my fingers as I meet my brother's stare. "I'm making this torture bearable by jamming this straw into my eardrum."

It'd be less painful than enduring them nag in-person. I can handle the hateful text messages, but this, showing up unannounced… that's a no.

Aspen yanks the straw from my grip and tosses it behind her where my eyes follow.

"Pops will trip and fall," I note dryly.

Aspen and Maverick might think I was acting reckless, but I wasn't.

"I promised I would take care of him," I bite out at my brother as Aspen retrieves the straw and tucks it into her purse. "I made one mistake."

"A mistake that could have gotten you killed!" Unlike the relaxed nature of my brother, Aspen always brings the passion, even if I'd rather she just send a text with a million exclamation marks like my sister-in-law, who is currently out with Pops getting ice cream while her husband and Aspen nag me about one fucking mistake from a week ago.

"It won't happen again."

I don't feel the need to explain or even make them feel better by coming up with an elaborate excuse. The bottom line is it happened, I was irresponsible, and I've since fixed the issue.

"You can't make a promise like that."

Exhaling, I drop my head, reading the line inked on the inside of my forearm as a reminder. My power is perfected in weakness. "You're right, Asp. I can't make that promise, but I can assure you that Pops and I are fine, and we're both getting more rest."

Maverick's jaw clenches. "Ainsley and I would love to see Pops more often."

Leaning back and settling in for yet another long debate, I raise one leg and rest it on a knee. "Then visit more. No one says you have to limit visits to holidays."

That's not quite true. Maverick and Ainsley visit more than a few times a year, but he's not about to make me feel guilty about moving Pops clear across the country.

"Don't play with me, little brother. You know what I mean. You're in the prime of your life—"

"Yes!" Aspen chimes in. "I'm fielding trade offers daily. Think about your future, Cooper."

I am. "My future is here in Nevada with Pops."

Maverick blows out an exasperated breath, raking a hand through his hair, leaving it disheveled. "It's my turn to look after him, Cooper." His voice is edgy. He's losing his patience, which means absolutely nothing to me. Maverick might be my big brother, but my ruler, he is not.

"Pops isn't a merry-go-round, Mav. You don't get a turn. He's happy here. I'm not shipping him back to Georgia just because you both think I can't handle my career and Pops at the same time."

"That's not what we think at all." Aspen's voice is calm as she tries to diffuse the tension between Maverick and me. "We know you can take care of Pops. You've been doing it all your life. But what your brother is trying to say is that he wants to help you. We both do."

What she's politely explaining is that they want me to focus on my career and live the bachelor life of a Major League pitcher.

Inhaling, I take a sip of my water on the table, contemplating my next words. Their concern comes from a good place. "I appreciate the offer," I respond, directing my words to both of them. "But we're fine."

"You fell asleep at the wheel and crashed your car!" Maverick snaps, and I'm underwhelmed. "I wouldn't call that fine." He spits the last word like it disgusts him to say it.

I shrug my shoulders, admittedly a little sore from last week's accident. "I wasn't hurt."

Neither was the ditch I finally crashed in.

My brother snorts. "So you're saying you blew that game last night for shits and giggles?"

"Can I not have an off day?"

"No. Mediocre pitchers have an off day. The Closer doesn't."

The Closer.

It's a name I haven't been able to shake. A few years ago, when I started my career in the Majors, I basked in the intimidation the name carried. Now, though, the stress of living up to a reputation I created years ago feels like a noose around my neck, smothering me breath by breath.

"I had an off day," I glare at Maverick. "It happens."

"Not to you."

Groaning, I lean my head back and stare at the ceiling. This conversation or intervention, whatever they want to call it, is grating on my last damn nerve. "He's not moving back to Georgia."

"Maybe we should ask Pops what he wants?"

Aspen's question has me on my feet in a matter of seconds. "He wants to stay here with me."

"Does he? Have you asked Pops if he misses home? If he misses Georgia?"

I shoot a glare at Maverick. We haven't traded blows since we were teenagers. That's liable to change if he keeps pushing the issue of Pops moving back to Georgia with him.

"No one misses Georgia, Mav. Stop trying to make this situation into something it's not. Pops and I have a routine. He has friends here. You're not dragging him back to Georgia and sticking him in another assisted living facility."

"He has friends?"

"Yes. Why do you seem so shocked?"

Maverick does a sweep of my and Pops's home with a critical eye.

I know what he sees, a one-story, newly built cape cod style home, minimally furnished with foam taped to every sharp edge I could find. In essence, it looks more like I have a toddler than a grandpa in his late seventies. "Is the nurse you hired working out?"

I nod, not wanting to speak the words.

"And he's doing his rehab?"

"Of course he is."

"Who takes him?"

I roll my eyes.

"When you're on the road, I mean. Away games and all that." He waves his hand like he can't bother to remember the correct terms, which is really the least of what I should let annoy me right now.

"Cooper?"

I was over this conversation when I saw their rental car in the driveway.

"Are you going to answer me or just stand there clenching your fists?" Maverick smiles. "Do you want to hit me, little brother?"

I'm glad I can serve as the source of his amusement today.

"We do his therapy on the road. We only have one nurse, and her contract stated no travel."

An audible gasp goes through my living room.

"Cooper!" Aspen clutches her heart. "Please tell me you don't mean you take him with you?"

Folding my arms across my chest, I level Aspen with a flat look. "That's exactly what I mean. What else am I supposed to do?"

"Hire another nurse," my brother muses. "The words assisted living come to mind."

I snap. Fuck both of them. "He will never live in one of those places again. That's how he fell and broke his hip in the first place. I won't have it happen again."

"He fell because he had a TIA. It wasn't because someone at assisted living was negligent." Maverick stands and steps closer to me. "Let me help you. You can't do this alone. It's not good for you—"

I open my mouth to argue that Maverick has no idea what's good for me when Aspen jumps in. "It's not good for Pops, Coop. Think of how much he's being set back by missing physical therapy appointments while you're attending away games. He needs stability. Maverick and Ainsley can give him that."

"No."

I don't have to explain myself.

"Don't be stubborn, Cooper."

This time it's me who steps closer, now eye to eye with my brother. "You don't get to tell me what's good for him. You weren't there. You don't know what we've been through."

I don't need to spell it out for Maverick. He might have wanted to stay home and help when Pops suffered a stroke, but Pops wouldn't hear of it. He forbid Maverick from coming home from college and looking out for us. I know it crushed him, but looking after Pops was always my job, even if Pops thought he didn't need the help.

Maverick holds my gaze before finally blowing out a breath. "Then at least allow him to stay with the nurse when you're away. So she can get him to therapy appointments, and you can focus."

It'll be a cold day in hell before I allow anyone to take care of Pops without me present. But I know what stubborn looks like, and my brother won't get the hell out of my house unless I concede to something. He and Aspen didn't come all this way not to get what they wanted. They aren't built to lose. But neither am I.

Thoughts of the nightmare intervention from three months ago play out in my head until my knuckles turn white against the leather-wrapped steering wheel.

His caregiver is going to leave…

I can feel it.

Reaching over, I dig through the glove box and find a warm energy drink and pop the top, taking a big gulp. It's three in the morning and from her texts, it sounds like I have a long night of groveling ahead. I just need a little energy to—

Slamming on the brakes, I swerve, barely missing the inconsiderate prick stopped in the middle of the off-ramp.

Dammit!

I can't do this. Not a-fucking-gain. The last thing I need right now is another accident in the wee hours of the morning. Maverick wouldn't give me the chance to explain again. He'd just invoke his older brother prerogative and move Pops without my consent.

And that can't happen.

All I need to do is offer this asshole a sincere apology and then be on my way.

Chapter
THREE

McKinley

"**A**re you insane?"

The sudden and inconsiderate honk startles me back against the tailgate, where I can't catch my footing (thanks, blinding toe pain) and fall to my knees.

"Get off the fucking road! This isn't a parking lot."

Aww. He's so sweet. "This is a rest area, no?" I doubt he appreciates my sarcasm probably about as much as I appreciate being blinded by his fancy LED lights.

Sitting up, I mentally do a pain assessment.

Toe? Throbbing nicely, if not a lot more than earlier.

Knees? Yeah, those scuffed up beautifully.

Elbows? They'll live. Actually, they need an award for saving my chin.

"Are you drunk?" The angered voice grows closer. As in, right behind me.

With sharp reflexes honed from many years of street-savvy survival, I grip the wrench from my shorts and whip it out like a sword.

"Don't come any closer," I warn, steadying the metal weapon. "I don't want to hurt you, but I will."

In the glow of his headlights, I swear the stranger's mouth twitches.

"I'm not joking. I have no reservations about defending myself."

The man in the dark suit puts his hands up, showing me his palms. "I believe you."

His voice is rough, as if he's been yelling at someone or raging at a rock concert. Given his suit, I'm going with a Wall Street yeller. "Can I help you get your truck off the road?"

My first reaction is no. Lu and I will be just fine. Better than fine, actually. Lu was moving at a good pace until Mr. Impatient nearly ran us over.

"You can stay in the cab and steer," he adds, nodding to my hands. "With your wrench."

He's definitely smiling.

"That's okay." I wave him off *with* my wrench. "I got it handled."

He studies my dirty hands wrapped around the handle of my metal ass-whooper before gazing behind me to where I assume he's getting a nice look at my bare feet that match my overall look of… well, a mess.

"Clearly," he muses. "My mistake."

So, not like a hero, he turns, shoving his hands inside his pockets, and walks back to his car.

Okay then.

It's not like I might have been convinced if he'd asked a few more times.

The annoying stranger settles into his seat, leaning back like he's readying for a nap, and then has the audacity to give me a thumbs up.

This mother—I will not stoop to his level.

If that's how it's going to be, then fine. I've never been shy. Having some stranger watch as I struggle to push Lu to the shoulder will be nothing new.

Okay, so it's new, but I never back down from a challenge.

In theory, having this dude sit in his car is probably safer than him hovering in my face, being all rude.

Setting my trusty wrench on the ground, I pull myself to a standing position and a deep, devil of a pain, shoots through my toe. I groan, which is terribly inconvenient when trying to appear badass.

"You can always go around me," I yell, chancing another look at the stranger and noticing he's no longer reclining. Instead, his fingers drum along the steering wheel, his face sporting a frown so deep it should have its own shadow.

"You could always let me help you."

It's really not that attractive that he yells out the window sarcastically. Honestly, I could do with more of a reserved stranger at the moment.

"No thanks."

I'm no dumbass (Thank you, Netflix documentaries).

Turning back to Lu, I put my hands on the tailgate and shove—hard. And mother fluffer if the pain doesn't send me back down to the pavement, and Sarcastic Stranger opens his door, thinking I need help.

"I just need to check something under the truck." I give the undercarriage a brief glance. "So," I drawl, buying a few seconds to catch my breath, "What are you doing on the road at three a.m.?"

I should have expected he would lose his cool.

"Are you serious right now?" I don't take his yelling personally. Like me, he's probably tired.

"I need just a breather. Don't worry, I'll be out of your way in no time."

The stranger's hand slaps against his car door before raking it through his hair, leaving it gloriously mussed. "I'm on my way home." Surprisingly, he sounds less angry than I expected. "My flight landed a little while ago." He points behind him as proof there is an airport a few exits south.

"Business or pleasure?"

"God help me." Kicking the car door wider, he heads my way with labored stomps.

Scrambling, I lunge for the wrench, but a heavy hand captures my upper arm and holds me still.

"I'm not going to hurt you."

Says probably every serial killer. But call me the next victim because my dumb ass actually believes him.

And after tonight, I can live with that risk.

What I can't live with is his grip on my arm.

Dropping his stare, I settle my gaze on the hand wrapped around my arm. "Excuse you."

He doesn't get the subtle hint, and rather than apologize, he reaches to the ground, grabbing —"Don't touch my wrench!"

The potential killer ignores my demand, standing up straight and holding my gaze. "I expect to come away from this insanity with no broken bones," he says all authoritatively.

I make no promises.

And after the long staredown, he finally shoves the wrench forward. "Take it."

I snatch it without hesitation.

"Now, can you please get in the truck? I need you to steer." His fingers are still wrapped around my arm when he helps me to my feet.

I feel myself nodding, whispering a *thank you* I'm not sure he hears since he turns and slips off his jacket, tossing it over Lu.

Heaven help me.

This stranger and his forearms… Why did he have to roll up his sleeves, revealing hills of muscle beneath inked skin? He has a tattoo that reads: My Power is Perfected in Weakness and heaven help me, my vagina tingles. His power? Perfected in weakness? Just sign me up. Gah, why do tattoos bring out my inner ho? It's not like I love tatted men over non-tatted men, but forearms? That shit is better than a six-pack of abs. Call me crazy, but I can—

"What are you doing?" Those same brawny arms grab me by the shoulders and pull me upright.

Huh. Who knew his hot forearms would send me to my knees in a haze of drool?

"Are you going to steer?" Bad Attitude snaps. "Or do you still think I'm going to decapitate you with my travel razor?"

I snatch out of his hold. "That's awfully descriptive," I accuse. "Have you been thinking about doing—"

"Get in the truck!" No amusement is mixed with his words, but that's probably because it's started misting, and his fancy button-down is now getting wet along with, well, all of him. Which isn't terrible, in my opinion.

"Right. Yes, I'm sorry." I start for the driver's door, forgetting about my broken toe and scuffed knees. "Ow."

"You're hurt." His gaze goes to my foot, still hovering a few inches off the pavement.

"I'll be fine."

What's that saying? Never be weak prey in front of the hunter?

Placing my foot back on the ground, I pointedly ignore the shooting pain and walk the remaining few feet and get in the truck. "I'm ready when you are, ho—homie."

Holy hell, I really have lost it. I just about called the man, hottie. To his face!

Luckily though, he seems to have not heard me while he leans his shoulder against Lu and shoves with far less effort than I gave.

And God bless Lu and her ornery self, she moves as if she's alive and not blown a gasket or some other insanely expensive part that likely will cost me a day's pay.

I steer the old girl to the shoulder and put her in *park*.

"I'll call you a tow." I jump at his voice at my window. Gah, what is he? A damn ninja?

"Thanks." I offer him a kind smile. "But you don't have to do that. I can call them."

He looks at the sky before sighing. "Can I give you a ride home then?"

Stubborn killer or a decent guy? The jury is still out, so I won't take any chances. "That won't be necessary. You've done enough already."

This super sexy muscle in his throat twitches and sue me, I want to touch it. "At least let me take you to the ER then." He tips his chin down. "And have someone look at your… foot."

Ha! "I drive a 1955 pickup that breaks down more than it runs. Does it look like I can spare the money for the ER to bandage my toe and offer me a painkiller? No. Besides, you can't do anything for a broken toe." I wave off his concern. "I appreciate your help getting to the shoulder. Go home and get some rest. It looks like you could use it."

I try. I try not to look at the saturated shirt clinging to his chest and hugging every inch of the muscles I failed to notice earlier. This man not only has hot forearms, but Stranger Hottie's chest and abs are next-level muscles. These ripples take years and the assistance of a personal trainer and money. Too bad his personality is a little prickly.

"I insist."

I gotta admit, he's sweet in his own hateful way though.

"Oh, well, in that case, let me get my purse."

It's adorable when he nods, not picking up on my sarcasm. "I'm joking. I'll be fine. Go home."

For someone who was in such a hurry earlier, he sure is dawdling now.

But no bother, I'm used to his audience at this point. Snagging my phone off the console, I google the nearest tow truck company, and dial.

"Yeah," the guy on the phone answers sleepily.

I turn and smile at the stranger still hovering at my door, damp in his expensive suit. I keep the phone on speaker so he can hear that I have help coming and he can scurry along now. "I need a tow. I'm parked off exit 227. On the shoulder. You can't miss me. I'm in a red pickup—"

"A beat-up, red pickup," Hottie Stranger adds unhelpfully.

I narrow my eyes. "That's not nice."

He shrugs, undeterred. "Just trying to give the man a more accurate description."

An accurate description, my ass…

"Yeah, so it'll be a while. I'm the only one working tonight."

"Define a while."

"Uh, Monday?"

I look at Hottie. "Did he just say Monday? As in two days from now?"

"Yep."

"It's really tacky to be smug, especially when you know I've clearly had a shitty night." Yeah, I'm talking to Wet Shirt with the bad attitude.

"My offer still stands." He shrugs like he wants to get hit.

"You could call Uber," the tow driver adds.

This is stupid. I'm totally going to die tonight.

"Or you could just grab a coffee and drag your ass out of bed and tow my truck!"

I deserved him hanging up. Really, I lost my cool at the end. I can admit that, albeit not gracefully. "Ahh!" I stomp my good foot on the floorboard and throw my head back against the seat. "Tonight can kiss my as—"

"Get out." My door creaks and my eyes fly open with it.

"Pardon me?" I know he didn't just demand I get out of my car.

"Get your wrench. I promise you can hit me if I do anything shady—which I won't." He does this little cross his heart thing that would be downright adorable if I wasn't mad. "But please hurry. I, too, have had a day that can kiss my ass."

I grin, and it's totally stupid since I'm considering getting into a stranger's car. But now that I look at Hot Forearms, like really look at him, I see the dark circles under his eyes and the hoarseness in his voice.

Dammit.

Why does he have to make me feel guilty, standing out here like a gentleman in the rain?

I look at the stranger, a million scenarios going through my head about how this night will end. "You promise you won't kill me?"

With all the seriousness in the world, his gaze locks with mine. "I promise."

Apparently, beautifully frightening eyes do it for me because I feel myself nod and roll up my window and step out. "I just need to grab my tree in the back."

"Your tree?"

In his defense, he tried to hide the sudden fear—which I appreciated.

"Yeah, my tree." I gaze at his car, still idling and blocking any oncoming traffic. "I think it'll fit in your back seat."

His eyes widen. But I don't bother explaining. I just need this day to be done.

Pausing at the bed, already reaching for Psalms, a big body presses mine into the truck. "Let me."

He gets no objections from me.

"Should I be the one who needs a wrench?" he teases, handing me the tree with a hint of a grin that does not make him look totally kissable. "Since I'm *not* the one covered in dirt, barefoot, sporting a broken toe with a half-dead palm tree in a coffee can."

"You caught me on an awful night," I offer by way of explanation.

My savior, the stranger, gives me one long look before offering me his arm to lean on. "I can understand that. I'm Cooper, by the way."

I take his arm and look up, noticing the slight stubble on his face. "I'm McKinley, by the way." I tighten the grip on my tree and pinch my fingers together for a visual measure. "And I might be a little crazy."

His returning laugh is rich with raspy goodness, but he tames it quickly. "I appreciate the warning. Now get in the fucking car."

Chapter
FOUR

Cooper

Arching my brows, I glare at her folded arms and stiff body laced with blatant refusal.

"I won't ask you again," I tell her seriously.

"And I will not hesitate to smack that bossy attitude right out of you if you can't ask nicely."

Is she serious? Is this day serious?

First, I endured a six-hour flight, only to land and be met with forty-eight texts between my grandfather and his caretaker. And now, I can't even get home to solve that clusterfuck of a mess because I'm stopped on the interstate with a woman who looks like she battled a grizzly and won. "Seriously?" I ask her, just in case I'm misinterpreting the situation. "You're broken down on the side of the road with what looks like gangrene taking hold of your toe and you want to delay getting to safety because I didn't say please?"

"Yes, I think a little pleasantry wouldn't kill you."

It might.

I glance around, taking in the streetlight illuminating nothing but pavement. Maybe someone else will come along and help her? I've had enough headaches today. Adding one more would just be persecution.

"Can't you—" Interrupted by a phone call, I glance at the screen and sigh, holding up a finger to the wrench-wielder. Maybe she'll tire of waiting and get in the car. "Hey, Pops."

The sound connects to my car's Bluetooth and booms through the speakers. "She's doing it again!"

I groan and flop down into the driver's seat. Not again. "Doing what, Pops?"

"Changing the channel!"

Inhaling, I breathe deeply and turn to the side, catching the curious gaze of the stranded woman easing into my passenger seat.

Thank God.

"Surely, she thought you were asleep," I add, keeping my eyes trained on the leaves falling into my car as McKinley turns and pushes the half-dead tree onto my floorboard.

"It doesn't matter if I was asleep! This is my house!"

Technically, it's mine, but I'm in no mood to hear about how many times he had to wipe my ass and share the last Oatmeal Cream Pie with me while growing up.

"I understand," I tell him, lowering my voice in hopes it deescalates the situation somewhat. "All I'm saying is if you were asleep, she wouldn't think you were exactly watching the TV."

For fuck's sake.

"I'm still listening, dammit!"

Do I blame Cynthia for trying to catch up on her shows while Pops slept? No. I'd have done the same. But since they've all but stabbed each other with forks tonight, I'm not going to take sides. The fact is, Cynthia is the only night nurse I've been able to keep for longer than forty-eight hours, thanks to Pops and his surly attitude. I can't afford to piss her off and deal with yet another search for caretakers.

But then again, I'm the one who deals with Pops more often than not, so if he wants Cynthia to sit there and stare at him while he sleeps, then who am I to tell him it's weird. I just need peace and fucking quiet. Every away game is a nightmare when I leave the two of them together.

"Pops?" The feminine voice to my right has me whipping my head around. "Is that you?"

I slice at my throat, my eyes wide, begging her to hush. Please don't tell me she's one of the fifteen nurses that quit.

"Mac?"

Ah, fuck. She is.

"Macaroni!" Pops shouts, his voice instantly changing from hateful to something softer, something more… happy. "What are you doing with Coop?"

Macaroni?

I look at the woman in my passenger seat, grinning and buckling her seatbelt. Guess she's coming along without a please after all.

"I didn't realize he's *your Cooper*. Lu broke down again, and Grumpy Grandson came to my rescue."

Grumpy Grandson? "Is that what you call me?"

I can't believe this shit. McKinley, wrench-wielding-Aphrodite, knows my grandfather, and she's not a scorned caregiver? No way.

"Only when you're in one of your moods," Pops assures me, getting a chuckle out of McKinley that suggests otherwise.

And then it hits me. His seat buddy. "You're Mac? The one he buys a pickle and Mountain Dew for at every home game?"

She nods. "He's my bestie."

And the one Pops cares more about seeing than watching me pitch. "I thought you were a guy."

She shrugs. "And I thought you were a titty baby."

A what? Did she just say she thought I was a titty baby?

I can hear the blood whooshing through my ears as Pops smothers a laugh. "You have a lot of explaining to do, you old fart." I can't believe he's been bashing me at games.

"Yeah, yeah," he poo-poohs my warning. "Where are you taking Mac?"

I don't hesitate. "Home."

"Bring her here!" He sounds like a little kid and not the seventy-six-year-old man that he is.

"She's hurt. I'm sure she wants to go to her house since it's three in the morning. You can have a playdate later."

"Hurt? Mac! You alright, my girl?"

McKinley's quick to jump in. "I'm fine. Just a minor scratch. Just another run-in with the devil. I'll tell you more about it tomorrow night at the game if you'll be there."

She looks at me, and I nod.

He'll be at tomorrow's—or tonight's—game. He wasn't at the last one because Cynthia said she couldn't keep up with him, and it was only a matter of time before he fell down the steps and rebroke the hip he had replaced several months ago.

Since I promised Maverick I'd keep him safe, I couldn't allow him to find out the old geezer beat me in a game of Scrabble, which had me owing him visits to the ballpark.

"I'm not waiting until tonight. Cooper, you bring her here so I can lay eyes on her myself."

There's no point in arguing with him, but there is a pesky situation Pops isn't considering. "You know," I say, already throwing my car in *drive*, "some might call me a celebrity, and bringing strangers to the house would only result in future restraining orders."

McKinley scoffs, but Pops beats her to it. "Some may think you're full of yourself. Bring my girl and your antisocial self home." He lowers his voice. "Then fire Cynthia."

"I'm not firing Cynthia."

I'm not dealing with another intervention.

Pops clears his throat, obviously not happy with my answer on not firing Cynthia. "We'll discuss it later."

We won't. No matter if I think Cynthia is better suited for a patient with a lot less sarcasm than Pops, the facts remain the same: Aspen and Maverick require we keep a nurse while I'm on the road and out on the field. If we fire Cynthia, Pops will have to return to Georgia. And though Pops may be a pain in my ass sometimes, he's my friend, the man who took me to practice after Mom died and Dad decided he had better things to do than to raise two boys.

Pops is family, and I'll never abandon family, even if that means I'll one day quit baseball to take care of him. It's the least I can do for the man who didn't abandon me when I needed him the most.

I glance at the girl in my passenger seat, still holding the wrench in her lap. "What do you want to do?"

Just because Pops wants her to come hang out doesn't mean she wants to do the same.

She bites her lip and her eyes glisten in the passing streetlights. "It's been a really rough day."

I nod, about to tell Pops another time when she adds, "I'd like to see Pops."

"Told you, hard-head. Bring her to me."

I totally ignore the smug old man on the phone and stare at the girl who, now that I really look at her, has a tremble in her hands. "Home it is."

Chapter
FIVE

Cooper

"Coop! Where are the bandages?"

I'm surprised I understand Pops's question, considering he asked it with a mouthful of Pop-Tarts while he hovered over an open jar of pickles on the counter.

Who eats Pop-Tarts and dill pickles?

I shake my head at the sight of Pops clad in his pajamas, standing next to a haggard McKinley, looking like I dragged her behind the car rather than in it. As tempting as it was earlier, she was relatively quiet on the way home.

"It's okay. I don't need a bandage," McKinley objects, slurping pickle juice straight from a cup.

"Follow me."

She side-eyes Pops, as if silently asking if it's safe. Considering my poor attitude tonight, I can't blame her.

"Please," I add, hoping that will quicken her pace and my pursuit of sleep.

With a twitch of her lips, McKinley shoves the last bit of pickle down and follows me through the hall, her limp more prominent than earlier. "Are you in pain?"

Her voice is quiet and not nearly as aggressive when she threatened to harm me on the exit ramp. "I'm fine."

"Your toe looks broken," I note, as if there's no way she could be okay.

"Probably."

No tears, no sobs. Just acceptance that her toe is probably broken.

I stop mid-stride and turn back, giving her the look I give Pops when he insists he doesn't need my help getting out of bed. "After you shower, I'll wrap your toe and give you a painkiller."

My tone doesn't leave room for debate, yet her mouth opens like that's precisely what she intends to do. But this time I'm prepared, taking her by the arm and guiding her to my bedroom, silencing her argument as she takes in the scene in front of her.

A king-size bed, unmade on one side, clothes half hanging off the hamper, an open suitcase I've yet to unpack, and an open book on the nightstand. "I wasn't expecting guests," I admit, closing the suitcase and ushering her into the master bathroom, flipping on the light. At least the bathroom is in better condition than my room.

"I imagine it's hard not being home a lot," she notes, fingering the lilac-patterned hand towel on the rack. It doesn't fit the decor at all, but it belonged to my mother.

Grabbing a fresh towel from the cabinet, I hang it on the rack and turn on the water. "I had a housekeeper for a while, but I let her go." Which was after she used a cleaner I specifically asked her not to use. It left the floor slick and Pops slipped.

"I noticed the padding on the table corners." She doesn't say it like it's weird.

"Pops had a stroke when I was a kid. The blood thinners cause even the smallest of scratches to bleed."

"I know," she whispers.

And it hits me, she *does* know.

A few weeks ago, I had Pops escorted down to the clubhouse after a home game, his arm was dressed with a bandage. He said the chair had a piece of metal protruding from the armrest. Immediately,

I was on the phone with maintenance, but Pops said Mac had already taken care of it.

"I never thanked you for taking care of him."

She shrugs. "You don't have to thank me."

As the steam fills the bathroom, my gaze stays transfixed to the field-green color of her eyes. Mac isn't who I expected would have beers with an old man while watching the game.

"I really don't need a shower." She clears her throat. "I didn't mean to intrude, I just had a bad day, and it was nice to see a friend. It's late and—"

"Any friend of Pops is welcome here."

At least it sounds sincere and less dickish than before. Which… is awkward. I don't even know Mac, and the last time I had a woman in my bedroom was… too fucking long ago.

Focus, Coop. You need sleep.

Quickly, I turn back to the bedroom and root through my suitcase, finding a pair of clean sweats and an undershirt.

I set them on the counter. "They'll probably fall off your hips, but it'll work for tonight."

Her mouth opens, and I quickly step back and close the door. I'm not in the mood for more arguing.

Leaving McKinley to shower, I head into the living room and address Cynthia for the first time since the text extravaganza. "I have to be on the field at three."

She needs no further direction as she stands. "I'll be here." It sounds like she'd rather not, but I pay her well enough to endure.

And well enough not to thank her as I close the door and glare at the old man in the recliner. "We're gonna talk about this tomorrow."

"Psh." He waves his hand at me, his poo-poohing gesture. "That tone doesn't scare me, boy."

At seventy-six, he'll always be the man who washed my mouth out with soap when I told him to go fuck himself one time.

I rake my hands through my hair. "Fine," I give in. "But if you run Cynthia off, you're dealing with Maverick. I'm not taking the heat again."

"You forget, I changed your brother's sheets when he dreamed of using the toilet. *Neither* of you scare me."

And this is why life is so fucking complicated.

"Why don't you head on to bed since the Devil Woman is now gone." I use his nickname for Cynthia, which gets an amused grunt.

"You sure? You got Mac?" He acts like we need to carry her to bed or something.

"Yeah, I got her."

"All right." He eases from the chair and stands, wobbling a little. "Don't you help me," he all but growls when I take a step toward him.

I stick my hands in my pockets, fighting the urge. "You get on my fucking nerves," I note as he walks past me toward his bedroom, sneaking me a grin.

"Ditto, my boy. Don't go being hateful to Mac, she hits."

She hits…

I wonder if he's witnessed her actually using the wrench she keeps, but I decide not to ask. Honestly, I don't want to know what all she and Pops do while unsupervised. "Good night, old man," I mutter.

For the next half hour, I pick up around the living room, setting out a clean bowl and instant oatmeal on the kitchen counter just in case Pops wakes before me. We long since established he isn't allowed to use the stove—it's only been recently his balance has started stabilizing.

"Did Pops go to bed?"

I look up from the half-dead palm tree I'm currently watering. "Uh, yeah. He did."

McKinley's eyes stay fixed on the tree for a minute before she glances at the bowl on the counter. "You need any help?"

She seems a lot calmer now that she knows I'm not a highway killer. "Nah," I say, setting down the cup I was using to water the tree she seems ridiculously attached to. "Let me get you a bandage and show you to the guest room." If I don't get sleep soon, I'll be benched for tonight's game. Coach is a real stickler about rest—a rule I break daily.

McKinley follows me to the room in front of Pops's. "Through there." I crack open the door. "I'm just gonna grab you a bandage."

This time, she doesn't argue, and I take the opportunity to grab not only a bandage but a pain reliever from the medicine cabinet as well. When I return to the guest room with a bottled water and supplies in hand, she's sitting on the bed, her legs hanging over the side as if she isn't sure she wants to stay. "I've been thinking."

I hand her a pill and the water and kneel at her feet. "About?"

"What are you doing?" Her eyes go wide.

"I'm wrapping your toe." Showing her the bandage, I tip my chin in the direction of her foot. "Before you make it worse."

Attempting to scramble further up the bed and away from my grasp, she hurries out, "Oh no, that's okay."

Unlike her, I have nothing broken to impede my grip as I pin her legs to the mattress.

"This one time," I start, hoping to relax her, "Pops took my brother and me to the bowling alley. I couldn't have been much older than twelve."

She struggles for a minute before she finally gives in. "Maverick, my brother, decided it would be fun if we could have a competition on who could throw the heaviest ball."

My hands trail along the smooth skin of her legs, my eyes holding hers, daring her to move. "I decided that rather than tiring my arms by increasing the weight of the ball with each throw, I could go with the heaviest ball."

Opening the wrapper of the gauze, I chuckle, remembering. "Maverick was so pissed and wanted to go first, knowing I would win." She lets out a hiss as I ease under her toe, looping the gauze.

"Anyway, like most brothers, we started wrestling, and the ball slipped."

She watches my hands as I tape her big toe to the one next to it. "And it broke your toe?"

I laugh. "No, it broke my brother's. Pops was so mad he made me Mav's bitch for a week. As you can imagine, my brother enjoyed his broken bone immensely."

McKinley laughs, and it's soft and feminine. "So that's how you know how to wrap a broken toe like a pro, huh?"

I shrug. "Amongst other injuries."

"Do you get hurt a lot? Playing baseball, I mean?"

Applying the last piece of tape, I look up at her, sitting back on my heels. "All done."

Nodding, she smiles hesitantly. "You aren't going to ask me how I broke it?"

"Pops told me you hit. I'm assuming you kick too."

She situates herself against the pillows, smothering a grin. "Sometimes."

Yeah, there's trouble written all over this girl, and no matter how delectable she looks in my clothes, I can't afford another distraction.

"Goodnight, Mac."

Chapter
SIX

McKinley

Woosah.

Woo—

"Are you even listening to me?"

Mr. Ear Hair's fingers snap in front of my face, the worn lines on his forehead deepening while he levels me with a glare. A glare that I've been able to ignore with grace. Quite impressive if I do say so myself. He's lucky I slept like a damn rock in Cooper's guest bed. Who has memory foam for guests? Hell, I don't even have a guest room.

"Look, lady, you don't need that much skill to cook a hot dog—" The dismissive hand-wave adds a little flair to his words. "—but, this is the third time you've charred my frank into something unrecognizable. You'd think you would at least get it right once." He shakes his head, his mouth puckering as he tsks. "Your boss must be desperate for help. I'd never let such incompetence stay on my staff."

The words bite, but not as much as they did the first time he said them. The first time I *accidentally* burnt his hot dog.

"My apologies, sir. Please let me swap your insufficient wiener for one less… ugly." I force a smile that I hope conveys the giant *fuck you,* I'm thinking.

Honestly, I didn't intentionally burn his hot dog, but when he snapped his fingers after ordering, adding a clipped, "Hurry the fuck up," slapping a hundred-dollar bill down on the counter… Well, I certainly wasted no time shoving the dry, crispy meat in a bun.

Mr. Ear Hair—a fitting nickname for one so pleasant—is a season ticket holder in my section at Landon Field, home to the Vegas Tides baseball team. I don't know what exactly Mr. Ear Hair does for a living, but he likes to remind me he's uber-successful by paying with bills that I don't have the change to break. He's so kind though (insert sarcasm here) and waits while I leave my cart to beg a neighboring cart for change—a no-no, per my boss, Ted—all the while pleasantly checking his watch with a shitty grin as the customers behind him groan and leave my line for another.

Obviously, Ear Hair does this on purpose.

And for that fact alone, he gets a burnt wiener. Every. Single. Home game.

One day, he'll more than likely complain to Ted. And more than likely, I'll get fired. But that's one day's problem. Today, I'm simply reveling in the fact that Mr. Asshole Ear Hair had to walk back to my cart, wait in line twenty minutes, and miss the sixth-inning home run hit by the Tides—his favorite team.

With that bit of payback in my back pocket, I can endure his condescension and the disdainful look he's giving me right now.

"Do you think you could actually hurry this time so I don't miss any more of the game?"

I manage a nod. "Anything for you."

Fucker.

I hope the next Tides's player hits a home run right at his forehead. Not hard enough that it causes brain damage, but hard enough that it knocks some decency into him.

Counting back his change, I level him with a fake smile. "Enjoy the game." *Encourage someone to take a bat to your car later*, I want to say. Though, I find a wrench is much more effective than a bat. It's lighter weight, fits in my purse, and Lyle, the head of security, doesn't think it's a weapon. He's had to give me a ride home a few times, so he knows how temperamental my truck can be.

Ear Hair turns away without so much as a thank you. I would never expect a thanks, but a *fuck you* would be nice occasionally. Ted, the owner of Backdoor Sliders, the concession stand right behind home plate, doesn't take too kindly to using the f-word. He wouldn't hesitate to ban Ear Hair with that sort of foul mouth. Which is probably why Ear Hair relies on his condescending repertoire of words.

"Tell me you spit in his food." Pops's gentle voice has me looking up, a genuine smile emerging since I shared a bowl of oatmeal with him and eventually accepted the Uber ride to work. Cooper, who only came out once, sporting dark circles under his eyes, muttering a nearly incoherent, "Good morning," had not only stayed awake and washed my clothes but ironed them too.

Who owns an iron anymore?

I was grateful though—maybe a little too grateful since I borrowed his sweats for another night. Victoria's Secret has nothing on oversized sweatpants that smell like soap and man.

Don't worry, I'll give them back when I go back for my tree. The Uber driver wasn't having Psalms in their back seat. Pops offered to plant sit for me.

Getting back to Pops's question about spitting in Ear Hair's food, I finally answer. "Not this time. Though, I can't say I haven't thought about it more than once."

At the last home game, I had literally given myself a pep talk that spitting was revolting and very unladylike. But those words didn't stop me from glancing around for witnesses as I rationalized Ear Hair deserved it.

However, it was Brenda, my foster mom's voice, that sliced through the noise, telling me I was giving Ear Hair power over my life by allowing his actions to control my reaction. "Power is given, Mac," she used to say. "No one is born with it."

I didn't bring up the royal family and their birthright of power because she scared me sometimes with these "mom" looks. But I got what she was saying. She meant only I could give Ear Hair the power to make me feel undervalued. I truly got what she was saying. I did. But letting a nasty comment go without retaliation is easier said than done. But I'd done it, settling instead to burn Ear Hair's hot dog. It was a small win, but satisfying all the same.

"No one would have blamed you," Pops says, standing behind the counter, Cynthia, his nurse, looking on with a severe case of resting bitch face.

I wave him off. "Ted would have blamed me," I answer with a shrug. "One complaint of spitting and I would be out of here."

While spitting in Ear Hair's hot dog would have made me happy, losing my job wouldn't. My landlord finds it exhausting chasing me down for the two months of rent I still owe. Combine that with an assload of medical bills and nothing but a fridge full of air and expired milk, I'm the poster child for debt and poor decisions times two.

"Thank you for the pickle and Mountain Dew. You didn't have to. You already let me bum a night over at your house." I don't tell him I'm only allowing myself one caffeinated beverage a day now. He'd look at me funny, and I'm not ready to have that conversation yet. Pops and I might be close, but there're some secrets I'd like to keep a little longer.

My much older bestie levels me a look, those thick gray eyebrows slanting toward his nose. "Hush."

He sounds a lot like his grandson with that bossy attitude sometimes. "You ready for your lemonade?" I grab a souvenir cup, already knowing the answer. Sometimes I'd sneak and have a beer with him, but we'd time it for later in the game when most of the fans leave to beat traffic.

I press the button on the dispenser, topping it off before handing it over. "Here you go." I wave off the cash in hand. "Your money is no good here, old man. You know that."

Those gray eyes beam back at me in approval. "Come over when you get a break." He motions to the aisle seat on the same level as my cart. "I'll get rid of the demon woman."

With his southern accent and his cute little jersey, I'd love nothing more than to scoop him up and take him home with me. It's been so long since I felt like I had someone on my proverbial team, someone who cared about my day and asked if people were nice to me.

The last person was Griffin, but I messed that up—royally. I can still feel his arms wrapped around me as I cried and snotted into his flannel shirt. Not once did he recoil or shove me off. He just held me tighter and patiently waited for me to get it all out. And when I did, I ruined everything.

And now…

I can't even think about it. Brenda would be so disappointed in me. I'd let my emotions rule my decisions. I did the day she died and every day since then. Through grief, I allowed myself to be nurtured by the things that made me feel better. Shopping. Food. Whiskey. And Love.

All those things controlled my life and took over every dream I had growing up. Everything I promised Brenda I would continue in her absence went to utter shit once she was gone. I was lonely, scared, and very much heartbroken. So I did everything I could think of to get rid of those pesky feelings. I shopped and maxed out my credit cards. I gained ten pounds and visited every restaurant in the area. I drank until I ran out of cash, and loved without abandon or sensibility.

All that comfort inevitably left me broke, jobless, and in debt up to my eyebrows. I didn't go to college. I didn't chase any of the dreams I once had. I just existed. And for the last year, that was enough for me. I still had Griffin… until I didn't. Until I messed that up too. Now it's too late. Too late to apologize and tell him I was sorry for being inconsiderate. I just wanted the pain to stop. I just wanted to feel wanted again.

Shaking off the memories, I muster up a smile and promise Pops I'll be over in a little while. "If you need a refill," I tell him, "holler, and I'll come over to you so you don't have to get up."

It's the very least I could do for him and his grandson's kindness last night.

You'd think most people watching a baseball game would be full of joy at seeing their favorite team or player live, but that's not always the case. Some fans use the concession stand as a way of decompressing. They need a beer to settle down or something to stave off the hangry until their team has a comeback inning. You'd think I'd be their hero by providing that relief, but not so much. Usually, by the time they get to me, they are pissed, hot, and tired of watching their team get their asses kicked inning after inning.

Not that the Tides have been terrible this year, but compared to last year's title-winning season, they aren't doing so hot, which upsets the fans who paid a small fortune for their tickets. Nevertheless, I wouldn't give up this job for the world. Running a concession stand might not be a brag-worthy career, but it feels like home. A type of comfort food that gets me through the day.

I took this job because of Griffin. He suggested it because he loved the Tides, and we never had the money to go. Heck, I didn't even like baseball until Griffin—hence the reason I didn't immediately recognize Cooper when he stopped to help me push Lu off the road.

Baseball was Griffin's thing, but I've learned that I enjoy it, too.

Griffin thought memories always outweighed tangible items. And I guess, I've let that one trait of his manifest into something unhealthy. I took it a little too far. Getting this job just so we could get a discount to games when we should have been paying rent and buying groceries. But we were addicted to drowning our aches in the sound of the crowd and nothing, not even money, stopped us.

Until now.

Until Griffin ended our trips to the Tides's games without asking me.

Sure, we made some mistakes—me especially. I took advantage of Griffin's kindness and used his adventurous energy to soothe my pain. Griffin was the distraction I needed after Brenda died.

We could have worked it out. Our argument didn't need to cost us our relationship.

But it doesn't matter now.

Griffin took the choice from both of us.

"Thanks, Lyle. I appreciate it."

My favorite security guard blushes and opens the door for me to pass through. "You clean that knee when you get home."

I go for a smile, the giant scuff still oozing a little blood from when I was shoved from behind on the escalator, hitting my knees and reopening the wound from last night. It was an accident, just two idiot teenagers roughhousing, but since my toe is still throbbing like a mother, my balance just wasn't on point and I lost my footing. Lyle had been waiting at the top and immediately spotted my injury and insisted he walk me out. I didn't have the heart to tell him that my car isn't out here, and I planned on hobbling home.

"Lu still giving you trouble?" He looks around the employee lot, probably realizing I'm not parked in my usual spot.

"Yeah, I've got a ride though, so don't worry that pretty little head of yours." He dodges my hand when I go to rub his bald head.

"You sure?"

I nod at the man who needs to get home to his wife and new baby. "Yep. She'll be here any minute." I make a show of looking around, trying to spot my imaginary ride. "Now, go on before Lauren throws your dinner in the trash for being late again."

Lyle grunts, remembering the last time he ended up eating a sandwich for dinner. The Tides went into extra innings and he didn't get home until after one a.m. His wife had just had their daughter and was sleep-deprived, and didn't give a damn Lyle was working late. "All right. Well, see you tomorrow then."

The Tides are home for the next ten days, meaning I'll be working ten days straight without a day off. Which, having something to keep me busy might not be a bad thing. After my altercation with Chris, and Lu's inevitable bill coming, I need all the money I can get. A part-time job might not be terrible either.

Lyle waves goodbye, and I watch as he folds into his car and drives away.

Here's the thing: I'm not a martyr. I'm not. I know I could call Pops and he would force Cooper to give me a lift home, but I don't want to. Chris, as awful as he may be, was right. I was a drain on Griffin's life and finances. It wasn't like I meant to be a mess. I wanted to pay my debts when I over-indulged after Brenda's death. I wanted to pay my rent, but I just couldn't. Grief is a hard thing to understand, and it manifests differently for everyone.

I haven't had good luck with family. I thought I had turned it around though, living with Griffin, laughing, going on adventures. Griffin helped me as much as he could with my debt, but neither one of us made much money. But we were happy, and that meant more to me than it did to him.

I crossed the line of friendship and family and drained the happiness from Griffin's soul. Finding him on the sofa… I'll never forget the way he looked so peaceful, like an angel dreaming of somewhere better. A place with no debt, no mistakes, and no unwanted ties.

I'll never make someone feel like they have no escape. Though, I realize Griffin had his own demons; I didn't help him by adding more stress to our already shitty circumstances.

Long story short, I'm owning up to my mistakes. I choose to keep a ratty truck that breaks down. Therefore, when she's out of commission, I will walk or take the bus. I won't allow my problems to be anyone else's. That's why I didn't want Cooper bandaging my broken toe. I kicked that sign in flip-flops. I probably broke a bone, and I should have to endure the pain and wrapping that comes with such poor decision-making.

So I set out for the three-mile walk to my apartment with my trusty wrench snug inside my shorts.

Chapter
SEVEN

Cooper

A yearly salary of twenty-five million dollars and I'm on my knees, begging. "I swear, he didn't mean it."

Cynthia, an impatient woman, glares down at my kneeled position. "I'm sorry, Mr. Lexington, but this was the last time."

"He won't do it again." I fight the urge to reach out and grab her scrub pants.

"That's what you said yesterday." Her eyes pinch as if to say, *and look where we are now.*

"I know, and I'm sorry. I'll talk to him again. Just please—" I glance back at Pops who's lounging in his easy chair as if this whole charade isn't transpiring in front of him. I turn back to Cynthia, pleading for her forgiveness and patience. "Please don't go. I need to be on the field in half an hour."

She takes less than a minute to think it over. "No."

"Please—"

With one swift turn, Cynthia steps over the threshold, but not before turning back with one pointed remark. "If I were you, Mr.

Lexington, I'd spare yourself the headache and send him to a nursing home."

And… Pops was right. She is the devil.

Standing, I dust off my knees and re-tuck my shirt that'd come loose. "We appreciate your time, Ms. Sparks. Your last check will be mailed to your residence."

With a curt, but polite nod, I close the door on caregiver number who-the-fuck-is-even-counting.

"I told you she was a devil woman, but you didn't listen."

"I didn't listen?" My shock is replaced quickly when I see the grin on the old man's face. "Really, Pops? A deer cam? You couldn't have just asked her if she moved it? Did you have to mount a hidden camera?"

He shrugs, flicking his gaze back to the TV. "Consider it similar to a Nanny Cam. Besides, she was stealing from me."

"Arthritic cream?" I try keeping my voice down as I push off the door and point to the pain relief cream clutched in his hands. "Why would Cynthia steal your cream?"

A half-smile plays on his lips. "Why does anyone steal?" He shrugs. "For all I know, she was stealing my arthritic cream and auctioning it off on eBay as "The Closer's private toiletries.'"

I roll my eyes at the name and the crazy notion that she was auctioning off a five-dollar tube of generic muscle relief. "That's ridiculous."

Pops sits up in his chair, grimacing. "What's ridiculous, my boy, is that you think you're still in high school, pitching on Georgia's clay mounds. When are you going to realize everything you have, even discarded tissue, is worth something? You're The Closer."

"Don't call me that."

"But that's who you are to the world."

I can see this conversation is going nowhere. "I understand you were just looking out for me, Pops, but Cynthia was taking care of you while I was away at games. Games like the one I need to be 'closing' in a little over three hours. What do you suggest we do now?"

If you ever needed evidence of the light coming on in someone's eyes, I should have taken a picture of Pops's. "I could go with you— without the devil," he offers.

"No." Absolutely not. "No one can watch you."

"I've recovered." He stands like that's proof of his recovery. "Besides, Mac'll be there."

I motion to the half-dead palm tree still sitting on my kitchen table. "Mac can't even keep a house plant alive. You expect me to believe she'll be able to work *and* keep an eye on you?" I want to ask him if Mac plans on picking up this monstrosity anytime soon, but I don't. One issue at a time.

Pops shrugs. "I don't need sunlight, just water. I think she can manage that while working, don't you?"

Heaven help me. "No, actually. I don't think she can manage." Does he not remember Mac's broken toe, dirty clothes, and skinned knees? If anything, Pops would have to look after her.

"Relax, Coop." Brushing past me, Pops pats me on the shoulder as if I'm some puppy. "We'll be fine."

I can feel the anxiety rising. "What if you fall?" And I can't get to you?

"What if you shit your pants on the mound?"

"Pops."

"Cooper," he mimics. "Just because I let you pretend to be the adult in this house, doesn't mean you are. I've raised you from when you thought underwear was optional. The way I see it, you either let me hang out with Mac or call your brother who will chew both of our asses like the big ol' bore he is."

"Are you blackmailing me?" Surely, the old man isn't stooping that low.

"Nope, just telling you the facts. Which is that you just shuffled Cynthia out the door—" He looks at his watch. "—and are due on the field in twenty-two minutes." He pauses, letting those issues sink in nice and low. "I'd say you're out of options, sport."

Unbelievable.

"Fine." I all but growl, running a hand through my hair. "Grab your things." Pops grins, and I point a finger at him. "But if Maverick asks, you had a great time with Cynthia at the park, and you will not, for any reason, leave Mac's side."

"Deal."

"I'm sorry, what?" McKinley cups her ear with her hand. "Could you repeat that? I'm having a hard time hearing you over the crowd."

This was the worst idea I've ever agreed to.

Narrowing my eyes, I try focusing on anything but McKinley's tits as they push against the t-shirt sized too small. "The gates haven't opened. There is no crowd." More accurately, there won't be crowds for another two hours.

Right now, players are dressing, doing pre-game meetings before batting practice. And vendors… well, they should be getting their carts prepped, but it seems like Mac is enjoying torturing me, so I'm late getting downstairs.

"Come on, Grumpy Grandson, let me have this little victory. How many people can say they saved The Closer?"

"Never mind." I turn and bark at Pops that he can sit in the family box with some of the players' wives. I don't know them and haven't even bothered making friends, but surely, the old man can woo them with his sarcastic charm.

A hand latches on to my arm. "Okay, I'm sorry. No more teasing. I can look after the old geezer." She shrugs and flashes me a smile, revealing a dimple on the right side. "It'll be like any other day except She-Devil won't be side-eyeing me, chanting out spells."

"She chants spells?" Who the hell did I hire?

McKinley, as bad as she is at asking for help, can't hold in her laughter. "I'm joking about the spells, but the side-eye and bitch-face are true."

"Did she ever say anything to you?"

Two brows arch. "Why?"

Why is right, Cooper? What do you care if Cynthia said something awful to Mac? She isn't your friend.

"Just curious."

Mac removes her hand from my arm, and I use the opportunity to secure my own hands in my pockets.

"I really appreciate you looking after Pops. I promise I'll find a replacement soon."

"It's not a problem. Besides, I owe you both anyway." Her voice seems less excited than when I walked up to her cart, practicing the word *please* the whole way. She made me say it six times before I got pissed off.

"We're not keeping score."

She hitches a shoulder, giving me her back as she walks behind the cart. "Sure we are. You helped me, and I don't like being indebted to anyone, therefore, I am helping you to even the score."

Why? Why is this his best friend? Why couldn't it have been one of the other players' fathers? Why is it this eccentric little spitfire that I want to spank and toss over my shoulder like a caveman?

"Go to work, Cooper. We'll be fine." She dismisses me with a wave of her hand that has me grinding my teeth. "I'll bring Pops downstairs when the crowd clears."

And for the first time since meeting her, I don't argue, because… fuck! I can't go into the locker room with a hard-on.

Pissed off doesn't accurately describe what I'm feeling right now as I jog through the open corridors. Mac specifically said she would bring Pops down when the crowd cleared. Did she? No. Is Pops answering his phone so I can yell at him? No.

I knew leaving him with her was a terrible idea.

Rounding the terrace-level seats, I spot Mac's cart, and of course, it's empty.

"Are you fucking serious?" I shout into the empty stands.

"You looking for Mac?" I whip my head around and find a guy emptying the trash can. "She's on the field."

I glance to the open space, and I'll be damned if it isn't Pops stretched out on the grass, Mac next to him, as they eat what looks to be a Costco-sized tub of popcorn.

"Thanks," I mutter, tipping my chin at, clearly, the most helpful person at the park today. "I appreciate it."

I take the back corridor, which connects to another, before

swiping my badge and entering the outfield where pain in the ass number one and two await me.

"Seriously, though. You shouldn't have tripped him."

I stop at the edge of the field at Mac's laughter. "Had you not started babbling nonsense, I think he would have punched you."

Pops takes a swig of his soda. "Nah, guys like him are all bark. He only wants to pick on pretty women, not crazy old men that would shove a bat so far up his ass, it'd tickle all that ear hair of his."

Mac rolls on the ground, holding her stomach as she snorts every other breath in laughter. "I love you, old man."

Pops grins at this mess of a woman. "Maybe next time he'll think before he tries embarrassing you again."

Wait, what? Who embarrassed Mac? And what in the fresh hell did Pops do to him?

I think it bears repeating that I knew leaving Pops and Mac together would be a disaster. And from what it sounds like, I could have been picking them up from security today instead of on the field, which is currently being littered with popcorn.

"Please tell me I'm not getting sued." I advance toward the two troublemakers and they immediately sober.

"Oh, hey!"

I cock a brow, refusing to wave as she did.

"We were waiting for you—"

Pops chimes in. "And then I had to pee."

"So we headed to the bathroom."

"And got sidetracked by popcorn?" I add, filling in the rest of their story.

McKinley shoves the tub toward me. "It was freshly popped. They were going to throw it away if we hadn't intervened."

She shoves the bucket closer, and reluctantly, I dip my hand in and toss back a few pieces.

"Good, right?"

I nod but don't admit that I almost moaned swallowing. How long has it been since I've indulged in empty carbs? Years? Hell, I can't even remember, it's been so long.

Dusting my hands off on my pants, I offer Mac a clean one and help her to her feet. "Thanks for keeping an eye on the old man."

Pops mutters something about not being an infant that I ignore.

"I hate to ask you again, seeing as I'll now owe you a debt, but would you mind—"

"Tomorrow isn't a problem. I have to be here anyway and well…"

She looks at Pops and grins, sticking out her hand, helping him up like I did for her. "Today was the best day I've had in a very long time."

Chapter EIGHT

McKinley

One game turned into three. And I was loving every minute of spending my days with my best friend at my side. I'd even moved a chair behind the cart, so Pops and I could talk freely and heckle Cooper when he marched up to the mound all badass, like he didn't get smacked on the back of the head daily.

For the first time since Griffin's death, I felt like I had most of my old life back. But like any high, a low always follows, and today, mine swan-dived to its eternal death.

"I want to speak with your manager."

A muscle in Ear Hair's cheek twitches—I bet it's an asshole too.

Inhaling, I raise my head and face him like the lady I'm not, signaling Pops not to approach with our Slurpees from the neighboring cart (Coop doesn't need to know). "He's not available."

"You're lying."

True. I am lying, like a MOFO, 'cause no one is in the mood to be fired today.

Ted, the owner, is a reasonable man, but not when someone is as loud as Ear Hair. His voice draws unwanted attention that Ted will have no other option than to deal with me. At least that's what he's said before. It's about the company's reputation apparently.

I take a deep breath and swallow back all the cuss words bubbling up in my throat. "Look, I apologize for your wait, but like I explained, we sold out of hot dogs." I motion to the empty bin in front of Pops's chair, where the hot dogs usually are. "If you could just be patient, our sister company is on the way with more."

That's reasonable, right? A few minutes wait? It's not like he's going to die in sixty seconds if he doesn't get his wiener before the seventh inning.

A noise, much like a person who wants his ass whooped, hisses across the counter. "Get. Your. Boss. Now." His fist bangs on the aluminum ledge.

I flinch, taking an extra second to steady my voice before I respond, "Okay, just a moment, please."

Another moment.

He won't wait on his hot dog, but he'll wait on my boss so he can complain. That makes total sense, right?

I don't know what I ever did to this guy to cause this much hatred, but I swear, if this was my stand, I'd have a big yellow sign that said, *No assholes. Violators will be advised to go fuck themselves.*

"Finally," Ear Hair mutters to the guy behind him who, from the looks of it, hasn't been paying attention. That's a relief. The fewer people who witness my dismissal, the better.

"I just need to text him," I tell Ear Hair, pulling my phone from my pocket and dialing, a wave of nausea hitting me like a Tsunami.

Oh no. Not now. Not in front of Jerk Face.

But it's too late. Nothing, not even the palm slapped over my mouth stops the explosion of vomit that plows through my fingers, finding the most deserving target, and splattering the entire front of Ear Hair's jersey.

"Are you fucking serious?"

I'm afraid so, Shit Head.

Chancing a look, Ear Hair's face is red with fury. Dammit. "I'm so, so sorry. I've been sick and—"

Each word he forces out is laced with hatred. "Get. Your. Boss."

Right. Ted. He'll be seriously unimpressed with my customer service today. "Sure, I'll be right back."

Pushing away from the stand, I grab a paper towel and wipe my face before walking toward Pops. "I need you to stay in your seat and not move until Cooper calls for you, okay?" I don't need Cooper pissed off at me too.

Pops wraps his arms around me, his hands still full of Slurpee, and squeezes. "I'm so proud of you, kiddo. Upchucking in that prick's face was better than me tripping him any day." He pulls back and eyes me seriously, his grin turning to one of concern. "Take this Slurpee. I'll have a ginger ale waiting on you when you get back."

I almost cry taking the drink, but I don't because if I cry, it will upset Pops, and who knows what Pops would do to Ear Hair. And Cooper, he might actually need to worry about a lawsuit. No, I need Cooper and Pops calm. "Promise me you'll wait for Cooper to come and get you?"

Tears sting the back of my eyes. I'm totally failing at this keeping Pops calm thing. "I need to go get my manager, but if I get—" I almost can't get the words out. "If I get fired and can't make it back, text Cooper to come and get you. Tell him I'm sorry."

I don't like making promises I can't keep, and the thought of being fired and not seeing my best friend sends a rolling wave of unshed tears I have to fight to keep back. "You promise, don't you?" I know he's a stubborn ass.

"Yeah," he says absently, looking over my shoulder at where I left Ear Hair covered in vomit. "I promise. You tell Ted to call me."

I nod, but I would never involve Pops, who I'm sure intends to involve Cooper, to save my job. I know that sweet old man, and I can't allow him or Cooper to stick their neck out for me like that. Again, I made this mess, and I will suffer the consequences, and in the process, not owe Cooper another favor. I like being ahead on the favor meter.

"I'd kiss you, but I'm afraid that would be utterly disgusting," I tell Pops with a watery laugh. "How 'bout an air-high-five instead?"

Pops doesn't return the laughter. Instead, his gaze volleys between me and Ear Hair and the audience my projectile vomiting drew.

"You're feeling better though?" he finally asks.

"Yeah, I am."

In more ways than one. Even if I lose my job, the memory alone of Ear Hair's mouth opening in shock as chunks of this morning's pickle landed on his cheek will be worth it. He had it coming, and while I'd rather have seen him get puked on by someone else, I can live with just knowing he finally got what he deserved.

"Go get your boss, kid. I'll still be here when you get back." Pops says it so confidently, so sure that I won't get fired, that I almost believe him.

"See ya later, old man."

With one final look at my friend, I walk down the corridor to the management offices where I'm sure I'll find Ted and a nice pink slip that will send me on my way. But at this point, I'm just going to roll with whatever happens. It isn't like my life has been this exceptional story that I'll one day tell my children. It's just another day on Survival Island.

Pulling out my phone, I bring up my texts and type out a quick message to Cooper, who reluctantly gave me his number after the first day I kept an eye on Pops.

I might get fired. I made Pops promise to wait for you, but you know how he lies.

I don't expect an answer. Cooper is out in the bullpen, waiting to see if they need him to pitch the last inning. So far, the Tides are up by four runs, so I doubt they'll use him. Secretly, I hope he doesn't have to go out tonight. He looked exhausted when he walked Pops to his seat earlier. I think he could use a week or so of sleep. Who knows, it might improve that crabby attitude of his.

At the manager's office, I take a deep breath, readying myself to be ripped a new asshole while I literally take the walk of shame out of the ballpark since I still can't afford to pay for Lu's repairs.

You got this, Mac. You have control of how Ted makes you feel. Don't give him the power to make you feel bad for upchucking on a man that deserved way more than that.

My phone buzzes, and I look down and see that Cooper actually texted me back during the game.

Why would you get fired?

Eh. That's not a story I'd like to discuss over text.

Ear Hair is tired of me being prettier than him. It was inevitable. I text back, grinning, but he doesn't let it go and fires off another response quickly.

I'll find out one way or another, he threatens.

Do I care if Cooper finds out that I puked on Ear Hair?

No.

My bigger concern is him finding out why I puked in the first place. Not that I'm hiding my situation. I'm not. I'm just not ready to admit what I did to put myself in this position to begin with.

A cold sweat of shame coats my skin as I stare at his text. I might not know Cooper as well as his grandfather, but I still have some dignity left, and I'd rather not admit to a man who made all the right life decisions that I'm a complete and utter fuck-up.

Inhaling, I look up at the sky and hope Griffin is up there, happier than he was here, then sigh, tapping out my response.

I'm sure you will, but not through me. Make sure you sneak out early so Pops doesn't try pushing through bodies to get to you.

He doesn't text me after that, and I'm glad. I need all the leftover energy to get through this discussion with Ted.

Chapter
NINE

McKinley

Ted fired me.

Big time.

He even threw his drink against the wall. I can't blame him. Someone caught the epic puke showdown on video, and it went viral before I even opened his office door to explain what happened.

Honestly, I expected it. Ear Hair is a loudmouth. Even if Ted had kept me around, Ear Hair would have just found another way to get me fired.

It's fine.

I'll be fine.

I'm sure I can find another job.

I used to waitress for a while before I started working at the stadium. I didn't hate it, though my toe would after an eight-hour shift. But like Griffin always used to tell me, this too shall pass. Hopefully, though, it passes quickly, and I find a decent-paying job and health insurance. So far, all the jobs I've worked at didn't offer healthcare coverage. It was okay since I stay pretty healthy, but now… Well, now, I probably need it.

That's not entirely accurate. It's not so much probably but more of a definitely need it type of thing.

But I'll figure it out. I always do.

"Get in." The deep and very pissed-off voice jerks me to a halt as the familiar black Audi screeches to a stop next to me. "Now."

Leaning down, I glance through the window and find the scowling Closer.

"Did you get Pops?" I completely ignore that hate-glare and the order he barked out.

"He's with a friend. He'll give him a ride home."

Oh. "That's shocking."

"Do I need to repeat myself, McKinley?"

Am I in the mood to give him a hard time? Um, yeah.

"Yeah, I think so. I'm having this issue with my right ear. I think it might be—ahh!"

Before I even realize it, Cooper is out of the car, his hand around my upper arm, guiding me toward the passenger seat, not hard, but definitely aggressive. "People are going to think you're kidnapping me!" I look around to see if anyone is taking pictures.

"Are you shitting me?"

He seems to be in a really, *really* foul mood. Worse than I've ever seen from him. "Okay." I sigh, holding one hand up in surrender. "I'll get in the car, but you're letting me give you gas money."

Those dark eyes, the color of steel, hold my gaze, widening ever so slightly as if I have rendered him speechless. "Can we agree to those terms?" I'm no mooch. I refuse to let this man keep coming to my rescue.

Cooper doesn't answer, only shakes his head and bends to lift my foot into the car before he slams the door so hard it rattles.

When he's settled and his breathing is more even, he puts the car in drive and pulls out of the lot. "I live that way." I point to the left.

He glares at me before flicking his blinker, indicating he's turning left. At least that's a good sign. He isn't taking me to his house so I can face him and Pops at the same time.

"Were you really planning to walk home?" he finally bites out.

I'm thinking being sarcastic would only further infuriate him. "Yes. Lu isn't ready after all."

His grip tightens on the steering wheel. "Pregnant and with a broken toe, you were going to walk three miles to your house?"

So many thoughts run through my head. How did he know I lived four miles from the field, but more so… "How did you know I was pregnant?"

He scoffs. "My sister-in-law is pregnant. Earlier in her pregnancy, she threw up all day for weeks—harsh, violent puking. It scared the shit out of my brother so much that he took her to the emergency room three times a week until it stopped."

His brother sounds adorable.

"I don't throw up very often," I admit. "Today just happened to be one of those times."

"Where's the father?"

If it wasn't for the pain in my chest, I would have reacted differently, but alas, such is not the case. "I don't think that's any of your business."

Cooper scoffs and takes the curve a little too sharp. "What man allows his pregnant girlfriend to not only walk home but walk home pregnant with a broken bone? I hate to tell you, Mac, you have shitty taste in men."

His comments hurt my feelings all for eighteen seconds before I snap. "Stop the car. I want out."

"No." His dark chuckle only serves to piss me off more.

"I'll jump," I threaten with absolutely no intention of doing so. I'm not a fool. I might be angry with the father of my child, but I would never intentionally hurt the little one growing inside me.

Abruptly, Cooper yanks the car to the shoulder. Those big forearms still clad in his uniform flex as he reaches over and covers my seatbelt buckle where I can't get to it to let myself out. "You will not jump from this car, nor will you threaten your life in my presence ever again."

We lock gazes, each of us glaring before Cooper finally sighs and releases my seatbelt, raking his hands through his hair. "I'm sorry," he says after a minute. "It's been a rough couple of days, and I'm tired and—"

"Worried," I supply, reaching over and taking his hand from his hair. He has really pretty hair, all sandy and beachy. If I saw him on the street, I'd think he was a surfer and not a professional pitcher.

"Yeah." His words sound breathy, and I feel bad for adding to his stress today.

"Pops will be okay. I'm sure you'll find another nurse."

His head bows and I could swear he's praying. "McKinley?"

"Yeah?"

"Are you having this baby alone?"

I don't like the pity in his voice. "And if I am? Are you going to tell me I'm irresponsible and should have gotten my life together before bringing a baby into this world?"

My chest heaves and my eyes burn. I will not be shamed for my decisions, no matter what. "I'm not having an abortion, if that's what you're going to suggest."

"What?" Cooper's eyes widen, and he reaches across the console as if he intended on holding my hand, but then thinks better of it and puts it back in his lap where it belongs. "Did someone say that to you?" He swallows. "That you weren't capable to handle a baby?"

I appreciate him phrasing it better than I did.

Offering the only answer I can think of, I shrug. "I know I don't have my shit together like most twenty-two-year-olds, but this baby is mine—the only family I have. I might not be the richest mom or even one who knows how to work a car seat. But I'll learn." A tear drops onto my hand. "And I'll love this baby with everything I have. I won't disappoint him or her."

At least I will try, so far I'm sucking pretty hard at this mom thing.

I glance at Cooper and see his jaw clenching. What did I say to piss him off now?

"You're going to be a wonderful mother," he finally says.

Immediately, I ruin the sweet comment. "How can you say that? You don't even know me."

The soft line of his lips flattens before he lets out a pained sigh. "I know enough."

"Sure you do. You're just saying what I want to hear."

I've been around enough men to know that they have an uncanny ability to always say what a woman needs to hear to get her into bed.

"Pops always talks about you," he starts, the harsh lines of his cheekbones softening. "At first, I was jealous." He chuckles and slides me this boyish look. "I thought you were a guy who drank with Pops during games. I thought he preferred a beer with you over one with me."

"I like beer—or I used to—and your Pops. He's nice to me." I think of the squishy old man and smile. He is more than nice to me. He treats me like I am family, like he genuinely cares about me.

"He told me how you guys met."

Frowning, I remember that day. "Those boys needed their asses beat."

Cooper grins. "The way I heard it, they got what they deserved."

I pat the wrench tucked away in my purse. "They took advantage of an old man who dropped his wallet. The least I could do was get his wallet back while adding a few bruises."

Pops had been ordering in my line. It was the first time he had come to a game, and he was a little unsteady. His nurse was no help at all—though he probably forbid her to help. Anyway, when he went to pull out cash to give me, he fumbled and dropped his wallet. Two brats walking by swiped it off the ground. I thought they would give it back, but they took off running.

"Pops said you chased them down."

I did. "I also threw my wrench, catching one in the back where I could wrestle the wallet away. That's when Lyle ran up and grabbed the little shits, though." I could have gotten another smack in, but Lyle wasn't having it. "I don't like thieves."

Cooper nods, a hint of a smile trying to break through. "But you liked Pops and gave him a drink on the house."

I'm not sure what he wants me to say here. I felt terrible…this man, who hobbled with a cane, got robbed in front of my concession stand. I felt like I had to show him we aren't all assholes.

"When we got home that day and Pops told me the story, I had his seat moved closer to your stand. I knew then you'd always look out for my grandfather. And at the time, when we were new to Nevada and didn't know anyone, it was good to know he had a friend."

Another tear slips down my cheek.

"So hear me now, Mac. I know the person you are in here." He places his hand on my heart and I drop my head, smothering more tears into my shirt. "And no one with your kindness will ever make a terrible mother. Whether you're in the ideal circumstances to have a baby is nobody's business." His thumb catches a rogue tear, and it only makes me cry harder.

"Thank you for saying that," I finally say, gathering myself and sitting up, "but I'm still giving you gas money."

Chapter
TEN

Cooper

She was going to walk home… Pregnant!

Never have I wanted to strangle someone for being so fucking stubborn. Why didn't she tell me or Pops? Aren't they supposed to besties? Isn't that what pregnant women do? Share their news with their best friends? Why did she keep it a secret?

Because she's got a past… I think to myself. A past that she doesn't share with anyone, not even Pops.

But Pops wouldn't care that she's pregnant. Neither would I. Though I'd like to have some stern words with her about walking home in her condition and doing stupid shit like trying to push her truck onto the shoulder the other night.

"Why is your knee still bleeding?" I eye the new bandage, ignoring the gas money comment. She and I both know that won't happen. I don't need her money, nor do I want it. She's been taking care of Pops; I'm in her debt. "Are you picking the scab?"

She looks at me utterly horrified. "No! What am I, four?"

I shrug. "Then why are you still bandaging your knee? Scrapes need air to heal."

"If you must know," she huffs. "I fell again. Now, there's a gash on top of the scrape."

"Are you normally so accident prone?"

I've pulled back onto the road, and she turns from the window, her cheeks still wet with tears. "No, but ever since, you know—" She points to her belly, "—I've been a little off."

I nod like I understand, but I don't. The only thing I know about women and pregnancy is that it makes my brother's heart condition flair up constantly. My sister-in-law, Ainsley, jokes that Maverick is so clingy she might file a restraining order just to have a moment alone.

My brother is the calmest person I know, and if a pregnancy upsets him to the point of insanity, I shudder to think what a woman goes through.

"When is the baby due?"

Her posture stiffens at my question.

"Am I not supposed to ask that?"

Ainsley is an over-sharer, so I don't know what's an appropriate question to ask a pregnant woman. All my knowledge has been provided through her random stories.

"No, it's fine," she says finally, giving me this smile that says it's not fine at all. "The thing is, I don't know. I haven't been to the doctor yet."

I fight off the urge to snap out a hateful *why*. I go for, "Oh," instead.

She sighs, and it's heartbreaking. "I've only known for a couple of weeks, and…" She bites her lip. "Obstetrician visits are expensive. So are hospital charges and anesthesia, which I won't get because I can save four grand just enduring a little pain during delivery."

My stomach clenches at the thought of her enduring more pain. Visions of my mother suffering in the months before her death flash through my mind. I can't bear anyone—let alone a single woman—enduring pain. "Are you saying you don't have insurance?"

She laughs, but it lacks sincerity. "That's what I'm saying. And now, I don't have a job. Kind of slows down the whole saving thing—which I was doing—I care about my baby; I'm just broke as fuck right now."

"I can make some calls—"

She doesn't let me finish. "Hold on, cowboy. Don't start with all that bossy chivalry. I'll just use the free clinic close to my house. I'll make an appointment now that I'm not working ten days straight, and there's no hope that I'm getting into a private practice now."

I don't know that much about free clinics. The care is likely the same but… "Are you planning to walk to this appointment?"

Her eyebrows rise. "Don't make me lie to you."

It takes everything I have not to slam my hand down on the steering wheel.

"Don't look at me all Closer-y either." She waves her hand in my face.

"What exactly is Closer-y?" I use her term and feel stupid for even saying it.

"You know," she squints her eyes, narrowing them while her lips purse and her forehead wrinkles, "all menacing. I see how you look at those batters when you come in to save a game… with the shadows over your face and no twitch or anything… It scares the shit out of them. No wonder they can't hit a pitch."

"Are you saying I scare you?" And that I'm a good pitcher? Dammit, I'm smiling now, and that's the last thing I want to do. This conversation is serious.

"Oh, no. I mean, sure, sometimes. Though, I do feel like there's a level of psycho in you just waiting to jump out and kill me—"

"I could say the same about the woman who carries a wrench and threatens good samaritans on the side of the road." I think it's important she realizes carrying around a wrench doesn't scream normality.

She shrugs. "I never claimed to be sane. I find hiding who I am is a waste of time. The day I stopped caring what people thought of me was the day I stopped being disappointed in people. It isn't like my mom is going to hear through the grapevine about what a wonderful, normal woman I've become and come back, telling me she made a huge mistake by giving me up." She shrugs. "There's freedom in not caring, and in that freedom, I find peace."

Even though she says she doesn't care, it's not what her face, or the tear that escapes, relays at all. "You're adopted?"

She swipes at the wetness on her cheek. "No, I wasn't. I aged-out of the foster care system."

"I'm sorry."

"Don't be. I had a wonderful foster mother."

I swallow, feeling the tightness spread to my grip on the wheel. "Do you still see her?"

She shakes her head, pointing at a side road. "This is my turn."

Rounding the curve, we stay silent until she finally adds to our earlier conversation. "Brenda, my foster mother, wanted to adopt me, but back then, I still rode that cloud of hope that my mom would come back for me. I didn't want my mom feeling like I betrayed her, you know?"

I can relate. "When my mother was diagnosed with MS, my father decided he was done with me and my brother too. He dropped us off at Pops's and never came back. For years, I had hope he'd return, that he was just grieving, but as the days went on and Pops packed my lunch, tucked me in, and read me a story, I realized my life had changed without my consent. It was okay though, I had all I needed with Pops and my brother. My father could go fuck himself. "

"Brenda died a couple of years ago." Her voice trembles. "If I could go back in time, I'd tell her yes, that she could adopt me." She scoffs, but it sounds watered down. "She was the best mom and I never told her."

"I'm sure she knew." I reach over and put my hand over hers. "Parents have a way of knowing. At least that's what Pops tells me."

"You're really close to him, aren't you?"

I nod. "I went through a spell of being angry that I couldn't play ball because my mom was sick and my dad was always working. I blamed my crappy season of Little League on the fact I only made the practices when Pops could drive down from Atlanta to take me, which wasn't too often. It wasn't until my mom got really bad that Pops came down and rented a house. It was then my dad dropped Maverick and me off and never came back. We moved back to Atlanta with Pops until he could sell his house and move us back home. The new house had a big back yard where Pops never missed an evening of catch."

Her hand flips over and she squeezes mine. "I'm sorry about your mom."

"It was a long time ago."

"Still." She shrugs. "Time doesn't heal all wounds."

True, but… "Are you hungry?"

"What?" She stares at me, confused.

"I have to make dinner for Pops," I explain. "I'm sure he'd love for you to join us, considering he threatened me before I left."

That gets a genuine smile out of her. "He threatened you?"

I grin. "He worried when you didn't come back. I found him hobbling down to the administrative offices looking for you."

Her mouth flattens. "I told you he lies. I specifically told him to wait for you."

She's not telling me anything I don't already know. "He's a stubborn old man. Has been for years."

"Agreed."

She seems a little lighter now, since the heaviness of our conversation has shifted, so I take that as a yes to dinner and turn the car around, heading home.

"You need any help in there?"

McKinley is sitting cross-legged on the floor, her knee is wrapped, along with a new bandage on her toe that she insisted she do herself. I didn't argue. Honestly, I thought if I did, I'd yell, which would then make Pops yell, so it was just better that I start cooking dinner.

"No thanks, I got it."

She ignores me, which I sense is an ongoing trend, and comes to my side. "What are we making?"

I feel my brows rise. "*We* aren't making anything," I say. "You're our guest."

And wearing my boxers and t-shirt, smelling like me—thanks to her washing her hair with my shampoo. "When will your truck be ready?" I try for a subject change.

Her grin immediately falls. "Oh, uh. Tomorrow, I think."

She's lying.

"What was wrong with it?" Is it me or is the girl cagier than a hamster?

"The radiator." She turns away and walks over to her malnourished palm tree and rubs over the leaves.

"You have enough money to cover it?" After her story in the car, the thought of her using the money for vehicle repairs instead of medical care has me nauseated.

"Yep, sure do. Thanks for checking." Her tone is so clipped I almost laugh.

"Good. Pops and I will give you a ride over there in the morning."

"That's okay, the shop isn't far from my house, I can walk."

"With a broken toe?"

She turns and puts a hand on her hip. "Yeah, with a broken toe. I'm a woman, I don't feel pain like men. I'll be fine, Closer. I don't need you to come save me—" She stops and grimaces. "Again. I don't need you to save me again."

Why does it send me into a rage that she totally refuses to acknowledge she could use the help? It's not that I'm some kind of savior, running around and saving damsels in distress, but she's Pops's friend, and friends, even the stubborn ones, are taken care of where I'm from.

"I'm not trying to save you," I grit. "I'm simply pointing out that it would be more comfortable if you just accepted a ride instead of walking with a broken toe."

I mean, that is what a sane person would do, right? Take a ride?

"I understand, and I appreciate your concern, but I'll be okay."

"We'll see."

She folds her arms, daring me with a glare. "We sure will. I don't need—or want—your help."

But she's going to get it all the same. "Water your damn tree." I point to the green coffee can filled with water and fertilizer I bought the other day like a psycho. Who buys fertilizer for a friend of the family's tree? "I'm tired of trying to keep it alive too."

Chapter
ELEVEN

McKinley

"How could you?"

Do I care Cooper lives in a nice neighborhood where screaming in the front yard is considered tacky? Do I care that he let me sleep in his guest room another night?

No. No, I don't.

"I owed you a favor for watching Pops this week."

I point a finger at his smug face, ignoring the scruff and the smirk. "It was only three games, not a week. Dammit, Cooper! I was only up by two favors!"

I know it sounds ridiculous, but it's how I live my life. Being burned a few hundred times does that to a person.

Cooper shrugs. "Okay, so now we're even."

"Oh," my voice rises as he gives me his back, walking inside the house, his pajama pants riding low on his hips, "we are so far from even! You put me back in the negative!" In debt!

Chasing behind him, he turns faster than I was expecting. "I helped a friend."

"Ahh!"

I've reverted back to just screaming out in frustration because that's exactly how a mature, mom-to-be should act. Ugh.

"Keep your voice down." Cooper grabs me by the arms and pulls me inside his bedroom where, from the looks of it, he didn't sleep last night.

"Look, I'm sorry. But I wanted you to have reliable transportation." His gaze settles on my bandaged toe.

"It feels better," I mutter. "But I specifically said I didn't want or need your help." Is he hard of hearing or just stubborn?

"I heard you, and while I don't understand your rationale, I was hoping to ask you for another favor."

Oh. "I'm listening." Anything to not be indebted to this man.

"I've been unable to find another caregiver to watch Pops, and we only have a few home games left before I need to travel again." He scrubs both hands over his face, looking seriously exhausted. "I made my agent and brother a promise that I wouldn't take Pops with me and cause him to miss therapy appointments."

"When's his therapy appointment?"

Cooper waves his hand away. "I made it for when I'm home. The point is, I can't leave Pops alone while I'm at away games."

My heart sinks. This is my bestie. "I would stay with him, but I have to look for work."

"Work for me then."

I choke on air. "Hell no. I'm not working for you." Mr. I-Can't-Respect-Boundaries.

"Why not?" he whispers, his neck flush with color. "You're currently in need of employment, and I need someone to help me with Pops. It's a win-win for both of us."

Shaking my head, I walk to his bed and plop down. "I'm not a caretaker. I don't know how to do it. What if I mess up?" I mean, he does know who he's asking, right? I can barely keep Psalms alive. Though, it seems much happier on Cooper's kitchen table than in Griffin's back yard.

With eyes the color of a stormy sky, Cooper stalks toward me. At first, I think he's going to snatch me off the bed, but then he—holy shit—drops to his knees, pushing his upper body between my thighs.

"McKinley, I'm begging you. Pops loves you, and there is no one I would trust more. Unlike Cynthia, you'll look out for his best interest."

I'll admit, he is incredibly sexy on his knees, and honestly, those pleading eyes have me wavering, but… "I can't. I'm sorry. With the baby and just the disaster that I am…" I stop. No need to self-deprecate any further. "I don't want to let either of you down."

"I'll pay for your obstetrician visits." His eyes hold mine.

"Absolutely not. I won't let you pay for something that is not your problem."

He swallows, pausing for just a moment. "Marry me then."

I spring from the bed, barely registering that I nearly knock Cooper backward. "Have you lost your mind?"

"Let me explain," he says quickly, knowing I'm about to sprint out of here like an Olympic track star. "I have health insurance—fantastic health insurance."

"Now is not the time to brag about all the awesome perks professional athletes get, Cooper." Seriously.

"And," he continues, as if I didn't speak, "if we were to get married, my wife could use it for all her obstetrician visits. I already pay for it; therefore, you wouldn't be taking a dime from me."

His chest is rising and falling quickly. "Mac, please."

He called me Mac, and it sounds absolutely adorable.

The workaround is tempting. I bet he has that good insurance with the low or no copays.

"We could get divorced after the baby is born or when you find another job."

There's something to be said about Cooper's tenacity here. "Coop," I try keeping my voice low, so Pops doesn't overhear. "You're a professional pitcher. For all you know, you could meet the next Mrs. Lexington next week at a game. You don't need to be tied down to me." Because I got knocked up.

If possible, Cooper's back straightens even more as his hands grip my knees. "I don't care about the next Mrs. Lexington. I care about Pops. Please, Mac. I'm begging you. You're all Pops and I have left. If you don't agree to watch him, my brother and I will argue, and Pops will have to make peace between us."

His jaw twitches and his eyes take on a glassy look. "Pops will go back to an assisted living facility, so neither of us will get our way. He'll stay Switzerland, and I'll never get to see him because of my travel schedule."

Damn. Fucking damn. But he's not finished yet. "I know it seems rash, but I don't know how many more years I have left with Pops, and I refuse to abandon the man who gave up his career to raise me."

"You're cheating," I tell him, fighting off the tears.

His hands move up my thighs like he's trying to get closer and pulls me to his body. "Please, McKinley. I'm willing to give up my career to care for Pops, but we both know he won't stand for it." He swallows thickly, baring his soul. "If I don't find a solution this week, I'll lose him either way—we'll both lose our best friend."

I throw my head back, my mind racing as fast as my heart. "Would I need to live here?"

Cooper pauses. "I think it'd look better for the insurance that my wife lives with me in the same house."

This is insane, but with Cooper's offer, I could take care of my baby, and I wouldn't have to sit in my apartment all summer pregnant as hell, and sweating more than enough to water Psalms. But the added bonus? I'd be able to keep my best friend and Cooper. He's like a mint on my pillow. It looks fancy and smells delicious, but it'll wreak havoc on my hips.

"I'm messy." I motion to his bed. "Like way worse than you."

Something like relief shines in his eyes. "I can live with that."

"I snore too."

His smile is why women and men alike scream when his picture flashes on the jumbo tron as he jogs across the field to the mound. "I don't sleep much, anyway." I flash him a stern look. "You should, you look like you could use a weekend in bed." That same smile widens, and I realize how it sounded. "Not in bed like that, but in bed, like to do actual sleeping." Oh my gosh, none of this is coming out right. "I'm sleeping in the guest room. No arguments about that part of our deal."

He nods, choosing not to comment with his preference, which I'm sure is a big hell no to me in his bed. Men like Cooper Lexington don't need a growing pregnant woman stealing all the pillows and snoring in his ear while he rests. "I'll work for free," I insist.

Those tired eyes narrow. "No."

"I'm not taking your money, Coop. You're already kind enough to let me use your health insurance, which, I imagine, will cost you a little more to add me to your policy. The least I can do is hang out with my bestie for free."

I know a little about insurance from when I researched it on the internet. Single policies are most definitely cheaper than family policies.

"And what happens when you have the baby?" His voice has a hard edge to it. Guess the moody Cooper is back. "You're just going to walk away after our deal with no money to support yourself?"

How dare he assume I haven't thought about that. "Of course not! I'm going to find another job. With the money I'm saving by using your insurance and staying here, I can work part-time and save. In six months, I should have a good stash of formula, diapers and all things baby related." Being broke is not new to me, he need not doubt my savvy abilities.

"I don't get home until late, and on away games, I'll need you to stay with Pops all day and night."

Duh. "I know that. Part-time means working *part* of the time. I'll tell my future employer I can only work overnight."

I swear he chokes on a yell before settling with a gritty, "Overnight? As in the dark without a reliable car?"

"Well, since you had Lu fixed, she's now reliable. But should she decide she needs another breather, my legs—and all other humans'— work in the dark just as much as they do in the light. I have my wrench, I'll be fine. Don't you worry your pretty little head."

His lips flatten as his hands tighten around my thighs. "You'll call me or an Uber if you break down." At least he didn't insist on me driving his car.

"What is it with you always trying to save me?"

His smile should be outlawed. "It's what I do for a living."

"Well, I don't need the assistance of a closer." Let's start a pool of how many times I have to say this exact phrase. "Besides, criminals are scared of crazy people, aka me. I'll be fine."

Cooper's head falls forward where it hangs close to his chest.

"Are you praying?"

"Yes."

Yes? "What are you praying for?" I've never seen anyone pray other than on TV. Call me a little fascinated that this hunk of a man, still on his knees, is actually praying.

"For patience," he mumbles, his head rising, and his eyes leveling me with a stare that is quite scary. "Because I'm seconds from telling you I don't give a fuck what you want. You will be walking nowhere, and if I catch you walking anywhere, you'll be sorry."

Oh, well, that was unexpected. "What kind of punishments—I assume they will be punishments—would make me sorry?"

He never wavers. "I'll tell Pops."

This time, I intentionally shove him, but his hateful self is ready for it. "That's bullshit."

That charming and deadly grin emerges once again. "You wouldn't want to worry an old man more than necessary, would you? Especially once he finds out you're pregnant."

"You can't tell him, Cooper." The words come out in a panic. "Please, promise me. He can't know." His forehead creases and I add, "Not yet, anyway. I'll tell him before I start showing. Just let me be the one who tells him."

Cooper's face smooths, all the lines of confusion disappearing when he says quietly, "He won't be disappointed in you. No one will be. I promise."

Like a child, I hang my head. "You don't know that." Pops knows I'm financially unstable. Admitting that I got myself knocked up amid all my hardships, doesn't exactly scream responsible adult who just signed on to take care of him.

I know I told Cooper I stopped caring what people thought of me a long time ago. But that's only part of the truth. Some people, the really important ones, matter to me. It matters what they think and how they treat me.

I already messed up with Griffin and Brenda. All I have left is

Pops. His opinion, so far, is untainted, and I'd like to keep it that way. I'm not ashamed I'm pregnant. Well, I guess in a way I am. I know the old stigma of women having babies out of wedlock has all but been eliminated. But it isn't the same for me.

I sigh, finding this part of our conversation more exhausting than the marriage negotiation. "Just let me tell him, okay?"

After a minute, Cooper nods, but he doesn't look happy about it.

"I promise, I won't hurt Pops. I'm gonna tell him, I just want to find the right time." Clearly, I will grow larger and it will be painfully obvious. But it's whatever. I can't change the facts. All I know is Cooper Lexington just offered me a way to take care of the little nugget inside me. We're going to be okay—at least for now. We'll worry about later, another day.

"Coop?" A knock at the door reminds us we aren't alone, and Pops is ready for breakfast.

"We're coming," he barks out, giving my knee another squeeze. "We'll figure it out."

We won't. This is my issue, not Cooper's, but either way, I'll keep my promise. I won't hurt Pops. "You—"

"Thank you," he cuts me off, his gaze filled with humility. "I'll never be able to repay you for stepping in and living a lie to keep Pops here. It means more than you know."

I have an inkling about how much it means to him. What grown man, with more money than sense, asks someone to marry him just to keep his grandfather close? A loyal man. A man hell-bent on repaying his grandparent's sacrifice for him. Cooper Lexington has the money and ability to put Pops somewhere lavish, but he wants him home, with him, for as long as he can. If that doesn't make my heart swell to the size of both my boobs, nothing will. This man is every parent's dream. I can only hope I raise my child like Pops has raised Cooper. To know he would give up his career—everything—to take care of his Pops is… Whew girl, don't go falling in love with this man.

"Well, just so you know," I say, clearing my throat. "You can change your mind on the offer anytime. I won't be offended. Well, maybe a little, but I'll get over it quickly. But I'm sure you can find a reputable caregiver. I can even help you find her."

"Pops and I want you."

Pops and I want you.

If that didn't destroy my heart completely, then him taking my hand, still on his knees, his eyes closing as he kisses the fourth finger on my left hand and asking, "McKinley, will you marry me?" would have finished the job.

"I don't have a ring, but obviously it's the first thing I will do tomorrow before the game."

Something fuzzy warms me from the inside out. So much that it worries me I won't let this man and his Pops go at the end of my pregnancy. I can't go through losing another family. I just can't. "No need in wasting money," I suggest. "I think I have something that will work at home." I don't, but Cooper doesn't need to know that.

"Okay." He seems skeptical, but that's okay. I would be too if I were him. I have no freaking idea what I'll be able to scrounge up, but this man is too good—too giving—for me to accept a ring that would likely amount to my annual salary. We can get this done cheaper with no one getting attached.

Psh. Who am I kidding? This deal is going to kill us all.

Chapter
TWELVE

Cooper

"I lied to my sister-in-law."

McKinley blinks several times, her mouth pulling down into a frown as she stands at the front door of her apartment. "Okay… Am I supposed to say she deserved it or that I'm highly disappointed in you? It's too early in the morning for me to make big decisions."

"And here I thought Pops would be the biggest pain in my ass this morning." Especially when he spent a solid thirty minutes accusing me of calling Ainsley to babysit, so I could, "chase a piece of tail."

McKinley glares, and I release a breath and try again. She isn't the only one moody in the morning. "No. That's not what—" The door slams in my face before I can finish.

On any other day, this would piss me off. But today, I don't have time to deal with McKinley's shit, so I charge in right behind her, calling out into the bare living room. Surprisingly, it isn't full of dead houseplants like the one still sitting on my back deck. "Mac?"

"Go away and come back in a few hours."

I follow the muffled groans down a narrow hall, coming to a stop and finding McKinley face down on a twin bed. She turns her head when she hears me enter. "What is it with you and not following directions? Seems like pitchers would be good at that kind of thing."

"What is it with you and slamming doors in your guest's face? Seems like a stadium hostess would be more hospitable."

She cracks one eye open. "You're not a guest."

"I'm not?"

"No. You're…" She waves her hand like she's dismissing me, but I know it's because she's still half-asleep and can't find the words.

"A phenomenal pitcher?" I suggest with a grin. "Patient? Sexy? Prompt?"

She lets out a scoff, which sounds more like a moan. "You know the great thing about being unemployed, Cooper?"

I don't answer. I'm quite sure she meant the question rhetorically.

"The wonderful thing about being unemployed is that you no longer have to get up at the ass crack of dawn if you don't feel like it. Unwanted guests or not."

Heaven help me. "You're not unemployed. I thought we discussed this last night."

"Not employed in the traditional sense, yes. But still… Your flight doesn't depart until two o'clock today, and I would've had half the morning to sleep in, but nooo, you had to interrupt Steve Irwin and me on a sea-scape mission to hug koala bears."

"Who's Steve Irwin? And why would you be looking in the sea for koala bears?"

"I didn't say the dream made sense, Cooper—just that *you* interrupted it."

For fuck's sake. I've really lost my mind asking this woman to marry me.

"Apologies to you and Steve, but we have a pressing matter at the courthouse—which is a wedding-scape mission, just in case you're wondering what to wear. White is the traditional color."

McKinley pulls a pillow over her head, her golden hair fanned around her like a halo—which is absolutely absurd since this girl is no angel. "Let's do it when you get back from Cincinnati."

I snatch the pillow, tossing it to the floor before rolling McKinley onto her back. "You need an OB appointment ASAP. With Ainsley here, we can squeeze in this wedding and solve both our problems before lunch."

"How romantic." She glares.

"I try."

She scoffs. "Can I at least shower first?"

I step aside, allowing her room to slide off the bed and literally—I repeat, literally—crawl to the bathroom and kick the door closed behind her.

"I'll just wait in—"

"Can you water down a Mountain Dew for me? Put it in one of those tumbler thingies."

I pause, looking at the closed bathroom door. "Water it down?" I don't touch the confusion on what a tumbler thingy is. The more urgent question is why she would want a watered-down soda.

The door is suddenly wrenched open, leaving a narrow opening just large enough where I can see her bare shoulders and an annoyed look. "Pregnant women should limit their caffeine intake to one drink a day. I was planning on giving up Mountain Dew, but since you woke me up with an attitude, I'm thinking for your safety, I should have at least a half of one. So—" she manages a pinched smile, "—pour half the can in a cup and fill the other half with water... Please."

Gross.

"And don't make that face. I know it's disgusting, but it's either that or murder you in the car."

I fight off a grin. "Understood."

Before Mac can shut the door in my face, *again,* I walk away, finding her small kitchen easily and locate a cup (not a tumbler thingy) in her cabinet before opening the refrigerator, housing two cans of Mountain Dew and a jar of pickles. No milk. No leftover takeout. Just Mountain Dew and pickles—dill to be exact.

Why does she only have the two items in her refrigerator? Heaven only knows. All I know is I don't have the headspace to ask her about it today. Maybe tomorrow. Better yet, I'll just tell Pops and he'll ask her. My guess is she eats out a lot and doesn't bother with leftovers.

Regardless of her eating habit mystery, I pour the Mountain Dew as she requested, taking a few minutes to check on Pops and Ainsley.

"Yel-low," he answers on the second ring.

"Ainsley hasn't burned the place down, has she? You know where the extinguisher is, don't you?"

Pops belts out a laugh. "Ains! Cooper said you can't use the stove."

"Pops!" I hiss. "That's not what I said!" Well, not verbatim anyway. My sister-in-law isn't known for her cooking skills. What she is known for is nearly burning down her apartment building when she and my brother were in college. That's how they met. She needed a place to stay, and he was the only one crazy enough to let her sleep over.

"Cooper!" Ainsley comes on the line, laughter in her voice. "I heard you were getting laid. Done already?"

"You sound more like my brother every day." I tsk, fighting a grin. "Such a shame. You were working your way up to being my favorite sister-in-law."

"I'm your only sister-in-law."

I take a sip of the drink in my hand, forgetting that it's Mac's watered-down soda, and choke.

"Are you alright? Is your date suggesting a gag and strap-on? Say the word, and Pops and I will come rescue you."

Clearing my throat, I look up at the ceiling, noting several water stains. "As much as I appreciate you and Pops having my back, I'm good."

"She's definitely making him uncomfortable," Ainsley whisper-shouts to Pops who, I imagine, is right next to her. He would never miss listening in.

"I'm not uncomfortable."

Why did I call again?

"Sure you aren't, pookie. That little growly thing you're doing… only happens when you're being The Closer."

"That makes no sense."

"Sure it does. The Cooper at Christmas is fun and snarky. The Cooper at the stadium has a baseball bat up his ass."

"Goodbye, Ainsley. Thanks for watching Pops for me." Pops shouts over her laughter that he isn't a toddler, but I ignore both their asses and hang up. I have enough insanity to deal with here.

Taking a few breaths, I head back into McKinley's bedroom, and I'm immediately met with, "Oh good, I need your help."

My gaze follows the sound until I locate the source.

There, on her knees, water dripping down her back, McKinley looks up at me from the floor in her open closet. "I can't find my white dress."

I notice the pile of clothes she's kneeling on. "My guess is it's in that pile."

She smiles, but I can tell it's forced. "Can you like, for one second, not be you? Pretend you're my butler who I pay well to find my dress, so we can get to the courthouse faster?"

Finally, she makes some sort of sense.

I haul her up by her arms and shove the watered-down drink in her hand. "Finish getting ready." It's not a suggestion, which she thankfully heeds. She merely tips the cup to her lips and walks backward a few steps before closing the door and leaving me to the mess that is her closet.

Five minutes into the search for her dress, I've found eight socks (all different patterns) and dozens of shirts, but no white dress. "I don't think it's in here," I holler.

"It's there, trust me. Check the top shelf."

The top shelf looks just as bad as the floor, cluttered with shoe boxes, clothes, and other random things like a tennis racket. "Do you play tennis?" I call out, inspecting the pink-handled equipment.

"What?"

McKinley opens the door, her forehead wrinkling until she sees the racket in my hand. "Oh. That. No, I don't play. I use it to swat the bees."

"Bees?"

She nods slowly, giving me this look like I'm the only idiot who doesn't swat bees with a racket. "Carpenter bees. They love the railing on the back balcony." She tips her chin to the sliding glass doors that I hadn't noticed before.

"Why not just buy a fly swatter?"

Her eyes roll, and I'm too intrigued to care. "What for, when I have a perfectly good tennis racket?"

"That you don't play with."

"Correct." She says the word slowly like this makes all the sense in the world. "Ooh! You found it!" She rushes past me, still clad in a towel, and grabs something white from behind my head cheering, "Attaboy, Coop!" before disappearing back inside the bathroom.

Attaboy? What—"Why is the shower running?" This day couldn't possibly get any weirder.

"I'm getting rid of the wrinkles. Have the rest of my Mountain Dew and relax. I'm almost done."

Part of me wants to know how she's getting rid of the wrinkles by turning on the shower, and the other part of me just needs a moment to process the insanity of this morning.

I slide the racket back onto the shelf, planning to take McKinley up on her offer and finish her Mountain Dew, when a shoe box—teetering on the edge—falls, spilling half the contents on the floor.

Fuck.

Squatting down, I gather the… napkins? Why is she keeping napkins in a shoe box? I flip one over. The logo on the front is from the concession stand she used to work for—Backdoor Sliders—but the back side is a drawing of a stick woman with a baseball diamond behind her and the words: *We'll go to all the home games. He'd like that*, at the top.

I pick up another, and it's more of the same with a stick figure drawing, though this one is on a swing. *We must have a tire swing in the back yard.*

"Dammit!"

Her shout startles me. I barely have enough time to gather the rest of the napkins and put the box back when she opens the door.

"I need your help… again. Zip me up? I've put on few extra pounds of baby, and this fabric isn't quite forgiving."

I swallow, trying hard to divert my eyes to hers and not the swell of her breasts spilling over the top of her dress. "Okay."

"Don't make this weird, Number Fifty-Four. You're about to become my husband…" She grins. "Until delivery do us part."

Apparently, my behavior confused her.

I tap her nose like one would a child, before taking her by the shoulders and spinning her around, pushing her up against the wall. "Best you know now that being a gentleman is a skill I haven't yet mastered."

She gasps, her hands flat on the wall as I take the zipper at her back between my fingers, leaning in closely, her heated skin beneath the cotton as I grip her hip for leverage. "Now, suck in."

Her hair shifts as she holds her breath, giving me a whiff of something tropical, something fruity. Something… completely edible.

Get it together, Lexington. Just because this girl is taking your last name, doesn't mean her body belongs to you. That wasn't part of the deal.

Ugh. I fight the raging erection pushing against my jeans, painfully noticing the fabric stretching tight over McKinley's body. "All done," I tell her, stepping back.

Don't look at her tits. Just don't.

Too late.

"Thank you." She shrugs, looking down. "I might not be able to see a baby bump, but my waist sure feels one."

If she thought that sentence would kill my boner, she was sadly mistaken. It only made it worse. "Let's go."

Chapter
THIRTEEN

Cooper

The courthouse is busy when we arrive and check-in, signing several forms and handing over our IDs and birth certificates.

"The team will want you to see a psychologist," Mac mutters, her knee bouncing while we wait our turn to be called back. "They'll think you knocked me up."

I sigh, looking to the ceiling. "I don't care what people think, and my contract doesn't require me to tell the team when I decide to get married." Just Aspen, my agent. And well, that's an issue for another day.

"You should! You're a celebrity." McKinley faces me, her eyes wider than when the woman at the desk asked us if we wrote our own vows—I assured Mac we didn't miss any "homework," as she called it.

"Be quiet. I'm not a celebrity. We'll be fine." I cover her mouth and hold it there for a moment before she pries it off.

"OMG! We need a prenup!"

Yeah, Aspen is going to nut-up with that one. But I didn't have the time nor the energy to explain it to her without admitting that Cynthia quit, and the woman from Pops's favorite concession stand was keeping an eye on him. Oh, yeah, and I was marrying her, even though I've only known her for a few days.

Yeah, that would have ended with another intervention and a straitjacket.

I might not know McKinley, but I don't have to. If Pops trusts her then I trust her, even with my assets. But whatever. If she takes me for half at the end of this deal, then it'll have been worth it to see my Pops happy and watching my games. We'll just chalk it up as the most expensive caregiver ever. I don't need a mansion or ten cars that I rarely drive. All I need is enough to keep Pops and me content—even a coaching position at a high school could do that for me.

I didn't become a professional pitcher for the money. I became a pro because it was my mother's dream for me, and no matter how short my career may be, I'll always know I achieved what she worked so hard for me to do.

"Hold on, we can fix this." McKinley holds up her hand like I was about to bolt, then roots around in her purse (she left the wrench in my car, thank goodness), locating a pen and an old grocery receipt that she flips over. "I, McKinley Parks," she starts writing, "forgo all assets and money that Cooper Lexington has and will acquire during our marriage. No matter the reasons for our divorce, McKinley Parks isn't entitled to ANYTHING. If—when—the marriage dissolves, both parties will walk away with no argument, keeping only the money and assets they brought into the marriage."

It's cute how she tries to sound professional.

"Signed, McKinley Parks."

She pushes the paper toward me and cuts me a look that says I better sign without argument. It's not legal, she has to know that.

"I'll forge your name, don't play with me. You might think all this chivalry and shit is cute, and I'll admit, it has some charm, but I can't let you be a complete moron. Pops means too much to me to lose him because you hate me."

"This document will never hold up in court."

She shrugs. "You don't know that. Besides, it'll keep us both honest."

It's like talking to an alien.

"Fine." I sign my name, drawing out an annoyed sigh, and slide the receipt back to her.

"Thank you." She stands and snatches up the paper.

"What are you doing?"

This time it's her that slaps her hand over my mouth. "Shh. The couple over there is complaining about how loud you're being. I'm just going over there to apologize."

But she doesn't. Instead, she congratulates the couple on their upcoming nuptials, and then she asks them to witness our prenup receipt.

God, help me.

If I thought this ceremony was going to be traditional, I would have been delusional.

"Do you have the rings?"

"Oh." Mac looks back at her purse sitting in the chair. "I do." She holds up a finger. "Give me just a minute. I'm sorry."

She drops my hand and sprints over to her bag, bringing out… You've got to be joking.

My eyes widen, and I look at the judge, afraid he might actually ask me what the fuck is in her hand. But he has a better sense of humor than me, fighting off a grin as McKinley steps up and faces me, two black pieces of plastic clutched in her fingers.

"Are those zip ties?" I try to appear like this level of crazy doesn't scare me.

"Uh-huh." She smiles tightly. "If they can hold Lu's bumper, they can hold this marriage together."

Tomorrow, I will appreciate the thought, but today, I'm just shocked as fuck as the judge resumes, instructing each of us to recite vows and zip tie our "rings" on each other's fingers.

"I now pronounce you husband and wife. Mr. Lexington, you may kiss your bride."

Hesitation should not be in my wheelhouse. I'm a closer, the best reliever in the bull pen. Being put in stressful situations is my Kool-Aid. But right here, in the middle of the judge's chambers, my palms start sweating as I reach for my bride, slipping my arms around her hips and pulling them flush with mine. "I'm—"

McKinley's arms loop around my neck, her lips pressing gently against mine. Her warmth… well, I just react. Gripping her hips, I waste no time taking advantage of her silence…and compliance. Maybe it was zipping that dress, watching as my own hands hid the body my eyes lusted after. She wasn't mine, not in the sense a normal wife is to her husband, but tell that to my body. To the way my fingers dig into her hips—hips that will bear a child that is not mine. A mouth that will one day marry another man after we divorce. A mouth that can't help but pop off with outlandish comments and argumentative retorts. Yeah, my mind might know this marriage is a sham, but my body—my tongue, using her surprise to slip in, claiming her intimately in front of witnesses—knows we're in deep. This isn't a kiss meant for a first date or a deal between friends. The feel of her hands tangling in my hair as she moans deep in her chest is intimate—primal. This is a kiss shared only between a husband and a wife.

And I'm… I'm fucked.

A throat clears. "Congratulations, Mr. and Mrs. Lexington. You may pick up your certificate at the front desk."

We finally pull back, McKinley dabbing at her lips, her eyes widening as she stares at me. "Yes, thank you, Your Honor."

With zip ties on our fingers, we grab our certificate, walk out of the courthouse to the car and shut ourselves inside, both of us silent on the way home.

"Hurry!"

"What do you want me to do? Chew it off?"

Half an hour into our marriage and we're already fighting.

"If you have to," she answers. "But we have to get these rings off before Ainsley and Pops get back from the movies!"

She's hysterical and rightly so.

"Cooper, he can't find out this way."

I wiggle the zip tie around her finger. Apparently, I zipped it a little too tight. "He won't find out, I promise."

It's a lie, since I can't remember where the fuck I put the scissors.

"Who doesn't have scissors?" She turns, her eyes glistening as she looks back at me through the mirror.

"Soap and water aren't going to get it off," I tell her, as she proceeds to empty the soap dispenser on her finger.

"Then maybe I can use it to drown myself!"

"Now you're just being dramatic."

"Find the scissors, Cooper!"

I throw my hands up. "I'm looking!" Apparently, I can't remember where I put the damn things when I caught Pops using them to pry off a bottle cap. He bleeds easily, and the last thing I needed was for Cynthia to be glued to a soap opera while he bled to death in the kitchen. So I claimed I lost them and kept forgetting to buy new ones at the store.

"They're here somewhere," I tell her when she starts to cry.

"Cooper! You here?"

We both stop, our gazes meeting in the mirror. "It's okay," I whisper. "I have a plan."

She shakes her head, panic filling her eyes. "Just cut off my finger. I won't need that one anyway."

I grab the hand towel and turn off the water. "Did I hurt you when you were stranded on the freeway?"

"No, but this is different."

Taking her hand, I wrap the towel around it, drying it thoroughly. "Today is no different. You trusted me then when you didn't even know me. I'm asking you, as Pops's grumpy grandson, to trust me now."

She smiles at the nickname she and Pops have for me.

"Can you do that? Will you trust me?"

I need to be at the airport in a few hours, so the timing of what I'm about to do isn't ideal, but it's better than the alternative.

"I trust you." Her voice is soft, not as panicked as it was a second ago.

"Good." I nod, taking her hand in mine, allowing our rings to face out.

Her eyes widen.

"You promised to trust me."

She shakes her head, her eyes watering just a little as I pull us from the bathroom and into the living room, where Ainsley and Pops await.

"Mac? I didn't know you were here."

"Yeah," Mac answers, fidgeting and trying to pull her hand from mine, but I don't let her. "Cooper and I went to check out this senior center. I thought—"

"Are those wedding rings?"

Leave it to Ainsley to sniff out a scandal.

McKinley goes stiff as the room falls silent.

Guess who can't sleep in the guest room now that everyone thinks we're married?

"Surprise," I tell the two nosiest people in my family. "We would have invited everyone, but our timeline was moved up."

Inhaling, I cast my Pops a smile and take one for Team Lexington. Aspen can't know I married Pops's bestie because I needed help caring for him, and Pops can't be disappointed that Mac is pregnant out of wedlock. I'm his grandson, he'll always forgive me because that's what grandparents do.

"We're pregnant." I place my hand over McKinley's stomach just as her knees buckle, but I'm fast, stepping in front of her and placing a kiss on her lips. "Keep it together," I whisper, holding her tightly until she engages her legs.

"You're what?"

So Pops sounds a little pissed. It's fine. I'm grown and not the teenager he gave the birds and the bees speech to.

"Pregnant," I repeat. "McKinley and I are having a baby."

"But you just met!"

I shrug, turning and flashing Ainsley a cocky look. "What can I say, I have super sperm."

"You're a super liar is what you are," Pops adds. "You told me you didn't know who Mac was until last week when you helped her."

"You're right. I lied."

Mac squeezes my arm, and I catch the subtle shake of her head and the tears streaming down her face.

"I asked to keep our relationship a secret. I didn't want it to affect your friendship, so we kept it between us. I'm sorry."

My chest aches as my Pops narrows his eyes, his hand gripping the arm of the recliner. "You could have told me—you both could have. I'm not a fucking child!"

"I know that, and I'm so sorry. It was a mistake, and one lie turned into five, and then it was just too late to stop."

"Are those zip ties?"

I sigh and cut Ainsley a look of annoyance. "They're symbolic. Much like the stuffed sea lions you sleep with."

She nods, understanding that weirdness comes in all forms. "Congratulations! Welcome to the family!" Poor McKinley isn't ready when Ainsley rushes her, pulling her into a hug and spouting off a zillion questions as she drags her into the kitchen, more than likely about to burn them something for lunch.

When the girls are out of range, Pops cuts me a look of disapproval. "You're lying."

I flop down in the armchair next to him and grin. "Prove it."

Chapter
FOURTEEN

McKinley

He's dead—or he will be in the next thirty seconds.

Pops will be upset, but surely he will understand that his grandson asked for it in epic proportions.

"Put the wrench down before the neighbors call the cops."

I hadn't realized that when I slipped outside, I had grabbed my wrench from my purse, intent on a) seeing what in the fresh hell my new husband was doing outside, avoiding his family and leaving me to answer ten billion questions, and b) killing him so the focus would be off my pregnancy with "Cooper."

"I'd be doing your neighborhood a favor by ridding them of an epic liar!" I raise the wrench in the air, and Cooper merely flashes me a look of boredom.

"I didn't lie." He steps on the side of the shovel. Did I mention the fucker is outside with his shirt off, digging a hole for my tree— the same tree he insisted was dead and not worth saving? Well, he is, and it's super hard to concentrate on arguing with him when all the muscles on his torso flex with each shovel of dirt. "I told you to trust that I had a plan."

Instead of launching the wrench at him, like I'd prefer, I toss it to the ground. Honestly, he's right, the neighbors will more than likely call the police, and the last thing I need is to explain why I'd like to whoop my husband's ass before he heads to the airport. I doubt they'd find it as excusable as I do.

"I didn't know your plan was to tell Pops I'm pregnant!"

He bounces on the shovel, pulling up dirt and shifting it to the side of the hole. "You were afraid that Pops would be disappointed in you." He shrugs, wiping the sweat from his forehead with his arm, the words on his tattoo drawing my attention, yet again, to those dang muscles. "Now he isn't. He's disappointed in me for knocking you up. Problem solved."

"Problem not solved! You lied to Pops. He's your grandfather."

"And you're my wife. By our vows, my duty above anyone else is to my wife. No one will be disappointed in you, not while I'm your husband."

Well, damn.

I certainly can't kill him now, can I?

"Coop," I whine, sitting down in the plush grass. "You can't say things like that. Our marriage isn't like other marriages."

He flashes me this grin that is completely adorable and full of boyish charm. "Don't I know it. If our marriage was like others, you'd be face down on the bed in Cabo right now. Your mouth would be far too preoccupied to argue with me."

And they say chivalry is dead… "You know what I mean. We have a deal."

He pauses, leaning on the top of the shovel, his brow arched. "And we have vows. At no point do I plan to break either one."

Talking to him is pointless and downright unhealthy for my broken heart. That steady beat in my chest does not need to fall in love with this man and his ridiculous obsession with honoring our deal *and* vows. My heart won't be able to take another blow like that. I have to focus on becoming the person I need to be for the little one inside of me.

I hang my head, knowing when to retreat. Obviously, Cooper

doesn't plan on budging, and no matter how aggravating he might be, I'm grateful. "Thank you."

"I'm sorry, I can't hear you. Can you speak up?"

I take it all back. He's a nightmare dressed in delicious forearms and a six-pack of abs.

Lifting my head, I glare at my husband, who is all too happy to antagonize me like I did him when we first met. "Thank you. Although I think you made a seriously stupid mistake by claiming to be this baby's father, again, I'm eternally grateful. I'll make it up to you. I promise I'll tell Pops the truth soon."

For a moment, Cooper just stares at me, searching for something that I'm not sure he finds in my gaze. "Whatever you want," he finally says, tipping his chin at Psalms next to me. "Want to get the hose and give it some water?"

I try—and fail—not to grin. "I thought you said it wasn't worth saving?"

He walks over and squats down in front of me, wrapping his hands around Psalms's trunk, his gaze holding mine. "I changed my mind."

"You changed your mind?"

Don't fall in love. Don't fall in love.

"You can too, you know?"

"What? Change my mind?"

He nods. "Anytime. There is no rule saying you can't."

I watch him, digesting all his cryptic words while he stands, planting my tree in his back yard where, unlike me, it'll grow roots.

"I can't believe you and Cooper checked out a senior center. It's not like I'm a child in need of daycare."

Pops is ornery. After Ainsley bid us goodbye three days ago, claiming she couldn't afford any more IOUs if she was late getting home, she and Cooper left for the airport, but not before Cooper shoved enough cash in my hand and told me to catch up my rent or move out, but to handle it before he got back home.

If that wasn't enough to push me over the edge, leaving me with nothing but time and a crotchety old bestie would have.

"Who said you needed a daycare?"

I take a bite of the pickle I confiscated from Cooper's fridge. Apparently, he ordered groceries from his hotel room and had them deliver an extra six jars of pickles. Yes, six. Who was I to waste his money?

"I was simply trying to get you laid, but if you don't appreciate it, then we can just go back to the house."

So now I'm lying to Pops, but Cooper had mentioned we visited a senior center while we were out getting married a few days ago, and since Pops and I were just sitting awkwardly with each other, I figured it couldn't hurt finding us something to do.

"Don't be like Cooper," he scolds. "He's already on my shit list for the other day. You're teetering on the edge with this senior center garbage."

"It's not garbage, and besides, how many games of Uno can we play before we fall into a coma?"

"It looks like we've pulled into a graveyard," Pops mumbles.

"Don't say that. You're the same age as these people. Being around people your own age is healthy." I motion to the group of gray-haired ladies lingering outside in rocking chairs. "Who knows, you might find someone who catches your eye." I can feel his glare beaming into the side of my head. "Don't tell me you're shy."

"I'm not shy," he bites out. "I've had girlfriends before."

I turn slowly, my brows raised.

"I have. Don't look at me like that. Just because I'm old doesn't mean my bed hasn't stayed warm."

Cooper would have gagged at his statement, but not me. Pops isn't my grandfather; he's my bestie. "Really? Maybe you could teach me a few things then?"

I'm totally baiting him and totally forgetting I'm married to his grandson.

Pops scoffs. "I'm not looking to be kicked out."

"Kicked out? Cooper would never kick you out."

Those silver brows arch while he gives me a pointed look. "And here I thought you were the smarter one."

I fight back a smile. "You think I'm smarter than Cooper?"

Pops grunts and lumbers out of the car, his weight leaning on the cane. "I said thought, not think. Clearly, your actions today have changed my opinion." Nodding to the group of elderly men and women, he makes his point.

"I'll have you know Cooper endorsed these outings too."

Pops scoffs. "That's what I'm saying. I knew he was a moron, but I thought you had better sense than that."

He's nervous, and for that fact alone, I don't take offense to anything that comes out of his mouth. I've been there. When I was little, bouncing around from foster home to foster home, new school to new school, I developed a method. It was called being antisocial. I wouldn't speak to anyone or participate in any activity because, what was the point? In six months, I would be in another school. Establishing friendships wasn't worth my time, and therefore, wasn't worth my effort. So I treated everyone as if they were visitors in my life.

Eventually, that behavior changed, thanks to my foster mother and her infinite patience. So Pops can lash out all he wants, but I'll still be here—waiting patiently for him to come around. Because that's what friends are for.

"Well," I say, blowing out a breath, and tying up my hair as if I'm readying to spar. "I'm sorry you feel that way. I guess I'll just have fun without you."

Ocean blue eyes, the exact color of Coop's, roll. "I'm not a four-year-old. You can't play those mind games with me."

I grin and place a kiss on his cheek. "Stay out of trouble while I get my fun on."

Without waiting for his response, I skip off toward the group, spotting the program director and waving him down. "Logan!"

He turns, flashing me a smile before he pats another member on the shoulder and jogs over to meet me. "So glad you could make it."

"Yeah, me too."

I feel an angry presence behind me. "Pops and I are really excited to participate."

Pops mumbles something that sounds like *liar*, but I ignore it, keeping my smile on Logan.

"Good. Come let me show you both around before we get started."

"We'd love that. Thank you."

As Logan leads the way, I take a step back and slip my arm under Pops's. "You better be careful," he chides, both of us taking slow steps.

"Be careful? Why?"

Pops scoffs. "Cooper has never been good at sharing."

Pulling us to a stop, I whip my gaze at the old man babbling nonsense beside me. "Are you suggesting that Cooper would be mad that I smiled at Logan?" Cooper did say he took his vows seriously. Not that I'm flirting with Logan. He's the program director and was nice enough to let us check out the facility on short notice.

Pops shrugs, and it sends a shot of aggravation down my spine. "I'm not flirting. And if I *were* single—I'm not—I wouldn't be interested in someone like Logan." Because I kind of have a thing for grumpy saviors who call me every night to check on things and insist he hear the deadbolt lock while he's on the phone.

"I would hope not," he says, dryly. "Logan hangs out with old people all day. That's weird."

A laugh bursts out of me. "Are you calling me weird?"

He shakes his head. "Not at all."

"But I hang out with you all day."

Like we aren't talking about people his own age, he answers, "But I'm not old." He pauses, scanning the clusters of groups. "And I'm cool."

Shaking my head, I start walking. "You're right. You're absolutely right. We'll hang out just a little while, then we can head back home and do cool kid things like spy on the neighbors with your deer cam."

Pops grins, wholeheartedly agreeing with that plan. "Thank goodness. Now you're acting like the woman I know."

We follow behind Logan, who leads us to the Hawaiian-themed garden set up where the trees have all been wound in white lights. Tables are set up around a sandpit complete with grass skirts. "You think they really buried the pig in the sand?" I ask Pops.

He shrugs. "I have no idea. I told you old people are crazy. For all we know, there could be several sets of dentures buried in that sand.

I think you guessing a pig is a little presumptuous, given our current company."

I bite my lip. "I thought you were going to give them a chance?"

"I said no such thing." He looks at the zip tie still stuck on my finger.

"Cooper wanted us to make the rings."

His lips thin. "Cooper is as crafty as a ball sack."

He knows I'm lying.

Folding my arms, I hold his accusing stare. "Maybe you don't know your grandson as well as you think you do."

"And maybe you think I'm a senile bastard."

I grin. "Maybe not a bastard…"

Pops barks out a laugh and thankfully leaves the conversation alone, steering us to one of the tables where we stay for the next hour, watching as the residents mingle, some even trying their walkers out with a hula routine.

I nudge Pops in the ribs. "Want to try hula? We could hip hop it up."

"No."

"Are you sure?"

"Yeah, I'm—"

"Good, I'd hate for you to break a hip." A smooth voice interrupts Pops, filling me with tingles I should not have in a back yard with residents who could be my great-grandparents.

Chapter
FIFTEEN

McKinley

I look up, and I swear the sun followed Cooper, lighting up his golden hair as if he were a real-life angel. "I thought you weren't going to land until tonight?"

That's so not excitement in my voice.

Cooper shrugs. "Rain canceled our last game."

And he didn't go home to rest. He came here.

"Thought I'd come supervise you two."

He looks around at the party, which is in full swing, if you can call a bunch of eighty-five-year-olds barely swaying to the music a party in full swing.

"What, you thought they'd spike the pineapple juice?" Pops says, his eyes going to a particularly fancy lady with pearl earrings, laughing in the hula line.

"Actually, I thought *you* might spike it and be banned for life."

Pops scoffs. "It's what you deserve after all the times I got called to the office for your bullshit at school."

"Pops!" We both hiss out his name as a warning.

"Don't swear," I say, looking around to see if anyone heard him.

"Why not? What are they going to do? Wash my mouth out with soap?"

Cooper shakes his head. "They should. You've been a real pain in the ass this week."

Pops waves us away, his eyes still tracking the lady in pearls. "Dance with Mac so I can get some damn peace."

He's still a little testy about me bringing him here. That's fine. He needs a little while to adjust.

I look at Cooper and flash him a smile. "Shall we have our first dance as husband and wife?" I hold out my hand. It's not like we had a fake wedding reception too.

Cooper looks at Pops, as if he's setting an example or realizing he has to play along to make this whole shotgun wedding thing seem realistic before flashing me a smile. "It'd be my pleasure, Mrs. Lexington."

"How fancy," Pops scoffs. "Don't embarrass her."

Cooper and I both ignore his comment and turn, leaving him with his fixation on the lady in pearls.

"I'm surprised to see you here," I say, just as Cooper pulls us to a stop in the middle of the grass, far enough away from the residents that we won't knock anyone down, but still close enough that we don't look weird dancing in a random spot.

"Well," he says, spinning me around, not following the hula beat at all. "I had to make sure you both didn't end up in jail." He dips me and I squeal, watching as his eyes light up. "You two, together, are trouble. You two with a wrench and a cane…are a felony waiting to happen."

That smile of his face is lethal. Even my flighty heart isn't immune.

"I'm offended," I lie, just as he pulls me up and into his chest.

That damn smile peeks out again. "No, you're not."

"I should be." I fight off a grin.

"You should," he agrees, stepping back and leading me around the grass like he actually knows what he's doing.

"Where'd you learn to dance?" I peer down between the foot of space between us, his feet moving effortlessly in a pattern.

"My brother."

I pull us to a stop, my eyebrows nearly to my hairline. "Your brother?"

Dropping my hand, his finger skims up my bare arm and stops at my chin before he pushes my jaw closed. His feet start moving, and for a moment, I think he isn't going to answer me, but again, he proves me wrong.

"You already know my mother died when I was young and Mav—" "He swallows harshly, and I almost tell him that he doesn't have to explain, but my curious nature wins out, and I keep my mouth shut, waiting for him to finish.

"Maverick never cared about dances or anything. In fact, he never went to one school function. But one night we were talking—he was in college then—I told him I was attempting to learn to dance from the internet, so I didn't look like a fool with this girl I was dating." He flashes me a smile, but this time, it's fake. "Back then I was cool. Captain of the baseball team and had an on again, off again girlfriend… The world was at my fingertips."

He spins us again to prove he's mastered this whole dancing thing.

"The last thing I wanted to do was embarrass myself, and well, my brother knew I didn't know how to dance." He shrugs. "So he shows up one night with a threat and a promise that we'd never speak of what was about to happen. Then he showed me how to dance."

A laugh has me hiding my face in his chest. "You danced together?"

His own rumbling of laughter joins mine. "We did, and it was as awkward as you can imagine."

Images of him and his brother, locked in each other's embrace, sends me into another fit of laughter. "I wish I could have seen it."

"No, no you do not. It was bad. Maverick doesn't drink, so we were both sober as nuns." He shivers. "No siblings should ever be that close."

"But he did it for you."

"He did. He's a decent brother when he wants to be."

Sounds like he's more than just a decent big brother.

"I always wanted siblings," I admit softly. "Real ones, you know? Not foster ones—though some weren't all that bad."

A muscle twitches in Cooper's cheek. "They weren't nice to you?"

"Most of them were, yeah." He goes in for another dip. I don't squeal this time. "But with foster siblings…" Pausing, I try to figure out how to say this. "I don't form attachments. I'm only loyal until the next time I'm moved. No one is permanent in my life."

I watch as my words sink in, but Cooper never makes a face or realizes why we can never be. He might be honoring this marriage for now, but I'm a risk he cannot afford to take. I'm not like his brother. I don't even know if I have that attachment trait. Well, I guess I can get attached—somewhat. Griffin proved that. But even then, he still left me.

Nothing is permanent in my life.

"You say that as if it's a warning."

I can't tell if he's being serious or not.

"I say it as if I don't understand what it feels like to have a big brother drive down from college and be awkward with me."

That's the truth.

He nods. "Maybe you could borrow mine sometime."

I burrow my head in his shoulder and smile. "Maybe."

It's all I can offer not to ruin the moment. Especially when Cooper turns us and whispers, "Look."

I pull my head up quickly and immediately miss the smell of mint and leather. "Ah!" It's all I can do not to clap. "He's talking to her!"

Cooper chuckles. "I wouldn't call it talking yet. More than likely, he's saying something completely inappropriate that will get him pepper sprayed."

Watching Pops tuck one hand in his trousers, leaning on his cane like Papa Pimp, I smile. "You're probably right, but by the blush on her cheeks, I'm wagering she likes his brand of inappropriate."

Cooper's groan is loud enough that I'm sure Pops's hearing aids pick it up. "How long is this thing again?"

He spins us around so I can no longer watch as Pops gets his flirt on. "Three hours."

"Three hours? It might as well be a decade." His voice is whiny, like seeing his Pops hit on a woman really bothers him.

"Do you not want Pops to find a friend?"

Cooper stops dancing. "He has a friend." His brows rise. "You."

I wave him off. "I know, but I mean like a lady—"

The hand that throws a hundred-mile-an-hour-fastball slaps over my mouth. "Do not use those words around me."

"Okay," I mumble around his hand. "No lady talk."

He drops his hand and I immediately pick up where I left off. "I thought you wanted Pops to branch out?"

There has to be a reason that he tensed beneath my hands and it's not because of the word lady.

"I do, but he's still recovering. He can't be out living it up like a college kid."

Ah, I see what's going on here. "You're scared he might want to move out."

Cooper scoffs. "No. That's not it at all. I just worry about him."

That he does. Probably more than he should, considering he's the grandson and not the grandfather. But if anyone can understand loving a parent unconditionally, even when you know it's time to let go, it's me.

We do a final spin. "Are you thirsty?"

Not really, but I nod anyway because I know he wants out of this conversation. "Sure." I take his hand and let him lead me to the table of refreshments and cute little coconut cups.

"You two looked like you were having fun out there." A gray-haired lady, with only a handful of wrinkles, ladles out a cup of punch and hands one to each of us. "How long have you two been married?"

I smother a laugh, just as Cooper clears his throat and responds, "Only a few—"

"—Fourteen months."

I nearly give myself whiplash as I stare wide-eyed at Cooper.

Did he—Yes, he just told this woman we'd been married fourteen months, which is so not true.

His gaze travels to my barely-there baby bump. His words from the other day come back to me, *I'll never let anyone be disappointed in you. Not while I'm your husband.*

This man. This freaking annoying man is lying, once again, to save my dignity. This lady will eventually see my stomach grow, and Cooper is already laying the groundwork so no one will whisper about me for getting pregnant out of wedlock.

And yes, I know this is the twenty-first century, and women can have babies without husbands, but I can't help the way the guilt gnaws at me. Because I didn't plan this baby, and my decision to have him or her destroyed everything good in my life. That doesn't mean I don't love this baby. I do. I want the world for him or her, but I'm not proud of how I got here—how I got to be a mother. So Cooper softening the blow and saving me from more disappointment in myself… means everything.

The woman smiles and points to Cooper. "I can always spot young love when I see it. You too will have many years ahead of you."

My smile falters, but I'm quick to turn to Cooper. "Unless he leaves his dirty socks next to the hamper again. Then, I might smother him in his sleep."

Totally not true, since Cooper is far more organized than I am, but he barks out a hearty laugh anyway, his drink sloshing over the side.

The woman just stands there, not smiling or laughing. Just standing stock still.

I elbow Cooper in the ribs like, see what you did? Your damn hot as fire laugh gave her a heart attack.

He elbows me back and sets his cup down. "If you'll excuse us? Clearly, we have marital problems we need to work out."

My mouth drops open, and he cuts off any remaining argument with, "Isn't that right, sugar plum?"

I'm definitely smothering him with yesterday's socks. I think we can all agree that it would be for the greater good.

Plastering on a fake smile, I meet this sweet lady's still frozen face. "Sure, hun. Let's join Pops and his lady friend. I'm sure they would like some company."

That shuts him up, and he drops that gorgeous smile. "Thank you for the punch," I say, adding a little wave. "It was delicious."

We hustle away, both of us quiet until Cooper breaks it by dropping my hand and adding, "I'll see you and Pops at home."

I don't even have time to argue or ask why he had a change of heart. All I can see is his low-hanging head, his shoulders slumped as if I offered to burn his glove.

"Where's Coop going?"

I turn my gaze to Pops who suddenly appears at my side. "Home. He said he'd meet us there."

"You two fight?"

I shake my head, watching as Cooper's car pulls out of the parking lot.

"I'm sure he's just being a vagina." Pops pats a hand on my shoulder. "Don't worry about it. Let him work it out."

I guess I have to. He didn't really give me a choice in the matter. But then again, earlier, I pretty much said I don't get attached, so maybe he feels like there's no point in sharing anything with me.

Perhaps he'll call his brother.

Perhaps he's just tired.

Perhaps… I care more about him than I thought.

Chapter
SIXTEEN

McKinley

It isn't so much that Cooper's been ignoring me for the past week; it's more like he's kept his distance. Was it because I talked about not settling down? I don't know. But something during that conversation with the woman at the senior center had him sprinting to the car and burying himself in everything but talking to me.

He's talked to Pops, watched game footage, cooked, and even helped me clean the kitchen, but talk to me? That'd be a no.

So why am I dragging my tired ass from the bedroom and stepping outside in the back yard where my sweet and antisocial husband is throwing a ball in the dark? Because I'll use any excuse to force him out of his silence.

"You know," I say, leaning against the doorframe, "you'd probably locate better pitches in the daylight."

I can't see him when he returns, "You shouldn't be up this late."

"And you should be asleep. You've been awake for more than twenty-four hours now." Does he have no concept of sleep?

"I slept on the plane."

"And I won the lottery yesterday. Don't bullshit me, Lexington. In the two weeks I've been with you, I rarely see you sleep."

I can hear his heavy sigh as the weight of the ball hits the grass. "That's because you pass out during the evening news."

This man. I fight off a grin as Cooper approaches me. "The baby zaps a lot of my energy."

"I'm sure." He climbs the steps of the deck and is in my face, crowding me before I can think to take a step back. "Yet, you're out here spying instead of resting." His nose brushes mine, his breath smelling of alcohol and mint. It's intoxicating, and I find myself tilting my head back, this crazy little groan slipping out.

"How do you smell so good sweaty?"

I can't even be mad the question slipped out. It's a valid question. As sweaty as I've seen Cooper, he's never smelled awful enough to have me turning my head and begging him to shower before the morning sickness kicked in.

His breath tickles my forehead as he drops his head to mine, slipping his arm around my hip and pushing me through the threshold. My muscles go limp while he manhandles me into the kitchen, his head still bowed, his breath dancing along my heated skin as he whispers, "Deodorant. Now, go to bed."

My head snaps up at his words, and I shove him away. "These pregnancy hormones are making me crazy."

The deep rumble of his laughter does not help the fuzzy tingles (most likely the baby is farting) bubbling around in my stomach.

"I find that hard to believe."

"Are you saying I was crazy before the baby?"

A boyish grin emerges and dammit, it's sexy. "I didn't say that."

"That's what you implied." I'm no fool. I also know it's true, but Cooper doesn't need to be right all the time or assume that I didn't just have pregnancy-brain when I groaned at his closeness and asked why he smelled so dang good.

Brenda said always to leave a little mystery. She swore men were born to be hunters and gatherers. "Give them the hunt of a lifetime, Mac, and they will gather every piece of you and cherish it for all of eternity."

At the time, I thought she was on the "good meds" as she battled ovarian cancer in her final days. But now, I think she might have been on to something. Especially as Cooper's grin morphs into a frown as he gets his first look at me in the light. His gaze roams from the top of my breasts to my knees.

"That's my shirt."

I grin, happy that he's the uncomfortable one now. "Actually, this shirt is *ours*. Until delivery do us part, remember?"

If I could give myself a high-five, I so would have. Instead, I focus on the frown my husband can't seem to shake. "But it's my jersey."

Looking down, I finger the navy buttons. "It's easy to take off."

His eyes widen.

"I get hot at night." I shrug. "Happens when another human is inside you." Cooper doesn't move or say anything, and it's making me feel a little awkward. "I mean, you have like twenty of them or something. Can't you just ask them for another one, let me borrow this one for a while?"

Is he really that upset that I borrowed a jersey? "The other button-downs you have aren't as loose as this one."

Finally, Cooper snaps out of it. "Keep it."

"Thank you." I think. "I'll make sure I give it back at the end of… you know."

He pushes past me. "Yeah, I know. Go to bed."

The next thing I know, his bedroom door clicks shut and he's gone.

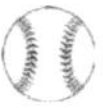

The next morning, Cooper went for a run and took up his strategy of effectively ignoring me again. I'm starting to think he might have a split personality or just a bad case of an attitude problem.

"You're home today, right?"

Bad Attitude is lounged on the sofa, his head hanging low in a dark pair of sweatpants and a t-shirt. He looks grumpy and oh so snuggly. Not that I want to snuggle with him, I'm just saying he could sell the shit out of some sweatpants if a company ever needed a boost in sales.

"Coop?"

Is he asleep? I think so.

Finally! After our encounter last night, I couldn't sleep and ended up just lying there, listening as his door creaked opened and the TV in the living room turned on, playing back footage of a game.

The man has a problem with insomnia. I don't buy that shit that I fall asleep and don't catch him sleeping. This—him asleep on the sofa mid-afternoon—proves it. He doesn't sleep, and these little cat naps are all he manages. No wonder he needed help with Pops. The man works himself to death; between watching game footage, practicing his throws, working out, taking Pops to therapy, and cooking for us all, he has no time left—especially for sleeping.

Walking over, I lean down and gently touch his shoulder. He jerks upright, his eyes wild and heavy. "Hey," I say, calmly. "I'm sorry to wake you. I just wanted to make sure you'd be home all day today. I have a doctor's appointment this afternoon. I tried to make it for the morning before I had to take Pops to his senior program, but they didn't have any openings."

Still in a daze, Cooper nods, answering my question, while scrubbing his hand over his face. "Yeah, I'll be here."

Now I feel terrible, even though I need this appointment and looked at Cooper's calendar ahead of time, making sure he had a day off to pick up Pops from the senior center, but still. Maybe I could reschedule. "So you don't mind picking him up from the senior center?"

"I got him. Go to your appointment." His voice is thick with sleep.

"Okay," I say. "It's over at three, and if I get out early, I'll pick him up." It's my job after all.

"I'll get him. Don't worry about it."

"Thanks." I mean it. If it wasn't for Cooper slipping me a temporary insurance card the other night and handing me a list of OBs his teammates' wives recommended, I would never be here with an appointment reminder on my phone. "Go back to sleep."

And like the stubborn ass he is, he stands and shakes his head. "That's okay, I need to get up and prepare lunch."

"I can do it before I leave. My appointment isn't until two."

Cooper pauses, seeming to consider my offer.

"Go take a nap, Cooper." For heaven's sake. "I'll handle the lunches." I know what Pops likes for lunch probably better than he does. "Besides, making food is my forte."

A hint of a smirk emerges on Coop's face. "Except for hot dogs."

I laugh out loud. "Yes, except for hot dogs." Honestly, I can make a hot dog; it's just I got distracted watching the game or dealing with Ear Hair. I could have done better if I tried.

"Alright, if you don't mind doing the lunches, I'll take a quick nap." I could add that I was right last night, but he looks exhausted, and honestly, I just want him to take care of himself like he takes care of me and Pops. I shoo him off. "Please, go sleep. You've been cranky as fuck this week."

He rolls his eyes. "I have not."

"The lack of sleep has made you delusional."

"I'll set my alarm," he says, ignoring me as usual.

"I'll wake you up before Pops and I leave," I insist. "Rest on your day off."

The man isn't a machine. He needs sleep, and not just naps here and there. He works far too much.

Cooper narrows his eyes like he isn't sure about sleeping that long. Like it's a crime that one naps at ten-thirty in the morning on a weekday.

"Go to bed before I tell Pops you only slept for three hours last night."

He jerks at my threat, which was a total guess, since I fell asleep before him, and he was already up with Pops this morning, discussing trade deadlines and free agent stuff that I didn't understand.

I feel the smirk when I whisper, "I know what you do at night, my dear husband. Now off to bed." And to capitalize on his shock, I grab his upper arm, which isn't as authoritative as when he does it to me given our height difference, lead him to his room and push him down to sit on the bed. I don't miss that he could have very easily jerked away from me, but he lets me bully him into taking a nap.

"Sweet dreams." I kiss him on the forehead to be funny, but when his hands go around my hips, it gives us both pause. My breath hitches and my heart thumps inside my chest as we stand there quietly, absorbing the situation. After a moment, I realize that Cooper is probably waiting for me to get the hell out of his face, so I step back, and he lets me as his arms fall to the mattress.

I give him a smile that says everything is fine, and I promise I'm not trying to make him my baby daddy. "I'll wake you up in a couple hours."

He doesn't acknowledge me, just tracks my every move as I walk to the door and gently shut it.

"Hubs." I giggle at the nickname as I gently shake Cooper awake. "It's noon. Pops and I are headed to the senior center."

It only takes a couple of shakes before Cooper's eyes fly open. "I can take him," he says drowsily.

"I'm sure you can, but Pops and I hate your taste in music. He can only endure one session with you today." I cross my heart with my finger. "His words, not mine."

Rumpled and looking incredibly adorable, Cooper sits up, his hair an utter wreck. "Both of you can kiss my ass."

Don't tempt me.

What the hell?

Did I seriously just think that I could kiss this man's ass? Who am I? Is this baby trying to find a daddy from within?

No, no.

We cannot get attached to Cooper Lexington and his incredible ass. No way. He's a ballplayer who travels a lot and can get traded a million times over the course of his career. We, little one, need to lay down some roots somewhere, and that can't be with someone who will never stay in one place very long. We're not about that life anymore. We want nothing to do with any more adventures.

"I gotta go." Without another word, I turn and holler at Pops to get his old legs moving. I am not sticking around to analyze what just happened. Sleepy Cooper can get himself together and get his signature grumpy on, so we can go back to normal.

Chapter
SEVENTEEN

McKinley

I drop Pops off with minimal grumbling since Grace—the lady in pearls' real name—was there. She was wearing a yellow dress, too, and yellow happens to be Pops's favorite color. At least, that's what it looked like when his eyes widened, barely waving goodbye to me as I signed him in.

I'm proud of him though. The old man needs a woman he can fawn over and tell her all his stories about back in the day. I know that old buzzard, and he definitely doesn't miss an opportunity to tell anyone about his mischievous grandsons.

Pulling into the parking lot of the OB's office I picked from Cooper's list, I note there is not one shitty car (I'm sorry Lu) in the entire lot.

Ugh.

I knew I should have googled more physicians and looked at the Google Earth images. A doctor is a doctor. I don't need a celebrity one that will probably cost Cooper's insurance a lot more money than a normal people one. Maybe not, though. I don't know how these things work.

I whip into a space in the back and pull out my phone to text Cooper.

This doctor's office is too fancy. Will they charge you if I cancel and find another one?

It doesn't take him long to respond.

Go to your appointment.

Ugh. Look at Mr. Fancy over here thinking I'm being ridiculous when he is used to this treatment. My fingers fly over the keyboard as I hit send.

Regular—non-celebrity—people don't use these offices. I bet they have a dress code.

This time, his response is almost immediate.

Go to the damn appointment, or I'll tell them to come out and get you. That's the power of "celebrity" people's doctors.

I swear my mouth drops to my chest as I type out a response.

Seriously? They will come out here?

I can imagine the smugness laced in his response.

Want to test it and see?

No, I absolutely don't want to test the power he might have with this office. I can almost picture him calling the front desk and telling them his wife needs help getting out of the car. I would be mortified if they came out in their fancy matching scrubs with a fancy wheelchair and found me, a celebrity wife, in beat-up, old Lu.

Yeah, I'm not about to see what he can do with a phone call and his celebrity-ness.

Getting out of the car, I grab my purse (with the wrench inside) and lock the doors, firing off one last text to my annoying husband.

Fine. I'm going in, but if I'm thrown out because I didn't wear pink on Thursday, it'll be all your fault when I cry.

I mean it too. I'm not a crier, but if someone scoffs at my ripped, unbuttoned jeans, covered by a loose, flowy tank top and asks me to leave, I will cry.

Who wouldn't?

I already don't belong being married to a wealthy ballplayer and living in his quaint, but extravagant house. I belong with the regular people. Not the ones who go to medical offices that look like art museums with their fancy architecture, glass walls, and chandeliers.

Taking a deep breath, I push open the glass doors and come to a halt. The open-floor plan with sage green antique-looking furniture and aged tables throughout stare back at me. And yes, there is a massive chandelier in the center. Two of them, actually. Am I at a doctor's office or the she-shed of Reese Witherspoon?

"Hi, how can I help you?" I glance to the woman at the desk and, thank heavens, she's not wearing pink. Instead, her scrubs have printed storks carrying pink and blue bundles.

Okay, so this might not be so bad after all.

"Hi," I say, fumbling around in my purse for the card Cooper gave me. "I have an appointment at two. McKinley Parks—I mean, Lexington."

"Hi, Mrs. Lexington. We've been expecting you."

She doesn't even need to look at her schedule. That's one of those fancy things I was talking about. I've never been to a doctor's office where the front desk receptionist didn't have to look at their schedule.

"I'll just need you to fill out this paperwork." She hands me a clipboard and pen.

"Do you need my insurance card?" I want to be sure I don't get a bill for this or mine and Cooper's arrangement will all be for naught.

"Yes. When you finish your paperwork, you can bring it up here with your ID as well."

Okay, good. "Thanks." I start for the chairs in the center but then turn back. "Mr. Lexington and I are recently married."

"Congratulations."

I cringe. "Thanks, but I haven't had a chance to change my ID."

The girl behind the counter laughs. "You don't need to explain. Clearly, he's kept you very busy."

Come again?

But then I get what she's saying. I'm pregnant. "Yes, yes, he has." I smile, not bothering to correct her incredibly wrong assumption.

I walk away before I can word vomit anything else, find a seat and begin filling out this stack of paperwork that asks me questions about my family history, which I have no clue about. Then there's this birthing plan stuff that scares the shit out of me. Do I want an enema? OMG. Is there a possibility I will poop giving birth?

I skip through most of the questions because really? Who knows the answers to these questions when you're still in shock that you're pregnant in the first place?

When I think I've answered the most important questions like how I'm going to pay, leaving the father's name blank, and doing the best I can with the medical history, I walk up to the desk with my insurance card and ID in hand.

"You've finished already?"

I smile, and it's fake as shit. "Yeah, I think I need to take some of it home to work on."

Dana, at least that's what her name tag says, laughs. "That's fine. I'm sure you want to discuss it with Mr. Lexington."

Oh, Dana. That's the last thing I will be discussing with Mr. Lexington. He will never know if I'm choosing to receive an enema or just yolo-ing it and letting the shit fall where it may. Maybe literally.

"Absolutely," I lie. "He can't wait."

I think she knows I'm being sarcastic, but her smile never wavers as her gaze travels to my paperwork, looking it over. "Oh, I'll just need Mr. Lexington's social security number for insurance purposes."

"Oh." Shit. Mr. Lexington is not my real husband, and I highly doubt he's up to sharing his social security number with me. But she needs it to file the insurance. "Okay. Let me just call him."

I fumble around with my phone, my palms already sweating as it rings.

"Hey," he answers, sounding better than he did earlier. He must have downed a few energy drinks.

"Hey." Why am I so damn awkward right now? "So, I'm at the office..."

"Uh, huh."

Ugh. He sounds exasperated already. "And they need your social security number for the insurance." I whisper the last word like the criminal I am.

"Okay. Do you have a pen?"

I shake my head. "I'm just going to hand the phone to Dana, and she can get it from you." This man has done too much for me, and I'm not going to invade his privacy like that.

A noise, something like a huff, goes through the phone before I hand it to Dana. She looks super eager as she takes the phone, her voice changing ever so slightly as she speaks to him, taking down his number. "Will you be joining Mrs. Lexington today? We encourage both parents to attend the first appointment while we go over what to expect during the pregnancy."

I choke and try to mask it with a cough.

Please, God. Don't let Cooper faint or tell this lady this is not his baby. I can handle a lot of things, but I'd rather these people draw their own conclusions from my lack of information on the form. Not from my husband shouting it out and embarrassing me, especially since I already insinuated to Dana that Mr. Lexington and I bumped uglies for weeks after saying I do.

But Cooper wouldn't do that to me. Would he?

"I understand, Mr. Lexington. Thank you for the information." Dana hands the phone back to me and I… freak out. I don't know what Cooper said to Dana, and I really don't want to know. So instead of thanking him, I just hang up and smile at Dana. "He had to go to practice. He's always so busy."

If she thinks I'm crazy for not telling my superstar husband that I love him and will see him later, she doesn't let it show. And I appreciate that immensely.

"We'll call you back in just a bit. Here's your unfinished paperwork, if you want to add more while you wait."

Sure. Like that's gonna happen, but I take the papers anyway and shove them in my purse.

It's about fifteen minutes later when another nurse (not in pink either) calls my name, but I don't answer because she says McKinley Lexington.

"Mrs. Lexington?" she confirms when I finally approach after her third call.

"Yes, I'm sorry. I zoned out. I need a nap." I use Cooper's excuse.

"No worries. Follow me and we'll get your vitals."

We go through a range of tests that include weight—which I refuse to look at—and blood pressure, and they take like a million tubes of blood before I am led into the doctor's office where a nice man with glasses and gray hair sits.

"Hi, Mrs. Lexington. I'm Dr. Montgomery. I'll be your physician during the course of your pregnancy."

I reach my hand out and shake his. "It's nice to meet you, Dr. Montgomery."

"Is Mr. Lexington joining you today?"

Dammit. Do all husbands join their wives on their first visit? What if they have to work, or what if I was artificially inseminated and had a bad case of girl power?

I smile sweetly at the doctor. It's not his fault for noticing that I am married (or at least confused as to why I'm wearing a zip tie on my ring finger) and assuming Mr. Lexington is the father. "He's not. Unfortunately, he had to work."

"Oh, okay. Well, we can always catch him up on another visit. Or we can all have a Zoom call. I have a lot of patients whose husbands are professional athletes."

Yep, there's that fancy shit again. If this was any other facility, they'd be like, "You can catch him up, or we'll fill him in if we have time at your next appointment." I highly doubt they do Zoom calls around their patients' work schedules.

"That's very kind of you, but I can fill him in when I get home."

I should just tell him. This man is going to see my vagina more than any other man has. We should have an honest and upfront relationship. But I can't. I don't want to acknowledge what I did yet. I just want to love this baby, keep it healthy, and raise it the best I can. I don't need a man or a lot of money to do that. But still, I don't want to reveal that Cooper married a woman who is pregnant with a child that is not his. I won't do that to him, and in turn, I don't have to acknowledge what I did.

"Okay, if that's what you—" A knock at the door stops Dr. Considerate. "Come in."

Swear to God, if I wasn't sitting down, I would have fainted like those women did back in the 1920s.

"Mr. Lexington. I'm glad to see you were able to make it."

I eye my husband who's in athletic pants and a t-shirt. His ass was working out. Did he seriously stop and come here… to do what? Wave hi?

"I thought you had to work?" I say with clenched teeth and tight lips.

"I got out early. I thought your appointment was later."

He is so fucking lying, but my heart does this little fist bump like he saved the day. And I'll admit just having someone with me during this stressful appointment does help. I wish it were Pops or Brenda, but I'll take my husband, the hero, as an alternative.

Cooper closes the door behind him and sits in the chair next to me, stretching his legs out in front.

"You really didn't have to come."

I don't care if Dr. Montgomery hears me. He'll just think I worry about Cooper's career over, you know, a little thing like this not being his baby.

"I know."

Clutching my purse, the wrench heavy in my lap, I glare at my husband. "Well—"

"Now that we're all here, let's get started."

Chapter
EIGHTEEN

Cooper

Getting started, by Dr. Montgomery's definition, meant hundreds of questions that turned McKinley's face a shade of red and made her look as if she suddenly had a fever. She waved her hand panicked-stricken and turned to me, mouthing she was sorry several times.

Honestly, I'm fine. More than fine, actually. After grabbing a couple of hours of sleep, I'm feeling better—or was—until her worried texts started coming through, forming an anxious knot in my stomach I couldn't get rid of.

Ever since our dance at the senior center, I've been a little off.

I'm quite sure it's McKinley's fault, throwing me off my routine and invading my life. But it wasn't until we danced that I realized how much I'd royally fucked up.

This marriage of ours was rushed, without any thought about how it would affect either of us in the long run. I was too focused on the short-term issues. Pops and I needed help, and so did Mac. It just made sense to enter into this deal.

But then, holding her in my arms, watching as the center's

activities' director kept watching her… suddenly, my problems seemed to double in size. I now know what jealousy feels like, and I wasn't expecting such a rush of feelings for someone I barely knew.

Someone who loves my Pops and went through a lot of effort finding him something to do with his downtime.

Someone who smiles and laughs like each day is a new day, and the world didn't take a massive shit on her for no reason.

Someone who doesn't kiss my ass, but rather prefers threatening to kick it on a daily basis.

Someone who refuses to ask for help, though we all can agree she needs it more often than not.

Someone who wore my unbuttoned jersey to bed, where it fell to the tops of her thighs, and sent me to bed with a painful boner that took hours of looking at game footage to lose.

Someone who bears my last name but isn't really mine… she's only mine—as she keeps reminding me—'until delivery do us part.'

How did I get here?

Could I really not find another caregiver in time?

No, I couldn't.

Especially when Pops's face lit up seeing Mac. This marriage gives him the opportunity to spend his days with his best friend, when he wouldn't normally get to see her. He's not shut in the house, miserable, with only the noise of the television to keep him company.

This was the right thing to do. I can handle losing Mac at the end of the pregnancy. It's not like she's suddenly going to catch feelings. She made that quite clear from the start, and that should make me seriously happy—not bothered by the comments she makes or the dance we shared.

I'm not a jealous man. I'm more than confident in my abilities to, not only please a woman, but keep her. But I don't have time anymore. It's been years since I've had a girlfriend. But here I am, stressed as fuck, in an OB's office.

"I'll show you guys to a room where we'll do an exam and ultrasound."

Mac looks straight on as if she's in a trance.

"Hey." I touch her shoulder, and I notice her eyes are watery. "I'll wait outside, okay?"

"You can come in with her, Mr. Lexington. We encourage the fathers to see the babies too. It helps with the bonding process."

Mac makes a noise low in her throat that sounds a lot like a groan, and I pull her into a hug like any good husband would do. "I appreciate that, Dr. Montgomery. Can we have just a minute alone, though?"

I need to see what the fuck is wrong with my wife. Where is the woman who teased me last night?

"Absolutely. When you're ready, you can come here to room two." He points to the door just ahead of him. "Mrs. Lexington, there's a gown on the table for you to wear."

Mac makes another noise and nods into my shirt, clinging desperately to me as Dr. Montgomery disappears down the hall.

"Look at me," I tell her, grasping her chin in my fingers. "These people don't matter, neither do their opinions." I take a wild guess as to why she's suddenly meek.

"I know they don't," she snaps, a bit of life coming back to her.

"Then why the panic attack? Pops claims nothing scares you."

She blinks and a rogue tear drops onto my hand. "Pops lies."

"I agree." I chuckle. "But I don't think he's lying about this. Where's that girl who threatened to hurt me with her wrench the other night?"

McKinley looks small and delicate while she sucks in her bottom lip. "She thinks this pregnancy suddenly feels too real."

"Our shotgun marriage didn't make it feel real enough for you?"

After all, that's why we're married. So she could get insurance, without me paying out of pocket for her medical expenses.

A slight grin emerges. "I like a little craziness in my life. Our marriage just felt like a blind date gone right." She shrugs, and I find myself repeating the phrase, blind date. How many blind dates has she been on?

"I don't know, I just didn't think I'd feel so much… guilt. I swear it weighs heavier than the wrench stuffed in my purse."

What the fuck? I drop her chin and snatch the purse off her shoulder. "Why are you still carrying around that damn wrench?"

"Because I don't have the patience to wait for a gun permit?" she offers, teasingly. Her smile is what lures unsuspecting men into her insanity.

God, help me.

"I'll hold your—" I shake my head, "—your wrench and wait outside while you go in there and do your thing, Aphrodite."

I don't bring up the comment about guilt. The office hallway isn't a place to discuss whatever weighs on her mind. But rest assured, I won't forget to ask later. Maybe the next time she spies on me in the middle of the night.

"Okay." She nods.

"Okay?" I make sure before I turn her and gently nudge her toward the room. She takes a few steps and looks back.

"Hey, Coop?"

"Yeah?"

"Why did you come?"

I eat up the few steps between us. "I find it absolutely irrelevant to discuss this now."

"Irrelevant is my second language," she returns, flashing me this smirk that shows off a dimple in her left cheek.

It's more like sarcasm is her second language.

Luckily for her, I speak it fluently. "Fine, I felt confident someone would report the rusty death trap in the parking lot. I figured you might need a ride home when Lu was towed." I grin and she shoves at my shoulder, and I take the opportunity to grab her hand. "Our deal might be unconventional, Mac, but our vows were not. I honor my promises."

Her chin quivers, and I wipe a tear from her face, adding, "We're a team, right?"

She nods. "But you've been ignoring me."

"I ignore everyone."

"Not Pops."

I sigh. "That's because he won't let me."

"Why can't that work for me too?"

I shift my weight, remembering last night. "Trust me, you get my attention plenty." And because this conversation can't end fast enough,

I turn her by the shoulders and give her a little swat to the ass. "Now get in there. I have to pick up another pain in the ass soon."

"Will you stay with me? I'm not scared or anything, I just—" She doesn't turn around to face me, only the slump of her shoulders tells me how desperate she must feel to ask for my help.

"If that's what you want."

She nods only once, and I step forward, opening the door and reaching out behind me, so she can take my hand and follow me through the door where I pull to a halt.

In the center of the sterile-feeling room stands a frightening table equipped with stirrups. "I can see why your palms are sweaty," I note, dryly.

McKinley snatches her hand away. "My palms are not sweaty! Must be yours."

Tearing my gaze from the monster table, I level her with a serious look. "My hands don't sweat, it's bad for business."

She rolls her eyes. "I've seen some shitty pitches you've made. You can't tell me your hands weren't sweaty when those throws veered off behind the catcher."

"No wonder you were fired. Clearly, your focus was elsewhere."

"Yep, watching The Closer almost not save a game."

"Now, you're exaggerating."

Under severe stress, and before I learned to manage the lack of sleep, she might have been correct, but I haven't thrown a wild pitch in quite some time. It's why I'm one of the highest-paid closers in the league.

"And you're delusional." She smirks, her earlier fear of this room all but forgotten with our bantering.

"And you're stalling," I chide, eyeing the pink gown folded on the table. "I'll wait outside while you change."

Just because we are husband and wife doesn't mean I'm entitled to see her body—even if I want to. Like really, really want to.

Mac pauses, swallowing hard. "Maybe you could just turn around?" Her eyes drop to the floor as if she hates asking me to stay.

"If that's what you want."

I came as her husband—to ease her anxiety. If she'd prefer me to stay, then I will, no matter how uncomfortable I might be.

"I'd like that."

I nod once, pulling my hat lower on my head and turning around, facing the wood-grained door. I hear rustling and then nothing. "Okay. You can turn around now."

I give myself a few seconds to breathe and not be a total man by imagining her naked body hidden beneath the thin gown held on by only a few strings.

It doesn't work, though, because when I face her, the gown hangs off her shoulder, and her bare legs and healing knee demand my eyes to drift along her entire body, up to her unrestrained breasts and nipples, hard against the thin fabric.

It's an absolute nightmare when my dick twitches.

I shouldn't react to her body. She's carrying another man's baby. A man that I'm not sure she isn't still in love with. She hasn't bashed him or even mentioned his name. And here I am at the first doctor's appointment with her, without knowing anything of her past.

Oh, God, what am I doing? What have I done?

I must look panicked because McKinley grabs my hand. "I'm sorry for worrying you earlier. I'll be okay if you want to leave. I understand this is weird and really freaking awkward. I appreciate you coming and playing the role of the dutiful father-to-be. I'll tell the doctor soon, so you don't have to do this anymore."

And now I feel like a complete asshole…

"I'm fine," I lie. She doesn't need to know I'm freaking out because I'd love to pull those ties at her side and watch the fabric fall open and bare her body to me—my wife's body.

Never have I imagined that word *wife* would have such a powerful effect on my dick. Had I known the word would keep my dick in a constant state of hardness and my mind swimming with territorial tendencies, I would have told Aspen to send as many caregiver applications as she could my way.

But it's too late now; McKinley is my wife. More than likely for a year, until she's on her feet with a healthy baby in tow. And until I can find Pops a caregiver he can tolerate. The boners and caveman behavior will just have to be dealt with as quickly as possible.

"I can stay, and then we can go pick up Pops," I offer in return.

It sounds like we're already raising a child together, and I guess we are in a sense—a crotchety child that won't hesitate to smack me in the back of the head if I were to tell him that.

The tense lines in Mac's face relax, and I know she just needs a friend. I can't imagine how my mom dealt with doing everything alone for me and my brother. Though my father was present occasionally, it was only when it benefitted him. A soccer game with potential clients in the bleachers? He was there. The day I had a 104 fever and my mother rushed me to the emergency room? Nah, he preferred text updates that he never answered.

McKinley's baby's father might be absent, but I promised her that I would be with her in sickness and in health. We may have married for the wrong reasons, but I will honor our vows until we dissolve them.

"Okay."

"Okay."

Now that we've gotten the awkward out of the way, I head to the table and grab her discarded clothes and carry them to the chair in the room, placing them in the seat. I try ignoring the silk bra and matching underwear but fail, while returning to her side and searching for a distraction.

"Let me help you up." I find the sheet on the table and grab it. "I'm sure the doctor will be here soon."

Extending my hand, McKinley looks at it for a moment and then takes it, her palm's definitely sweaty as I guide her forward and help her up onto the table.

When she's situated, the paper crinkling under her as she adjusts the gown, I shake out the sheet and drape it over her legs, so she's fully covered. "Thank you," she says, her voice trembling.

"Anytime." But I hope it's not often.

"Hey, Cooper?"

"Yeah?"

"When we get in the car, will you say something rude that pisses me off?"

I can feel my forehead wrinkling.

She chews on her cheek. "I just need—"

The knock at the door stops her mid-sentence, and she grips the sheet, a wave of fear thickening the air around her as she swallows and calls out, "You can come in."

Knowing this will be just as painful for her as it will be for me, I stand there in a state of uncertainty as the doctor and female nurse come in, dragging a machine behind them.

"Alright. Let's check on this baby."

McKinley looks at me with wide eyes.

Stepping to the table, I grab her hand like a husband and a first-time father would do. Her grip is tight as we both watch as the doctor opens drawers, turns on the light by McKinley's legs, and pulls out these huge Q-tip things and a bottle of clear liquid.

"That looks terrifying," I whisper.

"I'm sure it does to you. Men aren't known to handle pain well."

"Ha. Ha. I'll have you know—"

The doctor pulls out another torture device from a package and lays it on the table. It looks like a duck's bill and has me immediately shutting up.

McKinley's right; men aren't meant to endure shit like this.

I groan, and McKinley squeezes my hand like it's me who is suffering. But, then again, I need it since the next sentence out of the doctor's mouth stops my breathing.

"All right, Dad, if you'll help Mom put her feet in the stirrups, we'll get started."

Chapter
NINETEEN

Cooper

McKinley and I both freeze.

"I wasn't expecting to participate," I mutter, earning a grin from my wife.

"I think it's only fair you do something. I'm the one giving up bladder space and cute underwear. What's a little assistance with stirrups?" She glances down at the bulge in my pants. "Unless taking a few steps will be a problem for you?"

I force a grin, my teeth clenched as I will the boner away while the doctor and nurse wash their hands. "You seem to be feeling better," I note, taking a step closer.

McKinley chuckles, holding her foot in the air for me to take. "I am. Though now, I'm a little worried about you. You look *very* stressed."

I narrow my eyes, grabbing her ankle. "I can assure you, I'm fine."

A sly smile, inappropriate at a time like this, widens on my wife's face. "Are you sure? Because I'm pretty sure you just said sweaty hands were bad for business and your hands…"

Fuck. "—Aren't sweaty," I assure her, placing her foot in one of the stirrups before repeating it on the other side.

She shrugs and lies back, scooting down the table. "Whatever you say. Oh, will you fix the sheet while you're down there?"

While I'm down here… between her spread legs…

Swallowing, I step forward and place my palms over the sheet at her knees, meeting her gaze. If I don't do this, I'll blow our ruse.

McKinley scoots down the table, her eyes on mine as I pull the sheet lower, covering her as her knees open, creating a space for the doctor to look at the most coveted part of her.

God help me, I step forward, gripping her knees and preventing them from opening any farther.

"Okay, Mom and Dad. Let's get started."

The doctor approaches my side, but something wholly possessive has taken over me. I can't move—I'm glued to the floor, my hands clenching Mac's knees.

"Coop." Mac opens her hand, somehow sensing my struggle. "Hold my hand?"

Her fingers beckon me toward her, but my hands don't move from her knees. Why can't I move?

"Don't worry, Mr. Lexington, I'll be quick." I glance at Dr. Montgomery, offering me a patient smile. Hopefully, I'm not the only husband who feels like he could tear this room apart with another man seeing his wife's… my hands clench on Mac's knees. This was a really bad idea. Not just marrying Mac but coming here, watching another man see what's mine…

"Cooper." Mac sits up on the table and grabs my wrist. "Let go. It's okay."

This is very much *not* okay. At least not for me. Mac is not my *real* wife, yet, for some crazy reason, I feel unhinged.

"We'll give you two a moment." The door clicks shut and Mac and I are left staring at each other.

"What are you doing, Lexington?"

A muscle in my jaw clenches, and I'm positive it's the reason I can't answer her.

"You do know babies don't come from storks, don't you?"

I flash her an expression she knows all too well and roll my eyes, still not speaking.

"You're going to have to move so the doctor can look… down there."

"I'm fine," I tell her, which only makes her burst out laughing.

"Well, great. I'm happy to know you're fine and acting completely sane right now."

"Very funny." I step away, raising my hands from her knees, showing her my palms. "I'm going to wait—" There's a quick knock at the door before it opens, Dr. Montgomery entering with another doctor and the nurse.

"Mr. Lexington, this is my colleague, Dr. Cameron. She's going to take over for me. I have an emergency at the hospital."

He flashes me a wink and I'm absolutely horrified. "I'm sorry. I didn't mean…"

He claps me on the shoulder. "Believe it or not, this happens a lot. We'll ease into it." Turning, he faces Mac and smiles. "I'll see you at your next appointment."

Mac, the traitor, chuckles and waves. "I promise to leave him at home."

With that, Dr. Montgomery steps outside, closing the door behind him, leaving me with three grinning women. "Mr. Lexington, if you'll—"

"My apologies." I step up to the head of the bed and grab Mac's hand, ignoring the stupid face she's making.

"And here I thought it'd be me who embarrassed us at the fancy office."

I don't even make eye contact as the doctor lifts the sheet and settles between Mac's legs.

"Breathe, Cooper."

"I'm glad you're enjoying my discomfort," I grit.

"Immensely. Who would have thought the big bad Closer would be so uncomfortable in an OB office?"

"He was going to look at your—" I look to the doctor between her legs, busy doing heaven knows what and passing a brush-looking thing to the nurse.

"Pussy," she whispers. "Again, that's how babies—"

I cover her mouth. A) Her saying the word 'pussy' made me rock-fucking-hard, and B) I'm tired of her sarcasm.

"I know how babies are born."

I'm not stupid, just possessive as fuck. And it's irrational, which makes all this so much worse.

"Everything looks great, McKinley." The doctor stands, pulling down the sheet and taking off her gloves. "I'm going to leave you in stirrups while I do the breast exam, and then we'll do the ultrasound, okay?"

A breast what?

"It's okay," Mac whispers, probably seeing the 'holy shit' look on my face.

I nod, swallowing quickly and breathing through my nose as the doctor moves to the other side of the table and unties the gown.

Oh fuck. I shouldn't be here. I should—"Honey."

Mac's voice snaps me out of the panic. I meet her green eyes, holding them as the doctor bares her breasts. A pink pert nipple flashes into my vision, and I can't help but notice her tit is the perfect handful.

The doctor moves and presses around, and I have to shift on my feet, smothering a quiet groan. "Should we take Pops out for nachos? He's been mentioning he misses mine at the stand."

My initial reaction is that the only thing I want to eat is my wife's pussy and cover her breasts with my mouth and rid all the thoughts of another woman, doctor or not, touching her. But that would be crazy since we're not together in that way. But telling my dick that is a different story. Currently, he could hammer a nail in the wall with how hard it is.

"Darling?"

I shake off the thoughts and focus on Mac. "Dinner?" she repeats.

I nod my head. "Dinner is fine."

Her smile widens. "I have just the place. Pops will love it."

I nod my head. I can appreciate her distracting me from her tits. "Sounds good."

Mac squeezes my hand and the doctor, blessedly, covers Mac's chest. "Swap places with me, Mr. Lexington."

Fuck. "We have to do the other one too?"

I'm thinking I need to forego dinner and spend a night locked in the shower until my dick is too tired to even twitch.

The doctor laughs. "This is the last one."

Everyone is a freaking comedian today, which is fine, I suppose. At least it got Mac out of her funk and more relaxed.

Well, it did. Up until the nurse dims the lights and rolls the ultrasound machine closer.

"All right, McKinley. You're gonna feel a little pressure and warm gel."

Dr. Cameron pushes the device along Mac's stomach, bringing the screen to life.

Mac gasps and squeezes my hand.

"You okay?" The doctor peers over the sheet, and Mac nods. "Okay then, if you'll both look to the screen."

Instinctively, I turn and see the fuzzy black and white picture with a bean-shaped black spot in the center.

"See that right there?" The doctor's free hand touches the screen, directly on the bean shape. "That's your baby."

I grin, looking down at Mac, since she hasn't said anything, and see that her eyes are screwed shut. "Mac?"

With her lips pinched shut, she shakes her head, a tear slipping down her cheek. "Open your eyes. Look at the baby." I lean over and place a kiss on her forehead, but her eyes never open.

"I can't." Her arms loop over my neck and holds me to her. "Please don't make me."

"Never," I promise her, this time kissing her cheek. I don't know what happened that made her not want to see the baby, but now is not the time to discuss it. I imagine Mac will have many more times to see the baby before it's born. "I'll watch for you."

The last comment has her sobbing into my shirt at which point Dr. Cameron assures me that mood swings and bouts of crying are normal for pregnant women. What she doesn't confirm is if it's normal that pregnant women don't want to see their baby on the ultrasound. But, then again, I'm a man. What do I know about carrying babies?

Dr. Cameron goes on to show me the heartbeat and the baby's

measurements at twelve weeks old before she prints out the images for Mac and me to look at when she isn't so emotional.

"You guys are getting a Christmas baby," Dr. Cameron announces, turning on the lights.

Mac sits up and nods, her eyes still red and swollen. "Thank you."

Dr. Cameron pats her leg. "The hormones will level out, I promise. The good news is you and the baby are both healthy." She steps back and offers me her hand. "Congratulations, Mr. and Mrs. Lexington."

"Thank you." I shake her hand and wait for her and the nurse to clear out before shutting the door, leaning against it, and flashing Mac a half-smile. "I don't know if all this baby talk has made me hormonal or what, but I'm suddenly craving a pickle."

"I like pickles," Mac confirms through a sniffle.

"Really? No kidding?"

She laughs. "Where's my wrench?"

"Where it belongs." I approach the table and offer her my hand. "Let's get you out of this contraption, yeah?"

She smiles, and it only serves to make her cheeks puffier. "I'd like that."

My stomach knots and I touch the swollen skin under her eyes, drying what I hope is the last of her tears for the day. "No more crying either. It makes me feel weird."

She nods, a tiny hint of a grin emerging. "Weirder than getting a boner while your wife gets a vaginal exam?"

"Ew. Don't call it that."

"What about a pootinanny exam?"

I belt out a laugh. "What the hell is a pootinanny?"

Mac pulls her feet from the stirrups, allowing them to dangle. "A cooch."

"Oh my word. Just stop. I'm sorry I even asked."

Pulling her gown lower, I help her off the table, like a gentleman, and change the subject. "I'll wait for you outside."

Before I can turn away, Mac grabs my shirt. "I'll never be able to thank you for today." She shakes her head. "For everything."

"It's not a big—"

"It *is* a big deal, Cooper Lexington. You are a hotshot professional athlete, you deserve your first marriage to be to a young woman with nice tits, an influential family, and a stomach flatter than this table. I'm sorry you wasted your first marriage on me. I'm sorry that my stomach will grow to the size of a beach ball with another man's baby that everyone will assume is yours. You don't deserve this, but I'm beyond grateful you're giving me this opportunity to get myself together. I don't know how I'll ever repay you, but I will, somehow. I promise."

You would think she would be out of tears, but another sneaks down her cheek, and I sigh. "Hush and get dressed. I'll be waiting outside."

I'm not telling her how stupid her observation is. I didn't waste anything. McKinley Parks is one of the kindest souls I've ever encountered. She took care of an old man who's rude to nearly everyone. She loves plants—though she's not very good at keeping them alive. But she tries at everything she does. She's passionate, and whatever pain she's been through with this pregnancy, I hope the man who walked out on her knows I plan on making him pay for every tear she cries. No one fucks with my family. Especially my wife.

Closing the door behind me, I come face to face with Dr. Cameron. "I forgot to mention to McKinley that she should be taking it easy, no heavy lifting, riding rollercoasters, you know, common sense stuff."

I pause. I never thought of the things Mac wouldn't be able to do. Did she realize that? We're going to have a talk about that damn wrench in her purse.

"Got it," I tell the doctor, but I'm lying.

What if Pops needs help getting up? Mac shouldn't be the one to do it.

Great.

This whole arrangement just got a lot more complicated.

Chapter
TWENTY

McKinley

It's been a month since the ultrasound incident. The good news is, Cooper didn't latch on to what happened and hound me like a Labrador for more information. Instead, he made good on his promise and took me for a pickle, which was mouth-gasmingly delicious. The bad news is now Cooper has to die. Yes, even sweet men must have expiration dates.

"Do not get off the plane tonight. You won't live to see tomorrow if you do."

Cooper's voice is muffled as I imagine he's covering the phone, since I'm basically shouting at him at the top of my lungs. "Calm down. You're being dramatic," he argues.

I'll show him dramatic… "We had a deal, Coop! I thought you took your vows seriously?"

He drags in a ragged breath and tells someone in the background he'll be back in a few minutes.

"Don't tell them you'll be back. Tell them goodbye because once I get my hands on you…"

"Mac, you're blowing this way out of proportion."

How dare he? "Me? Pops is just as pissed off as I am!"

"I'm sorry, but—"

You know what? Fuck him. We're married, and per our vows, I have just as much say in this as he does.

I hang up on Cooper, cutting off whatever excuse he was about to use. I don't want to hear it. He made a promise and he's not going to renege. If I wasn't good enough, then he shouldn't have offered to marry me.

"Pops?"

I call out to the living room, where the TV is blaring at levels so high the neighbors could follow along.

After a few seconds, the TV is muted followed by a wary, "What did the traitor say?"

And this is why Pops will always be my bestie. "He said I was being dramatic. Can you believe that?"

Pops walks over to where I'm standing by the door. "It's Cooper we're talking about…"

"True. What do you think we should do?" I nod to the front door where the problem awaits.

Pops shrugs a shoulder, a conniving grin emerging. "I'm thinking Mrs. Lexington has just as much authority as Mr. Lexington."

My brows rise. "That she does. And I'm thinking it's about time she started using said authority."

"That's my girl. Show Cooper who's boss." He raises his palm in the air for a high five.

I wait to slap it, narrowing my eyes. "But should he explode and be the scary Closer Coop, you better have my back, old man."

"You know I got you." But he lowers his hand as if reconsidering what he's suggesting I do.

It's too late, though. Even if Cooper detonates in a fit of fury, I'll match his anger with my own. Who does he think he is?

With one last look at Pops, I wrench open the door and confront the woman who showed up at nine o'clock on the dot with a warm smile and a death wish.

"My apologies, Ms…" Yeah, I didn't catch her name. "After

speaking with Mr. Lexington, he offers his sincere apologies and two weeks of pay for the hassle, but we no longer require your services."

The woman, bless her, looks so confused, and rightfully so. Cooper was out of his mind hiring a nurse to help—get this—me and Pops. Me! As if he didn't marry me for the sole purpose of re-paying me with his celebrity insurance in return for caring for Pops while he's away at games. The nerve!

"I'm sorry. I know Mr. Lexington is an asshole. He's in a twelve-step program for it, but clearly, he can't get past step one in realizing he has a problem."

And that's knowing we had a deal.

"I'm…" The nurse shakes her head, at a loss for words.

"I know, honey. Just feel sorry for us. We have to live with him on a daily basis. You head on home now, and take these next two weeks of paid leave and enjoy yourself. I'll be sure to pass on a giant fuck you to Cooper for you."

"Oh no, that's—"

I pat her on the shoulder and step back. "It's okay. I'll be polit-ically correct when I pass on your best wishes. You have a wonder-ful day. Thanks again for tolerating my husband and his crazy antics. You're truly a saint."

At that, I cast, what I'm sure is a very nice woman, a smile and close the door, turning to face my partner in crime. "You didn't re-start the show without me, did you?"

Pops flashes me a toothy grin. "Never."

I didn't murder Cooper when he landed. Instead, I fell asleep, only waking up when I needed to pee and to turn off the TV in the living room.

I should have known he would still be up—still watching game footage like he does every night he's home.

"You need sleep," I tell him, picking up the remote and hitting pause.

His gaze lifts from the screen, slowly trekking up my body,

lingering on my bare knees, and hovering at the hem line of the t-shirt I borrowed from his drawer.

"Are you worried about me, Mrs. Lexington?"

His words have a hard edge to them, and I don't realize what he means until I respond, "Yes. I made vows too."

"So, you can take care of me, but I can't take care of you? Is that how this marriage is going to go?"

Ah. So this is why he's sitting here looking like he tasted something sour. "Look, it's late, and I don't feel like getting pissed off at you again."

His brows rise. "You're pissed off? Imagine my fury when the nurse I hired to assist you and Pops calls me and says, Mrs. Lexington doesn't require my services,' and good luck in my program."

I smother a grin and move closer, standing in front of him and extending my hand to help him up. "What can I say? You like to pick the crazy ones."

He ignores my hand. "You infuriated me today."

Shrugging, I drop my hand. "Then you felt an ounce of what I felt when you betrayed me."

"I didn't betray you, McKinley." He sighs. "What are you going to do in a few months when you can't pull Pops off the ground if he falls?"

"I can handle it."

"What if you can't and you fall and hurt the baby? I can't—"

Stepping forward, I run my hands through my husband's hair, tilting his head up and forcing him to look at me. "I know you like to bear the weight of everyone's problems, Coop, but you don't have to anymore. Pops and I can manage ourselves. His balance is ten times what it was a month ago. His therapist says thanks to our activities at the senior center, Pops has gotten much stronger. We'll be okay, Cooper. Just worry about you for a little while—like catching up on some sleep."

I note the dark circles under his eyes. "Did you even sleep at all while you were away?"

His hands go to mine, tugging them from his hair and placing them at my side. "This looks better on you," he murmurs, skimming his fingers between the fabric of his shirt and the tops of my thighs.

I swallow, willing away the attraction I've developed for this gorgeous, aggravating man with sandy hair that looks like he's fresh out of a sunscreen commercial. I can just picture him with a longboard, remnants of surf in his hair and the waves pounding at his feet.

Cooper Lexington is stunning. Boyish, yet magnificent, and humble in the way he honors his responsibilities and family. Most people in his position would be arrogant and cold to their grandfather, having no qualms about sending them to a nursing home once they were successful in their career.

But not Cooper.

If I've learned anything from living here with him and Pops, it's that family is everything to Cooper. Whether it's his brother calling him after games to discuss the plays or his sister-in-law calling to give him updates about the growing baby in her belly and his brother's health, Cooper is present and involved, proving just how much his family means to him.

And after each call and each outing with Pops, he disappears into his room. Once, after a lengthy call with his agent, he retreated into his room and didn't come out for quite some time. Just as I was going to check on him, Pops stopped me and said Cooper needed privacy.

I still don't know what he does in there, but I know his family's burdens weigh on him. I don't want to be another one of his burdens, contributing to his exhaustion.

"You're right," I whisper, moving my hands back to his hair where I wanted them, tilting his head back, staring into those deep blue eyes ringed in red. "This shirt does look better on me."

Gripping my shirt, his legs fall open and he yanks me between them.

I don't have to look down to see that he's hard, his length pulsing against my thighs, anxious and starved. "Why do you fight me about everything?" His hands go to my thighs, wedging between them.

My head bows forward. "You make it too easy," I mumble, fighting the urge to ease lower and grind down on his hands.

"I do, huh?" His hands roam down my legs and away from where I want him the most. "Guess I'll have to work on that."

This is why he gets threatened on days ending in y.

"I think what you need to work on is—" I yank his head back and trail kisses along his neck, eliciting a deep raspy groan as I add, "—being more tolerable."

A slight rumbling fills the air between us. "What more do you want from me, McKinley?"

I kiss his cheek, my chest pounding. What more do I want? I think the better question is what on earth am I doing kissing my husband, craving his hands on me?

Hell, mere hours ago, I wanted to beat him, and now, I can't keep my hands to myself. Maybe it's the hormones? Maybe it's the fact that he's taken care of me, even when I didn't want him to. Perhaps I'm attracted to hard-headed men.

The truth is, Cooper Lexington—despite being annoying—is a good man—a man that doesn't deserve a wife carrying another man's baby. A man that cares for everyone but himself.

A man that I feel certain will ruin me for all other men who come after him.

A man I shouldn't fall in love with.

"I want you to touch me," I finally admit, taking my husband's hand, my voice quivering with nerves, and pushing it at my center. I can't change our deal or my past. All I can offer him is the truth of what I want. "Touch me like you'll touch the real Mrs. Lexington one day."

Chapter
TWENTY-ONE

McKinley

Cooper's breath hitches as he leans forward. "You *are* the real Mrs. Lexington. In every way that matters."

"You know what I mean. I've never been touched as someone's wife, and after we… you know, divorce…" I swallow, my gaze settling on the floor as I open myself up to my husband, allowing the feelings I've developed for him to spread into my heart where they don't belong. Because in the end, I can't keep him; he deserves better. I take a breath. "I want to know what it feels like to be loved by all of you."

Our arrangement is temporary, but the effect he's continued to have on me—the proof that all men aren't selfish assholes—will never leave me.

Cooper doesn't give me time to respond before his powerful hands, his tattoo, confirm just how much dominance he has in my weakness at the moment.

As soon as his fingers apply pressure to the extremely sensitive bundle of nerves at my center, I melt, gasping as I tighten my grip on his hair.

"Look at me, sweetheart."

With his free hand, he lifts my chin as my skin heats under his caress, tingling with each pass. The man's hands definitely have more skills than just throwing strikes. "Oh shit." I lean forward and clutch his shoulders. "These hormones are no joke. My entire body feels like a livewire." I suck in a breath, my knees weakening. "I normally don't—"

His fingers stop. "Don't finish that statement. I don't want to hear how my wife normally responds to another man's touch."

Huh?

Leaning back, I meet his eyes, which are aflame with something primal, and drag my fingers down his cheek. "That's not what I was going to say." With my index finger, I apply pressure to his lips, but he doesn't open his mouth.

I can respect the gesture. Guarding your heart is no small matter. Just because he used that word again—wife—doesn't mean he loves me. For all I know, Cooper is just honoring his promise in this deal and taking care of my needs—all of them.

"As I was saying—before you so rudely interrupted—I normally don't feel like I could orgasm just by being touched."

"Then no one has ever touched you properly." His tone isn't clipped like before, and I wonder what exactly I said to make a difference.

"Does that please you?" I ask, and he surprises me by opening his mouth, allowing my finger to slip in easily. "Oh, wow." My back arches and my head tips toward the ceiling. "You're…"

"Your husband?" He growls from around my finger, giving it one farewell lick before guiding it down his chest, over his sweats, before resting on the massive bulge between his legs.

"I was going to go with incredible, but husband works too." Especially the way he says it all raspy and revered. It clenches something deep inside my belly that I'm quite sure isn't the baby.

"I want to see what's mine," he tells me straight-faced with a lust-filled look in his eye. "I want to see what *only* belongs to me."

Before you think that dominant ownership is totally not sexy, I challenge you to say that after your husband demands to see your body with this look in his eye as if he would slaughter anyone that even blinks at you. Trust me, you'll reconsider your views.

"Don't make me wait, Mrs. Lexington. I've been more than patient with you."

His fingers slip underneath my panties, fingering the wetness with leisurely strokes. "You're distracting me," I whine, gripping his hand just in case he decides to stop.

"Then you better get that shirt off *my* body." Two fingers slide into me, a delicious bite of pain making me gasp as he stretches me.

Under his heated stare, I strip off his shirt and toss it to the floor in a matter of seconds. So fast, I forget how my naked four-months' pregnant body might look to a man like Cooper. A man that could have any woman he wanted. I take a step back, ready to grab my shirt to cover myself.

"Where are you going?" His powerful legs squeeze me, preventing me from backing up and retrieving my shirt.

"I don't know what I was thinking. I'm…" Instinctually, my fingers trail over my stomach, delicately tracing the swell at my hips.

"You're what?" His brows rise as his legs loosen from around me. "Sorry?"

I don't know if it's his tone or the rejection that hurts worse. Either way, the pain from mine and Griffin's fallout rears its ugly head. Isn't that what he did to me when he said we weren't family—reject me? I don't know what I was thinking stripping off my shirt like I was still the McKinley from last year.

"You should be sorry—" Cooper admonishes, guiding me backward so he can stand. "Seeing the swell of your tits as you laid against that exam table, your legs parted—" his eyes lock onto mine, "—has had me in a constant state of hardness ever since."

He yanks my hand from my stomach and uses it to palm his erection as his head lowers and his tongue takes a leisurely swipe against my nipple that has him and I both moaning.

"You should be sorry that I daydream about using your mouth for other things than spatting out crazy ramblings."

I would comment that I don't ramble, but his mouth captures my nipple between his teeth, nipping slightly before sucking gently.

"I am—" My knees give out, and my hand loosens from around his solid cock.

"Don't you dare let go of me." He pulls away and I reach for him, but he blocks me, claiming my hand as he kisses the top, paying extra attention to the zip-tie wedding band that I gave up trying to get off. Let's be real, I kind of love it. And the fact that Cooper hasn't taken his off… Yeah, I'm not removing mine.

Those full pouty lips hover over my skin, his eyes laser-focused on the ring representing our union. "But what you should be sorry for the most, Mrs. Lexington, is that the thought of a child growing inside the swell of your abdomen—the evidence of such a miracle widening your hips—"

"Oh gosh."

Cooper lowers to his knees, his hand dropping mine as it traces a line down to my belly button. "Oh, Mrs. Lexington…" His large hands that grip a baseball and throw it at a cool one hundred miles per hour span the swollen part of me before he leans down and places a kiss right in the center. "Nothing turns me on more than the sight of my pregnant wife carrying a child."

And why has he been single all these years?

"Cooper," I drawl, leaning over him, "you make me feel like someone else."

Not the girl that makes poor decisions and doesn't have her shit together.

"You are someone else now." He tsks, his mouth trailing lower until he finds the centermost part of me and kisses there too. "You're my wife."

Oh, that word. *Wife*. When he says it, it doesn't feel like a deal we made in the heat of his panic. Oh no, when Cooper Lexington says *wife*, he says it like there is no end to our arrangement, like somehow, the rules have changed.

"I—ah."

He slips a finger, then two, inside of me, pumping them in and out before he adds pressure with his tongue, circling my clit until my legs begin to shake.

"Tell me," he drawls, coming up for a breath. "Tell me that you're my wife."

At that, his fingers curl and press the rippled flesh inside of me, my muscles clenching and bearing down as his tongue flicks against my swollen nub, tearing an orgasm from the deepest part of my soul.

"Oh, shit."

My breath is ragged when he finally lets up, removing his fingers and dragging them up my body as he stands. "You deny me?"

What? "I would never." Okay, so I would, but right now, I'm not sure what he's talking about.

"Tell me that you're my wife."

Oh, that. Yes, well, he distracted me. He can only blame himself for that.

Standing straighter, my chin only reaching his collarbone, I look up at the man that just made my body sing like it had far too many vodka shots on karaoke night. "I am your wife, Mr. Lexington."

His gaze heats under the weight of my stare as he slips his two fingers, the ones he used to bring me to euphoric bliss, into my mouth and demands, "Push down my sweats."

Oh hell. Fun time is not over.

Grasping his hips, I keep my eyes on him, still sucking his fingers, tasting myself as I lower, taking his pants down with me.

"Good girl." He walks us backward and pulls his fingers from my lips. "Now, ride your husband until I tell you to stop."

Did my vagina just fist bump me? Like is that what that clenching was I felt deep in my belly?

Cooper sits back on the couch, his knees widening as his dick pulses against his stomach.

He offers me a hand, and I waste no time climbing onto his lap. "Guide me in," is all he says as I settle myself over him, his eyes tracking my every movement as I take him in my hand and nudge him to my entrance.

I have very little experience with men. Clearly, I'm not a virgin, but before this little one came along, I'd only been with one other man. But Cooper is not like the other guy in size. His cock is swollen at the tip, the girth significantly wider than the entrance he seems to think it'll fit in.

"Sit."

I'm thinking that asking him to say please would not be ideal since, more than likely, I wouldn't be able to wait for him to answer. Whether this hurts or not, I want nothing more than this man and all of his bossy honor inside me. Right. Freaking. Now.

Gripping his length, I ease down, marveling as Cooper's head goes back, the muscles in his neck straining as he swallows a tortured-sounding moan.

"I knew you would feel like this," he says between breaths, clutching my hips and pushing me all the way down until he's firmly seated inside me. "Look at me." He grips my chin and gives me a long agonizing look before crashing his mouth to mine, exploring, tasting, and owning every piece of me.

If my husband is setting out to destroy me, he's doing a damn fine job of it, because when he knots his fingers in my hair, his other hand settling on my backside, lifting me up and down guiding me to his preferred pace, it doesn't take long for both of us to shatter.

Chapter
TWENTY-TWO

"Hey, Lexington!" I toss my shades onto the passenger seat before shutting the car door and nod to my neighbor who's wiping down his Hummer in his driveway. "Mike." The pinched expression he's wearing stops me. "Everything okay?"

He glances to my front window. "You dating a stripper or something? She's had the music turned up for the past two hours."

I'm not the most neighborly guy, so Mike not knowing I'm married isn't surprising.

"I'm sorry?"

He tips his chin in the direction of my house. "Her music has been really… stank today."

"Stank?"

One of the first things you learn when you play in a stadium packed with thousands of screaming fans is how to tune out everything. Honestly, I rarely pay attention to any chatter around me.

"Yeah, stank," he clarifies with a grunt and a face like he's constipated. "Like it has this stank beat you can grind to." He does this hip motion, which concerns me. What the fuck has Mac been doing today?

"Ah," I return. I still have no idea what he means, but now that he's brought up the noise, I can make out the bass rattling my front windows. "My apologies for the noise," I offer, ignoring the stripper comment. Aspen wouldn't be thrilled if I got arrested for giving my neighbor a black eye.

"No apologies needed," he says all too happily. "I've enjoyed the show."

Maybe Aspen is the forgiving type?

Whipping around, I note the open blinds and a set of hips popping to the same beat drumming against the windows.

I'm gonna kill her.

Then I see another set of hips, and I groan, not bothering to acknowledge Mike further before sprinting to the house.

"Seriously," I bark, coming through the front door and yanking the blinds closed. "You're both dancing to hip-hop music."

McKinley stops, her chest glistening with perspiration in a sports bra. "The therapist says movement is good for Pops's range of motion."

I look at Pops who just shrugs. "I told her I didn't have any rhythm." He takes a few steps away from me and what I'm sure is an enraged expression on my face. "I'll just be in my room if you need anything. You two play nice now."

I look at McKinley in nothing but leggings and a sports bra. "Where the fuck is your shirt?"

Immediately, her fun-loving expression morphs into one that's annoyed.

Guess how much I give a shit if she's mad?

"Probably in the fucking laundry since I barely have any clothes that fit me anymore." She holds up a finger. "Don't even suggest me wearing maternity clothes. They are ugly and as long as I can squeeze into your shirts and my leggings, I'll be fine."

With a long, lazy look, I don't bother hiding, I step up to her rounded belly, pushing against the waist of her leggings. She's radiant while pregnant. So much that as each week goes by, I find myself more and more attracted to her changing body. I can't keep my hands off her, much less her growing belly and the baby inside it.

She calls it obsessive. I call it *mine*.

I step forward, eyeing the flush in my wife's cheeks. "No one sees this but me," I grind out, effectively acting like a straight caveman when I caress her belly.

I'm addicted to this woman. So much so that I can't pitch, concentrate, or even attend a post-game meeting like I'm obligated to do. All I can think about is how fast I can get home and corner my wife in the laundry room and make her moan so loud she has to bite my shoulder to keep Pops from hearing.

You could say I'm royally screwed.

McKinley grins, her earlier frustration subsiding easily as she fingers the light dusting of hair on my jaw. "Now look who's acting crazy."

She's hilarious.

"You're wearing off on me," I admit, pulling her hand from my cheek and pressing my lips to the palm. "Please tell me the old man has an event he can go to."

She grins. "Poor baby," she coos. "It's been a long road trip."

It has, and when she palms my length in her hand, I'm all but reminded that I've been away from her for five excruciatingly long days.

"I need you." It comes out as a plea.

"Later," she promises, kissing me on the mouth. "Pops has a date in a couple hours with Ms. Grace." Her eyebrows waggle. "Don't act like you're about to vomit, Coop. He's excited. So go help him dress while I find something to squeeze into."

Now that I can get behind.

"I could help you first," I offer, pushing against her delightful hands.

"As much as I'd like that, we'll be late, and Pops is already nervous enough."

"Is that why you had him doing hip-hop? As a distraction?"

A sneaky grin emerges. "Maybe. Maybe I was just in the mood to dance."

"Maybe you're just in the mood to get fucked."

Her laugh is infectious. "Go help Pops before he leaves you out of the will for not helping him get his groove back."

It took about an hour for me to rid McKinley's horrific words out of my head. Unlike her, I don't have the sharing is caring type of relationship with Pops. I don't care if he ever gets his groove back, and if that's his goal, I'd hope he'd do it behind closed doors like me.

"Cooper, your face is going to freeze like that. It's not like we dropped him off at a brothel. It's a picnic for goodness' sake. It's not like he and Ms. Grace are going to have a leisurely romp on her newly quilted blanket in front of the rest of the senior center."

"Gross, Mac. You keep making it worse."

"And you keep acting like a baby losing his papaw's attention."

I pull into a parking space and turn in my seat. "What the hell is a papaw? And why are you sounding more and more like Pops?"

"He's been teaching me some southern slang for when we git to go to your brother's for Thanksgiving in the fall."

I groan. "No one but Pops says git."

She bursts out laughing. "Why not? I kind of like it. I think when I have this baby, I'm gonna use git all the time." Her nose scrunches as she points a finger at me, her eyes narrowing. "Git down from there, Billy! Git away from that hot stove. Git your ass home before dark!"

Pops has created a monster.

I sigh and open the car door, finding my wife far too fuckable for it only being mid-afternoon. "Come on, Ellie Mae, let's git you a baby book."

Mac frowns. "You know I can just google anything I want to know about the baby, right? You don't actually need to waste money buying me a book."

"So last night when we were on Zoom, and I asked you if you felt the baby kick yet…"

"And I said no because the baby is only the size of a pear." She puts her hands on her hips. "No one can feel a pear-sized baby kick yet, Cooper."

And this is why we are here. "Per Google, our baby is the size of an artichoke now, not a pear. At eighteen weeks, you should start feeling him or her kick anytime now."

She shoots me a glare. "My wrench is under the seat. Don't make this date turn bloody. I sort of like you and would hate for you to serve me divorce papers in a jail cell."

There she goes again, reminding me of our expiration date.

At least she didn't catch my slip of calling her baby ours.

I step forward, clasping her cheeks between my hands, and planting a kiss on those ridiculously pouty lips. "Hmm… I don't know. Conjugal visits sound kinky."

Pulling us inside the bookstore, I bark at McKinley to pull every baby book off the shelf and stack them in my arms. She rolls her eyes the entire time until we leave and stop at the ice cream shop where she orders a dill-flavored cone with cotton candy ice cream (I know, I gagged too) and asked for a pen. She tried to hide writing another mystery phrase on the napkin, which I'm starting to think is like her own version of a bucket list.

It wasn't until after we picked up Pops, and his refusal to divulge any details of his date (thank goodness) with Ms. Grace, that McKinley's frown returned.

"Why are you holding your book so far away?"

Turning my head, I look at my wife holding a baby book, dressed in another one of my t-shirts, since she refuses to wear maternity clothes. "I don't need to hold it as close as you do."

She leans over. "Are you saying you have super vision?"

"Maybe." I lie back and get comfortable again with one of the baby books we purchased today.

McKinley closes her book and flops back on the bed.

"Do you not like the book?"

I know she's in some form of denial about the pregnancy. She may want to take care of herself and the baby physically, but emotionally, she's not connecting, and I want to know why.

I thought maybe the baby books would help. Seeing a hand-drawn image would feel less scary than the one on the ultrasound.

"Mac?" I glance over when she doesn't answer me. "Are you okay?"

She sucks in her bottom lip, her gaze focused on the ceiling. "Do you think I'm a bad person?"

Closing my own book, I set it on the nightstand and roll to face her, taking her hand and pressing a kiss to the top. "I think some would call you a saint for the sole fact that you're best friends with Pops."

"I'm serious."

"Me too."

Finally, she pulls her eyes from above and fixes them on me. "What if I told you that I've considered giving this baby up for adoption?"

Every muscle in my body clenches. "I'd think you were selfless for putting the baby's needs above your wants."

A tear falls down her cheek. "But what if you knew that I'm too selfish to give it up? Even though he or she deserves a mom so much better than me."

"I'd say you're mistaken."

She shakes her head. "You don't understand. Through this whole pregnancy, I've been selfish, thinking only about what I wanted. I didn't think about how the father would react or even his desire to have children. All I thought is I finally have my own family."

"And now?" I press another kiss to her hand.

"And now, living with you and Pops, I know this baby deserves more than just me."

Chapter
TWENTY-THREE

McKinley

He left a napkin on the table, with his nearly unreadable handwriting, claiming:

We'll go sledding every winter.

How did he know about the box?

"Where's Cooper?" I ask Pops, while he sips on his third cup of coffee this morning.

"At a workout or an ass-kissing. Maybe both. I can't remember."

Not my husband. He would never abandon his morals or self-respect by kissing anyone's ass.

"Don't tell me you're starting to get all girly on me and miss your husband when he's away now."

This ridiculous man and his passive-aggressive jealousy.

"Don't make me leave you at a fire station, you old coot. I simply asked a question—I didn't break down in tears and track his phone."

Pops chuckles, never taking his eyes off the morning news.

"There's my girl." He motions to the whiteboard in the kitchen. "Cooper always writes down where he is in case of an emergency."

I don't know that my wanting to interrogate him as to why he left me a note on a napkin like the very ones I keep in a shoebox qualifies as an emergency but… oh no.

I sprint for the closet in the bedroom, ignoring Pops's questioning stare as I toss the mounds of clothes off the shelf and onto the floor.

"Please tell me he didn't look," I mumble to myself, finding the shoebox in the back, and slowly lifting the lid, seeing the dozens of napkins scattered about.

I take one out, reading it quietly to myself.

We'll get snow cones every Friday during the summer.

Smiling, I put the napkin back and pluck out another.

We'll celebrate our birthday week instead of just one day.

The notes all seem to be there. If Cooper read them, he left no evidence of his crime. Nothing is bent, nothing seems to be missing. Just the crazy promises I started writing when I found out I was going to be a mom and have a family of my own.

Brenda, my foster mom, said every family should have traditions, and since all I had to go on were Brenda's traditions with me, Griffin, and Chris, I figured I'd start some of my own. Though the whole thing has gotten out of hand.

As of now, there are probably two hundred napkins in this box. No way will I remember them all. Besides, some of them are just plain unrealistic. At the rate I'm going, I won't be able to afford birthday weeks or even a snow cone every Friday. I'll be lucky if I can find a job by the time this kid is old enough to eat a snow cone.

But it's still a possibility.

Brenda would say *one can always hope.* I didn't love when she used the phrase because, generally, she only said it when we wanted to do something and it was looking like we weren't going to have the money for it.

I thought it was her cop-out.

But now, carrying a child of my own, I understand the phrase a little more. It wasn't that Brenda didn't want to give us everything— she just couldn't at that time. But she always hoped one day she would be able to.

And that's what happened to me while I was watching the baseball game that one evening as it poured down rain, leaving only a handful of fans left in the stand. I knew I didn't have what it took right now to be a great mom to this baby. I couldn't take care of myself, much less a little one, but eventually, I would.

One day, I'd be able to give him or her everything I ever wanted in a family.

A swing.

A snow cone.

A birthday party.

I had hoped we would be a family and have a picturesque life.

But then he didn't want the baby. He didn't want to be a family with us.

He wanted to travel and see everything alone. He didn't want to spend his money providing for me or a little one. He wanted to live free—and we weren't in that plan of his.

So even though I still add more traditions to the box on occasion, my heart isn't in it like it was before.

Maybe he was right, maybe we weren't meant to be parents.

I put the lid back on the shoebox. Even if Cooper looked at the notes, I doubt he understood them. For all he knows, it's just crazy ramblings. Which they are. Because what kind of mother can't look at the image of her baby on an ultrasound?

Not a good one.

I tried. I really thought I could be a good mother, but maybe sometimes people just aren't wired the same. I don't deserve this child. This child deserves someone who can do all those traditions I placed in the box. Someone that won't have to work double shifts just so she can pay the rent and groceries.

This baby deserves a mom who can look at him.

I shove the shoebox onto the shelf, but it won't push back.

What the heck?

I move more clothes (that I don't wear) and spot another shoebox. Oh no.

My hands shake as my fingers graze the edge of a shoebox with a sports logo for cleats. Easing the box down, I take a few deep breaths as I slide to the floor, placing the box on my lap. A note is attached to the top: **For when you're ready.**

I can guess what's inside—the ultrasound images of my baby. The very ones I couldn't look at in the office.

Am I ready to look now? Can I look at the image of our baby and not cry about what could have been?

The image of the last time I saw *him* flashes through my mind. The look of relief on his face…

I shake my head.

No, I can't. Not yet. I'll try again another day when the guilt isn't so raw.

Standing up, I put the box back, pushing it gently into place when I notice something white sticking out of the side.

It can't be.

A boyish smile comes to mind as I picture my husband, thinking he's cute putting this box up here. I snatch the napkin through the small opening, immediately frowning when I open it up and read the note.

We'll always have huge jars of pickles for when your mom gets hangry.

Oh no.

I toss the napkin and flick open the top of the box grabbing a handful, reading each one aloud until I get through them all. That's when the tears fall.

We'll catch fireflies in our hands.

We'll blame all farts on Pops.
We'll always kiss your mom goodnight.

We'll tickle your mom when she's moody.

I'll always be here for both of you.

"I'm not going in there."

Hitching a shoulder, I push up my sleeves. "You will or the people in this parking lot will witness me dragging you." After the cry-fest of the century, my husband came home with a smile and a new jar of pickles.

The smile was his first mistake. His second mistake… refusing to read my note, which would clearly show I was right and that he needed glasses.

Cooper lifts a brow, a tiny hint of a smirk playing at the corner of his mouth as he leans over the hood. "You couldn't possibly drag me. I'm way too heavy."

And way too argumentative. "We wouldn't be here if you'd just read my note."

He narrows his eyes. "I did read it. I don't see why I failed your stupid test just because I wouldn't read it aloud."

Because if he would have read it aloud, he would have read *you can't see for shit*. Clever, right?

Striding around the car, my steps purposeful and sure, I reach the driver's side, where Cooper is standing, and smother a smile when Cooper holds up his hands. "Don't play, Kin."

Kin.

It feels… warm—like that ratty old electric blanket I used to sleep with every night until it caught fire.

"I still have the note in my pocket. All you have to do is read it to me, and we can play sword and hoot before Pops's activity is over." I take another step closer to the car where my husband appears to be all-casual, like he isn't nervous. All I need to do is reach out and just—

Cooper sidesteps me, avoiding my grab easily. "Stop making up names for my dick and your pussy." The smile he flashes me is boyish and absolutely adorable. One would even say it's panty-melting.

The way it puffs up his cheeks, hiding the strong jaw that lies underneath… completely charming.

"You're going in that office, Number Fifty-Four. One way or another." I'm not allowing a cute grin to distract me. "You need your eyes checked."

Seriously, who does he think he's fooling?

"You can't see. Anyone around you for more than five minutes can tell."

His arms fold across his chest, his smile disappearing with the clenching of his jaw. "I'm a Major League pitcher."

"You are." I nod slowly, as if now we need a psych consult too. "A *professional pitcher* who can't see up close." I smirk as I watch his nostrils flare with my last retort.

I take a step closer, but this time, he doesn't move back. "There's no shame in wearing glasses, Cooper. Lots of players do."

"I'm not ashamed," he snaps. "I don't need glasses."

We agree he's lying, right?

"Then you won't mind proving me wrong by having the ophthalmologist check out that amazing twenty-twenty vision of yours."

His lips flatten and it's seriously cute. "You're not funny."

"Actually—"

"Why is this so important to you?"

His voice is laced with concern. Whether it's from me butting into his personal life or for fear of me telling someone about his secret vision troubles, I don't know. Either way, he needs to know the truth. "You work so hard." I step close enough that I could grab him if I wanted to. But I don't. He needs to do this on his own. "You wouldn't read my note in front of me because you'd have to hold it out to see it."

He flinches, and I move my hand to his cheek. "You take care of everyone else but yourself. Have your eyes checked, Coop. Make life just a little bit easier." Swallowing, he looks over my head at the door to the ophthalmologist's office.

"It'll only take a minute," I add. "Isn't it worth it to check?"

I take little gratification when he tips his chin, agreeing. "Fine. But when you're wrong—" his eyebrows arch in a challenge, "—because you will be wrong—you'll owe me a hoot and sword marathon."

He steps around me and I grin—I'm so not going to be wrong. I've never been more sure about something in my entire life. "Deal," I say with far too much enthusiasm, skipping to catch up and swatting that firm booty of his just like I've seen his teammates do on the field.

Cooper stops abruptly, and I plow into him with my excited momentum.

"Did you just spank me?" His eyes are wide and he tries to school his expression into something more shocked.

Spoiler alert: he doesn't fool anyone with that fake aghast look.

Instead, he fights off a wicked grin and attempts to narrow his eyes.

He looks ridiculous.

Scowling, I ignore the adorableness that is Cooper and pull back just enough so that I can rub my poor boob which took the majority of the impact. "Please," I scoff. "If I'd spanked you, you'd know it. That was merely a juicy high five."

His lips tip at the corner. See? What did I tell you? He wasn't shocked. "Is that right?"

I nod. "I like to keep our marriage interesting."

"You definitely do that."

I can't tell if he means that in a good way or not.

I'm going to go with good.

"Come on, Professional Pitcher, we're going to be late." Taking him by the elbow, I lead him toward the door. We get halfway when he stops. "What n—" I stop mid-question when he removes my hand from his elbow, preferring to hold my hand instead, our zip-tie rings on full display.

Chapter
TWENTY-FOUR

Cooper

"I think it's tacky you're still holding a grudge two weeks later. I told you the glasses look hot on you."

Running my hands through my hair, I glance at my wife, hanging on to the seatbelt like a life vest.

"This is your normal twenty-week appointment. In no way did I have anything to do with the timing, just because you forced me to go to the ophthalmologist."

She narrows her eyes. "Seems an awful bit like retaliation."

"McKinley."

"Cooper."

"You're being ridiculous. We're going inside and getting the ultrasound." At the word ultrasound, her eyes turn glassy. "I promise, I'll go next week."

I lean over and unbuckle her seatbelt, easing it off her shoulder. "We aren't rescheduling, nor are we going to cry."

She shakes her head, panicked. "I can't promise the tear thing. Last night, Pops and I were watching wrestling and that toilet paper commercial came on—Don't look at me like I'm crazy, Cooper! It was the one with the bears." She smacks me on the arm as I fight a grin. "It was sad!"

I highly doubt it was that sad, but since her smack was pretty hard for a pregnant woman, I'll drop it. "I believe you. Bears always choke me up too."

The green of her eyes sparkles in the sunlight. "You're a smartass is what you are, Cooper Lexington." She opens her car door, seemingly less nervous than a few minutes ago. "Scary Closer my ass…"

Never have I enjoyed picking on someone as much as I do McKinley. And yes, the crying at the commercial bit is, for the most part, incredibly funny, but I'd be crazy not to admit that some nights she's sobbed so hard, I was scared something was definitely wrong. I had to hide in the bathroom just so I could call my sister-in-law for advice—which went as well as you could have expected. She burst out into heaving laughter and handed the phone to my brother, who assured me that it's perfectly normal and that Ainsley likes to cry at street signs—especially the ones that say deaf kid in the area. He said she has a complete meltdown and wants to get out and personally stop cars in the neighborhood that go faster than the posted twenty-five miles per hour.

Anyway, a woman's hormones are no joke. They go from a sobbing mess to a wrench-wielding psychopath who threatens if you leave the toilet seat up one more time, you won't need to stand anymore to pee. Needless to say, lesson learned.

I've also learned that when she asks me to help her with the dishes, she means now. Not when I finish film. She means I better hit pause instantly and get my ass up to help her. Even Pops has suffered. Let that old man leave another napkin on top of his plate. We've been told we don't have a maid or a busboy that enjoys separating the trash from dishes.

No shit, the last few weeks have changed my and Pops's entire outlook on pregnant women.

"Come on, Cooper. Let's get this over with."

Locking the car, I slip on my hat and meet her at the front of the car. "You gonna look this time?"

"Maybe."

I tug her lip free of her teeth. "Just consider it. If you can't, maybe tomorrow?"

I've never pushed her on this issue, and she's never volunteered the information about what troubles her. Although most days we seem like a normal couple, other days, she reminds me that we have a deal. I think it's her way of validating that she doesn't need any rescuing or even a shoulder to cry on—unless it's a toilet paper commercial.

McKinley nods, and I take her hand. "If you start to feel like you can't handle things," I pull out my earbuds and sleep mask from my back pocket, "you can use these." I shrug. "They help when I need to rest on the plane."

Something like relief flashes across her face right before she throws her arms around my middle. "I love the shit out of you and your insomnia, Cooper Lexington!"

She tenses. "I'm sorry. I meant I love you like I love pickles and air conditioning."

"I don't keep the house *that* hot." I pull her beside me, letting the love comment go. I'm sure she didn't mean it. "The units outside are going to frost over if you keep the thermostat at sixty degrees."

She side-eyes me. "It's not me. It's this little heater inside me." She lets out a little whine. "It's cooking me from the inside out."

I shake my head at her ridiculousness. She can't be that hot, but I don't dare verbalize it for fear she might shank me with a pen inside her purse. The wrench is finally too heavy and it, too, causes her to overheat with its weight.

"You know," I droll, trying to ease into the subject of this appointment. "After today, we won't have to call the little heater an *it*. We'll know if it's a boy or girl."

McKinley's hand clutches mine. "What if I don't want to know?"

I pull her to a stop and lift her chin that's already quivering. "Then we'll keep on with 'It' or 'little heater.'" Nodding, she inhales, and I pull her into a hug, resting my head over hers.

She sighs. "I kind of like surprises anyway. Besides, I don't want to cry anymore."

I squeeze her firmly but not tight enough to smash her belly.

"Then don't. You deserve this baby. Enjoy creating a life, something that some people would love to do."

And that was the wrong thing to say. "Do you think I'm selfish?"

"No, absolutely not. Every woman deals with pregnancy differently. No one knows what you've been through, Mac. I may not understand it, but I can respect your reactions and decisions."

I rub soothing strokes down her back. "It's not my place to judge you. Ever. And if anyone else ever judges you in my presence, they'll wish they hadn't."

She snorts. "Your hands are worth millions."

I pull her back and touch her cheek. "My foot isn't though."

McKinley didn't cry, but she didn't look at the scan or listen to the heartbeat either.

"Are you upset with me?"

I shake my head. "I'm not mad."

"Are you disappointed I couldn't watch?"

I raise my brows. "Are you?"

She doesn't answer me, and that's fine. Honestly, I'm still in shock from it all. Seeing the baby inside my wife move on the 3D ultrasound, the tiny thumb shoved between the tiniest lips as it rolled and kicked to find a comfortable position was the most incredible thing I've ever witnessed.

I was entranced.

I'd never seen something so amazing, so absolutely pure. And I won't even lie, I was grateful Mac wore the eye mask since she would have seen me wipe away a tear. I might not be this baby's father, but something happened in that darkened room. Something otherworldly as I watched—amazed at the life inside my wife.

All I wanted in that moment was to be that baby's father—which is insane. I'm the equivalent to this baby's long-lost uncle, and in four months, after the holidays, I'm likely to never see Mac and this baby again. Sure, she'll probably text me a picture or two occasionally, but it won't be enough.

Losing her—and this child—will devastate me.

"Why not?"

The day has not gotten any better.

When we arrived home, Mac locked herself in the bedroom, telling Pops she was tired and needed a nap. Pops and I proceeded to play a game of poker to pass the time before dinner when I mistakenly answered a call from my nosy sister-in-law.

"Because, Ains. She wants the sex of the baby to be a surprise." Like my brother, when Ainsley Lexington wants something, she will annoy the fuck out of you until you break or cry.

"Where's the fun in that? I say we have a joint gender reveal party. Mav and I can fly out this weekend. Right, Mav?" My brother grunts out a non-answer that neither sides with me nor Ainsley. "Come on, Coop. Promise you'll talk to her about it?"

"I'll talk to her, but don't get your hopes up, okay?"

"Eep! This is gonna be so fun! I say we do an aquarium theme!"

Maverick chuckles in the background but doesn't tell his wife that her idea is a little too unique for our tastes. Instead, I hear Ainsley gasp and mumble something before she hurries me off the phone with, "Convince her!" before hanging up.

"That's going to be a shitshow," Pops says from his chair.

Don't I know it. "Ainsley's Mav's problem."

Pops grunts. "Maverick would dress up as a sea lion if that woman asked him to. He's ruined forever."

We both share a small chuckle as McKinley opens the bedroom door and lumbers out, her face red and slightly swollen.

"You hungry?"

She nods and goes to sit on the sofa next to Pops, who has also learned to never ask if she's been crying or take note when her hair is wild and looks like a nest of some sort.

"I'm kicking Coop's ass in poker. You want to join us and make him feel worse about himself?"

McKinley's laugh has me relaxing.

It was torture not knocking on the door and talking to her about what happened today in the office. It was also torture not looking in the envelope the nurse gave me, which contained the sex of the baby. She thought Mac might change her mind once she settled down a bit. I agreed, and like my sister-in-law, I'm impatient to learn if it's a future ballplayer kicking around in there.

"Are BLTs okay?" I ask from the kitchen. "Pops picked it."

"Yeah, BLTs sound good, actually."

I want to ask her if she wants to take an antacid first, since tomatoes and just about everything acidic give her heartburn, but I refrain. She seems delicate right now. So I'll give her time and let her know that Ainsley says if you get crazy heartburn, it's a sign the baby will have a lot of hair.

Finishing up, and adding one more sandwich to the tray, I head over to the coffee table and set it down. "Thank you," McKinley says, her voice sounding stronger than earlier.

"You're welcome."

We eat, chit-chatting a bit before we deal another hand of poker and rib each other, until Pops announces he's off to bed. I use the opportunity to straighten up before sitting down to watch game footage.

"Where're your glasses?"

I glance up and see McKinley's hands on her hips and a scowl on her face. Guess someone is feeling better. "The bedroom."

"Why aren't you wearing them?"

I sigh and scrub a hand down my face. "Let's not do this, Mac. You're not the only one who had a tough day."

It wasn't something I had allowed myself to admit. Seeing the baby fucked me up. I haven't been right since the appointment. I understand Mac had a day much worse than mine, but it's not like I'm not affected by all this too.

The cushion shifts and a hand comes over mine. "I'm sorry."

"It's okay. We're both tired."

Her voice comes out pained. "I'll sleep in the guest room tonight. I know you aren't getting much sleep when I get up ten times a night to pee."

I do wake up several times at night, but that's not the reason I feel run down.

"I'm fine."

Leaning back, she pulls me with her, the remote in her hand, pushing play. "Who are you most concerned about tomorrow?"

I point at the player up to bat. "Camden. He was just called up from the minor leagues four weeks ago."

"Seems like he'd be easy to sit down then."

By sit down, she means to strike out. "Not really. Those guys are the most dangerous. We don't have as much footage to study as we do older players."

"Can't you study the minor league footage?"

She pauses the screen and stands up, striding closer to the TV. "Like here, with his foot placement. He's obviously crowding the plate. Can't you just pitch him inside and back him off the plate? Why are you smiling like that?"

I shrug. "You sure know a lot about pitching."

"Well, when your husband is the Closer, you start to think he might need some help sometimes too."

She sucks in her cheek, chewing on it.

"Are you embarrassed?" Because her talking to me about how to pitch a batter and then looking sheepish like she didn't want me to know she was studying players, has my dick pudgy.

"No."

She cocks a hip, accentuating the swell of her stomach, and my dick stands at attention. "Come here."

She stands there, not moving. "Why?"

"Do you want me to have to ask again?"

I don't know who she thinks I am, but when I ask her this question, she seems to not want to test me. She takes a few steps forward, and I open my legs, beckoning for her to stand between them, which she does, albeit hesitantly.

"I want to see you." I tug at her t-shirt and she grins.

"Without your glasses, you won't be seeing shit."

Technically, she's wrong. I only need help with reading up close.

As long as her tits are within squeezing distance, I won't need to see, but I understand what she wants. Control.

"Fine."

If she wants me to wear them, then she'll have to traipse her fine ass to my bedroom. "I suppose the lack of movement means you want me to get them?"

"If you want me to wear them."

I lift the edge of her shirt with my finger and drag it down her skin. "Oh, shit. Why does that feel so good?"

I'd like to think it's my skills of touching a woman, but it's more likely her hormones are in overdrive. Per my brother, his dick nearly cried the other day because they both are beyond exhausted, keeping up with Ainsley's sexual appetite.

Gripping McKinley's shirt, I pull her down until her soft thighs meet the hardness between my legs. "I think we can manage without the glasses, don't you?"

Her tongue sweeps across her lips. "Yeah."

Yeah is fucking right. "Now, let me see you."

Placing my other hand at her hip, I drag both palms up her sides, her shirt catching on my wrists and ruching up, causing her breath to hitch. Leaning up, I tilt my head to meet her gaze. "You feel incredible."

I continue up her sides and her hands stop mine. "I might feel incredible but I don't look very—"

"Do not finish that sentence." I'm up and pushing her back, her foot catching as she stumbles, but I hold on to her. "I'm tired of it, Mac. I'm tired of this self-deprecating, self-pitying thing you've got going on here lately."

I don't give her time to argue, I simply pull her behind me to my room where I kick the half-full suitcase from the door, and stand with her facing the mirror. "I love you like baseball," I tell her, brushing the hair off her shoulders.

"Don't say that."

"Why not? You said you loved me like pickles and air condition-ing earlier."

Her lips purse. "Because… I…"

"Because you might love me more than Mountain Dew too?"

She nods. "I've tried not to."

And that's exactly what I needed to hear. My wife's walls are finally breaking down. I smooth the lines of her chin. "Do you think I look hot with my nerdy glasses?" I try for a smile. We can discuss details later.

McKinley grunts out a laugh. "Are you serious?"

"Absolutely. I need to know if you still find me sexy with glasses."

It's a long minute as she searches my face, looking for something. But finally, she takes a breath and relaxes under my hands. "I do."

I nod. "Then why can't you see what I see? Who has told you that you were less than absolute perfection?"

Her eyes turn glassy, and it's the last thing I want. "No tears. Not yet, anyway. Let's save them for the gut-wrenching bear commercials."

She sniffles but looks to the ceiling, composing herself before she meets my gaze head-on.

"Good girl," I praise, lifting her shirt slowly, allowing myself my fill as the fabric hitches over the swell of her tits. "Now, don't take your eyes off my wife."

She's reluctant, but she eventually nods and looks past my shoulder, keeping her eyes there. "My hair's a mess," she notes.

"Your hair is slept in," I correct her, "and it's still gorgeous."

She moans at my comment, and I use the distraction to raise her shirt to her neck. "Lift your arms for me."

She does, and I slip the fabric up and off, tossing it behind her. "Keep them up." I kiss the side of her neck, just behind her ear, and she groans, tipping her head to the side as I unclasp her bra. "You can lower your arms now."

Slipping the straps off her arms, I bend and place a kiss to each swell, taking a moment to suck each nipple into my mouth.

McKinley's hands go to my hair. "I'm okay if you keep going," she tells me breathily, her thighs squeezing together, trying to create the friction she needs.

It's then, when I know I have her good and compliant, that I drop to my knees, giving her a full view of her half-naked body in the mirror. "Oh, no. What are you doing?"

Chapter
TWENTY-FIVE

McKinley

He's kneeling at my feet.

This man, powerful with a ball, arms swollen with muscles I didn't even know existed, drags my sleep shorts and panties down with his tight grip.

"Look at my wife, McKinley." His voice is thick and raspy. "Tell me how beautiful her eyes are."

My hands go to his shoulders as I steady myself for him to slip the panties off my feet.

"I—I don't know what to say."

I'm not so sure about this little sex game. I was rather hoping he'd bend me over the bed and tell me how much I got on his damn nerves today and punish me with his amazing dick, not make me stand in front of his full-length mirror and tell him how beautiful my eyes are.

His palm comes up, slipping through my thighs. Oh, good. Maybe he's let this shitty foreplay game go. "Yes," I tell him, nodding eagerly and trying to ignore the enormously round belly and boobs that have grown into a new bra size.

Spreading my legs, because I'm a considerate lover like that, I give him access to my center.

"Is this what you want?" he teases.

I nod. "Badly."

He doesn't move any closer though. "My hand is soaked."

No shit. Did I not just say that I very much wanted his hand to work me like he does those balls? I've had a really shitty day and I'd very much like him to remedy that as fast as he possibly can.

"Would you like for me to show you how wet you are?"

Honestly, I couldn't give a fuck less. I can feel it pooling between my legs. I don't need a demonstration, just his tongue or his fingers will do. Hell, at this point, he could use a loofah and I'd probably still get off. That's how horny I am right now.

"Sure," I whine. I'd do anything to get him to move where I need him the most.

He rises as his gaze holds mine, and then—bless this man—a lone finger slips inside me.

"Oh shit." I fold over, using his shoulder as support while he proceeds to ease that same finger in and out until my legs are shaking, and then it just… stops.

"What are you doing?" Standing up, I pull him up with me. "Are you punishing me for today?" I already beat myself up enough about not seeing my little peanut on the ultrasound. I don't know why I can't bear to see the image—I just can't.

"Do you think I'm not concerned? That I'm not scared that I'll be that terrible mother who never bonded with her child and won't even be able to look at him or her when I deliver?"

Cooper sits back on his heels. "We're not discussing that now. I'm not punishing you. But in order for me to give you what you need, I need something in return."

"Anything." Except an explanation. I can't have alcohol, and those types of discussions require it.

"I want you to tell me how beautiful my wife is."

My breath hitches. He might as well have asked me to name all forty-five presidents. It's not that I don't find myself attractive, I do.

Sure, there are definitely areas in need of improving, but I'm not totally disgusted with myself. At least not with my pre-pregnant self.

Seeing myself pregnant doesn't carry the same excitement I see on social media as other women who mark each week of growth with a baby bump picture.

They don't feel the shame I do—the shame that I destroyed one life for another.

"Mac, baby?"

I blink away the tears and focus on my husband humbly kneeling at my feet, so ready to serve me—to please me, if only I could just give him what he wants.

An answer.

"I can't."

His head inches closer to my center as he looks up at me with those deep blue eyes. "You can't what?"

"Tell you what you want to hear."

That I'm stunning, my skin glows with radiance, my hair long and silky. I can't tell him how beautiful I feel as he beholds me in reverence as if I'm the most exquisite prize. No, I can't tell him any of those things because I don't deserve to feel this way.

Cooper presses a kiss to my center, the heat of his mouth setting my skin ablaze. "Oh, wow."

He pulls back, taking all the blissful pressure with him. "I think you can tell me what I want to hear, Mrs. Lexington. In fact, I think you want to tell me everything that's amazing about my wife." He sheaths a long digit inside me once more, and the pressure is blissful torture when he demands, "Tell me how magnificent she is on the inside and out."

This man is a real-life prince, full of everything good in this world.

"She thinks her husband makes her a better woman."

Cooper smooths his hands against my thighs. "Before you, I only bowed for one other," he says, "and his law is clear about how I should love my wife."

He places a kiss to my swollen stomach and stands, stepping behind me and pressing on my upper back to ease me forward until I'm able to grip the mirror on each side.

"Do you want to know what God says about how a man should love a woman, McKinley?"

I nod, enraptured by his passion.

"That I shall love my wife like he loves me—willing to sacrifice my life for hers." He nudges my legs apart, his eyes locked on mine in the reflection as he lowers his pants, his erection painfully swollen, while he twists my hair in his hands. "For a husband's body belongs to his wife and hers to him."

My eyes roll back as Cooper paints an image of ownership—of a love unmatched by any mortal love.

"And they will not withhold themselves from each other."

I don't have time to brace for the delicious intrusion as Cooper plunges inside me, my breath caught in a gasp as he ruts in and out of me like a husband who can't get deep enough inside his wife.

Cooper is manic as his hands rake over every inch of my exposed flesh, nipping and lavishing it like he's a starved man.

If you would have asked me my thoughts on marriage a year ago, I would have said it was something you did when the fun wore off and you needed a roommate to pay fifty percent of the bills. Never would I have told you that I've never felt so honored, so wholly full that the thought of divorcing my husband makes me physically sick.

If Cooper Lexington was trying to break me, he just did.

"Look at me." One hand wraps around my waist while his finger presses against my clit.

"I want you to see what I see." His free hand grips my chin, forcing my eyes on him, a beautiful angel. "I see a woman so full of light that even hardships can't dim her spirit. I see her body swollen with a miracle that I'm not deserving to experience. I see a woman who loves all people without fault, even though she considers herself less than."

My knees go weak as he pumps furiously from behind. "But she would be wrong."

Tremors start in my legs, my muscles clenching in my lower belly.

"Because my wife is nothing short of extraordinary."

His finger presses harder on the tight bundle of nerves at my core. I can feel he's close, he's waiting on me, and when he whispers

reverently in my ear, "It's an honor to call you mine," I explode, with him following behind me.

I don't bother covering up as I roll over, propping my head on my hand. "I've heard an orgasm is the best way to fall asleep quickly."

He grins, just barely, just enough to be boyish, his eyes a lot more awake than they were a few minutes ago. "It seems like you're trying to give me a reason to stay awake." He nods to my tits against the sheets.

"I'm just wondering why you're still awake after—" I shrug and grin, "all that hoot and sword play."

He barks out a laugh, and I'm quick to use it to my advantage, scooting in close and pressing a soft kiss on his lips while trailing a finger down the scruff of his jaw. "What causes your insomnia?"

He chooses to ignore me, his mouth opening slightly as he kisses me again, urging me closer as his tongue slips in—foreign, yet so comfortable.

After a moment, I pull back. "Let me be a good wife. Tell me how I can help your insomnia."

I realize I'm being a hypocrite. I want Cooper to let me help him with his problems, yet I fight him at every turn when he tries to help me with mine. "You've been so kind to me by taking on my burden and pretending to be the father of my baby, without even knowing what exactly happened to the father."

He shakes his head. "It doesn't matter."

But it does.

Even when I couldn't look at my baby on the ultrasound, the ultimate sin of a mother, Cooper didn't look at me any differently. In fact, he acts like I'm more amazing than anyone he's ever encountered.

But we all know Cooper is just a big old softie. I mean, come on, he takes care of his grandfather for goodness' sake. He worries about everyone but himself. I also know he's been paying my rent on my apartment. Pops and I went one day, so I could pay down some of the back-rent, but the landlord just seemed confused, telling me that

I was all caught up, which was clearly wrong since I've been staying with Cooper since we married.

"It matters to me, Cooper. It matters to me that you would tarnish your reputation by pretending to be the father of my baby. It matters that my husband, who takes care of everyone else, refuses to take care of himself."

The man that the media doesn't know and batters fear, pulls me close. "You matter to me, Mrs. Lexington, and that's the only thing you need to remember."

"I'm not dropping the matter. Not until you tell me what keeps you up at night."

He sighs. "Everything. I don't know."

"Oh, well, now everything makes so much sense."

If he thinks I won't be persistent, then he better brace himself. I cut him a look. "Do you worry about Pops?"

It's the most logical choice.

"Sometimes." He frowns.

"But…"

I pull at the blankets, a warning in my eyes that my boobs will soon be covered if he doesn't speak up.

"It started after Pops had a stroke." He stops my hands, tugging the covers back down so he can palm my tit.

"And," I prod, earning an exasperated look.

"And I was young. The only man who has ever given a shit about me nearly died from a blood clot. Life became real—a measured timeline. I didn't want to waste a minute with Pops or years in college when all I wanted to do was play baseball and shoot the shit with my crotchety, old best friend."

I almost argue that statement, but since he's opening up, I let him have the BFF comment.

"So I started packing in everything I could into the hours I had. I would never let Pops see how much time it took me to pre-plan meals or clean up the house. It didn't matter. I could handle everything."

His hand gives my tit a firm squeeze. "I never needed that much sleep anyway, but when I knew I wanted to play pro ball, I knew I would have to sacrifice time and sleep if I wanted to keep Pops and baseball in my life."

"Not that I don't love the old man or find you completely endearing, but don't you have a brother?"

"I do, and he'd drop everything for me and Pops."

"So why don't you let him help you?"

Cooper lets out a deep breath. "Because he's sacrificed enough for us. It was my turn to take one for the team."

Chapter
TWENTY-SIX

Cooper

"Last call for bets."

McKinley—as predicted—gave me a big, fat, *hell no* when I finally asked her about the joint gender reveal party, which disappointed Ainsley about a fraction of a second before she got sidetracked with the idea of a poker-themed reveal and hung up on me.

It's a ridiculous theme, I know, but it makes my sister-in-law seriously happy.

"You want to re-up your bet?" I ask, carefully watching for any signs of distress.

I wasn't sure McKinley would even want to come considering she was thirty weeks pregnant and stayed hot and uncomfortable on most days. But she insisted on supporting Ainsley and Maverick, though she doesn't know either of them very well. "It's important to you, therefore it's important to me," she had said when I offered up her staying home and Pops and I going to Georgia alone.

"No, I'll stick with what I have." McKinley flashes me a smile that seems genuine.

She's been busy since we've arrived. Ainsley pulled her away, threatening to cut me if I didn't let go of Mac's hand and allow her to show off her new sister-in-law. But now that Ainsley is firmly secured in Maverick's arms, his hands resting protectively around her belly, I have my wife back to myself.

"Do you need to re-up yours?" she returns, as we watch Ainsley motion to a blackboard, where a running bet of the baby's sex is displayed.

"Already did." Grinning, I add, "My brother expects nothing less than to win a bet against me."

She chuckles. "What do you think the baby is?"

Over the course of this extremely lavish back yard party, I've seen Mac's smiles go from fake to real. She's actually enjoying herself. And when Maverick and Ainsley sit down at the poker table, a deck of playing cards between them, her smile at the excitement of the reveal is wider than I've ever seen it.

"It's a girl."

My brother, though I love him dearly, has thrived since Ainsley came into his life; he deserves nothing less than the headache of looking out for women who will defy him every chance they get.

"I think it's a boy," McKinley offers with a shrug. "But I'm just guessing."

"We're all guessing—or at least hoping—Mav gets what he deserves."

The crowd goes quiet when Maverick picks up the cards and deals out two cards to each of them. Though Mav's game of preference is poker, it looks like he and Ains are playing blackjack.

"All right, you two," Sebastian, Maverick's best friend, announces, a clear green visor sitting atop his head. "Pick up your cards and turn the applicable ones over."

Sebastian rigged the cards, per Ainsley's specifications, so they could flip them over, each with handwritten words that will let them know the baby's sex.

"Ainsley."

My sister-in-law smothers a smile as she lays down the card where the word "It's" is scribbled onto the white of the card in black Sharpie, something my brother does to her all the time in forms of IOUs. "Hit me, Bash."

Sebastian slides a card to Ainsley, face down on the felt table. She puts her palm over it, waiting.

"Mav."

Unlike the times Maverick plays real poker, his face isn't stony or hard. Instead, his eyes flick back and forth between Ainsley and the card in his hand. He taps it on the table and tosses it, face-up, to the center with the word "A" scrawled out in the same handwriting. "Hit."

Again, Sebastian slides another card, this time to Maverick. "On my count, show your cards."

Everyone starts counting down from five, and McKinley's hand tightens in mine, her breath hitching just as the crowd gets to one and Maverick and Ainsley flip over their cards, revealing in pink Sharpie the word, "Girl!"

"You were right!" McKinley jumps up and down and throws her hands around my neck as my brother kisses his wife then the little girl in her belly.

"I can't believe you were right!"

I chuckle and kiss the space underneath McKinley's ear. "I had a fifty percent chance of being right."

She swats my shoulder. "You know what I mean. I could have sworn your scary brother would be having a boy."

"My scary brother is just a big, old softie," I tell her, which has her turning, watching as my brother ignores the entire party, insisting on kissing his wife and whispering in her ear things I doubt any of us want to hear.

"Their baby is really lucky to have them as parents."

I pull her back to stare into her eyes. "I'm sure their child is lucky, but even if it were just my sister-in-law or just Maverick raising that child, it wouldn't mean that she would be loved any less. Perfect parents don't exist, Mac. Neither do perfect families. Just because we've been fed that families are made up of a mom and dad, two kids, and a dog, doesn't mean the fantasy is for everyone."

I touch her stomach. "This little one is just as lucky to have a mom who would marry a stranger just to make sure he or she stayed healthy." I push my forehead to hers. "That tells me this child's mom would sacrifice whatever she had to make sure he was taken care of. That's what love is all about. That's what being a parent is made of. Love and sacrifice. Don't let others' lives twist you into thinking you're somehow not good enough because you didn't fall into a specific bucket the media said you should be in."

"You really believe that?"

I kiss her mouth. "Every word."

"Cooper?"

The bedroom door opens, and I lift my head.

"Oh, I'm so sorry. I'll come back later. I didn't mean to disturb you."

"It's fine. I was finished." Pulling myself up from where I had been kneeling, I turn to face her. "What's wrong?"

She stares at me for a moment, hesitating. "Were you—never mind. If you're not busy, I'd like to see you and Pops outside."

It's been a week since we've returned from my brother's. Mac has been somewhat reserved, but for the most part, pretty normal. Except now. "Sure, I'll get Pops and meet you out there."

Mac nods and mutters a quiet, "Thank you," before disappearing.

It takes me a few minutes to convince Pops to pause the evening news and slip on some shoes, but he eventually does, and we join Mac outside as the sun begins to set.

"All right, Macaroni. We're both out here sweating our balls off in this heat. What is it that you need to tell us that you couldn't do in the air conditioning?"

It's then I realize this is no laughing matter as I spot two shoeboxes in front of Psalms, my wife's head bowed.

"You don't have to do this," I tell her, realizing what she's about to do.

"Yes, I do. Pops deserves to know the truth. You both do."

Pops flashes me a concerned look. "What's she talking about, Coop?"

McKinley steps forward and takes my grandfather's hand, a lone tear streaking down her face. "Your grandson is an extraordinary man."

Her voices cracks and I take a step toward her.

"Don't," she warns. "Let me do this."

Standing still, watching the pain etched in my wife's expression as she stands there alone is one of the hardest things I've ever had to do.

"Pops, this baby is not Cooper's. He didn't knock me up."

The old man scoffs. "No shit."

Mac rears back. "You knew? How?"

Pops turns his head, side-eyeing me. "Because before you, that boy hadn't seen pussy since prom."

"Pops!"

"Don't act all offended, Cooper. You haven't left my side since I woke up in the hospital and found you on your knees, praying at my bedside. You've made it your personal mission to be up my ass so much, neither of us can get any."

I groan, fighting off scarring images of a naked Pops. "I still could have been getting laid at away games—" My eyes go to Mac and find her grinning. "Not that I was. I'm just saying it's possible."

Pops grunts. "No, it isn't. I check your phone all the time. The only calls you make are to me, Aspen, Ainsley, and Mav." He shrugs. "And now, Mac."

"You've been checking my phone?" I cannot believe the lack of privacy in this house.

"What else am I supposed to do? I can only take so much of The Weather Channel."

"I don't know, find a hobby."

"I have. I enjoy combing through my grandson's lack of texts and videoing unsuspecting thieves with my deer camera."

"I don't even know what to say to that other than checking my phone is highly inappropriate."

Pops shrugs. "Just as inappropriate as you and Mac lying to me about why you got married."

I open my mouth and close it. What can I say other than he's right—which he does not need to hear right now.

"You're right," McKinley adds, her voice trembling. "We should have never lied to you. I'm sorry. I never wanted to disappoint you. You've been such a good friend all this time, and the thought of losing you scared me into silence and letting Cooper take the blame for my situation."

"Aww, Mac." Pops pulls McKinley in his arms. "You could never do anything to lose our friendship. We're family."

McKinley starts crying, and it takes all I have to let Pops comfort my wife. "But—" She sniffles. "You don't know the rest."

"You're talking to a man that raised two boys. Nothing, sweetheart, could be as bad as some of the shit they put me through." Pops flashes me a grin. "Ain't that right, Coop?"

"I plead the fifth." McKinley doesn't need to know all the dumb shit Maverick and I did as teenagers.

"Come on, let's sit down." Pops leads Mac back over to Psalms where the two boxes await. "Coop, grab us some chairs."

I do, dragging two from the deck and sitting them in front of Mac and Pops.

"I owe you both an explanation," McKinley says, sitting stiffly.

"No, you—"

"I do, Cooper. You can't always protect me. You deserve to know who you're living with, who you protect on a daily basis."

I'm so in love with this woman that she could be a serial killer and I'd still protect her. Though, I have to admit, I am curious to know everything about who she is and what's happened in her life to shape the person she is today.

McKinley pulls in a shaky breath, and I lower myself to the ground, kneeling in front of her. "Nothing you can say will make me love you any less."

A sob bursts from her chest. "I killed my baby's father."

TWENTY-SEVEN

Cooper

"I'm sorry. You what?"

Pops seems to have recovered his speech faster than me.

"I killed him," she repeats, her head buried in her hands. "Griffin and I lived at the same foster house."

"How'd you kill him?"

McKinley lifts her head, the tears ceasing for just a moment. "Pops! Hush."

"You used the wrench, didn't you?"

Mac chokes. "No, it wasn't the wrench."

"I take it back, I can be disappointed in you, Macaroni."

Heaven help me. I look at McKinley, rubbing soothing circles over her thigh. "Ignore him."

Mac smiles, Pops's crude statement seemingly lightening the tension. "Brenda, my foster mom, was my high school teacher. She had fostered Griffin and his brother, Chris, for years, until she took me in too. Griffin and I immediately hit it off, preferring to spend our time together on what Griffin called adventures—which were basically hikes in the woods where he pretended to see waterfalls and historic landmarks." She shrugs, her voice cracking with emotion. "Griffin swore when he got older, he would hike every mountain and visit every monument. And for a while, he did, dropping out of school, and leaving me Lu when I turned sixteen. I didn't speak to him much after that, as he worked odd jobs, only calling me whenever he could pay his phone bill."

She takes a breath and looks me in the eyes. "Then Brenda got sick. Chris was older than Griffin and just a few years earlier, had received a scholarship to college and spent all his time there. I was alone as my last family member wasted away from cancer."

"I'm so sorry you had to go through that," I tell her, taking her hand as she hiccups.

"One day, after Brenda decided to stop treatments, Griffin called. I cried and begged him to come home. He never told me where he was, just promised he would come. And two days later, he showed up on Brenda's doorstep with a duffle bag in hand. He helped me with Brenda, staying at the house and working with a landscape company during the day."

I look over at Pops and notice him wringing his hands as McKinley continues.

"I dropped out of school after that. Brenda was conscious only a few hours a day. Had she known, she would have made Griffin drive me back to school and sit there so I didn't leave. But she never found out. Because she died a few days later with no one but me at her side."

McKinley chuckles, swiping at a tear. "I went crazy after that. I got the job at the stadium and spent every dime I had as Brenda's house was foreclosed on, forcing Griffin and me into an apartment until he was able to save enough money to buy a house. That's when he brought home Psalms. He said the palm tree is known for its fibrous root system. When some die, new ones grow in their place to keep the tree strong. He told me I would grow new roots after Brenda and stand tall in the storm, bending but not ever breaking—just like Psalms." She squeezes my hand, tears welling in her eyes. "I want you to know that I never meant to ruin his life. I was so sad after Brenda, I guilted him into staying in Nevada instead of going back to his adventures."

"I'm sure he wanted to take care of his friend," I say.

"He did. At least at first, but then he started partying, popping pills, and drinking. Initially, I thought he just needed a break from the pain of losing Brenda, since I was still spending every dime I had shopping and racking up debt. We were devastated by her loss."

She bites her lip, her hand trembling in mine. "And then one night, we both had a few too many drinks and I…"

"Asked him to pork you until the sun came up," Pops supplies, making McKinley snort.

"Essentially."

"And you got pregnant."

She nods, her bottom lip red and swollen under her teeth. "He didn't want the baby."

"But you did?"

"Yes. I felt like something truly wonderful had come out of our pain."

"And he didn't agree."

Her breath hitches and she begins to cry, her words so full of agony that it tears through my chest. "He said I should have never begged him to come back. He said—" She heaves, a vicious sob erupting. "He said I'd ruin his life if I had this baby."

Standing, I pull her from the chair, wrapping my arms around her as she cries into my chest. "I thought he was just upset—that he would come around eventually."

Another set of arms wrap around us as Pops adds, "Sounds to me like he deserved a wrench to the ass."

Mac lets out this cry-chuckle. "He struggled with an abusive father growing up. I knew that he never wanted children, yet I didn't take his fears into consideration."

"He didn't have to parent this child if he didn't want to." I don't know Griffin, but I do know that one good parent can enrich a child's life more than two bad ones. Take me and Pops. I achieved everything I ever wanted in life with my grandfather. Not my father or mother, but my Pops. I know for a fact, families can thrive with one parent.

"I know," she says, "but to him, he was only perpetuating a cycle of bad genes."

"So you killed him?"

I pull back and level Pops with an exasperated look. "Could you stop?"

"What? I want to know if we need to bury a body or leave the country before the baby is born."

I hadn't thought about that. What if Mac is running from the law?

Mac sniffles, pulling her head up to flash Pops a sad smile. "I found Griffin on the couch one evening when he wouldn't answer my calls. He looked so peaceful…"

I tighten my grip around her as she slumps in my arms.

"There were pills on the coffee table and an empty bottle of alcohol in his hand. I was too late to help him. The doctors said it was an anaphylactic reaction to one of the medicines."

I hold her tightly. "You didn't cause this, sweetheart."

"But I did. If I could have just handled being alone with Brenda… if I hadn't asked him to come back. If only I wouldn't have gone to his house that night."

She snakes a hand through our bodies and palms her stomach. "If I hadn't been so selfish and wanted to have this baby, Griffin would still be alive. I chose one life over another."

"No, your choice had nothing to do with what happened to Griffin."

Mac shakes her head. "I made a promise that I would never accept help from anyone again. I would handle anything. My choices would never affect someone again. And then…" Her cries turn hoarse.

"And then I made you get in the car on the interstate."

She nods. "But then I heard Pops and thought I could just use a friend. Chris was selling Griffin's house, and I needed to get Psalms out of there before he banned me from the property. And now my decisions have affected both of you."

Her knees give out and Pops steps back, letting me take her to the ground and pull her into my lap. "Unlike Griffin, we wanted to be part of those choices, McKinley. We love you."

"I love you both too. I really tried not to, but you both were just so damn persistent."

Pops scoffs, and Mac reaches out for his hand. "You were one of those new roots, old man. You made my awful job bearable, and when you left me your number on that napkin when Ear Hair left me crying… You gave me hope for the first time in a very long time."

So that's where she started the whole napkin thing.

"And you," she turns back to me, "you snooped in my closet and found my box."

"It fell when I was looking for your dress on our wedding day," I admit. "It was an accident."

"An accident that turned into you creating your own box." She dares me to deny it.

"I did." I smooth her hair back. "It seemed like a really cool idea that I wanted to be part of, but I was scared it would freak you out."

"Oh, it definitely would have."

"That's why I waited until…" I need to choose my words carefully, but McKinley beats me to it.

"Until you made me fall in love with you."

I hold back a grin, fighting the urge to just carry her back into the house and make love to her until her tears dry. "I don't know if that was exactly my intention, but yeah, I guess so."

"I don't know what y'all are talking about."

McKinley looks at me, then at Pops. "I'd like to look at my baby now," she says. "With both of you."

I lean in, planting a kiss on her lips. "We'd be honored to share this moment with you."

Letting go of McKinley's hand, Pops grabs both boxes and hands them to me. I put the one McKinley put all her notes in on the ground next to me, handing her the one containing my notes and the images of the baby from the ultrasound.

She lifts the lid, sifting around the many napkins I grabbed from all over the country when I was away at games, writing on them all the things I wanted to do with her and the baby she's carrying.

"Do you want me to open it?"

McKinley's fingers tremble at the sealed envelope.

"I'm scared," she finally admits. "I'm scared he or she will hate me for what I did to their father."

I place my hands over hers. "What you did to this baby's father was love him so much that you carried a weight that wasn't yours to carry. Keep his memory alive, Mac. Tell this baby of their father's adventures and the passion he had for the outdoors. Tell them about his failures and successes, but don't forget to tell them about their mother, who sacrificed everything just to bring them into this world happy and healthy."

A tear streaks down her face.

"Promise me, Mac. Promise me that you'll love their mother like they will."

She nods her head, and I slide open the envelope, pulling out the picture, my gaze noticing the rounded cheeks, the small fingers, and the typed words above it.

With the picture clasped between my fingers, I watch as my wife takes the image with trembling fingers, giving it one look before raising her head, her gaze locked on mine before she bursts into tears.

"It's a boy."

Chapter
TWENTY-EIGHT

McKinley

Cooper's baseball season ended in early October, with the Tides not making the playoffs.

You would think that would have my husband moping around the house in a crappy mood. But nope, he's channeled all his energy into something far worse.

Me.

"What did I do for you to hate me so much?"

Cooper rolls his eyes, the shiny new tattoo on his left forearm catching my eye for the millionth time this afternoon.

Ugh. Could he have not tattooed a mermaid or a baseball or something less captivating?

Of course not. My husband likes to be cryptic and ink *Give Me A Sign* down his arm—another phrase to keep me up at night.

What does it even mean?

Give him a sign for what?

A pitch? A life choice? His marriage to me?

Surely, that's just my hormones talking.

Ever since I fell apart in Cooper's arms and Pops grumbled that all my crying was giving him indigestion, things changed between all of us.

You could say there was less tension at home, but I don't know if tension was ever a real problem. Secrets and stubbornness were the problems in the Lexington household. Once the secret was out about Griffin and me, as well as the purge of the guilt, my heart seemed to ease up—at least on me. That's not to say all my heartbreak and guilt went up in a cloud of rainbows, though. It didn't. I still cry when I think of this baby never meeting Griffin, or when I'm grieving the lost opportunity Griffin could have had to change his thoughts on becoming a father. It's all still terribly raw and tragic.

But instead of allowing my pain to manifest into denial, my husband gathers me in his arms, handing me a stack of napkins and two pens. We write all the things we think Griffin would have wanted to do with his son once he saw him. Crazy things like climb Mt. Rushmore. But then we get realistic and scale it back, writing something like watching *Hocus Pocus* on every Halloween. The napkin promises help—even though now we have three shoeboxes instead of two.

"Stop being dramatic."

At some point, I decided to grab that flashy new tattooed arm and grip it with all of my strength. "You can't open that door."

My stupid-sexy husband's lips twitch like this is all seriously amusing—which it isn't.

"Come on, Kin. It's not that bad."

Says the man who never gets nauseated when he pitches in front of thousands of fans.

"How would you know how bad it is? Have you had a baby before?"

He takes my hand, prying it off of his as if it were as simple as peeling off a sticker. "Have *you* ever had a baby before?"

I narrow my gaze. "I'm thinking you should ask the coach if there are more practices you can do at the field. All this time together has made you snarkier—and not in a hot way."

I've rubbed off on the man, and it's not charming at all. How does he put up with me being thirty-five weeks pregnant?

"We're going in."

I throw myself in front of the door. "How 'bout this? We go home…" I slip my hand under his t-shirt, feeling his abs. "We get naked, and you can read the book to me instead."

The man that really is a pain in the ass, leans in and presses a kiss to my lips. "That sounds absolutely delightful."

Finally. Why didn't I just suggest nakedness before?

"And we'll do it just as soon as this class is over."

Whoever said marriages consisted of compromise, clearly needs to give Mr. Lexington here a recap.

"Cooper," I sigh, "be serious. I was caught up in the moment when the doctor suggested this class. I was all excited about seeing the baby in 4D, but now that the excitement has died down, I think the doctor was just trying to weasel more money out of you. I mean, really, women have been birthing babies for centuries. It can't be that complicated. More than likely, it's like having a stomach virus—my body will naturally push the baby out as soon as he's overstayed his welcome."

Cooper tries—and fails—not to laugh. "While your birthing description sounds absolutely horrible, I agree. I'm sure your body will know exactly what to do to birth this baby. But I don't think it's a terrible idea for you to learn a few techniques to improve your pain management and overall experience, do you?"

Why is he ridiculous? "Isn't that what the good insurance is for?" I pop a hand on my hip. "So they can give me the good pain meds?"

"What happens if forty women go into labor at the same time and you have to wait on those good pain meds? Wouldn't you want to know some tips to help ease your pain?"

Never marry someone who makes sense. "Maybe."

"Maybe?"

"This isn't funny, Cooper. Stop smiling. You're a celebrity, not the knocked-up, broke girl sitting in a class with a bunch of women who lick their husband's toes after hot yoga with their besties."

He chokes, and honestly, I don't move to help him. I think we can all agree a little fear is good for this man. "Why would they lick their husband's toes?" He finally manages to get out between coughs. "Is that like a new thing I've been missing out on?"

Ugh. He's insufferable. "All I'm saying is I'm not like those women in there." So I've still not mastered the whole 'married to a celebrity' thing. Especially since I'm due in about a month, and Cooper hasn't mentioned long-term arrangements or permanent rings—which is okay. I don't want him to stay with me just because he feels sorry for me. Just because I love his ridiculous ass doesn't mean he's ready to spend forever with me. Sure, we write future plans on the napkins, but I think we can all attest that Cooper Lexington will do anything to take care of the people he loves or the people his Pops loves. So I'm not getting my hopes up in case some twenty-pound, non-pregnant Barbie catches his eye, and he decides to move on. I mean, I'd hate to kill her and live a life on the run with my newborn, but it is what it is.

"Look, Coop. I might have an uppity doctor, but I'm still a fraud. Maybe we could just reschedule for a different class? Maybe one in my old neighborhood?" Hello, insecurity. It's nice to see you again.

Cooper's jaw clenches.

"You're going to chip a molar, and I'm not going to lie, I will film any crazy thing you say under anesthesia when you have it fixed." It would be the best Christmas gift for Pops.

"McKinley…"

Uh oh. His sense of humor has left for the day.

"You *are* one of 'those' women. You belong in this class just as much as they do." He grasps my chin between his fingers, tilting my head up so I can't look away when he grins. "You may not lick my toes when I get home, but you are just as uppity as they are."

This man… "Psh."

I try pulling away, but Cooper holds me still. "You belong with me. For all these women know, we fucked every day for hours until I put a baby inside you. You are my wife, and more of a woman than anyone in there."

And this is why I don't let him shower alone anymore. He needs naked hugs. Lots of them.

"Now, we're going into this damn Lamaze class, and then we'll stop for ice cream."

Seriously? "You could have just mentioned ice cream at the beginning." I press a kiss to his lips. "If you get me two scoops, I might even give you one of those fancy toe licks—" I act like I'm actually considering such a thing before adding, "Or we could just have some pregnancy sex."

Cooper shakes his head, a hint of a grin playing on his lips before he turns me in his unyielding grip and opens the door.

I go stiff in his arms, which earns me a swat to the backside, right before he guides me inside. "See?" I whisper, taking in the hardwood floors, yoga mats, and far too much crepe paper for grown-ass women. "Yoga and toe kink."

Cooper masks his laugh with a cough as a woman—who is not pregnant—approaches us. "You must be Mr. Lexington. We're so honored you could join us."

Because clearly, she's here for the eye candy and not all those helpful tips Cooper was lying about. I knew this was a bad idea. It reeks of money and stature in here—except for the crepe paper, which seems cheap and way out of character for a place like this.

"My *wife*—" Cooper tugs me out in front of him, his arms wrapping around my waist, his hands spanning flat against my belly. The traitor child inside me kicks; clearly, he's another Closer fan, "—and I are really happy to be here."

The woman, who I suppose is the instructor, glances at my finger where the black zip tie sits. *Yeah, lady, we like to slum it with plastic rings. Gasp!* "Well," she clears her throat, attempting to smile but failing, "please have some refreshments and acquaint yourself with the others. We'll start soon."

She shuffles away, and I immediately pinch Cooper's arm. "Just because I was right, you can lick my toe after this hot yoga class." Lamaze class my butt… Celebrities don't need Lamaze class. They have scheduled C-sections with added tummy tucks.

Okay, that was ugly of me. Some celebrities may need Lamaze, but not *this* class. I haven't seen this many toned bodies in one place since I went inside the gym to use their bathroom last week.

"Come on, let's see if they have pickles," Cooper suggests, knowing good and damn well I'll go along with anything if there is a possibility of pickles. Who knows, since celebrities love low-calorie snacks and pickles have zero fat, they may have some.

Cooper pulls us to the table of refreshments, where there are several husbands and wives, but no pickles.

"Do you know any of these people?" I whisper.

He leans down, whispering back, "No, I didn't pay the monthly dues, so I haven't been introduced yet."

He wouldn't let me bring my wrench for this exact reason. First, he brings me to this uppity Lamaze class, and second, he makes me mingle with women who basically have diamonds the size of stars on their fingers.

And now he's being sarcastic.

"Apart from what you might think, all rich people don't know each other," he says seriously, stopping in front of the bottled waters and handing me one.

"Well, excuse me if I thought maybe you had some teammates here." Isn't that how he found the doctor's office?

"If I did, I—"

"Lexington?" A guy several years older steps in front of Cooper, extending his hand for Cooper to shake. "I'm Caulder, I'm a client of your brother."

Cooper stands taller, like he can't be as antisocial as he wanted. "It's nice to meet you."

"Your brother brags about you every chance he gets."

I find it funny that Maverick looks so scary yet brags about his "little" brother's accomplishments. The way they all are so close sends a pang through my chest. I used to think Griffin and I were close, but after seeing Coop and his family, I'm starting to think my definition of *close* was highly lacking.

"When are you due?"

I turn to a woman who thinks it's okay to interrupt my eavesdropping on my husband and his conversation with… I forgot his name. "Christmas," I state flatly, turning back to the refreshment table.

"Oh. You should have the doctor induce or schedule a C-section a couple weeks before. I'd hate to miss Aspen that time of the year."

"Aspen? Like the place?" Surely we aren't talking about Cooper's agent here. I highly doubt she prefers to spend her Christmases with clients.

The woman scoffs, fingering her platinum necklace. "Of course. We never miss a year."

How delightful. "I think we'll manage."

She shrugs. "Just trying to warn you. With our first child, I was two weeks later than my due date. And after forty-eight hours of labor, I finally had our son—with my husband at the airport."

The tragedy she must have endured… Wait. "He left without you?"

She looks around, probably scanning for her crappy husband. "I'm going to give you a little advice. When you marry professional athletes, remember it's all about them and what they need." She glances at Cooper, and my gaze follows, noting him engaged and actually smiling at that guy whose name I can't recall. "They work six months straight; when it's the off-season, you're either there when they need you, or someone else will be."

My mouth falls open, and she flashes me a fake smile full of pity. "Get the C-section and go to Aspen. Otherwise, you won't need to worry about baby number two."

Just when I thought Ear Hair was the shittiest male on the planet. Now, this lady is saying that the majority of players are assholes too? Is that what Cooper does or did? Will he fill his bed with someone else when I'm healing for six weeks?

No, surely not. Cooper isn't like that. Except, I really don't have to worry about what happens after Christmas, now do I? Unlike that crabby lady, I have a contract, one that ends with delivery.

I should give her advice to always get a contract—it ensures you won't have a broken heart.

"All right, mommies and daddies. Finish up and have a seat on the mat."

I watch as the unhelpful lady wiggles her fingers and scurries off, pulling her husband off the phone.

"You ready for this?" Cooper's voice is a welcome distraction.

"No. I'm thinking we should get rich people diarrhea." I wave my hand, looking up at the ceiling like it's going to be written there. "Oh, what's the word?"

"Dysentery?" Cooper suggests like the amazing man that he is.

"That's it! Yes, we need to get dysentery and get out of here. Maybe we can have a quickie before Pops needs to be picked up."

Cooper turns me in his arms. "Did someone say something to you? You seem upset."

Do I? I thought I was nailing this whole 'blending in' thing. "Not really. Nothing I didn't already know anyway."

That these are not my people—not that Cooper is a ho, though, I don't really know that for sure. We've only been married for a short time.

Cooper stares at me a beat longer before sighing and pulling me to a mat in the back. "Come on, if you hate it, we can get diarrhea and go home."

I look at the man who has literally changed my life and take his hand, allowing him to pull me to one of the yoga mats.

Cooper Lexington is a good man and an even better husband. I don't know if he has the professional athlete mentality like ol' girl suggested, but I know he'll kill himself in order to take care of the people he loves.

"Oh, wow." Cooper stops abruptly at the edge of the mats, and I have to move around him to see what caused him to stop.

"Well, this has certainly taken a turn," I note, noticing all the wives getting on all fours. "You sure this is a Lamaze class? I mean, surely they aren't about to turn off the lights and just start fuck—"

Cooper turns and covers my mouth with his hand. "Just thinking of you on all fours is giving me a semi."

My gaze drops between us, and I note the bulge in his pants.

"This isn't funny," he says when I can't contain my grin.

" Mr. and Mrs. Lexington, is there something wrong?"

I look at the tense lines in my husband's face, the bulge in his pants showing no signs of disappearing. Now's my chance to get out of this nightmare. "Tell her we have the rich people's diarrhea, Coop, and I promise, I'll get on all fours at home."

He groans, no doubt warring with his morals of making me learn stupid tips or plowing me from behind. "We can't just walk out."

"Are you sure?" I ask. "Because I don't have any underwear on, and if I get on all fours, you'll be staring at my slit through these thin leggings and not be able to do anything about it for two hours."

Cooper's hands grip my arms as he leans over me.

"Mr. and Mrs. Lexington, is everything okay? Please come join the class on the floor."

I cup Cooper one more time, squeezing what was a semi that is now a full-blown stiffy. "What's it going to be, Mr. Lexington? Torture or pleasure?"

He needs no more enticing as he flips me around, ushering us to the door, his voice loud when he yells, "I'm sorry. We have dysentery!"

Chapter
TWENTY-NINE

Cooper

"**I**'m going to crack the quartz."

I turn from the stove, where I'm currently basting the turkey for tonight's Thanksgiving meal, to my wife who I have perched on the island, merely serving as the phone holder and my own personal eye candy. "You're fine."

"I'm as big as the entire island. It's no longer cute for me to sit up here like I'm only a hundred pounds."

Drying my hands, I walk over to the most beautiful woman in the world, wedging my body between her legs. "I disagree."

Lifting her (technically my) shirt, I press a kiss to her belly, the little one inside now up to four pounds per our last ultrasound. The doctor said the baby is formed to perfection. The only thing we are waiting on is for the lungs to finish maturing and the baby to put on weight. Delivery cannot come fast enough. I can't wait to hold the little one in my arms. The hiccups, the kicks, every little thing this kid does is nothing short of amazing.

"You're biased." McKinley laughs.

"That I am." It's ridiculous how hard I've fallen for this woman.

"You two better not be contaminating the food!" Pops hollers from the living room. "I don't want to have to change out of my pajamas."

He mutters something else about not wanting to eat at the Chinese buffet like we did last year when Ainsley smoked up the kitchen by burning the pumpkin pie.

"Hush, old man. Be grateful you're even being fed at this point with all the snoring you did last night." Between Mac getting up ten times to pee and Pops snoring like a steam engine, I might have pulled in four hours of sleep, which is rare anymore since McKinley has been helping out and baseball season is over.

"Cooper, I will still wash your mouth out with soap for lying. You aren't too big."

I chuckle, turning to my wife and meeting her grin. "Give me a kiss so I can get back to the food and shut him up."

She leans down, grasping my face between her hands while she presses her lips against mine. "You say the sweetest things sometimes."

She's being sarcastic which is nothing new.

"You know I love you."

Her lips purse. "Uh, huh."

I'm not disappointed she doesn't say she loves me back. Honestly, McKinley has been through a lot this year, and I want her to heal. I know she loves me, even if she isn't ready to admit it to herself.

With one last peck, I turn back to the stove and continue basting what I hope is a decent-tasting turkey when my phone rings.

"It's Aspen," McKinley notes, holding it out.

"Just put it on speaker." I need to get this turkey back in before Pops decides to risk it and not wait until it's cooked all the way through.

"Cooper?"

"Hey, Aspen," I say over my shoulder. "What's up?" I don't ask why she's calling me on Thanksgiving. My agent sleeps about as much as I do.

"Okay, so do you want the good news or the greatest news?"

I can literally feel her excitement coming through.

"Uh, surprise me." I'm more focused on opening the oven and not dropping this turkey on the floor.

"Ugh! You're just as bad as your brother about showing emotion. Come on, Coop! This is big! Pick one!"

The turkey slides to one side and I barely have time to catch it. "Asp? Can I call you back in a minute?" If I ruin dinner, I will never hear the end of it.

"Are you fucking serious right now?"

She doesn't give me time to answer, which is probably for the best since I would have said, "Yes, I'm absolutely serious."

"Never mind. You know what? No, you can't call me back. If you don't hear our exciting news, I will get my ass on a plane and come over there and shove my shoe so far up your as—"

"The good news," I blurt out, shutting the oven door.

"That's better," she says after a beat. "So, you know how I said you had interests sniffing around your free agency?"

I glance at Mac on the counter, her face expressionless. "Yeah."

"Well, my dear, you had several offers. Eight to be exact!"

The squeal at the end of Aspen's sentence makes me grin. We've talked about a trade before, but with Ainsley due any day now and having a family of my own, I told Aspen I was interested in coming home. "I'm assuming that you're happy with a couple of offers then?"

"Oh, I'm more than happy with a couple. I'm freaking ecstatic. How does forty-mil a year sound?"

I stop mid-sip. "Forty million a year? For a closing pitcher?"

Closing pitchers make decent money if they are good, but forty million a year is considered prime. You're at the top of your game for this kind of money.

"Yes!" Her scream that follows sounds as if she's bouncing up and down.

"For how many years?"

"Ah! That's the better news. It's a five-year contract!"

A five-year contract? "That's almost unheard of!"

"Right? But there was a bidding war. Your skills are needed by many teams, my friend. Those teams need a pitcher to come in and save their pitiful run leads. They need a closer, and the best one on the market right now is you."

Her words take a minute to sink in. This deal is everything I've ever wanted in life. "Wait, what team had the winning offer?"

"Eek! I thought you'd never ask. That's the greatest news! It's here!"

My stomach clenches. "Here? As in Atlanta?"

"Yes." I can hear the annoyance in her response. Aspen is excited about this deal, and I'm giving her nothing. "Here in Atlanta. You know, where your home and family are," she whines. "Cooper, why aren't you telling me how amazing I am and how you want to give me a bonus?"

Because my wife is sliding off the island, her face tight. "Mac, wait." She waves me off.

"I'm gonna check on Pops while you finish your call."

She's upset, understandably. I haven't talked to her about it, but really, I haven't thought much about it. Aspen and I broached the topic after the awful intervention. At the time, I shot down everything she suggested, but a new contract during free agency? That was happening whether I had help with Pops or not. There was no harm in being open to all offers and locations.

"How long do we have to respond to the offer?"

A very much offended scoff sounds in my ear. "Are you serious?"

I rake a hand through my hair. "I need to talk to Mac. With the baby coming and—"

"Mac will love it in Atlanta. Besides, we'll be here to help you and her with the baby. Not to mention Maverick and Ainsley miss Pops. Don't be greedy, Cooper. Share the old man and the baby. You can't keep them all to yourself. It's not fair to your family."

Her comment hits me right in the heart. I know keeping Pops away from my brother and sister-in-law isn't ideal. I know they miss him and Pops misses them too. Aspen is right, I have been selfish. All I've cared about is keeping Pops safe, keeping my partner in crime with me so that I'm not alone. I didn't consider that my brother would want to recoup lost time with Pops while he was in college. But he's never said anything.

"He didn't want you to be alone. He wanted you to be happy, and if living with Pops was the answer, then he'd never tell you otherwise. Maverick has Ainsley, and you had no one other than Pops."

I didn't realize I had wondered that last part aloud as Aspen answers me, sending a sickening feeling through me.

"Maverick will always be your big brother. He's always gonna look out for your best interests, Coop." She pauses for a second and then delivers the final blow. "Maybe it's time you return the favor and look after him some."

Fuck.

I want to scream. I want to throw this baster against the wall and put a dent in the sheetrock. It'll make me feel better. Anything to forget that I've been selfish with the only family Maverick has left too.

"We have a week to give them an answer."

Bile rises, and I know today is going to be awful. "When would I have to report to Atlanta?"

"The first of February. But, Coop?"

I inhale, bracing myself for another blow. "You should come earlier to let McKinley pick out a house and spend the holidays with your family. You know, get things settled."

I know this. I do. But things aren't as simple as Aspen thinks. "Okay. I'll let you know my answer by the end of the week."

She doesn't respond immediately, and I think that's because she's disappointed I didn't accept on the spot. It's a great offer. Six months ago before I married Mac, it would have solved all my problems. But now… not so much. "All right. But don't make me fly over there and kick your ass. Don't be stupid. This is a once in a lifetime deal."

I know. "Did you tell Maverick?"

I don't know why I care if she told my brother. Well, I guess I do. The last thing I want to do is choose between him and Mac.

Aspen sighs thick and heavy. "Maverick doesn't know yet. I'll only tell him if you make the wrong decision."

Aww. How sweet of my agent to cross lines of professionalism if I choose incorrectly. "I'll get back to you." Inhaling, I look to the ceiling. How the fuck am I supposed to deal with this? "And, Asp?"

"Yeah?"

"Happy Thanksgiving."

She sounds resigned and not nearly as happy as she was when she first called. "Happy Thanksgiving, Coop."

After agreeing to pass along Aspen's love to Pops, I head into the living room, only to find Pops watching TV alone. "Where's Mac?"

"In the bedroom. She said she was tired."

More like pissed, but it's about time Mac and I have this discussion. We might have agreed to end things at delivery, but things have changed.

"Mac?" I rap on the door once and open it, finding Mac in the bed, curled up on her side.

"Not now, Coop. I don't feel well."

Do I know she's lying? Sure. But I don't want this conversation to end in a fight.

"Alright, but we need to talk about this. I'm a professional ballplayer. Sometimes I have to go where the contracts are."

That comment has her turning over. "I haven't forgotten."

"Then talk to me. Clearly, our relationship is different now."

"Is it?"

I rear back. "What is that supposed to mean?"

McKinley sighs, pulling the blankets onto her. "I don't know, I—"

My phone rings in my hand, and I almost don't answer it, but it's Maverick, and Ainsley was due a week ago. "I gotta get this."

McKinley nods, rolling back over like the interruption was a welcome relief.

"Mav?"

My brother's breathing is frantic like he's running or having an SVT spell. "Mav? Everything okay?"

"Something's wrong with the baby."

Chapter
THIRTY

Cooper

'm throwing clothes in a bag while Pops secures us airline tickets
home to Georgia.

"Cooper?"

I shove another pair of pants in my suitcase, never looking up.
"Are you packed?" I don't have time to finish the contract discussion
with McKinley. My brother needs me.

"Um, no."

I pause, finally looking up and noticing McKinley's red-ringed
eyes. "Why not?"

McKinley swallows, picking up a shirt off the bed and folding it.
"I think you and Pops need to go without me this time."

"No—"

She holds up her hand. "I can't fly this far along."

Oh. Fuck. "Is that a thing?" How did I not know that?

Mac laughs. "Yes, it's a thing."

My face must show my stress since Mac comes around the bed
and puts her arms around me. "I'll be fine. Besides, someone has to
eat all this food you cooked."

"Maybe we could rent a car?" I suggest.

"Cooper, no. Your bother needs his family as soon as you can get there. I refuse to delay you getting to him and Ainsley."

My chest tightens at the thought of Mav driving himself crazy with worry alone in a waiting room.

"Got the tickets, Coop! Let's go!" Pops appears in the doorway.

"Where's your bag?"

Pops looks at me weirdly. "I told you I would get the tickets. What have you been doing in here this whole time?" He looks at my open suitcase. "Packing a month's worth of clothes?"

Mac laughs. "Come on, old man. I'll get you a bag." She plants a kiss on my cheek, and if I'd known it would be the last one I'd receive from her, I would have made it last.

Pops and I arrived at the hospital just in time to see my brother emerge from the nursery in blue scrubs. "Mom and baby are doing great," he tells us, his forehead damp with sweat.

We don't even congratulate him. "How are you?" Pops asks, examining his oldest grandson with a scrutinizing gaze.

Mav shrugs. "I kept it together." He doesn't deny he had an episode.

My brother suffers from a heart condition known as supraventricular tachycardia which, more often than not, is brought on by stress.

Pops grabs Maverick's arm, putting two fingers on his wrist.

"Pops," Mav argues, just as a big body barrels out of the nursery, pointing at Mav.

"You," the guy demands, pointing at an empty chair in the waiting room, "come here."

Maverick groans. "I already told you I'm fine, Boss. Besides, the old man already crawled up my ass, I don't have room for two."

Pops grunts and I realize, "Boss," is Maverick's father-in-law. It's been a while since I've seen him. "He looks a lot bigger than I remember," I tell Mav as Pops drops his wrist, seemingly accepting Mav's pulse rate.

"Lexington, you must have thought I fucking asked you."

I smother a laugh when my scary older brother's head drops and his shoulders slump as he drags himself over to his father-in-law and sits like the good little boy he is. "Don't laugh at him," Pops scolds, pulling us over as Maverick fills us in on what happened with Ainsley and the baby.

"The doctor said it was a placental abruption. She started bleeding and—"

"We'll talk about it later," Boss interrupts, as Mav begins to break out into a cold sweat. "You hear me? Everything is okay. Ainsley and the baby are fine."

I don't know what happened in the delivery room or what my brother went through, but I do know whatever it was, has Boss keeping a protective hold on my brother—a hold that makes me and Pops feel like terrible family members.

"Look who wanted to check on her daddy?" Ainsley's mom emerges from down the hall, a pink bundle wrapped in her arms.

I look at Pops. "You're a great-grandfather now. Does that make you feel ancient?"

Pops's eyes never leave the little girl who is sucking on a pacifier that takes up the majority of her face. "It makes me feel like smacking my grandchild with the big mouth."

Chuckling, I lead Pops to the chair next to Maverick as Ainsley's mom lowers the baby into my brother's arms. "Congratulations, Mav, she's beautiful."

Maverick nods, his eyes taking on a glassy appearance.

"I'm going to check on Ains. Make sure he breathes," Boss says, clapping me on my shoulder as he passes.

"Will do."

When Ainsley's parents have disappeared, I take the chair on the other side of Maverick, both me and Pops hovering over the little girl.

"You gonna tell us her name, son?"

After a moment, my brother raises his head, tears welling in his eyes as he says, "Her name is Vienna."

Pops sucks in a breath. "You named her after your mother."

After Pops and I checked on Ainsley, who was more worried about Maverick than herself, we headed to Maverick's house and commandeered the guest rooms with Pops immediately opting for a nap and me a phone call to my wife.

"I'm sorry our first Thanksgiving was a shitshow."

McKinley sounds tired. "It's fine. I haven't had a Thanksgiving in two years, so I didn't miss it."

Her nonchalant tone stuns me. "Are you okay? Is something wrong?" Obviously, we parted on less than ideal circumstances with talks of relocating back to Georgia. And after being with Maverick, feeling like the shittiest brother in the universe, I'm even more inclined to take Atlanta's deal. But I can't do that if Mac won't come with me.

"I'm fine, just tired. How's Pops? Was he excited about seeing his first great-grandchild?" Her voice breaks on the last word.

"He's happy to see Mav and boss him around," I tell her honestly. At least she knows where I get the bossiness. "But he's probably more excited that Mav named his daughter after our mother—Pops's daughter."

"Oh, wow. What an honor. I'm guessing you guys are going to stay for a while, huh? Help with the baby and all that?"

My chest tightens, and for some reason, a bad feeling settles in the pit of my stomach. "I suppose Pops will want to, but I had planned on coming home. I need to start painting before the nursery furniture is delivered."

It took nearly the entire pregnancy to convince Mac to let me buy furniture for the nursery. She was insistent she had the money and only needed a few things since the baby will only, "eat, sleep, and poop," for a while.

"Oh. Well, I don't think we need to worry about painting. The tan color already in the guest room is fine."

"I don't mind painting the room, Mac. It's not like I have a lot going on right now." Being the off-season, I don't have daily practices with the team.

"I know, but…" she pauses, dragging in a breath, "I don't want to move to Atlanta, Cooper. My home is here in Nevada with… well, it's just here. I want to raise my baby here."

Her baby, not ours.

"Okay, no big deal. I have other offers—none in Nevada though."

"That's not what I'm saying. Look, I'm tired, and I'm sure you are too. Let's both get some rest and talk about it tomorrow," she suggests.

I rake my hands through my hair. No way will I be getting any sleep tonight. "Sure. Sleep well."

She mumbles out a quiet, "You too," before hanging up, leaving me feeling like life just took a shit on the past six months of my marriage.

Unlike home, Maverick's kitchen feels empty.

"What do you need?"

I whip around from the cabinet and face my brother. "Why aren't you at the hospital?"

Maverick groans, and I notice the shadows under his eyes. "My wife says I'm too stressed being at the hospital, so she and my mother-in-law sent me home for some 'rest.'" He rolls his eyes, pulling out a container of coffee grounds. "I'm forbidden to come back until morning." Scoffing, he measures out a few scoops. "Like I'm going to sleep here when my wife and daughter nearly died not even twenty-four hours ago."

I take a seat at the kitchen table. Clearly, he's making enough coffee for both of us. "Where's your watch?"

His eyebrow's arch. "Are you trying to mom me, baby brother?"

"No." I chuckle. "I'm just asking a question." My brother never goes without his watch.

"It's in my bag. I had to take it off. Ainsley keeps checking the data."

Which means the "data," aka his heart rhythm, is not good. And the last thing he wants is his wife knowing that tidbit of information and stressing even more. "Wives can be a little…" I search for the word.

"Bit of a pain in the ass?" Maverick supplies with a grin.

"Well, I was going to say nosy, but I think your term fits better tonight."

Maverick hits a button on the coffee pot and pulls out a chair. "What's going on, Cooper? Why are you up and not asleep? You've had a long day. Everything okay at home?" He arches a brow like he already knows things are not okay at home, which is crazy, because for all Maverick knows, my shotgun wedding to Mac was an act of wild love. Apart from a congratulations and an 'I hope you know what you're doing' conversation after the nuptials, Mav and I haven't discussed anything else about my marriage with McKinley—which I appreciated.

"Yes." I sigh, rubbing at the tense muscles in the back of my neck. "No? I don't know, man. Sometimes I think I understand women, and other times, I feel like I'm trying to remember a password I didn't create."

Maverick chuckles. "Are you saying you're now locked out for trying too many times?"

I shake my head. Trying too many times is not the problem. "Atlanta offered me a contract," I tell him. "But I don't think McKinley wants to move."

Thoughtful, Maverick nods a few times as he gathers his thoughts. "As your older brother, I would love to see you and Pops more often, but I'll understand if you don't take the deal. You're a married man now and have to do what's best for your family."

It's a sweet sentiment. But what my brother doesn't know is that said marriage is set to end in three short weeks.

McKinley

A week has passed since Pops and Cooper left for Atlanta, which should have left me with a lot of quiet time, but that hasn't been the case. Instead of taking time to digest the whole moving and contract thing, Cooper has kept my phone and mind busy with tons of pictures of him and baby Vienna. He even sent some of Pops with a big silly grin on his face as he awkwardly cradled the newborn to his chest.

I miss them terribly. So much that I haven't been able to sleep without watching the news for hours on end after stuffing pillows under the covers, so it feels like I'm not alone in the bed.

When did I become a person who didn't enjoy a whole bed to herself?

Apparently, when I got used to sleeping next to Cooper and his delicious body heat.

Why did he have to be a free agent this year? Why not next year? We'll have been together longer and things won't be so complicated. I won't need him as much then. Is it unreasonable that I'm scared Cooper will only stick around until his hero complex wears off?

Taking a look around the packed living room, I note all the boxes that Cooper just *had* to order. I told him we only needed a bassinet for the baby, but he insisted on a full nursery. He also insisted he put it together instead of paying extra—which I'll admit, my cheap heart loved.

But now when I look at the boxes, all I feel is guilt.

Guilt that Cooper has called dozens of times to check on me, and has gone above and beyond what's sane and had dinner delivered to me every evening.

I don't deserve him.

Not like Maverick and Ainsley deserve each other. They deserve to have Pops and Cooper cooing and cuddling their baby until they throw them out for overstaying their welcome. They don't deserve Cooper's attention divided between me and them.

My phone dings, and it's the second time in the past five minutes.

All the flights are delayed due to the ice storm. I might rent a car.

It's Cooper—again—talking nonsense. No matter how much I tell this stubborn ass that there is no reason for him to come home now, he doesn't listen, always giving me ridiculous excuses like he's scared I'll trip or Pops thinks he left on the iron. Just bullshit for him to have an excuse to come home and corner me alone, so we have to talk about the future and the possibility of moving.

My fingers fly over the keyboard as I insist, once again, that he wait out the storm and come later in the week, but before I can hit send, a knock comes at the door. With my belly being downright enormous, it takes me a few tries to get up.

"I'm coming! You don't have to keep banging. I hear you!"

If Cooper called in a welfare check, I'm going to beat his ass like it's never been beaten before. He's crossing the line now.

I wrench open the door. "Tell him I'm fin—"

My mouth snaps closed as I narrow my eyes at the asshole in front of me. "How did you find me?"

Chris, Griffin's real brother, and my foster brother, flashes me a smile that is more like a sneer. "Believe it or not, my wife was reading some trashy tabloid and recognized you." He huffs. "I should have known you'd move on and find another sucker to take care of you."

If I wasn't scared I'd lose my balance, I'd kick him straight in the balls. Instead, I step back and start to shut the door. "Goodbye—"

He slaps his palm against the door. "As much as I'd like to say I came to see you, I didn't."

Always the sweetheart. "So what do you want?"

I should have known Chris seeking me out would not be good, especially when he grins, the lines around his mouth looking very Grinch-like. "I came to give you this." He hands me an envelope that has unused postage still on the front. "I found it while I was cleaning out Griffin's house—we close next week—thought you should read it."

The envelope looks simple enough, but it's the address that has me asking, "Who's Sarah?"

"No one now—thanks to you." With that, Chris steps back, offering me a glare that translates how much he hates me. "I hope your new husband realizes what a monster he married."

"I'm not a monster." My voice cracks as I fight back the tears welling in my eyes.

Chris arches his brow. "Oh yeah? Let's ask Griffin what he thinks? Oh, wait—we can't because you killed him. You destroy, Mac. You always have. Griffin and I were close until you came to live with Brenda. You tore our family apart—you took everything from me."

"I… I'm so—"

"You're not sorry. You always get what you want—no matter who's in your way. You don't deserve this life." He steps back and gives the front of the house a once-over. "You don't deserve a new life when you ended his."

I can't even wait until he pulls out of the driveway before sliding down the doorframe and pulling out the letter, tears streaming down my face, hot and angry.

Dear Sarah,

You finally got tired of waiting for me and disconnected your phone. I don't blame you—I deserve to lose you. After all, I promised when I got Mac settled, I'd come back for you, and I didn't. Just know I wanted to do it all with you—the sleeping under the stars, bathing in the rivers, living off the land with nothing but each other to fill the time. I wanted it all with you.

But things at home have changed.

I made a mistake.

I have no other excuse than that I missed you so bad it killed me each day when I was away, and I fucked up, Sarah. Really bad. McKinley is pregnant, and no matter how much I regret allowing it to happen, I have to do the right thing. I have to be the father mine never was.

I'm so sorry, Sarah. If I could go back in time... well, I still would have come home. McKinley needed me, but I should have let you come along and meet her. I should have put you first, and I'm sorry.

Maybe in another life, we'll find each other again.

All my love,
Griffin

The letter is dated the night he died. He was going to be a father and give up his love all because I acted irresponsibly and sought his comfort when I should have just handled things on my own.

If I would have known Griffin was in love, and had his own family, I would have never asked him to come home. I didn't need Griffin to help me with Brenda. I could have done it. Eventually, I would have gotten better—found a job and a place to live. I didn't have to call him to come home.

Big, fat tears drip down my cheeks as the guilt of Griffin's death rises up to choke me. Chris is right; I destroyed our family. Instead of just handling my problems, I let them bleed out and become my entire family's problems.

Griffin was happy. He had a life. A girlfriend that he loved. And I made him give it all up because I needed a what? A hug? Someone to hold me through the tears? Someone to tell me it was going to be okay?

But it wasn't okay.

Griffin wasn't okay.

Chris wasn't okay.

They had escaped their past, and I dragged them back and ruined all of their progress.

I am a monster.

But I don't have to be. I can stop the bleeding. I can protect the ones I love. Pops and Cooper don't have to go down with my sinking ship.

With tears in my eyes, I unlock my phone and see several texts from Cooper.

Pops wants to stay with Maverick a little longer. I'm going to rent a car and come home.

He's coming home to make sure I'm okay—which clearly, I'm not. Cooper can't see me like this. He'll stay for me just like Griffin did.

I made this mess, and whether or not it crushes my entire soul, I'm going to fix it.

Because Cooper deserves a wife who isn't selfish. One whose belly is stretched with *his* child. He deserves someone to save him.

I didn't save Griffin.

But I can save Cooper.

He asked for a sign, and while my fingers tremble across the screen, I stay strong and give him one, texting him the greatest gift I can offer—a way out.

I want a divorce.

Chapter
THIRTY-TWO

McKinley

I moved out of Cooper's house and back into my old apartment that smells like feet and stale crackers.

It's not like I wanted to, but Cooper left me no choice when the neighbor from across the street came over and handed me a napkin with a look of pity in his eyes. "Do you need anything?" he had asked me. I shook my head and took the napkin.

"I'm sorry my husband thinks everyone is at his beck and call," I'd returned, shutting the door gently in his face.

Honestly, I figured Cooper would resort to such measures after he sent about forty-five texts that I didn't answer, choosing to turn my phone off, so I wouldn't be tempted to answer one of the one hundred and twenty calls from him and the sixty-two from Pops. Hell, the man even had Aspen and Maverick calling me. My poor phone was overheating, and my heart was breaking.

I couldn't take any more.

So I turned it off.

And I cried.

And I cried more.

I cried so much I went through two shirts before just getting into the shower and sobbing until I was too tired to even move. But then the neighbor showed up with the napkin that read:

You better have your wrench handy because I'm coming for you.

It's a threat that says I can try to fight him off, but he'll just keep coming. Like with everything else in his life, Cooper Lexington is a relentless mofo when he wants something.

So I had to hide.

And while my apartment isn't much of a secret, it was the best I could do being thirty-seven weeks pregnant and barely fitting behind Lu's steering wheel. All I took with me is what I brought to the marriage (as agreed upon in the hastily written prenup), which was nothing except Psalms (who I could not bear to uproot from his happy place), Lu, and my shoebox. Well, I take that back. I took the shoebox Cooper made for me as well. I figured he wouldn't miss it after the divorce.

Oh, and I took the bassinet too (What was Cooper going to do with it?) It was ridiculously heavy, but the neighbor, as stalkery as he was, offered to load it into Lu. Which was fantastic at the time but sucky when I realized he wouldn't be able to unload it.

But nevertheless, I managed, opening the box in the bed of Lu's truck and separately taking each piece inside until I had a mound of parts in the center of the living room, no closer to having it put together than I was solving world hunger.

It just can't be done. At least by me. Whoever said you could do anything with instructions and YouTube was sadly mistaken because no matter how many times I rewatch and reread, I still can't manage to get this damn thing to stand up without falling.

Maybe my baby won't mind sleeping in the bassinet's box? It's big enough, I think.

Fine. I'm not going to allow my baby to sleep in a box. I'll finish putting it together, eventually. Like maybe when the contractions hit. That way I can occupy my hands and scream out F-bombs for both.

I stand, taking a moment to stretch as I eye the monstrosity, which should be a bassinet, in front of me. One wheel is attached to a bent pole that I may have taken the wrench to a few minutes ago.

It'll be fine. Maybe all Cooper's timely rent payments will have softened the landlord, and he'll take pity on me.

I think of the hateful old man that isn't cute like Pops.

Nah. He won't help, but that's okay. I said I was going to take care of myself, and I will.

Starting tomorrow.

Lumbering to my bedroom, I fall back onto the mattress, since my stomach muscles are as good as dead (not that they were spectacular before the pregnancy) and hit my hand on the edge of the box.

"Oww." I slip the offended finger into my mouth and eye the two shoeboxes sitting on my pillows where I may or may not have been sleeping with them last night.

It's been a rough twenty-four hours since moving out and telling Cooper I wanted a divorce. The little guy kicked me all night like, he too, was pissed off we left the comfort of Cooper's bed and amazing air conditioning.

"It's gonna be okay." I rub my belly, my eyes never leaving the shoebox. "I can be your mommy and your daddy. I might have to YouTube a few things or read that damn book all the way through, but I'll make sure you grow up healthy, happy, and somewhat normal, considering your mama is a psycho."

The kid doesn't answer me with kicks like he does when he hears Cooper's voice, which is okay because I think Cooper's voice is much sexier than mine too. I start getting antsy when I hear it, but for entirely different reasons.

Reasons that I don't need to think about right now because I told him I wanted a divorce, and I meant it. Cooper can come here and threaten me, but I'm still going to sign those divorce papers because Pops deserves to be in Atlanta with both his grandsons and his new great-granddaughter.

Besides, the reason Cooper hired me in the first place was to help him with Pops during away games. With him moving to Atlanta, closer to Maverick and Aspen, he'll have that. He doesn't need me anymore. And technically, once I have this baby, I won't need his celebrity insurance or this shoebox full of traditions I'll never get to do with Coop and his bossy self.

Eyeing the shoebox, I slide it to me and flick off the lid with my fingers, rooting around in the sea of napkins until my hand hits something hard. What the—? Rolling over, I pull myself into a seated position and dump the box, scattering the dozens and dozens of napkins until I find it.

A thumb drive with the Tides' logo taped to a napkin. Carefully, I unfold it and read.

And read it again. And again. Until the tears start flowing. "Fuck you, old man!" I shout into my bedroom, clutching the napkin with two stick-figure men and one woman holding a tiny stick-figure baby in her arms. Down below, it reads:

Pops, Mac, Baby Macaroni, and Coop
Est. On a dreary night in August, thanks to Lu

The words burn the back of my throat. Thanks to Lu breaking down that night, Pops, Cooper, and I all became family—at least for a short time. That old man and his charm…

I flip the thumb drive over in my hand, taking note of the beautiful navy color and… words written super small down the back.

Family isn't born, it's created.

The floodgates to my tear ducts break, and I can't get to Brenda's old laptop fast enough, shoving the device in and closing all the notifications for updates as I wait for it to load, and then…

"No."

Hot and angry tears fall as the small grainy video from Pops's deer cam comes on screen. My belly is the size of a small walrus as I sleep against Cooper's chest, drooling as if I'm dreaming of pickle ice cream. Cooper isn't asleep, though he should have his ass whooped for being up at two in the morning. But that's not what I'm angry about. The tears streaking down my face are because my Closer reaches out and grabs a book *and* his glasses. His glasses!

Dammit if he doesn't look sexier than Clark Kent could ever

dream of being, as he sets a children's book on top of my belly and begins to read to our—I mean, my baby.

"Ben knew he wasn't like the other kids," he read aloud. "He didn't know how to hold the bat or throw the ball, but he was willing to try—because he would never hear the crack of the bat or the thud of the ball when he caught it for the first time in his worn glove. Ben knew that in order to play, he had to be brave enough to fail."

Stupid, stupid tears drip down my chin as I watch my husband read, rubbing my belly as tiny, unborn feet kicked against my skin, making the book go up and down with the motion. My little baby responded to Cooper's voice. He loves Cooper and Cooper loves him.

And I took them away from each other.

Not intentionally, no. I would never be that cruel, but yet… that's exactly what I'm being, as I watch the smile on my husband's face when he spans his big palm over the tiny kicks. "You hear me in there, buddy?"

Oh, gosh. He's talking to the baby.

"Daddy can't wait to meet you."

I smother a cry as the baby inside me kicks.

The baby loves Cooper, and my husband, well, I think he fell in love with this baby before he fell in love with me. Cooper may not be this child's biological father, but that doesn't mean he loves him any less than one would.

Just like Brenda.

She might not have carried me in her womb, but that didn't mean she didn't love me like a daughter. Am I really going to take the choice away from Cooper? From this little one inside me? Griffin would want his child to grow up with a father, even if that father wasn't him.

I think Griffin would be happy I found a good man that will love and do anything for his child. And if I learned anything through this whole ordeal, it's that we can't choose who gives us life, but we can choose who to spend that life with.

And I choose to spend it with a man who makes me crazy—crazy in love with his bossy ass. The little one cramped inside me? Well, he chooses Cooper too—this video proves it.

Who cares if I'm a mess? Cooper is bossy and will gladly tell me how to fix it. I just need to get to him before he changes his mind and lets me go for good.

Chapter
THIRTY-THREE

Cooper

"Have you ever wanted to kill Ainsley? Like, blister her ass until she can't walk?"

My brother arches a brow. "All the time."

"So it never gets any better over the years?"

"Afraid not."

Great. "What am I supposed to do now?"

"Just take my car. I'll call in a favor for a rental."

After we came up empty with flights to Nevada, I tried rental car companies, and guess what? They were out too. Between the holidays and the storm, they didn't have one car I could rent to get back to my pain-in-the-ass wife and tell her where she can shove her divorce.

"Sure you'll be able to get another?" I don't want to leave Maverick with only one car with Ainsley, the baby, and Pops.

"Yeah. If I need something, Boss will loan me his." Oh. I forgot about his father-in-law.

"All right, if—" My phone buzzes mid-sentence. "It's Mac," I tell him.

"Maybe she came to her senses?"

I look at the phone. How many times did I call her? "Doubtful." But since I'm a sucker for all things McKinley Lexington, I answer anyway and am immediately greeted with yelling.

"The bassinet is fucked, and it's all your fault."

Mac's voice is loud and nasally. "Are you crying? What's going on? Are you okay?"

"Of course I'm crying, Cooper! And don't think for one minute I won't take it out on you and that sneaky old man when I get there."

What? "I need a minute," I mutter to Maverick, who waves me off. I'm sure he's been in this position before.

"What do you mean when you get here?" This woman is going to make me prematurely gray. "Where are you, McKinley?"

She makes this exasperated noise. "Technically, I'm in Arkansas."

"Arkansas!" I nearly explode. "In Lu?"

"What else am I supposed to drive? I'm too pregnant to fly, which I think is bullshit."

Heart racing, I start looking for Maverick's keys. Where did he put them?

"Cooper? You there?"

I can feel my jaw clench, barely able to grit out the words, "When I get to you…"

"You won't do a damn thing but tell me you're sorry for making me cry and drive without air conditioning when I'm cooking from the inside out."

"Maverick!" I can't form more words—let alone wonder why she's so hot when there's literally ice on the roads.

"You can't stop me from coming to Georgia," she says, sniffling. "If you refuse to divorce me, then we're still married, and I'm coming home to kick my husband's ass."

"Mac," I pace around Maverick's office, "pull into the next hotel you see. I'll come to you, and we can talk."

"No. My arms—just like my legs—work just fine. I'm coming home, Cooper Lexington, and you have no one to blame but yourself. You had your chance to divorce me, you didn't."

"I don't want to divorce you!" I'm losing my cool, and I don't know why. It's not like I haven't tried to tell her this or send her a hundred texts and voicemails, trying to convince her. "You were the one who wouldn't listen!"

I can hear the smile in her words. "Honestly, Cooper. You knew what you signed up for. I'm stubborn, you knew this."

"This is serious, McKinley."

"And I'm seriously coming home. Tell any woman there I have a wrench, and I'm not scared to use it—after I pee though because, damn, this heavy-ass kid is sitting on my bladder."

I love her, and yet, if I could reach through the phone, I would strangle her. "I would have come to you."

"I wanted to see you and the new baby. I wanted to spend time with my family. Not tomorrow. Today."

"You're also due in a few weeks!" I fell in love with a crazy person.

"You of all people heard the doctor say that first-time mothers are usually late. Besides, last checkup, I was still pregnant as ever with no baby movement. He is happy all wadded up in there."

I groan. "Please let me pick you up."

"No. I have something to tell you, Mr. Lexington, and for once, you aren't coming to my rescue."

I take a seat in a chair, my head in my hands as my brother pokes his head in. "You all right?"

"No."

"You're fine, Cooper. Tell Maverick to enjoy his family."

I pull my head up and level my brother with a look. "My wife, due at anytime, is on her way here in a truck that should be scrapped for parts."

Maverick cringes. "Let me know if you need me." At least he understands. Apparently, the Lexington brothers enjoy crazy women.

"Thanks."

Maverick leaves, and I focus on my wife. "What did you need to tell me?" Why am I'm entertaining her?

"I love you." There's no hesitation in her voice as she says the words clearly. "I loved you when you almost hit me with your car and never apologized."

I grunt out a laugh.

"I like my men unapologetic. And you, Cooper Lexington, never apologized for stealing my heart or my baby. The kid loves you more than me, and he hasn't even taken his first breath yet."

My heart bangs against my ribs as I think of the baby I slept with every night, his kicks against my back like my mini alarm clock.

"He loves you, Mac. You're his mother—the one who has made all the sacrifices to bring him into this world."

Sniffles come through the phone. "You never told me you read to him."

"It never came up."

"Cooper."

"McKinley."

And we're back to being us.

"I love you," I tell her seriously. "And I love anything that is part of *you*."

"See?" Her voice cracks. "This is why I'm in the car, coming to hit you and then hug you."

"Because I love everything about you?" I fight off a smile.

"Yes. I don't know why you love me or why you find my beach-ball stomach sexy, but I'm tired, Cooper. I'm tired of fouling off pitches. I'm ready to strike out now."

Her use of baseball terms stirs my dick.

"I'm tired of fighting you."

"Thank fuck."

She laughs, and I'm sure my comment is inappropriate, but dammit. "Seriously, I haven't been able to sleep, all I do is worry about you and the baby."

"Psh. Of course, you haven't, hardhead. When I get there, you can have sex with me, that way you can nap, and I can encourage this freeloader to come on out so you can hold him some too."

"I think I can handle that." I've missed this—the banter, her smile, her pussy.

"Good, but I'll need a shower first because I'm disgustingly sweaty."

I shake my head. McKinley might like her men unapologetic, but I like my women the same.

"If you pulled over, you could shower at a hotel while you wait on me to dirty you up again."

Her laugh is genuine. It's been over a week since I've heard it. "Cute but—oh no. No, no, no."

"What?" I'm on my feet, already heading toward the family room looking for Maverick. I should have left the minute I knew she was on the road.

"Lu… uh…" She almost sounds embarrassed. Almost.

"Tell me what's happening."

"Calm your tits, Lexington. Lu just needs a breather. At least she managed to get us over to the emergency lane this time."

"This isn't funny, McKinley." Grabbing a set of keys off the counter, I don't bother telling anyone where I'm going. All I can think is that I won't be able to get to McKinley for hours, no matter if I manage to catch a flight or drive.

"Where are you going?" I'm jerked to a stop by a hand on my shoulder.

"McKinley is broken down somewhere in Arkansas. I'm going to get her."

"I'm fine," I hear her hollering through the phone to Maverick, who still hasn't let go of my shoulder.

"You won't make it today," my brother notes, unhelpfully.

"I can if I don't stop." Shrugging off Maverick, I meet Pops's eyes across the room. "I'm going to get our girl."

"About fucking time." He stands. "I'll go with you."

"No, I can't stop ninety-five times for you to pee."

"Meh," he mutters but sits back down. He knows he pees more than a toddler. "Bring back dessert then. The pecan pie is a little…"

I look at my brother and grin. "Burnt?" Ainsley, bless her heart, is not a baker.

Maverick rolls his eyes. "I made the pie, fuck you very much."

"Then it was terrible," Pops adds. "At least Ainsley can claim exhaustion from dealing with your baby. You have no excuse."

Pops is just kidding. A little.

"Behave," I tell the old man. "I'll be back soon."

"Be careful."

I nod, watching as Pops's face lightens with knowing I'm bringing his girl back to him. He's been extra ornery since Mac has been avoiding us. Even with Ainsley and the new baby, he hasn't been as sarcastic as he is when he has his bestie.

"Coop?" McKinley's voice is off. "You should probably hurry."

"What? What happened?" I'm already pushing toward the front door, my brother on my heels.

"I'm driving," he barks, and I don't argue. Whatever gets me in a car the fastest.

"Mac!" I lose it when she doesn't answer me. "What's going on?"

Her next words are my greatest fear—I'm not going to make it in time. "My water broke."

Chapter
THIRTY-FOUR

Cooper

"**W**hat do you mean your water broke?"

Hysteria is not a good look on anyone, let alone someone who is supposed to come into stressful situations and save them. But that's the thing, I can't help McKinley from this far away.

"I mean, never mind. It was a false alarm. Everything is fine. Just stay there. Lu will catch her breath, and we'll be back on the road in no time."

Maverick swerves onto the highway, breaking several posted speed limits. "You're lying." I know her tones of voice now. She might have once been able to convince me she was fine, but I've been with her through highs and lows for the past six months. I know when my wife is scared.

"Mac? Baby? Listen to me—"

"No, no, no. You listen to me," she starts all bossily, her voice quaking through the phone. "I will not have this baby alone. I've been alone all my life, and I refuse to go through this without my husband."

My chest tightens, and I have to look out the window to find a focus. "You're not alone," I tell her. "I'm coming, but you can't wait on me."

"Yes, I can—I am waiting on you. Labor takes hours. You'll make it."

If my brother wasn't next to me, I would yell, but that would be counterproductive as Mac seems set on waiting, and Maverick doesn't know that the baby isn't mine. Discussing this in front of him will only blow our story. I promised I wouldn't go back on my word, and I won't. Mac's secret will die with me. Besides, that baby inside her *is* mine, no matter whose DNA it carries.

After a few deep breaths, I lean my head against the window, preparing for a long debate.

"Don't breathe all bossy like that, Cooper. I don't even want to hear it."

Breathe bossy? How does one breathe bossy?

"This baby is coming out of my body, and he—like you—will learn that we wait for Mommy to be ready. And I'm not ready, Coop." The spunk in her words wane. "I'm not. I thought I was, but I'm not. I'm so not ready to have a baby. I couldn't even put the bassinet together. I fucked it all up."

Seriously? She's basing her parent-readiness on baby furniture? "I'll handle the bassinet."

Her breathing is heavy, and she goes quiet for a second. "Mac? You okay?"

"No." She starts crying, the pain in her voice ripping apart my insides. "These contractions hurt. It's so not like that Lamaze lady said. Breathing is not fucking helping."

Shit.

I look at my brother and put my phone on mute. "Mac's having contractions."

My brother, the no-bullshitter looks at me, his mouth firm. "Call her an ambulance before she has the baby on the side of the road."

He's right. *He is*, but he didn't hear the fear in her voice. "Cooper?"

I take the phone off mute. "I'm here. Is it over?"

"I think so." She sounds so weak, so vulnerable. I can't bear to tell her. So I do what husbands are supposed to do for their wives—I protect her, even if it's without her consent. "Where are you, baby? Can you drop me a pin, so I can put it in my GPS?"

With a teary, "Yes," she sends me her location, and I immediately forward it to Maverick and put the phone on mute.

"Send an ambulance to that location."

If she hates me, she hates me, but there is no way I am risking her and the baby's safety because she's stubborn.

Another contraction hits Mac, and I hear her breathing through it when she shouts, "I don't hear you breathing, Cooper!" It makes me smile. I may not have been the one to fill her body with a baby, but I'll happily pick up the job of being yelled at to get it out.

"Hee, hee, hee, hoo," we chant together, giving Maverick time to call an ambulance, keeping his voice low so Mac doesn't hear and try to do something stupid like walk somewhere else.

"That one hurt a little worse," she finally says, regaining her snark. "But they are far enough apart that it'll be fine. At least that's what that stupid book you made me read said."

The asshole rears its ugly head. "They don't sound far apart to me."

"Well, I didn't ask for your—or your watch's—opinion on the matter."

I grit my teeth, knowing she's scared and in pain. "Please let me call someone for you." I don't want to surprise her and piss her off when she's finally speaking to me again. If she would just consent for an ambulance, it would save me a grovel session later.

"No, you'll be here in like eight or so hours. I'll be fine."

And this is why I yell. She makes absolutely no sense, and she knows it.

"Mac." I sigh, not knowing how else to negotiate with her. "This is serious."

She sucks in a breath. "Don't you think I know that? I—"

I can hear sirens.

"Please tell me you didn't call them." She's crying, and I feel like such an asshole that I can't be there to hold her.

"I didn't." Exhaling, I add, before she can say anything, "But Maverick did."

"Why?" She's sobbing, her breath catching as another contraction hits her.

"Because I love you, and I vowed to always look out for you and the baby—even if it pisses you off."

"Well." She blows out a breath, and I find myself doing the same. "I." Another breath. "Am."

"I know you're mad, but I couldn't live with myself if something happened to you."

"I don't want to have this baby in a strange hospital… alone."

The sirens are closer, and I try lightening the situation with a joke. "But at least we have that good insurance. You shouldn't have to pay anything regardless of what hospital."

I do, actually, have co-insurance, but she'll never know that. For all she knows, I have no copays or deductibles. I'll take care of any expenses for her and the baby.

"Don't make jokes. This is serious. I'm about to have this baby, without our uppity doctor." She's serious.

"I'm sure I can call ahead and ask for the uppity-est doctor they have on staff," I tease.

A sob bursts through the phone. "I want you to come save me now."

Something in my chest tightens to the point I can't take a breath.

"I know I said I didn't ever want or need your help, but I do. Having you beside me this whole pregnancy made everything a lot less scary because I knew you would protect me, even if I didn't want you to—because that's what you do, right? Save games and people?"

My throat clogs with emotion, and it takes me a second to work through it. "I'm coming, baby, but I won't make it to you in time. But you're strong. You carry a wrench, remember?"

She lets out a half-hearted laugh.

"You're so strong… I wish I could take credit for saving you, but I have never saved you, Mrs. Lexington. I've just had a front-row seat this whole time, watching as you saved yourself."

"Stop lying, Cooper! It's not sexy."

I'd laugh if she weren't serious.

"I've failed at everything. I couldn't even look at the ultrasound pictures! What if I can't look at the baby? What if I can't soothe his crying?"

Her own crying increases before the sirens stop. "Oh, God. They're here."

"You're okay. Take your wrench and go with them. I promise, I'm coming."

"Can I call you?" She sounds so defeated, so alone that I want to stomp on Maverick's foot and make him go faster.

"You'll be sorry if you don't."

That gets a laugh out of her. "You always threaten me with that, yet I've never seen you follow through."

"I've been keeping a tally. I figured the baby didn't need to suffer with you."

"So you're saying when I've delivered…"

I grin. "You'll pay your dues."

I hear the emergency crew talking to her. "Tell your husband to meet us at Baptist Health."

A choked cry is all she manages before I add, "I'll be there. Call me when you get settled."

She doesn't answer, and I don't dare hang up. Even when I can hear them loading her into the back of the ambulance and asking her dozens of questions about the pregnancy. Her voice seems steady as she answers, but then they ask for her home address.

"Cooper," she calls. "Tell this man where home is."

"I can't wait on you, Mav!"

Maverick, unlike me, is calm and collected as he waves me off with a laugh. "Go, I'll meet you in there."

We drove through the night to get to Mac in eight hours with me on FaceTime, holding my breath with her through each painful push. Thankfully the nurse dug through McKinley's purse, finding the wrench, and the phone charger, so I could watch in helpless awe as my strong and beautiful wife pushed our son into the world all on her own in a room full of strangers.

I watched as the tears streamed down her face when they placed him on her chest as she sobbed, kissing his chubby little cheeks. My heart couldn't take it. I wanted nothing more than to be there with them and enjoy the moment, but I knew Mac needed a moment with our son. A moment that was just them. She needed to be able to look at that baby without guilt. She needed to see that he might have been part of Griffin, but he was part of her too.

She was not a failure.

She was a woman, beautiful and dedicated to raising that baby with everything she was. The journey for her to get to this point might have been long, but it was worth it, so damn worth it.

"Mac?" I knock on room 402, the one Mac told me she and the baby were in.

"Come in." Her voice sounds tired. That's fine. I'm here now, and she can rest while I hold the baby.

The room is dark when I push the door open and find my wife in bed, with a lamp lit on the bedside table, illuminating the swaddled baby in her arms.

"Hi." I take a seat on the mattress, careful not to jar her in case she's sore.

She grins. "I guess you want to meet your son, huh?" She's teasing, but it doesn't stop the tears at seeing her okay, at hearing the healthy baby cooing in her arms as I lean over and kiss the top of her head. "I very much would like to meet my son."

And like I had never felt love before, my wife lifts her arms, kissing the striped hat on the baby's head, and places him in my arms.

Everything pauses.

I don't breathe or swallow when the tiny boy in my arms, his eyes the same shape as his mother's, looks up at me.

"Levi Lexington," my wife whispers, "meet your daddy."

Epilogue

McKinley

"Hand Mama the wrench and close your eyes. I gotta kill Daddy before dinner."

I level the little boy at my side with a look that dares him to argue, which he ignores.

"Daddy said you're not supposed to be carrying a wrench anymore."

I squat down so I'm eye to eye with Griffin's mini-me. "Levi, don't you want a new daddy?" Glancing at the strange vehicle in the driveway—a Mercedes that clearly isn't mine—I growl. "One who doesn't have a death wish every other Friday?"

Unfortunately, Levi, like everyone else who gets to know Cooper, is his biggest fan. "Daddy also said that making death threats when the baby can hear you isn't nice."

Cooper is such a manipulator.

"Did he also say that it's his fault I'm always pregnant?"

What did Cooper do when Levi finally went to school? The asshole knocked me up again. Jacob came four years later, which leads us to that time Ainsley and Maverick offered to watch Pops and the boys for us so that we could have a date night.

Spoiler alert: Cooper knocked me up again.

This time though, we're having… another boy. Don't get excited. I'm surrounded by men who are replicas of my husband. You'd think I'd have one that was Team Mom, but nope, it's still just me and Pops against Cooper and his brood.

But he's done it now. Telling me he was running behind at the stadium and couldn't stop to pick up dinner. Dinner, clearly, is some ball bunny in need of a DILF.

Not today, sister.

If Mr. Lexington can't be with me and all these dang kids, then he will die. No questions, no explanations, no nothing but a wrench to the balls, ensuring he will never impregnate another woman or charm her into marrying his sweet adulterating ass.

"Daddy said not to get upset when you talk loud and don't make sense. He says the baby makes you crazy sometimes."

And there is reason number two that Daddy is getting his ass beat. "Never mind. I'll get the wrench myself."

"Pops!" The little traitor runs to the front door. "Tell Daddy to run!"

I sigh and look up at the Georgia sky. Yep, you heard right. The Georgia sky. Cooper didn't hesitate to sign the contract for Atlanta when I agreed to move. The next week, before I could change my mind, movers showed up, and Cooper had us packed in the car. If the man has learned anything, it's been not to give me time to think about my decisions.

"You threatening people already? It's not even eight o'clock." The old man at the door grins, pulling Levi close. "Don't worry, kiddo, we hid the wrench the last time Daddy left the toilet seat up."

Cooper almost died then too. Nothing—and I mean nothing—makes getting up ten times a night to pee better. But falling into the toilet bowl because your husband—on the one time he gets up to pee—forgets to put the lid down… That's grounds for murder or until death do us part.

I had to stop with the delivery do us part. I felt sure it was the reason Cooper kept knocking me up. He needed to make sure I didn't change my mind and leave with Levi.

Don't roll your eyes at my comment. I know when I've been replaced.

The moment Cooper held Levi, I knew I wasn't getting that kid back. The Closer took one look at those chubby little cheeks and was ruined.

I knew I could never divorce Cooper at that point. Not that I would have, I'm just saying, I knew then that no man would ever look at my child like Cooper looks at Levi. He doesn't just look at him like a stepfather looks at his stepson.

No, Cooper looks at Levi like it's his face staring back at him. Not one hour has passed when Cooper has ever shown preference with our boys. Not one. To him, they are all equally his. Granted, we tell Levi about Griffin, and Jacob about his Uncle Griffin. We don't keep secret Griffin's role in bringing Levi into this world and making us a family. For all the pain that came with losing Griffin, getting to raise his son has been an absolute joy.

At night, Cooper and I sit with Levi in his bed and tell him bedtime stories, consisting of all the silly things Griffin used to do when we were kids. Levi knows he has two daddies. One that died before he was born and the other one that loved him from the moment he saw him on the ultrasound.

"You need some help getting Jacob?" Pops hollers across the yard.

I narrow my eyes at the old man. "Well, if I plan on stabbing your grandson with my keys (how dare they hide my wrench), I do."

Pops chuckles. "Coop! She's home, and she's stabby again."

I watch as my bestie and my first-born disappear into the house before I shuffle to the car where I left the door open in my haste to kill Cooper and his girlfriend, and look at the baby in the back seat, sucking aggressively on a pacifier. "Should Mommy key the girlfriend's car?"

Jacob doesn't answer, and that's quite all right, he's only eighteen months old. I'm in no hurry for another man in this house to sound like my husband.

"You know that's not my girlfriend." Crazy muscled arms wrap around me. "You know Pops would have killed me first."

I shrug, refusing to turn my head to look at him. "That's why Pops is still my favorite."

The scruff on his face scratches my cheek as he nuzzles me. "Don't lie in front of the baby. It sets a bad example." He palms my belly, the nearly-identical black wedding ring (we had to cut them off a few times when his hands would swell from pitching) made from a zip tie still sits on his finger. I refuse to let him buy us real ones.

I said it once and I'll say it again, if they can hold Lu together, they can hold our marriage together. And Lu, well, she still takes up a space in the garage, even though I never get to drive her anymore (see seating capacity with a shit load of kids.) But she still runs… sometimes.

So, we can't get rid of the rings because Lu is still being held together. Pitchers know you can't change routines that work. When you're pitching great, you don't change anything. Translation: I still love Cooper, and he's not dead yet. Best to be wise and not fuck with changing the rings. I don't care what the rest of those baseball wives think.

"I'm going to set a terrible example when I kill whoever is in that house with you," I tell him.

He pulls away and flashes me a smile, grabbing Jacob from his car seat. "We'll get the shovel ready."

Okay, something smells fishy here. "Who's in the house, Cooper?"

The man who I love dearly, but want to kill daily, simply responds with, "See for yourself."

"I don't know if I should kiss you or smother you."

I'm exhausted when I finally come to bed, finding two boys lying across my husband with their great-grandfather asleep in the side chair.

"I'm thinking a kiss sounds better right now."

I flop down on the bed and rub down Jacob's back. "Why did you call Chris?"

My husband, the sneak, shrugs. "He owed you an apology."

That he did, but it was still a shock to see the man, who crushed my heart with only a few words, sitting at my kitchen table. "You let him see Levi too…"

"He needed to see the wonderful person he was leaving behind because of anger. He needed to see his brother's legacy."

For the billionth time, my eyes well with tears since seeing Chris. "He begged for my forgiveness," I tell him.

"And did you give it to him?"

I nod. "Do you think that was the wrong thing to do?" I mean a few sweet apologies don't change a raging asshole overnight.

Cooper leans up and presses a kiss to my lips. "Life's too short, Mac. Don't live it with regrets."

This man. This stinking man… "I love you," I tell him. "Even if you're the reason I'll never fit into a size two pair of jeans again."

He chuckles and it jostles Levi on his chest. "Mama?" the sleepy little boy calls out.

"Go back to sleep, baby." I rub his back, but his little head pops up anyway as he blinks at his daddy. "Did she say yes?"

Cooper smiles, and I'm immediately on edge. "What's he talking about, Cooper?"

"Just say yes, Mac, so we can all go to bed. My back hurts sitting in this chair." Pops, who is now awake, aims a glare at me.

"Well, maybe I would if y'all weren't so damn—dang sneaky tonight. What is going on?"

Levi sits up, seeming wide awake now. "Can I give it to her before she cries?"

Cooper ruffles his hair, and I don't bother correcting Levi that I'm not about to cry, I'm about to lose my shit. "Yeah, give it to her."

The little cupid who brought me and his daddy together crawls over to my side of the bed and reaches under my pillow, bringing out…

"Oh, no! No, Cooper. You'll jinx it." Now I am crying as Levi opens the black box, revealing a diamond ring.

Cooper slides Jacob up his chest. "McKinley Lexington. I did you a great dishonor by not proposing to you properly six years ago." He rocks the little boy gently. "I still can't properly propose, but you know what? You don't deserve the same proposal everyone else gets. You deserve all your boys piled up in one room, witnessing me asking you to stay married to me forever by sliding the platinum ring—that will never bend or break either—over your finger while you promise me a lifetime."

Levi takes the ring out of the box, his expression bursting with excitement. "Can I put it on her finger now?"

Cooper's gaze never leaves mine. "Not yet. Not until she promises me forever."

Levi's little groan has me rolling my eyes at Cooper. He stooped really low this time involving the boys. He knew there'd be no way I would say no to that little face.

"What if we jinx it?"

My husband pulls me closer. "Nothing will ever come between me and my love for my wife—especially superstition."

Well, when he puts it like that, and my little prince and Pops start clapping, there's nothing left for me to say except, "All right, Mr. Lexington. You can have my forever."

Did you love 21 Rumors? Do you want to binge more of my stories? Check out my box set, Commander in Briefs and fall in love with the grumpy men of the McCallister Jameson Foundation.

Click here and subscribe to my VIP listing to be notified of all future release dates.
https://geni.us/GZ3uPKV

Love *21 Rumors*? Want to read more from me? All of my books are standalone and are free in Kindle Unlimited.

Acknowledgments

A wise man once told me if you want to *impress* people, tell them of your successes. If you want to *impact* people, tell them of your failures.

Well, I'm here to tell you my first marriage was an absolute failure. I made mistakes out the wazoo and regretted so much. What I didn't regret is the experience and the two wonderful little girls that came out of the deal.

But it took me a long time to realize I didn't have to be the perfect wife or the perfect mother, all I needed to do was learn from the mistakes I made along the way. The Closer was a cleansing story for me to write. I went through the same shame and heartache, but in the end, I found a good man who loved and cherished even the bad qualities in me.

To all my readers who may find themselves in the same position I was, this book is for you. Take solace in knowing you are not a failure. You're not alone in this journey. Blessings are right on the other side of this pain. Stay strong and believe. Good things are coming your way.

Okay, so now for the hero roll call. In no particular order, these are the people who stood beside me as I wrote this book, deleted this book, cried, laughed, threatened to quit, and encouraged me to tell this story how I wanted. I couldn't have done it without Jaime, Becky, Sarah P, Sarah S, Aundi, Keri, Melody, Ri, Autumn, Jessica, Amy, Catherine, Rebecca, Stacey, and Letitia. Thank you all for riding this roller coaster with me.

YOU ARE THE TRUE HEROES.

Other Books

21 Rumors

A Romantic Comedy Series—All novels are standalone and feature different couples with crossover characters

IOU
The Pretender
The Closer

The Commander Legacies

A Second-Generation Contemporary Series—All novels are standalone and feature different couples with crossover characters

Rebellious

Commander in Briefs

A Contemporary Series—All novels are standalone and feature different couples with crossover characters

Pitcher
Commander
Gorgeous
Drifter
Interpreter

<u>**In the Hands of the Potters**</u>
<u>A Contemporary Series—All novels are standalone and feature</u>
<u>different couples with crossover characters</u>

The Potter

Come hang out in my Facebook reader group, Kristy's Commanders, for exclusive content and sneak peeks of my newest releases.

Sign up to receive updates on all my new releases and participate in juicy giveaways.

Check out my website and purchase signed copies of your favorite paperback.

Follow me!

Amazon:
www.amazon.com/author/mariekristy

BookBub:
www.bookbub.com/authors/kristy-marie

Instagram:
www.instagram.com/authorkristymarie

Facebook:
www.facebook.com/authorkristymarie

Twitter:
www.twitter.com/authorkristym

Goodreads
www.goodreads.com/author/show/17166029.Kristy_Marie